KANSAS

Four Prairie Romances
Dusted with Faith

Tracie Peterson
Judith McCoy Miller

BARBOUR BOOKS
An Imprint of Barbour Publishing, Inc.

ISBN 1-58660-278-0

All Scripture quotations, unless otherwise noted, are taken from the King James Version of the Bible.

Published by Barbour Books, an imprint of Barbour Publishing, Inc.,
P.O. Box 719, Uhrichsville, Ohio 44683, www.barbourbooks.com

Printed in the United States of America.

KANSAS

BEYOND TODAY

Tracie Peterson

Bud and Cora, Fred and Casey, Pete and Kay,
and all the other alias names they go by;
with special thanks for the home they've provided,
the love they've poured out, and the son they've shared with me.

Chapter 1

On the way home from town, Amy Carmichael closed her eyes and rested her head against the edge of the jostling wagon. She was trying desperately to ignore the animated, nonstop rambling of her twin sister, Angie.

Physically, Angela and Amy Carmichael were identical. Considered too tall by most of their peers, the girls measured at exactly five feet, ten inches. Their stature was the only thing their friends could find to criticize, though, for the twins' perfect features and tiny waists had been the envy of all. Now, at nineteen, with dark hair the color of chestnuts and brown eyes like velvet, the twins were envied more than ever.

On the outside, the twins were a beautiful matched pair, so much alike that they confused even their friends. But on the inside. . .

"You're not listening, Amy," Angie commented with a pout.

"No, I suppose I'm not. I'm really tired, Angie." Amy tried to adjust her sunbonnet for the tenth time. She pulled its shade over her eyes, squinting at the October sun that felt as hot as any summer day. She tucked a strand of hair beneath the bonnet, glad for the air's slight crispness that hinted that colder weather was coming.

"Just look at the dress Alice sent me," Angie whined.

Amy sat up and tried to show some interest. Angie was profoundly proud that their older sister Alice had broken away from the frontier prairie life to live in a big city back east. Their sister understood Angie's passion for city life and often sent Angie hand-me-downs from her city finery.

Amy, on the other hand, had little or no interest in the clothes Alice sent. She'd rather be in calico or homespun any day. In consideration of Angie's feelings, however, Amy reached out and touched the shiny, pink satin. "It is lovely, Angie. You'll look quite the city girl in this."

"Oh, I know," Angie gushed, "and won't the boys be impressed?"

Amy grimaced. "Where in the world will you wear it for them to see?"

"Why the barn raising, of course!" Angie continued to chatter away, while Amy waved to one of the neighbors in the wagon behind theirs.

As they made their way home, Amy looked often over her shoulder at the small parade of wagons behind them. She smiled. The harvest had been a good one this year. The corn, sold today for a record price, combined with August's summer wheat, guaranteed that the residents of Deer Ridge would head into winter fully supplied with not only their homegrown foods but also store-bought goods and money in the bank; such security was a rarity indeed.

Things had gone so well in fact, that the twins' parents, Charles and Dora Carmichael, were planning a barn raising to erect a much needed live-stock barn.

"What do you think he'll look like?" Angie questioned, continuing to rub the satin against her wind-burned cheek.

"Who?" Amy asked, wondering if she'd missed part of the conversation.

"The circuit rider, of course. Think of all the wonderful places he's been. I get goose bumps just imagining all the things he's seen. It must be truly spectacular to travel to new places all the time." Angie sighed dreamily. "Don't you ever think of what it'd be like to live back in the city? Don't you ever want to make plans for the future, Amy?"

Amy smiled. "A future beyond today?"

"Oh, bother with that," Angie said in frustration. "I remember Grandma always saying that, and I hated it then too. A person has to make plans."

"Why?"

"Just because they do." Angie's lips pressed together. "Besides, you're making plans for the future. You just don't know it. You're already rearranging the house in your head, just to accommodate the barn raising and the circuit rider's stay. Now don't tell me you're not, because I know you, Amy Carmichael."

Amy shrugged her shoulders. Arguing with her twin was pointless, so she said nothing at all.

Angie didn't care. She continued chattering as if the conversation had never taken a negative turn. *That is the best thing about Angie,* Amy thought as she half-listened to her twin; Angie'd argue her point of view, but she wouldn't run it into the ground by fighting.

"Amy," she said now, leaning forward as if to share a great secret. "I heard Mama say that the circuit rider used to live in Kansas City! Imagine that—Kansas City!"

Amy rolled her eyes. Between the satin dress and the circuit rider, Angie was completely daffy. Amy watched while Angie's fingers slid back and forth over the smooth material; she could tell that Angie's fascination with the gown was reaching the point where she would soon sink into an absorbed and silent contemplation. She would be imagining, Amy knew, what she would look like in the dress, what accessories would complement it, how she should do her hair when she wore it. Amy smiled and sighed; she welcomed the silence.

While Angie dreamed of the party that would follow the barn raising,

Amy, as her sister had predicted, calculated the work that would be involved during the day of labor.

Barn raisings were real celebrations, and the entire community would turn out to help. The plentiful harvest, coupled with the news of the circuit rider, made the best of reasons to celebrate.

Amy hadn't realized how much she missed regular church services, what her father referred to as the "calling of the faithful." Now they would have a regular circuit rider, and even if he only came every three or four weeks, it was better than nothing at all.

The small community of Deer Ridge had often contemplated building a church and hiring a full-time minister, but nothing had ever come of the plans, much to Amy's disappointment. She remembered the community meeting to decide which they would build and support first—a church or a school. With the many large families supplying donations of felled logs and other building materials, the school easily won.

Amy sighed as she remembered church services back in Pennsylvania. They'd left the civilized East, though, and moved to the wild prairie of western Kansas when she and Angie had been only seven.

Their older brother, Randy, had been elated at the prospect of an adventure. At seventeen, Randy saw this as an answer to the future. Pennsylvania farms were hard to come by, and most of the land near his parents' home was already being farmed. Randy had known he could continue farming his father's land, but he wanted to make a stake for himself; homesteading in Kansas offered him the best chance.

Twelve-year-old Alice, though, had been miserable, just as Angie had been. They hadn't wanted to leave Pennsylvania. Alice had cried herself into the vapors and had to be put to bed, while Angie had whined so much that she received the promise of a spanking if she didn't settle down.

But despite the trepidations of two of the Carmichael daughters, the family farm was sold and the remaining possessions loaded into a canvas-covered wagon.

Unlike her sisters, Amy thought the whole thing great fun. She loved to run alongside the wagon on the way to their new promised land and hated being made to ride inside with the weepy Alice and whining Angie.

The memory made Amy feel cramped now as she sat squeezed between the supplies for the barn raising. "Pa?" she called up to the wagon seat in front of her where her father handled the team. "I'd like to stretch for awhile. Would you stop so I can jump down?"

"Sure." Charles Carmichael smiled. Amy was so much like him—always moving, eager to be doing rather than watching.

Amy scrambled down, and because of the slowness of the heavily loaded wagons, she was easily able to keep pace on foot. Once again, she twitched her sunbonnet back in place. "Pa?"

"What is it, Amy?"

"I was just wondering if you knew anything about the circuit rider. Is he young or old?"

"Can't rightly say, but the district minister said he'd be on horseback. I can't imagine him being too awful old, if he's going to cover all this territory on horseback," Charles answered thoughtfully. "It'd be a might taxing on an older feller."

"And he'll be there for the barn raising and stay the night at the farm with us?" Amy already knew the answer, but she wanted to check the grapevine information she'd received from her sister.

"Yup. It's all settled, and ain't we the lucky ones? New barn and a man of God all in the same day. Ain't we the lucky ones?"

"More like blessed than lucky," Amy's mother, Dora Carmichael, put in from the other side of her husband. "Carmichaels don't hold no account in luck."

Charles laughed. "That's for sure, Ma. We'd never have gotten this far on Carmichael luck." The three of them laughed at this, though no one was really sure why. The Carmichaels had enjoyed a good life with many choice blessings, yet something in her father's words had amused them all.

No one who lived on the prairie ever chalked much of anything up to luck. Out here, surrounded by such a vast expanse of wilderness, human beings seemed to dwindle right down to the size of ants. They needed their belief in a pattern made by God, a design that He could see from up above, to give them strength; the thought of luck and chance spoiled the image. Maybe that's why they'd laughed. Whatever the reason, Amy was grateful for the laughter and the love.

Three weeks later found the farm in a frenzy of preparation for the barn raising. The entire community would turn out to help the Carmichaels put up their new barn, as well as celebrate the harvest and the arrival of the circuit rider.

Dora Carmichael spent hours sweeping the farmhouse floor. The Carmichaels were one of the few families in the community to have a puncheon floor, and Dora prided herself in keeping the long thin boards shining with a glow that rivaled even the finest city homes. Normally, once a month she would scrub the floor with a splint broom made from a piece of hickory—Dora always declared that this was the only way to "gussy up" the worn wood—but now with the circuit rider due to stay the night in the Carmichael house, Dora worked that broom until her arms ached.

The Carmichael farmhouse was by far the largest in the community. It was made now of logs and stood two stories high, but it hadn't always been so. The soddy house had come first. Amy remembered her disappointment the first time she'd seen their new home. It had been made of grass and mud, and the thought of living in a dirt house made Alice and Angie bawl. Amy didn't care for it any more than her sisters, but she looked past the sod and saw her father's pride.

Charles Carmichael had stood proudly with his hands on his hips, the hot Kansas sun at his back, and sweat dripping down the side of his face. He was dirtier than Amy had ever seen him, but the promise of the future had shown clear in his eyes, and his smile was as wide as the Smokey Hills River itself. He had built his family a house; now it was up to them to make it a home.

Right then Amy decided to work extra hard to make each day pleasurable for her parents. And that was when she decided to adopt her grandmother's attitude of one-day-at-a-time, looking no further than that day for trouble, because tomorrow was sure to have even more time to plan for problems. *And now,* Amy thought with a smile, *what with getting ready for the barn raising, I have plenty of work to keep me from worrying about anything that might come later on.*

"Amy!" Her mother's call made Amy hasten to pull up yet another bucket of water from the well.

"Coming, Ma." Amy hurried back to the house, slopping water on herself as she ran. She was careful to leave her boots at the back door as she entered her mother's freshly scrubbed kitchen.

"Just put the water on the stove and help me put these curtains up." Dora Carmichael motioned Amy toward the stove.

Amy poured the bucket of water into a large cast-iron pot and put the bucket outside the door. Wiping her wet hands on her apron, she reached up to help her mother place the red calico curtains at the kitchen window.

"Looks real good, Ma." Amy stepped back to get a better look. "That calico made up real nice for curtains."

"Well, it's not too bad if I do say so myself. Especially considering the fact that this was your sister's dress, just last week."

"Don't tell her, and maybe she won't fuss," Amy laughed. Angie fought to have less homemade things in the house and more store-bought luxuries.

"I just can't understand that sister of yours. Never could understand Alice either." Dora sighed. "Don't they ever stop to think that somebody had to make those things the store buys and resells?"

Amy laughed and put her arm around her mother's shoulders. "Angie only thinks about which one of her beaus she's going to marry and what big city she'll go live in. I don't imagine she thinks about much more than that."

The late October temperatures were unseasonably warm, and the window stood open to let in the steady southerly breeze. The calico caught the wind and fluttered like a flag unfurling. "They sure do look nice, Ma," Amy repeated.

The twentieth of October found the Carmichaels' homestead overrun with friends and family. Amy and Angie's brother, Randy, was the first to arrive. His growing family was seated in the bed of the wagon behind him.

Amy helped her nephews, Charlie and Petey, from the wagon bed before taking her two-year-old niece, Dolly. Her very expectant sister-in-law Betsey smiled at her gratefully.

"How have you been feeling, Betsey?" Amy questioned as the pregnant woman scooted herself to the back of the wagon.

"I've definitely been better. I think it would have been easier to ride bareback than to sit another mile in this wagon."

Amy laughed at the rosy-cheeked blond and offered her a hand down, but Randy came and easily lifted Betsey up and out, placing a loving kiss on her forehead before he set her feet on the ground. At the sight of her father offering kisses, Dolly reached out her arms and said, "Me too!"

Everyone laughed, but Randy leaned over and gave Dolly a peck on the cheek. "Now, Lilleth Carmichael, I expect you to mind your manners today."

The little girl cocked her head to one side, as if confused by the use of her Christian name instead of the nickname her brother had given her. Then four years old, Petey had been unable to pronounce "Lilleth," and so he announced that he would call her "Dolly," because she looked just like a baby doll he'd seen in Smith's General Store. From that point on it had been official, and Lilleth became Dolly.

"Come on, Betsey. Ma's already got a comfortable spot picked out for you under the cottonwood tree," Amy said. Taking hold of Betsey's arm she led her to the waiting chair.

The farmyard was soon a riot of people and livestock. Randy and Charles had picket stakes already set up for the horses, and the wagons were used as tables or places to sit when taking a break from building.

Amy was to be in charge of the children, thus freeing the women to quilt, cook, and visit. Some of the more ambitious ladies were even known to get into the act of helping with the construction. Why, Cora Peterson sometimes shinnied right up to the roof supports to put in a few well-placed nails. She said it kept her young, and at seventy years of youth, nobody was going to argue with her.

As the sun rose above the horizon in a golden orange glow, the final preparations were taken care of. Tents were quickly erected for the purpose of neighbors spending the night, thus saving them the long trip back to town, only to turn around the next day and return to hear the circuit rider preach at the Carmichael farm.

Tables bowed from the weight of food, and the array of tantalizing, mouth-watering delights was never to be equaled. Amy had to laugh, knowing that the overflowing plenty was not even the main meal but for the purposes of snacking only. Huge cinnamon rolls and fresh baked breads lined the tables, along with jars of preserves and jams of every flavor, as well as a variety of butters: apple, peach, and even plum. Someone had thought to bring several long rolls of smoked sausage, which were quickly cut into slices and eaten between bread before the first log was in place. All in all, everyone deemed it a great day to build a barn.

Chapter 2

"The preacher's a'comin! The preacher's a'comin!" The children ran toward the two approaching horses.

The excitement was uncontainable among the Deer Ridge residents, and even Angie stopped flirting with Jack Anderson. Another of her boyfriends, who just happened to be Jack's brother Ed, rode into the farmyard with the biggest man anyone in Deer Ridge had ever laid eyes on.

Amy was out of earshot, and so she missed seeing the circuit rider as his six-foot, six-inch frame bounded down from his huge Morgan horse. Angie, on the other hand, was ready and waiting.

"This is Pastor Tyler Andrews," Ed Anderson told them. Ed was the town's bank teller and the one person Angie figured had a pretty good chance of getting her out of Deer Ridge.

"Howdy do, Parson," Charles Carmichael said, taking the man's mammoth hand in his own.

The giant man smiled. "Please call me Tyler." His voice was rich and warm. "Pastor and Parson sound much too stuffy for friends." Taking off his hat, he revealed sweat-soaked golden curls. Angie thought they were divine.

She batted her thick black lashes while her dark eyes slid appraisingly over Tyler. He dwarfed everyone around him, but his brown eyes were welcoming and friendly.

Without warning, Angie reached out boldly and took Tyler's arm. "You simply must meet my mother, Dora Carmichael. Oh, and over here is Mrs. Stewart. Her husband owns the bank. And this is Mrs. Taggert—her husband is Doc. He's that man over there in the dark coat." Tyler had to laugh as the tall, willowy girl fairly pulled him through the mass of people, completely ignoring Ed Anderson.

If anyone in Deer Ridge was surprised by Angie's outburst, no one said a thing. Angie was always livening up things, and today wasn't going to be any different. She had a way about her that endeared her to people about as quickly as she annoyed them. Angie, though, never had any hard feelings; she was simply being Angie, and most people understood that.

Only a handful of people missed getting introduced to the massive preacher by Angie. Most of them were under the age of ten, though, and the only adult not yet privileged to make Tyler's acquaintance was Amy.

Amy had taken the children to play hide-and-seek and red rover in the orchard. She loved the children best. They were demanding, but their wants were simple. They continually asked for drinks and help to the outhouse, but Amy found them easier to be with than the adults. She could simply play with them all morning, and they accepted her just as she was. At the noon meal, the weary and worn-out children would join their folks and be ready to nap in the afternoon.

"Watch me, Amy! I'm gonna jump out of this tree," eight-year-old Charlie called to his aunt.

"If you break your leg, don't come crying about it afterwards," Amy called over her shoulder as she hoisted Dolly to her other hip. She was glad she'd chosen to wear her older blue gingham for playing with the children, since Dolly was taking turns chewing first on the collar of the dress and then the sleeve.

"Poor baby," Amy said as she smoothed Dolly's downy brown hair back into place. "Are you getting new teeth? I bet Grammy has some hard biscuits for you to chew on. We'll just see if she doesn't."

Amy put two of the older girls in charge of watching over the others and went in search of a teething biscuit for Dolly. As she rounded the corner of the Carmichaels' two-story log home, Amy could see that the barn was already sporting a frame on three sides. She glanced around, wondering if the new minister had arrived. Spying her mother, Amy made her way to inquire about the preacher and the biscuit.

"Dolly needs a teething biscuit, Ma," Amy said, trying to pull her collar out of her niece's mouth. "Those back molars of hers are causing her fits."

"There's a whole batch of hard biscuits on the table in the house," Dora answered and reached up for her granddaughter. Dolly would have none of it, however, and turned to bury her face in Amy's hair.

"You ought to tie your hair back, Amy," Dora suggested. "She has your hair a mess."

"I tried putting it back three times," Amy answered. "It keeps coming free, mostly because of a little boy named Petey who thinks it's fun to snatch my ribbon." Amy laughed. Betsey and Dora laughed too.

Amy turned to go to the house when she remembered the circuit rider and turned back. "Is he here yet, Ma?"

"Who?" Dora asked, wondering if her daughter was finally taking an interest in one of the community's eligible men.

"The circuit rider, of course. Who else did you think I was talking about?"

"Oh, no one in particular." Her mother smiled. "I was just hoping, that's all."

"Now, Ma. Don't get started on me and husband hunting. I'll know when the right man comes along. He just hasn't come along yet. So is the preacher here or not?"

"Sure is. See that spot of gold on top of the east edge of the barn frame?"

Amy craned her neck to see the man her mother was pointing out. She could barely see him, but he was there, and she felt satisfied just knowing it.

"I'm sure glad he made it. It's going to be fun having a preacher and regular church services again."

"We haven't done so bad with the home services," Dora said, supporting her husband's perseverance in holding some type of Sabbath service for his children and grandchildren.

"Of course not, Ma. I just think it will be nice to get together with the others. Is he nice? What's he look like? I can't really see him too well from here." Amy strained to get a better look without being too obvious.

"Well," her mother answered, "I must say your sister was certainly taken with him. Angie latched onto him first thing, so you'd best ask her if you want to know what he's like. I just barely said hello before Angie was dragging him off again." Dora laughed and added, "About the one thing I could tell about him is that he's a big man. Taller than your pa and shoulders broad as a bull."

"That's for sure." Betsey struggled to get into a more comfortable position.

Amy decided not to seek out the new preacher. After all, if Angie had already set her cap on him, what chance would the poor man have of freeing himself up to meet the likes of Amy?

I don't need to meet him now, Amy decided, going back to tend the children. *I'll get to hear him preach tomorrow and maybe even tonight. Let Angie make a fool out of herself. It seems to give her such pleasure.*

Amy was enjoying the children so much, she was surprised when someone rang the dinner bell.

"You children run on now and find your folks," she said. "It's time to eat—and I heard tell somebody brought cherry cobbler for dessert." She steered the children in the direction of the lunch tables.

She managed to deposit Dolly into Dora's arms with only a few complaining whimpers from Dolly, and then she went to make sure the other children made it back to their mothers. She glanced around again for a glimpse of the preacher, but he was seated among a huge group of people, and she couldn't get a good look at him. She would just have to wait to satisfy her curiosity.

"So that would make you thirty-one years old," Angie said, after mentally calculating the figures she'd just heard Tyler recite.

"That's right, Angie." Tyler grinned. He liked this young woman, so lively and vibrant. She seemed to pull everyone around her into an atmosphere of celebration. "I've been riding the circuit for seven years, with most of my time spent in Missouri. My folks live outside of Kansas City."

"Kansas City!" Angie squealed. "Oh, do tell me what Kansas City is like. I want so much to go there. Have you been to any other big cities? I want to hear about them too!" Angie rambled on, giving Tyler no time to answer.

But before the meal was finished, Angie had managed to learn a great deal about life in Kansas City. She also knew that Tyler Andrews had become a minister after losing his bride of several months to an influenza epidemic.

Stuffed from the heaps of food ladled onto his plate, Tyler excused himself to clean up. Meanwhile, Ed and Jack Anderson had taken as much ignoring as they could tolerate from Angie, and as soon as Tyler got to his feet, they came to reclaim her.

Tyler listened to Angie fuss over the two men and laughed to himself. He shook his head in wonderment, nearly running over Charles Carmichael.

"Pastor Tyler," Charles said, unable to bring himself to use only the man's first name. "I hope you're finding everything you need. The conveniences are behind the house, although I'm sure you could've figured that one out. Feel free to walk around." Charles patted his full belly. "I think I'll take a little nap while the others rest."

"Thank you, Mr. Carmichael," Tyler said.

"No, no," Charles protested, "just call me Charles. Everybody else does."

"Only if you'll call me Tyler."

Charles laughed and stuck out his right hand. "It's a deal, Tyler. Although never in my life have I called a man of God by his first name."

"Then it's about time." Tyler shook the man's hand vigorously. "Formalities hold little account with me. We're all one family, after all."

"That we are. That we are," Charles agreed and went off in search of a place to rest. He was going to like this new preacher; he could tell already.

Amy placed the two full buckets of water on either end of the yoke. Careful to avoid spilling any of the precious liquid, she hoisted the yoke to her shoulders. She carried the water to a huge caldron, normally used for laundry and soap making, and dumped it in. After several trips to the well, she lit the kindling and logs beneath the pot so that the water would heat for washing the dishes.

Satisfied that the fire was well lit, she went back to hauling water. She hummed to herself, enjoying the temporary quiet in the aftermath of lunch. The final two buckets hoisted at last to her shoulders, she was startled to find the weight suddenly lifted. She whirled around.

Her mouth fell open as she stared up at Tyler Andrews's giant form. After several seconds, she stammered, "I, I, ah—" She couldn't think of anything to say.

Tyler grinned. "You amaze me, Angie. I wouldn't have thought a little lady like you could've raised this thing, much less carry it very far. How in the world did you manage to give your beaus the slip?" He chuckled, amused by the stunned expression on the face of the woman he thought was Angie.

Amy felt her legs start to shake. What in the world was wrong with her? She hoped she wasn't coming down with a spell of ague, or malaria, as some of the city doctors referred to it. It ran rampant at times, and while Amy and Angie had been lucky to avoid it, Amy knew her mother suffered severe bouts of it.

She struggled to find something to say and finally blurted out the only thing that came to mind. "You must be the circuit rider. I'm glad you decided to come to Deer Ridge."

Tyler looked at her strangely for a moment. What kind of game was Angie playing now? She'd nearly broken his arm dragging him from person to person this morning, and then at lunch she flirted with him unmercifully. Now, she acted as though she'd never met him.

Amy felt her heart pounding louder and faster, until she was certain Tyler could hear it from where he stood. She put her hand to her breast as if to still the racing beat. Tyler Andrews was as handsome as any man she had ever met.

When Tyler just watched her, his brows knit, Amy suddenly realized that he was confused. Apparently, though not surprisingly, Angie hadn't told him she had a twin sister. Amy took a deep breath. "I'm sorry, you must think my manners are atrocious. I'm Amy Carmichael, Angie's twin sister."

A broad smile crossed Tyler's worried face. "That's a relief. I thought for a moment you were touched in the head. You know, too much sun."

Amy smiled. "No, just not as forward as my sister. Sorry if we confused you. We're really not up to mischief." She heard her own words, and she thought her voice sounded normal enough, despite the alien feelings inside her body and the clutter of confusion in her mind. "Well," she added with a grin, "at least I'm not up to mischief. Once you get to know us, you'll be able to tell us apart. We may look alike, but that's about it."

Tyler laughed out loud. "So there are two of you—and I'll eat my hat if you aren't identical."

"We are that, Pastor," Amy agreed and added, "in a physical sense. We do have our differences, though, believe me."

"I can see that too."

Tyler had forgotten about the weight he still held, but Amy noticed the water and motioned for Tyler to follow her. "You'll burn your muscles out good, standing there like that, Pastor," she said. She wondered whether she should take one of the buckets and ease his burden.

"Just lead the way," he answered, "and please don't call me Pastor. I've just worked through that with your pa, and finally he's calling me Tyler. I'd like it if you'd call me that too." He followed Amy to the caldron.

She took the pails off the yoke hooks and emptied them into the caldron before answering. "All right, Tyler." She smiled a little, tasting the name for the first time. "And you call me Amy."

Tyler placed the yoke on the ground and extended his hand. "It's a deal."

Amy held out her hand, and Tyler took hold of her small tanned arm with his left hand as his right hand grasped her fingers. The touch of his warm hands made her shiver. "There's a chill to the air, don't you think?" she said, despite the warm sun that beat down on their heads. She thought she saw a glint of amusement in Tyler's eyes.

What in the world was wrong with her?

Chapter 3

Despite the jittery feeling that ran along her nerves, Amy found herself comfortable in the company of Tyler Andrews. She showed him around the farm, pointing out things she loved the most.

"There's a path down past the old barn that leads to our orchards," she told him, guiding him back to the construction site of the new barn. "But I can show you later." She noticed that a few of the men were already back at work, and while she was enjoying her time with Tyler, he was probably anxious to get back to the company of men.

In reality, nothing could have been further from Tyler's mind. He was delighted at his good fortune and Amy's company. He'd ridden the circuit for over seven years, always embracing each new community, always enjoying his service to God. But in the back of his mind, he had always had the desire to settle down. That desire had made Tyler carefully consider each and every community that he pastored—as a possible home.

Now, as he watched Amy Carmichael speak in her soft, quiet way about the life she loved here on the plains, Tyler began to think he might see the possibility of a lifetime partner—and maybe even a home.

Amy brushed back a loose strand of brown hair and took her red hair ribbon out of her apron pocket. "I tried three times to retie my hair—and each time one of the ornery boys I was caring for this morning pulled it from me and left my hair disheveled. I do apologize for being so unkept." Amy tied the ribbon in place. "Now that the children are napping, I should be safe."

Tyler chuckled, and Amy was surprised to see a strange look of amusement spread across his face. His laughing brown eyes caught the sunshine and reflected flecks of amber in their warmth. There were tiny creases at the corners, betraying his love of laughter.

What manner of man was this preacher? So full of life and laughter. So comfortable and happy to share the small details of life on the farm. Amy smoothed down the edges of her dress collar, now hopelessly wrinkled from Dolly's chewing; she didn't even feel the hand that reached up and pulled loose her hair ribbon.

As the chestnut bulk fell around her face, Amy gave a gasp of surprise. She looked up to see a mocking grin and arched eyebrows, as Tyler dangled her ribbon high above her head.

"Boys will be boys no matter the age, Miss Amy," Tyler said and then put the ribbon in his shirt pocket. Amy started to protest, but Tyler had already moved away to retrieve a hammer. She stared after him, long after he'd climbed the ladder to help her father.

"Better shut your mouth, Amy, or you'll catch flies in it," Angie teased. "Isn't he wonderful!" It was an exclamation, not a question, and Angie fairly beamed as she continued. "He spent lunch with me and told me all about his life. Do you know, his parents still live near Kansas City, and they go to the opera and the symphony. Can you imagine it, Amy?"

"No, I truly can't," Amy admitted. The things that attracted her twin held little interest for Amy, and while she hated to hurt her sister's feelings, she couldn't lie.

"If I were to marry that man," Angie continued, "I could probably live with his parents in Kansas City, while he rode the circuit. Wouldn't that be a dream? Everything in the world at your fingertips!"

"For pity's sake, Angie. The man just arrived in Deer Ridge, and already you're acting as though he's proposed." Amy didn't want to admit the twinge of disappointment she was feeling. Her sister was used to getting her own way when it came to men. Most of them simply fell at her feet whenever she batted her eyes, and now Angie was contemplating the new minister as if he were a prized hog at the local fair. Amy shrugged her shoulders.

"Things move pretty fast among frontier folk," Angie mused with a coy smile. "But, I think I would like to get to know this Tyler Andrews better. I'm going to see to it that he dances at least half the dances with me tonight. I'll bet I can have him proposing before the night is over."

"Angie!" Amy gasped. "You don't even know this man. You surely don't love him, so how can you even think of trying to snag him into marriage?"

"I can love anybody, dear sister. In fact, love is the easy part. I haven't met a man yet that didn't make me feel happy and loved."

"What about the man?" Amy asked and noticed the smile leave Angie's face. "Don't they deserve to be loved by their wives?"

"Well, don't get vulgar about it." Angie feigned a shocked expression. She hated it when Amy revealed a flaw in her ideals, and now she tried to distract her twin by deliberately misunderstanding. "Of course, whatever is expected of a wife would come along with the marriage. I'm sure it can't be too unpleasant."

"You know very well I'm not talking about that," Amy said with a blush. "I'm talking about caring and supporting. That's the kind of loving I'm talking about."

Angie tossed her precisely placed curls. Unlike her twin, she had little trouble keeping her hair pinned, despite the number of suitors that followed her around the farm. "You are such a bother, Amy. I don't want to argue with you, so let's just drop it for the time. I like Tyler, and he likes me. If something more comes about tonight, then it must be meant to be."

With that, Angie bounced off in the direction of the newly arrived Nathan Gallagher. Nathan was Deer Ridge's only lawyer and the third of Angie's more serious boyfriends. Amy shook her head and sighed. Sometimes her sister could be infuriating.

By nightfall the barn was completed, with the exception of some indoor work, and it was as fine a structure as any farmer could ever hope for. Its completion signaled time for supper, and everyone knew what would follow that—the dance!

Amy was busy with kitchen work, but she found her thoughts still caught by Tyler. She couldn't help but remember the way his eyes seemed to laugh even before his face cracked a smile. She had already memorized each feature of his handsome face, she realized, and she nearly found herself tracing its lines in the potatoes she was mashing before the clatter of pans behind her brought her back to reality.

She looked around her to see if anyone had seen how silly she was acting, but the bustling group of older women seemed to scarcely notice her presence. Most of the other women Amy's age were outside, enjoying the company of the young men. Through the open window, Amy could hear Angie's exuberant laughter. No doubt she had cornered Tyler again and was working him into her snare.

Amy threw down the potato masher. Why did Angie have to be like that? Trying to ignore the sound of her sister's joy, Amy took the large bowl of potatoes to the table and fled to the safety of her room.

After an hour or more had passed, Amy rejoined the festive crowd. She had changed her grass-stained dress and now wore a soft muslin gown that had been dyed a shade of yellow. The dye was made from goldenrod plants, and the color was called nankeen. The gown was simple, with gathers at the waist and a scoop-necked bodice that had been trimmed with handmade tatting. The bodice was a bit snug, as the dress had been made nearly three years earlier, and it accentuated Amy's well-rounded figure and tiny waist.

She had pulled back her hair at the sides and pinned it into a loose bun at the back of her head. Tiny wisps fell stubbornly loose, framing her heart-shaped face, but Amy felt satisfied with her appearance. She shouldn't let Angie's zeal for life annoy her—and she certainly shouldn't let her irritation make her miss the fun of the evening.

Amy stepped into the yard just as the fiddles began tuning up for the dance. Her father had hung several lanterns from poles and trees, and their light cast a hazy glow over the party. The light was so soft, so muted, that Amy felt as though she were in a dream.

She couldn't help but hear Angie's vivacious voice, though. Her twin stood with several girls her own age, telling them about the pink satin gown she wore. Amy sighed and turned toward the dessert table to help the older women cut pies and cakes.

"Amy!" a voice called out from the sea of people.

Amy was surprised to see Jacob Anderson, younger brother of Ed and Jack, pushing his way toward her through the crowd.

"Hello, Jacob." Amy smiled. "I didn't know you'd be here tonight. I thought you were still in Hays."

"I wouldn't have missed a chance to dance with you. My, don't you look pretty tonight. How come you won't marry me? We could run off to find our fortune in gold. You know they're pulling nuggets as big as sows out of the Rockies. We could have it all, Amy." Jacob took hold of Amy's elbow. "Come over here where it's quieter and talk with me a spell."

"Oh, Jacob," Amy sighed. "I have a great deal of work to do. Ma counts on me to help out, seeing's how Angie's always so preoccupied." She allowed Jacob to lead her to the back of his family's wagon and accepted his hands on her waist as he lifted her to sit on the edge of the wagon bed. "I can't stay long."

Jacob stood in front of her, his boyish face illuminated by the glow of a lantern that had been mounted on the wagon. "You know how I feel about you, Amy." He took hold of her hands. "I can't stand not being around you, and when you're not around, you're all I can think about."

Amy shook her head. Poor Jacob. He wasn't at all interesting to her. He was only a year older than her and so immature with his wild dreams of gold in the Rockies. "How you do go on, Jacob Anderson. How come you aren't taking after Angie, like your brothers?" Amy smiled, hoping to lessen the seriousness of Jacob's face.

He smiled sheepishly, not wanting to admit that he had been interested in Angie, but his brothers had threatened to skin him alive if he so much as dared to speak with her. "Don't you think your sister has enough beaus?" he said instead. Amy was every bit as pretty as her sister, and she was always kindhearted, listening to his gold-rush stories. That made up for a lot, Jacob reasoned.

Amy pulled her hands gently from his. "Jacob," she began, "you know I'm not interested in being courted by you. Why do you keep after me like this?"

Jacob pushed a hand through his blond hair and shrugged his shoulders. "I keep thinking it can't hurt to try. Sooner or later you're bound to come to your senses. Why you're already older than most of the unmarried girls in the county." He grimaced as he realized what he'd said. "I'm sorry, I didn't mean it like it sounded."

Amy laughed and pushed herself off the wagon to stand eye to eye with her suitor. "I know you didn't, Jacob. Don't worry, I'm not Angie, and I couldn't care a fig how old I am. I won't marry anyone until I'm in love and know that it's the man God wants me to marry."

Amy left Jacob to contemplate her words and joined her mother at the food table. An array of pies, cakes, cookies, and fruit breads lined the long wooden planked table. Amy noticed that here and there someone had placed a cobbler or custard dish, and someone had even gone to the trouble of making a tray of fruit tarts.

"Did I see you with the youngest Anderson boy?" Dora was ever hopeful that Amy would find someone who interested her.

"Yes, Jacob proposed again, in a roundabout way." Amy laughed. "And, I told him no, in a most definite way."

"One of these days, Girl, you're going to have to settle down with someone." Dora reached out to caress her daughter's cheek. "But until you do I'm mighty glad to have you here with me. You're a blessing, Child, both to me and to your pa."

"I could never doubt that for a minute!" The masculine voice belonged to Tyler Andrews, and Amy felt her face grow hot with embarrassment.

"I've been looking all over for you," Tyler said with a grin, amused that Amy was so self-conscious, while Angie had boldly flirted with him through a half dozen reels already. "Come share a dance with me, and let me see if twins dance differently from one another."

Amy laughed. "I don't dance nearly as well as Angie. In fact, I quite often avoid the activity if at all possible." Her heart pounded in an unfamiliar way, and she noticed her mouth suddenly felt dry.

Tyler wouldn't be put off. He surprised both Dora and Amy by coming around the table to take Amy's hand. "I won't take no for an answer. Now, if you'll excuse us, Mrs. Carmichael, I intend to waltz with your daughter."

Dora Carmichael nodded and smiled as Tyler fairly dragged Amy toward the other dancers. Amy flashed a look over her shoulder at her mother. Dora shrugged in amusement at the stunned expression on her daughter's face.

"Maybe," thought Dora aloud, "just maybe he's the one." The thought gave her a great deal to contemplate as she watched the new circuit rider take her daughter into his arms.

Amy stiffened at the touch of Tyler's hands on her waist. She felt her hands go clammy and wished she'd remembered to bring her handkerchief with her. She was glad for Tyler's towering height, because usually she had no choice but to look directly into the eyes of her dance partner. With Tyler, however, she was granted the privacy of his chest.

"Relax, you'll do just fine," Tyler whispered into her ear.

But instead of relaxing, Amy felt a shiver run up her spine. Her stomach did a flip, and she felt weak in the knees. "I don't think I can do this," she murmured beneath her breath.

"Of course you can," Tyler said with knowing authority. "Look at me, Amy."

Amy's head snapped up at the command. Tyler's face was only inches from hers, and the look he gave her seemed to pierce her heart. She'd seen looks like this before, but usually they were intended for her sister.

She swallowed hard and unknowingly tightened her grip on Tyler's hand, as she stepped on his toe. She frowned. "I told you I wasn't any good at this."

Tyler laughed and whirled her into the flow of the other waltzers. "You dance perfectly well, Miss Carmichael. I fear it's my inept skills that caused your misplaced step."

"How gallant of you, Sir," Amy said, playing the game.

"My pleasure, Ma'am," Tyler teased, and Amy found herself relaxing almost against her will.

When the dance ended, Tyler suggested a walk. "You did promise to show me the orchards."

"I did?" Amy tried to remember. "Oh well, come along then."

Tyler took hold of her arm and allowed her to lead. As they passed from the warm glow of the lighted farmyard into the stark brilliance of the moon's light, Amy felt her breath quicken. She chided herself for being so childish. *Next thing you know,* she thought, *I'll be swooning!*

Tyler's large, warm hand securely held her arm to keep her from stumbling. He had no way of knowing, of course, that Amy knew this land as well as her own bedroom. He was being chivalrous, as she'd noticed him to be with everyone. Tyler Andrews, she told herself, was simply a gentleman; the caring way he treated her meant nothing special.

Familiar laughter rang out, and Amy and Tyler saw a very busy Angie talking nonstop to a group of four or five men. She was flitting about inside a ring of suitors as she made promises for upcoming dances.

"That sister of yours is something else," Tyler commented. Amy's response stuck in her throat. She'd always wished she could be more like Angie, and now even Tyler seemed to be as captivated with her twin as most men were. But before she could reply, Tyler continued. "You two are so different. Such a contrast of nature. I thought twins were supposed to be alike."

Amy giggled. The sound touched Tyler's heart with the memory of another tenderhearted woman. A young bride who'd only lived as his wife for a few months before losing her life to influenza.

Seeing Tyler's frown, Amy's laughter died. Her worried look made Tyler say, "I'm sorry. For a moment you reminded me of my wife."

"Your wife!" Amy nearly shouted the words. "I didn't know you were married." She was gripped with guilt for the thoughts she'd been having. Thoughts about how nice it would be to be married to Tyler Andrews. Now she'd coveted another woman's husband.

"I was married." Tyler put Amy's racing thoughts to an abrupt halt. "She died over ten years ago. We'd only been married four months when she caught influenza and died."

"I'm sorry." Amy truly meant the words. She'd seen a great deal of death here on the stark, lonely plains of Kansas.

Tyler smiled the sad sort of smile Amy knew people to get when remembering something bittersweet. "Don't be. She was a frail thing, and she was ready to meet God. I've learned not to mourn but to rejoice because I know she's happy and safe. It was her fondest desire that I not wallow in self-pity and mourning. She even made me promise to remarry."

"I see."

"Losing her made me realize the void in my life. It was then that I decided to become a minister. Circuit riding just seemed to come as a natural way for me, what with the fact that I wasn't tied to one spot. It's been a good life, but I can see the time coming when I'll be ready to settle down to one church and one town." Tyler didn't add the part of his heart that said "and one woman."

"It would be wonderful if you could settle in Deer Ridge," Amy said, not thinking of how her words might seem to Tyler.

"I was just thinking that myself." Tyler smiled at Amy's blunt honesty. "What about you, Amy? Do you have any plans for the future?"

Amy laughed, the sound like music in the night. "You mean beyond today?"

Tyler felt his heart skip a beat as Amy leaned back against the trunk of an apple tree. Her face was lit by the white glow of the moon, and Tyler decided he'd never known a more beautiful woman in all his life.

"That was the general idea," Tyler whispered in a husky tone that was barely audible.

Amy smiled up at Tyler, knowing he didn't understand the Carmichaels' family joke. "I've learned to take it a day at a time. There's too much that's unpredictable in life. My grandmother used to tell me, 'Never make plans beyond today!' " Her voice was soft, almost hypnotic, and when she fell silent, Tyler stood completely still, captivated by the moment and the feelings he had inside.

The night was unseasonably warm, and the sweet scent of apples still clung to the ground and air around them. Amy couldn't understand why her chest felt tight every time she tried to breathe deeply. Or why, when she looked at Tyler looking at her the way he was just now, she felt moved to throw herself into his arms. What kind of thought was that for a good, Christian girl?

Used to speaking her mind, Amy suddenly found herself blurting out a confession. "I don't understand what's happening to me. I feel so different. Ever since you appeared at the well, I just feel so funny inside."

Tyler refrained from smiling at this sudden outburst. He was amused to find a woman so innocent and unaware. Surely she must feel the same way he did. After ten years of loneliness, Tyler felt a spark of hope.

Amy frowned as she contemplated her emotions, and Tyler couldn't help but reach out and run a finger along the tight line of her jaw. At his touch, she relaxed. His fingers were warm, and she stood very still, hoping he would not take his hand away.

"Tyler, I. . ." Her voice fell silent, and she lost herself in his eyes. The moment was too much for either one of them, and Tyler pulled her against his huge frame, bending her ever so slightly backward to accommodate his height.

When his lips touched hers, Amy found herself melting against his broad, muscled chest. Molded there against him, Amy thought she would die from the flood of passion that filled her. *Was this love?* she wondered as his mouth moved against hers.

Tyler pulled away only enough to look deep into Amy's eyes. Amy suddenly realized that she'd wrapped her arms around Tyler's neck; the impropriety of romancing the district's circuit rider made her pull away.

"I'm so sorry." She backed out of his arms and found herself up against the trunk of the tree. "I didn't know, I, uh. . .I didn't mean to do that."

Tyler laughed and pulled Amy back into his arms. "Well, I did," he said and lowered his lips to hers one more time.

Chapter 4

Sunday morning dawned bright and clear, and the temperature remained warm. Friends from far and wide crawled out from tents, where they had slept on pallets on the ground, and lifted their faces to the sunlight. As the sun rose higher over the brown and gold corn shocks, the shadowy fingers of night disappeared.

Amy watched from her bedroom window. She'd had to spend the night with her sister, because Angie's room had been taken by several of the elderly women in the community, and Amy had had to endure Angie's account of Tyler's life until the wee hours of the morning. She couldn't explain to her twin that Tyler had kissed her, nor could she explain the feelings he had stirred inside her heart.

The fact was, Amy didn't know what to say or think. After all, Tyler Andrews was the new minister, and Amy was nothing more than one of his flock. Or was she?

When Amy finally came downstairs, she could tell by the way people were gathering up their breakfast dishes that the hour was late. Angie had long since departed, anxious to find Tyler and see how he'd fared the night before. Amy was glad she'd chosen to linger upstairs. She felt apprehensive, almost fearful of facing Tyler. What must he think of her after she had wantonly allowed him to kiss her, and not once but twice?

Amy didn't think she could sit in the congregation with family and friends, listening to Tyler Andrews preach, when all the while she was thinking of his kiss. Somehow, she must have led him on; after all, he was a man of God, and surely he had better self-control than she did. Tyler would have no way of knowing how grieved she was by her actions the night before, and Amy longed to apologize.

Amy purposefully avoided the busy kitchen and chose instead the quietness of the back sitting room. *Dear God,* she prayed silently, *I don't understand what happened last night, and I don't understand the way I feel. I'm truly humiliated at the way I acted, and I ask You to forgive me. I asked You long ago to send a strong Christian man into my life, a husband I could love for a lifetime. And,* she felt tears form in her eyes, *if Tyler Andrews is the man You have in mind, please show me. I don't mean to be a naïve and foolish child, Lord—but like Pa sometimes says, "I need a good strong sign—one I can't miss." Please, God, please don't let me feel this way toward Tyler if he's not the one. Amen.*

Someone began ringing the dinner bell, signaling the time to gather for the services. Amy made her way out the back door of the house and around to where the residents of Deer Ridge were congregating.

She spied Tyler in the crowd, shaking hands and sharing conversation with just about everyone. She also noticed Angie standing to one side of him, her eyes eating up the sight of him in his Sunday best. Amy could almost hear Angie's thoughts as she eyed the cut of his stylish black suit. The string tie he wore at the neck was secured with a tiny silver cross, and beneath the creased edge of his pant legs, his black boots were polished to a bright shine. All in all, the massive man was a fine sight.

Amy tried to slip past Tyler and Angie without having to speak, but Angie didn't let her. "I saved you a seat, Sleepyhead," Angie said, taking hold of Amy's arm.

Tyler turned to Amy. Her long brown hair was neatly pinned up, and the wispy strands that fell in ringlets worked with the high-necked collar of her blouse to form a frame for her face. He looked at her for several moments before she allowed herself to meet his eyes.

"I thought you'd sleep right through breakfast!" Angie said. "And you tossed and turned so much last night, I thought I was going to have to kick you out of bed to get any sleep."

Amy turned crimson as she caught sight of Tyler's grin. She wanted to run to the safety of the house, but Angie's grip on her arm was firm, and her twin was already rambling on. "I never knew you to get so worked up over a get-together. I swear you mumbled all night long and fairly thrashed me to death."

Amy could no longer stand it. She turned to Angie and with very little charity, flashed her a look that produced instantaneous silence from her twin. Tyler wanted to laugh out loud but didn't want to add to Amy's embarrassment. He loved the innocence in her eyes, and the knowledge that she'd spent as restless a night as he had gave him even more confidence that she was the woman to end his searching. Confident that God would show him in time, Tyler knew he could wait. After all, he'd waited this long.

"Ladies, if you'll take your seats, I'll start the service," he said with a tender glance at Amy.

Amy immediately relaxed. His look was almost apologetic. She couldn't figure out if the apology was for her sister's comments or for his actions the night before, but either way, he was kind to care. Amy had never known a man to be so considerate of her feelings.

The congregation fell silent when Tyler stepped forward. He'd refused to stand in the back of a wagon, as one person had suggested, for he knew he needed no extra height while he preached. Instead, he'd asked only for a small table upon which he could place his Bible.

Amy couldn't help but notice the way he cradled the beloved book. She could tell by the way he caressed the cover with his large calloused hands that this Bible meant the world to him. It was clearly his life's blood, and confirmation came in the powerful words which followed.

"People without God are nothing," he began. "They have no purpose, no destiny—no life. They are useless in matters of importance, and worthless tasks are all they know." The words rang out loud and clear, and no one, not even the children, said a word.

"People without God don't know which way to walk or where they're bound. They don't have even the slightest solid path to follow, and they are lost from the one road that matters." Tyler's intense stare moved from person to person. As he made eye contact with the community people, he could see whose lives were saved and whose weren't by the looks on their faces. Some met his stare with a confident nod; those were souls who'd clearly accepted the truth of the Word. Others seemed to squirm uncomfortably at the contact he made; these knew the truth of the words but weren't following them. One or two stared in disinterest and seemed preoccupied with other things; these souls were not yet open to the urging of God's Spirit, or they'd chosen to ignore Him altogether.

When Tyler's eyes fell upon Angie, she straightened up in her seat and gave him a sweet smile. And then his eyes moved on to Amy. She was fairly on the edge of her seat, so hungry to hear the Word preached that she was oblivious to the fact that this was the same man who'd held her so intimately the night before. When Tyler's gaze met her eyes, he saw the need there. A need for God's Word—a need to hear the truth reconfirmed, over and over. A woman after the heart of God.

Tyler pulled his eyes from her face before continuing. "Jesus said in John 14:6, 'I am the way, the truth, and the life: no man cometh unto the Father, but by me.' " Tyler paused to let the words sink in.

"Think about it, folks. Jesus made it real plain to the people of His time. But not only that, He made it simple and clear for the people of our time and for those whose time has not yet come. He's the only way. He's the only truth. He's the only life!"

The richness of his booming voice seemed to penetrate Amy, and she began to tremble from the very power of the hand of God upon this man. Tyler Andrews was clearly God's chosen servant. Several people around Amy murmured an "amen" or "hallelujah," but Amy remained fixed and silent. At that moment, she longed only to be nourished by the Word.

"You all have a purpose in life," Tyler was saying, "and if you aren't living that purpose, you're missing a very special pleasure that God has reserved just for you. Some of you know that purpose; others don't. Some of you share a common purpose, and others of you are fixed upon a solitary path. But that purpose, that way God has established for you, leads everyone in the same direction. It leads to His arms and to His very heart. It leads you home."

The silence that fell was nearly deafening. Amy felt a warmth spread through her body as she thought of walking home to God. Yes, that's exactly how it was to be a Christian. You had a definite direction and a path that was sure. Then at the end of your way, you got to go home to the Father—your very own Father.

"Do you know the way home?" Tyler asked the congregation. "Is your path clearly marked? It's a simple step to the right path, and your Heavenly Father is waiting at the other end of the road. He's waiting for you to come home."

Tyler offered salvation through Jesus to the residents of Deer Ridge, and Amy was deeply moved by the sight of grown men weeping in their acceptance. Women who'd struggled under the heavy burden of the loneliness and tension of prairie life gave up their loads and placed them at the feet of God.

After Tyler closed, the congregation lingered to sing and praise God. People gave their testimonies, stories Amy had never heard, stories which blessed her heart and gave her hope and reason to also praise God. This was why the calling of the faithful was so important. This was the fellowship of God's people that she had so sorely missed. These were her brothers and sisters, and how dear they were to her, how rich the love she felt for each one.

The gathering turned into a celebration again. After the services, leftovers from the night before were joined with a few new foods, and lunch was served. While they ate, the residents of Deer Ridge urged Tyler to return to their community as soon as possible.

"We've missed having a man of God in our town," the schoolmaster, Marvin Williams, said, shaking Tyler's hand. "When you come back, we'll use the schoolhouse for the services." There was a hearty confirmation from the crowd that had gathered around Tyler.

Tyler took out a small black book and pencil. "I can be here in three weeks on a Saturday. That's when I'll be back in this part of the district again."

"Then it's settled," someone called out from the group. The murmured affirmation was enough to confirm the entire matter.

As families began to pick up their belongings and wagons were repacked, Amy couldn't help but feel a sadness to see them go. Sometimes the isolation of the prairie wore heavy on her soul.

Rebuking herself for her attitude, Amy realized that she'd have little time to feel sorry for herself with all the work left to do to get ready for winter. Mentally, she began a list.

November was always butchering month. The men would be getting together to butcher the hogs. This was planned for the first true cold spell, and Amy knew that wouldn't be far off. Then there was the matter of the apple preserves, jellies, and butters that she still needed to put up before the apples went bad. Then they'd can some of the meat, smoke the rest, and make soap with the fat.

Amy moved around, picking up messes wherever they caught her eye, and continued to think of the things she needed to take care of in the weeks to come. She was so lost in thought that she hadn't been aware of Tyler's watchful eye.

When she looked up, though, her eyes immediately met his. He stood casually against a cottonwood tree, arms folded across his chest, a gleam in his eye. Amy glanced around, wondering where Angie was and why she wasn't captivating Tyler's attention.

A smile spread across Tyler's face, as if he could read her thoughts. She blushed and quickly lowered her eyes to the work at hand. Tyler, however, wouldn't allow her to get away that easy.

"I'd like to have a minute or two alone with you," he said, taking the dirty plates from her hand. He placed them back on the table and turned to her. "That is, if you don't object."

Amy felt her pulse quicken. "Of course I don't object," she answered. Her hands were trembling as she wiped them on her apron and allowed Tyler to direct her away from the crowded farmyard.

"I suppose you'll be leaving soon." She hated to say good-bye, but she knew it was inevitable.

"Yes," Tyler answered.

They walked past the new barn, and Amy realized that Tyler was leading her back to the orchard. As soon as they were well away from the noisy neighbors, he slipped his hand from Amy's arm and into her hand. They continued to walk in silence for several moments until they came to the spot where they'd kissed the night before.

"Amy." Tyler paused to look down into her face. "I have to say something to you before I go."

Amy felt her stomach tighten, and her legs began to tremble. "All right."

He abruptly dropped his hand and turned away from her, as if he had something to say that was painful and distasteful. Amy twisted her hands together, burdened by the thought that perhaps he wanted to reprimand her for the night before. She waited, head bowed and hands clenched, while Tyler seemed to contemplate something of extreme importance. When he finally turned back to her, Amy couldn't bring herself to face him. She kept her head lowered.

He reached out and gently lifted her face. When he did, he saw her cheeks were damp with tears. "What's this all about?" he whispered softly.

Amy choked back a sob, certain that God was going to tell her Tyler Andrews was not the man for her. "I, uh. . .I'm sorry," was all she could manage to say.

"Sorry? For what?"

Amy began to wring her hands, but Tyler took one of her small hands in each of his larger ones. "Have I offended you?" he questioned gently.

"Never!" Amy dared to look up into his compassionate eyes. The worried expression she saw there touched her heart, and silently she wished there was an easy way to apologize.

"Then what's the trouble?" Tyler asked.

"I was just afraid that I'd offended you," Amy finally managed to say.

Tyler chuckled softly. "And how, my dear Amy, do you imagine you might have accomplished this offense?"

Amy swallowed hard, unable to concentrate on anything but the touch of his hands on hers. "I thought maybe you brought me out here to talk about last night."

"I did."

"Then I was right. I'm really sorry about acting so loose with you." Amy licked her lips nervously. "I'm really not generally so forward. In fact, mother worried that I'd never take an interest in anyone. Honestly, that was my first kiss." Amy's honesty was telling Tyler a great deal more than she'd expected.

She continued to try to make amends. "Just please forgive me. I know you're a minister and all, but I guess I was just, well. . ." Her words drifted into silence. She really had no excuse for what she'd done.

"You think I brought you out here for a comeuppance? Is that it?" Tyler asked in a serious tone.

"Yes." Amy hung her head.

Tyler gently brushed his finger against her closed lips. "I'm responsible for what happened last night," he whispered. "Yes, it was a bit forward, and I, not you, am the one who should apologize." He broke into a broad smile. "But I am glad that I was the first one to kiss you, and," he added with a certainty that caused Amy to tremble anew, "I intend to be the only one who has that privilege."

Amy stared openmouthed for a moment, but then the real meaning of Tyler's words sank in. She smiled, realizing Tyler wasn't upset with her at all.

"You look so charming when you smile," he whispered, tracing the line of her jaw with his finger. "Then again, you look wonderful even when you aren't smiling."

Amy cocked her head slightly to one side and put her hands on her hips.

"Just what are you up to, Tyler Andrews?"

"I just wanted a chance to tell you a proper good-bye." He grinned.

"Good-bye, then," Amy said with a hint of laughter in her voice. She started to walk away, but Tyler reached out and pulled her back. Amy couldn't suppress a giggle. Her heart was suddenly light; Tyler was obviously as interested in her as she was in him.

"Oh no, you don't," he said. "You must be a more mischievous person than I thought. I thought Angie was the manipulative one, always teasing with people's feelings and such."

Amy stiffened and felt her muscles go rigid. Her smile was replaced with a look of serious intent. "I wasn't teasing with your feelings, Tyler."

"I know," he replied soberly and added, "and neither am I."

"Three weeks is a long time," Amy murmured.

Tyler took her face in his weathered hands and looked deeply into her eyes for what seemed an eternity. "Three weeks is just a heartbeat, Amy. Just a heartbeat."

Chapter 5

By the end of the first week, Amy had put up seven quarts of applesauce, fifteen quarts of apple preserves, and twenty-four pints of apple butter. She also helped her father and mother with the butchered hogs. She stuffed sausage casings until she thought she'd drop, and she helped her mother hang so much meat in the smokehouse that not a spot was left to put even one more ham. When all that was done, she and her mother canned enough meat and vegetables to bulge the pantry shelves.

The second week she missed Tyler more than she had the first, but Amy plunged into anything that kept her mind occupied and her hands busy. She ripped rags into strips and braided them into rugs, then worked in a fury through her mother's great pile of mending, much to the amazement of everyone. She counted the days down and then dissected the days into hours and counted those too.

Taking advantage of a clear but cold day, Amy was boiling a kettle of lye for soap when Angie came sashaying through the yard.

"Ma wants me to see if you need any help." Angie pushed out her lips in a pout.

Amy knew better than to solicit Angie's help. Angie was hopelessly clumsy at most every household task. Ma had said on more than one occasion that they'd all be lucky if Angie did move back east to a big city with servants.

"No, Angie. I was about to add the grease, and you know how careful I have to be with the amount. I'd rather just work alone."

"Good," Angie said with a sudden smile. "Do you realize that Tyler will be returning in little more than a week? I've asked Ma to help me make a new skirt. I needed one anyway, but I think it will be glorious to wear it for Tyler the first time."

Amy bit back an angry retort and poured grease into the caldron. She couldn't stand the way her sister was acting these days. Most all their lives the twins had been comfortably close—not like people thought twins ought to be, but close enough. They really had very little in common, but still a bond had tied them together. Now, though, that bond seemed to be fraying.

"And Betsey said she heard him telling Randy that he was quite taken with me," Angie said, dancing around the caldron to keep warm.

Amy's head snapped up. "What did you say?"

"I said, Tyler told Randy that he was quite taken with me," Angie repeated.

"He said that?" Amy nearly forgot to stir the soap.

"Well, he didn't use my name, but Betsey said that Randy was certain he meant me." Angie ignored the look of displeasure on Amy's face.

Amy wiped the perspiration from her brow and continued to work over the fire. She was certain Tyler hadn't meant Angie. How could he after the things he'd said? She wished she could ask Angie for more details without arousing suspicion, but Angie would pick up her interest in a flash. Besides, Amy reminded herself, Tyler had voiced his own interests, and they certainly did not include Angie.

Angie was growing bored with Amy's lack of attention. "I'm going back into the house. Ma will be here to help shortly," she finally said and turned to walk away. Then she stopped abruptly and came back to where Amy was working with the wooden tubs for cutting the soap. "I almost forgot, Ma said that we'll need about ten dozen bars of hard soap. She wants to give some to the Riggses since Anna Beth is due to have her baby any day. All the women in town have agreed to take care of something, and we get to provide soap."

Amy nodded and tried to mentally calculate how much rosin she'd need to add to make the soap set up and how much soft soap she'd have left over for their other house-cleaning needs. "Tell Ma by my best calculation that'll leave us with five barrels of house soap."

Angie nodded and went on her way, while Amy still worried about Angie's attraction to Tyler. She'd never really cared before about her sister's flirtatious ways, but now with Tyler in the picture, her sister grated on her nerves like fingernails on a slate. What if Angie ruined everything for her? What if Tyler ended up liking Angie's fun-loving nature more than Amy's quieter one? Maybe she should tell Angie that she cared for Tyler. Maybe then Angie would leave well enough alone.

Amy remembered then a verse from the Bible: "The Lord shall fight for you, and ye shall hold your peace." The words of Exodus 14:14 seemed to haunt Amy throughout the day, and by nightfall she was thoroughly convinced that she should hold her tongue and say nothing to her sister about her feelings for Tyler.

When only two days remained until Tyler's return, Angie made an announcement that stunned Amy into an even deeper silence. "I've decided that I'm going to marry Tyler."

Amy slapped the bread dough she'd been about to place into pans onto the floury board and began to knead it some more. She thrust her fingers deep into the soft mass again and again; Angie had stirred an anger inside her that Amy didn't want to acknowledge.

"I see," she managed to say at last.

Angie pulled up a chair, certain her sister would want to hear all the details. "His parents still live in Kansas City, and that's perfect for me. I could go and live with them, and maybe I could even convince Tyler to get a big church in the city and quit the circuit. I just know I'd love Kansas City."

"What about Tyler?" Amy found herself asking against her better judgment.

Angie laughed. For her, the situation was as fun as a good game of croquet. "Why, I'd love Tyler too. What did you think, silly goose, that I'd marry a man I didn't love? I think Tyler is one of the greatest men I've ever known, and I just know we'd be right for each other."

Just then Dora Carmichael entered the kitchen to find Amy nearly destroying the bread dough. "Amy, what in the world are you doing?"

Amy looked down at the sorry mess. "Sorry, Ma, I was a bit preoccupied."

Angie flashed Amy a look that demanded silence regarding their discussion, and Amy said nothing more.

"Mercy," Dora said as she pulled out a chair and sat down. "I'm feeling a bit peaked."

Amy placed a hand on her mother's forehead. "Ma, you've got a fever. You go on up to bed, and I'll bring you some sassafras tea." Amy pulled her mother to her feet.

"I hate to leave all this work to you girls." Dora knew full well the load would fall to Amy.

"Nonsense, Ma. You're sick, and you have to get to bed before the shakes set in. Do you think it's the ague?" Amy remembered her mother's bouts with the sickness.

"Can't rightly say that it feels that way, but time will tell. Better get the quinine anyway." Dora headed toward the stairs. "Angie, you make yourself helpful," she called over her shoulder.

Angie grimaced. "Ma must think I don't do a thing around here," she pouted, but Amy had no time to care. She had to tend to her mother, for she knew that prevention was crucial here on the frontier. If they were to have any chance at all of heading off a bad bout of ague or a serious fever of some other nature, Amy knew they'd need to work fast.

When Saturday morning arrived, Dora was still sick. She'd suffered with the shakes and fever for over two days, but Amy felt certain her mother was getting better now. The only problem, however, was that this was the day Tyler would preach in Deer Ridge, and Amy could not leave her mother alone.

When Charles came in to check on his wife, Amy assured her father that she'd see to everything. "Just go on to the services, Pa, and tell everyone hello for me." Amy tried not to sound too disappointed.

Angie had already put a deep dent in Amy's sense of well-being by prancing through the house wearing her new blue plaid wool skirt. Every other word was Tyler this and Tyler that and Amy thought she'd scream before the buckboard finally pulled down the drive for town, with Angie securely blanketed at their father's side.

When her mother was dozing comfortably, Amy went to stoke the fire in the stove. She couldn't stop the tears that flowed down her cheeks when she thought of missing Tyler's service. How cruel life was and how unfair.

She tried to pray, but her heart wasn't in it. Instead, she found herself whispering over and over, "Help me, Father, to understand. Help me to understand."

By midday, Dora was feeling well enough to sit in a chair for awhile and take some beef broth. Amy knew this was a good sign and tried to feel more cheerful. She tried to chat lightheartedly with her mother, but Dora could sense that something was amiss. Amy assured her mother that nothing was wrong.

When the hall clock chimed four, she helped Dora back to bed and went downstairs to tend to the other household needs. Soon, she heard first the wagon, then Angie's animated laughter. Amy was anxious to ask her father what Tyler had preached on and hurried out to the barn, meeting Angie halfway.

"How's Ma doing?" Angie's voice was filled with real concern. No one could accuse Angie of not loving her family, despite her absorption with her own self.

"Much better," Amy answered. "She's napping now, but she was up earlier and even ate a little."

Relief passed across Angie's face. "I think I'll peek in on her and then I'm going to bake some muffins," she said and walked past her sister toward the house.

"Why in the world would you want to bake muffins, Angie? You know you hate to cook."

Angie whirled on her heel and put her finger to her lips, indicating that Amy should be quiet. Amy cocked her head slightly and then realized that her father was talking to someone in the barn. Angie hurried into the house, while Amy made her way to the barn in time to find her father and Tyler sharing a hearty laugh.

Amy's mouth dropped open. She had no idea he would accompany her father back to the farm and she looked down at her dress, realizing that it was stained and smudged from the ashes in the fireplace. She knew she must look a fright, but Tyler smiled warmly at her as though he'd genuinely missed her.

"How's your Ma doing?" Charles asked Amy when he'd finished hanging up the tack.

"Much better, Pa. She's resting but wanted to see you when you got home." Amy tried to keep her voice even. In truth, her nerves were rattled, all because of the smiling giant who stood behind her father.

"You've done a good job by your Ma, Amy. I'm deeply grateful for your love of her," Charles said, reaching out to give his daughter a warm embrace. "I'm going to go see your Ma now. Tyler, if you need anything, I'm sure this little lady will be happy to accommodate you."

Amy blushed a deep scarlet, and when her father was out of earshot, Tyler let out a hearty laugh. "Well now," he said with a teasing tone, "how about accommodating me with the same kind of greeting your Pa got?"

He crossed the distance between them and lifted Amy into the air to whirl her in a circle. "My, but I've missed you. How in the world can you stand there so calm and quiet? I wanted to give out a yell when I saw you there."

Amy had to laugh. "Put me down, Tyler." She said his name with pleasure. How she loved this man! Now that she saw him again, she admitted the fact to herself. She chided herself that she might be feeling a mere childish crush, but her heart told her otherwise.

Tyler allowed her feet to touch the ground, and his hands left her waist. How he'd missed her! But had she missed him too? Tyler couldn't help but wonder. She seemed interested enough; she always responded positively to his touch, and she was honest to a fault. He knew he'd have only to ask her how she felt, and she'd no doubt spill her feelings. *But could she love me, could she really love me,* Tyler wondered to himself, *the way I love her?*

"So." Amy pulled away from Tyler's hold. Somehow she felt safer with some distance between them. "Why did you come to the farm today? I suppose Angie wouldn't have it any other way."

"Your sister does make it hard to say no," Tyler laughed.

Amy frowned, and Tyler couldn't help but notice the furrows that suddenly lined her forehead. She had been all laughing and smiles one minute, and now she looked sad, almost miserable. Tyler had no way of knowing that Amy was contemplating Angie's plans to marry him.

A scream came suddenly from the house. Tyler and Amy whirled and ran across the yard. Smoke was pouring out of the kitchen door, and Angie stood screaming for help.

"Something's burning!" she exclaimed, nearly hysterical. "Oh, Amy, do something!"

Tyler and Amy shared a brief look, then Amy moved past her sister into the smoke-filled kitchen. "Didn't you think to check the oven before you fired up the stove? I had your supper warming there, and now it's burned." Amy threw a look back at Angie. "Don't just stand there crying, Angie, open the windows." She looked past her sister to the towering man who stood behind her and added, "Tyler, would you go upstairs and tell Pa what happened? I'll take care of this." She took a potholder in one hand and covered her mouth with the other in order to ward off the smoke.

In a few minutes, Amy returned outside to deposit the hopelessly burned food. Angie soon joined her after opening the windows to let out the smoke. After the smoke had cleared, Amy went to work fixing them something else to eat, while Angie took the opportunity to court Tyler.

Amy tried not to feel angry about things, but it was difficult. She kept worrying that Angie was using Tyler and that somehow he would come to care more about her twin than about Amy. She attacked a ham, slicing off thick pieces to fry on the stove, all the while considering how frustrated she felt playing second fiddle to her more rambunctious sister.

When she had mixed up a batch of muffins, she started to relax a bit. If God wants you to have Tyler for a mate, she reminded herself, no amount of interference from Angie will matter.

Outside, Amy could hear the wind pick up and felt a chilly blast, cold enough to merit closing the windows. Placing the muffins securely into the oven and checking to make certain the temperature wasn't too hot, Amy went around the house closing the windows.

She had just walked into the front parlor when she heard Angie's voice. Apparently she had taken Tyler to the front porch swing in order to share her heart with him. "It must be wonderful to see so many different places, but don't you ever get lonely, Tyler?" Before Tyler could answer, Angie asked him a second question. "I mean, don't you ever think of getting married again?"

Amy felt her ire rising at her sister's brazen behavior. Angie was being totally improper, even if Amy had wondered the same things.

Tyler's laughter caught Amy's attention, however, and she found herself eavesdropping to hear the answer to Angie's questions. Did Tyler get lonely? Did he want another wife? Angie wasn't as patient as Amy, and she prodded Tyler to speak. "Well?"

"I do get lonely, Angie. These open prairie plains are enough to do that to any man. And, yes, I do plan to marry again."

"I see." Angie thought a moment and then said, "Why don't we go into the parlor, Tyler? I'm getting a chill out here, what with the sun going down."

Amy heard the creak of the porch swing as its occupants got up. She had no recourse but to leave the parlor windows open and go out the back way. She wasn't about to have Tyler or Angie catch her listening to their conversation.

She hurried to the kitchen and pulled the golden brown muffins from the oven. They were plump, just barely crisp on the tops, and Amy knew they were some of the finest she'd ever made. She hurriedly placed them on the table and added bowls of plum jelly and freshly churned butter. Then she turned her attention to the ham steaks and put some potatoes on to boil.

Soon the table began to take on the look of a proper supper, and Amy felt satisfied that she'd worked through her anger. She loved her sister and hated to think anything could come between them.

Amy was just about to call her family to supper when her father appeared in the kitchen doorway. Behind him were Tyler and Angie.

"It's getting mighty late, Tyler. Why don't you plan on staying the night with us?" Charles Carmichael invited.

"Oh, do say yes, Tyler," Angie gushed. "I do so want to hear more about Kansas City."

Amy glanced up, her soft brown eyes betraying her own desire for Tyler to stay. With a chuckle, Tyler sniffed the air. "How can I pass up the opportunity for such great cooking and company? My schedule's pretty tight, but I'd be happy to stay. Thank you."

"Well, it's settled then." Charles smiled. "I'll ready a room for you."

Chapter 6

Amy had more than her fill of Angie's fussing over Tyler. Angie hadn't really done anything improper, but Amy felt jealous of the control and confidence her twin boasted.

After clearing the supper dishes and putting the kitchen in order, Amy decided to retire to her room and leave Tyler to Angie's wiles. Going quietly to check on her mother first, Amy found that Dora was feeling much better. She gave her mother a dose of quinine and a drink of cold water and then sought out the sanctuary of her room. She was contemplating her feelings for Tyler and the promise she felt God had given her about waiting, when a knock sounded at her door.

"Yes?" Amy called.

"Amy, Carl Riggs is downstairs," said her father's voice from the other side of the door. Amy opened the door to reveal his worried face. "It's the baby, Amy. Carl thinks that Anna Beth is dying in childbirth. He needs you to come midwife 'cause Doc is out of town."

Amy smiled, trying to ease her father's worry. "Of course I'll go, Pa. But every man I've ever known thought his wife was dying in childbirth. It's probably nothing at all."

Charles placed his hand on his daughter's arm. "Carl says there's a great deal of blood, Amy."

Amy's expression changed immediately. "I'll get the birthing bag. Will you saddle the horse for me?"

"I can take you in the wagon if you like."

"No, there won't be time. I'll have to ride like all get out as it is." Amy pulled on a heavy coat she used for outdoor chores. "I'll be downstairs in just a minute."

Charles nodded and hurried to saddle the horse for his daughter.

Amy grabbed what her mother had dubbed "the birthing bag." It held the supplies the Carmichael women had found useful over the years during childbirth chores. Amy knew it had a collection of herbs for easing pain and bleeding, as well as the routine tools necessary for bringing new life into the world.

She fairly flew down the stairs and ran headlong into Tyler. She was startled to find his hands reaching out to steady her.

"I think I'd better come too," he said solemnly. "If the woman is truly dying, she may need me too."

Amy nodded, her eyes worried. "It doesn't sound good anytime there's a lot of bleeding." She glanced around the hallway for Mr. Riggs. "Where's Carl?"

"He went with your father to the barn. Come on, and I'll carry this for you." Tyler took the birthing bag.

Angie stood by the door, looking helpless and without purpose. Amy turned to her, realizing her discomfort. "Angie, you'll need to care for Ma. I gave her the quinine just a few minutes ago, but you might want to look in on her shortly." With those few words, Amy redeemed her sister's obvious lack of nursing skill. With that behind her, Amy lifted her skirts and ran for the barn.

The Riggses lived in a two-room soddy about two miles from the Carmichael farm. Amy was off her horse and flying through the soddy door before the men had even managed to dismount. "Anna Beth," she called as she entered the bedroom.

Amy was shocked by the blood-drenched sheets and bedding. Anna Beth had to be bleeding a great deal to have soaked through the quilted blankets that had been placed on top of her.

"Amy Carmichael," a weak voice called out, "is that you?"

"It is, Anna Beth. Ma's sick in bed, so I'm here to help you with the birthing. We need to get these wet things off you." Amy started removing the quilts as Tyler and Carl entered the room.

"Dear God," Carl moaned at the sight of the blood.

"Carl, I need you to get water boiling on the stove. Then I want you to cut me some strips from any extra sheets you have. It's really important. I know you'd rather be here with Anna Beth, but I need you out there." Amy motioned toward the kitchen. "Can you do it?"

Carl nodded, almost relieved to leave the sight of his dying wife. Tyler stood fast in the doorway. "What can I do to help?"

"Oh, Tyler, we need to get her out of all this blood. Can you lift her while I cut the nightgown away?" Amy pulled the last of the bloody quilts away.

"Just show me what to do."

Anna Beth's weak voice barely whimpered a protest as the contractions ripped through her abdomen. Amy could tell by the flow of blood that the birth of Anna Beth's child would also be the death of her.

"Anna Beth," Amy called to the barely conscious woman. Amy shook her head, for in truth Anna Beth was barely a woman. Anna Beth Riggs was only sixteen, but on the frontier adulthood came early, and birthing was the ultimate arrival of womanhood.

Amy wiped the woman's head with a cool cloth. She knew she could do very little for her. Amy's only real hope was to save the baby and pray that God would help the mother. But in order to accomplish even the delivery, Amy was going to have to pull the child from the birthing canal.

"Anna Beth, your baby is having a hard time being born. I need to help him," Amy said softly. She glanced up to meet Tyler's intense stare. He seemed concerned for Amy's well-being, as well as for the dying woman. Amy shook her head at him, for her own feelings could not possibly matter at a time like this.

"Amy, save my baby, please! Do whatever you must," Anna Beth whispered and then turned to Tyler. "Pastor, will you pray for us?"

"Of course, Anna Beth." Tyler took hold of the woman's hand. "Father, we lift up your daughter, Anna Beth. She's fought a hard fight, Lord, and we ask that You ease her burden and give her rest. We ask for the safe delivery of her child and Your healing touch upon both. Steady Amy's hands to do what she must, that we might all bring You glory. In Jesus' name, amen."

Amy felt warmed by the prayer. She placed a hand on the struggling woman and patted her reassuringly. "Anna Beth, you just rest a minute. I need to talk to Tyler and tell him what I need him to do. I'll just be right at the end of the bed, so you won't be alone." The woman nodded, and Amy motioned Tyler to the foot of the bed.

"This won't be easy, Tyler. I'll need you to hold her down and still. I'll have to reach up inside and pull the baby down. It's not a pretty sight, and it won't be pleasant work. Can you help me? I know Carl won't be able to stand it."

Tyler took hold of Amy's upper arms and held her firmly for a moment. "I'll stay by your side no matter the cost. You can count on me to be there for you." Tyler's words somehow seemed a promise of something more.

Amy nodded. "We must work fast, or we'll lose the baby too. It may already be too late."

Tyler and Amy took their places at the bedside, and Amy explained to Anna Beth that she had to hold as still as possible. "Tyler is going to help you, Anna Beth. It won't be very easy for you, and it's going to hurt." Anna Beth nodded and accepted Tyler's hands upon her shoulders.

Amy rolled up a washing cloth and gave it to Anna Beth. "Bite down on this." Obediently, the woman heeded her instructions.

At Tyler's nod, Amy went to work. For the first time since their arrival, Anna Beth screamed, and then she lost consciousness. Amy worked unsuccessfully to rotate the breech-positioned baby and finally managed to pull the child out, bottom first.

The baby boy was stillborn.

Amy glanced down at Anna Beth, who was just starting to stir. The blood was flowing even harder now, and Amy knew no amount of packing would ever keep Anna Beth alive.

Anna Beth's eyes fluttered open. She looked first to Tyler, then at Amy. Amy pulled out a soft flannel blanket that Anna Beth had made for her baby and wrapped the child lovingly in its folds. She talked gently to the baby, as if it were alive.

Tyler stood by in utter amazement, not certain what Amy was doing. He watched in silence as Amy washed the tiny, red face of the infant and smoothed back the downy black hair on his head.

"Anna Beth," Amy said as she brought the infant to his mother. "Your son is a might worried."

Anna Beth perked up at the words that she had a son. "What is it, Amy? Can I hold him?"

"Of course you can." Amy placed the small bundle in Anna Beth's arms. "Does he have a name?"

"Carl Jr.," Anna Beth whispered, trying feebly to stroke the baby softness of her son's cheek.

"Anna Beth," Amy whispered as she stroked the woman's hair, "Carl Jr. is afraid to be without you. He wants to know if it would be all right to go on to heaven and wait for you there."

Tears fell down Anna Beth's cheeks, but Amy's remained dry. Her eyes revealed her pain, however, and Tyler longed to take her away from the death scene in the Riggses' bedroom.

"That would be fine, little boy," Anna Beth murmured to the baby. She cupped his cheek with her hand. "Mama will be right there. You go on ahead. Mama's coming soon." She glanced up and smiled at Amy. Her eyes were filled with a sad knowledge, but also with peace. "Thank you, Amy." She pulled her son close and closed her eyes. She sighed, glad that the pain was over. And then Anna Beth joined her son in heaven.

For several moments, no one said a word. Amy continued to smooth Anna Beth's hair, unmindful of her action. Tyler reached out and took Amy's hand from across the bed.

" 'Yea, though I walk through the valley of the shadow of death, I will fear no evil: for thou art with me,' " he recited.

Amy looked up into Tyler's eyes, grateful for his comforting presence. This was only her second time to deal with death in childbirth, and it wasn't any easier than the last time.

"Thank you, Tyler," she said. Letting go of his hand, she squared her shoulders. "I'll get the bodies ready for burial. Will you tell Carl?"

"Of course."

Nearly two hours later, Amy and Tyler left the stunned Carl and rode back to the Carmichael farm. They'd both tried to convince Carl to come back with them, but he wanted to be near his family. He'd requested that Tyler perform the funeral the next day, and Tyler readily agreed.

At nearly two o'clock in the morning, they made their way across the open prairie. Amy was quieter than ever, and Tyler knew her mind was on Anna Beth and the baby.

"Childbirth is a risky thing," he said. "I sometimes wonder how a woman can bear a normal delivery, much less as much pain as that woman had to endure tonight."

"It's the joy of the child to come," Amy said absently. She smiled sadly. "I know I'm not a mother, but I've heard enough to tell their story. I think maybe it's the things that cost the most pain that are the things most worth having, the things that bring us the most joy."

"You believe that to be true about children?" Tyler's question seemed louder than he'd intended, somehow amplified by the vast expanse of the open plains.

"I suppose I do," Amy murmured.

"You only suppose? Don't you plan to have children, Amy?" After what they had witnessed tonight, he wouldn't blame her if she said no.

"Beyond today," Amy said, "I don't have any plans." She tried to laugh, making light of her lifelong doctrine.

"Maybe that's because you've never had the right person to plan with."

"Maybe," Amy admitted. "But I feel God wants me to just take a day at a time. I think it keeps me better focused than looking at the big picture."

"What do you mean?"

Amy pulled her coat collar around her throat. The night had turned cold, and a shadowy ring had formed around the moon. The air tasted like snow.

She could tell that Tyler's eyes were still on her. He was waiting for an answer to his question, and throwing caution to the wind, Amy decided to be honest with him. "Angie always has plans a plenty. She revels in them like some people glory in a large account of money. Angie knows what she wants in life, or at least she thinks she does. She wants to live in the city and have the world eat out of her hand. And believe me, Tyler," Amy paused to look at Tyler's silhouetted profile, "she's used to getting what she wants."

"But what about you?" Tyler asked, frustrated by this talk of Angie when Amy's feelings were what concerned him. "What do you want?"

Amy smiled. "I want whatever God wants for me. I'm not always very patient, but I know His promises are rich. I don't want to miss out on a single one of His gifts."

Tyler's mouth curved. "That's a bit evasive, don't you think?"

"Perhaps."

The lights from the front room of the Carmichael farm were now in view. Just a few more minutes and they would be home. Amy felt the weariness deep in her bones. She felt as if she could sleep forever.

Silently, she braved a glance at the man who rode by her side. She was surprised to find him watching her with an unreadable expression on his face. Amy offered a weak smile.

"I'm glad you were with me tonight," she whispered and turned toward the barn.

Tyler sat back thoughtfully in the saddle. *She is quite a woman, this Amy Carmichael,* he thought to himself. In his heart, he knew she was much more to him than just another member of his flock.

Chapter 7

Charles Carmichael took one look at their faces and then shook his head sadly. He took his daughter's hand in his. "You gave it your best, and God was with you, Child. You mustn't blame yourself."

Amy leaned against her father and sighed. "I know, Pa. We tried to talk Carl into coming home with us, but he didn't want to leave them."

Charles nodded. "I don't think I would've left your Ma either. He'll have to work through this in his own way. No one can grieve for you, Amy. No matter how many others shed their tears, the pain is still your own. We'll keep him in our prayers, and I'll ride over tomorrow and see how I can help."

"Thanks, Pa." Amy was too close to tears to say anything more.

With the horses cared for, Charles led them back to the house. "I'll show you where we put your things, Tyler." Tyler nodded and gave Amy a quick glance before following her father up the stairs.

"Don't forget to turn down the lamp, Amy," Charles called over his shoulder.

"I won't. Good night, Pa." Almost as an afterthought, she added, "Good night, Tyler."

In the empty downstairs, the silence fell around her like a cloak. Amy felt drained and cold in the aftermath of what had taken place. She went to the front room and stoked up the fire before easing her weight onto the sofa. Staring into the flames, she felt her composure crumble.

Tears fell down her cheeks until she was sobbing quietly into her hands. Why did bad things happen to people who loved God? It seemed so harsh. So unfair. Why, if a person put their trust in the Lord, didn't He relieve their suffering and keep them from the horrors of the world?

Without warning, Amy felt herself being swept to her feet. Tyler's warm fingers took her hands from her face. Staring up at him with red eyes, Amy's tears began anew.

"Hush, it will be all right." He pulled her into his arms. Amy laid her face against his broad chest and sobbed.

Her tears raged for several minutes, while Tyler waited patiently for her to regain control. He stroked her hair and whispered over and over in her ear that it would be all right. The words, though plain and simple, were a comfort, not only for what they said but because of who said them.

"I'm sorry," Amy murmured, finally feeling able to speak. Tyler's arms were still around her, and she wasn't ready yet to pull away from the safety she felt there.

"Don't be." Tyler pulled her with him to sit on the sofa. "You can't bear the pain for all the world."

"I try so hard to be strong. I want so much to be of some use to God," Amy whispered. "I guess sometimes I'm just not cut out for His work."

"Nonsense." Tyler's firmness surprised Amy. "God knows what each man and woman can bear. He knows how your heart breaks for those who suffer—but He knows too how He can use that pain in you to do the work of His kingdom. If your heart wasn't so tender, the Lord wouldn't be able to use you so much."

"It just seems so unfair." Amy allowed Tyler to pull her head against his shoulder. "There's a part of me that wants to cry out and ask why this thing has happened. There's even a part of me, I'm ashamed to say, that questions how God can allow folks to suffer so."

Tyler smiled, though Amy never saw it. Hadn't he himself had those questions, those doubts? "That's pretty normal, Amy. Everybody wonders at something, sometime."

"I don't know, Tyler." Amy pushed away to look him in the eye. "I feel so helpless. Life out here is so hard. Sometimes I wonder if Angie doesn't have the better idea—escape to the city and live a more protected life." Before Tyler could say a word, she continued, "But then, I see a sunrise across the open prairie or hear the coyotes when the moon is high, and I know I could never leave it. For all its unmerciful hardships, I'm at home here, and here I'll stay."

The words brought a flood of emotion to Tyler's heart. For a moment he'd feared she'd tell him she planned to move away with the first man who offered her an easier life in the big city. Hadn't he just listened to that very plan from her sister's lips earlier in the day? Now, he felt relieved by Amy's declaration. He was more certain than ever that Amy Carmichael was the woman God intended him to marry.

Amy started to wipe her face on her apron but then noticed the blood stains. "Christ spilled His blood for us," she whispered. "Although He was a man, I think He must have understood the pain a woman feels in childbirth. He knew what it was like to bleed, to feel pain, to die while giving life to another. So why do I feel so discouraged and sad? That should be enough."

"It is enough," Tyler agreed. "Enough for our salvation and reconciliation with God. But although our eternal life is safe and assured, that's no guarantee we won't run into pain and hardship in our everyday, physical life.

Like everyone, we must endure hardships and trials, just as Jesus said we would. Remember?"

Amy frowned for a moment, trying to remember what Scripture Tyler might be quoting. She shook her head when nothing came to mind and waited for Tyler to enlighten her.

"Jesus was preparing for His death when He told His disciples in John 16:33, 'In the world ye shall have tribulation: but be of good cheer; I have overcome the world.' He made it real clear that we will have trouble in this life of ours. But the good news is that He's already overcome anything the world can throw at us."

"That's all fine and well." Amy's lips pressed tight together. She sighed and then burst out, "Of course He overcame the world. He was God. He had the power and the ability to overcome anything He chose. I know it sounds selfish, but how does that help me? I still have to go through the trials and heartaches. How do I comfort myself or find ease from the pain when it's Jesus that has overcome, not me?"

Tyler read the agony in her eyes. He touched her face gently. "Because He overcame, we have the power to do the same. When we accepted Him as Savior, He came into our hearts. He became one with us, and now we share in His life. We share His suffering—but we also share His triumph. That's why He told us to be of good cheer. We're a part of Him now, and that means we've already overcome. We just don't realize it sometimes."

Amy stared thoughtfully into the fire for a moment before nodding her head. "Of course," she whispered. "That makes so much sense. How could I have thought He was being a braggart, when He was simply trying to bolster the disciples' courage?"

Tyler nodded. "That's right, Amy. He knew we wouldn't be able to bear the load alone. When He died on the cross, He bore the pain of the entire world. He knew all about Anna Beth and her little boy. And He knew how you would hurt tonight. He's already taken that load onto Himself. All you have to do now is let Him have it. You have to let go of the pain you're feeling." Tyler smiled. "It's a funny thing, but sometimes it's almost harder to trust God with the hard things in our life than it is to trust Him with the happier things. Believe me, I know."

Amy smiled and sat back against the sofa. "You make it so easy to understand. I think that's why I've missed having church and a regular minister so much. I read the Word every day, but so often its meaning eludes me. Thank you for being patient with me, Tyler."

"I think, Amy, that when it comes to you," Tyler reached for her hand, "that I have an infinite amount of patience." He looked into her face. "Maybe we could pray about this together."

"Yes, please." Sudden joy leapt up from the depths of Amy's pain. How often she had dreamed of a man with whom she could pray about the sorrows and troubles of the day. A man who truly sought God's heart for the hidden answers and meanings to life's questions.

They prayed together silently, and then each shared their petitions aloud. Amy felt as though a revival of sorts was taking place just for them. For hours, in spite of the fact that dawn was fast approaching, they sat and prayed, talking about the mercies of God and their hope for the future.

Finally, Amy couldn't stifle a yawn, and Tyler pulled her to her feet. "Come on, Sleepyhead. You've had a busy night, and you'd best get some sleep. From the sounds of the wind outside, I wouldn't be surprised to find a foot of snow on the ground by morning."

Amy had to laugh as she cast a suspicious glance at the mantel clock. "It's going to have to snow mighty hard and fast in order to meet that demand. After all, it's nearly morning now."

Tyler chuckled and pulled her along with him toward the stairs. "It could snow three feet by daylight, and I wouldn't care one bit. I think I might rather enjoy being snowed in with you, Amy Carmichael."

Tyler's words very nearly came true. First light greeted the Carmichael farm with a raging blizzard that dumped snow on top of snow, burying everything in a blanket of white.

Dora was up and feeling better when Charles returned from the barn and morning chores. "My," she exclaimed, brushing snow off his shoulders, "but you look frozen clear through!"

"It's a bad one out there." Charles shook the worst of the snow from his coat before hanging it up on the peg by the back door.

Angie burst into the kitchen all smiles and sunshine. "Good morning." She nearly sang the words. Glancing around for Tyler and Amy, she suddenly frowned. "Where is everybody?"

"Well, part of us are right here," Dora chided her daughter. "As for your sister and the pastor, I don't know."

"Well, I do." Charles stepped out of his wet boots. "They didn't get back until late last night. Anna Beth and the baby died."

"Oh no, Charles." Dora's stricken expression matched her husband's heavy heart. "Poor Carl. And poor Amy, having to deal with that alone. I should have been with her."

"She was pretty upset," Charles agreed, "but you know Amy. She held her ground. I wouldn't bother to wake up either one of them." He turned his eyes meaningfully toward Angie. "They need their rest."

Angie's lower lip threatened to quiver into a pout, but noting her father's stern expression, she managed to shrug her shoulders and leave well enough alone. Dora quickly put her daughter to work making bread, lest Angie change her mind and go about some type of noisy task. Angie was unhappy about the arrangement, but in light of her father's presence, she did as she was told.

Much to her surprise and pleasure, Angie found her patience rewarded when Tyler popped his head into the kitchen doorway nearly an hour later.

"Smells mighty good in here," he said with a grin toward Dora.

Dora was pushing bacon around the frying pan and looked up with a smile. "I thought you might be hungry. We've already eaten so you just make yourself comfortable at the table and tell me what you'd like to eat."

Tyler did as he was told and soon found Angie at his side. "Would you like some coffee?" she asked sweetly, eager to please.

"Sure would," he replied.

Dora barely managed to find out what Tyler wanted to eat, because Angie immediately monopolized him. Dora thought privately that their conversation seemed more like an interrogation than a conversation, with Angie in the role of interrogator.

At last Angie fell silent and sat looking dreamily at the man while he shoveled in forkfuls of Dora's scrambled eggs and potatoes. He squirmed a little under her steady stare, wishing she would turn her eyes somewhere else, but he didn't want to hurt her feelings. When she began her interrogation again, he tried to answer her questions when he could; if he didn't know the answer, she seemed just as content to move on to yet another subject.

At last, with hearty praise for Dora's fine cooking, Tyler moved from the kitchen. He allowed Angie to lead him to the front room where he'd spent most of the night talking to Amy. He couldn't help but think of her when Angie spread out her red calico skirt on the sofa and beckoned Tyler to join her there.

Leaning against the mantel, Tyler laughed. "I swear, Miss Angie, you have more energy than a woman ought to have."

Angie giggled and took his words as a compliment. "I do believe," she said, "that it's the company of one particular circuit rider that brings out the best in me."

This was the comment that a bleary-eyed Amy overheard from the doorway. She had thought to greet them both, but instead she backed away. Going to the kitchen, Amy found her mother taking fresh baked loaves of golden bread from their tins.

"Morning, Ma."

"Amy!" Dora set the pans aside. She hurried to her daughter's side and embraced her. "I'm so sorry about Anna Beth. I wish I could've been there to keep you from bearing that alone."

"I wasn't alone," Amy replied softly. "But I wish you'd been there too. I keep thinking that maybe it was my lack of experience that kept me from saving them."

Dora pulled back with a shake of her head. "No. You have no power over life and death, Daughter. Only God has that. Besides, you've helped in more births than I can even name. Sometimes, no matter how skilled we might be, there's just nothing we can do. Anna Beth was a mere girl. Obviously, the whole thing was too much for her. We have to trust she and her baby are both in God's hands."

Amy nodded. "Tyler stayed with me and helped. I was sure glad he was there. He helped me afterwards too."

"Oh?" Dora felt hope flicker once again. She noticed the underlying softness to Amy's voice.

Amy nodded. "We stayed up and talked quite awhile last night. Pa had shown Tyler to his room, while I decided to sit a spell and think on things. Pretty soon, though, I was blubbering like a baby—and Tyler was there to comfort me."

Dora hid her smile. "I see."

"Oh, Ma." Amy had a look in her eyes that left her mother no doubt as to her daughter's heart. "The best part was that he knew just what to say and then he prayed with me. Not just a short little prayer, but he really prayed. We must've talked to God for over an hour before we got it all said."

Dora squeezed Amy's shoulder and offered her a chair. Saying nothing, the two women sat down at the table, and Dora reached out her hand to take Amy's. Through the hallway drifted Angie's laughter, causing a frown to form on Amy's lips. Glancing up at her mother, Amy suddenly felt a kindred spirit with the woman who'd given her life. Dora smiled sympathetically, yet it was something more than just that.

"You know, don't you?" Amy questioned. "You know what I'm feeling inside."

Dora nodded. "I've waited long enough to see you feel it. I knew when love came to you, it would come like a rushing wind that knocked you off your feet and took away your breath."

"That's just how it is too," Amy agreed. She found comfort in the fact that her mother knew her so well. Angie's boisterous laugh sounded again, and Dora patted Amy's hand.

"Don't give it a second thought," she reassured. "If God is for you, who can be against you?"

Amy nodded, finding comfort in her mother's words.

Hours later, the storm still showed no signs of abating. Tyler donned heavy boots and clothes to help Charles with the chores that wouldn't keep, while the womenfolk worked to keep the house warm and made sure that hot food and coffee were waiting.

Amy tried not to feel angry when Angie managed to control Tyler's time. She even bit back an angry remark when Angie set the table for dinner and placed Tyler between herself and Charles.

But by the time dinner was over, Amy had more than enough of Angie's brazen behavior and blatant designs. After washing the dishes, Amy managed to slip unnoticed to the back parlor. She sat down and considered her feelings in silence.

"I don't mean to be jealous, Lord. It's just that I can't hold a candle to my sister. I wish I could have more confidence like Angie, but it's just not me," she whispered aloud.

No, it isn't you, a voice seemed to whisper to her heart. Amy sat back and closed her eyes. Was God trying to speak to her? She relaxed for a moment, listening to the gentle silence, before feeling the need to say more. "Forgive me, Father. I'm sorry for being so mean tempered. Forgive me." She felt a peace spread throughout her body. She wasn't Angie, and she'd never be as lively and vivacious as her sister, but that didn't mean God hadn't given her qualities of merit that were all her own—qualities that she already knew attracted Tyler.

"All right, Father." She folded her hands in her lap. "What do I do now?"

Chapter 8

"Are you avoiding me?"

Amy's head snapped up, surprised that Tyler had managed to get away from Angie long enough to seek her out. She tried to choose her words carefully before replying.

"No," she answered finally. "I just figured your attention was pretty well taken." She bit her lip, immediately wishing that she'd said something else.

"Your sister does have a way about her, doesn't she?" He laughed and came closer to where Amy sat.

"She always has," Amy replied rather flippantly. The anger was starting to surface again, making her feel she was a miserable failure after all her efforts to put her bad feelings aside.

Tyler suddenly became aware of Amy's feelings. She was obviously put out with the way Angie had monopolized his time. Why hadn't he seen it before? Reaching out, he pulled Amy to her feet and encircled her in his arms.

"Don't you know yet?" he whispered.

"Know what?" Amy's voice was a bit breathless. His actions had taken her by surprise.

"It's you I care about, not Angie. It's you who's captured my heart." Tyler's eyes pierced Amy's facade of strength. Her mouth formed an "O," but no sound escaped her lips. The sheepish curl of Tyler's lips widened into a full-fledged grin. "That's what I like best about you, Amy. You're unassuming and so innocent. You have no idea what you do to me. Why, just one look at those big brown eyes and my heart does flip-flops inside. I love you, Amy."

Amy was grateful for the arms that held her. Her knees felt like jelly, and she was certain that she swayed noticeably at Tyler's declaration. "I think I'd better sit down," she said weakly.

Tyler stared at her with concern. "Did I say something wrong?" His worried expression steadied Amy's legs.

"No," she managed to say, her voice so hoarse that it sounded nothing like normal. "You said something very right."

"I had hoped you felt the same way. I know we're moving things pretty fast, but I feel like we've lived a lifetime of experiences in the few short times we've spent together. After last night," Tyler sighed, "after last night, I knew. I knew without a doubt that I loved you."

He'd said it again. Amy felt a wash of excitement and wonder flood over her. "I still think I'd like to sit down," she whispered, and with a smile that lit up his eyes, Tyler assisted her back into the chair.

Amy was elated by Tyler's words, but in the back of her mind a nagging doubt crept in to spoil the perfect picture. Angie! Tyler immediately noticed the change in Amy and pulled up a chair to sit directly in front of her. "You might as well tell me what's on your mind, 'cause I'm not going away until you do."

Amy grimaced and nodded. "All right," she said with a sigh. "It's Angie. She fancies that you're the one man who can get her away from small-town life. She's set her cap for you, I'm afraid, and a more determined force you will never have to reckon with."

Tyler rubbed his chin thoughtfully and shrugged his shoulders. "I'm honored that she thinks so highly of me, but it doesn't matter. She's a nice girl, and I realize you look a great deal alike, some might even say identical, although I've noticed some differences. Anyway, Angie's not for me. I've no desire to live in the city. I've done that, and it chokes the life out of me."

"But don't you see," Amy pleaded, "this thing will be between us. I love my sister, and I don't want to hurt her. She'll think I worked against her, knowing what she had in mind for you, and that I stole you away from her. I can't have that kind of rivalry between us. I've fought too long and hard to avoid it."

"Is that why you don't have any other suitors?" Tyler asked softly.

"Yes, I suppose it is. The one man in this town who's paid me the slightest attention has only done so because his brothers forbid him to chase after Angie. You see, they both want her for themselves and refuse to have another rival for her attention." Amy couldn't believe she was sharing all of this with Tyler.

"I just don't want her hurt, Tyler," she stressed. "Angie's just being Angie, and she really isn't trying to hurt me. She's just so used to me backing away from her conquests and leaving her to her designs."

"And what about this time?" Tyler asked with a raised brow. His face held a look of amusement that eased Amy's tension.

"This time, I'm not backing away," she replied in a whisper.

"Good," Tyler countered, "because I wouldn't let you if you tried." He reached out to hold her hand. "I can deal with Angie."

"How, without hurting her and making this an issue between sisters?"

"Leave it to me," he answered lightly. "I've had to deal with hundreds of mamas and their daughters. All who have set their strategies toward seeing me married. I've fought them off this long; I reckon I can handle one very lively Angela Carmichael."

Amy shook her head with a sadness in her eyes. "I don't think it will be that simple, Tyler. She's got a tender heart, in spite of her outward appearance of invincibility."

"Trust me, Amy. I will work this thing out so that it's Angie herself who loses interest. She'll cast me aside quick enough when she learns that I've no intention of living in the city or even moving close to one. When I make it clear that the open Kansas prairies are my home, she'll no doubt find a way to ease herself away from me."

Amy's face lit up. For the first time since this problem developed, she saw a way around having to battle with Angie for Tyler. "It just might work," she smiled.

"Trust me," Tyler said with a wink, "it'll work."

Amy made herself scarce for the rest of the day so that Tyler would have time to speak with Angie. Because of the storm's relentless tirade, the entire family was trapped inside the house through the whole long day; Tyler would surely have plenty of opportunities to get his message across to Angie.

When supper time came, Amy joined her mother in the kitchen to help prepare the meal. Angie wandered in, seeming rather dejected, and Amy felt certain that Tyler had made his plans known to her.

"Angie, you can set the table while Amy cuts this bread," Dora said, noticing that Angie was just moving about aimlessly.

Angie did as she was told, setting the plates absentmindedly on the red-checkered tablecloth they used for everyday. Soon, Dora was calling the men to supper, and Amy found herself privileged to sit beside Tyler, while Angie quietly ate her dinner beside their mother. Apparently, Tyler's plan had worked.

After supper, everyone gathered in the front parlor to talk and share stories of days gone by. Charles and Tyler shared a game of checkers, while Amy and Dora worked on quilt blocks. Angie excused herself to her room, much to everyone's surprise. Everyone except Amy, who knew that her sister had seen her dreams defeated in one swift blow. Her heart ached for her, and silently Amy prayed that God would send a man for Angie. One who would understand her needs and love her.

The wind died down around eight-thirty, and Amy found herself so tired that she too decided to excuse herself. Dora put aside her sewing and, with a nod to her husband, expressed her desire to also retire.

Charles stood and put a loving arm around his wife. "It's been a real joy having you here, Tyler. I'd like nothing better than if we could find a way to keep you on full time as our parson. I intend to speak to the townsfolk and see if they aren't of the same mind. Do you suppose you might be interested in settling down in a tiny town like Deer Ridge?"

Tyler cast a quick glance at Amy and then smiled broadly at Charles and Dora. "I might be persuaded."

Charles laughed. "Somehow I thought you might be willing to consider it." With that, he and Dora went upstairs, leaving Amy and Tyler to follow.

Amy took one of the oil lamps and handed it to Tyler. "In case you want to read," she said and moved to extinguish the other lamps.

With nothing more than the soft glow from the fireplace and the lamp which Tyler held, Amy turned to study him for a moment. "Thank you," she finally said. "Thank you for caring and helping Angie through this."

Tyler moved forward and put an arm around Amy's shoulders. "I simply told her the truth," he answered. "I told her my heart could never be in the city."

Amy smiled knowingly and climbed the stairs with Tyler at her side. At the top, they stood for a moment before Tyler placed a brief kiss on Amy's mouth.

Amy felt a happiness like she'd never known, and her expression clearly revealed her heart. Without words, she went to her room, while Tyler moved in the opposite direction to the guest room.

"Thank You, God," she whispered against her closed bedroom door. She hugged her arms to her breasts and smiled, knowing that tonight's dreams would be the sweetest of all.

By morning the weather had cleared, leaving pale blue skies and sunshine against the snow-white prairie fields. Huge drifts of snow had piled up against the house, barn, and fences. Anything that stood out as an obstacle to the blowing snow found itself insulated in white.

Tyler shared morning devotions with the Carmichaels before announcing his departure. Amy was happy to see that Angie was acting more like herself and smiled when her sister spoke of the Anderson brothers for the first time in weeks. Tyler was happy to see the recovery of Angie's lively spirit as well. He'd felt confident that he could disinterest Angie in him as husband material, but like Amy, he was worried that she might somehow place the problem between her and her sister.

"When will you be back our way?" Charles asked, while Dora began clearing the breakfast dishes from the table.

"I plan to spend Christmas here," Tyler replied. "That is, if you think folks around here will approve."

Charles laughed. "I think they'll more than approve. It'll be our first

Christmas with a real parson in charge. I'll see to it that plans get made for a real celebration. We'll have the kids put on a play or something, and the ladies can all make those goodies we enjoy so much."

"I'll look forward to it then," Tyler said enthusiastically.

"Where are you headed after you leave here?" Dora asked. "I'd be happy to pack you some food for the road."

"I'd appreciate that, Dora. I promised to stop by the Riggses' place for the funeral. With this snow, I doubt many folks will be able to get away, and it will be difficult at best to make a proper grave. I want to offer Carl as much help as I can."

"Of course," Dora replied. "I don't imagine we'll be able to make the funeral." She glanced up to see her husband shake his head.

"I don't see how," Charles agreed. "I'm still not sure what kind of damage the storm has done. If we can, we'll go over later on and see what kind of help we can offer."

Amy remained silent throughout the exchange. She hated the idea of Tyler leaving, and yet what else could he do? That was his job, and if she were to marry him, it would be a big part of her life as well.

The thought of marriage to Tyler made Amy smile, and without her realizing, the attention of everyone in the room turned toward her.

"Looks like Amy's already a world away," Charles laughed.

Dora nudged her husband good-naturedly. "Now, leave her be, Pa. She's just daydreamin'."

Amy blushed and lowered her head. No doubt they all knew full well what she was thinking about. Angie was the only one who seemed not to notice.

"Well, I for one will be glad when winter is over," Angie declared, moving to wash the dishes.

"Winter's just set in, Angie," her father mused. "You'd best just set your mind for a few more months of cold."

Tyler laughed and got to his feet. "I'd best get a move on."

Dora set about to make sandwiches for him to take along, while Amy packed some gingersnaps and sugar cookies. She was glad for some task to occupy her hands; otherwise, she feared she'd just sit and twist them until everyone knew she was upset and asked her why. Surprised by the flood of emotions that threatened to run out of control, she silently prayed that she'd not cry when Tyler departed.

When the moment did arrive, everyone bid Tyler farewell and managed to inconspicuously disappear, leaving Amy and Tyler alone.

"I'll miss you," Tyler said, pulling on his heavy coat. Amy nodded, afraid to speak. She lifted her eyes to his and saw the love shining clearly. Mindless of proper manners, Amy threw herself into Tyler's arms and clung tightly to his broad frame.

"It won't be that long," Tyler whispered against her buried face. "And when I come back, I intend to ask you something quite important, so you'd best be ready to give me an answer."

Amy lifted her face to his and nodded. "I'll be ready," she replied. "I promise."

Chapter 9

Amy felt a giddy anticipation in the days that followed Tyler's departure. She missed him terribly, yet she felt as though she shared a private secret with him. Over and over, she remembered his words to her when they said good-bye, and she was certain that when he returned, he would ask her to marry him.

The snow kept them homebound for five days, but then a warm southerly breeze blew in and melted most of the drifts. Soon, soggy brown puddles were all that remained. During the thaw, the twins' older brother Randy arrived to announce the birth of his new son.

"He's a big one, for sure," Randy boasted. "I measured him myself and he's pert near twenty-three inches long."

"My," Dora remarked in amazement, "he is good-sized."

"Congratulations, Son." Charles gave Randy a hearty slap on his back. "How's Betsey doing?"

"She's fine. Tired, but fine. Doc was there this morning and said she needs to get plenty of rest. Other than that, he thinks both of them are good and strong."

"I'd be happy to come keep house and tend the children," Amy offered her brother.

"I was kind of hoping you might say that," Randy said with a smile. "I know it'd be a real peace of mind to Betsey. She doesn't trust me in her kitchen."

At this the family laughed. Even Angie teased him good-naturedly, "You must take after me."

"Naw," Randy teased right back. "Nobody is as bad as you are in the kitchen. At least I can make coffee."

Amy smiled, remembering the day Angie had filled the house with smoke when she had tried to impress Tyler with her culinary skills.

"He's got you on that one, Angie," Charles laughed. Then turning to Amy, he said, "You'd best get your things together."

Amy nodded and hurried upstairs. She was grateful for the job that awaited her, knowing that it would keep her mind occupied until Tyler returned.

She calculated the days left until his return, then she smiled again. Maybe she'd even be married before the year was out! The idea warmed her like a toasty quilt. She hugged her arms around herself, imagining what Tyler would say when he saw her again, then she laughed out loud at herself when she realized what she was doing.

"I'm always telling folks to take one day at a time—but ever since Tyler's come into my life, it's all I can do to keep from dreaming away my days," she said aloud. "Maybe Tyler was right. Maybe I found it easy to keep from planning beyond today, because I had no one to plan for or with."

She threw the things she would need at Randy's house into a a worn carpet bag. Then she headed downstairs to join her brother. She determined in her mind to take life one day at a time, just as she always had before she met Tyler, but her heart was already rebelling at the idea.

In the weeks that followed, Amy found that caring for Betsey and the baby was the easy part of her responsibilities. The hard part was keeping Charlie, Petey, and Dolly amused. Blustery winter weather confined them to the house, and out of boredom they insisted on constant attention.

Amy tried to fuss over each one of them. She took great joy in getting to know the newest Carmichael, baby Joseph, whom everyone already called Joey, but she tried to remember that the needs of the other children were just as important as the baby's. Dolly, used to being the youngest, had her nose slightly out of joint when it came to sharing attention with her baby brother. She didn't want to give up without a fight the important job of being the family baby.

Amy soothed her niece by telling her it would be far more fun to help with Joey than to cry over the attention he got. Dolly was a bit young to understand logical reasoning, but Amy found a sugar cookie usually helped matters greatly.

Petey and Charlie were intrigued with the ruddy-faced bundle, but the attraction wore off quickly. Soon they were begging to bundle up and go outside, then they tracked in mud and snow from their outdoor adventures.

Before long, Betsey was up and around, and the need for Amy to stay lessened with each passing day. Finally, when Christmas was only a week away, Amy bid them good-bye and headed home.

"Only a week," she told the horse on their journey to the Carmichael farm. "Only one more week and Tyler will be back."

The horse flicked his ears and plodded faithfully along the soggy prairie. Amy gazed out across the fields and sighed. The land was so open here, so vast and empty, yet life was only asleep; Amy knew when spring arrived the prairie would come to life once again.

Even the gray skies overhead could not dampen her spirits, and Amy found herself humming a tune. She loved thinking about a life with Tyler.

She wondered where they would live and whether she would travel with her husband on his circuit. *Most circuit riders ride alone,* she thought and frowned at the lengthy separations their wives must know.

Maybe Pa will talk the town folks into giving Tyler a job right here, she thought. *Especially if we're married.* The idea pacified her concerns, and Amy's thoughts turned to what she'd do once she arrived home.

She rode into the yard just before noon and found an animated Angie awaiting her. They walked together to the barn, but when Amy prepared to unsaddle her horse, Angie reached out to stop her.

"I was hoping you'd ride into town with me," Angie said. "I haven't done much Christmas shopping, and now there's only a few days left."

Amy froze, realizing that she'd not prepared anything for Tyler in the way of a Christmas gift. What should she do for him? Should she make something or purchase some trinket at Smith's General Store? Her mind raced with ideas, totally blocking out Angie's ramblings.

"You aren't listening to me!" Angie exclaimed at last.

Amy stroked the horse's mane and sighed. "Sorry, Angie. I was just thinking about what you'd said. I managed to make something for Ma before I left, but I don't have a thing for Pa or you." She carefully didn't bring Tyler into the conversation.

"Then you'll go with me?" Angie asked hopefully.

"Sure." Amy smiled. "Let me get my money and a bite to eat, and I'll be ready."

Angie flew into the house to tell their mother what the girls had planned. Angie even made a sandwich for Amy in order to hurry things along.

The girls rode side by side, saying little until they neared the small town of Deer Ridge. To call it a town seemed a bit of a boast, but it was all they had, and Amy loved it. The handful of buildings made up what folks affectionately called "Main Street." On one side stood the general store and bank, along with several smaller establishments, including the barber shop and Doc Taggert's place. On the opposite side of the street was Nathan Gallagher's law office, the livery stables, and blacksmith's shop, and farther down from this was the new school building. Opposite the school building at the other end of town was the hotel/boardinghouse.

Smith's General Store was the main attraction for the small community, however. Folks gathered here to discuss the weather and crops, new babies and deaths, and whatever else came to mind. Socializing wasn't an everyday occurrence; it was a luxury, and if one had to make the trip into town, he or she had the responsibility of bringing back all the news that bore repeating.

Tying their horses to the hitching post, Amy and Angie pulled their coats closer as a blast of frigid prairie wind pushed them along. "Pa says it's going to snow tonight for sure," Angie said with a shiver.

"He's usually right about those things," Amy replied and added, "so we'd best get to it and get back home."

Angie paused for a moment outside the clapboard storefront. "Uh, Amy," she said hesitantly.

Amy turned and eyed her sister suspiciously. "What are you up to, Angie?"

"Nothing," Angie hedged. "It's just that I saw Nathan go into his office across the way, and I thought, I mean. . ."

"Go on and see him." Amy shook her head. "You and I neither one will enjoy this trip if you don't attend to all of your beaus. I'm sure Ed Anderson will be slighted if you don't make the rounds to the bank as well."

Angie laughed and gave her head a toss. "I don't care if he is. He hasn't been to see me in over a week."

"And Nathan has?" Amy teased.

"Well, no," Angie admitted. "But Nathan's practice keeps him busy."

Amy had to laugh at the idea of an abundance of law work in Deer Ridge. "The idea of a railroad spur coming this way is the only thing that keeps Nathan Gallagher busy. Tell them all hello for me," Amy replied. She left Angie contemplating her words.

Inside the store, the potbellied stove was nearly glowing red from the hearty fire that Jeremy Smith had built to keep his customers warm. Several of the community's prominent members stood discussing important matters when Amy entered. The gentlemen tipped their hats, and the only other woman, Mrs. Smith, came quickly to Amy's side.

"Land sakes, Child, whatever are you doing out on a day like this? Come get warmed up." The gray-headed woman pushed her way through the men, dragging Amy with her to the stove.

"Angie and I needed to do a bit of last-minute shopping. You know," Amy whispered in the woman's ear, "for Christmas."

Betty Smith nodded and shared the excitement of the moment with Amy. "Who are you still shopping for?"

"Pa and Angie," she said right away, and then with a quick glance around her to make certain no one could overhear, she added, "and the new pastor."

Betty smiled, revealing two missing teeth. "I heard tell he'd spent a deal of time out your way. Is there something I should know about you and him?"

Amy blushed and lowered her head. "No, but when there is, I'll let you know."

"Why, Amy Carmichael!" the woman exclaimed a bit louder than she'd intended. Ears around them perked up, so Betty pulled Amy away from the crowd and toward the back of the store. "I'll bet your ma's plumb tickled pink. She's always a frettin' that you'd never find anyone to settle down with."

Amy felt her face grow even more flushed. Did everybody have to know her business? Seeing her discomfort, Betty began showing Amy some of the trinkets they'd stocked with Christmas in mind.

"That silver mirror is pretty," Amy said and immediately thought of Angie's love of primping. "I'd imagine my sister would like that very much."

"Where is Angie?" Betty asked, setting the mirror aside.

"Oh, you know Angie. She had to make the rounds."

Betty laughed, because she did know Angie and her love of flirting with half the town.

Amy continued to shop for the next half hour or so before finally settling on the mirror for Angie and a brass-handled jackknife for her father. Buying a gift for Tyler proved to be an easy task when Amy spied the newest collection of books. Tyler had mentioned his love of reading, and with this in mind, Amy quickly sorted through the stack and picked out Dickens' *A Tale of Two Cities.*

Thumbing through the book, Amy remembered her father telling about a series of public readings which Charles Dickens had performed in America. The man had taken the country by storm, and his works were quite popular.

Tucking the book under her arm, Amy glanced around to see if Angie had returned. Most of the other customers had filtered out, and now, with the exception of the self-appointed Mayor Osborne who was in a heated argument with Jeremy Smith, the store was empty.

"Betty?" Amy called into the back room where she'd seen Betty take her other purchases.

The woman emerged with two brightly wrapped packages. "I thought this might dress them up a bit," she said proudly. "And don't be fretting that I'll charge you, 'cause I won't. I just happened to have it left over from my own things."

"Oh, Betty, it's wonderful. Thank you!" Amy held out Tyler's book. "I'm going to take this as well. I'd be happy to pay for it to be wrapped."

"This for the pastor?" Betty asked with a grin. Amy nodded and waited while the woman disappeared into the back to wrap the book.

When she'd paid for her things and Angie still had not appeared, Amy could do nothing but try and find her sister. She tucked her gifts into one of the saddle bags, then made her way across the street to Nathan Gallagher's office.

Opening the door to the law office, Amy peeked in. No one was in the outer room, and she saw no sign that Angie had ever been there. Amy started to step out when she heard voices coming from the other room. Thinking that Nathan and Angie were talking in his office, Amy quietly moved to the door and started to knock.

Her hand was nearly against the wood when she heard Nathan's voice bellow, "I don't care what you think! We'll take the bank money on Christmas morning when that fool of a pastor is teaching the town about charity and love."

Amy's heart pounded harder, and she froze in place. Her hand was still lifted to knock, but for some reason she couldn't bring herself to move.

"Gallagher, you're a hard man," a voice commented. "I guess I'll take my share and be on my way. You can do this job on your own."

"Have it your way, but go out the back door. I don't want anyone seeing you." Nathan's voice was clearly agitated. "Oh, and here." Amy heard a clinking thud as something hit the floor. "Don't forget your money."

The other man grumbled, and then she heard the sound of a door being opened and closed. Amy hadn't been able to bring herself to move, but she suddenly realized what a precarious position she'd placed herself in. She backed away slowly from the closed door.

She'd made it halfway to the front door, when she stumbled into a spittoon and sent it crashing over with a resounding clang. Nathan was through the door in a heartbeat, staring dumbfounded at Amy. He tried to decide for a moment whether she was coming or going, but Amy didn't give him any time to figure it out before she turned to run for the door.

He was on her before she'd taken two steps, gripping her wrist with his steely hand and dragging her back to his office for privacy.

"What are you doing here, Angie?" he asked, mistaking her for her sister.

"I, I. . ." Amy tried to speak, but the words wouldn't come.

"What did you hear?" Nathan shoved her into a chair.

Amy shook her head. "Nothing. I came here to find my sister."

"What would Amy be doing here?" Nathan frowned and then his eyes narrowed. "You're not Angie." His words seemed to hang forever on the air.

"Yes," Amy finally admitted. "Angie and I were shopping, and she said she was coming to visit you. I was just trying to find her so that we could go home." Amy timidly came up from the chair, only to have Nathan whirl around and slam her back down.

"Stay there!"

Amy trembled, but she did as she was told, while Nathan moved quickly to lock his office door. She cast a quick glance toward the back door, knowing if she could somehow make it there, she'd be safe.

Nathan came back to where she sat, putting himself between her and freedom. He rubbed his jaw for a moment and stared at her, his hard eyes boring into her face. "You know, don't you?"

Amy tried to look innocent and shook her head. "Know what?"

"Don't play games with me, Amy. You aren't going to ruin my plans. I can't have you out there bringing the town down on me. You overheard my plans, or you wouldn't be so afraid of me."

"I wasn't afraid until you grabbed me and dragged me in here," Amy said angrily. "I don't know why you're treating me like this, but when my Pa and brother find out, you won't have time to worry about any plans you've made." She prayed he'd be convinced that she hadn't overheard his conversation with the now absent stranger.

Nathan moved away from her, thinking. As a lawyer, part of his job was to study men and what they had to say, determining whether or not they were telling the truth. He had to admit, Amy Carmichael was either a very good actress or she truly hadn't overhead his plans. Still, if she hadn't heard him talking, why was she running from him?

When Nathan turned his back to retrieve a drink he'd poured earlier, Amy bolted for the back door. She had managed to get it open before Nathan slammed her against it.

"I won't say anything!" Amy exclaimed without thinking. Nathan was twisting her arm behind her so violently that she thought she'd pass out from the pain.

"I thought you didn't know anything," Nathan sneered. "How can you say anything about something you didn't hear?"

Amy knew he'd caught her, and she hung her head in dejection. "What are you going to do with me?"

"That, my dear, does present a problem," Nathan said, pulling her back to the chair. "I have no desire to kill anyone over a matter of a mere several thousand dollars. Still," he paused to push her into the seat, "I won't have you mess this up for me."

Amy said nothing, waiting and watching while Nathan contemplated her fate. "I suppose," he continued, "if I can keep you out of the way until after the job is done, I won't have to kill you."

Amy blanched at his statement, making Nathan laugh. "Don't worry, little Amy. You just cooperate with me, and I'll figure this out. Otherwise—well, let's just say, it won't be a Merry Christmas at the Carmichaels'."

Chapter 10

Amy struggled against the ropes that bound her hands and feet. She tried to yell, but the gag Nathan had placed firmly over her mouth muted any sound that came from her throat.

Quieting for a moment, Amy listened to hear if Nathan was still in the building. He had dumped her in the storage closet with orders to keep quiet or else. When he told her he had to get her horse out of sight, Amy knew he meant business; she could hardly believe this was the same man who had courted Angie. "Please," she had tried to say through the gag, but Nathan locked the closet door and left her alone in the darkness.

He had tied her hands tightly behind her back so she would have no chance of freeing herself. Nevertheless, Amy worked at the ropes until her wrists were chafed and sore. She felt her eyes fill with tears, but she refused to give in to her misery. Somehow, she had to get out of this.

Angie finally made her entrance into Smith's General Store, only to find Amy already gone. Betty assured her that Amy had gone in search of Angie when her shopping was completed, so Angie took the time necessary to finish her own Christmas shopping, certain that Amy would return any minute. When she didn't, Angie started to get worried. After paying for her things, Angie went outside and looked up and down the street.

The sun was already well to the west, and Angie knew they'd stayed a great deal longer than they should have. Noticing Ed Anderson as he came out to lock up the bank, Angie ran toward him.

"Ed, have you seen Amy?" she asked breathlessly.

"Angie!" Ed grinned. "Why didn't you tell me you were coming to town?"

"Didn't know myself until just today," Angie replied. "I'm looking for Amy. She rode in with me to do some shopping, but now I can't find her."

Ed laughed. "Deer Ridge isn't that big. She must be around here somewhere. Did you check over at the post office—or maybe Miller's Hotel? You know how Mrs. Miller likes to visit."

"You mean gossip—and no, I hadn't checked there." Angie smoothed her hair and smiled up at Ed, but her lips were still tight with worry. "I was visiting with Mrs. Miller earlier myself. Maybe Amy and I just crossed paths."

"That's probably it," Ed agreed. "Would you like me to walk with you over to the hotel?"

The worry eased from Angie's face. Ever the flirt, she batted her eyes and extended her arm. "I would simply love it!"

Passing by the store again on their way down Main Street, Ed noticed the solitary horse that stood outside. "You girls didn't ride double, did you?"

"What are you talking about, Ed?"

Ed pointed toward Angie's horse. "You said you rode in together. Did Amy ride her own horse?"

"Yes, yes, she did," Angie replied. She shrugged her shoulders. "Maybe she was mad at me for taking so long, and she got tired of waiting for me. I'll bet she rode on home without me. That would figure."

"Sure would." Ed laughed. "I guess the joke's on you for taking too much time visiting around the town."

Confident that this was true, Angie allowed Ed to help her up onto her horse. "She's probably already home sitting safe and warm in front of the fireplace."

"If you give me a minute," Ed said, "I'll go saddle up my horse and ride part of the way home with you. I promised Ma I'd bring out some supplies tonight for her baking, so I've got to go that way anyway."

Angie's face lit up, and her frustration with Amy disappeared. "I'll wait right here for you."

Dark had nearly fallen by the time Angie finally rode into the farmyard. She'd had the most wonderful time with Ed, and she was still wearing her dreamy expression when her father met her in the barn.

"I was beginning to get worried," Charles said, helping her from the saddle.

"I'm sorry, Pa. I took time to try and find Amy, and before I knew it, the sun was sinking lower and lower. Ed Anderson rode out as far as the creek with me, so I didn't have far to come alone."

"Alone?" Charles frowned. "Where's your sister?"

Angie's mouth dropped open. "You mean she's not here?"

"No." Charles's voice was flat. "What made you think she was?"

"We separated in town because I went to see Mrs. Miller at the hotel. She'd promised to make me some lace as a Christmas present for Amy. I stayed too long I guess, 'cause when I headed back to the store, Amy was already gone. I went to look for her after I finished my shopping, but I couldn't find her anywhere." Angie twisted a curl around her finger nervously. "I saw Ed Anderson locking up the bank, so I went and asked him if he'd seen Amy. He hadn't, but he offered to look for her with me. That was when we noticed her horse was gone."

"Amy's horse was gone?" A frown lined Charles's normally cheerful face.

Angie nodded. "We figured she'd gotten mad at me for taking so long and had headed home on her own. That's why I came on home myself. I thought she'd be here."

Charles was already pulling the saddle off Angie's horse. "You give this horse some feed and water. I'm going back into town to look for your sister. Tell your ma what happened, but try not to tell it so as she worries too much. Amy's probably still looking for you, so there ain't no reason to get her frettin'."

Angie nodded. She was starting to feel anxious for her twin. Amy was not the type to act irresponsibly, Angie realized, and she should have known Amy would never have gotten mad and left her. Angie quickly cared for the horse and hurried inside to tell her mother what had happened.

Amy knew it was only a matter of time before Nathan returned. She pondered what he might do with her in order to keep her from spilling his plans. She still couldn't fully comprehend that the handsome, young lawyer planned to rob the town of its harvest money.

Without even realizing what she was doing, Amy began to pray. *Lord,* she thought, *I need help out of this one, for sure. Please send someone to rescue me. And keep me from the harm Nathan Gallagher plans for me. Please,* she added, *help me not to be afraid.* It was only a brief prayer, but it strengthened her spirits, and Amy began to have hope that she would somehow escape.

Waiting there in the dark, her mind turned to thoughts of Tyler. He would be arriving any day now, and Amy wondered if he would be the one to find her. She fell into a daydream where Tyler rode up to Nathan's office and pulled her out of the closet into his strong arms. *How terribly romantic,* she thought and had to laugh at her nonsense.

She'd no doubt be home long before Tyler returned. But thinking about that was just as romantic, for then he'd ask her to marry him, and she would of course say yes. She fell deep into another daydream.

The sound of someone entering the law office caught her attention. She began to pound her feet against the floor and threw her shoulder against the wall of the closet. The door to the closet swung open, and light from a lantern blinded Amy's eyes for a moment. "Quiet down—or else," Nathan whispered harshly.

Amy sat still while her eyes adjusted to the light. Nathan placed the lamp on the floor and began searching his pockets for something.

"I've decided to take you out of here," he said while pulling a handkerchief from his pocket. "I have a problem, though. I can't very well parade you down Main Street, now can I?"

He laughed at Amy's expression and continued. "I paid a visit to Doc Taggert. Well, actually to his office. You might say I allowed myself entrance through the back window in order to retrieve this." He held up a corked bottle of liquid.

Amy shied away, trying to scoot back against the closet wall. She was only too certain of what Nathan had in mind. He uncorked the bottle and poured a liberal amount of the contents onto his handkerchief before continuing. "This way, it will be a lot easier on me and you both."

Amy shook her head furiously. She kicked at Nathan when he moved closer to her. Her strangled protests couldn't make it past the gag, but Nathan understood their meaning well enough.

"Don't fight me, Amy. I can't let you spoil this for me. I've worked too hard and too long on this. You're a good girl, and I don't want to hurt you. Now just cooperate with me, and it'll all be over in a short time."

Amy felt a scream rise up inside her, only to die as Nathan pulled her forward. He held the cloth firmly against her face, and in spite of her thrashing from side to side, the chloroform did its job. Amy had a burning sensation in her nostrils and throat, and then the darkness overtook her.

She came awake slowly, almost like she'd been a part of some strange dream. She lifted her aching head and tried to focus on the images around her, but nothing made sense. Dropping her head back, she waited for a few moments, hoping her head would clear before she tried to lift it again.

Her lips felt sore and dry, and she ran her tongue across them. She remembered the gag then—it was gone! With that memory, everything else came back to her. She was lying on a bed somewhere, and she swung her legs over the side, realizing that the ropes had been cut from her hands and feet. She sat up, her head swimming.

Her head pounded with the echo of each beat of her heart, and her throat was scratchy and sore from the chloroform. When she could finally focus a bit better, she noticed a small table across the room from the bed. On it, a lantern offered the room's only light.

Amy got to her feet slowly, testing her weight against her wobbly legs. When she felt confident she could stand, she walked to the table and inspected the items on top of it. Nathan had left her a jar of water, a loaf of bread, and the light.

Looking around the room, Amy surmised that it must be a dugout or root cellar. She climbed the two dirt steps that led to a wooden door and pulled at the handle to open it. It wouldn't budge—but then she really hadn't expected it to. Heaving a sigh, she stepped away and took a more careful inventory of the room's contents.

There was the makeshift bed she'd been lying on, the table, and nothing else. Overhead was the dirt and grass ceiling that was typical of dugouts, but with no stove and no hole in the roof for a flue, Amy decided this must be someone's deserted storage cellar.

She returned her gaze to the table, then again to the door, and at last sat back down on the bed. She was trapped without hope, and the silence of her prison broke her like nothing else could have. She lay back on the bed and began to sob.

Chapter 11

Charles Carmichael pounded on the door to the general store. After several moments, Jeremy Smith's scowling face appeared in the window.

"You know we're closed," he called from behind the glass.

Charles was undaunted. "Jeremy, have you seen Amy?" he bellowed.

His expression erased Jeremy's scowl. He opened the door and shook his head. "Not since earlier when she was shopping."

The lines in Charles's face grew deeper. "She's missing," he said heavily. "I've looked all over for her. I covered the miles between here and home as best I could, but I didn't see any sign of her anywhere. I was hoping she'd be somewhere still in town."

"I'll get my coat and a light," Jeremy said. He knew no one would be able to rest until the young woman was found.

"I'm going to ride out to the Anderson place," Charles said. "If they haven't seen anything of her, then I'll bring George and his boys back with me to help with the search. Would you get the men together here and wait for us?"

"Sure thing, Charles. We'll be waitin' for you right here."

Confident that Jeremy would help, Charles mounted his horse and rode as fast as he dared to the Anderson farm. Snow was beginning to fall as he dismounted, but Charles barely noticed. He charged toward the house, ignoring the barking dogs, but the commotion brought George Anderson to the door before Charles could knock.

"Charles!" George exclaimed. "What are you doing out here on a night like this? A guy would have to be pert near crazy to brave the winds tonight."

"You haven't seen Amy, have you, George." Charles's words were a statement rather than a question. He wiped the snowflakes from his face and took a deep breath. "She went into town with Angie and never came home."

By this time Ed and Jack had joined their father at the door. "I thought she'd ridden out ahead of Angie," Ed said. "I helped Angie look for her until we noticed her horse was gone. We figured she'd gone home."

"If she headed toward home," Charles said, fear making his voice gruff, "she never made it. I've got Jeremy Smith getting the men together in town. I wanted to ask. . ."

"No need to ask, Charles," George interrupted. "Boys, get your brother, and tell your ma what's happened."

Ed and Jack quickly returned with Jacob, closely followed by Emma Anderson. "Is there anything I can do, Charles?" Emma asked.

"Pray," Charles suggested. "Just pray for her safe return. I know your prayers will be joined by an awful lot of others petitionin' God for the same thing. I just have to believe that Amy will be safe in our Father's hands."

"I know she is," Emma said firmly. "And I'll be praying for both her and for you men as you search." She reached out to squeeze Charles's hand, then watched as her family prepared to leave with Charles.

"Bar the door, Emma," her husband told her as they left. "We don't know what's amiss, and there's no sense taking chances." He kissed her lightly on the cheek, picked up his rifle, and followed his sons outside.

Alone in the cold, damp room, Amy shivered and hugged her arms around herself. She was grateful she still wore her heavy coat, but she was still cold. She pulled the thin bed blanket around her to add to her coat's warmth and tried to breathe slowly and calmly. She could do nothing now but wait. Surely Nathan wouldn't just leave her here to die; after all, he had provided food and water for her.

She got off the bed and paced back and forth across the room, trying to warm herself by moving around. Her thoughts turned to home, and she bit her lip while her eyes burned with tears. Her parents would be frantic, and Angie would blame herself. Amy breathed a silent prayer that God would ease their worry, and she asked again for a speedy rescue.

She tried to focus on pleasant thoughts and not give in to the fear and hopelessness of her situation. She was uncertain how long she had been unconscious, and she wondered what day it was. *Days might have already passed,* she told herself, *and rescue could be very near.* Clinging to that hope, she ate a small piece of the bread, allowing herself no more than a brief swallow of the water. She knew rationing could be essential, because she had no guarantee that Nathan would return to supply her with more.

As the hours dragged by, she spent most of her time praying and remembering. The air grew colder, and she feared she might freeze to death before anyone could find her. She felt more and more sleepy, but she knew sleeping could be dangerous in the cold, and so she forced herself to stay awake by reciting Bible verses and singing hymns.

"Father," she said aloud. Even the sound of her own voice was welcome in the silence. "I need a miracle. I don't know what's happening out there or even where I am, but You know, and I know You're watching over me. Please let them find me in time, Lord—and if not, then teach me how I can help myself get out of this." She didn't add a closing "amen," for she knew her prayer would continue again when the stillness became too much for her once more.

Tyler approached the Carmichael farm with the giddy excitement of a schoolboy. He'd arranged to have three weeks away from his circuit, while another rider took his place during his absence. During those three weeks, he intended to make plans with Amy for their wedding.

Snow covered the ground now, and Tyler was reminded of the storm that had kept him at the Carmichaels' long enough to share his true feelings with Amy. He smiled to himself, thinking of how worried she'd been about her sister's feelings. That was one of the things he loved most about Amy. She was always looking out for the folks around her before ever considering her own needs.

Without stopping at the house first, Tyler went directly to the barn. He cared for his horse and then ran across the yard to the house. Slightly breathless, he knocked on the door. A red-eyed Dora opened it.

"Tyler!" she gasped in surprise. Her face twisted with emotions that Tyler could not identify, and then she turned to her husband. "Look, Charles, it's Tyler."

The skin on the back of Tyler's neck prickled when he saw how haggard both of Amy's parents were. They ushered him into the kitchen without a word and motioned him toward a seat. When Dora and Charles had sat down with him, he leaned toward them, waiting for them to speak.

"What is it?" he asked finally. He knew in his heart he wasn't going to like the answer. "Has something happened to Amy?"

Dora began to cry anew, and Charles put his face in his hands. "She's gone," he said. The sorrow in his muffled words made Tyler believe she was dead.

"Dear God," he breathed, feeling his own heart break. "What happened? How did she. . .?" He fell silent, unable to utter the word.

Dora instantly realized what he was thinking. "She's not dead, Tyler! At least we pray to God she's not."

Relief washed over him, but the sick feeling that filled his stomach refused to leave. "Then what are you saying?"

Charles leaned back in his chair and shook his head. "She's been missing ever since she went into town with Angie. They went Christmas shopping four, no, five days ago, and Amy hasn't been seen since."

Tyler's heart pounded in his ears, nearly drowning the words Charles spoke. "We got a search party together," Charles continued, "but there wasn't a clue anywhere. It was like she simply disappeared off the face of the earth."

"Is anybody else missing?" Tyler asked.

"No," Charles replied. "Everyone else is accounted for. None of her friends have seen her. Even her horse has disappeared."

"Her horse?"

Charles nodded. "She and Angie both rode horseback into town. When Angie saw that Amy's horse was missing, she presumed she'd ridden home without her. Angie's beside herself. She blames herself for not sticking around and waiting."

Dora sighed. "I've tried to talk to her, but she won't even open her door."

Angie tossed fitfully in her bed. She'd tried to sleep, but whenever she closed her eyes, a cold foreboding settled upon her, and she felt a misery that she'd never known. People often said twins were bonded to one another, and although she had never experienced it before, Angie couldn't help but wonder if what she was feeling now was actually the echo of Amy's suffering.

The knock at her bedroom door brought her upright in the bed. "Leave me be, Ma," Angie called in a ragged voice.

"Angie, it's Tyler. Please open the door and talk to me."

Angie swallowed hard and felt a trembling start at her head and go clear to her toes. Her mother had already told her how much Amy cared for Tyler. She'd also told Angie that she was quite confident Tyler cared deeply for Amy. Angie couldn't help but believe Tyler would blame her for Amy's disappearance. "And why shouldn't he?" Angie muttered to herself.

"Angie," Tyler persisted. "Please open the door. It's not your fault that Amy is gone—but you may be the only one who can really help us find her."

At these words Angie jumped to her feet and threw open her door. "How?" She stared into Tyler's face. "How can I possibly help her?"

Tyler studied the young woman before him. She was the image of his Amy, but in some ways she was different as well. The differences were especially clear now after the days of worry and grief Angie had spent alone. She had dark circles under her eyes, and her face was gaunt and pale.

Tyler put his arm around Angie's shoulders. "Come downstairs, and let's talk."

Angie nodded and allowed him to lead the way. When she saw her parents waiting in the kitchen, she nearly turned to run back to her room, but Tyler's grip was firm.

They look so old, Angie thought, taking the chair Tyler pulled out for her. *Do they hate me for doing this to them? Will they ever forgive me for leaving Amy?* Angie buried her face in her hands and sobbed.

"I should have never left her. This is all my fault, and you all hate me now."

Dora looked at her in stunned silence, while Charles nearly dropped the cup of coffee he'd been nursing.

"Nobody blames you, Angie," Tyler said. "Nobody except yourself."

Angie looked up at him with tear-filled eyes. "I feel like Cain in the Bible," she cried. "I was my sister's keeper, and now. . ." She couldn't say any more and put her head on the table to cry.

Tyler put his arm around her. "Father," he prayed, "please comfort Angie in her pain. She feels responsible for her sister, but we know that isn't the case. Help her, Lord, to see that her parents love her a great deal and that no one holds her accountable for Amy's disappearance. Father, guide us to Amy and show us the way to bring her home. In Jesus' name, amen."

Angie's tears slowed, and finally she leaned back in her chair and sighed. Her father reached out and covered her hand with his own. Taking in another deep, ragged breath, she steadied her nerves. "What do you want to know?" She lifted her face to Tyler's imploring eyes.

"Just start from the beginning and tell me everything," he said with a smile of hope. "Don't leave out anything, no matter how insignificant it might seem."

Sometime later, Tyler rode into Deer Ridge. He wouldn't rest until he'd questioned people himself, and so he made his way to where several of the townspeople stood talking in a cluster in front of the store.

"Howdy, folks." He climbed down from his horse. "I heard about Amy and was hoping to help locate her." He wasted no time with formalities.

"I think Injuns took her," the hotel owner, Mrs. Miller, stated firmly.

Cora Peterson scoffed at this. " 'Tweren't no Injuns, Bertha. Don't you ever think Injuns got better things to do than snatch up white folks? Might as well blame the Swedes."

"Well, it could've happened," Bertha Miller sniffed. "It hasn't been that long since Little Big Horn. They might be feeling riled at white folk, and Amy might just have been in the wrong place at the wrong time."

At this Cora's husband Bud stepped in and waved the woman away. "Don't get her started on Little Big Horn, or we'll never get to hear what the preacher has to say."

The crowd smiled, in spite of their worry, and even Bertha seemed to relax a bit. Tyler was grateful for the break in the tension he'd known since first learning of Amy's disappearance.

He talked with the folks for a few more minutes before heading into the general store. At the sound of the front door being opened, Jeremy Smith came from the back room. For once the store was strangely void of activity. *Maybe,* thought Tyler, *people are too tense to relax inside the store the way they would normally.*

"Good to see you, Parson," Jeremy Smith said, extending a hand over the counter.

"It's good to be back although I had hoped for more pleasant circumstances," Tyler replied.

Betty Smith joined her husband, fear clearly etched in the weathered lines of her face. "Pastor Andrews." She greeted him with a nod.

"I'm glad we're alone," Tyler said, glancing around him. "I hoped you could give me the details about the day Amy disappeared. I promised her folks I'd help look for her."

Betty's eyes misted with tears. "You know, she bought you a Christmas present." The words were out before she realized it. "I'm sorry. I shouldn't have spoiled the surprise, but. . ."

"It's all right, Mrs. Smith." Tyler smiled. "I know Amy would understand, and I promise to be surprised." Tyler was deeply touched to think that Amy's thoughts had been on him.

He stayed long enough to listen to the Smiths tell every detail they could remember. When the couple fell silent, Tyler mulled the information over for a moment and then asked one final question.

"You say she was going to look for Angie when she left here. Where might she have thought to find her?"

"My guess," Mrs. Smith answered, "would be that Amy figured she was visiting her beaus. Ed Anderson would have been over at the bank, and Nathan Gallagher's office is across the street."

Her husband nodded in agreement, and Tyler took a deep breath. At least he had a place to start.

Chapter 12

Talking to Ed Anderson revealed nothing more than Tyler already knew. Ed went over every detail patiently, even though he'd already told his story a dozen or more times to the Carmichael men. He understood Tyler's anxiety because Charles had told him in confidence that Amy and Tyler had feelings for one another. Ed tried to offer Tyler comfort, and he promised he'd continue to search for Amy as his time allowed.

Tyler picked up his hat and coat and headed for the door.

"You know, Tyler," Ed said, returning to his desk, "Nathan Gallagher has been pretty quiet about this whole thing. You might want to see if he knows any more than I do. If he'll talk to you."

"I was headed over there now," Tyler said. "I'll stress the need for his cooperation."

Ed smiled at the towering pastor's back. No doubt he would get his point across to Mr. Gallagher.

Tyler let himself into the law office and tossed his hat and coat on the nearest chair. "Hello!" he called.

Nathan Gallagher came from his office with a look of surprise. "You're the circuit rider, aren't you?" He looked Tyler up and down.

"That's right," Tyler responded. "I'm also a good friend of the Carmichaels. I'm trying to help them locate their daughter."

Nathan stiffened slightly. "I see. And just what has that to do with me? I've already told Mr. Carmichael I know nothing about Amy's whereabouts."

Tyler was taken aback by the man's cool manner. Everyone else had greeted him with somber cooperation and earnest concern, but Nathan Gallagher seemed not only indifferent to Amy's plight but almost angry at the interruption.

"Folks tell me that Amy was last seen looking for her sister," Tyler said. "Everybody knows that Angie has a number of gentlemen callers, one of which is you. I figured it might be possible that Angie came to see you the day Amy disappeared—and that Amy might have come by here looking for her." Tyler leaned against the wall in a casual manner, making it clear to Nathan Gallagher that he intended to stay until he got some answers.

"It's true that I've called on Angie before," Nathan acknowledged. "But Angie didn't come to see me that day. Amy wouldn't have any reason to come here without Angie."

"She would if she were looking for her sister," Tyler said. "That would be a logical thing to do, now, wouldn't it?" His eyes were intense, watching Gallagher's reaction.

If the lawyer thought he was good at reading people's expressions, then Tyler Andrews was a genius at it. He noticed the way Nathan's eyes darted from side to side to avoid his own, and he saw the way Nathan's hands fidgeted in his pockets.

Nathan shrugged, feigning nonchalance. "I guess that's reasonable, but Amy didn't come here. I told her father that, and now I'm telling you."

"I'm just trying to find her," Tyler said calmly. Inside, however, he was boiling at Nathan's lack of concern.

"Well, I believe you've done all you can here," the lawyer said firmly. "Now if you'll excuse me, I have work to do."

Tyler allowed him to return to his office without another word. Something told him that Gallagher knew more than he was saying, but Tyler could not force him to reveal what he knew. Frustrated, Tyler pulled on his coat and hat and retrieved his horse from the front of the general store. Then he turned toward the Carmichael farm, eager to see if Randy or Charles had learned anything more.

When at last Tyler arrived back at the farm, he felt more discouraged than he'd ever felt in his life. Amy was out there somewhere, maybe hurt, definitely scared, and he couldn't help her. He wanted so much to let her know that he cared, that he would always care, but he had no leads, no answers to the questions that could help him find her.

When he approached the house, his heart jumped. Amy's horse was tied out front alongside another that he didn't recognize. Had she been found? God surely must have heard his prayers. He nearly flew off his horse and into the house.

"That's Amy's horse!" He pushed into the kitchen without so much as a knock.

Randy Carmichael stood against the stove warming his hands. "I found it in Hays," he said without looking up. "The livery owner said a man came in several days ago and sold it to him, tack and all, for twenty dollars."

"Did he get a description of the man?" Tyler asked.

"He did," Charles said, coming in from the other room. He nodded down the hall. "Dora and Angie are pretty upset by this. I told them to leave the discussion to us."

Tyler nodded. "It's probably best." He turned to Randy and asked again about the man.

"Livery said the man was about six foot tall," Randy answered. "Heavyset, scraggly red beard, and hair down to his shoulders. He wasn't dressed well, and the livery owner was surprised when he only wanted twenty dollars for the horse. The man told him that he just needed to unload the animal and that twenty was plenty. That's when the livery man got suspicious."

"Was anything missing?" Tyler asked. "Was there any sign of what might have happened?"

Randy shook his head and took the cup of coffee his father handed him. "No, even the Christmas gifts Amy bought were safely stashed in the saddlebags. There was no sign of blood or anything else that might give us a clue."

"Well, then, she wasn't taken for the money," Tyler thought aloud.

"You think she was taken then?" Charles asked, pouring a cup of the steaming liquid for Tyler.

Tyler nodded. "More so now than ever. If she'd gone out ahead of Angie and gotten hurt or lost her way somehow, the horse would have come on home. Nobody is missing in town, but that still leaves the area surrounding it. Were any of the local men interested in Amy? I mean, would they have taken her by force?"

"Naw." Charles shook his head and made a face, as though the thought was ridiculous. "We've been here a long time, Tyler. Ain't no one round here who would try to get a woman that way. Besides, I don't know anyone who was even interested in Amy. You know how it is between Angie and Amy. Angie's always courting, and Amy never was. The only one marginally interested in her was Jacob Anderson, and he's been most devoted to helping us look for her."

"If someone did take her," Randy began, "and I'm inclined to believe someone did, what reason could they possibly have had? What purpose would it serve to take Amy?"

"That's what I'm trying to figure out," Tyler replied softly. He took a long drink from the mug and set it on the table. "By my calculations there is only about an hour on the day Amy disappeared that her whereabouts was unaccounted for before Angie noticed her horse was gone. The time from which Amy left the store until Angie began looking for her was only forty-five minutes, maybe an hour at best. Somewhere in that hour is when Amy was taken. Since no one remembers seeing any strangers in town, Amy had to have been taken by someone familiar to her. Maybe she was even talked into helping someone she knew well and went willingly with them."

Charles rubbed his jaw, then looked at his son. Randy nodded; Tyler's words made sense.

"So what do we do from here?" Charles asked.

Tyler rubbed his own stubbly chin for a moment, noticing absently that he needed a shave. "We make a list," he finally said. "We make a list of everyone in the area. Then we plot the names on a map. You take part of it, Charles,

Randy a part, and I'll take another part. I'll stick to the town, since I'm not all that familiar with the outlying farms. You and Randy can divide your lists with someone you trust, like the Andersons. Then we'll go door to door, farm to farm. We'll question everybody and leave no stone unturned."

Charles frowned. "That might make our neighbors feel we don't trust them to come forward with what they know."

"They'll understand." Tyler drained the coffee from his cup, then added, "They won't be offended if you remind them that should this have happened to one of their own family members, you'd expect them to do the same."

"I'll get some paper," Charles agreed and left the room.

"I'll get the horses into the stable," Randy offered, "and then I'll help you map this thing out."

Tyler tried to ignore the anguish in his soul. He had forced his voice to remain calm and even while he talked with Randy and Charles, but inside he was gnawed by a fear that said if Amy's horse had turned up as far away as Hays, then Amy too could be long gone from Deer Ridge.

Running a hand through the waves of his hair, Tyler decided not to say anything to the family. No sense taking away what little hope they had. Tyler would keep the fear to himself that with each passing day, Amy was getting further and further from his reach. He whispered a prayer and sat down at the table, prepared to work.

Making the list and map took them most of the evening. When it was completed, Tyler divided it in thirds, with the larger of the shares going to Charles and Randy.

"I'm heading home." Randy stuffed the paper into his pocket. "I'll be back early, and we can get started then."

"We'll be ready," Charles replied and bid his son good-bye.

The silence that fell between Charles and Tyler was numbing. Each man wanted to comfort the other, but neither had any words for what they were feeling. Each bore a burden so heavy that the weight drained them of energy. Finally, Charles reached out and placed his hand over Tyler's. Tyler lifted his eyes and saw the tear-stained cheeks of a worried father.

"If God be for us," the pastor whispered, "who can be against us?"

Tyler spent a restless night in the Carmichaels' spare bedroom. He could hear Dora crying off and on from down the hall, and from time to time Angie joined in from the privacy of her own room. A verse from the Bible came to Tyler, the verse that describes Rachel weeping for her children and refusing to be comforted. The verse so haunted Tyler that at last he got up and opened his Bible to Jeremiah 31:15.

"Thus saith the Lord; A voice was heard in Ramah, lamentation, and bitter weeping; Rachel weeping for her children refused to be comforted for her children, because they were not."

Tyler shuddered, but then he found the Lord leading his eyes on to verses 16 and 17, and the words he read now brought him hope.

"Thus saith the Lord; Refrain thy voice from weeping, and thine eyes from tears: for thy work shall be rewarded, saith the Lord; and they shall come again from the land of the enemy. And there is hope in thine end, saith the Lord, that thy children shall come again to their own border." He read the words silently, then again aloud.

A weight lifted from his shoulders, and he fell to his knees in prayer. First he offered thanksgiving for the Scriptures God had led him to, then he began to petition his Father for Amy's safety.

When Randy arrived the next morning, the entire family gathered for Tyler to lead them in devotions and prayers. He shared the precious verses he'd read the night before. "We must put our hope in God," he reminded them. "He is our only hope right now, but He won't let us down. He is the only One who can reach out and help Amy. We must put her in His hands." Tyler waited for them to absorb his words, and then he added, "We can trust Him with Amy's life, for He loves her even more than we ever will."

At these words, Dora seemed to sit straighter, and even Angie lost her mask of fear. A light had been given them in their darkness, and they stood at a crossroads that would lead them to a wondrous peace of mind.

"You're right, Tyler," Charles said finally. "We've been fighting this thing too hard on our own. If we're to ever get anywhere, we must let God work it out." Angie, Dora, and Randy nodded in unison.

After breakfast the men readied their horses and prepared to leave. Dora and Angie stood by helplessly watching, until Angie could no longer stand it.

"Can't I go along and help?" she asked her father.

"No, you'd best stay here. We still don't know what we're going to find out there. I'd rather you be here to care for your mother." Charles gave Angie's cheek a gentle stroke.

"But it's awful just waiting here," she protested.

Dora nodded. "Feels like we're not doing our part."

"Somebody should be here," Tyler said before Charles could reply. "In case Amy makes it home on her own. If you're both here, then Angie can ride out and let the rest of us know."

"I suppose that makes sense." Dora put her arm around Angie. "And," she added softly, "we can continue to pray."

Angie saw the wisdom in their words, and though she longed to be at some other task, she agreed that they needed to stay at the house.

"We'll be back by dark," Charles said, mounting his horse. The cold leather creaked and groaned as he settled his body in the saddle. "Looks like it might snow again, so you'd best stay inside."

"What about the chores, Pa?" Angie questioned.

"We took care of everything before you ladies got up. You just stick indoors and stay warm," Charles instructed. He hated to leave them alone, but he knew he had to trust God to watch over them if he was to go look for his other daughter. He gave Dora a loving look, then turned his horse to follow Randy and Tyler across the yard.

"Kind of like leaving the ninety-nine," he murmured aloud.

"What was that?" Tyler questioned.

Charles smiled and pulled up even with Tyler. "I was just thinking that leaving them here is like the shepherd who leaves the ninety-nine to go look for the one."

Tyler returned the smile with a nod. "That it is. I guess now we know just how precious that one can be."

Chapter 13

Tyler stood in the center of Deer Ridge's Main Street and stared down at the list. He decided to start with Miller's Hotel, since six of the people on his list resided there. He spoke first to Mr. and Mrs. Miller and then was happily received by Marvin Williams, who was enjoying his holiday break from teaching.

Marvin, however, knew next to nothing about the entire affair, and so Tyler moved on to Nathan Gallagher's room. He knocked, but receiving no answer from the other side of the door, he again moved on. He could pin Gallagher down at his office later, he decided.

The town barber and dentist, Newt Bramblage, was also absent from the hotel, but Mrs. Miller reminded Tyler that he'd probably be happy to answer any questions while giving Tyler a shave.

The only other resident was an elderly woman who rarely left her room. The woman had a delicate constitution, and so as not to upset her unduly, Mrs. Miller questioned her for Tyler. The woman, not surprisingly, had no knowledge of Amy Carmichael's whereabouts; she went still further, however, and insisted that since she was not given to gossip, she would have nothing to share in the future, even in the unlikely event that she should fall privy to such knowledge.

Tyler thanked the Millers and moved on down the street to where Doc Taggert was shoveling snow in front of his building. "Doc," Tyler called and climbed down from his horse. He tied the reins and offered to take over the shoveling if Doc would speak to him about Amy. He finished the remaining work quickly, and Doc invited him inside for coffee and biscuits.

"My wife Gretta always worries that I'll starve before I come home for lunch." Doc smiled. "Then she wonders why I don't have much of an appetite at supper."

Tyler laughed and helped himself to the offered refreshment. "I'll happily share your misery." He bit into a fluffy biscuit.

"I don't know what I can do to help you." Doc took a seat behind his desk. "I don't believe I saw Amy at all the day she disappeared."

"Did you work in your office that day?"

"Sure did," Doc replied. "I was here pert near all day. I'd just gotten in a shipment of medicine and had to inventory it before I could close up and go home. I was just leaving when—say, wait a minute."

Tyler leaned forward. "What is it, Doc?"

"I didn't see Amy that day," Doc said thoughtfully, "but I did see Angie."

"Oh." Tyler sat back hard against the wooden chair. The disappointment was clear on his face.

"Yes," Doc remembered. "She was just crossing the street and heading into Nathan Gallagher's office when I was locking my front door."

Tyler leaned forward again. "You saw Angie going into Nathan's office?"

"That's right."

"How did you know it was Angie? I'd think from a distance it would be pretty hard to tell the twins apart. I'm not sure even I could do it. What made you so sure it was Angie and not Amy?"

Doc shrugged and scratched his jaw. "I guess I just assumed it was Angie. After all, Amy wouldn't have any reason to visit Gallagher. He's not at all her type. Besides, everybody knows Angie considers him one of her more serious gentlemen callers."

"But—" Tyler opened his mouth, then closed it again. His eyes narrowed, and he took a deep breath. "You're sure it was the same day that Amy disappeared?"

"Positive."

Tyler grabbed his hat. "Thanks, Doc. I think you have helped me a great deal."

Without another word, Tyler hurried from Doc's office. He left his horse behind and walked to Nathan's office. Nathan had insisted that he'd not seen Angie or Amy on the day Amy disappeared—and now Tyler had proof that he'd lied.

"Gallagher!" Tyler slammed the office door behind him.

Nathan came from the inner office with the same look of surprise that he'd worn the visit before. "What in the world is going on, Preacher?"

"Doc Taggert says he saw Angie come here to visit you the day Amy disappeared." Tyler's voice was flat.

Nathan's mouth hardened. "He's mistaken, Andrews. I told you that I didn't see Angie that day."

Tyler stepped forward, barely able to control his temper. "Doc was sure about what he'd seen."

"Doc is an old man." Nathan laughed. "He simply has his days mixed up. Angie never came to see me that day." Nathan's voice was confident. The more time that passed, the closer he was to accomplishing his goal of robbing the town on Christmas. Without a clue to Amy's whereabouts, Andrews was simply grasping at straws.

"I'm going to get to the bottom of this." Tyler's tone left Nathan little doubt that he would do just that.

"Well, you aren't going to get to the bottom of it here," Nathan replied.

Tyler backed away, fearful that if he remained within punching distance of Nathan, he'd lose control and flatten the man. "I'll be back." He looked at Nathan for another moment, his eyes dark with anger.

"You do that, Preach." Nathan crossed his arms across his chest and smiled. "I'll be here—and I won't have any more information for you then than I do now."

Tyler stalked out of the office and climbed into his saddle with a growl that made his horse's eyes roll. Tyler knew that Gallagher was keeping something from him, but he had no proof. His only recourse was to head back to the farm and question Angie. Perhaps she'd lied about seeing Gallagher for fear her folks wouldn't like her forward actions. Maybe she had seen him and covering that up made her feel even guiltier about Amy. Tyler shook his head and urged his mount forward. He would have to question Angie in private and promise to keep her secret.

Amy forced herself to wake up, but the effort cost her every ounce of determination she had. She was weak from lack of food and numb from the growing cold. She had no idea how much time had passed, so she tried to concentrate on the present moment only. She could not anticipate the future, and remembering the past now only made the present seem worse. She was no longer living even one day at a time; instead, she knew if she was to survive, she must live moment by moment.

She wasn't worrying anymore about whether Nathan would steal the harvest money. Now she thought only of whether or not he would free her before she succumbed to cold and thirst.

Each minute seemed as long as an hour. She still had a little water left, but she was afraid her thirst would drive her to swallow the remaining drops in one gulp. Again and again she reached out to take the jar in her hand, but each time she forced herself to put it back on the table. She had to make the water last. Without water, she would surely die.

With each passing moment, the room seemed smaller, as though the walls were closing in on her. She tried the door over and over, and shouted until her voice was hoarse. The longer she considered her plight, the more certain she felt that Nathan intended to leave her to die. Finally, her desperation drove her to action.

"My only hope of getting out of here is through the roof," she said aloud. She took the lamp and water from the table and put them on the floor. Next, she looked around the room, trying to figure out where the roof might be the weakest and easiest to penetrate. She moved the table to one side and gingerly tested it to see if it would hold her.

The table wobbled, but it held as Amy put her full weight on it. Weakly, she climbed to her feet on the tabletop and then had to duck down to keep from hitting the ceiling overhead. She pulled at the cold, packed dirt with her hands until she cried out from the pain. The dirt was frozen by the winter's cold, and Amy's numb fingers were no match for it.

Glancing around the room, Amy looked for some tool to make her job easier. She found nothing that looked promising, though, and so she continued to labor with her hands. God would give her strength, she reminded herself. "God is my strength," she whispered again and again while she scrabbled with her numb hands at the frozen ceiling. "God is my strength."

Tyler pushed his overworked gelding to gallop across the prairie until they reached the Carmichael farm. He dismounted quickly and left his mount in the barn. He knew he should care for the horse, but the snow was coming down heavier than before, and time was of the essence. He patted the patient animal apologetically and turned toward the house.

Before he could reach the door, Angie burst through it. "What is it? Did you find her?" she cried. "Mother is sleeping, but I can wake her."

"No, Angie." Tyler pulled her into the house with him. "I have to talk to you alone. It's very important."

Angie's brow wrinkled. "Me? Why me?"

"Sit here with me." Tyler pulled one of the kitchen chairs out for Angie.

Angie did as he asked, but her apprehension mounted with each silent moment that passed. Finally, Tyler found the right words to begin.

"Angie, I know this might be a delicate matter to broach, but if it weren't so important, I assure you I would never question what you told me before." Tyler took a deep breath. "Doc Taggert and I talked this morning. It seems he remembers you going to Nathan's office the afternoon Amy disappeared."

Angie shook her head. "I already told you that I didn't see Nathan that day. I spent my time with Mrs. Miller. I let Amy think I was going to go calling on some of my beaus—but that was just so she wouldn't suspect the Christmas present for her I was planning with Mrs. Miller. Mrs. Miller can tell you I was with her the whole afternoon."

"Yes, she did say that." Tyler sighed. "Look Angie, I'm not calling you a liar—I'm just desperate to know the truth. If you went to Nathan's and felt ashamed—or if you were concerned about your folks—or one of your other beaus—catching wind of it, I promise to keep it to myself. It's just that when I questioned Gallagher about it, he swore to me that he'd not seen you either.

And yet he acts suspicious about the whole thing. I need proof that he's lying to me."

"You think he's hiding something?" Angie asked in surprise.

"Could be. Is he hiding your visit?" Tyler's tone was gentle. "Is he protecting you, Angie?"

Angie shook her head vigorously. "No! I did not go to see Nathan Gallagher that day. I would have if I'd had time after I finished with Mrs. Miller, but I lost track of the time. By the time I returned to the store, Amy was already gone. I figured she'd be back soon, so I finished my shopping. When she still hadn't come back, I decided to find her. I stepped outside the store and saw that her horse was still there, so I knew she was nearby. That's when I went to talk to Ed. . . ."

"Wait a minute, Angie," Tyler interrupted. "You just said that when you came out of the store, Amy's horse was still there."

Angie looked at him in astonishment. "Yes! Yes, it was there! That's why I went to ask Ed if he'd seen her. He was outside locking up and—oh, Tyler, what does it mean?"

Tyler got to his feet. "I don't know yet. What I do know is that Doc is confident that he saw you entering Nathan's office."

"But I didn't," Angie insisted.

"If you didn't," Tyler took a deep breath, "then it had to have been Amy that Doc saw!"

"Of course." Angie's eyes narrowed thoughtfully. "And if Amy went to Nathan's to find me, and Nathan swears he didn't see either of us, then he's lying. And that means he probably has done something with Amy."

"That's just about the way I figure it," Tyler muttered. "Tell me, Angie, has Nathan said anything to you about leaving town?"

Angie started to shake her head and then stopped abruptly. "He did say he wouldn't be here at Christmas. I remember, because I asked him to accompany me to your service and the festivities afterwards, and he told me he couldn't."

"Did he say where he was headed?" Tyler moved closer to Angie and put his hands on her shoulders. "Think hard, Angie. Did he give you any idea at all?"

Angie thought for moment and then shook her head. "No. He just told me he couldn't escort me and left it at that. I wish I could be more help." She sniffed back tears. "That lying, no-good skunk. He better not have hurt my sister. I just wish there was something I could do to help her."

Tyler put his arm around her and patted her shoulder. "It's all right, Angie. You've given me more to go on than anyone else. You've at least pointed the way. Now listen to me carefully. I want you to wake your mother and tell her what we know. Then I want you to ride out and find your father. It's snowing again, so dress warm and ride quickly."

"What do you want me to tell him?"

"Tell him to find Randy and meet me in town. Since Nathan's still in town and Christmas is tomorrow, he must be planning to make his break tonight. We'll have to be there to follow him and hope that he'll lead us to Amy."

Angie dried her tears and agreed to Tyler's plan. "I'll send them, don't worry about a thing. Just please, please find Amy."

"I'll do my best," Tyler promised, heading for the door. "You just do what I've told you and keep praying."

Chapter 14

Tyler went straight to Nathan's office, but he found it dark and the door locked. He glanced down the darkening street to the boardinghouse, wondering if Nathan had taken refuge in his room or if he had fled town altogether. Tyler could only pray that he'd not find the latter to be the case.

"Pastor Andrews," a voice called from behind him, and Tyler turned to find Jeremy Smith.

"Evening." Tyler's manner was preoccupied.

"Gallagher's gone home for the night," Jeremy said, gesturing toward the locked office. "I saw him leave not ten minutes ago for the boardinghouse."

Tyler let out all his breath at once. "I guess I'll talk to him later," he said and started for his horse.

"Pastor," Jeremy called out, "you will be giving us a service tomorrow, won't you?"

Tyler turned and saw that several other people had joined Jeremy. "Yeah, Pastor," another man added, "the family's sure been looking forward to Christmas morning services."

Tyler had nearly forgotten his promise to preach. His worry for Amy was shutting out all other thought. "I'll be there," he replied, knowing that his voice lacked its normal enthusiasm.

"Good, good," Jeremy said, satisfied that the matter was settled. "The kids are going to put on a play for us, and I've got sacks of candy to give them after you preach. It's going to be a lot of fun for them. I know you're mighty worried about Amy, but I wouldn't want to spoil things for the young 'uns."

Tyler agreed that they should not spoil the festivities, but his heart wasn't in his words. He knew only God could mend the hurt that bound him inside.

Excusing himself, he pushed past the men and got on his horse. "I'll see you all tomorrow morning." He rode out past the hotel, casting a suspicious glance upward at the second-story windows.

He maneuvered his horse into the shadows of nearby trees and dismounted. From where he stood, he could watch the boardinghouse, and he realized that he might learn more by waiting for Nathan to move than by questioning him further.

Grateful that the snow had let up, Tyler decided to board his horse at the livery and stake out the boardinghouse from the livery loft. From there, he would have a view of everything around, and he'd be able to spot Randy and Charles when they made their way to join him.

If the livery owner thought the new pastor was strange for wanting to sleep in the loft, he made no mention of it as he accepted Tyler's money.

Tyler saw to his horse's care and feed, then threw his saddlebags over his shoulder and made his way up the rough ladder to the loft. Tossing the bags aside, Tyler eased the heavy wooden shutter open just enough to peer down the road. All seemed quiet. Only the soft glow from the windows of the surrounding homes broke the fall of darkness.

Tyler studied the boardinghouse a moment longer, noting the side stairs that led to the second floor. Gallagher would have to come out one of three ways, Tyler surmised. Either by the front or back door or these side stairs. Whichever he chose, Tyler was ready.

Tyler was prepared for a lengthy stay, but within a half hour, he was rewarded by the appearance of Nathan Gallagher on the side stairs. He watched as Nathan moved away from the hotel and came toward the livery. Tyler wondered if Nathan had chosen to depart Deer Ridge now. Easing away from the window, Tyler heard the livery door open below. He held his breath.

After a moment, crawling at a snail's pace on his hands and knees, he eased his six-foot-six frame to the edge of the loft. Looking over, Tyler flattened himself in the straw and watched the dark hatted head below. Nathan seemed to be waiting for someone to appear. He checked his watch several times and paced the floor below, making the horses stir.

Tyler could hardly force himself to remain still. He kept thinking of Amy and wondered if Nathan had hurt her. Every time her brown eyes and smiling mouth came to mind, Tyler had to bite back a growl. He wanted to throttle the man, but he knew Gallagher's type wouldn't respond to force. *Lord, I need patience and steadfastness,* Tyler prayed. Feeling the cold bite into his skin, he could only hope that Nathan would lead him to Amy soon.

The back door to the livery swung open then, and a man appeared in the shadowy light. Tyler saw that he matched the description of the man who had sold Amy's horse.

"Gallagher?" the man called, and Nathan stepped into the light.

"Here," he replied. "Did you do the job?"

"You paid me to do it, didn't you?" the man growled. "Still can't figure selling a fine piece of horseflesh like that for only twenty dollars. Why, the saddle alone. . ."

"I don't want to hear what you think," Nathan interrupted. "That's precisely why your brother isn't working with us any more. Because he thought too much."

"Well, what do you want me to do now?" the man asked.

"Come back to my room with me. We'll take the side stairs and no one will see you." Nathan motioned the man to leave the way he'd come.

Tyler wished he could follow them, but he knew he wouldn't have enough cover to get close enough where he could be out of sight and still hear the conversation. All he could do was watch the two men walk away, knowing full well that one or both of them knew where his beloved Amy was hidden.

The men had no sooner disappeared into the hotel than Tyler spotted two riders approaching. He figured they would be Randy and Charles, and he bounded down the ladder to meet them in the street before they could go in search of him.

The Carmichael men were anxious for whatever news Tyler could share. He told them what little he knew, including the whereabouts of the man who'd sold Amy's horse. He and Charles had to grab Randy's shoulders to keep him from storming over and calling the man into the street.

"It won't get Amy back," Tyler insisted, while Charles kept a firm grip on his son's arm.

"Tyler's right," Charles said. "You can't just barge in over there and spill your guts. If Tyler is right, and Nathan plans to make some move between now and the morning, we'll be here to see what it is."

"Each of us needs to stake out a different spot," Tyler suggested. "I'll bet Doc would let one of you use his place."

"We'll work that out, Tyler," Charles agreed. "You stay here, and we'll do what we have to."

"If anyone sees or hears anything that bears notifying the others about, don't waste any time. We may only have minutes to act." Tyler's voice was grave.

Randy nodded and swallowed his anger. "I hope your plan works."

Tyler looked first at Randy and then Charles. "I pray it does too."

Loneliness settled over Tyler after Charles and Randy had gone. Whenever he was near Amy's family, he felt at least a small link with her; but now nothing distracted him from the image of Amy cold and afraid somewhere, perhaps hurt, needing him. . . . Nothing could comfort him.

No, that wasn't true, he realized as he settled himself in the loft again. God was with him, and God was with Amy. That was comfort enough.

An hour passed before the scraggly looking man reappeared on the side stairs of the boardinghouse. Tyler watched the darkness, straining to see where the man would go next. He was surprised to see him return to the livery.

Without thought for his safety, Tyler perched himself on the edge of the loft landing and waited for the man to appear. The door groaned as it was pushed open and then closed with a thud. The man had taken only two or three steps when Tyler jumped from the loft and threw his full weight against him. Delivering a well-placed blow to the burly man's face, Tyler knocked him nearly senseless.

Tyler quickly bound the stranger's hands and feet, hoping he could finish before the man's head cleared. His task accomplished, Tyler maneuvered the heavy man to one side of the livery and went for a bucket of water to revive him.

The frigid water made the man jump, and his eyes flew open. "What the—" The man noticed Tyler for the first time. "Who are you, Mister?"

"I'm Tyler Andrews, the circuit rider for these parts. I'm also the man who hopes to marry Amy Carmichael as soon as she's found," Tyler replied.

The man shook his head. "Don't know no Amy Carmichael." He reached his tied hands up to his bruised jaw. "Why'd you do this? Sure don't seem like a very parsonlike thing for you to be doing."

Tyler studied the man carefully. He seemed to be genuinely surprised that Tyler would have any interest in him. "I know you're working with Nathan Gallagher. And I know you sold Amy's horse in Hays."

"I did sell a horse for Gallagher," the man admitted, "but I didn't know who it belonged to. He just told me to get rid of it quicklike, and I did."

"It doesn't matter." Tyler drew closer. "What does matter is that you'd best tell me where Gallagher has Amy, and you'd best tell me right now."

The man shook his head. "I'm telling you, Mister, I don't know any Amy. There ain't been any woman involved in my dealings with Gallagher."

Tyler grabbed the man by the collar and yanked him forward. "Then you'd best tell me what you and Gallagher are up to, and let me judge for myself."

The man's eyes narrowed, as if he were considering Tyler's words. "I don't reckon Mr. Gallagher would like that," he finally replied.

Tyler's face twisted. He tightened his grip on the man and slammed him back against the wall. "I don't reckon Gallagher's going to take the beating that you are when I go across the street and retrieve Amy's pa and brother. Of course, that's going to be after I get done with you myself. After that, I figure you'll be right glad to go to the gallows."

The man blanched. He wasn't getting paid enough by Gallagher to take the gallows for him—especially if Gallagher had done in some woman in the process of setting up his scheme. Looking into the preacher's face, the man met his deadly stare. What he saw there was more than enough to unnerve him.

"I'll talk," the red-headed man declared. "I ain't going to hang for something I ain't done."

"You'd best get to it then." Tyler voice was ominously calm.

"Gallagher plans to rob the bank tomorrow morning," the man replied. "He has the combination to the safe, and while the town is celebrating Christmas at the school, he's going to let himself in and clean out the harvest money."

Tyler nodded. The man's explanation made everything fall into place. Somehow, Amy must have overheard Gallagher's plans. That was why he had taken her hostage. At last her disappearance was starting to make some sense.

"How do you and your brother figure in this?" Tyler asked, surprising the man with his reference to his brother.

Rather than question the preacher, though, since the huge man seemed to be feeling a might testy, the red-haired man hurried to answer his question. "We arranged to get Gallagher's stuff out of town. Then we were to act as lookouts while Gallagher took the money. We aren't involved in any killings, though, and I never did see any woman. That's the God's honest truth, Preacher."

"Gallagher never said anything about a woman overhearing his plans? He never told you that the horse belonged to Amy Carmichael?"

"No, Sir, he never told me nothing. He got mad at my brother and told him to git. Told me I could have his cut if I wanted to keep on with the plan. It sounded like easy money, so I told him I would. When he told me to take the horse to Hays, he just told me to get rid of it without a scene and to take whatever I could get without haggling the price. I did that and came back here to let him know and get ready for tomorrow."

Tyler realized the man was most likely telling the truth. He studied him for a moment before speaking. "So you aren't supposed to see Gallagher again until tomorrow?"

"I ain't supposed to meet up with him until after the job's done," the man admitted. "I'm supposed to wait between the bank and the school and make sure no one interrupts Gallagher. After that, I'm supposed to ride out and meet him at the river."

Tyler nodded. "Good enough. I'm going to have to lock you up, but maybe once this is done with—and if Miss Carmichael is found unharmed—just maybe the judge will go easy on you since you cooperated with me."

The man grumbled at Tyler's plan, but he knew he had nothing to bargain. He nodded weakly and resigned himself to captivity.

Tyler locked the man in the tack room and hurried to find Charles and Randy. He located Charles first, and together they went to retrieve Randy. He quickly explained to them what he knew.

"Look," Tyler said, the excitement clear in his voice. "Gallagher plans to rob the bank tomorrow while we're having Christmas services. We've got to play this thing out carefully and give him no reason to believe that anything is amiss. Most likely he'll be ready to use Amy as insurance for his plans."

"What'll we do?" Charles asked cautiously.

"We'll act as though nothing has changed," Tyler said. "Randy, you go on home to your family and, Charles, you do the same. Get everybody up and around for the services and bring them on in, just like you planned."

"We can't just pretend nothing's happened," Randy protested.

"Of course we can." Tyler's firmness hushed Randy's objection. "It's the only way we can smoke Gallagher out of his hole."

"The Andersons will need to know," Charles said. "They've been so good to help look for Amy. I know they'd want to be in on this."

"Good. In fact," Tyler had a sudden thought, "we'll need Ed to be inside the bank before Gallagher gets there."

"What do you have in mind?" Charles asked. He looked at the preacher and shook his head, and his lips curled a little. "Never would have thought no parson could be as mean as you are."

"Even Christ got angry enough to physically throw the money changers out of the Temple," Tyler answered. "When He saw true evil, He was just as 'mean' as I feel today."

"What do you have in mind?" Charles repeated.

Tyler smiled, feeling assurance for the first time. He'd finally nailed Gallagher down. "Well, I see it like this. . . ."

Chapter 15

The sleepy people of Deer Ridge emerged from the warmth of their homes and made their way to the schoolhouse for Christmas morning services. Tyler stood outside the school welcoming the families as though nothing was amiss. He saw pain and fear in the eyes of some of the people and wished he could ease their minds even a portion.

Wagons came rattling in from the farthest reaches, and those who dared to make the snowy trip were anxious to seek the warmth of the school building. Dora and Angie Carmichael arrived well bundled in the buckboard, with Charles riding alongside. Close behind them were Randy and his family in their wagon, with Randy's horse tied to the back. Tyler nodded to the two Carmichael men and felt a calm assurance that everything was falling into place.

He cast a quick glance down the street to where the bank stood. Ed Anderson had taken up his place there some hours earlier, and Tyler knew that the other Anderson men were waiting out of sight in order to lend a hand in the capture of Nathan Gallagher. All was progressing as planned.

"Let's hurry inside, folks," Tyler called to the gathering crowd. "We've got a good fire going in the stove, and Brother Smith has kindly furnished hot cider for everyone."

The children clapped their hands at this, and the adults offered brief smiles of gratitude. Tyler knew their discouragement and worry. Wasn't his own heart nearly broken? Didn't his own mind strike against him with torturous thoughts that Amy might already be dead?

Please, Father, he prayed silently, *help me be strong for these people. Help me to help them through this. And be with Amy wherever she is. Let her know that help is on its way—that we haven't forgotten her.*

Amy struggled to climb again onto the table. She had little strength left to even walk, much less to put forth the energy required to knock a hole in the roof. She had no way of knowing how much time had passed, but in spite of the care she had taken, she was out of water now, and the lamp was nearly out of oil.

Always before, Amy had forced herself to ignore her dilemma and to concentrate instead on the task at hand. Minute by minute, she reminded herself that she could lie down and die or fight to escape. Up until this moment, she had always chosen quickly to fight. Now, however, she was tired, cold, hungry, and completely defeated in spirit.

"God," she whispered in a hoarse voice, "I know You're here." She felt like crying, but tears had long since stopped coming. "I've got nothing else to give, Lord. I'm spent, and we both know it."

Just then a huge clod of dirt worked loose from the roof and fell, striking Amy across the face. The pain it caused was brief, but the sunlight it let in was stunning.

Amy stared up in disbelief at the small hole. Bits of snow came in with the dirt, and Amy instantly reached out to pull a handful of the moist whiteness into her mouth. Her lips and tongue seemed to suck up the snow immediately, and eager for more, Amy reached out again and again.

The stream of sunlight offered only shadowy light to the room, but it was enough to encourage Amy. She felt as though God had spoken to her directly, and she worked at the hole with fresh strength, scraping and clawing, until all of her fingers were cut and bleeding.

But she was too weak to work for very long. When her legs would hold her no longer, Amy let herself sink down on the tabletop to rest. After a moment, she rolled from its surface and took herself to the bed, hoping to regain even a little more strength so that she could continue her work.

She closed her eyes and felt the air grow colder. She hadn't thought about the fact that by making a hole in the roof, she would lose what little warmth she'd maintained in the dugout. Opening her eyes, Amy glanced up at her handiwork, then sat up abruptly. Her newfound hope ebbed into despair. The hole was hardly more than eight inches across, too small to do her any practical good. All of her hard work had rendered nothing more than this!

She began to sob, though her eyes refused to produce tears, and she slumped down again on the bed. Hopeless despair filled her heart, and all reasonable thought left her mind.

"I'm going to die," she cried. "Oh, God, I can't bear this!"

Her body was spent, and she had no energy left to urge her on. For a moment longer she struggled to call forth the will to fight, but then at last she gave up and offered God her life, praying that death would be quick and painless.

The exhaustion of the past week had overtaken her, and she had no strength left to fight death any longer. Without even bothering to pull the filthy cover around her, Amy let her mind drift into dreams of her family and Tyler.

It must be close to Christmas, she thought. *Will they still have the Christmas service? Will they sing the old songs?* she wondered.

Strains of music rose through her memories. The haunting melody of "Silent Night" brought her tired mind peace. "All is calm, all is bright." She mouthed the words. "Sleep in heavenly peace." *Yes,* she thought, *I will sleep in heavenly peace.*

Tyler stood at the front of the schoolroom for only a moment. He looked out at the community gathered there, and then he made a brief statement. When he had finished, stunned silence echoed through the room.

"You must help us," Tyler beseeched the crowd. "Amy Carmichael's life depends on it. I don't mind telling you good folks, her life has come to mean a great deal to me."

Several couples exchanged brief knowing smiles before they turned back to the preacher, awaiting further instruction. Moments later the congregation joined in song. The music rang out loudly as Mrs. Smith played a donated piano, and the gathering did their part to assure anyone listening from outside that the service was well underway.

Meanwhile, Tyler hurried out the back door and came quietly around the school to where his horse was hitched. In one fluid movement, he pulled the reins loose and mounted the animal's back. Then, without making a sound, he pushed the horse into a gallop across the snow-covered plain.

Nathan heard the singing and knew his time had come. He smiled and congratulated himself on the simplicity of his plan. He was Morgan Stewart's lawyer, and Morgan Stewart was the bank's owner and the only one besides Ed Anderson who had the combination to the safe. That is, he was the only one until he hired Nathan as his lawyer. Then he had allowed Nathan to keep the carefully guarded secret in a confidential file with Stewart's other important papers.

The whole thing had been too simple, Nathan laughed. He'd only had to place himself in the community for a couple of years and earn their regard and trust. Then when the opportunity of a good harvest presented itself, Nathan knew his time had come.

He threw the last of his belongings into already bulging saddlebags and made his way down the side stairs of the hotel. *I will miss Mrs. Miller's apple dumplings,* he thought, *but with thousands of dollars in my keep, I can no doubt buy tasty apple dumplings elsewhere.*

He went to the livery and saddled his horse, loading his bags before leading the animal down the empty street. The bank sat there like an unguarded jewel, and Nathan felt his pulse quicken.

Down the street, the townspeople broke into yet another Christmas carol, oblivious to the evil that lurked just steps away. At least that's what Nathan presumed.

Quickly, he hitched the horse behind the bank. He looked up and down the empty alleyway, and then with great caution, he picked the lock on the bank door and let himself in.

With the door closed behind him, the singing voices were muted. He steadied his nerves with a deep breath and moved toward the safe. One step, then two, and everything was quiet, just as it should be. But as he lifted his foot a third time, a voice stopped him cold.

"Hello, Gallagher." Ed Anderson sat ever so casually to one side of the room, contemplating the revolver he held in his hand.

Nathan's eyes narrowed, and he whirled on his heel, his own gun quickly drawn from his coat pocket. "Anderson!" He leveled the pistol.

Ed seemed unmoved. His sober gaze never wavered. "Where's Amy?"

Nathan had forgotten the girl, and now he nearly laughed. "Somewhere you'll never find her."

"Now, that doesn't seem to be a very reasonable way to act," Ed said.

Nathan sneered. "Drop your gun, Anderson. I have a quicker hand than you, and I won't hesitate to shoot."

"Oh?" Ed raised a brow. "Then you won't mind when the whole town is alerted by the noise?"

Nathan realized Ed was right. He paused a moment to rethink his plan. "Where's the money?" he asked, noticing that the safe was open.

"Where's Amy?"

But Gallagher refused to give in, and Ed realized he'd have to draw him out. "Look," Ed began, "we know you're using Amy as your protection. I realize that once you leave here, you'll go get her and force her to ride with you so that none of us will follow."

Nathan smiled smugly. Anderson had just given him his new plan of action. "That's right. If you try to stop me, Amy will die."

"I kind of figured that." Ed's voice was cool. "I just figured maybe you'd strike a deal. Like I give you the money, and you give me Amy. Maybe we could have a trade-off down by the river."

"No," Nathan refused firmly. "I'm not a fool to fall into a predictable plan like that. You'll give me the money now, and you won't follow me—or you'll never see Amy Carmichael again!"

Ed got to his feet and took a step toward Gallagher. The look on his face was threatening, and Nathan waved him back with the gun. "If I have to, I'll shoot you—whether the town hears me or not. When they come running, I'll just tell them that I stopped you from robbing the bank. Of course, you'll be dead, and dead men tell no tales. Then where will your precious Amy be?"

"All right, Gallagher," Ed said between his clenched teeth, "you win."

"Of course I do. Now, give me the money and leave me to ride out of here. Remember, I'll have the girl, and there won't be anything to stop me from killing her."

Ed nodded and motioned to the safe. "The money's still inside."

"Get it," Nathan commanded and stepped back. "But first, lose that gun."

Ed looked angrily at Gallagher for a moment and then put the gun down on the desktop. He crossed the room to the safe and pulled out two full money bags.

"Put them on the table by the door," Nathan motioned, and Ed did as he was told. "Now, get down on your belly and don't even think of following me. Not if you want me to release the Carmichael girl unharmed."

Ed began to get down on the floor. "What assurance do I have that she hasn't already been harmed?" he asked.

"None." Nathan leered. "But what other choice do you have?"

Ed shrugged his shoulders and lay down on the floor. He waited until Nathan had grabbed up the money and exited the bank before raising his head. Then glancing around cautiously to make certain Gallagher wasn't waiting for him, Ed got to his feet, pulled on his coat, and ran out of the bank.

He mounted his horse and circled the building. Gallagher was long gone, much to Ed's relief, but the tracks in the snow pointed the direction he'd fled, and Ed knew that his brothers and Amy's family would already be tracking the man. Hopefully, he'd lead them straight to Amy.

Chapter 16

Amy's mind registered sounds, but she told herself she was dreaming. She thought she heard a horse's whinny and the sound of movement on the ground above her, but try as she might, she couldn't push herself to investigate.

She forced her eyes open, only to be blinded by a flood of brilliant light as the door creaked open. She waited, uncertain whether she was dead or alive. Either way, she could only wait, helpless, for whatever happened next.

She felt herself being lifted, and for a moment she wondered if God had come to take her to heaven. The thought comforted her, and she waited limp in the arms that bore her, hopeful that she'd find her celestial home on the other side of the door.

Instead, cold air hit her face, and Amy roused ever so slightly. Trying to focus on the face overhead, she felt a deep foreboding. This was definitely not her heavenly Father who carried her.

"You didn't expect me to come back, did you?"

Amy shook her head, not in reply to the question, but because she was unsure of the words. Her mind was so muddled, clear thinking so beyond her strength, that she could only bide her time.

"The whole town has been looking for you," the voice said. "Especially that fool Andrews."

Amy's foggy mind grasped at the thought of Tyler Andrews. His name was like a lightning bolt, jolting her with energy. She remained silent, however, feigning the near unconscious state that she'd been in before. She still didn't have enough energy to fight this man, but no longer was she apathetic, ready to give up.

"Now," the voice spoke again, "everyone in town is going to have a little more to say about Nathan Gallagher."

Nathan! Of course, now Amy remembered. Nathan had brought her to the dugout. She forced her mind to remember the events, and through the clouds she pulled together bits and pieces. *Yes, yes,* she thought, *I remember; Nathan planned to rob the bank.*

All of a sudden Amy found herself slammed stomach side down against the back of a horse. Just as quickly, Nathan mounted behind her and half pulled her body across his lap.

"They won't be so inclined to do me in," he said with a laugh, "when they see what's at stake."

"I wouldn't count on that, Gallagher," a voice called.

Nathan whirled his mount around to meet the angry faces of Tyler Andrews and Randy and Charles Carmichael.

Tyler could barely maintain his seat at the sight of Amy, half-dead, sprawled across Nathan's lap. He gripped the reins so tight that both hands were balled into gloved fists. More than anything, he would have liked to strike those fists against Gallagher's head.

Randy Carmichael was feeling none too patient either. He moved his horse forward a step. "Let her go, Gallagher."

Nathan laughed and revealed his pistol. "I can easily shoot her," he replied, cocking the hammer. "And I will if you try to stop me from riding away from here."

"But then," Tyler's voice was steady, "you'd have no hostage. And instead of bank robbery, you'd be facing murder."

Nathan shrugged. "I don't intend to rot in any prison either way."

The sound of Tyler's voice had cleared Amy's head a bit more. She moved it ever so slightly to get an idea of her circumstances. The tiny movement caught Tyler's eyes, but Nathan seemed not to notice.

I've got to keep him talking, thought Tyler. "Look Nathan," he began, surprising Charles and Randy with the smooth, open way he spoke, "this doesn't have to end badly. You know what you've done is wrong, but a lot of people have gone astray besides you. You know that God offers forgiveness and new life to all those who ask, no matter what they've done. Why not start over?"

"I don't need a sermon, Preach," Gallagher said.

Tyler moved his horse closer, his eyes never leaving Nathan's. "It's more than a sermon, Nathan, and you know it. If you died right now, you'd have to face God. Are you ready to do that? Are you ready to risk eternal damnation and separation from God?"

"I don't intend to die right now," Nathan said evenly.

"But you will if you don't hand Amy over," Randy promised, his voice tight.

Nathan shrugged. "But then you'd be responsible for her death."

Amy stiffened at the words being bandied over her head. Tyler's horse came forward another pace, making Nathan's horse prance nervously.

"Stay where you are, Andrews," Nathan demanded. "I know what you're trying—and it's not going to work."

"I'm not above begging." Tyler's voice was offhand. "I don't want you to hurt her. I care a great deal about her. In fact, I love her and want her to be my wife."

Nathan laughed. "How touching. But I could care less."

"I guess I've pretty well figured that out." Tyler tried to control his temper. "Point is, I can't help trying. A man such as yourself must surely be in a position to understand that. After all, you're also facing a most precarious situation."

"I've had enough of this," Randy interrupted. He narrowed his eyes. "Gallagher, you let my sister go now, or you'll have to deal with all of us."

"I thought I already was dealing with you," Nathan said, unmoved by Randy's declaration. "I seem to be managing satisfactorily." He grinned.

"Not quite." Ed Anderson came out of the trees. His brothers, Jacob and Jack, followed. Now six horsemen surrounded Nathan. Slowly he began to realize that he was losing the battle.

"God can still save your soul, Gallagher." Tyler edged the huge Morgan he rode another step forward. "But right now, you're the only one who can save your hide."

Nathan's horse shied at the Morgan's nearness and whinnied nervously. Tyler refused to back off and pressed his luck. Nathan quickly brought the gun up from Amy to level it at Tyler, just as the Morgan nudged his head against Gallagher's mount.

Amy took that opportunity to dig what was left of her ragged fingernails into the horse's side. Nathan's mount reared. While Nathan fought to hold onto the reins, Amy slid backward off the horse. She used every ounce of her remaining energy to roll to the side. After that, she could do nothing more than lie there and await her fate.

Without warning, Tyler leapt across his horse, knocking Nathan to the ground. The pistol fired harmlessly into the air as it flew from Nathan's hand. Within seconds, four other men were helping to restrain Gallagher, while Charles Carmichael jumped to the ground and lifted Amy into his arms.

"Pa?" she whispered. Her throat was raw, and her voice was barely audible.

"I'm here, Amy," he answered with tears in his eyes. "You're safe now."

Tyler was at her side immediately. He pulled off his coat and wrapped it around her shivering body. In Amy's confused state of mind, she found his worried expression almost amusing, but the overgrown stubble of his beard amused her even more.

"You need a shave." She croaked the words against his ear.

Tyler lifted his head and laughed loud and hard, though tears shone in his eyes. Even Charles had to join in the laughter. "That's my girl," Tyler said, lifting her in his arms.

Randy left Nathan to the capable hands of the Andersons. They'd already agreed to be responsible for getting Gallagher to Hays. Ed was the one witness who would be able to confirm the bank robbery, and the others would no doubt be called upon if needed at a later date.

"Merry Christmas, Sis," Randy said, laying a hand on Amy's dirty cheek. Tears gleamed in Randy's eyes too.

"Quite a present," she replied weakly.

"Let's get her to Doc," Tyler said, heading for his horse with his precious cargo.

"I can take her," Randy offered. He reached out his arms, but his father's hand pulled him back.

"I think you'd have a fight on your hands if you tried to separate them now," Charles said softly.

Randy nodded. "I suppose you're right. If it were Betsey. . ."

"Or Dora," Charles interjected. "There comes a time when fathers and brothers have to step aside. Now, come on, let's get back to town."

Tyler held Amy close, whispering endearments and encouragement all the way back to Deer Ridge. She snuggled against the warmth of his coat, thanking God silently for sending help in time to rescue her from Nathan's plans.

She opened her eyes briefly and gazed up into the haggard face of the man she'd come to love more dearly than life. With a smile, she whispered, "I love you, Tyler Andrews."

Tyler shook his head with a grin. "You're something else, Amy Carmichael. You endure all of this, and now you want to finally get around to telling me that you love me?"

"Just thought you'd like to hear it," she smiled, closing her eyes.

Tyler leaned down and placed a kiss against her forehead. "You bet I want to hear it. I want to hear it every day of my life for the rest of my life!"

The entire town was waiting and watching for the riders to return. When they caught sight of Tyler's huge horse, they strained their eyes to identify the bundle he held. Cheers went up when Randy and Charles moved ahead to announce that Amy was alive but extremely weak. Charles handed his reins to Randy and went quickly to Dora and Angie to assure them that Amy was safe. There were tears of joy on their faces as they followed arm in arm to Doc Taggert's office. In hushed conversation, the town's people gathered behind them and followed in the street to gather outside the doctor's office.

Tyler waited outside with Charles, while Dora and Angie went inside to be with Amy while Doc Taggert examined her.

"Where's Gallagher?" Jeremy Smith asked the question everyone wanted to know.

"The Andersons are taking him to Hays," Tyler replied. His mind was not on the question, though. He had been reluctant to leave Amy's side, and now he ached to know if she would be alright.

"Then he's alive?" someone else called out.

Randy moved through the crowd with Betsey at his side. Their children were being tended back at the school by one of the townswomen, while baby Joey was safely tucked in the crook of his mother's arm.

"He's alive," Randy said, coming to stand beside his father. "He could just as well be dead and so could Amy, if it weren't for Tyler's patience." A smile crossed Randy's face. "Good thing for Gallagher, 'cause patience ain't exactly one of my own virtues."

The crowd laughed, and then Charles hushed them all. "I want to thank all of you for your help in finding Amy. We're stuck out here so far from everybody else in the world that we've truly become one big family. Without working together, we'd probably all perish."

Murmurs of agreement went through the crowd before Charles could speak again. "Truth is, and you folks need to understand this, Tyler Andrews saved this town from disaster. See, Gallagher didn't just take Amy, he planned to clean out the bank as well. Amy overheard his plans, and that's why he kidnapped her."

The exchange of looks between the people varied from anger to plain shock. Their hopes and dreams were pinned on their savings and earnings.

"Look, I know you folks feel the same way I do about having a full-time parson around these parts. I think we pretty much owe that to Tyler, and I'd like to propose we hire him on as Deer Ridge's first pastor." Charles sent a beaming smile toward the man he knew would one day be his son-in-law.

Cheers from the crowd confirmed that Deer Ridge's residents felt the same way the Carmichaels did.

"It's the least we can do," Jeremy Smith said to the crowd. "We wouldn't even have the money to last through the winter if it weren't for Andrews getting wind of Gallagher's plan."

"That's right," Mrs. Smith agreed enthusiastically. "I think Pastor Andrews is just what this town needs."

Tyler held out his hands to quiet the enthusiastic response of the people before him. "I appreciate the offer," he said.

"Well, what do you say?" Amos Osborne, Deer Ridge's self-appointed mayor, questioned Tyler. "Will you pastor our community? I'm sure I speak for all the folks here in saying we'd be most honored to have you stay on. We might even be able to build a church in another year or so—that is, if we get another good year behind us." Everyone nodded in unison and waited for the towering man to speak.

Tyler's heart was touched, but his mind was on Amy. "I'll pray about it," he replied.

Just then Angie appeared at the door with a smile on her face. "Doc says Amy is half-starved and dehydrated. But she didn't suffer much from the cold, and he says she ought to be just fine in a few days."

Tyler reached out and gave Angie a hearty hug at the news.

"Whoa, Preacher," someone called. "You got the wrong sister!" Everyone laughed, and Tyler's face reddened.

"Don't worry," Angie laughed. "I'll pass that hug on to the right one." With a wink, she turned and went back into the building.

Bit by bit, the crowd dispersed and regathered at the schoolhouse where the festivities for Christmas started anew. Once Tyler was certain Amy was out of any real danger, he agreed to return and preach the service he'd promised. The atmosphere was one of genuine love and happiness, with each and every person knowing just how far God's protection and love had extended to them that Christmas.

The kids made clear that they considered the holiday theirs, and after their simple play about the shepherds seeking the Christ child, they lined up to receive candy from the Smiths. Soon the entire affair burst into a full-fledged party, with sweets and goodies spread out on a lace tablecloth. Someone brought out a punch bowl and cups, and soon everyone was toasting the day and the man who they hoped would stay to become one of Deer Ridge's own.

Finally, Tyler led them in a closing prayer. "Father, we thank You for the gift of Your Son. We can't begin to understand the sacrifice You made on our behalf, but we praise You for Your love."

Several people murmured in agreement before Tyler could continue. "You've watched over this town in a most wondrous way this day—and in a very unique and special way You brought us all together. For awhile, we forgot our differences and divisions. For a very precious time, we were able to stand here before You, knowing with surety that Your gift was given equally to us all. In that gift we are given hope, forgiveness, and eternal life. Thank You, Father. Amen."

There were few dry eyes in the room when Tyler finished. Beyond a murmured thank-you or pat on the back, no one said a word to the young pastor as he left the school. They all knew where his heart was hurrying him.

Chapter 17

Amy restlessly pushed back her covers and started to sit up. She'd been in bed four days now; because of her mother's continual care, she was very nearly herself again. In spite of this, however, no one seemed inclined to let her out of bed.

"Oh no, you don't, young lady." Her mother came into the room with a tray of food.

"I can't just lie here eating all the time," Amy protested. "I'll get fat and lazy!"

"You could do with a little more meat on your bones." Dora laughed. "As for lazy, that will be the day pigs fly."

Amy giggled and sat back reluctantly against the pillows. "I truly feel fine, Ma."

"I know." Dora put the tray across her daughter's lap. "You just let me pamper you a bit more. Soon enough, if I have that young preacher of yours figured out, you'll be gone from this house and my care—so let me enjoy it while I can."

Amy frowned slightly. Since the day after her rescue, she had not seen Tyler at all. She'd asked her father about him yesterday, but Charles had shrugged his shoulders. Perhaps Tyler needed to tend to business, he told her.

"You can just wipe that frown off your face," Dora commanded good-naturedly. "Tyler will be back."

"I hope so." Amy's voice lacked confidence. She glanced down at the tray on her lap; it held a bowl of beef stew, two biscuits, and a glass of milk. "Didn't I just eat an hour ago?" she asked with a laugh.

"Just be quiet and eat." Dora tucked the covers around her daughter. "I used Cora Peterson's recipe for the stew. I seem to recall that was your favorite."

Amy took a mouthful of the thick stew and nodded. "Mmm, it's perfect."

Dora smiled at this announcement and turned to leave. "Now, if you need anything at all, just ring." She nodded at the bell by Amy's bedside.

"I promise." Amy tried to give the stew her attention. When her mother had left the room, though, Amy sighed and pushed the tray back.

"Where are you, Tyler?" she whispered into the silent air. She didn't want to eat or rest anymore. She wanted to talk to Tyler. She needed to hear his voice and know that everything was truly all right.

Boredom was her enemy, and Amy wanted nothing more than to be up and about. At least if she were back to her regular duties, Tyler's absence wouldn't be so noticeable.

After ten or fifteen minutes, her mother reappeared. She gave the tray a glance and frowned. "You haven't eaten much of it." She looked at Amy for a long moment, then she surprised her daughter by going to the closet and pulling out a long flannel robe. "Here." She handed Amy the robe and took the tray. "Put this on, and I'll let you sit at the window."

Amy's smile stretched nearly from ear to ear. This was the first time her mother had agreed to let her get up for any reason other than the absolute necessities. Hurriedly, in case her mother changed her mind, she thrust her arms through the robe's sleeves.

Dora put the tray on the table by the window. "Now, seeing as how I'm being so nice to you, oblige me by eating a little more of this." She went back to help Amy to her feet. "You promise to just sit here now?" Dora settled Amy in the chair. "No big ideas about trying to get up on your feet?"

"Of course not." Amy smiled.

Dora sniffed and looked at her daughter suspiciously. "You just mind what your mother says, Girl." Her voice was stern, but the corners of her mouth curved up.

A knock at the bedroom door made them both turn. Charles peeked his head inside with a grin. "I found someone wandering around the yard below, hoping to get a chance to talk with our Amy," he teased. Pushing the door open wide, he revealed a grinning Tyler Andrews.

"Tyler!" Amy jumped to her feet.

"Sit back down!" Dora commanded. "You promised."

Amy obediently did as she was told, but a slight pout on her lips told them all that she wasn't happy about it.

"Now, if you promise," her mother stressed the words, "to stay put, we'll let Tyler visit you for a spell."

Amy nodded and made the sign of an "X" over her heart. "Cross my heart," she said solemnly.

Her parents and Tyler laughed. "I guess that's the best we can hope for," Charles said. "I'll get you a chair, Tyler," he added. "Be right back."

Dora smiled and exited the room quietly. Meanwhile, Amy tried to keep herself from leaping across the room into Tyler's arms.

"You shaved," she said with a grin.

"I was told it was quite overdue." Tyler returned her grin.

Charles entered the room with a kitchen chair, then just as quickly left. Tyler brought the chair to the table where Amy's food still sat untouched.

"You'd best eat that." He pointed to the stew.

"I'm not hungry," Amy said softly.

Tyler frowned. "You're still not feeling well?"

Amy made a face. "I feel fine. But Ma's been feeding me every five minutes—or so it seems. All I've really wanted to do was get up and. . ." She stopped abruptly and looked deep into Tyler's warm gaze.

"And?" Tyler prompted.

"And talk to you," she admitted. "Where have you been? I was beginning to get worried that I'd have to saddle up and come looking for you."

Tyler reached out and took hold of Amy's hand. He looked down at her fingers and then gave them a squeeze. "I'll never be far from you. I promise."

Amy felt warmth spread from her hand, up her arm, until it finally engulfed her whole body, leaving her trembling. "I've missed you," she whispered. "I never even had a chance to thank you for all that you did. Pa told me you were the one who figured things out. He told me that without your devotion to the search, I'd most likely have died."

Tyler said nothing. He knew the words were true, but they seemed unimportant just now. "I had to find you," he whispered.

"Yes," Amy said. A hint of amusement played at the corners of her mouth, but she made her voice carefully serious. "Mrs. Smith told me that she accidentally told you about your Christmas gift. I suppose it was necessary to find me in order to be sure you got it."

Tyler looked surprised at her words, almost taken back for a moment, and Amy laughed. "Don't be so serious, Tyler. I was teasing."

Tyler shook his head and smiled sheepishly. "I guess it's going to take me awhile to get used to the idea that you're really here with me safe and sound—and even a little obnoxious. I was so afraid I'd lost you."

Amy smiled, but her eyes misted at the expression she saw on his face. "But I'm all right now, thanks to you and Pa and everyone else. God watched over me. Even when I gave up hope, He stood fast and provided for my rescue. I won't spend the rest of my life having you look at me that way." Her voice was firm.

Tyler pulled his hand away. "Look at you what way?"

"Like I'm about to disappear into thin air. Or," she lowered her voice to a whisper, "die."

Tyler considered her words for a moment. "I know you're right. I have to learn to trust your safety to God. But you did disappear into thin air—and you came awfully close to dying. Gallagher would have left you there in that soddy if we hadn't interfered. I don't think you could have survived much longer." He shook his head, his eyes dark.

"I know." Amy reached to take back Tyler's hand. "After what happened to your wife, I can understand how you must feel. But we are all in God's hands. And you must let go of your worry. I want to get on with my life. I want to make plans."

Tyler's face relaxed, and after a moment his mouth curved into a smile. "What? Beyond today?" he teased.

"Yes." She looked up at him. "You were right. It's easy to take one day at a time when you have no one to plan for a future with. Now that I have you, I find my head just bursting with plans. But I don't think it can be all bad to make plans. Even Proverbs says that we can make our plans, counting on God to direct our path. I'll still try to live one day at a time. I don't want to miss even one of the wonderful blessings God has given me in the here and now. But while I'm doing that, I'm also going to look forward to the days to come. Just so long as our plans for the future are grounded in God's Word."

"Then maybe you'll need this." Tyler pulled his well-worn Bible from his coat pocket. He handed the book to Amy and watched as she gently ran her fingers across the cover. "Merry Christmas."

"I don't know what to say." Amy looked up at him with tears in her eyes. "I can't take your Bible." She blinked the tears away and saw now the amusement in Tyler's eyes.

"Well, you're right," he said. "I won't be able to get along without that Bible very well. That's why I have a confession to make."

"Oh? And what might that be?" Amy's voice was suspicious.

"The Bible is just a part of your Christmas gift."

"And what might the rest of my gift be?" Amy leaned forward.

Tyler shrugged, then held out his arms. "Me. It's a package deal. To get the Bible, you have to take me too. We kind of go together."

"I see." Amy hugged the Bible to her.

"Will you marry me, Amy Carmichael?" Tyler's voice was serious now.

"Of course I will." Amy breathed out a heavy sigh. "I was beginning to wonder how I was going to propose to you, what with you taking so long to ask that particular question. All this talk about Bibles."

Tyler laughed and got to his feet. He started to pull Amy up into his arms, and then suddenly he stopped and pushed her back down. "I forgot. You promised your ma you'd sit."

Amy frowned, but Tyler quickly remedied the situation by pulling his chair close to hers. Leaning over, he pulled her against him with one hand and lifted her face with the other. "I love you, Amy." He lowered his mouth to hers, his lips both gentle and firm.

Amy melted against him. She felt her heart nearly burst with love. When he pulled his lips away at last, she opened her eyes slowly and met his amused stare.

"When?" she whispered.

"I beg your pardon?"

She narrowed her eyes at him, but his golden hair beckoned her fingers, and she reached up to push back a strand before she answered. "You know very well what I mean, Tyler Andrews." She pursed her lips primly. "When can we get married, Parson?"

Tyler grinned. "I'll have to check my schedule and see when I can fit you in. Pastoring is a mighty big responsibility, you know. It might be a spell before I can get back to these parts and. . ."

Amy jerked away from his arms. "Don't tease me, Tyler Andrews. If I have to, I'll hitch up the team and drive us to Hays myself." She sighed and then added firmly, "I've never been pushy about anything in my life—until now. But I'm beginning to think Angie may have been right all along. She sees a thing she wants and goes right after it. Well, now I intend to do the same."

Tyler's raucous laughter filled the air, bringing Charles and Dora to the doorway.

"What's going on?" Charles gave Tyler and Amy an amused look.

"Your daughter," Tyler said, still laughing, "is threatening to hitch up the team and drive us to Hays so we can get married. I was just picturing the sight in my mind. Barely off her deathbed, clad in her nightgown, hair all wild and crazy behind her," he paused, and Amy turned crimson at his description, "and she's going to drive us to Hays."

"It's always the quiet ones who'll surprise you," Charles advised Tyler. With an arm around his wife, Charles added, "And I speak from experience."

Tyler laughed all the more at that, and even Dora couldn't help but join in. Soon, Amy gave up trying to be serious and chuckled in spite of herself. With Tyler Andrews for a husband, she had no doubt she would always have laughter in her house.

From that moment on, Tyler and Amy spent many hours together planning and preparing for their wedding. Tyler shared with her his prayerful consideration of the town's offer to become the full-time pastor, and Amy rejoiced when he decided to accept the job. She'd happily follow him anywhere, she knew in her heart; but she loved Deer Ridge and her family, and she was glad to stay close to all that she cared about.

She soon learned that Tyler's absence during her recovery had included a trip to Hays, where he had managed to find another preacher who would not only take over Tyler's circuit but also returned to Deer Ridge with him. With the other preacher officiating, the wedding was to take place on New Year's Day. Amy couldn't imagine a better way to start the new year.

When the day came at last, she stood proudly beside the huge man. The drawn, nervous look on his face almost made her giggle, but her own nerves weren't much more settled than Tyler's appeared to be. She listened carefully to the words spoken by the circuit rider, and then she repeated her vows. Without a doubt in her heart, she promised to love, honor, and obey this man she loved so much.

Tyler's voice was firm and grave as he repeated the same vows. When he took her hand and placed a small gold band on her finger, tears of joy and wonder slid down Amy's cheeks.

Then the ceremony was over. Tyler pulled her into his arms, kissing her in front of the entire community. With a loud voice, he declared to one and all that they were joined in God's sight and in love.

The community cheered heartily as the ceremony concluded. They congratulated the young couple until Amy thought her hand would be permanently numb from shaking the hands of so many people.

Charles and Dora came to greet their children, and Amy smiled radiantly when they called her Mrs. Andrews. Angie in her wedding finery, a new gown of blue taffeta which had come from Hays, danced rings around everyone. The entire community was convinced that she'd be the next to marry. The only question was which one of her many suitors Angie would finally settle on.

"We're mighty glad to see you up and around, Miss Amy," Jeremy Smith said when his turn came to congratulate the newlyweds. He turned then to Tyler and broke into a broad grin. "And we're mighty happy, Preacher, to know we'll get to hear your preaching every week and not just once a month."

Tyler pulled Amy close. She lifted her face to see the look of pride and joy in her husband's eyes. "Deer Ridge will be a good place to call home," he replied, looking down into Amy's face. "A right fine place to plan a future."

Amy smiled. "You mean a future beyond today?" she whispered.

The joke was lost on Jeremy, but Tyler smiled as he looked down at Amy and nodded. "You can count on it, Mrs. Andrews." He gave her a wink. "I'm planning on spending a good long time with you beyond today. A whole lifetime, in fact."

THE HOUSE ON WINDRIDGE

Tracie Peterson

Prologue

Windridge Ranch, Kansas
January 1, 1863

The pathetic cries of a newborn continued to split the otherwise heavy silence of the day long after the sheet had been pulled up to cover the infant's dead mother. The baby's hunger and misery seemed to feed her wails, despite the housekeeper's attempts to soothe and comfort the distraught child.

Gus Gussop had already borne the pain of hearing the housekeeper tell him his wife was dead. Now he faced the hopelessness of trying to satisfy a newborn—his wife's departing gift. Running his hands through his chestnut hair, Gus felt pain more acute than any he'd ever known. The tightening in his chest gave him cause to wonder if his heart had suddenly attacked him. He prayed it would be so and that he might join his beloved Naomi in eternal rest.

The baby's high-pitched cries intensified, causing Gus to storm from the room. "Find some way to shut her up!" he bellowed over his shoulder.

Slamming the door to the bedroom he'd shared with Naomi, Gus made his way downstairs to the front door. But he'd no sooner reached it than he heard the approaching footsteps of his good friend and ranch foreman, Buck Marcus.

"I'm deeply sorry for you, Gus," came Buck's apologetic voice.

"What do you want?"

"You can't be going out there now," Buck reminded. "Did you forget we're in the midst of a blizzard? Ain't no visibility for miles, and you'd surely freeze to death before you made it ten feet."

"Well, maybe I want to freeze to death," Gus answered flatly, turning to scowl at the red-haired Buck. "Leave me be."

Buck nodded at the order and took his leave, but when Gus turned back to the massive front door, he knew the man was right. For a few minutes, all Gus could do was stare at the highly ornate oak door—stare and remember. He'd paid a handsome sum to have the door designed with stained glass and detailed woodcarving. Naomi had been so very fond of pretty things, and this door, this entire house for that matter, had been Gus's gift to her for having a good nature about moving to the Flinthills from her beloved home in New York City.

He turned and looked up at the beautifully crafted oak staircase. Wood came at a premium in Kansas. For that matter, with a nation at war against itself, everything came at a premium. But Gus had found ways around the inconvenience of war. The beautifully grained oak had been meticulously ordered and delivered over a two-year period, all in order to give his wife the best. The wood floors and heavy paneling in the library had been equally difficult to come by, but Gus had successfully managed each and every problem until he had exactly what he wanted for his impressive ranch house.

The house itself had been designed out of native limestone and stood atop the hill Gus had affectionately named "Windridge." They said the wind in Kansas was the reason that trees seldom stayed in place long enough to grow into anything worth noting. And while Gus had made his home on Windridge, or rather on the side of this massive hill, he was of the opinion that this was true. For miles around, they were lucky to find a single stubborn hedge tree or cottonwood. The rolling Flinthills stretched out as far as the eye could see, and the only thing it was good for was grazing cattle.

Gus had built his empire, constructed his castle, married his queen, and now it all seemed to have been in vain. She was dead. Naomi had died in the house he had gifted her with upon their marriage, died giving birth to their only child.

"What do I do now?" Gus questioned aloud, looking up the stairs.

At least the baby had quieted. He had never once considered Naomi might die in childbirth. She seemed such a healthy, vital woman that to imagine her dead over something women did every day seemed preposterous. After all, they were only an hour away from Cottonwood Falls, and should there be any need for a doctor, Gus knew it would be easy enough to get one. But on the last day of the year, a blizzard had set in, making travel impossible. The storm had now raged for over twenty-four hours, and snow piled in drifts as high as the eaves on the house. The stylish circular porch was covered in ice and snow, and no one dared to set foot outside without a rope secured to him to guide him back to safety.

A line had been tied from the house to the barn and to the bunkhouse, but other than checking on the livestock, which had been crammed into every possible free spot in the barn, the men were ordered to stay inside, out of danger. This he could order and see performed to his specifications. But Naomi's labor was another matter entirely. It had begun in the midst of the storm and was so mild at first that Katie, their housekeeper, had thought it to be a false labor. But then Naomi's water broke, and Katie informed him that there would be no stopping the birth. The child simply would not wait until the storm abated.

Things went well for a time. Katie had attended many area birthings due to her experience growing up with a midwife for a mother. It didn't seem they had anything to worry about. But then the baby came breech, and Katie said the cord seemed caught up on something. She fought and worked her way through the birthing, praying aloud from time to time that she could save both mother and child. Standing at Naomi's side, offering what assistance he could, Gus had heard the prayers, but they didn't register. He still refused to believe that anything could mar the happiness he had shared together with Naomi.

But as the hours passed and he watched his wife grow weaker, he knew those prayers were very necessary. There seemed to be nothing Katie could do to ease Naomi's suffering. She instructed the young mother-to-be, and Naomi heeded her, performing whatever task she was told to do. Katie had her out of the bed at one point to squat in order to push the child down. But nothing seemed to work the way it should, and Katie soon began saying things that Gus didn't want to hear.

"We may lose the baby," she had told him. "We may lose them both."

Gus had gone to the door then, just as he had a few minutes ago. He had planned to fight his way through the storm to the doctor's, if necessary. But one look outside, and Gus had known there was no hope of leaving Windridge. He prayed the storm would abate. Prayed his child might be born safely. But never did he pray that Naomi might not die. It was unthinkable that such a thing could happen. It simply didn't fit Gus's plans.

But the unthinkable did happen.

Shortly before midnight, Jessica Gussop arrived as a New Year's Eve baby. She cried out in protest as Katie lifted her from her mother's body. She cried in protest when Katie cut the cord, and she cried in protest when Naomi, after holding the child and kissing her tiny head, had died.

He could still see the look in Naomi's eyes. She knew she wasn't going to make it. She smiled weakly at Gus, told him she loved him—that she would always love him. Then she whispered Jessica's name and closed her eyes.

Gus shook his head, trying to force the horrible scene from his mind. It just couldn't be true. They were all mistaken. He would go back upstairs now, and Naomi would sit up in bed and call his name.

He reached for the banister.

It was possible. They could be wrong.

Sorrow washed over him, and he knew without a doubt there had been no error in judgment. Her presence was gone from Windridge. There was nothing upstairs for him now. Naomi's body was there, but not the lighthearted laughter, not the sweet spirit he had fallen in love with.

She would never sit up. She would never call his name.

He turned and walked away from the staircase and passed through large double doors that slid open to usher him into the walnut-paneled library. This had been his refuge and sanctuary whenever the events of the day proved to be too much. Now, it only echoed the sounds of his heavy steps as he crossed to the desk where he did his book work.

She was gone. There was nothing left. Nothing to hope for. Nothing to live for.

He pulled open a drawer and saw the revolver that lay inside. He could join her. He could settle it all with one single bullet. The idea appealed to him in a way that went against all that he believed. He had shared a Christian faith with Naomi, had served as an elder in the church at Cottonwood Falls, and had always remembered to give God the glory for all that he'd been blessed with. To kill himself would directly violate God's law. But to live violated his own sensibilities.

Gus heard the cry again and knew that before he could settle his own affairs, he would first have to do something about the baby. Jessica. Naomi had called her Jessica, and Jessica she would stay. He hadn't cared much for the name—had teased Naomi, in fact, about calling any daughter of his by such a fancy name. Bible names were good enough for the Gussop family. But then Naomi had reminded him that Jessica came from the masculine root of Jesse—the father of King David. So it was to be Jessica for a girl and Jesse for a boy. Gus had liked that idea. He'd liked it even more when Naomi, the granddaughter of a highly respected preacher in New York City, told him that Jesse meant "the Lord exists" and she liked very much to think that God would prove His existence through the life of this child.

"I see His existence, all right," Gus muttered. "The Lord giveth and the Lord taketh away." He refused to finish Job's ancient proclamation by blessing the name of the Lord.

"I can't raise a baby without a mother," Gus said emphatically. He slammed his hands down on the desk, then sent the contents flying with a wide sweep of his arm. "I can't do it! Do you understand!" he bellowed. "I won't do it!"

He shook his fist at the ceiling. "You can't expect me to do it without her. You can't be that cruel. You may give, and You may take away, but You can't expect me to be happy about it—to go about my business as if nothing has happened."

Silence. Even Jessica's cry had quieted. Gus looked down at the mess he'd made and slammed the desk drawer shut. First, he would see to the child. There would no doubt be someone who would take her and raise her to adulthood. Especially given the fact that upon his death, Jessica would inherit everything he owned. That would make her an attractive package to prospective parents. But who should he approach on the matter?

Katie, his housekeeper, was hardly the one to saddle with such a responsibility. At twenty-five, the thing that most amused Katie was Buck, and even though the man was thirteen years her senior, a May wedding was already in the works. No, it wouldn't be right to put Jessica off on Katie and Buck. Buck had been a friend to him long enough that Gus knew the man wanted no part of owning a big spread of his own. He'd told Gus on more than one occasion that if he died tomorrow he would be happy being Gus's hired man and friend.

Gus considered neighbors and friends in town, but no one struck him as having the right combination of requirements for raising his child. And those requirements were very important to him. Just because he didn't feel capable of seeing to the needs of his daughter didn't mean he wouldn't take those needs into consideration while choosing her guardian.

After several torturous days of thinking through all the possibilities, Gus had eliminated all names except one. Harriet Nelson. Harriet was the maiden aunt of his deceased wife. The woman had practically raised Naomi, and as far as Gus was concerned, she made the perfect choice for raising Naomi's daughter. But Harriet lived in New York City, and exchanging letters or even telegrams would take days—maybe months. Gus didn't like the idea, but it seemed his only recourse.

Then, too, Jessica was too young and sickly to travel. Katie had tried to find a proper source of nourishment for the child and had finally come up with sweetening and watering down canned milk. At least the poor babe could stomach the solution. Which was more than could be said for the other dozen concoctions that had been tried.

Taking pen in hand, Gus began the letter to Harriet. He explained the death of Naomi first, offering Harriet his condolences in recognition of her position as adoptive mother to his wife. Then he told her of Jessica. He described the child who'd been born with her mother's dark brown eyes, despite the fact that Katie had never heard of any infant being born with other than blue eyes. She also had her mother's dark brown hair, although there wasn't much of it. He described her as a good baby, telling of the trial and error in finding something to feed her. Then he concluded the letter by expressing his desire that Harriet take over the rearing of his daughter. He made no pretense about the issue.

I find that I am ill-equipped to care for an infant on a prairie ranch. The housekeeper has done a fine job, but with her own upcoming wedding, I hardly can rely on her for such assistance in the future.

Harriet, you are the only one to whom I would entrust this job. The reflection of your ability was clearly displayed in Naomi's character. I know you would raise the child to be a good Christian and to occupy herself with godly service. I know too that Jessica would be loved and pampered. Please understand, I am well aware of my own responsibilities. I would, of course, provide financially for the child and yield to your authority on matters concerning her schooling.

Please do not refuse me on this matter, Harriet. I know you planned a different life for Naomi, and apparently your choice would have been wiser. A Kansas cowboy and a prairie ranch were unworthy of a woman such as your niece, but I recognize my own limitations and would go so far as to say this is a matter of life and death. I would appreciate your speedy response on the matter.

Ever Your Faithful Servant,
Joseph Gussop

He reread the letter several times before finally sealing it in an envelope and penning the New York address to the outside.

There, he thought. *The job is done. I have only to mail this letter and receive her response and then—then I can put this all behind me.*

Buck came in about that time. "Boss, we've been looking things over as best we can. Looks like most of the stock survived."

Gus nodded. He had little desire to talk about the ranch or his responsibilities.

"There's something else I need to discuss with you," Buck said hesitantly.

"Then speak up," Gus replied, seeing Buck's apprehension. It wasn't like the man to skirt around an issue.

"It has to do with her."

Gus felt the wind go out from him. For days the only way he'd managed to get through the hours was to avoid thinking about her. It was one thing to mention her in a letter to Harriet, but another thing to consider what was to be done in the aftermath of her death. In fact, he had no idea what had already been done in the way of preparing her for her burial. He'd simply refused to have any part of it.

"All right," he finally answered.

"Well," Buck began slowly, "I built her, ah. . ." He faltered. "I mean, well, that is to say—"

"You built her a coffin?" Gus questioned irritably.

Buck nodded. "Yes, Sir. We took her out like you asked. But, Gus, the ground is too froze up for burial."

Gus growled and pounded his fists on the ground. "I don't care if you have to blow a hole in the ground with dynamite. I want her buried today." Buck nodded and without another word took off in the direction from which he'd come.

Several hours later, Gus heard and felt the explosion that signaled the use of dynamite. It rattled the windows and caused the baby to howl up a fit, but Gus knew instinctively that it would also resolve the problem. They would bury her today. Buck would say the words, given their inability to have the preacher ride out from town, and they would put her body into the ground.

Gus tried to think of everything analytically. First he would see to Naomi. Then he would see to Jessica's care. Then he would take care of himself.

Two weeks after the little funeral, Gus was finally able to post his letter to Harriet in Cottonwood Falls. And two months after that, with a strangely warm March whipping up one of the first thunderstorms of the season, Gus rode back from town, reading the missive he'd received from New York City.

> *Of course, you must realize I am hardly the young woman I was when Naomi was small, but I would be honored to raise Jessica for as long as time permits.*

He breathed a sigh of relief. She had agreed to take the child. He continued reading.

> *However, I do have my own requirements to see to such an arrangement. First, I desire final say over her upbringing. As you pointed out, you are hardly aware of her needs. I want no interference, no monthly visits, no constant trips back and forth between the desolate American desert and New York. I want the child to know proper society and schooling before she is exposed to the barbaric plains of Kansas. I also believe it will diminish any sense of loss in the child. In other words, if she is constantly looking toward her next trip to Kansas, she may well be unruly and unwilling to focus on her life here.*

Well, Gus thought, *that certainly wasn't a problem.* He wouldn't be around, but, of course, he couldn't tell Harriet that.

> *Secondly, I have devised the figures that I believe constitute the*

proper amount of money necessary to care properly for a child in New York City. She will be a child of social standing, and, therefore, the cost is higher than you might otherwise believe necessary. If you will note the second page of this letter, however, you will see I have detailed the information for you.

Gus looked at the page and noted that Harriet had indeed outlined the cost for food, clothing, schooling, supplies, toys, furniture, and a nanny to assist Harriet. It all seemed perfectly reasonable, even if it was a pricey figure. *Still,* he thought, *it didn't matter.* He wouldn't be around to argue or protest Harriet's judgment. He turned back to the first page of the letter and continued to read.

If these things meet with your approval, then I will expect to receive the child whenever you deem yourself capable of delivering her.

Gus breathed a sigh of relief. It was all falling into place.

Once he'd arrived at Windridge, Gus called Katie and Buck into the library and explained the situation.

"I'm sending Jessica to her mother's aunt in New York City," he said flatly, without a hint of emotion in his voice. His emotions were dead. Dead and cold, just as she was.

Katie spoke first. "What? How can you do this? I'm perfectly happy to bring her up for you, Mr. Gussop."

"Katie," he replied, "you and Buck are about to begin your lives together. There's no need to be saddling you with a ready-made family."

"But we don't mind," Katie insisted.

"Honestly, Boss," Buck added, and Gus would have sworn there were tears in his eyes.

"This is how it's going to be," Gus stated, leaving no room for further protest. "The Flinthills is no place to raise a child. The desolation and isolation would be cruel. There'll be no other children for her to grow up with, and the responsibilities of this ranch are enough to keep you both running from day to night. That is, unless you'd rather not stay on with me." Gus watched their expressions of sorrow turned to disbelief.

"Of course, we'll stay on with you," Katie replied.

"Absolutely, Boss. We're here to do our job, but more important, we're here because we're friends."

Gus nodded. He would leave them both a hefty chunk of money upon his death. They were faithful and loyal, and a man didn't often find friends such as these.

"I have a favor to ask," he finally said. "I need Katie to take Jessica to New York. You can go along too, Buck. Act as her escort. Mrs. Nelson is expecting the child, and the sooner we get started on it, the better. I'll go with you into town, and we'll purchase train tickets. I'll also draw out a substantial sum of money from the bank, and that will be your traveling money. I'll wire another substantial amount directly to Mrs. Nelson's bank account, so there will be no need for you to worry about carrying it with you. Will you do this for me?"

Katie broke down and started to cry, and Buck put his arm around her. "Hardly seems like the kind of thing we could refuse," he told Gus. "But I can't leave Windridge right now. You know full well there's too much work to be done. Those Texas steers will be coming our way in another month or two, and that last storm took out a whole section of fence. Not to mention the fact that we're breaking six new stock horses. I can't take the time away and stay on top of this as well."

"It'll be here when you get back," Gus assured him.

"No, Sir," Buck said emphatically. "Katie's ma and brother can go along with her. If you'll pay their ticket instead of mine, I'd be much obliged."

Gus didn't like the idea but nodded in agreement. "If that's the way you want it," he told Buck.

"It is."

And so it was nearly a week later that Gus watched the carriage disappear down the long, winding Windridge drive. He felt strangely calm as he watched them go. He knew he'd done the right thing. The very best thing for all parties concerned. Jessica would grow up never knowing either parent, but she would be loved and cared for just as Naomi would have wanted.

With a solemnity that matched the weight of the moment, Gus turned and stared at the house he'd created. Three stories of native limestone made a proud sentinel against the open prairie sky. It was her house—her home. She had loved it, and he had loved her. The memories were painful, and for the first time since she had died, Gus allowed himself to cry.

At first, it was just a trickle of tears, and then a full rush of hot liquid poured from his eyes. He couldn't have stopped it if he'd tried, and so instead of trying, he simply made his way to the library and closed the door behind him. He thought for a moment to lock it but decided against it. Someone would have to come in and take care of the mess, and there was no sense in having them have to bust down the door and ruin the house in order to do so. The house would one day belong to Jessica, just as it had belonged to her mother. He wanted to keep it neat and orderly for her. He wanted to offer her at least this much of himself.

He took a seat at his desk and pulled out his handkerchief. Wiping away the tears, Gus took out a piece of paper and began to pen a note of explanation for Buck. He'd already seen to his will when he'd gone into Cottonwood Falls for the train tickets. Everything would go to Jessica, with the exception of five thousand dollars, which was to be shared equally between Buck and Katie.

But this letter was an apology. An apology for not having been stronger. An apology for the problems he would now heap on his dearest friend.

I can't go on without her. The pain of losing her is too much to bear alone. If you can see your way to staying on and keeping up the ranch on Jessica's behalf, I would count it as my final earthly blessing. I have also arranged for you to be paid handsomely for the job. I just want you to know there was absolutely nothing you could have done to prevent this. I did what I had to do.

He signed the letter and left it to sit in the middle of his desk. He didn't want Buck to have a bit of trouble locating it. Then with a final glance around the room, Gus reached into the desk drawer and pulled out his revolver.

A knock on the library door caused him to quickly hide the gun back in its drawer. "Come in," he called.

Buck moseyed into the room as though nothing sorrowful had ever come to them. He held a pot of coffee in one hand and two cups in the other. "Thought you could use this just about now."

"I'm not thirsty," Gus replied.

"Well, then, use it to warm yourself."

"Ain't cold, either."

Buck put the coffee down on top of the note Gus had just finished writing. He stared hard at Gus for a moment, then put the cups down and took a seat. "I can't let you do it, Gus," he said so softly that Gus had to strain to hear him. "I ain't gonna let you die."

Gus stared at him in stunned surprise. "What are you talking about?"

"I know what you're doing, and that's why I didn't go with Katie," Buck said, quite frankly. "I know you've been putting your affairs in order, and I know why."

Gus said nothing. He couldn't figure out how in the world Buck had known him well enough to expect this action.

"See, I know what it is to lose someone you love. You probably don't know this, but I was married a long time ago. I am, after all, thirteen years Katie's senior. Anyway, my wife died. Died in childbirth, along with our son."

Gus shook his head. "I didn't know that."

Buck nodded. "Well, it happened, and I would have followed her into the grave but for the ministerings of my ma. She knew how heartbroken I was. Sarah—that was my wife's name—and I had been childhood sweethearts. We'd grown up side by side, and we'd always figured on marrying. My ma knew it would be like putting a part of myself in that grave, and she refused to leave me alone for even a moment's time. And that's what I intend to do for you." He shifted back in the chair and crossed his leg to fumble with his boot for a moment.

"See, I know you intend to kill yourself, Gus. But it isn't the answer."

"I suppose you know what the answer is," Gus replied sarcastically. He wanted Buck to storm out of the room and leave him be. He didn't care if Buck hated him or called him names; he just wanted to forget everything and go to be with his Naomi.

"I do know," Buck replied. "God will give you the strength to get through this. You may not think so, but He will. I'm going to stay with you, pray with you, eat with you, and I'll even sleep at the foot of your bed if it keeps you alive."

Gus gave up all pretense. "I don't want to live. You should understand that."

"I do. But you're needed here on earth. You have a little girl who needs you. You have friends who need you."

"I don't want to be needed."

Again Buck nodded. "Neither did I, but I had no choice, and neither do you. Do you really want to leave that little girl with the guilt that she somehow caused her ma's and pa's deaths? It's bad enough that she'll have to live with the guilt of her mother dying, but hopefully, some kind person will teach her that it wasn't her fault. But if you put a bullet through your head, she'll be convinced it was her fault."

"That's stupid. It wouldn't have anything to do with her," Gus answered.

"You and I might know that, but she won't. And, Gus, there won't be a single person in this world who'll be able to convince her otherwise."

Gus realized the truth in what Buck said. He felt his eyes grow warm with tears. "It hurts so bad to lose Naomi—to face a lifetime without her."

Buck nodded. "I know, and that's why we aren't going to face a lifetime. We're just gonna take one day at a time. I'll help you get through this, but you've got to be willing to try. For Jessica's sake, if for no other."

Gus thought about it for a moment. He didn't have the strength to do what Buck suggested, but neither did he want to burden his child—her child—with the idea that she was responsible for his death. "I just don't know, Buck. When I think about the years to come—and I know that she won't be there—it just isn't something I want to deal with."

"I understand. But like I said, we don't have to think about the years to come. We only have to get through today," Buck replied. "And we'll let tomorrow take care of itself."

In that moment Gus chose life over death. His heart was irreparably broken, but logic won over emotions. One day at a time, Buck said, was all he had to face. Just one day. If life proved to be too much today, he could always end it tomorrow.

Chapter 1

October 1890

Jessica Albright wrapped her arms around her nine-month-old son and frowned at the dark-skinned porter. He held her small traveling bag and held out his arms to further assist her departure from the train.

"If it pleases ya, Ma'am," he said with a sincere smile, "I kin hold da baby and hand him down to ya."

"No," Jessica replied emphatically. "No one is taking him."

The porter shrugged and then held up his hand. "I kin go ahead of ya. Then iffen you fall, ya'll fall against me." He smiled broadly and jumped down the steep steps ahead of her.

Jessica had no choice but to follow. She gripped the baby firmly against her breast and made her way off the train. The nine month old howled at the injustice of being held so tightly, and Jessica could only jostle him around and try her best to cajole him back into a decent temperament.

"Oh, Ryan, neither of us is happy with the arrangements," she said, glancing from her son's angry face to the crowd gathered around the depot platform.

"Miss Jessica," a voice sounded from behind her.

Whirling around, Jessica met the smiling face of a snowy-haired man. "Hello, Buck. Thank you for coming after us. I'm sorry for having to put you out."

"Wasn't any other way you were going to get there, short of hiring someone in town to bring you out. Besides, Katie would skin me alive if I refused. This your little guy?" he asked, nodding at the angry baby.

Ryan continued to howl, and Jessica grew rather embarrassed from the stares. She felt so inadequate at being a mother. Where her friends in the city had spoken of natural feelings and abilities regarding their children, Jessica felt all thumbs and left feet. "Could we just be on our way, Buck?"

Buck looked at her sympathetically. "Sure, sure. Let me claim your baggage, and we'll be ready to head out."

"This here bag belongs to the missus," the porter announced. Buck took up the bag, but Jessica quickly shifted the baby and reached out for it. "It has our personal things." Buck nodded and let her take it without protest.

"I'll go for the rest." He ambled off in the direction of the baggage car, and Jessica felt a sense of desertion. What if he forgot about her? What would she do then? She had very little money with her and even less ambition to figure out how to arrange transportation to her father's Windridge Ranch. *No,* she thought, it was her ranch now. Her father had died, and there was nothing more to be said about the situation. Still, she'd only been here on three other occasions, and the last time was over five years ago. She'd never know which way to go if she had to figure a way home for herself.

Ryan finally cried himself out and fell asleep, but not until his slobbers and tears had drenched the front of Jessica's plum-colored traveling suit. She couldn't do anything about it now, she realized. Aunt Harriet had always said that a lady was known by her appearance. Was her attire in order? Was her carriage and walk upright and graceful? Jessica felt neither properly ordered, nor upright and graceful. She felt hot and tired and dirty and discouraged.

"Here we are. This all you brought?" Buck asked, one huge trunk hoisted on his back, a smaller trunk tucked under one arm, and a carpetbag dangling from his hand. He turned to include the young boy who followed after him with two additional suitcases.

"Yes," Jessica replied. "That's everything."

Buck never condemned her for the multiple bags, never questioned why she'd needed to bring so much. Buck always seemed accepting of whatever came his way. Jessica didn't know the man half as well as she would have liked to, but Buck was the kind of man she knew would have made a wonderful father.

Buck stopped alongside a mammoth, stage-styled conveyance. Jessica watched, notably impressed, as Buck gently placed the trunk and bags up on the driver's floor, then paused to hand her and Ryan up into the carriage. She arranged a pallet for Ryan by taking his blanket and one of the carriage blankets and spreading them out on the well-cushioned leather seats, while overhead Buck secured the baggage on top.

The opulence and size of the carriage greatly impressed Jessica. No expense had been spared. In fact, it very much resembled an expensive stagecoach of sorts. The beautifully upholstered seats sported thick cushions, leaving Jessica with the desire to join Ryan in stretching out for her own nap. After four days on the most unaccommodating eastern trains, she found this a refreshing reprieve.

Blankets were positioned on a rack overhead, as well as a lantern and metal box that she presumed held other supplies. Outside, she heard Buck instruct the boy to hand up his cases, then figured he must have tipped the boy for his actions when she heard the child let out a hearty, "Thanks, Mr. Buck."

"You all settled in there?" Buck called out, sliding a window open from where he was on the driver's seat.

Jessica thought the window ingenious and nodded enthusiastically. "I'm ready. The baby is already sleeping comfortably."

"All right, then. We'll make for home. I know my Kate will be half beside herself for want of seeing you again."

Jessica smiled weakly and nodded. She could only wonder at what her reception might be when they learned she was coming to Windridge to stay.

Since Buck had pulled shut the slide on the window, Jessica felt herself amply alone and reached inside her purse to pull out a letter. She'd only received the missive a week ago, but already it was wrinkled and worn. Kate had written to tell her of her father's death. He'd suffered a heart attack, or so it was believed, and had fallen from his mount to his death. The doctor didn't believe he suffered overmuch, and Jessica had been grateful for that.

"We'd love to have you home, Jessie," the letter read. Kate was the only one who had ever called her Jessie. "Windridge is never the same without you. Now with your father gone and what with the death of your own husband, we'd like to be a family to you. Please say you'll come for a visit."

And she had come. She had telegraphed Kate before boarding the first available train, and now she was well on her way to Windridge.

But what would she do after that?

She stared out the window at the dead brown grass of the Flinthills. She had felt fascinated the first time she'd laid eyes on the place at the age of twelve. Her aunt Harriet had figured it was time for Jessica to make a visit to the place of her birth; and sent west with a most severe nanny, Jessica had had her first taste of the prairie and rolling hills where thousands of cattle grazed.

And secretly, she had loved it. She loved the way she could stand atop Windridge when her nanny was otherwise preoccupied and let loose her hair ribbon and let the wind blow through her brown curls. She liked the feel of the warm Kansas sun on her face, even if it did bring her a heavy reprimand from her nanny. Freckled faces weren't considered a thing of beauty, not even for a child.

Now she looked across the vast openness and sighed. *I'm like that prairie,* she thought. *Lonely and open, vulnerable to whatever may come.* A hawk circled in the distance, and Jessica absently wondered what prey he might be seeking. It could possibly be a rabbit or a mouse, maybe even a wounded bird or some other sort of creature.

"Poor things," she whispered. Life on the prairie was hard. Often it came across as cruel and inhumane, but nevertheless, it continued. It went on and on whether people inhabited the land or died and were buried beneath its covering.

Jessica felt she could expect little more than this.

Her own life had taken so many different turns from that which she had expected. She had married against her father's wishes. But because he was a man who had never taken the time or trouble to be a real father to her, his letter-written advice had held little sway with Jessica. After all, she scarcely knew her father. Harriet chose the man Jessica was to marry based on his social status and ability to conduct himself properly at social gatherings. It mattered very little that Jessica didn't love him. She was, Harriet pointed out, twenty-two years old. It was time to marry and take her place as a matron of society.

But society wasn't very accepting of you when you ran out of money.

High society was even less forgiving.

It grieved Jessica to know Gus Gussop had been right in his long-distance judgment of Newman Albright. Gus had called him a dandy and a city boy. Called him worse than that, as Jessica recalled. And Newman had been all of those things.

Harriet had died shortly after Jessica's marriage. With her death came the inheritance of a fashionable house and a significant amount of money. Newman refused to move them into the Nelson place. Instead he insisted they sell the place and buy a less ostentatious home. Jessica quietly agreed, having been raised to respect her husband's wishes as law. What she didn't realize was that Newman had managed to get himself deep into debt through gambling and needed the sale of the house to clear his ledgers.

He robbed her of both the fortune left to her upon Harriet Nelson's death and her father's wedding gift of ten thousand dollars. A gift Newman never bothered to mention. She found out about these things after Newman had died. Of course, by that time they were living in poverty, and Newman's only explanation was that Jessica's father had cut them off without a dime, and their investments had gone sour.

Upon Newman's death, Jessica learned the truth about everything. Things she'd much rather have never known. Part of this came by way of her father's request. Gus had sent a telegram asking her to be honest with him about her financial situation. When Jessica had given the pitiful statements over to her father via a long, detailed letter, Gus had written back in a livid anger that seemed to leap off the page and stab at Jessica's heart.

"That blackguard has robbed you blind, Jessica. He has taken the ten thousand dollars I wired to him, which was intended to go toward the purchase of a lovely new home, and has apparently wasted it away elsewhere. He's taken additional money, money he telegrammed requesting of me, and apparently has lost the fortune given you by Harriet."

Jessica knew it was true. By the time Newman's death darkened her life, Jessica knew he had a gambling problem. A drinking problem. A fighting problem. And a multitude of other sins that had destroyed any possible hope of her loving him. He was a liar and a cheat and an adulterer, and Jessica could find no place in her heart to grieve his passing.

He had stumbled home one morning after an apparent night in the gutter not far from their poor excuse for a house. His nose was red, and his throat raw, and he bellowed and moaned about his condition until Jessica, then in her eighth month of pregnancy, had put him to bed and called for the doctor. Within three days, however, her husband was dead from pneumonia, and Jessica faced an uncertain future with a child not yet born.

It was at the funeral for Newman that Jessica realized the full truth of his affairs. Not one but three mistresses turned up to grieve their beloved Newman. None of the women had any idea about the others, and none knew Newman to have a wife and child. One particularly seasoned woman actually apologized to Jessica and later sent money that she explained Newman had given her for the rent. Jessica wanted to throw the money into the street but was too desperate to even consider such a matter. As a Christian woman of faith, she knew God had interceded on her behalf to provide this money. To throw it away would be to ignore God's answer to her prayers.

It had been painful to admit to her father that she was living from day to day in abject poverty, but even more painful to endure his response. He had raged about the injustice, but never once had he suggested she come home to live at Windridge. Jessica never even mentioned the baby to him. She was too afraid of what his reaction might be. Instead, she did as he asked, providing the information he sought on her finances. Then she followed his instructions when a letter came informing her that he'd hired a realtor to move her elsewhere and had set up an account of money in a New York City bank so that she might have whatever she needed. Such generosity had deeply touched her. But still, he never asked her to come home.

That broke her heart.

Then her life grew even more complicated when her best friend, Esmerelda Kappin, began to suggest Jessica give Ryan over to her for raising. Essie, as Jessica had once affectionately called her friend, was barren. She and her husband had tried every midwife remedy, every doctor's suggestion, and still they had no luck—no children. Essie took an interest in Ryan that Jessica didn't recognize as unhealthy until her friend began to suggest that Ryan preferred her care to Jessica's. Then Essie's very wealthy mother appeared on the doorstep to offer Jessica money in exchange for Ryan.

Of course, Jessica had been mortified and from that point on began guarding Ryan as though the devil himself were after the child. The Kappins grew more insistent, showing up at the most inopportune times to remind Jessica that she was alone in the world and that Ryan deserved a family with a mother and a father.

Jessica looked down at the sleeping boy. He did deserve a father, but that wasn't to be. She had no desire to remarry. Perhaps it was one of the reasons she'd decided to come to Windridge. Running Windridge would keep her busy enough to avoid loneliness and put plenty of distance between her and anyone who had the idea of stealing her son.

The prairie hills passed by the window, and from time to time a small grove of trees could be spotted. They usually indicated a spring or pond, creek or river, and because they were generally the exception and not the normal view, Jessica took note of these places and wondered if their gold and orange leaves hid from view some small homestead. Her father had once prided himself on having no neighbor closer than an hour's distance away, but Jessica knew that time had changed that course somewhat. Kate had written of a rancher whose property adjoined her father's only five miles to the south and another bound him on the west within the same distance. The latter was always after Gus to sell him a small portion of land that would allow him access to one of Gus's many natural springs. But Gus always refused him, and the man was up in arms over his unneighborly attitude.

Jessica wondered at her father's severity in dealing with others. Kate told her it was because he'd never managed to deal with life properly after the death of Jessie's mother. But Jessica thought it might only be an excuse for being mean tempered.

Her conscience pricked her at this thought. She didn't know her father well enough to pass judgment on him. Her Christian convictions told her that judgment was best left to God, but her heart still questioned a father who would send away his only child and never suggest she return to him for anything more than a visit. With this thought overwhelming her mind, it was easy to fall asleep. She felt the exhaustion overtake her, and without giving it much of a fight, Jessica drifted into dreams.

Her first conscious thoughts were of a baby crying. Then her mind instantly awoke, and Jessica realized it was Ryan who cried. She sat up to find the nine month old trying to untangle himself from the blankets she'd so tightly secured him inside.

"Poor little boy," she cooed. Pulling him from the confines of his prison, Jessica immediately realized his wetness.

Looking out the window, Jessica wondered how much farther it was to the house. She hated to expose Ryan to a chill by changing him in the carriage. Wrapping a blanket around the boy, Jessica shifted seats and knocked at the little window slide. Within a flash, Buck slid it open.

"Something wrong?" he asked, glancing over his shoulder.

"How far to the house?" she questioned.

"We're just heading up the main drive. Should be there in five minutes.

Is there something you need?"

Jessica shook her head. "No, thank you. I'm afraid the baby is drenched, and I just wondered whether to change him in here or wait. Now I know I can wait and not cause him overmuch discomfort."

"Kate will probably snatch him away from you anyway. That woman just loves babies."

Jessica cringed. What she didn't need to face was yet another woman seeking to steal her child.

"Sure wish you'd told us about him sooner. Kate would have come east in a flash to help you out and see the next generation of Gussops."

She didn't bother to correct Buck by pointing out that the baby was an Albright. She thought of him as a Gussop as well. Despite the fact they both carried the Albright name, Jessica considered both herself and her son to be Gussops.

Buck left the slide open in case Jessica wanted to say something more, but she held her silence. She was nearly home, and the thought was rather overwhelming. Home. The word conjured such conflicting emotions, and Jessica wasn't sure she wanted to dwell on such matters.

"Whoa!" Buck called out. The carriage slowed and finally stopped all together. Jessica looked out and found they were sitting in the wide circular drive of Windridge. The house stood at the end of a native stone walk, and it was evident that her father had sorely neglected the property in the last five years.

"Well, we're here, Ryan," she whispered against the baby's pudgy cheeks. "I don't know about you, but I'm rather frightened of the whole thing."

Ryan let out a squeal that sounded more delighted than frightened, and Jessica couldn't resist laughing.

Buck quickly came to help her down from the carriage, and just as he had predicted, Kate appeared to whisk them both inside.

"Oh, my!" Kate remarked in absolute delight upon catching sight of Ryan. She reached arms out for the baby, but Jessica shook her head.

"He's soaking," she warned.

"Like that could stop me." Kate laughed and took the baby anyway.

Jessica felt a moment of panic, then forced herself to relax. *This is Kate,* she reminded herself. Kate, who had kept up correspondences over the years. Kate wouldn't try to steal her baby. Would she?

"What a beautiful boy!" Kate declared. "Come on. Let's get you in out of this wind and into a dry diaper."

Jessica glanced around and felt the breeze on her face. It invigorated and revived her. Somehow it seemed that city life had stifled her and drained her of all energy. Windridge had a way of awakening Jessica. It had begun with that first visit at twelve and continued with each subsequent trip home.

She finally looked back at Kate and found the woman was already ten feet ahead of her and heading up the stone steps to the porch. Drawing a deep breath, Jessica followed after the older woman, thinking to herself how very little Kate had changed. She now had a generous sprinkling of gray in her hair, and she wore small, circular, wire-rimmed glasses that gave her an almost scholarly appearance. But she was still the same old jolly Kate.

"You can see for yourself that the place has suffered miserably," Kate told her as they made their way into the house. "Your father wasn't himself for the last five years."

"Since my marriage," Jessica replied flatly, knowing full well that she had grieved him something terrible when she'd married Newman.

Kate stopped dead in her tracks. "Oh, Jessie, I didn't mean it that way."

Jessica shrugged. "But it's true. I know it hurt him. I wish I could take it back, but I can't."

"Don't wish for things like that," Kate admonished. "You'd have to wish this little fellow away as well. Everything comes with a purpose, and God turns even our disobedience into glory for Himself."

Jessica smiled. How good it felt to hear someone speak about God. Most of her friends in New York were into mystic readings and psychic adventures. They believed in conjuring spirits of dead loved ones and held all-night parties in order to satisfy their ghoulish natures. Jessica could have no part in such matters, even if the likes of such things were sweeping the eastern cities in a rage of acceptance.

She'd been told by a friend that Essie had purchased a charm to make Ryan love her more than Jessica. It was all madness, or so it seemed. Playing at what most considered harmless enchantments and magic spells had left Jessica desperate to find new friends. Friends whose faith was steeped not in manipulating people to do what they wanted but in seeking God and learning what He wanted.

"Did I lose you?" Kate asked, turning suddenly inside the foyer.

"Not at all," Jessica replied. "I was only thinking of how wonderful it was to hear someone speak of God again. I'm afraid all manner of strangeness is going on in the city, and I've been rather alienated from good fellowship."

"You'll have to tell me all about it," Kate answered, and Jessica knew she truly meant it. Ryan began to fuss and pulled at Kate's glasses in irritated fashion. "Come on, little guy; let's get you changed."

Jessica felt a momentary panic as the baby continued to cry. She fought her desire to rip him from Kate's arms. It wasn't Kate's fault that Essie had treated Jessica so falsely. Swallowing her fear, Jessica followed Kate up the ornate wood stairs.

Focus on the house, she told herself. *Look at everything and remember how good it always felt to come here.*

Inside, the house looked much the same as it always had. Kate kept it in good fashion, always making it a comfortable home for all who passed through its doors. She was, for all intents and purposes, the mistress of Windridge, and she had done the place proud.

"We've created a nursery for you in here," Kate announced, sweeping through the open bedroom door. "Your room is in there." She pointed to open double doors across the room. "Of course, you have access through the hallway as well."

Jessica looked around her in stunned amazement. A beautiful crib stood in one corner, with a cheery fire blazing on the stone hearth on the opposite side of the room. A dresser and a changing table were positioned within easy access of one another, and a rocker had been placed upon one of Kate's homemade rag rugs, not far from the warmth of the fire. There was a shelf of toys, all suitable for a baby, and yet another long oval rag rug on the floor where a small wooden rocking horse had been left in welcome. *No doubt,* Jessica thought, *Buck made most of the furniture, including the rocking horse.*

"It's charming here," Jessica said, noting the thin blue stripe of the wallpaper. "But really you shouldn't have gone to so much trouble."

"It wasn't any trouble," Kate replied, taking Ryan to the changing table. "I had kind of hoped that if I filled the place with welcome, you just might stay on." She looked over her shoulder at Jessica, her expression filled with hope. "We'd really like it if you'd give up the East and come home to Windridge. Would you at least think about it?"

Jessica nodded. "I've already thought about it. I had kind of hoped that you'd let me stay."

Kate's face lit up with absolute joy. "Do you mean it? You've truly come home for good?"

Jessica nodded. "If you'll have me."

Kate threw up her arms and looked heavenward. "Thank You, God. What an answer to prayer." She looked back to Ryan, who was now gurgling and laughing at her antics. "You're both an answer to prayer."

Jessica found her own room much to her liking. Delicate rose-print wallpaper accented by dusty rose drapes and lacy cream-colored sheers made the room decidedly feminine. Kate had told her earlier that the room had been designed for Naomi, and in spite of the feminine overtones, Gus had left everything exactly as Naomi had arranged it.

The massive four-poster bed was Gus's only real contribution to the room. It seemed a bit much for one person, but Jessica realized it had belonged to her parents and had always been intended for two. A writing desk was positioned at the window, where the brilliant Kansas sunlight could filter into the room to give the writer all possible benefit. A six-drawer dresser with wide gown-drawers was positioned in one corner of the room, with a matching vanity table and huge oval mirror gracing the space in the opposite corner. A chaise lounge of mahogany wood and rose print was the final piece to add personality to the room. Jessica could imagine stretching out there to read a book on quiet winter evenings.

The room seemed much too large for one person. But Jessica was alone, and she intended to stay that way. There seemed no reason to bring another husband into her life. How could she ever trust someone to not take advantage of her? After all, she was now a propertied woman—not just of a house, but of thousands of acres of prime grazing land. She would no doubt have suitors seeking to take their place as the master of Windridge. She would have to guard herself and her position.

But while she had no desire to bring a man to Windridge, she did want to bring people into her life. She wanted to share her faith and let folks see the light of God's love in her life. She didn't know exactly how she might accomplish this stuck out in the middle of the Flinthills, but she intended to try.

After changing her clothes into a simple black skirt and burgundy print blouse, Jessica checked on Ryan and found him still asleep. His tiny lips were pursed, making soft sucking sounds as he dozed. She loved him so much. The terror that gripped her heart when she thought of losing him was enough to drive her mad. Surely God would help her to feel safe again.

Jessica left Ryan to sleep and made her way downstairs. Her mind overflowed with thoughts about how she would fit into this prairie home, and she was so engrossed in figuring things out that she didn't notice the man who watched her from just inside the front door.

When she did see him, she froze in place on the next to the last step. Her heart began to pound. Was this some ruffian cowboy who'd come to rob the place? She forced herself to stay calm.

"May I help you?" she asked coolly.

He stood fairly tall, a good five inches taller than her own statuesque five-feet, seven. He met her perusal of him with an amused grin that caused his thick bushy mustache to raise ever so slightly at the corners. His face, weathered and tanned from constant exposure to the elements, appeared friendly and open to Jessica's study.

"You must be Jessica," he drawled as though she should know him.

She bristled slightly, feeling his consuming gaze sizing her up. His cocoa brown eyes appeared not to miss a single detail. "I'm afraid you have me at a disadvantage," she finally managed.

"I'm Devon Carter, your father's foreman for these past five years."

Devon Carter. She thought of the name and wondered if anyone had ever mentioned him in their letters, but nothing came to mind. Buck had always been foreman over Windridge, but she knew he was getting up in years and no doubt needed the extra help.

"I'm Jessica Albright."

His smile broadened. "Good to have you at Windridge. Heard tell you have a little one."

"Yes," she replied and nodded. "He's upstairs."

"Kate has done nothing but talk about you and the little guy for days," Devon said with a chuckle.

Jessica stepped down from the stairs and folded her hands. It seemed fairly certain she had nothing to fear from this man. "Is there something I can do for you, Mr. Carter?"

"Devon."

She eyed him for a moment before nodding and saying, "Devon."

"I just came up to the house to talk to Buck about the feed situation. You don't need to pay me any never mind."

"I see." But in truth she didn't. Was this man simply allowed free run of the house? Did he wander in and out at will?

"Oh, good," came the sound of Kate's voice from the stairs. "You've already met. Jessica, this man was a godsend to us. Your father took him on as a foreman when Buck said the workload was too much, and he's quickly made himself an institution around here."

Jessica turned to find Kate coming down the stairs with Ryan. The baby appeared perfectly content in her arms.

"You do go on, Katie," Devon countered affectionately. "Say, he's a right handsome fellow. It'll be good to have him around. Keep us all on our toes."

"I won't let you change the subject," Kate said, coming down the stairs with Ryan. "Gus thought of you as a son. You earned his respect quickly enough."

Jessica felt her nerves tighten. Her father had never treated her with much respect, nor, as far as she was concerned, had he thought of her as a daughter. How dare this stranger come into her home and earn a place that should have been hers?

She quickly reached for Ryan as soon as Kate joined them in the foyer. She didn't want to feel angry or hurt for a past that couldn't be changed, but it bothered her nevertheless. How could these two people act so nonchalant about it, knowing full well that she had suffered from the separation?

"What with the fact you've spent all your life in the city," Devon said.

Jessica stared up at him, not at all certain what had preceded that statement. "What?"

"I just told Devon that you plan to stay on at Windridge and take over your rightful place as mistress of the ranch," Kate replied.

Jessica looked at Kate for a moment while the real meaning of her words sunk in. It was true enough that her father had left her the ranch, but she'd not thought much about the fact that by moving in, she would become the mistress in charge.

"And I was just saying I hoped our simple way of doing things wouldn't cause you to grow unhappy and bored, what with the fact you've spent all your life in the city."

"I assure you, Mr. Carter," Jessica said rather stiffly, "that I will neither suffer boredom nor unhappiness due to the location. Other things may well come about to make me feel those things but not the address of my new home."

With that she set off with Ryan to explore the rest of the house. She felt an awkward silence fall behind her and knew, or rather sensed, that Devon and Kate were staring after her, but she didn't care. She wasn't prepared for the likes of Devon Carter. And she certainly wasn't prepared for her reaction to him.

Chapter 2

At thirty-two, Devon Carter was pretty much a self-made man. He held deep convictions on two things. One, that he loved Windridge and the Flinthills as much as any man could ever love a place. And two, that his faith in God had been the only thing to sustain him over his long years of loneliness and misery.

He dusted off his jeans, wiped his boot tops on the back of each leg, and opened the back door to the kitchen without any announcement. He found Kate busy at work frying up breakfast and crossed the room to give her an affectionate peck on the cheek. Kate had become a second mother to him, and he saw no reason that their closeness should end now that Jessica Albright had come home to claim her fortune, if one could call it a fortune.

"Morning, Katie."

"Morning, Devon. Did you sleep well in the garden house?"

"It was good enough," he replied. "Don't know how you and Buck ever managed to keep warm enough out there, what with the drafts and such."

"We had each other," Katie said with a grin. "Besides, nobody's lived out there in twenty years. Gus had us move up to the house when the quiet got to be too much. We brought the kids and all, and he never once complained about the noise."

"Well, I'm going to have to do some repairs to it today if I'm going to have a better sleep tonight."

"Why don't you just tell Buck what you need? That would be simple work for him, and I don't want him overdoing it by following you over the prairie searching for strays. He just doesn't have it in him anymore."

"Now, Katie, you're selling me short again," Buck announced as he came in from the pantry.

"Just being sensible," Katie replied, pausing long enough to turn over a thick ham steak from where it browned in a cast-iron skillet.

"Well, sensible or not," Devon replied, "the work still needs to be done. You want the pleasure, Buck, or shall I do it?"

Buck laughed, watching Kate pull down her wire rims just far enough to look at him over the tops. "I'll take care of it. You just give me some ideas on where to start."

"Will do." Devon turned then to Kate. "Table set?"

"Nope, you go right ahead and do the honors. Buck and I will bring in the food."

Devon nodded and went into the pantry where the fine china and everyday dishes were displayed in orderly fashion. He took down three plates then remembered Jessica and Ryan, as if he hadn't thought of them all night long, and added one more. He grabbed silverware and saucers and decided to come back for the cups after seeing that he was juggling quite a load.

He'd just finished laying out the arrangement and filling the saucers with cups when Jessica and Ryan appeared. She stood casually in the doorway, baby on her hip, looking for all the world like a contented woman. Devon smiled.

"Breakfast is nearly on."

She looked rather surprised as she took sight of the table. "Who else will there be?"

"Well, there's Buck and Kate," he answered, then added, "and me. Plus you and Ryan. That makes five."

"Oh," she answered, and Devon immediately wondered if she had a problem with the arrangement.

"Something wrong?" he asked.

"I'm just not used to, well, that is to say," she fell silent and shifted Ryan to the other hip, where he found her long chestnut braid much easier to play with.

"Jessie," Kate called out as she brought in a huge platter of scrambled eggs, "my, but don't you look pretty. I like that you've left your hair down. Reminds me of when you were a little girl."

Devon watched Jessica blush as Kate continued. "Do you know, Devon, this girl would defy her nanny and sneak out of the house to get to the top of the ridge. Once she got there, she'd pull out all her ribbons and whatnots and let her hair go free to blow in the wind. Anytime she got away from us, we could be sure to find her there."

Devon grinned and cast a quick glance at Jessica, who was even now trying to help her son into the wooden highchair at the end of the table.

"Here, let me help," Devon said, pushing Jessica's hands away. He made a face at Ryan as he positioned the boy in the seat and brought the top down around him. Ryan immediately laughed and reached out chubby arms to touch Devon's mustache.

"No, Ryan!" Jessica declared, moving back in position to keep her son from touching the cowboy.

"It's all right, Jessica. He won't hurt anything," Devon replied.

She glared hard at him. "I'm his mother, Mr. Carter. It's my place to decide what is right for him."

Devon saw the unspoken fury in her eyes, but rather than angering him, it made him want to laugh. *Better not,* he told himself. *That would really infuriate her.*

He waited until Jessica took her seat at the right of the highchair before considering that he'd positioned himself at the left. He liked kids. Liked them very much and had, in fact, planned on having several by this time in life. But life often didn't work out the way a person planned.

Katie and Buck took their places, and Buck offered grace over the food. He also added thanksgiving for Jessica's return, before putting on a hearty "amen" and directing everyone to dig in. If Jessica noticed that Buck was the one in charge of the meal, she didn't say anything. She sat opposite Buck at the end of the table, while Katie sat at his right and Devon at her right. One entire side of the table sat empty except for the food platters, and Devon wondered if maybe he should have arranged things differently. He was about to speak when Buck voiced a question.

"How did you sleep last night, Jessica?"

She put down a forkful of fried potatoes and smiled. "Very well, thank you."

"I told him a person could get lost in that big old bed of your pa's," Katie said, "but you know Buck. He said we could always send out a search party to find you."

They all chuckled at this, and Devon wondered if maybe the tension of the morning had finally subsided.

"Ryan also slept very well. In fact, it was his first time to sleep through the night without waking up to. . ." She reddened and stopped in midsentence.

Kate seemed to understand her discomfort. "He's a big boy now. Have you started him eating something more substantial?"

Jessica shook her head. "No, in fact, this is his first time at the table."

She hadn't noticed, but Devon had put several pieces of egg on the highchair tray, and already Ryan was stuffing them into his mouth.

"Well, it looks as though he thinks highly of the idea," Buck said with a laugh.

Jessica looked down in confusion and noticed the baby reaching for a piece of buttered toast. "No, Ryan!"

"He's fine, Jessica," Devon assured her.

"Mr. Carter, I don't appreciate your interference with my child," Jessica said harshly. "He's my responsibility."

"Around here, folks pretty much try to help out where they can," Devon countered, meeting her haughty stare. "I figured since you're staying on, I'd try to do what I could to fill in for the absence of his pa. I'm sure Buck feels the same way."

Jessica appeared speechless. She stared openmouthed at Devon and then turned to Kate and Buck. "And you think this is acceptable behavior?"

Kate laughed. "We don't hold any formalities around here. Ryan will be greatly loved and maybe even spoiled a bit, but those are good things, not bad. The ranch is full of dangers as well as benefits. You'll appreciate that folks are willing to keep an eye open for him."

"No, I'm not sure I will," she replied quite frankly.

"Jessica, you shouldn't worry about these things," Kate told her.

Devon watched her reaction and tried to pretend he was unconcerned with her hostility. But in fact, he was offended that she should be so put out with him. He was, after all, only helping. Maybe it was her upbringing that caused her to be so mulish about things.

"I'd appreciate it if we could change the subject," Jessica interjected. "And, I'd appreciate it, Mr. Carter, if you would leave the raising of my son to me."

Devon swallowed back a short retort and let it go. There would no doubt be time enough to take issue over these things. He felt deep gratitude when Buck did as Jessica requested.

"Well, since you've decided to stay on, Jessica, there are a few things you need to be aware of."

"Such as?" The woman's eyes were wide with a mixture of what appeared to be fear and pure curiosity.

Buck looked at Kate for a moment, and after receiving her nod of approval, he began what Devon knew he dreaded more than anything.

"It has to do with the financial affairs of Windridge."

"I see." She busied herself with her food, and when Ryan cried for another piece of toast, she calmly buttered one and broke off a piece for him.

"Well, anyhow," Buck continued. "Windridge is not in a good state. Gus got into drinking these last few years. About the time you. . ." He fell silent.

"Married Newman," Jessica filled in for him.

"Yes, well, when you got married, other things started happening around here as well. Your pa suffered a mild heart attack, and we had a round of viruses that took the lives of most our herd one year. One thing after another took its toll, and before we knew it, Gus was running pretty short on cash. After that, he just stopped trying. Wouldn't even keep up his partnership with the Rocking W down in Texas."

Jessica dropped her fork. "What partnership?"

Kate leaned forward to explain. "Your pa had an agreement to purchase cattle from a ranch in Texas. It was easier to get them that way, fatten them up here all summer, then sell them off in the fall—usually for a good profit. That way, we didn't have to worry about keeping them through the winter."

"I suppose that makes sense," Jessica agreed.

"Well, for the last three years or so, Gus let things get so far out of control that he couldn't even afford to purchase the steers. Jeb Williams, owner of the Rocking W, offered to spot him the herd. He knew Gus was down on his luck and knew he was good for the money, but Gus refused. He became more and more reclusive, spending most of his time nearby, but doing little or nothing."

"So you're telling me that we're broke?" Jessica questioned.

"Pretty much so," Buck replied. "Devon can give you better details on the matter."

She looked to him, and Devon thought from her expression that it had cost her a great deal to put aside their differences to pose her question. "What exactly is the situation, Mr. Carter?"

"There's not much in the bank. It'll get us through another winter, if the winter isn't too bad. There's only minimal livestock—a dozen milk cows, about the same number of horses, and the place is in a state of disrepair. We've tried to keep up with things, but it takes money to do so. Come spring, we'll be in a world of hurt."

"But I see cattle on the hills," Jessica replied. "Kate, you even mentioned the hands would soon be driving the cattle to Cottonwood Falls."

"They aren't ours," Devon told her instead of allowing Kate to answer. "We leased out the pasture without telling Gus. He mostly stayed in his room those last few months, and if he noticed the herd, he didn't say anything. The lease money is what we have in the bank."

"What are we to do?" Jessica asked, turning her gaze back to Buck and Kate.

"Well, there's a neighbor, Joe Riley, who'd like to buy a parcel of land that joins his property. It has a spring on it, and he's been after your pa for all these years to let him buy it. Your pa just felt mean about it, I guess," Buck replied. "Never did fully understand why that man refused to sell one little spring, but that's behind us now, and I don't intend to speak ill of the dead. He probably won't be interested until spring, but it's worth asking about."

"Then I thought I'd go down to the Rocking W on your behalf," Devon said rather cautiously. "I know Jeb Williams from the cattle drives I've helped with before coming to Kansas. I think Jeb might be willing to extend the same offer to you that he offered to your father. We could purchase a small herd from him—on credit—and fatten them up for a profit come fall."

"Of course," Buck threw in, "there's always a risk. Viruses, weather, insects, and all other manner of complications. It could end up that we'd lose our shirts in the deal and be unable to pay Williams back."

Jessica nodded, appearing to consider the matter. "I have an idea for the place," she said, surprising them all. "Back East, there is quite an interest in ranching and the West. Many people have never known much but the city—especially those in higher social classes."

"And your point would be?" Devon asked.

"My point is that opening resort ranches has become quite popular. They offer an unusual respite for travelers who otherwise live their lives in big cities. I have a couple magazines upstairs that talk about this very thing."

"Dude ranches," Devon said in complete disgust. "Your pa would sooner you sell the place in total."

"My father isn't here," Jessica reminded him. "And it appears that even when he was, he wasn't much interested in what happened with the ranch. The place is mine now, and I intend to run it as such. I realize I have a lot to learn, but I'm offering one simple solution. People could come here and take their rest. We have miles of solitude to offer them. We could feature carriage rides, hunting, picnics, and horseback riding—we could show them how a ranch actually works, and we could fatten them up on Kate's cooking."

"You forget," Devon replied, "the place would have to be fixed up first. There's a lot that needs to be done in order to make this a model working ranch. And that, my dear Jessica, takes money."

She frowned at him. "I realize it would take something of an investment to get things started. I didn't say the plan was without challenges."

"A plan? So do you figure to just move forward with this plan? Didn't you think it might be important to get the advice of those who know the place?" Devon questioned.

Kate and Buck stared on as if helpless to interject a single word. Jessica slammed down her empty coffee cup and countered. "I am not stupid, Mr. Carter. I am simply offering the idea up as a possibility. That is all." She glanced to Kate. "I also believe it would be nice to open the ranch up to hurting souls. People who need the quiet to escape and heal from whatever woe they have to face. As Christians we can minister to these people and share the gospel of Christ."

"Now you're suggesting we turn this into some sort of revival grounds?" Devon asked.

"And what if I am? Are you a heathen, Mr. Carter?"

"No, Ma'am. I accepted Christ as my Savior a long time ago, but I never once felt called to be a minister."

"Neither have I called you to be one, Mr. Carter." She stressed the formality of his name, and Devon cringed inwardly.

Ryan pounded the tray with his hands and fussed for something more to eat or play with. Devon handed the baby a spoon without even realizing what he was doing. Jessica scowled at him and merely took the spoon out of Ryan's hands. This caused the baby to pucker up, and as his bottom lip quivered, he began to cry.

"Now, do you see what you've done?" she snapped at Devon.

"I didn't make him cry. You're the one who took his spoon away."

"Ohhh," she muttered and handed the spoon back to Ryan. "You and I are going to have to have a more private discussion of this matter, I can see."

"You name the time and place," Devon countered, feeling completely up to any challenge Jessica could offer.

"The point is," Buck finally interjected, "Windridge is going to need some help. Arguing about it isn't going to make improvements around here."

"I think if we sink our remaining capital into spring stock," Devon replied, "we could have enough to sell off next year and make a good profit. Beef sales are doing just fine. The immediate need is for us to build back our capital—not to spend it on frivolous ideas that might never come to be worth anything."

"I disagree," Jessica replied. "And since I now own Windridge and you are just the hired help, I believe I have the final say."

Gasps from Kate and Buck came at the words *hired help*, but Devon held his temper in check. "I may be the hired help, but I was hired because I knew ranching. Your father thought enough of my skills to honor me with his trust. I think that should say something for itself."

"It says plenty, and so does the rundown state of this ranch. If you are such a good foreman, Mr. Carter, why do I arrive to find the place in such a state?"

Kate put a hand on Devon's arm. "Jessie, you don't understand all that has happened. Devon had little say about matters of finance. He is a good foreman for the ranch, knows cattle and horses, and is handy with repairs, but he didn't have any say over the money. Your father was the one who made all the decisions—bad and good."

"And he's gone," Jessica said simply.

"Not if you just pick up where he left off," Devon proclaimed without thinking.

Jessica stared at him for a moment. "I resent that implication, Mr. Carter. And I would further add that if you don't like the way I intend to do things and if you think it impossible to take my orders seriously, then I'd suggest you find another place of employment."

"No, Jessie!" Kate declared. "You don't even know what you're saying. Now I want both of you to calm down and stop acting like children. A ranch takes a lot of people to see it through. We can work at this together and build it up, or we can destroy it. It's pretty much up to us."

Jessica seemed to take heed of Kate's words and fell silent.

Devon threw down his napkin and got up from the table. "I have work to do," he announced and stormed out of the room. *Aggravating woman*, he thought. *Thinks she can just come in and solve the problems of the world by forcing us all into her mold.* He slammed the kitchen door behind him as he made his way into the crisp October morning.

Glancing skyward, he prayed. *Lord, I don't know why this has to be so difficult. I figured her visit would be trying, what with her being a city gal and all, but I didn't figure on her turning this place into a dude ranch. I need some help here, Lord.* He looked out across the broken-down ranch and sighed. *And I need it real soon.*

Chapter 3

Winter moved in with a harshness that Jessica had not expected. Living near the top of a high ridge caused them to feel every breeze and gale that came across the prairie. It also made them vulnerable to the effects of that wind.

Jessica tried not to despair. She knew that any plans she had for the ranch would have to wait until spring, so she tried to busy herself around the house. Her friendship with Kate also blossomed as the women worked together. Kate gave Jessica her first lessons in canning, butchering, and quilting, and out of everything she learned, Jessica thought quilting to be the very best.

"I think quilting is the only way to make it through the long, lonely winters," Kate told her one afternoon. "I've passed many a winter this way."

Jessica stared at the quilt block in her lap and sighed. "I just wish I was a better seamstress. My stitches are so long and irregular. I'm sure I shall never be able to make anything useful."

"Nonsense. We all had to start somewhere. You do a fine job embroidering, and if you have a way with a needle, you can certainly learn to quilt."

"What do you do with all the quilts you make?" Jessica asked.

"I give them to family, use them here, or just stack them up in the storage room."

"I'll bet folks back East would pay good money to have a beautiful quilt like that one," she said, pointing to the quilt frame where Kate worked.

"This old flower-basket pattern isn't that hard. Most folks could whip one up for themselves. Can't imagine they'd pay much of anything for my work."

"But they would. I have several friends in New York who would be very happy to purchase something like this. They don't sew—in fact, they're worse than me when it comes to putting in a stitch. They love beautiful things, and your quilts would definitely fall into that category," Jessica protested.

Kate stopped in her tracks. "You honestly think folks would pay good money to buy my quilts?"

"I do," Jessica replied enthusiastically. "Kate, if you were willing to part with some of your quilts, I could ship them back to my friends and see what kind of money they could raise. They could send the money, as well as some additional materials, and maybe if they talked to their friends and families, they would have orders for additional quilts."

"That might be one way we could raise some money for the ranch," Kate replied. "Of course, it wouldn't be like selling off a steer, but every little bit would help. Especially after so many years of waste."

Jessica paused and grew thoughtful. "Kate, what happened with my father? I mean, what caused him to start drinking?"

Kate stopped her work and looked sympathetically at Jessica. "I can't really say. I know he was never the same after Naomi died. He loved that woman more than he loved life. Buck feared he'd kill himself just in order to be with her. He just lost all desire to go on, and we did our best to keep him among the living."

"But he seemed so capable whenever I came to visit. And the ranch, I mean, it never looked like this."

Kate's expression took on a sorrow that immediately left Jessica feeling guilty.

"Your father had a number of things happen to put him into despair. The losses were just too much for him to bear."

"What kinds of losses?" Jessica dared the question, fearful of what the answer might be.

Kate pushed up her glasses and set her attention back on the quilting. "He lost a great deal of money, for one thing. I'm not really sure where it all went. I know he gave everyone a bonus, and when hard times came, we tried to give it back, but Gus wouldn't hear of it. Buck and I just gradually added it back into the purchases we took on for the ranch. Gus was always helping one friend out or another—never thinking that the money might not be there in the future.

"Then that summer, half the stock came down sick and died. That caused all kinds of problems. Drought came on us later that same summer, but we still had the fresh-water springs, so we didn't suffer for water like most folks. Just when things seemed to be getting a little better, a late summer storm set the prairie on fire and burned most everything in its path. The bad thing was, it wasn't just one fire, but a series of fires, and the cattle and wild critters had no place to run. For some reason we'd neglected plowing fire strips—those are wide breaks in the prairie where we don't allow anything to grow. They can be very useful in containing fires because when they reach those places, the fires just sort of burn themselves out. But that year we just didn't see to it properly.

"The fire killed whole herds in some areas. We spent over forty-eight hours toting water up from the springs and watering down everything in sight and plowing wide strips around the main homestead. We were able to save the house and most all the outbuildings, but nothing else. The house smelled like smoke for months afterward. We lost so much that I thought Gus was going to up and sell it off for sure. But he wouldn't sell—felt it was too important to stay on."

"Why?"

Kate shook her head. She seemed reluctant to speak. "I think Gus worried about all of us. You, included."

"Worried? In what way?" Jessica couldn't imagine that this powerful figure she'd always known as her father would be worried about anything.

"He worried about whether we'd be cared for. He worried about Buck and me having a place to live. He worried about you back East with that money-grubbing social dandy." Kate stopped and threw Jessica an apologetic look. "Sorry. I shouldn't have said that."

Jessica sighed and shook her head. "Why not? It's the truth. Might as well tell it like it is."

Kate turned up the lantern a bit, then went back to work. "Well, he worried about you. He always feared that sending you back East wasn't the right thing to do, but you must understand that he felt so inadequate to deal with you."

"Is that why he sent me in the first place?" Jessica asked flatly.

Kate halted her work and pushed away from the quilt frame. "Jessie, I know we've never really talked about any of this, but with your father gone, I figure it's all right to talk about it now."

"Then please do," Jessica encouraged.

"Your father intended to send you off to your aunt, then kill himself."

"What?"

"You heard me. He totally broke down with Buck and told him he had no desire to live. Buck had been your father's friend long enough to realize that he would feel this way. He stayed with your father through the next months. Sometimes he even slept in the same room with Gus—on those nights that were particularly bad. Buck would make a pallet on the floor of Gus's room and keep watch over him until he fell asleep. Those were usually anniversaries. You know, her birthday, her death day, their wedding day. Those were the worst for Gus."

Jessica nodded. It was easy to imagine the pain and suffering that those simple reminders must have put upon her father. It seemed funny that where Newman was concerned, Jessica felt only relief. Sometimes it made her feel guilty, but most of the time she was just glad to be rid of him. She tried not to hate him, because hating him seemed to make it impossible to love Ryan in full. And she wasn't about to jeopardize her relationship with Ryan. He was all she had, and no one would take him from her.

"When you married," Kate began again, "your father feared for you. I remember him hiring a man back East to send him a report on Newman's background and financial status."

"He did what?" Jessica questioned.

"He hired a man to check into Newman Albright. The reports that came back weren't at all flattering."

"He knew about Newman?" Jessica questioned, completely mortified that she'd not been able to hide the details of her married life from her father. She'd known that her father was aware of the gambling and the financial crisis Newman had heaped upon his family, but surely he didn't know about the mistresses and other problems.

"He knew it all. The women, the abuses, the baby. He made me promise to never say anything to you in my letters. It worried him sick sometimes. He used to talk to me about it—ask my advice. I told him if you felt like talking, you'd do it."

"But he never showed me any sign that he'd be open to my talking to him," Jessica replied angrily. "Even when he knew me to be widowed, he never asked me to come home."

"But you never gave any indication that you would have wanted to come home. You stopped visiting, even though you were old enough to make your own decisions. You up and married without even asking him what he thought—"

"Why should I have asked him?" Jessica interrupted. "He'd barely showed the slightest interest in my life."

"That's not true, Jessica. Your father had detailed monthly reports from your aunt Harriet. It was her rule that you not be allowed to come to Windridge before you reached twelve years of age."

"I didn't know that," Jessica replied, her anger somewhat abated. "I thought he didn't want me here. I mean, he's the one who sent me away."

"He sent you because he planned to end his life. Then when he finally had a reason to go on, you were well established with your aunt, and to force you to a life out here on the Kansas Flinthills seemed cruel. Besides, he'd signed an agreement with Harriet. Your father, if nothing else, was a man of his word."

"Would he have really asked me to come here? If Aunt Harriet would have been willing, would my father have brought me home?"

Kate shrugged. "Who can say? We have no way of reliving the past to see what other choices we might have made. You have to stop worrying about what might have been and focus on what is. You have a fine son and a failing ranch. It's the future that needs your attention."

"I realize that, but sometimes the choices for the future find their basis in the past," Jessica replied.

"True. I guess I can see the sense in that."

"Well, you ladies are gonna freeze to death if you don't stoke up that fire," Buck said, coming into the room with an armload of firewood. "I just put more wood on the fire in the baby's room."

"Is Ryan still asleep?" Jessica questioned.

"Yup. He didn't even stir," Buck replied. He put several thick logs into the massive stone fireplace and took the poker to it in order to help the wood catch.

"He truly seems to like Windridge. He's slept through the night ever since our coming here," Jessica said.

"Well, he is a year old now," Kate reminded them.

"It's so hard to believe," Jessica said. "When I think we've been here at Windridge for almost four months, I can't imagine where the time has gone. It seems like just yesterday we were sitting down to our first breakfast together."

"It only seems that way because you've hardly spoken two words to Devon since then," Kate admonished.

Buck chuckled but knew better than to join in the conversation. He quickly exited the room after replacing the poker against the wall. Kate watched him leave before turning her attention back to Jessica.

"You really should work out your differences."

"He wants to run my life—and Ryan's."

"He just cares about you and the boy. He's good with Ryan, and Ryan really seems to love being with Devon. Why would you deprive the child of such a meaningful relationship? Devon's a good man."

"Yes, I suppose he is, but I cannot have Ryan getting close to someone who may well be gone tomorrow."

"Why would Devon be gone tomorrow? He loves Windridge—loves it as his own."

"But it isn't his. It's mine!" Jessica protested, knowing she sounded like a spoiled child arguing over toys. "Devon has interfered in my son's life, and he tries to manipulate and run mine. He tells me constantly how bad the finances are, but he never has suggestions as to how we could improve things. In fact, I'll bet he'd even laugh at our idea to sell quilts back East."

Kate smiled. "I kind of laughed at that idea myself, so don't hold that against Devon."

Jessica put her sewing aside and went to the fire. The warmth felt good to her. "I don't want to hold anything against anyone, Kate. I just want to be given due respect. I want Devon to realize that I love this place too, and just because I didn't get a chance to grow up here doesn't mean I don't have Windridge's best interests in mind."

"So tell him that," Katie urged. "He's a reasonable man. He'll listen."

Jessica shook her head. "But what if he doesn't? What if he just wants to fight with me?"

Kate laughed. "What if you step out the door and the lion eats you?"

"What?"

"It's in the Bible. The foolish man refuses to go about his duty because he's afraid if he steps out of the house, a lion might eat him. There's a lot of things in life like that. We refuse to take steps forward because we're afraid something overwhelming will happen."

Jessica nodded. "I just don't know how to take that man. He's so, well, he's too confident of himself. He acts like he has all the answers, and nobody else can possibly have anything good to say."

Kate shook her head. "I've never known Devon to fit that description. He's confident—that much I'll give you. But honestly, Jessica, his confidence is in the Lord rather than himself."

The muffled sound of Ryan's cry came from upstairs. Jessica immediately went to the sitting-room door and pulled it open. "I think someone is telling us his naptime is over."

"I think you are right," Kate laughed. "It's time for me to be putting supper together anyway. Those men are going to be hungry pretty soon, and I'm starting to feel a mite caved in myself."

Jessica too felt a slight gnawing of hunger. "What are we having tonight?"

"Roast," Kate replied. "Left over from last night, but tonight I'll fix it up in a stew with biscuits."

"Sounds wonderful."

With that, Jessica made her way upstairs. She had nearly reached the nursery door when Ryan's cries abated, and she could hear the sound of a male voice from within. She paused outside the door, wondering if Buck had gone to check the fire and had accidentally awakened the boy.

"There now, Partner," came Devon's voice. "No sense in getting yourself all worked up. Ain't much good can come of it."

Jessica could hear Ryan's animated babble, as well as Devon moving around the room.

"Let's get you out of those wet clothes and into something more comfortable."

At this, Jessica could no longer stand idle. She burst through the door as though the house were on fire and stared daggers at Devon Carter. Her mind was flooded with thoughts of Essie Kappin trying to steal her son's loyalty by always insisting Jessica allow her to deal with the child whenever they were at the Kappins' for a visit.

"Just what do you think you're doing?" she protested. She came forward, grabbed Ryan out of Devon's arms, and maneuvered past him to the changing table. "Whatever possessed you to just allow yourself entry into my son's room?"

Ryan began to cry again, reaching around Jessica's tight hold toward where Devon stood rather stunned. Jessica hated that he was making such a scene. It was almost as if she were the monster having ripped him from the security of his parent, rather than the other way around.

"He was crying," Devon replied. "I figured he needed attention, and I was free for the moment."

Jessica plopped Ryan down on the changing table and set her mind on the job at hand rather than arguing with Devon. As soon as Ryan was changed and happily occupied on the rag rug with a toy, Jessica turned her full fury on Devon.

"I've told you before that I don't like having you interfere with my son."

Devon put his hands on his hips. His thick mustache twitched a bit as he frowned. "Jessica, this is a pretty isolated place. Don't you think we could agree to a truce of some sort?"

"No, I don't. I'm tired of telling you how I feel, only to have you ignore me." She hadn't noticed Ryan getting to his feet or the fact that he was walking, until he padded across the floor to Devon and took hold of his leg.

"Say, you did a right good job of that, little fellow," Devon said, clapping his hands.

Ryan laughed and let go to clap his own hands, only to smack down on his bottom. For a moment he looked startled, then he laughed again and got on his hands and knees as if to try the whole thing again.

Jessica, stunned that her son was walking, refused to allow him to make Devon the center of his attention. Devon was stealing her son away from her, and she could never allow that.

"If you don't mind," she said, snatching Ryan up protectively, "I'm needed downstairs to help with supper."

"I could watch him for you," Devon suggested.

Jessica could hardly believe he'd made the offer. He wasn't listening to her protests at all. Battling Ryan's squirming body, Jessica answered him as coolly as she dared. "You were hired to work the ranch, Mr. Carter, not the nursery." With that she left, refusing to give him a chance to reply. *Oh, but the man could be infuriating.*

Ryan began to cry, only furthering her frustration. One way or another, she would put an end to Devon's interference before he'd totally turned her son away from her. She would not have another situation on her hands where someone suggested her son was better off without her.

Chapter 4

Jessica spent the next two weeks feeling deeply convicted about her attitude and behavior toward Devon. Not only had he refused to share supper the night of their disagreement, but he had refused to share all subsequent meals from that night forward. Jessica knew the fault lay with her. She knew too that in order to deal with the matter and put things aright, she would have to be the one to do the apologizing.

She realized that Devon had meant only to be helpful, but her own insecurities regarding Ryan had caused her to act unforgivably bad. Sitting with her Bible in hand, Jessica felt hot tears trickle down her cheeks.

"I just don't want to lose Ryan's love, Lord," she whispered in the silence of her room. In the nursery Ryan already slept contentedly, but there would be no sleep for Jessica until she dealt with the matter at hand. Already she'd spent some fourteen restless nights, and her misery was rapidly catching up with her.

"I came here with such great expectations, Father," she began to pray again. "I thought there would be financial security and a place to belong. I have thought of the house on Windridge as my own special utopia since I was a small child. You know how I felt about it. You know I loved this place and always desired to be here. I just wanted everything to be perfect. I want to be perfect. The perfect mother. The perfect mistress of Windridge. But I fail and continue to fail no matter how hard I try."

She opened the Bible and found herself in the book of Colossians. " 'Put on therefore, as the elect of God, holy and beloved, bowels of mercies, kindness, humbleness of mind, meekness, long-suffering,' " she read aloud. Glancing past the desk where her Bible lay, Jessica peered out into the darkness of the night. Only the shadowy glow of lamplight from the cottage where Devon stayed could be seen on this moonless night.

"I certainly haven't been merciful or kind where he is concerned. Neither have I been meek or long-suffering, and I come nowhere near to being humble of mind. But, Father, I'm so afraid. I'm afraid of failing once again. I failed Harriet when I pleaded to come west. I failed when I married Newman. I failed even when I was born—taking the life of my mother and the joy of my father. If I fail here, then what is left to me?

"If I fail to be a good mother to Ryan, then someone will come along and take him from me. And if I fail to bring this ranch back into prosperity, then I might well lose the roof over my head. I want to make things perfect, but I feel so inadequate. My life has been so far removed from perfection, and now that I finally have some say over it, nothing seems to be going right." She sighed and added with an upward glance, "What do I do?"

She felt the turmoil intensify and continued to read from Colossians. " 'Forbearing one another, and forgiving one another, if any man have a quarrel against any: even as Christ forgave you, so also do ye. And above all these things put on charity, which is the bond of perfectness.' "

Jessica returned her gaze to the cottage. *I've not been forbearing or forgiving, and I certainly haven't put on charity. I've shown Devon Carter nothing but anger and resentment.* She thought of the close, affectionate manner in which Devon handled Ryan, and her heart ached. The situation tested every emotion within her. On one hand she feared Devon's involvement because of the Kappins. And on the other hand she feared Ryan's reaction to Devon's attention.

She couldn't provide Ryan with a father. Certainly not a father like Devon. Was it fair or right to allow the boy to grow close to Devon, when the man could pick up and go at any given moment? Kate said Devon would never do such a thing, but what if he grew tired of the failing ranch? What if he left them like so many of the other ranch hands had already done?

"Oh, Father, what am I to do? How do I show this man charity instead of fear?" Then a thought came to mind, causing Jessica to feel even more at a loss. Devon seemed perfectly willing to answer her questions, to take time out of his schedule to work with her on matters—at least those times when she had allowed herself to ask and seek his help. But the relaxed nature of Devon—his considerate and generous spirit—made Jessica uncomfortable. Devon clearly represented the kind of man she would have chosen for herself had others not interfered with her life.

"If Harriet hadn't thrust me into her social circles, demanding I choose a husband from the men of leisure who haunted her doorstep, I might have known true happiness. I might even have come here and met Devon Carter long before joining my life to Newman; then Ryan would be his son, and I would be his wife."

The thought so startled Jessica that she slammed the Bible shut. *I can't allow myself to think that way*, she scolded. *There is nothing to be gained by it. I can't take back the past. I can't bring my dead mother and father to life and start over under their care instead of Aunt Harriet's. I can't remake my life.*

The light went out in the cottage, leaving Jessica to feel even more deserted. Somehow, knowing that Devon was awake made her feel less alone. As if taking this as her own cue to go to bed, Jessica made one more check on Ryan, then turned down the lamp and crawled into the massive bed. Scooting into the very middle, Jessica could extend both arms and never touch the sides of the bed. How empty it seemed. How empty her entire life seemed.

I'll try to do better, Lord, she prayed the promise. *I will humble myself and go to Devon and apologize for my attitude and actions. I will even be honest with him about the reasons. But please, just go before me and help me to say the right thing. Don't let me make a fool out of myself—again.*

The next morning dawned with a promise of spring. The air felt warm on Jessica's face as she made her way out to what Kate called the garden house. The ground gave off a rich, earthy smell that made Jessica want to plant something. Maybe she'd talk to Kate about restoring the flower garden that used to grow along this walk. Kate had spoken of the prairie flowers and the delicate splotches of color that graced the hills when springtime was upon them in full. Kate said it had been Naomi's favorite time of year.

Standing just outside the cottage, Jessica gave a brief prayer for courage. She wanted to speak to Devon before breakfast in hopes that he might join them and ease the tension that had engulfed the house since Jessica's last outburst. She also intended to follow through with her promise to God and humble herself before this handsome stranger.

Knocking lightly, Jessica tried to plan what she'd say. She had continued to wrestle with her conscience long into the night, but somewhere around two in the morning, she'd finally let go of her fears and given them over to God. It wouldn't be easy to face her mismatched emotions, but somehow she knew God would give her the grace to handle things day by day.

Devon opened the door, stared at her blankly for a moment, then smiled. "And to what do I owe the pleasure of a visit from the boss lady?"

Jessica swallowed hard and tried to think of each word before speaking. "I've come here to apologize."

Devon crossed his arms and leaned against the door frame. "Apologize?"

Jessica nodded. "That's right. My behavior toward you has been uncalled for. I've known it all along, but I'm hoping you will give me a chance to explain."

Devon's expression softened. "Why don't you come in and tell me all about it."

Jessica nodded. "All right."

She entered the cottage for the first time, amazed at the hominess of the front room. A native stone fireplace took up most of one wall, while a big picture window that looked out onto a small porch graced yet another. A narrow pine staircase took up the south side, while an open archway made up most of the remaining west wall. A large rag rug, no doubt put together by Kate, lay on the floor in front of the fireplace, and a couch, upholstered in a sort of brown tweed, stood awaiting them behind this.

"Might as well sit over here," Devon said, leading the way to the couch. "It's really the only warm spot in the house. Buck and I are trying to find materials to make repairs, but it's rather slow going."

"If there's anything I can do to help. . . ," Jessica offered, letting her voice trail off.

"That's all right. I think Buck and I can handle it," Devon countered. "So you were going to do some explaining."

Jessica nodded. She gazed into Devon's dark eyes and felt a wave of alarm wash over her. Maybe coming here wasn't a good idea, after all. She looked away and clasped her fingers tightly together. "I know I've treated you rather harshly."

"Rather harshly?" he questioned.

Jessica took a deep breath and let it out. "All right. I've treated you badly, and I'm sorry. There's a great deal in my life that makes it hard for me to trust people. Especially strangers. From the minute I stepped foot on Windridge, you seemed to be everywhere, and frankly, it made me uncomfortable."

"I can certainly understand," Devon replied. "That's kind of why I've been trying to keep my distance."

"Then there's Ryan," she continued uneasily. Devon was a man. What would he understand of her motherly insecurities? She looked up and found his expression fixed with a compassionate stare. Maybe he would understand. "Do you know my story, Mr. Carter? How I came to live back East rather than on Windridge?" He nodded. "Well, it's left me with a very real void in my life. I never knew my parents—never saw my father until I was twelve. Even when I came here to spend a few weeks that summer, I still didn't see him much. He probably felt as uncomfortable as I did. Neither one of us knew what to do with the other one."

She paused as if trying to sort out her words. She wanted Devon to understand why she resented his interference with Ryan, but it seemed important to set up the conflicts from her early days in order to make her present days more clear.

"I never felt love for my father," she admitted. "I think I was afraid to love him. I certainly didn't want to give him another chance to send me away or to reject that love. My aunt Harriet encouraged neither shows of emotion nor words of endearment, and so I never felt loved in her home. I've been taught most of my life to bury my emotions, or at best, to shut them off. I tell you this because I would like for you to understand my difficulty in being open with my feelings."

Devon chuckled. "I thought you made your feelings quite apparent. You don't like me or my interfering with Ryan."

"No, that's not it," Jessica replied, looking at the dying embers in the fireplace. "I love Windridge. It's the only thing that couldn't reject my love." Her voice trembled slightly under the emotion of the moment. "I don't want my pride to keep this ranch from becoming a success once again. I don't want my feelings from the past creeping into the future of this place, and I won't allow myself to cause the demise of Buck and Kate's happiness, nor of yours."

"You don't have the power to put an end to Buck and Kate's happiness. Nor can you destroy mine for that matter," Devon replied, seeming most emphatic. "As for the success of this ranch, well, maybe the time has come to put an end to Windridge. There are folks out there willing to buy. Maybe you'd be happier back East or even in town."

"No!" Jessica said, looking back to see Devon watching her reaction with apparent interest. "I don't want to sell. If I gave you that idea, then I know I've failed to say the right words. Look, I mentioned the idea of a resort ranch only because it seemed to be profitable. We're only an hour away from the train. We already have a perfectly suited stagecoach, though why my father ever purchased such an elaborate means of transportation, I'll never know."

Devon laughed. "Gus got it in trade, to tell you the truth. One of the locals ran a stage line for about two months. He went broke in a hurry and then took sick. When he saw he couldn't keep it up, he asked Gus to trade him for some good beef stock so his son could start a small ranch. Gus agreed, and there you have it."

"Well, that does explain it rather neatly," Jessica agreed. "But don't you see? I envision the healing power of this ranch will draw others to its doorstep, just as it has me."

"But honestly, Jessica," he said, his voice lowering and his expression growing intense, "part of Windridge's healing is the isolation. You bring in a bunch of city folks and suddenly it's not so very isolated anymore. Folks will come with their strange notions and ways of doing things, and soon you'll find that Windridge is nothing like it once was. I'd hate to see that happen."

Jessica felt a bit defeated. She honestly tried to see Devon's point. Maybe he knew what he was talking about. Maybe she was the real fool in the matter. She reached into her apron pocket and pulled out several folded pieces of paper. "These are the articles I mentioned to you awhile back. All I ask is that you take a look at them."

Devon reached out to take them, his fingers closing over hers for a brief moment. The current of emotions seemed to leap from Jessica to Devon, and for a time he looked at her as if he could read every detail of her soul. The longing, the loneliness, the fearfulness, and the insecurity—Jessica worried that if she didn't look away quickly, she'd soon reveal more about herself than she'd ever intended. She dropped her hold on the papers and pulled her hand back against her breast as though the touch had burned her fingers.

Devon seemed to understand her discomfort, but to what extent, Jessica couldn't tell. "I'll look these over," he promised, tucking them between the cushions of the couch.

"I appreciate that. I also have another favor to ask you."

"All right."

She lowered her head and stared at her lap. "I would very much appreciate your help with the Windridge accounts. I've looked at the books, but I'm still not sure what I'm looking at."

Devon chuckled. "I can't say that Gus was the best bookkeeper in the world. He knew his system but seldom wanted to share it with anyone else. It wasn't until about a year before he died that I knew we were in real trouble. After that, things just sort of went from bad to worse. But in answer to your question, I'll be glad to do what I can. I do know the workings of this ranch—very nearly as well as Buck. I think together we can give some strong consideration as to what is to be done."

Jessica nodded. "Thank you. I do appreciate it. I know I've not acted with Christian charity, and God has quite seriously brought it to my attention." She glanced up to find him studying her. Her heart skipped a beat when he grinned at her.

"He's had to bring it to my attention quite often as well—not because of your attitude," he said, pausing, "but because of my own."

Jessica got to her feet. The intimacy of the moment was rapidly becoming quite noticeable. "I hope this apology of mine will mean that you'll reconsider and share meals up at the house again. Kate hasn't been herself since you stopped coming up, and I know you're staying away because of the way I acted."

Devon walked with her to the door. "That's not exactly true," he told her. "I also stayed away because of the way I acted when I was around you."

Jessica turned to look at him—wondering at his meaning—afraid to know the truth. Instead of asking him to explain, she realized she'd omitted a very important matter. "There's one more thing, and it comes very hard for me."

"By all means, speak your mind."

Jessica looked at him for a moment. She felt down deep inside that she could trust this man. That his motives were pure and his actions were not intended for harm. What she wasn't sure of was whether or not she could accept that her child would have needs in his life that she would be unable to fill—needs that would require a man's thought, perspective, and guidance.

"It's about Ryan," she finally said.

"I see."

Devon took a step back and looked like he might say something, but Jessica hurried to continue. "I was wrong there as well." He raised a brow but said nothing, and Jessica realized she'd have to explain further. But how much should she say? Would it be appropriate to tell Devon about Esmerelda and her mother? Would it be appropriate to explain her deepest, heartfelt fear that she might somehow lose Ryan to another?

She looked away, tears forming in her eyes. How could she explain? She scarcely understood the feelings she had. She felt so protective of Ryan, but not only for him, but for fear she would once again be denied love.

"I'm sorry," she whispered. "It's very difficult for me to speak about it."

Devon's voice was low and filled with tenderness. "Jessica, I know you're still grieving your husband's passing and all. I wasn't trying to take his place."

Jessica laughed and turned to meet Devon with her tears flowing freely. "It isn't that. Believe me, it isn't that at all." Her voice sounded foreign in her own ears. It came out as a mixture of a laugh and a sob all at once. "I didn't love Newman Albright, and he certainly didn't love me. We married because he was chosen by my aunt Harriet. I often thought afterwards that for all she did to sing his charms and merits, Harriet should have married him herself."

Devon reached out and touched her tear-streaked cheek. "Then what is this all about?"

"I might never have loved my husband, but I would die rather than lose my son," she answered, quivering under the touch of his warm fingers.

"I still don't understand what that has to do with me."

He looked at her with such intensity, such longing to understand, that Jessica had to close her eyes to regain her composure. "The only reason," she began, her eyes still tightly closed, "that I didn't want you interfering with Ryan—"

"Yes? Go on," he encouraged when she fell silent.

"I don't want you replacing me in his life," she finally managed, but the tears came again. "He's all I have." Her voice came out like a whimper, and Jessica hated sounding like a lost child. She knew it was better to be honest and face humiliation than to lie and go on dealing with her conscience.

To her surprise, Devon put his arms around her and gently pulled her head to his shoulder. No one had ever done this for her. Not once. Not even Newman. The action seemed so intimate, so loving, that Jessica broke down and cried in deep, heart-wrenching sobs.

Devon did nothing but hold her. He let her cry, all the time keeping his arms tightly around her. He didn't say a word or try to force answers out of her. He just held her. Oh, but it felt wonderful! It felt like something Jessica had been searching for all of her life. Warm arms to comfort and assure her that the world outside would not break in to hurt her anymore. Without even realizing it, she had wrapped her own arms around Devon's waist and clung to him as though in letting go, she might well drown in a sea of emptiness.

After a few minutes, Jessica felt the weight of her emotions lift. Her tears subsided, and she fell silent. She knew it was quite uncalled for to be standing there alone with Devon, embracing him so familiarly, but she was quite hesitant to let go.

"Feel better?" he asked softly, reaching a hand up to smooth back her hair.

Jessica sniffed in a most unladylike way and nodded. "I think so." She let go of him and wiped her face with the edge of her apron. "I'm sorry about losing control that way."

"Don't be," Devon answered quite seriously. "You don't have to face the world by yourself, Jess."

The nickname warmed her, where only weeks ago it would have irritated her. "I know. I know. The Bible makes that clear, but sometimes it seems God is so far away."

"I wasn't talking about God." She looked up to see Devon's eyes narrow ever so slightly as he scrutinized her. "God is there for you," he agreed. "I wouldn't presume to say otherwise. But I meant that we're here for you too. Katie, Buck, and me. We care about you, and we care about Ryan. And honestly, Jessica, I would never do anything to harm your child or to take him away from you. I do realize that there is more to this than you're telling me, but maybe one day you'll feel confident enough of our friendship to share it all. Until then, just know I care.

"We'll get through this, but we'll need to rely on one another. Ryan is starting to walk now, and there are plenty of dangers around the ranch. You'll wear yourself to the bone if you worry about having to watch him alone. Let us help you. We want to make your life easier, not harder, and certainly not more painful."

Jessica nodded. "I know that." She lowered her head and looked at the floor. What she would say next would come at considerable risk to her security. "Ryan seems so miserable without you around. I want you to feel free to play with him and be around him. I know he's already taken to you in a big way. I would even go so far as to say he loves you."

Devon reached out to touch Jessica's chin with his index finger. Lifting her face, he replied, "He loves you too, Jessica. That won't change just because other people come into his life. It's been my experience, the more love the better. People need to be loved."

Jessica felt his words cut deep into her heart. If she didn't clear out now, she'd start crying all over again. "Thank you," she whispered quickly and hurried to the door. Throwing it open, she looked back over her shoulder. "I'm sure Kate has breakfast nearly ready. You will join us, won't you?"

"You bet. I'll be up to the house in a few minutes."

Devon watched Jessica walk up the path to the big stone house. He felt an overwhelming urge to run after her and declare his love for her. Funny, he thought, he'd fallen in love with her almost from the start. At least he thought it was love. He certainly knew that it was something powerful and strong. He thought about her constantly and worried that she would give up on the ranch before he had a chance to convince her to take his help.

He had money in the bank. Not a lot, but enough to help the ranch. He would just do as Buck and Kate had done and start purchasing things as they needed them, and he wouldn't let Jessica know about it. Of course, Buck would know, and so would Kate. But he knew they would keep his secret. Kate had told him of their scheme to sell quilts. Maybe he'd offer to take some to Kansas City when he went there to buy cattle. He could always add some extra dollars to the amount he actually managed to make.

It was easy enough to formulate an idea about bringing in more cattle and maybe a ranch hand or two, but it was harder to decide how he would help Jessica to work through her inability to trust. He longed to help her feel secure in the house on Windridge. He wanted her to know that her home would be here as long as she needed it. That he would be here too, if only she would let him.

He thought of her fears of losing Ryan's love and realized rather quickly that with Jessica's very personal declarations of her life, he had become privy to the knowledge that she had never felt loved. Kate had loved her from the start and had said so on many occasions. But Kate had not been allowed to raise the baby of Naomi and Gus Gussop. A cold, unfeeling woman with social concerns had raised Jessica. The father Jessica had never known had no idea how to receive her or her needs when that unfeeling woman had finally allowed Jessica a visit home.

Even her husband hadn't married her out of love. And Devon found that particularly distressing considering his own growing feelings. He hadn't said anything about his interest in Jessica, primarily because he assumed she wouldn't be ready for such attentions. Now he realized she was not only ready for it, but she'd been ready for over twenty-seven years. She needed love. She needed the love of a good man.

He smiled and leaned against the doorjamb as Jessica disappeared through the back door of the house. "I'm a good man," he said aloud, a plan already formulating in his mind. His smile broadened. "In fact, I'm the only man for the job."

He looked up into the clear morning sky and felt the overwhelming urge to share his thoughts with God. "This was what You had in mind for me all along, wasn't it? I wouldn't have been happy with another woman, and that's why You didn't let me waste my life on Jane Jenkins."

He thought of the petite blond who'd appeared at the ranch less than two weeks before their wedding day to announce she was marrying someone else. At least she'd been good enough to bring back Devon's ring. The ring had belonged to his grandmother, and Jane knew how much it meant to him. She hadn't been totally without feeling.

"I can't stay out here in the middle of nowhere," she had told him that day so long ago. "I hate Kansas and everything that goes with it. I want to see the world and live in a big city, and I've found someone who feels exactly like I do. I hope you'll forgive me like you said you would."

Last Devon had heard, Jane was living just outside of Topeka. She had three kids, a cantankerous mother-in-law, and a husband who was seldom home due to his job as a traveling salesman. He felt sorry for her, knowing her dream had not been realized. At the time, her rejection had hurt him deeply; but as the months and years passed, Devon knew God had saved him from a miserable life.

"Thank You," he whispered. "Thank You for sending Jane out of my life and for bringing Jessica into it. Now, it's my prayer that You would show me how to help her. How to make her feel loved and safe."

He realized they would all be sitting down to breakfast soon, so he grabbed his hat and closed the door to the cottage. "It wouldn't hurt if You helped her to love me too." He grinned and tapped his hat onto his head. "Wouldn't hurt at all.

Chapter 5

One of Jessica's greatest pleasures came from horseback riding. Buck had suggested it one glorious April day, and Jessica found it a perfect solution to those times when the house seemed too quiet and the day too long. Of course, with Ryan now getting into things, those times were few and far between, but nevertheless, Jessica found it a wonderful time. Riding out across the prairie hills, she could think about the days to come—and the days now gone. She could plan her future without anyone barging in on her thoughts, and she could pray.

It also became an exercise in trust. She forced herself to leave Ryan in Kate's care and trust that nothing would happen to threaten her relationship with her son. It wasn't easy, but Jessica knew instinctively that it was right.

Now, having ridden to the top of the ridge, Jessica stared out across the rolling Flinthills and sighed. Flowers were just beginning to dot the prairie grasses. It reminded her of her mother. Kate had told her that this view had been Naomi's favorite because of the flowers and the contours of the hills and the glorious way the sunsets seemed to spill color across the western horizon.

Jessica wearied of the saddle and dismounted. "All right, Boy, it's back to the barn for you."

The horse seemed to perfectly understand her, and with a snort and a whinny, he took off in the direction of the corrals and barn. By letting the horse go free, she found that he always made his way back to the stable and to Buck's tender care. The first time it had happened totally by mistake when Jessica had dismounted and let go of her reins. Buck had worried she'd been thrown, but Jessica had assured him as she came running down the hill to recapture her mount that she was fine. Buck had laughed; so had Devon; and when they'd shared the scene with Katie, she had laughed as well. Buck said the Windridge horses were so spoiled and pampered, they'd return to the barn every time, and after that, it just became the routine.

Today, the wind came from the south as it often did, but with it came a gentle scent of new life. Flowers bloomed sporadically across the prairie, and Jessica reveled in the addition of color to her otherwise rather drab world. The fields had greened up, much to the delight of the cattle who seemed rather tired of hay and dried dead grass. Even the house itself seemed to take on a more golden hue.

Jessica sighed and reached up to take off her bonnet. She let down her hair and shook it free, grateful to feel the wind through it one more time. Kate said her father had called this God's country, and Jessica could well understand why he felt that way. Just standing there, watching the cattle feed, seeing the occasional movement of a rabbit or the flight of birds overhead, Jessica felt her heart overflow with praise to God. His presence seemed to be everywhere at once.

The land was so wholly unspoiled. The city had a harshness to it that she'd once accused the prairie of having. Both could be ruthless in dealing with their tenants, but while the prairie did so from innocence, the city made its mark in snobbery, class strife, and confrontation.

In the city, Jessica seldom knew a moment when noise didn't dominate her day. The activities were enough to cause a person to go mad. And it seemed the poorer you were, the higher the level of clatter. Street vendors called out their wares from morning to night. Children—dirty urchins who had no real homes—raced up and down the streets begging money, food, shelter. Poverty brought its own sounds: the cries of the hungry, the street-fighting of the angry, the con men with their schemes to make everyone rich overnight.

But always the needs of the children concerned Jessica. She had tried to do what she could, but there'd been so little, and she could hardly take away from her own child in order to provide for someone else's. When her father had started to provide for her once again, she had shared what she could with some of the others. Esmerelda had thought her quite mad. "Charity," she had told Jessica, "is better left to the truly rich." Essie thought Jessica's money could be much better spent on a new gown or toys for Ryan. It was easy now to see how harsh Essie could be when Jessica refused to play by her rules.

And there were so many rules. Not just Essie's but New York's rules as well. The rules of class—of not crossing boundaries, of staying where you belonged. Jessica had provided a dichotomy for her friends. She had been raised in the best social settings with Harriet Nelson and married a man who held rank among the well-to-do. But when their money was gone, so too were their friends. It seemed strange to suddenly find that she was never invited to parties or teas. Never visited by those she had once been bosom companions with. Essie had maintained a letter-writing campaign, but never once had the young woman come to visit after things had gone bad for Jessica. She hadn't even come to Newman's funeral.

But once Jessica's father stepped in to move her back to the proper neighborhood and reinstate her with financial resources, everyone flocked around. It was all as if Jessica had only been abroad for several years. In fact, Essie had once introduced her that way, telling the dinner guests that Jessica had enjoyed an extensive stay in Paris. It was true enough that she had done exactly that, but Essie failed to mention that Jessica had been thirteen years old at the time.

She let her gaze pan across the western horizon, while the waning sun touched her face with the slightest hint of warmth. She knew Aunt Harriet would have been appalled to find her in such a state, but to Jessica, it felt wonderful! She cherished the moment, just as she had when she'd been twelve.

"Thank You, Father," she whispered, raising her hands heavenward as if to stretch out and touch her fingertips to God.

"You make a mighty fetching picture up here like that," Devon said.

Jessica turned, surprised to see the overworked foreman making his way up the ridge. "I thought maybe you'd hightailed it back to civilization," she teased to ease her own embarrassment. "I've scarcely seen you in two weeks."

"There's been too much to do," Devon told her. "But you already know that. Kate told me you've been pretty busy yourself."

"Yes. We've finished up some quilts, and then Buck dug us up a garden patch."

"I saw that. Can't say this is good farm ground, but Kate's gardens generally survive. It's all that tender loving care she gives them." Devon took off his hat and wiped his brow with a handkerchief. "Feels good up here."

"Yes," Jessica agreed. Her hair whipped wildly in the breeze, and she felt a bit embarrassed to be found in such a state. It was one thing to know they could see her from down below the hilltop, but for Devon to be here with her made Jessica self-conscious.

She reached up and began trying to pull her hair back into order, but Devon came forward and stilled her efforts. "Don't do that. It looks so nice down."

Jessica laughed nervously and stepped away. "It's just something I do sometimes. Kind of silly, but it reminds me of when I was a little girl."

"Nothing silly about that."

"Maybe not," Jessica said, forcing herself to look away from Devon's attractive face to the start of a beautiful sunset. "The prairie used to make me lonely. I used to feel so small and insignificant in the middle of it all. The hills just go on and on forever. It reminds me of how I'm just one tiny speck in a very big world."

"What happened to change how you felt? I mean, you told me you wanted to stay here and never leave. Surely you wouldn't feel that way about a place that made you feel lonely and insignificant."

Devon had come to stand beside her again, but Jessica refused to look at him. "I never had many chances to visit here before getting married, but after the second visit, I had already decided that the prairie was growing on me. I went home to New York City and felt swallowed up whole. The lifestyle, the parties, the activities that never seemed to end—it all made me feel so forgotten."

"How so?" Devon questioned softly.

Jessica stopped toying with her hair and let it go free once again. "No one really ever talks to anyone there. You speak about the city, about the affairs of other people. You talk about the newest rages and the fashionable way to dress. You go to parties and dinners and present yourself to be seen with all the correct people, but you never, ever tell anyone how you feel about anything personal. It fit well with my upbringing, but I came to want more."

She finally looked at him. "I feel alive out here. I feel like I can breathe and stretch and let my hair blow in the wind and no one will rebuke me for it. I feel like I can talk to you and Buck and Kate, and you not only talk back, but you really listen."

"I can't imagine being any other way," Devon said. "But, as for the coldness of the big city, I do understand. I go to Kansas City once, sometimes twice a year for supplies and to sell off the cattle. I hate it there. No one seems to care if you live or die."

"I know," Jessica replied, admiring the way the sky had taken on a blend of orange, yellow, and pink. "And you certainly never get sunsets like these."

Devon laughed. "Nope."

"I know God brought me here for a reason. I know He has a purpose for my life, and I feel strongly that my purpose involves helping other people. That may sound silly to you, but I know God has a plan for me."

"It doesn't sound silly at all. I believe God has a plan for each of us."

"What kind of plan does He have for you, Devon?" she asked seriously, concentrating on his expression.

Devon shoved his hands into his pockets and stared to the west. "I don't guess I know in full."

"So tell me in part," she urged.

"I know God brought me to this ranch. It was a healing for me, so when you speak of it being a healing for other people, I guess I understand. I was once engaged to be married, but it didn't work out. Windridge saw me through some bad times. Now, however, I feel God has shown me the reason for that situation and the result."

"What reason?" Jessica questioned, truly wondering how Devon could speak so casually about losing the woman he apparently loved.

"I know God has someone else for me to marry. He's already picked her out."

"Oh," she replied, her answer sounding flat. She'd only recently allowed herself to think about Devon as something more than a ranch foreman. She'd actually given herself permission to consider what it might be like to fall in love and marry a man like Devon Carter. His words came as a shock and stung her effectively into silence.

"I don't like being alone. I see myself with a family of my own. Six or seven—boys, girls, it doesn't matter—and a fine spread to work. Ranches can be excellent places to bring up children."

He looked at her as if expecting her to comment, but Jessica had no idea what to say. His words only told her that one day he would go his way and leave her alone. Not only that but leave Ryan alone as well. A dull ache caused her to abruptly change the subject.

"I see Windridge surviving and becoming stronger. I think we have a lot to offer folks here. Have you had a chance to look over those articles I left with you?"

"I've looked them over. I have to say I'm not nearly as against the idea as I once was. It seems the ranch would mostly be open to the public during summer months, is that right?"

Jessica perked up at his positive attitude. "Yes. Yes, that's right. Late spring to early autumn might be the biggest stretch of time, but basically it would be summer."

"Ranches can be mighty busy during the summer," he commented.

"Yes, but that's part of the attraction. Folks from back East will come to see the workings of the ranch. You and your men would be able to go about your business, and the visitors would be able to observe you in action."

"They'd also want to ride and maybe even try their hand at what we do, at least that's what one of your clippings said," Devon countered.

"But only if we wanted it to be that way," Jessica replied. "It can be arranged however we see fit. No one makes the rules but us."

"I suppose it wouldn't be so bad if the rest of the year allowed us to get back to normal. The location does seem right for something like that. I suppose we could even fix one of the larger ponds with a dock and a place for fishing."

"What a good idea," Jessica replied. "Maybe swimming too."

Devon nodded. "Hmmm, maybe. Might be a bit cold. Remember, those aren't hot springs." He appeared to be genuinely considering the matter. "And you see this as a ministry?"

Jessica felt herself grow slightly defensive. "I do. I see a great many things we can share with people. Kindness and love, mercy, tolerance—you name it. I know it would be a resort, and people would pay to come here and rest, but how we handled their stay would be evidence of Christ working in our lives. They would see how we dealt with problems and handled our daily lives."

"One of the articles talked about taking folks out camping under the stars to give them a taste of what the pioneers experienced when they went west in covered wagons. You thinking about doing that?" Devon asked.

Jessica considered the matter for a moment. "I think at first it would be to our benefit to just keep small. We could advertise it very nearly like a boarding home for vacationers. We could offer quiet summers. Maybe fishing, like you suggested, and horseback riding. We could build some nice chairs for the porch, and Kate and I could make cushions; folks could go through my father's library and pick out something to read and just relax on the porch. I just want to make a difference in people's lives."

Devon stepped closer. "You've made a difference in mine. You and Ryan both."

She looked into his warm brown eyes and saw a reflection of something she didn't understand. His words sounded important, yet he'd made it clear that God had someone already in mind for him to marry.

"I need to get back." She turned to leave, but Devon reached out to touch her arm. "I meant it, Jess. And I'm starting to think that maybe a resort wouldn't be a bad way to get the ranch back up and running. Hopefully, this small herd we've taken on from the Rocking W will make us a tidy profit and allow us to get a bigger herd next year. You keep praying about it, and so will I."

Jessica nodded and hurried down the hill to the three-story stone house. She didn't know how to take Devon or his words. He always treated her kindly and always offered her honesty, but today only served to confuse her.

Quietly, she entered the house through the back door, hoping that she'd not have to deal with Kate. Kate would want to know how Jessica had spent her day. Kate would want to know what she and Devon had talked about. And there was little doubt in Jessica's mind that Kate would know they had talked. She'd probably observed them up on the ridge. Everyone would have seen them there. Buck. The ranch hands.

Jessica felt her face grow hot. She had very much enjoyed being with Devon, and she enjoyed their talks. But Devon had another woman in mind to marry, and Jessica knew the heartache of losing a man to another woman. She'd not interfere in Devon's relationships. She'd not ruin his chances at happiness with the woman of his dreams. The woman God had sent to him.

With a heavy heart, Jessica admitted to herself that she was gradually coming to care about Devon. She liked the way he moved, the way he talked. She loved how he played with Ryan and how Ryan's face lit up whenever Devon came into the room. Reluctantly, Jessica began to put her hair back up in a bun. "I'm being so childish and ridiculous," she muttered.

"Oh, so there you are. Guess who just woke up?" Kate asked, coming down the back stairs with Ryan in her arms.

Jessica had just secured the last hairpin in place. "How's Mama's boy?"

Jessica asked, holding her arms out to Ryan.

"Mamamama," Ryan chattered. "Eat." He pulled at Jessica's collar, and she knew he wanted to nurse. She'd only managed to wean him a couple weeks earlier, but he nevertheless tried to coerce her into nursing him.

"Mama will take you to the kitchen and get you a big boy's cup," Jessica told him, gently tousling his nearly hairless head. "Do you suppose this child will ever grow hair?" she asked Kate.

"I've heard it said you were the same way," Kate said chuckling. "I think you finally achieved those glossy brown curls when you were nearly two."

"I hope he doesn't take too long," Jessica replied as she retraced her steps to the kitchen. She thought for a moment she was off the hook until Kate, pouring fresh cold milk into a cup for Ryan, asked, "So, what did you and Devon have to talk about while you enjoyed that beautiful sunset?"

Jessica tried not to act in the leastwise concerned about the question. "We discussed the ranch. It consumes most of our talks. Devon is finally coming around to my way of thinking. He's not nearly so negative about turning this place into a resort ranch."

"I never thought you'd convince him, but he talked to Buck about it just yesterday. Buck said he actually had some good ideas about what they could do to make this place ready by next year."

"Next year? But Devon said nothing to me about next year. I figured I'd have to spend most of this one just convincing him to let me do it."

Ryan drank from the cup, finished the milk, then tried to pound the empty cup against the wall behind his mother. Jessica finally put him down on the floor and turned her attention back to Kate.

"Did he really say next summer?"

Kate smiled and pushed up her glasses. "He did. I take it that surprises you?"

"Indeed it does. He said only that he was starting to see some merit in the idea. I had no idea he was actually working toward a date."

"Well, he's found some extra capital to sink into the ranch. Then too we have the quilts to sell, and we can always busy ourselves to make more. Besides, Devon doesn't own this ranch—you do. If you want to turn it into a resort, you certainly don't need anyone's permission."

"Yes, but I want you all to be happy."

"Devon too?" Kate grinned.

"Of course. You told me I needed to consider his thoughts on the matter, and I have. I respect Devon's opinion. I know all of you understand the ranch better than I do, but nevertheless, I want to learn, and I want to keep everyone's best interests at heart. I've been praying hard about this, Kate. I'm not going to just jump in without thinking."

Kate reached out and gave Jessica a hug. "I knew you wouldn't. We want you happy though, and if turning this place upside down would do the trick, I have a feeling Devon would start working on plans to figure a way."

Jessica said nothing but turned instead to see Ryan heading for the stove. "No, Ryan! Hot!" she exclaimed and went quickly to move the boy to another part of the kitchen.

"Why don't you and Ryan go out on the porch and spend some time together?" Kate suggested. "I've already got supper well underway, and there's no need to have you both in here underfoot."

Jessica laughed. "Just when I started thinking I had become needed and useful."

Kate laughed. "Oh, you're needed and useful, all right. Maybe more than you realize."

Jessica picked up the boy and made her way to the front door and out onto the porch. The sky had turned deep lavender with hints of even darker blues to the east. Night was still another hour or so away, but already shadows fell across the hills and valleys. Jessica liked the effect and wished fervently she could draw or paint. It seemed a shame that something so lovely should go by unseen. This thought provoked another. She could always advertise the ranch to artists. Mention the beautiful scenery and lighting. Of course, many people would consider the scenery boring and anything but beautiful. Perhaps that wouldn't be a very productive thing to do. What if someone went home to complain about the falsehood of her advertisement?

As Ryan played happily with Katie's flowerpots, Jessica allowed her thoughts to go back to Devon. She couldn't help it. She didn't want to care about him, at least not in the sense of falling in love and sharing a life with him. She didn't like to think of the rejection that could come in caring for someone, only to have them not care in return.

Still, if she couldn't have him in that capacity, then it was enough to have him here on the ranch full time. He made a good foreman, and she prayed he'd stay on for as long as she kept the ranch. A gray cloud descended over her thoughts. What if he married and brought his wife here to Windridge? Jessica shuddered. She'd not like that at all. And then with Ryan already so attached to Devon, it might create even greater problems. What if Ryan wanted to be with Devon instead of Jessica? What if Devon's new wife attracted Ryan's attention as well?

Jessica shook off the thoughts and tried to remain positive. "I can't be given over to thoughts of what if. There's plenty of other things to worry myself with."

Ryan babbled on and on about the flowerpots. Some words came out in clarity, and others were purely baby talk. Jessica found herself amazed to see how much the child had grown over the last few weeks. It seemed he'd almost aged overnight. She didn't like to think of him growing up and not needing her anymore. She didn't like to think about him becoming an adult and moving away. What would she do when he was gone? Who would love her, and whom would she love?

Devon's image came to mind, but Jessica shook her head sadly. "That's not going to happen," she told herself again. "He has other plans, and they don't include me."

Ryan perked up at this and toddled back to Jessica. He pounded the flats of his hands on her knees. "Me. Me. Me go. Me go."

Jessica looked down at him, feeling tears form in her eyes. "I know you will," she told him sadly. "One day, you will go."

Chapter 6

"If we convert those two sitting rooms at the back of the house," Kate said one evening after dinner, "we could have additional bedrooms for guests."

"True," Buck replied, looking to Jessica and Devon for their reactions.

"It might even work better if Ryan and I took those two rooms and let our rooms upstairs be used for guests," Jessica replied. "I mean, that way the entire second floor would be devoted to guests, and the third floor would still belong to you and Buck."

"Maybe it would be better to give the third floor to you and Ryan," Devon said thoughtfully. "After all, Kate needs to be close to the kitchen to get things started up in the morning, and Buck needs to be close to the barn and bunkhouse."

"I hadn't thought of it that way," Kate replied. "Those two rooms would be more than enough for Buck and me. In fact, one room would be enough."

"No, now I wouldn't feel right about it if you and Buck didn't have your own sitting room for privacy," Jessica said firmly. "Having a house full of strangers will be cause enough to need our own places of refuge."

"I could give you back the cottage," Devon offered. "If you and Buck think you'd be more comfortable there, I could move into the bunkhouse."

"Nonsense," Kate said shaking her head. "You've already moved once; you might as well stay put." Jessica wondered what she meant by this statement, but the conversation moved along so quickly that she never had a chance to ask.

"Katie and I would be happy just about any place you put us," Buck stated. "I think those two sitting rooms are just perfect for us. It would eliminate running up and down all those stairs, and what with my rheumatism acting up from time to time, that would be enough to motivate the move on my part."

"Buck, you should have told me you were having trouble," Jessica countered. "I would have seen to it that you and Kate were moved long ago had I known."

"The exercise does us good," Kate said. "But I agree with Buck and Devon. Moving us downstairs into those back rooms would be perfect. That way, you and Ryan can have the full run of the third floor. You can set things up differently or keep it the way we have it. Either way, Ryan will have more room to run around, and there's a door to keep him from heading down the stairs when you don't want him to get away from you."

Jessica laughed. "No doubt he'll figure doors out soon enough."

"I think we could safely conclude," Devon said, pointing to a rough drawing he'd made of the house, "that we could have six rooms to offer to guests. We could even offer the bunkhouse's extra beds if someone wanted to come out and truly experience the life of a ranch hand. Those articles Jessica brought from back East said that some folks actually pay money to be abused that way."

He grinned and poked Buck lightly in the ribs. "A drafty room, work from sunup to sundown, dirt and grit everywhere, and the smell of sweat and horses and cattle—yes Sir, that's the kind of stuff I want to pay out good money to experience."

"You get to experience it for free," Jessica chided.

"But when we're back on our feet, I expect to be paid," Devon replied, looking at her in a way that made Jessica's pulse quicken. Oh, but he was handsome. She loved the way the summer sun had lightened his hair and tanned his face.

"I doubt that will happen for awhile. Every dime we make is going to have to go back into making the ranch successful again."

"I wasn't necessarily talking about being paid in money," Devon said, his lips curling into a grin.

Buck snorted, and Kate turned away, but not before Jessica saw her smiling. They were all so conspiratorial in their teasing, and sometimes Jessica felt oddly left out. She had come onto the scene after they were all good friends, and sometimes it made her feel very uncomfortable. Like they all knew a good joke and refused to tell her.

"Well, it's getting late," Buck said, getting up from his chair. "I suspect Katie and I should retire for the evening. You two going to church in the morning?"

"Planning on it. I figured to drive Jessica and Ryan. You two need a lift?"

"No," Buck answered. "I figure on preaching a bit myself. Those ranch hands of ours need to get some religion now and then. What with the fact that it'll soon be time to herd those prime steers of ours to market, I figure on giving them a couple of pointers on staying out of trouble."

Kate joined Buck, leaving Devon and Jessica alone in the front parlor. "See you both tomorrow. I figure on frying up a mess of chicken for the hands and for us as well. Anything else you're hungry for?"

Devon grinned. "How about some of your famous raspberry cream cake?"

Jessica threw Kate a quizzical look. "I don't think I've ever had that. Do you mean to tell me I've been here almost a year and never once had the opportunity to taste your 'famous' raspberry cream cake?"

Kate laughed. "It's only famous to Devon. But sure, I'll fix us up some. The raspberries came on real good this year. I'll bet those bushes down by the main springs are still bearing fruit.

"Maybe Jess and I could pick some for you after church tomorrow," Devon offered.

"Maybe you could just speak for yourself," Jessica added in mock ire.

"You two can work it out," Kate replied as Buck slipped his arm around her waist. "I'll see you tomorrow."

When they'd gone, Jessica turned back to find Devon still grinning at her. "What?"

"I don't know what you mean."

"You're looking at me oddly," Jessica replied. She liked the way he was looking at her but refused to allow herself to show it. Devon's weekly trips into Cottonwood Falls had convinced her that he had a girlfriend in town. She tried not to think about it, but it bothered her nevertheless.

Devon chuckled and got up from his chair. "How about a stroll to the ridge? The moon is full, and the air warm."

"I can't," Jessica replied nervously. She was desperately afraid of being alone for too long with Devon. Just thinking about the ride into town for church caused her stomach to do flips.

"Why not?"

"Well, I should stay close to the house in case Ryan needs me."

"Guess that makes sense. So how about just coming out on the porch with me? The upstairs windows are open. You'll be able to hear him if he cries."

Jessica realized that she'd either have to be rude and refuse or go along with the plan. "All right. Maybe for a little bit. Then I need to go to bed."

He nodded and allowed her to lead the way to the front door. Neither one said another word until they were out on the porch. Devon and Buck had made some wonderful chairs and a couple benches, and it was to one of the latter that Devon motioned Jessica to follow him.

Nervously licking her lips, Jessica joined Devon on the bench. She put herself at the far edge of the seat, hoping Devon would take the hint and sit at the opposite end. He didn't, however, choosing instead to position himself right in the middle of the bench.

"It's a fine night," he said. Suddenly he jumped up. "Say, wait here. I have a surprise."

Jessica couldn't imagine what he had in mind, but she obediently nodded and watched as he bounded down the porch steps and disappeared around the side of the house. When he returned, he was carrying a guitar.

"I didn't know you played," she said in complete surprise.

"I just got started last winter. I've been taking lessons in town from Old Mr. Wiedermeier. That man can pick up anything and make music with it."

Jessica smiled as she wondered if it was this, and not a woman, that had been taking Devon to town on Friday evenings. It made her heart a little lighter, and she suddenly found herself quite eager to hear Devon play.

He began tuning the strings, strumming one and then another, then comparing the two to each other. When he finally had all six in agreeable harmony, he began strumming out a melody that Jessica instantly recognized.

"Why that sounds like 'O Worship the King.' "

Devon laughed. "That's good. It's supposed to." He played a few more bars.

"Do you sing as well?"

"I don't know about how *well* I do it, but I do sing." He didn't wait for her to ask but instead began to harmonize with the guitar. Devon's rich baritone rang out against the stillness of the night and stirred Jessica's heart. How lovely to sit on the porch in the warmth of late summer and listen to Devon sing. She could easily picture herself doing this for many years to come. Seeing it in her mind, she imagined herself married to Devon with four or five children gathered round them. It made a pleasant image to carry in her heart.

"I don't think I've ever seen such a look of contentment on your face, Miss Jessica," Devon drawled.

Jessica realized she'd just been caught daydreaming. "I was just thinking about something."

Devon put the guitar aside and moved closer to Jessica. "I've been doing some thinking too. There's something I want to say to you."

Just then, the sound of Ryan crying reached Jessica's ears. "Oh, that's Ryan. I guess I'd better go."

Devon looked at her with such an expression of frustration and disappointment that Jessica very nearly sat back down. But her own nervousness held her fast. "I'll see you in the morning," she paused as if trying to decide whether or not she should say the rest, "and we can talk on the way to church."

With that she hurried upstairs, anxious and curious about what Devon might have had to tell her. Perhaps she was wrong about his trips into town. Maybe there was more than just the guitar lesson. Maybe her earlier feelings of Devon meeting up with a lady friend were more on target than she wanted to imagine.

By the time she'd reached Ryan, he'd fallen back to sleep and lay contentedly sucking his thumb. Jessica tidied his covers, gently touched his cheek with her fingers, and went back to her own room.

"There's something I want to say to you," Devon had said. The words were still ringing in her ears.

What could he possibly need to say?

Devon knew nothing but frustration that Sunday morning. He'd barely slept a wink the night before, and now the horses were uncooperative as he tried to ready the buckboard wagon. He knew it wouldn't be nearly as comfortable for Jessica and Ryan, but there were supplies he'd been unable to bring home on Friday night, and he'd need this opportunity to get them safely home before he headed to Kansas City with the sale cattle.

He kept rethinking what he'd nearly said to Jessica the night before. It should have been simple. Jessica was a widow going on two years, and by her own declaration she'd never loved her husband. It seemed more than enough time to put the past behind her and deal with Devon's interests.

"Say, after church you might want to ask Joe Riley if he still wants to buy that acreage on the western boundaries of Windridge," Buck said as he came into the barn. He saw the difficulty Devon was having and immediately went to work to see the task completed.

"I'll do that," Devon said absentmindedly. "I'll ask Jessica if she's still of a mind to sell. You know how angry she gets when we try to second-guess her."

"Still, she's a good-hearted woman," Buck replied.

"Yeah, I know that well enough," Devon muttered.

"You ain't gonna let that little gal get away from you, are you? There's plenty of fellows down at that church who'd give their right arms to be able to spend time with Jessie the way you do."

"For all the good it does."

"You feeling sorry for yourself, Son?" Buck questioned. "That doesn't hardly seem like you."

"Not sure I even know what's like me anymore," Devon admitted. He took hold of the horses' harnesses and led the two matched geldings from the barn. "I wouldn't have been of a mind to turn this place into a dude ranch ten months ago, but look at me now."

"You just see the wisdom in it," Buck replied. "Besides, ranching and courting are two different things. I know you have feelings for Jessie. Why not just tell her and let the chips fall where they will?"

"I tried to say something last night, but—"

"Here we are," Jessica announced, coming down the steps with Kate and Ryan directly behind her. Jessica stashed a small bag of necessities behind the wagon seat, then beamed Devon a smile that nearly broke his heart. How could a woman look so pretty and not even realize what she did to a fellow? She had a face like an angel. Long dark lashes, delicately arched brows. A straight little nose that turned up ever so slightly at the end, and lips so full and red that Devon was hard-pressed not to steal a kiss.

"We're all ready. Say, why are we taking the buckboard?" Jessica asked, letting Buck help her up onto the seat. She reached down and lifted Ryan from Kate's arms.

"Devon's picking up some supplies that came in on Friday. He didn't have the wagon with him when he went into town Friday night, so he secured them at the train station until he could pick them up today."

"No doubt someone will frown on his toting home necessities on the Lord's Day," Kate murmured. "But if we don't get some flour and sugar soon, not to mention coffee, we'll have a mutiny on our hands."

"No one will think anything about it," Devon said, climbing up to sit beside Jessica. The buckboard seat was very narrow and pushed the two people very close together. Devon could smell her perfume. "If they have a problem with it, they can answer to me." With that he smacked the reins against the backs of the geldings.

The trip into town passed by before Devon and Jessica could get past discussing how they were going to renovate the house for their guests. Jessica had all manner of thoughts on the matter, and it seemed she and Kate had made some definite decisions. Each room would have a color theme with quilts and curtains to match. And guests would share breakfast together, which meant the extra extensions for the dining-room table would have to be located and additional chairs ordered to match the existing ones.

Church hardly presented itself as a place to explain his feelings. Devon went through the motions of worship and even managed to focus his attention on the sermon, but over and over he thought of how he might share his feelings with Jessica. He was due to leave with the cattle in little more than two weeks, yet so much needed his attention, and very little time would be afforded him for quiet, romantic talks.

After church, Devon loaded up the ranch supplies while Jessica fed Ryan. Fussy and cantankerous from a day of being cooped up, Ryan seemed to do his level best to make life difficult for his mother. Jessica said he was teething, and she had it on Kate's authority that chewing a leather strap was the best thing to ease the pain. She'd brought one along just for this purpose and was trying to interest Ryan in chewing on it. Ryan just slapped at it and cried. Devon shook his head and finished securing two rolls of bailing wire before jumping up to take the reins.

"I imagine he'll be a whole lot happier when we get home," Devon suggested. He could see exasperation in Jessica's expression.

"I suppose you're right."

"You want me to hold him awhile?" he asked, seeing Ryan push and squirm while crying at the top of his lungs.

To his surprise, Jessica shrugged, then handed the boy over. Ryan instantly calmed and took notice of Devon's mustache. "Now, Partner, we're going to have to have an understanding here. I'm driving this here wagon, and you're going to have to help me." He showed Ryan the leather reins, and immediately the boy put them in his mouth.

"No!" Jessica began, then shook her head and relaxed. "Oh, might as well let him. I found him eating dirt yesterday. Guess a little sweat and leather won't hurt."

Devon laughed. "It could be a whole lot worse." He called to the horses and started them for home while Ryan played with the extra bit of reins.

Jessica watched them both for several moments, and Devon could sense she felt troubled by the situation. They rode in silence for several miles while Devon battled within himself. The selfish side of him wanted to just get his feelings out in the open—to express how he felt about Jessica and the boy he held on his lap. But the more humanitarian side of him figured it was only right to find out what was troubling Jessica.

"You're mighty quiet. You going to tell me what it's all about?" Devon finally worked up the nerve to ask.

Jessica looked at him blankly for a moment. Then he noticed there were tears in her eyes. She shook her head, sniffled, and looked away.

Ryan's head began to nod, and Devon figured it the perfect excuse to draw her focus back to him. "I think someone's about to fall asleep. You want to take him back?"

Jessica smoothed the lines of her emerald green suit and reached out for her son. Ryan went to her without protest, and Devon thought Jessica looked almost relieved. She cradled the boy in her arms, and Ryan willingly let her rock him back and forth. Within another mile or two, he'd fallen asleep without so much as a whimper.

Devon tried to figure out what Jessica's display of emotions had been about. He'd never been around women for very long. Even his mother and sister, who now lived a world away in Tyler, Texas, always kept to themselves when emotional outbursts were at hand. His mother had always said such things were not to be shared with their menfolk, but Devon disagreed. He worried about those times when his mother went off to cry alone. His father always seemed to be away working one ranch or another, always someone else's hired man. He seldom knew about his wife's tears or needs, and Devon determined it would be different with him—mostly because he knew how painful it was for his mother to bear such matters alone.

He could remember the time when his younger brother, Danny, had still been alive. Pa had gone off to work on the Double J Ranch, hoping to earn extra money before the winter set in. Danny had contracted whooping cough and died within a week of their father's departure. His mother had borne the matter with utmost grace and confidence. Devon tried to be the man of the house for her, supporting her at the funeral, seeing to her needs afterwards. But she would have no part of sharing her pain with him, and it hurt Devon deeply to be left out. When their father had returned, his mother had simply said, "We are only four now." Nothing more was mentioned or discussed. At least not in front of Devon.

Unable to take the situation without pushing to understand, Devon looked over at Jessica. He watched her for a moment before saying, "Please tell me what's bothering you."

Jessica continued to stare straight ahead. Her expression suggested that she was strongly considering his request. Finally she answered. "It isn't worth troubling you with."

"How about letting me be the judge of that?"

They continued for nearly another ten minutes before Jessica finally answered. "I can't hope that you would understand. It has to do with being a mother."

"I suppose I can't understand what it is to be a mother," Devon agreed, "but I do understand when someone is hurting, and you are obviously in pain."

Jessica nestled Ryan closer to her in a protective manner, and instantly Devon realized that her mood had to do with her insecurities over the boy. He'd figured she'd outgrown her concerns, but apparently she still carried the weight of her fears with her.

"Are you still afraid of losing his affection?" Devon finally asked.

Jessica stiffened for a moment, then her shoulders slumped forward as if she'd just met her defeat. "You can't understand."

"I only held him to help calm him down. You looked so tired, and Ryan was obviously tired; I just figured it might help."

"It did help," she said, wiping at tears with her free hand. "It's just that he's all I have, Devon. If I can't be a good mother to him—if I can't make it work between us—then I might as well give up."

"Give up what? Motherhood? You can't take them back once they're here."

"But there are those who would take them from you," Jessica declared.

Devon felt confused. Who did she fear would take Ryan from her? "You don't mean to suggest that someone might come after Ryan, do you? Someone from back East? His grandparents? Is that it?"

Jessica shook her head. "Newman's family is all dead. They died when he was a teenager. His only brother died some years after that. He'd never married, and therefore Newman was the end of the line."

"Then who?"

Jessica still refused to look Devon in the face. "There was a friend in New

York, Essie. She always offered to help me with Ryan. She always insisted on having us spend our days with her, and she never wanted me to lift a finger to care for Ryan. She made me uneasy, but I felt sorry for her. She was barren, you see."

Devon did indeed begin to get a clear picture of what must have taken place. "Go on," he urged.

Jessica ran her hand across Ryan's head. "One day she came to me with the idea of letting her and her husband adopt Ryan. She said it was impossible for me to give Ryan all he needed. She said she would make a better mother."

"She obviously didn't know you very well," Devon muttered.

Jessica turned and gave him a look of frantic gratitude. "She thought she did. I'm afraid I was rather harsh with her and sent her home with her suggestion completely refused. Two days later, her mother showed up on my doorstep. The woman was positively intimidating. She took one look at my home and condemned it. She said it would be a wonder if Ryan weren't dead by winter."

Devon clamped his teeth together in anger. He wanted to say something to counter the horrible insensitivity of the woman's actions, but he knew there was nothing he could do.

"She finally left, but then Essie showed up the next day and the next day and the day after that. Ryan adored her because she spoiled and pampered him. I began to fear that he loved her more than me, and when I sent her from my home for the last time, I had to forcibly remove Ryan from her arms. He cried and cried, and Essie cried and declared it a sign that she should be his true mother. I told her to never come back, and I slammed the door on her. Three days later, the letter came announcing Father's death. It seemed like an answer from God, and yet I would have never wished my father dead. I'd just about decided to beg him to let me return to Windridge anyway."

"But, Jess, she can't hurt you," Devon said, hoping his words would comfort her. "She's far enough away that she can't just drop in on you and make you miserable again. And Kate would never tolerate anyone storming into Windridge and threatening yours and Ryan's happiness. This Essie can't hurt you anymore."

Jessica said nothing for several moments. Then she shifted Ryan in her arms and looked at Devon with an expression of intense pain. "But you can."

Devon felt the wind go out from him. "What?" he barely managed to ask.

"Ryan adores you. He seeks you out, and he's drawn to you like flies to honey. I can't ignore that. I can't just look away and say it doesn't exist. Neither can I find it in myself to deny him."

"Why would you want to? You have nothing to fear from me. I'm completely devoted to the little guy. I wouldn't do anything to hurt him or you."

"Maybe not willingly," Jessica replied. She looked away, and Devon watched as she fixed her sight on the horizon where the house on Windridge was now coming into view.

Devon wanted to reassure her and thought for a moment about declaring his feelings for her, but it didn't seem right. Somehow he feared she would just presume he'd made it all up to comfort her. Feeling at a loss as to what he could say, Devon said nothing at all. He looked heavenward for a moment, whispered a prayer for guidance, then fixed his sight on the road ahead. Somehow, someway, God would show him what he was to do about Jessica and Ryan.

Chapter 7

Driving cattle had always been a loathsome chore to Devon. He didn't like the time spent with cantankerous animals on the dusty trail, and he certainly didn't care for being away from Windridge. Especially now. Leaving Jessica wouldn't be easy, and Devon tried to avoid thinking of how he would handle their good-bye.

The days passed too quickly to suit him, and before he knew it, Devon was giving instructions to the other four ranch hands, explaining how they would drive the cattle to Cottonwood Falls and from there board the train for Kansas City.

"I'll only need you as far as Cottonwood. You all get two weeks to settle any other business you have." He pointed to two of the cowhands. "Sam and Joe can take off after we get the livestock settled in the freight cars. Neil, you and Bob need to wait until the other two get back. Buck will handle the ranch until I return, which hopefully won't be any longer than two, maybe three weeks."

The men nodded, asked their questions, and waited for Devon to dismiss them to prepare for the drive. "We'll head out in fifteen minutes or so. Be ready."

The men moved off to collect their horses just as Buck ambled up. "Heard tell the Johnsons down Wichita way are working with a new breed," Buck said as Devon finished packing his bags. "You could go down that way before coming back here. You know, check it out and see if it would work for us."

"I suppose I could. But do you think that's the direction we want to go?" Devon questioned, not liking the idea of delaying his return to Windridge.

Buck shrugged. "It's just an idea. Heard they're getting an extra twenty to fifty pounds on the hoof. You can suit yourself, though."

"I'll give it some consideration. Maybe I'll find the same thing in Kansas City. Most folks in these parts are going to end up at the livestock yards there anyway. It just might work out I can get the information there."

Buck nodded. "That sounds reasonable."

Kate appeared just then, Ryan toddling behind her. "I brought you some sandwiches to take with you. I know you don't have that long of a drive, but those animals can be mighty slow when they take it in their minds to be that way."

"Thanks, Katie," Devon said, taking the basket she'd packed. "If we don't need them, I'll take some of them to Kansas City."

"Eat my sandwiches instead of Mr. Harvey's fine railroad food?" Kate laughed. "I can't imagine anyone making that trade."

"Then you just don't realize what a good cook you are," Devon replied. About that time, Ryan wrapped his arms around Devon's leg and started chattering.

"Horsy! Horsy!"

Devon laughed. He often gave the boy a ride on his knee, and it was clear Ryan wasn't about to let him leave until he received his daily fun.

"Okay," he said, reaching down to lift Ryan into the air. He swept the boy high, listening to his giggles, then circled him down low. Finally he stepped over to a bale of hay and sat down to put Ryan on his knee. "Now tighten those legs," Devon instructed, squeezing Ryan's legs around his own. "A good rider knows how to use his legs."

"You keep an eye on him for a minute," Buck called out. "I'm going to walk a spell with Katie and tell her good-bye properly."

"Will do," Devon called out, "but you won't be gone for more than a few hours."

Buck laughed. "To Kate, that's an eternity."

Devon, too, chuckled and returned his attention to Ryan. "You know, you'll be a right fine rider one day. I'll take you out on the trails and teach you all there is to know about raising cattle. You'll know more than your ma or anyone else in these parts, 'cause I'm going to show you all the tricks."

Ryan giggled and squealed with delight as Devon bounced him up and down on his leg. The boy had easily taken a huge chunk of Devon's heart, while the other portion belonged to his mother. The only real problem was finding a way to tell her.

Devon had fully planned to discuss his feelings for Jessica before he left for Kansas City. But the opportunity never presented itself. Jessica had been overly busy under Kate's instruction, and when she wasn't working at quilting or sewing or any number of other things Kate deemed necessary to her ranch training, Jessica was busy with Ryan. She almost always retired early, not even giving Devon a chance to suggest a stroll on the ridge or a song or two on the porch. The only time she went into town was on Sunday, and that was usually with Buck and Kate at her side. Devon had no desire to make his confession of feelings a public issue. Even if Buck and Kate already presumed to know those feelings, Devon wanted to get Jessica's reaction first.

"Well, Ryan, a fellow just never knows where he stands," Devon muttered.

Ryan seemed to understand and chattered off several strange words, along with his repertoire of completely understandable speech. "More horsy! Mama horsy."

Devon laughed. "I doubt Mama would appreciate the idea, Son." The word *son* stuck in his throat. He wished he could call Ryan son. He thought of Jessica's worries that he would steal Ryan's affections, but in truth, Devon worried that Jessica would take Ryan from his life. He already cared too much about both of them, and the thought of losing either one was more than he wanted to contend with.

Lifting Ryan in his arms, Devon rubbed his fuzzy head. "You've got to grow some more hair, Boy. You don't want to go through life bald." Ryan reached out and pulled at Devon's thick mustache. "Ah, a mustache man. Well, grow it there if you prefer," Devon teased, "but the head would be better for now."

He gently disentangled his mustache from Ryan's pudgy fingers, then gave the boy a couple of gentle tosses into the air. Ryan squealed once again, and the expression on his chubby face was enough to satisfy Devon.

"You take good care of your mama while I'm gone," Devon told him and hugged him close.

"Kate said you two were in here," called Jessica.

Devon looked up, almost embarrassed to have been caught speaking of her. He wondered how long she'd been watching. She looked to have been there for some time, given her casual stance by the open door.

"We were just having a talk," Devon said, putting Ryan down.

"Horsy, Mama," Ryan said, toddling off to Jessica's awaiting arms.

She lifted Ryan and held him close and all the while watched Devon. "Are you about ready to go?"

"Yup," he said casually, taking down an extra coil of rope from the wall. "Everything's set. We have to give ourselves enough time to make the train."

Jessica nodded. "Well, I hope you won't have any trouble finding everything we need."

"I shouldn't," Devon replied, wishing they could get beyond the chitchat.

Ryan began squirming and calling for Devon. The boy had not yet mastered Devon's name, so when he called out, it sounded very much like "Da da."

"Unt Da da," Ryan fussed, straining at Jessica's hold. She put the boy down, not even attempting to fight Ryan's choice.

The boy hurried back to Devon, inspected the rope for a moment, then raised his arms up and bobbed up and down as if to encourage Devon to lift him.

"It's easy to see how much he loves you," Jessica said, her voice low and filled with emotion.

"I love him too," Devon said, wondering how she would react to this. "He's a great little guy. It would be impossible *not* to love him."

Jessica nodded. "I just hope you take that love seriously."

"What do you mean?" Devon asked, wishing he could turn the conversation to thoughts of his feelings for Ryan's mother.

Jessica stepped closer and studied Devon before answering. "I just ask one thing of you, Devon Carter. Don't let Ryan get close to you unless you plan to be around to be his friend for a good long time. It'll be too hard for him otherwise."

At first, Devon wanted to reply with something flippant and teasing, but he could see in Jessica's eyes that she was dead serious. His heart softened, and he gave her a weak smile.

"I plan to be around for a very long time. I wouldn't dream of leaving Ryan without making sure he understood my reason for leaving. And since he'll be too small to understand much along those lines and will be for a good many years, I guess you'll both just be stuck with me."

"Just so you understand."

He rubbed the boy's head, kissed him lightly, and put him back on the ground. "I intend to always be here for Ryan," Devon stated firmly. He looked deep into Jessica's dark eyes—knowing the longing reflected there. He wanted more than anything to add that he would also be there for Jessica, but he could already hear Buck calling everyone to mount up.

"Guess you'd better go," Jessica whispered.

Devon took a step toward her, then stopped. There wasn't enough time to say what he wanted—needed—to say. "I suppose so," he finally murmured.

"You've got the list?" she questioned.

He nodded, almost afraid to say anything more.

"And you will be careful?"

Her voice was edged with concern, and Devon longed to put her worried mind at ease. He remembered that moment months ago when he'd held her while she cried. "It's a piece of cake," he replied. "The hard part is getting the critters to Cottonwood. After that, there's nothing to it but haggling the money." He grinned, hoping to put her at ease.

"I've heard about folks killed in stampedes," she countered. "And Kate says we're coming up to time for a tornado or two."

"We'll be careful," he promised, realizing that whether she spoke it in words or not, she cared about his well-being.

"You coming?" Buck asked as he poked his head into the doorway.

Devon caught his mischievous expression and sighed. "I'm coming."

Jessica had the distinct impression that had Buck not interfered, Devon might have said something very important. She sensed his desire to tell her something, but no matter how long she stood there in silence, he seemed unable to spit out the words. Of course she did no better. She had hoped to say that her concerns for Ryan were based on concerns she also felt for herself. She knew she was coming to depend too much on Devon. She also knew that she'd lost her heart to him, and that for the first and only time in her life, she was in love.

With this thought still weighing heavily on her heart, Jessica followed Devon from the barn, calling to Ryan as she moved back to the house. She picked the boy up and told him to wave good-bye to Devon.

"Unta go," Ryan began to whine. "Me go too."

"No, Ryan," Jessica said. "You have to stay here. We can't go this time."

Ryan continued to fuss, and Katie tried to still him with a cookie that she kept in her apron pocket for just such occasions. Ryan contented himself with the treat, while Jessica found no such consolation.

I should have told him how I felt, she thought. But her feelings were so foreign and new to her that she wasn't sure what she would have said to him.

"I should be back by the end of November," Devon called to them, bringing his horse to a halt just beyond the porch. "Don't worry though if I'm later than that. It may take some time to secure the freighters and collect all the things you ladies have deemed necessary to running a good resort."

"Do you have the money?" Jessica asked.

"I'll pick up most of it in Cottonwood Falls. I have the deed papers for Joe Riley's piece of land, and that will allow me to take his money for the land and add to what we have in the bank." He glanced over his shoulder and saw that Buck was already positioning the ranch hands in preparation for moving the cattle from the corrals. "I'd best get over there and do my job." He turned the horse and started to leave.

"Devon!" Jessica called out. She knew her voice sounded desperate, but she couldn't help it.

He stopped, looked at her quite seriously, then grinned. "What?"

Jessica swallowed hard and tried to think of something neutral to say. "I'll be praying for you," she finally managed.

Devon's grin broadened. "Thanks. With that bunch," he said, motioning over his shoulder, "I'll need it." He took off before either Kate or Jessica could say another word.

"Wonder whether he means the men or the steers?" Kate teased.

"Probably both."

Jessica brushed cookie crumbs from Ryan's face and headed to the front door when Kate called out, "Looks like we have company."

Turning, Jessica could see the faint image of a black carriage making its way up the Windridge road. "Who could that be?"

Kate shrugged. "I don't know. I'll go put some tea on and set out some more cookies. It's been so long since anyone's come calling at Windridge, I might not even be able to find a serving plate."

Jessica laughed. "Don't you go running off when whoever it is finally arrives. I don't want to have to entertain on my own."

"Maybe we could set up things in the quilting room," Kate suggested and Jessica nodded.

"Sounds perfect. That way, we'll be busy, and if the conversation lags, we can talk about the quilts."

Kate nodded. "Why don't you put Ryan down for a nap in the back room? Then he'll be close at hand and yet out of harm's way."

Jessica nodded and followed Kate into the house, after sending one final glance south where Devon and the rest of the ranch hands were organizing the cattle on the trail. Giving Ryan a drink of milk while Kate fixed the tea, Jessica made her way into one of the two rooms that were being converted for Buck and Kate's use. It had been Kate's idea to put another bed in for Ryan. It seemed senseless to run up and down the stairs all day, and Jessica quickly saw the sense in it. Kate had even suggested that maybe Jessica and Ryan would one day prefer the privacy of the cottage once the guests overtook the house. Jessica had quickly pointed out that Devon now occupied the place in question, but Kate had just shrugged and told her that God had a way of working those things out.

"But the way I'd like to see it worked out," Jessica told Ryan, "isn't likely to happen. Devon said God already has a wife picked out for him."

Ryan yawned and pulled at his ear. This was his routine signal that he was tired. Gently, she tucked him into bed and brushed his cheek with her fingertip. Ryan quickly realized she intended to leave him for a nap and decided he wanted no part of it. Jessica wasn't surprised at the display as he began kicking at the covers. Soon he was sitting up and fussing for her to take him.

"Ryan," she said in a stern voice. "You lie back down and go to sleep. When you get up, we'll go up to the ridge and see what we can see."

Ryan made no move to obey, so Jessica gently eased him back down and pulled the covers around him once again. "Now go to sleep and be a good boy."

"Goo boy," Ryan muttered in between his fussing.

"That's right," Jessica smiled. "You are a good boy, and Mama loves you."

She left him there to fuss and upon returning to the kitchen found that Kate had things well under control. "Is there anything you want me to do?" she questioned.

"No. Just relax."

Jessica looked out the side kitchen window, hoping to catch a glimpse of the cattle drive. She could just catch sight of the last two outriders, but Devon was nowhere in sight. She strained her eyes for some sign of his brown Stetson, but the hills hid him from view.

"You should have told him how you feel about him," Kate admonished. Jessica felt her face grow hot as she looked back to where Kate studied her. "It's pretty apparent."

"I didn't realize," Jessica admitted. "You don't suppose he knows, do you?" She realized her voice sounded high pitched, almost frightened.

"No, I don't suppose he does," Kate replied, turning back to putting cookies on the tray. "I think he's too wrapped up in his own feelings."

Jessica nodded. "I think you're probably right."

"Why don't you go check on our visitor? Ought to be up to the house by now."

Jessica did as Kate suggested, her heart heavy with thoughts of Devon being in love with another woman. When she opened the front door, she was surprised to find a smartly dressed woman making her way up the front steps of the porch.

The woman, looking to be in her late forties, carried herself with a regal air. Her golden blond hair, although liberally sprinkled with gray, was carefully styled and pinned tightly beneath a beautiful bonnet of lavender silk.

"Good morning," Jessica said, trying her best to sound welcoming.

"Good morning to you," the woman replied. "I'm Gertrude Jenkins, and you must be Jessica Gussop."

"Albright. Jessica Albright. Gussop was my maiden name."

"Of course. I remember Gus having quite a spell when you married."

Jessica felt her defenses rise to the occasion. "We don't get many visitors here, Mrs. Jenkins. Won't you come in?"

The woman smiled. "I used to come here quite often, you know, before Gus died. After he died, I went on an extended European trip. Couldn't bear to stick around here with him gone, don't you know?"

Jessica couldn't figure the woman out. She'd never heard of Gertrude Jenkins, much less in any capacity that endeared her to her father. She ushered the woman into the house and, rather than stopping at the front parlor, led her down the hall to the room she and Kate used for quilting. Kate already sat sewing behind the quilting frame, while Jessica's work lay on the seat of the chair nearest to Kate. It looked for all intents and purposes that Jessica had only moments before left the work in order to answer the door.

"Well, if it isn't Gerty Jenkins," Kate said in greeting. "I heard tell you were back in the area." Jessica watched the exchange between the two women, feeling the immediate tension when Gertrude spotted Kate.

"Hello, Kate," came the crisp reply. She glanced around the room and sniffed. "Well, if this isn't quaint."

"We've been working on quilts. We were just going to have some tea and cookies," Jessica offered rather formally. "I do hope you can stay and partake with us?"

Gertrude glanced to the small table where the refreshments awaited their attention. "I'm certain I can. Especially after coming all this way."

"Gerty lives on the ranch directly south," Kate told Jessica. "It's her drive you pass by on the way to church."

Jessica smiled and nodded. "I remember Devon mentioning the drive leading to another ranch."

"Devon? Devon Carter?" Gertrude questioned. "Don't tell me he's still here at Windridge."

"Of course he is," Kate replied before Jessica could answer. "He was like a son to Gus, and Jessica has come to rely on him as well."

Gertrude eyed Jessica rather haughtily as she pulled white kid gloves from her hands. "I suppose it is difficult when you know nothing of ranching."

Jessica could immediately see that Gertrude had no intention of being a friend. But her reasons for visiting in the first place were still a mystery.

Ignoring the comment, Jessica motioned to a high-backed chair. "Won't you sit down? I'll pour the tea."

"Cream and sugar, please," Gertrude stated as she took her seat.

Jessica nodded and went to the task. "Would you care for some of Kate's sugar cookies? They're quite delicious."

"If you have no cakes, I suppose they'll have to do," the woman replied.

Jessica served her and then brought a cup of plain tea to Kate. She tried to question Kate with her expression, but Kate only smiled.

"I suppose I should have visited sooner," Gertrude continued before anyone else could take up the conversation, "but I've only returned last week. A year abroad has done me a world of good."

"This last year has done us a world of good as well," Kate replied, continuing with her stitches.

Jessica thought the response rather trite given Kate's usual friendliness, but she said nothing. Instead, she tried to draw out the reason for Gertrude's visit. "I'm pleased you have found the time to call upon us," Jessica began. "I don't believe we've had a single visitor in the past year."

"Well, it really is no wonder. The place is in an awful state of disrepair."

"Oh," Jessica said, looking first to Kate, then back to Gertrude, "you must not have had the opportunity to look around you. We've been making steady progress throughout the year. We are, in fact, moving ahead with plans to turn

Windridge into something rather special."

"Well, it once was quite special," Gertrude said, flicking crumbs from her skirt onto the floor. "Do tell, what plans have you for the place?"

Jessica licked her lips and took the tiniest sip of tea to steady her nerves. "We're opening Windridge to the public. We are taking on guests next summer and becoming a working vacation ranch. A quiet respite from the city, if you will."

Gertrude appeared stunned. "Are you suggesting this place will become a spa—a resort? Here in Kansas?"

"Not only suggesting it, Gerty," Kate threw in, "but the plans are already in the works. Devon is bringing back the final touches in new furnishings and supplies."

"Was that him heading out with that scrawny herd?"

"Him and Buck and the others," Kate replied. "Only Devon is heading on to Kansas City. He figured we'd best keep the others here to keep an eye on things."

"Yes, but who will keep an eye on Devon Carter?"

Jessica perked up at this. "Whatever do you mean?"

"I simply mean, my dear," Gertrude began, "the man should not be trusted."

"Bah," Kate said in disgust. "Gus trusted him."

"Yes, and see where it got him."

"I don't think I understand," Jessica interjected, feeling the anger between the two women.

"Gerty is just showing her age." All eyes turned to Kate at this. "Gerty's daughter was once engaged to Devon, but she broke it off."

"She had to. There was simply no other choice under the circumstances," Gertrude said stiffly.

Jessica felt the tension mount. She silently wished Kate would stir the woman into another subject of conversation, but Gertrude remained fixed on her mark.

"Devon was seen with another woman in Cottonwood Falls. Of course, my poor Jane was devastated. They were barely two weeks away from their own wedding. It grieved her so much she stayed out the entire night and came home weeping in the wee hours of the morning."

Kate rolled her eyes, and Jessica was hard-pressed not to smile. Apparently Kate thought the story to be less than accurate, but Gertrude didn't seem to notice. "I was heartsick, and had her father still been alive, he would no doubt have gone to take Devon Carter to task for his behavior.

"Poor Jane cried until she was exhausted, then told me she had found Devon in the arms of another woman." Gertrude leaned closer. "He was kissing her, don't you know? Of course, Jane felt terribly misused. She was never herself after that and ran off with the first man who asked for her hand after Devon's terrible behavior."

"That wasn't exactly the story we heard," Kate muttered under her breath.

Gertrude glared at her but said nothing to support the idea that her version was anything but the honest facts of the matter.

"I simply wouldn't trust him out of sight, my dear. Gus and I discussed it on many an occasion, and while Gus felt the need to give the young man a chance, I always felt there was something rather shiftless about him."

"You let Jane get engaged to him," Kate threw out.

"Yes," Gertrude replied in a clipped tone, "but then every mother makes mistakes. I wanted Jane's happiness, and she was certain Devon Carter could give her everything she desired."

Jessica felt shaken and uncertain of herself. She wondered if the other woman Jane had found Devon with was the same one who now held his heart. "More tea?" she asked weakly.

"No, thank you," Gertrude replied, setting the cup and saucer aside. "I really should be going. I can see that you both have your hands full, and there's much that needs my attention at home. I do recall someone mentioning, however, that you have a child, Mrs. Albright."

"That's right. My Ryan is almost two. He's sleeping right now, or I'd give you a proper introduction. Perhaps Sunday at church?"

"Yes, perhaps so," Gertrude replied, getting to her feet. "I do suggest you heed my advice. Devon Carter is not all he appears to be, and if you have given him a large sum of money, it might well be the last time you see him or your funds." She glanced at Kate. "Good day, Kate. Mrs. Albright."

Jessica walked out with the haughty woman and paused on the porch. "Thank you for coming, Mrs. Jenkins."

"I felt I owed it to Gus. You know we were very close to an understanding. Had he lived, I'm certain I would be mistress of Windridge, and our ranches would join together to make a mighty empire."

Jessica did her best to show no signs of surprise at this announcement. She merely nodded and bid the woman good day.

Gertrude Jenkins climbed into her carriage and pulled on her gloves. "I suppose we will be seeing each other again soon. Don't forget what I said about Mr. Carter. It's not too late to send someone after him and change the course of events to come."

With that, she turned the horses and headed the buggy down the lane. Jessica watched for several moments, uncertain what to think or feel about the woman and her visit. Not only had Mrs. Jenkins discredited Devon, but she'd implied an intimacy with Jessica's father. An intimacy that suggested marriage. Jessica found it impossible to believe and thought to question

Kate about it, but it was clear the two women had nothing but disdain for each other.

With a sigh, Jessica decided it wasn't worth the bother. She trusted Devon to do what he said he would do. Closing the door behind her, Jessica decided to close out negative thoughts of her visitor. She had no reason to worry and refused to borrow the trouble that Gertrude Jenkins so expertly offered.

Chapter 8

The first week without Devon at Windridge left Jessica feeling listless and bored. Kate kept her occupied with canning and butchering, but at night Jessica had nothing to keep her from thinking about Devon. Not only that, but Ryan cried and called for him, leaving Jessica little doubt that her fears about Ryan's attachment to the cowboy were well founded.

Week two spent itself out with the return of Sam and Joe and the departure of Neil and Bob. Jessica worked with Kate to make lye soap. Kate told her there was no sense in paying out good money for store-bought soap when they had the hog fat and other ingredients on hand. Jessica hated the work but realized she was doing something important to keep Windridge up and running. Soap was a necessity of life—especially if you intended to keep guests.

By the third week, Jessica began to watch from her upstairs window for some sign of Devon's return. She mourned the loss along with her son and grew despondent and moody. Kate and Buck watched her with knowing smiles and tried their best to interest her in other things, but it was no use.

An early snow followed by a fierce ice storm caused Jessica to sink even lower. Now it was impossible to spend much time outside, and even horseback riding was curtailed. Making the hour journey into Cottonwood Falls was clearly out of the question, and so their boredom intensified.

Gertrude Jenkins's words kept intruding into Jessica's thoughts. She realized the older woman had planted seeds of doubt, and although Jessica was determined not to let them grow, Devon's delay seemed to bring about their germination. She wondered at Devon's past and why her father thought so highly of him. She wondered if Gertrude had known something about Devon that no one else had knowledge of. Maybe Jane Jenkins had truly seen Devon betraying her.

Jessica hated even allowing such thoughts, but as November passed and December came upon them and still there was no word from Devon Carter, she began to fear the worst.

"Buck says it looks to be nice for a few days," Kate told Jessica one morning. "He doesn't see any reason why we can't go in and participate in the ladies' Christmas quilt party."

"I don't feel like going," Jessica told Kate.

"I know. Which is exactly why we're going."

Jessica looked up from where she was busy washing the breakfast dishes. Kate had that determined look that told Jessica clearly she'd brook no nonsense in the matter.

"What about Ryan?" she asked, casting a glance at her son. At almost two years of age, Ryan was into everything, and it was too cold for him to travel the long distance into Cottonwood Falls.

"Buck is going to take care of him," Kate told her firmly.

"Buck?"

"Absolutely. He handled our own boys well enough. There's no reason at Ryan's age that Buck can't see to his needs. I've already talked with him, and Buck thinks it's a good idea. He knows how worried you are and how hard the waiting has been. Besides, Devon might even come in on the train while we're in town."

It was this last thought that made up Jessica's mind. "All right, let's do it."

Kate grinned. "I thought you'd see things my way."

But three hours later, Jessica wasn't at all sure that they should have come. The location for the sewing party rotated each year through the various families in the church and this time was at Esther Hammel's house. The living room had been cleared of furniture with the exception of wooden-backed chairs, a couple worktables, and several quilting frames.

This was an annual event for the women of Cottonwood Falls, and everyone took their duties quite seriously. One person came to help Esther set up the frames and worktables, while another was in charge of organizing the refreshments. Someone else held the responsibility of making sure the word got out as to the place and time, and yet another lady arranged a group of women to help with the cleanup.

Everyone brought food to the party, and Jessica was rather relieved to find that this was the only requirement she had to meet. Esther said that being as it was her first year to join them, they would go rather easy on her.

The women gathered, taking their places around the various work areas. Jessica and Kate were in the process of piecing some quilt tops together, so they took seats at one of the worktables rather than at the frames. Esther Hammel, a petite woman with fiery blue eyes and a knotted bun of white hair, saw to it that everyone had all they needed in order to work before calling the women to order.

"First, we'll pray. Then we'll gab." Everyone smiled and nodded, while Esther bowed her head. "Father, we thank You for this beautiful day and for the fellowship of friends. Bless our work to better the lives of those around us. May we always bring You glory and honor. Amen."

Jessica murmured an *amen,* but her heart and mind were far from the prayer. She had hoped to see Devon by now. She had imagined how they would meet on the road to Cottonwood, and he would surprise her with a caravan of goods and supplies that would leave no one doubting his honesty and goodness. But they had met no one on the road between Windridge and Cottonwood.

Buck had instructed Sam to drive the massive stagelike carriage for the women. That way, they could enjoy the warmth and comfort of the plush furnishings. Sam had family in town and was only too happy to go home to his mother's cooking while waiting for Kate and Jessica. It was also rumored that his parents' neighbors had a fetching daughter who seemed to have an eye for Sam.

Jessica had instructed Sam to check on Devon at the railroad station, just in case there was some word from him. She'd also told him to pick up the Windridge mail and to check with the telegraph office, just in case some word had come in that they'd not yet received because of the weather. She could hardly sit still through the sewing for want of knowing whether Sam had found out anything about Devon.

"So when I finish with this quilt," Esther was telling the women gathered around her frame, "I intend to donate it to poor Sarah Newcome. Her Elmer died two weeks ago, and they're dirt poor. She's got another baby coming in the spring, and those other three kids of hers don't have proper clothes or bedding. I figured this here quilt could keep all three of them warm."

"My Christmas project was to make and finish five baby blankets for the new mothers in the area," spoke another woman. "As soon as I get this last one quilted, I'll probably start on my spring projects."

The chatter continued until it came to Jessica and Kate's turn to speak. Kate seemed to understand Jessica's confusion and took charge. "Jessica and I have had many projects this year. The latest one, however, is to put together a number of quilts to give to the orphans' home in Topeka."

Jessica said nothing, realizing that Kate had indeed mentioned the project some weeks ago, but since that had occurred around the time of Devon's departure, she'd totally forgotten what they were working toward.

"The quilt tops we're working on today are for the girls." Kate held up her piece to reveal carefully ordered flower baskets. The colors were done up in lavender and pink calicos, with pieces of green and baskets of gold. "I think we'll have them put together by Christmas, but whether or not we'll be able to get them shipped north will depend on the weather."

At this the women made comments on the weather and how the early snow hampered one thing or another. The ice had been the worst, they all agreed, and for several minutes that topic held the conversation. Jessica sighed and worked to put together her pieces in an orderly fashion. There were only a few weeks left before Christmas. Devon should have been home already, and yet here she sat, with no word from him and no idea as to his welfare.

A knock on the front door sent Esther off to find out who might have arrived and caused Jessica to hold her breath in anticipation that the visitor might be Devon. Disappointment engulfed her, however, as the visitor proved to be Gertrude Jenkins.

"Sorry for being so late," Gertrude announced. "I had so much to take care of this morning that I just couldn't seem to get it all accomplished." Her gaze fell upon Jessica and Kate, and her pasted smile faded. "Well, if I'd have known you were planning on coming to the party, we could have shared transportation." Her voice sounded accusatory, as though Kate and Jessica had committed some sort of heinous crime.

"Sorry about that, Gerty," Kate replied without missing a beat. "We figured you'd still be all worn out from your travels abroad."

Jessica nearly smiled at this. She knew how artfully Kate had maneuvered Gertrude into her favorite topic. There'd be little more retribution for their lack of notification once Gertrude focused on her journeys.

"Oh, I suppose I'm still young enough to bounce right back from such things. I do admit at first I was quite exhausted, but a few days of rest and I felt quite myself again." She allowed Esther to take the pie pan she still held and then swept out of her coat and gloves and handed them to Esther just as she returned from the refreshment table.

"We were just commenting on the weather and our projects," Esther told her after seeing to Gertrude's coat and gloves.

Gertrude removed her ornate wool bonnet and set it aside on the fireplace mantel. "We suffered terribly from the ice," she admitted. "But as for my project, well, I simply haven't started one. I thought I'd come here and help someone else with theirs."

"Good," said Esther. "You can help us quilt. I've already told the girls, but my Christmas project is for Sarah Newcome."

Gertrude's chin lifted ever so slightly, but she said nothing as she took her seat at the quilting frame. After several moments of silence, someone finally asked her about her time in Paris, and the conversation picked back up with a detailed soliloquy.

"Of course," Gertrude said, eyeing Jessica suspiciously, "I was quite happy to arrive in Kansas City and make my connection for home." Without pausing for breath she added, "Speaking of Kansas City, has Devon returned with your supplies?"

Jessica felt the wind go out of her. She didn't know what to say that wouldn't provoke a new topic of conversation centered around the possibility that Devon had deserted ranks. Apparently this dilemma showed on her face, because Gertrude nodded and continued.

"I thought not. I hadn't heard from any of my hands that he'd made it back into town. Well, I certainly hope for your sake that he's at least notified you as to what's keeping him."

"No, Gerty, Devon doesn't need to check in with us," Kate responded. "He's family, and we trust him to be making the right choices. He left here with a long list of things to accomplish, and we don't expect him to return until he's able to negotiate everything to the benefit of the ranch."

"Yes," Gertrude said, taking a stitch into the quilt, "but then, he left here with much more than a long list."

The other women in the room fell silent. Jessica felt as though all eyes had turned on her to learn the truth. Swallowing her fear and pride, Jessica looked blankly at Mrs. Jenkins. "Yes, he also left with about one hundred head of prime steers."

Gertrude, not to be toyed with, smiled. "Yes, I suppose he'll be selling those for you in Kansas City."

"That's right."

The tension in the room mounted as Gertrude replied, "I suppose he'll be taking the money in cash."

Kate laughed. "Well, I certainly hope he doesn't take it in trade."

The other women chuckled. They appeared to know how Gertrude could be, as evidenced by the way they remained so obviously cautious at the first sign of her attack on Devon.

"I realize you believe the man can do no wrong," Gertrude said, continuing to focus her attention on Esther's quilt, "but you all know how I feel about him. You know how he hurt my Jane."

Unintelligible murmurings were the only response to this statement. Esther seemed to understand the pain it caused Jessica to hear such things. She smiled sweetly, giving Jessica the first sign of support from someone other than Kate.

"I believe the Carters to have raised a fine son," Esther began. "I knew his mother and father most of my life. When his father died and his mother and sister moved to Texas, I allowed him to stay here until he took up the position at Windridge. He showed only kindness and godliness while living in this house."

Gertrude was clearly offended by this and put down her sewing to stare angrily at Esther. "Are you suggesting that his actions with my daughter were kind and godly? Kissing another woman while only weeks away from marriage to another? No, Devon Carter is a deceiver. I only hope that his long absence doesn't signal yet another fault in him—that of theft."

"Devon is no thief!" Jessica declared, realizing how angry the woman had made her. "He has a job to do, and he will take as long as he needs in order to do it properly."

Gertrude turned a cold smile on Jessica. "Believe what you will, my dear, but actions have always spoken louder than words."

Jessica gripped the edge of her material so tightly that her fingers ached from the tension. Kate patted her gently, and Esther took up the cause. "Gerty, you'd do well to keep from being overly judgmental. You know what the Good Book says about such matters."

Gertrude appeared unfazed. "I know it says not to cast your pearls before swine. That's exactly what this naïve young woman has done if she has given her fortune over to Devon Carter. If she has any expectations other than to find herself devoid of the money given over to that fool, then she's more naïve than I think."

"I suppose the *Christian* thing to do," Esther suggested, "would be to pray for Devon's safe return."

Jessica felt like a lightning bolt had hit her. In all her worry and concern over Devon's whereabouts, she'd sorely neglected the one thing she could do to aid him. Pray. She'd fretted—given herself over to all manner of wild imaginings, talked about his absence—and now fought about it as well. But she'd not really prayed. Furthermore, she'd promised Devon that she would pray for him, and other than a quickly rattled off request for his health and safety, she'd not given the matter another thought.

"That's an excellent idea," Kate said. "Christian women should be more given over to speaking to God about matters rather than judging them falsely."

Gertrude glared at her, but Kate seemed unmoved by the obvious hostility that was directed at her.

From that point on, the day moved rather quickly. Jessica found herself actually enjoying the company of the women, in spite of the rather frustrating beginning to their day.

Later that afternoon, Esther stopped Jessica and Kate as they were preparing to leave. "Don't pay any mind to Gerty," she admonished. "The woman has a bitter heart. First, her daughter disgraces herself the way she did, then Gus refused her advances. She isn't likely to be a good friend to you, Jessica."

Jessica wanted to ask Esther about her father and Gertrude but decided it would make better conversation on the trip home with Kate. "Thank you for all you did," Jessica said instead. "I do appreciate it."

"That's what we older women do best," Esther said, patting Jessica's arm. "We have the privilege of not caring what others think about us because we're old enough to realize that the truth is more important than opinions. You stick with Kate, and she'll help you through this."

"I will," Jessica promised, already feeling much better.

"And one other thing," Esther added. "Your pa put a lot of faith in Devon Carter, and I put a lot of faith in your pa. He wasn't without his mistakes—sending you away after Naomi died was probably his biggest one. But he had a good heart, and he was smart as a whip. He could judge horseflesh and humans like no one I've ever known. He trusted Devon for a reason." She paused and smiled. "The reason—Devon is worthy of trust. Plain and simple."

Jessica smiled and nodded. "Yes, he is."

Devon pulled up his coat collar in order to shield himself from the cold winter wind. It seemed the wind was worse in the city than in the Flinthills. The tall buildings seemed to force the wind down narrow corridors and tunnels of roads and alleyways. He'd be glad to get home and knew he was long overdue. He'd thought to drop a postcard to Jessica and let her know about his delays, but always he figured he'd be leaving in a day or two at the most and would surely beat the thing to Windridge. What happened, however, was that one day turned into two and then into a week. And now Devon was clearly three weeks overdue and had sent no word to Jessica.

But there was a light at the end of the tunnel. Devon had finally managed to negotiate an order for the furniture needed at Windridge, and he'd arranged for the freighters to take the supplies out come spring. Then he'd taken it upon himself to telegraph his mother and ask her to speak on his behalf to Jeb Williams. This resulted in a telegram from Jeb himself stating he was more than happy to manage a deal between the Rocking W and Windridge. Devon felt as if he had the world by the tail. Everything was going better than he could have ever dreamed.

Now, as he made his way back to his hotel room, Devon decided the cold was a small price to pay. Tomorrow he would go to the train station, where he'd already made arrangements for those supplies he intended to take home with him, and board a train for home. How good it would be to see them all again. Especially Jessica and Ryan. He smiled at the thought of their birthday presents sitting back in his hotel room.

Kate had told him that both Jessica and Ryan shared their birthday with New Year's Eve. So along with baubles for Christmas, Devon had picked out toy soldiers for Ryan and a jewelry box for Jessica. He already imagined how he would place his grandmother's wedding ring inside the box and wait for her reaction when she realized that he was asking her to marry him. Turning down the alley where he always made his shortcut, Devon nearly laughed out loud. *She would be surprised to say the least,* he thought.

Halfway to the hotel, Devon felt the hair on the back of his neck prickle. He felt with certainty that someone had stepped into the alley behind him, but he didn't want to turn around and make a scene. He stepped up his pace but had gone no more than ten steps when a big burly man popped out from behind a stack of crates.

"I'll just be relieving you of your wallet," the man said in a surprisingly refined tone.

Devon felt a bit of relief, knowing that his wallet didn't contain much more than a few dollars. He'd secured his remaining money in the hotel safe, recognizing that it was foolish to walk about the city with large quantities of money.

He started to reach into his pocket just as the wind picked up. The gust came so strong that Devon's hat blew back off his head. He turned to catch it before it got away from him, but apparently the man who'd been following him took this as a sign of attack and struck Devon over the head.

Sinking to his knees, Devon fought for consciousness as the men began to beat him mercilessly. He thought of Jessica and how he wouldn't be leaving on the morning train. He thought of how worried she'd be when he didn't come back to Windridge. As his world went black, Devon Carter wondered if this was what it felt like to die.

Chapter 9

Christmas at Windridge came as a solemn affair. Jessica had no spirit for the holiday, and even Ryan moped about as though thoroughly discouraged at Devon having not returned. Kate and Buck had to admit that enough time had passed for Devon to have seen to all the responsibilities he'd gone to Kansas City in order to accomplish. They had very few words of encouragement for Jessica, and the house grew very quiet.

Jessica still tried to pray. She worried that Devon might lay ill somewhere in the city with no one to care for him. She fretted that he'd been unable to sell the cattle or that some other catastrophe had befallen him causing him to be unable to purchase the things they needed.

It was in a complete state of anxiety that Jessica decided to do a little cleaning. She started with Ryan's room, thoroughly scouring every nook and cranny in order to make certain it met with her approval. Then she started on her own room. She went through the closet, reorganizing her clothes and even managing to pull the feather tick and mattress from her bed in order to turn them. That was when she found her father's journal.

Surprised that a man like Gus Gussop had been given over to penning any thought to paper, Jessica felt nervous about opening the book. She felt intrusive, almost as if she were committing some kind of sin. Her father had never shared any part of himself with her—at least not in the way Jessica had needed him to share.

Finding Ryan quite content to play in his room, Jessica took a seat near the fireplace and began to read.

"It's hard enough to allow my thoughts to come to mind," she read aloud, "but to put them to paper seems to give them life of their own."

These were the opening words of her father's journal. Eloquent speech for a rough-and-ready rancher who'd sent his only child away rather than be faced with raising her alone. Then Jessica had the startling realization that the words written here were to her mother.

> *Naomi, you should never have left me to face this alone. You knew I wouldn't be any good at it. You gave me a child, a beautiful daughter, and left me to live without you. How fair was that? I never had anything bad to say about you, with exception to this.*

You were wrong to go. Wrong to die and leave me here.

Jessica continued to read in silence, unable to speak aloud the words that followed.

She's beautiful, just like you. I can see it every time she comes to visit. I see you in the roundness of her face, the darkness of her brown eyes. I see you in her temperament when she gets a full head of steam up, and I hear you in her laughter. How I loved you, Naomi. How I love our little girl.

Jessica wiped away the tears that streamed down her face. Why couldn't he have told her these things? Why couldn't he have been honest with her and kept her at Windridge? The injustice of it all weighed heavily on her heart.

These long years have been like a death sentence to me, and the only reason I write these things now is that the doctor tells me I'll be joining you soon. What glory! To finally come home to you after all of these years. I know a man is supposed to look forward to heaven in order to be united with God, but forgive me, Lord, if I sin in this thought: It's Naomi I long to see.

Twenty-seven years is a long time to live without the woman you love. Others have tried to fill the void, but there is no one but you, my beloved. I tried to take interest in other women, but they paled compared to you, and how fair would it have been to have made another woman live here at Windridge in your shadow?

Jessica bit her lip to keep from sobbing out loud. Ryan would be very upset to see her cry, and with him just beyond the open doors of the nursery, she knew he'd hear her and come to investigate. The words of the journal opened an old wound that Jessica thought had healed with time. She felt the pain afresh, remembered the bitterness of leaving Windridge while her father watched from the porch—no wave, no kiss good-bye, no word.

She saw the devotion he held for her mother, believed that devotion extended in some strange way to herself, but also knew the emptiness her father had felt. An emptiness he imposed upon himself in order to be true to the memory of someone who had died nearly three decades ago.

It was never fair that I should have sent Jessica away from here. Kate scolded me daily for weeks, even months, and finally she stopped, seeing that I would not change my mind and bring the child home. I wanted to. Once Buck helped me past the worst of it, I wanted to bring Jess here to Windridge, but Harriet would have no part of it. We'd signed an agreement, which she so firmly reminded me of anytime I wrote to suggest doing otherwise.

Jessica startled at the realization that her father had tried to bring her back to her real home. She felt a growing anger at the knowledge that Aunt Harriet had kept her from such happiness. She thought of the years of strange girls' schools, where the loneliness threatened to eat her alive. She thought of her miserable youth and the parties and men who stood at Harriet's elbow, hoping to be chosen as a proper mate for Jessica. If only her father could have found a way to break the contract and bring her home. If only she had known that he desired her to be with him, she would have walked through fire to make it happen. She would have defied Harriet and all of her suitors in order to be back on Windridge permanently.

Naomi, I never imagined you would leave me. I built an empire to share with you. Built you a house on Windridge and planned a lifetime of happiness here in God's country. When you went away, you took all that with you. Took my hopes, my dreams, my future. After that, there was no one. Not even Jessica, because Harriet wouldn't allow her to be a part of my life.

Jessica could no longer contain her sobs. She moaned sorrowfully at the thought that her father had longed for her return.

Then Jessica married. He was nothing, less than nothing. A miserable worm handpicked by your aunt. I should have remembered her choice of husbands for you and realized how far I fell from the mark. How upset she was when you ran off with a cowboy from Kansas. Jessica had no one to fight for her, and she didn't have your strength of mind. She did what Harriet told her to do and married that eastern dandy who did nothing but bleed her dry.

Harriet died and left them a fortune, but Albright squandered it on gambling and women. I had him watched, knew his every move, but because Jess loved him, I did nothing. I couldn't hurt her more by interfering where I wasn't wanted. Devon Carter helped me to see that it was no longer my place to fret and stew. Devon's a good man. He's a Christian and a finer son a man could not ask to have. I consider him the son we never had. He's there, just two doors down, whenever I need him.

Jessica suddenly realized that Devon had lived in the house prior to her coming to Windridge. She also realized, without having to ask Kate for confirmation, that Devon had moved out of his own accord in order to maintain the proprieties for Jessica and Ryan. She'd only been coming for a visit as far as they had known. Her decision to stay had caused Devon to have to move permanently from the house. It made her feel bad to realize that she'd sent him off like the hired hand she'd so often accused him of being.

> *I've given Devon a piece of his own land, some two thousand acres on the south side. I also gave him a bonus of five thousand dollars. I figured if Gertrude Jenkins and Newman Albright could bleed me for funds, I might as well leave money to those I love. Jess will get the house, of course, and all of what remains of Windridge. Although in truth, I've neglected it badly, Naomi.*

Several things came immediately to mind. First of all, Gertrude had taken money from her father, and from the sounds of it, she'd taken quite a bit. Jessica had known about Newman's indiscretions from her father's letters, but Gertrude came as a surprise.

But the most important thing that Jessica realized was that Devon Carter had his own money and his own land. He didn't need Jessica's pittance. He had no reason to run from Windridge and Kansas. He could have quit his position many times over and headed over to his own land and started a new life, but instead he stayed at Windridge—with her.

Warmth spread over Jessica in this revelation. Devon hadn't run away, taking her last dime. No, the delay was for some reason other than his alleged dishonesty, and with that thought, Jessica really began to worry. Perhaps he *had* fallen ill. Or maybe someone had done him harm. The possibilities were endless.

Wasting no more time with the diary, Jessica lovingly tucked the book beneath her pillow and went in search of Kate. There were several questions burning in her mind, and Kate would be the only one except Buck who could answer them.

Kate was in the kitchen mixing a cake when Jessica came bounding down the back stairs.

"Kate, I want the truth about something," Jessica announced.

Kate turned and looked at Jessica over the rim of her glasses. "As if I've ever given you anything else."

Jessica smiled. "I know you've been honest with me. That's why I know I can come to you now."

Kate seemed to realize the importance of the matter and put the mixing bowl aside. "So, what's on your mind?"

"Devon."

"Now why doesn't that surprise me?"

Jessica smiled. "Devon lived here in the house when my father was alive, didn't he?"

Kate nodded. "How'd you find that out?"

"My father kept a journal shortly before he died. He knew he was dying and wrote the words as if speaking to my mother."

"I never knew this," Kate said in complete surprise. "Where did you find this journal?"

"Under my mattress," Jessica replied and laughed. "Remember how you wanted to turn the mattress last spring, and we only turned the tick and said we'd see to the mattress come fall? Well, I finally remembered it and took it on my own initiative to resolve the matter. When I managed to pull the mattress off, there it was."

"Well, I'll be," Kate said in complete amazement. "If I'd just turned that mattress after Gus died, we'd have found it a whole lot sooner. Guess that's what I get for being a poor housekeeper."

Jessica shook her head. "Don't you see? This was exactly as God intended it. There was a hardness to me when I came to Windridge that would never have allowed me to deal with the words I read in that journal. God knew the time was right and knew too that I needed to read those words."

"What words?"

"My father talked of how he loved me," Jessica said, tears forming anew in her eyes. "He talked too of how he loved Devon as a son. How he gave Devon land and money. Devon is considerably better off than I figured, isn't he?"

Kate smiled. "I don't know how much he has left. He took a good deal of his own money and started using it to fix up Windridge."

"What?"

"He knew he couldn't just offer it to you, Jess. He knew you'd say no. So he just started buying things that we needed. And he figured to add a good portion of his own funds to whatever the steers sold for and just tell you that he got a really good deal."

"And here I thought Devon was an honest man," Jessica said, wiping her eyes and smiling.

"He didn't want to hurt your feelings or spoil your dreams. Took a lot for him to accept the idea of a resort ranch, but he did it because he knew what it meant to you."

"I only wanted to make something of Windridge without relying on others for help. Guess that was my pride getting in the way of reality," Jessica admitted. "And to think I called Devon the hired help."

"That was pretty hard on him. Gus had treated him like a son, then you came along and relegated him to one of the hands."

Jessica shook her head. "Why didn't you tell me?"

"Devon made us promise we wouldn't. Made us promise we wouldn't say anything about any of it. As much as I love you, Jess, I couldn't betray that promise."

"Papa's diary also said that Gertrude Jenkins and my husband had bled him for money. What do you know about that?"

Kate thought for a moment. "I don't know too much about his dealings with Newman. I know your husband would send telegrams asking for money, telling of one emergency or another. Gus always sent whatever he asked for, knowing that even if Newman spent it on something other than what he claimed, it would at least keep you from suffering."

"It didn't keep me from suffering," Jessica replied. "But if Papa thought it did, then I'm glad."

"I think he knew the truth," Kate replied. "He knew about a lot we never gave him credit for. As for Gertrude, well, she thought she was going to talk Gus into marriage. She's a poor manager of that ranch of hers, and Gus lent her sum after sum, all in order to help her keep afloat. She finally deeded the ranch over to him, although no one was supposed to know that but she and Gus. That's part of the reason why she took off for Europe. She didn't want to face the retribution of listening to what folks would have to say when they learned she'd borrowed against the ranch until Gus owned the whole thing."

"Why wasn't I told about this?" Jessica asked.

Kate took a deep breath. "Because Devon arranged to buy the land from Gus, and when Gus died, Devon gave it back to Gertrude. It's the reason she hates him so much. He told her he knew he didn't owe her anything, but that he couldn't bear to see her suffer, especially if there was the slightest chance that he had somehow caused Jane to look elsewhere for her happiness. He also told her the truth about finding Jane in the arms of a traveling salesman. Told her how he confronted Jane, agreed to forget the whole matter, and still planned to marry her. It wasn't the story Gerty wanted to hear."

"I can well imagine."

"Anyway, Gus never knew. He probably figured Devon saw the merit of the property because it adjoined the land Gus had already given Devon."

Jessica wouldn't have thought it possible that she could love Devon more than she already did, but hearing of his generosity and giving to a woman who hated him made her realize how deeply she admired and loved Devon Carter.

"This changes everything," Jessica murmured, wishing silently that there might be a way to win Devon away from the woman he knew God had intended him to marry. *Perhaps that is the reason for his delay,* she thought for the first time. *Maybe he's gotten himself married.*

"Not really," Kate replied, interrupting Jessica's thoughts.

"What do you mean?" Jessica asked.

"You love him, and he loves you."

She shook her head sadly. "No, he told me there was someone he cared for. Someone God had chosen for him to marry."

Kate started laughing. "Silly woman, he meant you. He told Buck as much."

"What?" Jessica felt her chest tighten and her breathing quicken. "Are you telling me the truth?"

"I thought we'd already established that I've never lied to you. Do you think I'd start now?"

"No, but, I mean—" A wonderful rush of excitement flowed over Jessica. "He loves me?"

Kate laughed even more. "It's pretty obvious to everyone but you two that you're perfect for each other. You need each other in a bigger way than any two people I've ever seen. Whether you go back to regular ranching or run a resort, you'll do fine so long as you do it together."

"He loves me," Jessica repeated. "And he loves Ryan." She looked up at Kate and saw the happiness in the older woman's eyes. There was no doubting the words she spoke. Devon loved her.

Chapter 10

Looks like it's gonna blow up a snow," Buck said, coming into the house. "I don't like the taste of the air. Wouldn't be surprised to see it shape up to be a bad one."

"Are we prepared for such a thing?" Kate asked.

"I'm having the boys bring up wood from the shed. We'll stack it high against the back of the house. That way, if we have a blizzard like the one the year Jessie was born, we won't have far to go for fuel."

"What about the hands?" Jessica asked, easily realizing the seriousness of the moment.

"They usually ride the storms out in the bunkhouse. We run a rope from there to the barns, and that way, they can keep an eye on the horses and milk cows."

Jessica nodded. "If it gets too bad, let's bring them up to the house. Better to use fuel to heat one place than two."

Buck and Kate exchanged a quick glance and smiled approvingly. "You sound more like your father each day," Kate told her.

Jessica laughed. "I would have thought that an insult at one time. Now, I take it as the compliment you intend it to be."

"I'll bring up extra fuel for the lanterns, and if you ladies think of anything else we need, you let me know," Buck said, heading back for the door. He opened it and looked outside. "Snow's already started," he announced.

"Then we'd best get busy," Kate told Jessica.

Ryan came into the kitchen about that time. His cheeks were flushed, and his eyes appeared rather glassy. Jessica immediately realized he'd been unusually quiet that morning. Picking up her son, Jessica could feel the heat radiating from his tiny body.

"Ryan's sick," she told Kate. "He has a fever."

Kate came to Jessica and held out her arms, but Jessica felt all her feelings of overprotection and inadequacy surface. "I'll take care of him," she said more harshly than she'd intended.

Kate nodded as if understanding. "I only wanted to see how high his fever was."

"You can tell by a touch?" Jessica asked, still clinging tightly to Ryan.

"You can when you've dealt with as many sick boys as I have. Remember,

I've nursed the bunk hands, my own sons, Gus and Buck, even Devon. You get a feel for it after a time." Kate put her hand to Ryan's head. "Feels pretty high. We'd best get him to bed and see what we can do to bring that fever down. Do you see any rashes on his body?"

"Rashes?" Jessica asked in a panicky voice.

Kate nodded. "I heard some of the Newcome kids were down with the measles."

"Measles!" Jessica's voice squeaked out the word. "He just can't have measles."

"Well, only time will tell. Let's get him to bed, and we'll work on it from there. Why don't you put him in the bed in our room? That way you won't have to run up and down the stairs all the time, and it'll be warmer here by the kitchen. If you like, you can sleep there, and Buck and I will take one of the upstairs rooms."

"Thanks, Kate." Jessica looked down at Ryan, who had put his head on her shoulder. It was so uncharacteristic of the boy that Jessica thought she might start to cry. She bit her lower lip and, knowing nothing else to do, began to pray.

The blizzard blew in with the full force Buck had expected and then some. Icy pellets of rain came first, coating everything with a thick layer of ice. Then sleetlike snow stormed across the hills, and visibility became impossible.

Jessica thought very little about the storm, except to occasionally worry about Devon. She had far too much with which to concern herself by keeping on top of Ryan's needs and easily relegated everything else to Buck and Kate.

By the second day of the storm, Ryan bore the telltale signs of measles. Tiny red splotchy dots covered his stomach and groin, and his fever refused to abate. Jessica found herself so weary she could hardly keep her eyes open, yet when Kate offered to relieve her, Jessica refused.

"You aren't doing yourself or Ryan any good," Kate told her. "I don't know why you can't see the sense in letting others help you." Kate's tone revealed the offense she took at Jessica's actions.

"I'm sorry, Kate. I didn't mean to make you feel bad. It's just that. . . well. . .he's mine, and it's my responsibility to see him through this."

"But if you kill yourself trying to nurse him back to health, what good will it do? I swear, the way you act, you'd think I was trying to steal your glory."

"What?" Jessica questioned, struggling to clear the cobwebs from her sleepy mind. "What glory is there in a sick child?"

"None that I know of," Kate replied. "But you seem to think there's some reason to keep anyone else from getting too close to that boy."

Jessica slumped into a chair and nodded. "I just can't lose him. He's so important to me. I don't want to lose him to you or Devon or sickness."

"Why would you lose him to anyone? Ryan knows you're his mother, and he loves you. Well, as much as any two year old can love. Jessica," Kate said, reaching out to touch the younger woman's shoulder, "you've been like a daughter to me. I always wanted to have a daughter, and I would have happily raised you for Gus. Let me offer you a bit of motherly advice."

Jessica looked up and nodded.

"Don't let fear be the glue that binds your relationship with Ryan. Fear is a poor substitute for love."

"But you know about the past. You know what Essie did when I lived in New York."

"Yes, but I don't see Essie around here. It's just you and me, and I'm not about to steal your child away from you. Don't you see, Jessica? The more you smother Ryan with protectiveness and isolate him from being able to love anyone but you, the more hollow and useless your relationship. He'll run the first chance he gets, just to give himself some breathing room."

"I know you're right. God's been working on this very issue with me. I guess I just let fear control me sometimes."

"Sometimes?" Kate questioned with a grin.

"All right, so fear and I are no strangers," Jessica said, smiling. "Kate, would you please watch Ryan while I get some sleep?"

Kate nodded and patted Jessica once again. "I would be happy to help."

Jessica nodded, made her way to the bed, and fell across it, not even bothering to undress.

Father, she prayed, *please heal my son. You know how much I love him and how lost I would be without him. I'm begging You not to take him from me.*

She felt welcome drowsiness engulf her. Devon's face came to mind and, with it, the thought that she needed to pray for him. *Watch over him, Father,* she added. *Please bring him home to Windridge.*

The snow let up, but not the wind, which kept the effects of the blizzard going on for days. The blowing snow blinded them from even seeing the top of Windridge. Jessica saw notable improvements in Ryan's health and forced herself to accept Kate's involvement in nursing him. It wasn't that she didn't dearly love Kate, but the fact was, Jessica still needed to let go of her possessive nature when it came to the boy.

Sitting at her father's desk in the library, Jessica thought back on the things Devon, Kate, and Buck had told her over the course of her time at Windridge.

"Folks need folks out here," Buck had once said. "It fast becomes a matter of survival." His point had been made in talking to her about selling property to Joe Riley. He needed a spring in order to assure himself of having water for his cattle and his land. Jessica could easily see that what Buck said made perfect sense. They were so isolated out here in the middle of the Flinthills that to be anything other than neighborly could prove fatal.

She stared into the fireplace and watched the flames lick greedily at the dry wood. Kate had said, "It's better to rely on folks than to die on folks." This was kind of an unspoken code of Kate's. "The prairie is no place for pride," Kate had added. "Pride not only goeth before destruction, it is the thing that stirs up strife and causes heartache."

Jessica knew it was true. Her own pride had nearly caused her to alienate Kate's affections. That was something she could never have abided. Kate was like a mother to her in so many ways that Aunt Harriet had never been. Aunt Harriet had raised her, but Aunt Harriet had never loved her the way Kate did.

Devon came to mind when Jessica thought about love. She loved him so much that it hurt to think about what tragedies might have befallen him. She planned to have Buck go into town and wire the livestock yards in Kansas City. They would have records of the cattle transactions and just possibly those records would include the name of the hotel where Devon was staying. It was Jessica's hope that they might learn something about Devon's whereabouts by starting down this path.

But the blizzard had put an end to that thought, and Buck felt certain more snow was coming their way. She felt her enthusiasm slip another notch. Life on the prairie was very hard—there could be no doubt about that—and it was quickly becoming apparent that Jessica could either accept that she could do nothing on her own, or she could perish.

"Don't be so sure you don't need anyone," Devon had told her once. It had startled her to have him read her so easily. She smiled when she thought of the halfhearted protest she'd offered him. She could still see the laughter in his eyes and the amusement in his voice when she'd told him he didn't know anything about her feelings.

"I may not know you or your feelings," he'd countered, "but I know pride when I see it. Pride used to be a bosom companion of mine, so I feel pretty certain when I see him. Just remember, pride isn't the kind to stick around and help when matters get tough."

Jessica chuckled at the memory. *He's so right,* she thought. *Pride only offers seclusion and a false sense of security. I have to let go of my pride and allow people to help me when I need it and to help others when they have needs. Otherwise, Ryan and I will never survive life at Windridge.*

"It's been two weeks," Devon heard someone say. His mind was lost in a haze of darkness, but from time to time someone spoke words that made a little sense. He strained to understand the words—fought to find the source of the words.

"His vital signs are good, but the fact that he's still not regained consciousness worries me."

"Any word on the man's identity?" came another male voice.

"None. We really should send someone around to contact the businesses in the area where he was found."

Devon floated on air and wondered why everyone seemed so concerned. Who was this person they couldn't identify, and what were vital signs?

"His injuries were extensive," the man continued, "but the bones seem to be healing just fine, and the swelling has gone down in his face. It's probably that blow to the back of the head that keeps him unconscious."

From somewhere in his thoughts, Devon began to realize they were talking about him. It startled him at first, but then it seemed quite logical. The next realization he had was of being in extreme pain. Something wasn't right. Somewhere in his body, someone was causing him a great deal of torment.

These thoughts came and went from time to time, but to Devon they seemed to transpire in the course of just a few hours. It wasn't until he heard one of the disembodied voices announce that if he didn't regain consciousness soon, he would die, that Devon began a long hard fight to find his way through the mire of blackness.

"Did you have a nice Christmas?" someone questioned.

"A very nice one, Sir," came the feminine voice in response.

Devon thought for a moment the voice belonged to someone he knew, but the thought was so fleeting that he couldn't force it to stay long enough to interpret it.

"The New Year's ball was superb," the woman continued. "I'd never been to anything so lovely."

"Yes, my wife loves the occasion. Of course, it's also her birthday," the man responded.

Birthday. Devon thought about the word for a moment. Someone he knew had a birthday on New Year's Eve. Without realizing what he was doing, Devon opened his eyes and said, "Birthday."

His eyes refused to focus for several minutes, but when they did, Devon could see the startled faces of the man and woman who stood at his bedside.

"So, you finally decided to join the world of the living," the man said in a stern voice that was clearly mingled with excitement.

"Where am I?" Devon asked, his voice gravelly.

"You're in the hospital. Have been for nearly a month," the man replied. "I'm Dr. Casper, and you are?"

He waited for Devon's response with a look of anticipation. The woman too looked down at him in an expectant manner. Devon stared blankly at them, trading glances first with the woman and then with the man.

"Did you understand my question?" the doctor asked. "I need to know who you are."

"I don't know," Devon replied with a hideous sinking feeling. He shook his head, feeling the dull pain that crossed from one side of his skull to the other. "I don't know who I am."

Chapter 11

The weeks that followed left Devon depressed and frustrated. His injuries were quick enough to heal, so why not his mind?

"How does that leg feel?" the doctor questioned as Devon hobbled around the room like a trained monkey.

"It's sore, but I've had worse."

"How do you know?" the doctor asked curiously. "Are you starting to remember something more?"

Devon shrugged. "I remember little pieces of things. I remember a room with a stone fireplace. I remember riding a horse out on the open range." He hobbled back to bed and sunk onto the edge of the mattress. "But I don't remember anything important."

"Those things are all important, Mr. Smith," the doctor told him.

"Don't call me Smith," Devon replied angrily. "Not unless you have proof that that's who I am."

"We have to call you something," the doctor replied. "Now, raise that arm for me."

Devon lifted his left arm and grimaced. Apparently his assailants had hit him repeatedly and kicked him as well. He had suffered busted ribs, a broken ankle, and a dislocated shoulder. His left arm had been continuously pounded, the doctor believed by boot heels, as had his face.

"It still works. Just not as well," Devon told the doctor.

"I'm sure in time it will all heal properly. Are you in as much pain today as you were yesterday?"

Devon shook his head. "No." He glanced up to find one of the nurses coming down the ward with a well-dressed man at her side.

"Dr. Casper, this man believes he knows our patient."

Devon perked up at this and studied the man for a moment. Was he a friend? A brother? Some other family member?

"Yes," the man said enthusiastically. "This is the man I've been searching for. He didn't have a beard when he stayed with us, but he's the same man. He's a guest, or was a guest, at our hotel. I'm so happy to have found you, Mr. Carter."

"Carter?" Devon tried the name. Carter. Yes, Carter sounded right.

"The assault this man received left him without much of a memory,"

Dr. Casper told the hotelman.

"No wonder you failed to return," the man said sympathetically. "When I heard about the poor man who'd been beaten in the alley not far from the hotel, I thought, perhaps this is Devon Carter. I knew you wouldn't leave without retrieving your things. After all, you left quite a bit of money in my safe."

Devon nodded. Yes, he remembered having a good amount of money. He closed his eyes and pictured himself handing it over to the man who now stood at his side. "I remember you."

"Good," the doctor said enthusiastically. "Seeing something familiar often triggers memory." He turned to the hotelman. "Did you bring any of his things?"

"No, but I can have them brought here immediately."

"Then do so," the doctor instructed. "Mr. Carter will need all the help he can get in order to remember who he is."

Nearly half an hour later, a boy appeared with saddlebags, two brown paper packages, and a large envelope. The man from the hotel stood at his side as though standing guard. "We have your things, Mr. Carter."

Devon nodded. It felt so good just to know his own name that knowing anything else would be purely extra. He took hold of the saddlebags and noted the carved initials *D.C.* He ran his fingers over the indentation, remembering vaguely the day he'd carved the marker on the bags. Reaching into one side, Devon pulled out his shaving gear and studied it for a moment. It seemed familiar, but nothing that offered him any real memory. Next, he took out an extra shirt and pair of socks. Nothing came to mind with those articles, so he quickly reached into the other side of the bag.

Here, he found receipts all dated from the middle of December. Some of the receipts were for furniture, and others were for homey things like lamps, curtain rods, material, dishes, and such. The kind of things a wife would have need and desire of. Did he have a wife? The same face kept coming to mind. At first she had appeared only in a hazy outline, but as time went on, the warmth of her smile and the sincerity in her dark eyes became clearer in his memory. Was this the image of his wife?

"Do you remember these things?" the doctor questioned.

"Somewhat," Devon replied.

"This," the man from the hotel said, "is the money you left with us."

Devon took the envelope and looked inside. There was a great deal of money, and it immediately triggered a thought. The money was intended for a special use. The money belonged to her. The woman in his mind. Perhaps it was a dowry. Maybe they were setting up house, and this money had come from her.

"Why don't you unwrap these packages? My nurse will be glad to rewrap them afterward, but perhaps they will trigger some memory."

Devon nodded and gently stripped away the paper on the first package. Toy soldiers. Devon felt mounting frustration at not being able to remember. Then to his surprise, the image of another face came to mind. It was that of a child. The fuzzy brown hair of the boy seemed to draw Devon's attention first. There was something important about this child. Then a horrible feeling washed over Devon. Was he not only a husband but a father as well?

"Here, try this one," the doctor said, helping to pull the paper from the other package. A jewelry box was revealed as the paper fell away. Devon stared at the box, feeling sure that he should remember it but having no real understanding of why. Had he bought this as a gift for the woman in his dreams? Had he left a family somewhere to worry and fret over his well-being? What if they were in danger because of his absence? What if they needed the supplies and goods he had procured?

"No," he muttered, handing the things over to the nurse. He stuffed the receipts and money into the saddlebag, then turned to the hotelman. "I don't suppose I gave you an address?"

"No, Sir, but you said you were from Kansas. You came to sell cattle."

Devon drew his legs up onto the bed and fell back against the pillow. "I think I need to rest," he told them all. He felt angry and frustrated. He had hoped that with the recognition of his own name, he might instantly remember everything else that he needed to know.

"Thanks for bringing my things," he told the hotelman. The man smiled and prodded the kid to follow him from the room. The nurse and doctor agreed that rest was the best solution and finally left Devon alone.

He stared at the ceiling for awhile, then rolled onto his side and stared down the corridor of beds. Several men moaned and called out for help. Others slept peacefully, and a few read. But all of them had their minds. All of them knew their name and recognized their own things.

Sleep finally overtook Devon, and although he passed the time fitfully, he actually felt better when he awoke. The light had faded outside, leaving little doubt that dusk was upon them. This time of day made Devon melancholy. He longed to be home—wherever home might be.

He thought of the dark-haired woman in his dreams. Thought of the child whose laughing face warmed his heart. He loved these people; he felt certain of that. They were important to him in a way he couldn't figure out, but he knew without a doubt they were keys to his past.

Supper came, and although Devon had figured nothing good could come of the meal, he found himself actually enjoying the beef stew. It wasn't as good as Kate's, but. . .

Kate? Was that the dark-haired woman's name?

Devon stared at the stew and forced an image. He was sitting in a stylish dining room. The dark-haired woman and little boy were sitting beside him, but there was also someone else in the picture. An older woman's face beamed a smile at him. She pushed up wire-rimmed glasses and asked if he'd like more stew. Kate. Katie! He actually remembered her.

This triggered other thoughts, and soon Devon found himself overwhelmed with people and events. Still, he couldn't remember the brown-haired woman's name, nor that of the child. Nor could he remember where he lived and where he might find the others.

"I've brought another visitor," Dr. Casper said as he approached Devon's bed.

The supper had grown cold, but Devon didn't care. "I've been remembering some things."

The doctor smiled. "Good! That's very good. This gentleman called for you at the hotel, and he knows quite a bit about your home. We thought you might remember him as well."

Devon looked at the man and nodded. "Yes, he does seem familiar."

"I am Mr. Whitehead. You ordered a large number of chairs and two bedsteads from my company. You also ordered several nightstands and dressers." The man chuckled. "You look a bit different what with the beard. You had the mustache, but the beard is new."

Devon nodded and smirked a grin. "Nobody seems to offer me a shave around here. You say I ordered furniture? I do seem to remember something along those lines, but did I say why I needed so much?"

"You were ordering them for your place in Kansas. You are planning a resort ranch at a place called Windridge."

The word *Windridge* triggered everything. Suddenly it was as if the floodgates to his mind had opened. He realized exactly who he was and who she was. "Jessica." He breathed the name and sighed.

Then, startling both the doctor and Mr. Whitehead, Devon exclaimed, "What day is this?"

"February 3," the doctor replied.

Devon rubbed his bearded face. "Get me a razor and some soap. I have to get home. I should have been there months ago."

The doctor smiled. "Are you certain you feel up to leaving us?"

Devon nodded. "I'm positive. Just get me my things. Oh, and I need to send a telegram." No doubt everyone would be worried sick by now. Especially Jessica.

"Well, it seems as though this is all working out rather well," Dr. Casper said. "I wouldn't have given you odds on pulling through that beating, but you're one tough man, Mr. Carter."

"I don't know about how tough I am, but I'm definitely a man with a purpose, and that gives a guy strength, even when all hope is lost."

When they left him to dress, Devon felt the overwhelming urge to get down on his knees and thank God for supplying him with the answers he'd been so desperately seeking. Stiff and sore from his inactivity, Devon ignored the pain and knelt beside his bed.

Thank You, Father, he prayed, feeling hot tears come to his eyes. *I was so lost, and I despaired of ever being found. But You knew where I was all the time. You knew what I needed, and You brought it to me. I pray with a heart of thanksgiving for all that You've done to rescue me from the hopelessness. Please keep Jessica and everyone at Windridge in Your care. Help them not to worry, and help me to get home to them quickly. Amen.*

Jessica awoke with a start. She went first to Ryan's bed and found the boy sleeping peacefully. All signs of the measles were gone, but he was still rather weak, and Jessica worried over him.

She watched him sleep peacefully and thanked God for His mercy.

"I've learned so much here at Windridge," she murmured. "Things I never expected to learn."

She thought of the diary her father had kept and went to take it up from the special place she'd given it on her fireplace mantel. Lighting a lamp, she sat down to reread the final entry in the journal. She continued to come back to this one entry, because while the rest of the book was written to her mother, this entry was written to her:

My beloved Jessica,

I can only pray that you will someday forgive me for sending you away. I have always loved you, will die loving you, but I know I am unworthy of your love. I've tried to help out where I could—tried to be there for you when you would let me, which, although it didn't happen often, happened just enough to give me some satisfaction.

Please know this, I never blamed you for your mother's passing. People live, and people die, and that's just the way things are. Only God chooses the timing for those things. Only God can give life, as He did in the form of my beautiful child, and only God can take life, as He did with your mother.

I'm sorry I can't leave you a legacy of memories spent here at Windridge, but I hope you'll stay on. I hope you'll come to love this house as much as your mother did. I hope too that you'll be good to Katie and Buck and Devon Carter. You don't know any of them very well, but they're good people, and I know they will care very deeply for you. When you think of me, Jessica, I hope it will be with something other than hatred and anger. Maybe one day you will actually think of me as I used to be when your mother was alive. Hopeful, happy, looking forward to the future and all that it had to offer.

Your Father

Jessica sighed and closed the book to cradle it against her breast. She felt warmed and comforted by its words. Now if only Devon would come home. If only they could have some word from him. Some hope that he was all right.

Getting up, Jessica walked to the window and looked across the snowy prairie. "Come home to me, Devon," she whispered against the frosty glass. "Please come home to Windridge."

Chapter 12

Warm southerly winds blew in and melted the snows on Windridge. The land went from white to dull brown practically overnight. Jessica marveled at the change. She could actually go outside without a coat, although Kate told her the warmth was deceptive. But Jessica didn't care. The heat of the sun felt good upon her face, and the warm winds blowing across the land would dry the ground and insure her ability to get to town again.

Jessica didn't allow herself to be concerned with what she would do once she actually got to town. She hadn't a clue as to how she would go about searching for Devon, but she knew the key would be in communication. She would start by telegraphing anyone who might have some idea of Devon's whereabouts.

Bundling Ryan up, Jessica decided a walk to the top of the ridge would be in order. The land was still rather soggy, but Jessica carefully picked her way up the hill while Ryan chattered about the things he saw.

"Bword," he cried out, pointing to a robin sitting on the fence post.

"Yes, that's a good sign," Jessica told her son.

"I want bword," Ryan said, trying to squirm out of her hold.

"No. Now stop it," Jessica reprimanded. "We're going up here to see if we can find Devon."

"Dadon," Ryan repeated.

Jessica smiled. No matter how much Ryan's language improved, Devon's name still came out sounding like some form of *Daddy.*

"Dadon comin'," Ryan said enthusiastically.

"Soon, I hope." Jessica wondered if she'd made a mistake by telling the boy they were looking for Devon. Now he would be constantly chattering about Devon, always asking where he was and when he'd come home. The measles had forced all of them to focus their attention on something other than Devon's absence, and even though Ryan had cried for Devon on more than one occasion, he seemed to accept that the man was gone from his life. At least temporarily. Now Jessica realized she'd probably stirred up the child's anticipation all over again.

"Dadon comin' to me," Ryan told her, patting his hand against her face.

Jessica kissed his fingers and laughed. "I pray he comes home soon." She trudged up the final few feet of the ridge, realizing as she did how much Ryan had grown since the last time she'd carried him up the hillside.

"Oh, Ryan," she said rather breathlessly, "you're getting so big."

"Wyan get big," he said, raising his arms high in the air. "Dadon comin' to me."

Jessica shook her head and grinned at the boy's enthusiasm. *Let him have his moment,* she thought. *It can't hurt to be hopeful.* Jessica stared out across the Flinthills and felt the longing in her heart grow stronger. He was out there somewhere.

"I don't know where you are," she whispered, her skirts bellowing out behind her as the wind whipped at them. She knew she couldn't keep Ryan outside for much longer and had just started to turn back down the hill when she spotted a wagon emerge from behind a hill.

Ryan saw the object as well and started clapping his hands. "Dadon comin'!"

Jessica felt her heart skip a beat as yet another wagon followed the first and then another. Four wagons in all, laden with crates and covered boxes, made their way toward Windridge. Then Jessica caught the outline of the two men in the lead wagon.

"Devon," she whispered, feeling absolutely confident that the man beside the driver of the wagon was her beloved Devon.

"Come on, Ryan, we have to get you back in the house."

"I want Dadon," Ryan protested as Jessica nearly ran down the hill.

Because the grass still held moisture, she slipped and nearly fell. "I've got to calm myself down," she said aloud and forced herself to walk more carefully.

Seeing the wagons come ever closer, Jessica forgot about taking Ryan inside. She forgot about everything but getting to Devon. She started walking down the dirt road, her pace picking up as the wagons rounded the final bend. She tightened her grip on Ryan. *Devon's home!* It was all she could think of.

He apparently saw her, because the wagon stopped long enough for Devon to jump down from the seat. He waved the driver on and walked toward them with a bit of a limp. *He was hurt!* she thought, and all sensibility left her mind. She began to run, mindless of Ryan, mindless of the drivers passing by in their wagons.

"Oh, Devon!" she exclaimed. His face registered surprise as she crossed the final distance and threw herself into his arms. "Oh, Devon, I thought you were never coming home." Then without thought, she kissed him. At first it was just a peck on the cheek, then another and another, and finally her lips met his and stopped. All rational thought had fled, and she kissed him passionately. Pulling away, Jessica suddenly realized by the look on Devon's face that she'd made a grave mistake.

Her enthusiasm waned, in spite of the fact that Ryan was now clapping and shouting Devon's name over and over. She did nothing for a moment, her gaze fixed on Devon. She searched his eyes for some sign of acceptance, but he only stared back at her as if trying to figure out who she was and why she'd just kissed him.

Thrusting Ryan into Devon's arms, Jessica turned and ran back to the house. He didn't even call after her. Jessica felt her face grow hot with humiliation. Kate must have been wrong about his feelings for her. She must have misunderstood Buck, or Buck had misunderstood Devon.

Jessica wanted to die. Wanted to crawl under a rock and never be seen again. What a spectacle she'd just made of herself. Running out there to Devon as though he was her long lost love.

But, she thought, *he is* my *love.* She might not be his, but he was her own heart's love. And deep down inside, Jessica knew she would never love another. If he couldn't return that love, then she would live the rest of her life alone. The thought terrified her.

"Is that Devon?" Kate exclaimed, stepping out the front door.

"Yes," Jessica barely managed to say. She rushed past, mindless of the shocked expression on the older woman's face. She couldn't stand and explain her humiliating actions to Kate. No, let Devon tell Kate how poorly she'd conducted herself.

Jessica stayed out of sight until suppertime. Kate had brought Ryan to the nursery for his nap, and although Jessica was just in the adjoining room, she didn't open the doors to speak to the woman; Kate, thankfully, didn't knock and ask her to.

She felt guilty for having neglected Ryan, but in truth her emotions were so raw and foreign that Jessica knew it would have been impossible to deal with anyone.

"I don't know what to do," she whispered, pressing her face against the cool pane of the window. "I made a fool of myself, and now I have to face them all at supper."

She heard Kate ring the supper bell, something the woman had come up with in order to call guests to meals. The tradition had been started early, all in order to see how and if it would work. The bell pealed out loud and clear, and Jessica cringed. She would have to go down. There was no other way.

She splashed water on her face and checked her appearance. She'd changed out of the skirt and blouse she'd worn earlier. The hem of that skirt had been laden with mud and grass, and the blouse had clung to her from perspiration. Now she studied her reflection and realized that the peach-colored gown made her look quite striking. The muttonleg sleeves made her shoulders look slightly wider, which accented her tiny waist. The gown was cut in a very simple style, with a rounded neckline and basque waist. The peach material had been trimmed in cream-colored lace and cording, and with Jessica's brunette hair, the effect was quite stunning.

She bit her lip and shook her head. It didn't matter. She had dressed for him, but it wouldn't matter. His feelings had obviously changed while he'd been away from Windridge. She would have to accept this fact and deal with her broken heart.

"Mama! Mama come!" Ryan called out to her from the nursery.

Jessica smiled and opened the door. "Yes, Mama is coming."

By the time they made their way into the dining room, the others had already congregated. Jessica hated making an entrance where everyone could stare at her, but she knew there was no other choice. She swept into the room, Ryan in her arms, and made her way to the table determined that no one would think anything was wrong.

"Here we are. So sorry for the delay," she announced, putting Ryan in his chair and taking her own place at the foot of the table.

"I thought perhaps you'd fallen asleep," Kate said, allowing Buck to help her into her chair.

Jessica could feel Devon's gaze upon her, but she refused to look at him. "Yes, well, I did rest for a time. Thank you for seeing to Ryan."

"Oh, I didn't see to him except to put him down for his nap. Devon wouldn't hear of it. He insisted that they had a lot of catching up to do."

Jessica could feel her cheeks grow warm. "Well, then, thank you." She refused to say his name. It was almost more than she could stand. Being so near to him yet knowing that he was put off at her behavior was too much to bear.

They blessed the meal, with Buck giving thanks for Devon's safe return. Then Kate started the conversation, asking Devon to explain his long absence.

"As I was telling Buck and Kate, earlier," Devon began, "everything went pretty well the first couple weeks. I had no trouble selling the cattle and arranging for most everything we had on our list."

Our list. The words sounded pleasant, but Jessica knew she could take no comfort in them. Devon merely thought of Windridge as being partly his own because her father had instilled that belief in the man. How could she blame him for his concerns about the ranch and what would become of it?

"They hit me hard and of course—"

"What?" Jessica nearly shouted, and for the first time her gaze met his. "Who hit you?"

Devon grinned. "I was just telling you that I got myself mugged in Kansas City. A couple fellows waylaid me in the alley not far from the hotel. Thankfully, the money was secured in the hotel safe, and those thugs only managed to get about five dollars. But they hit me hard on the back of the head, then proceeded to beat me. They thought they'd killed me, and why not? I was unconscious and bloodied up pretty good."

Jessica could only stare at him. Her throat tightened as if a band had been tightly wrapped around her neck.

"By leaving me for dead, they did me a favor. Someone found me and hauled me off to the hospital. I was in a coma for about three weeks."

"A coma." Jessica barely breathed the words.

Devon nodded. Ryan began calling for something to eat, and Devon reached over to hand the boy a piece of bread without stopping his story. "When I woke up, I hurt like all get out, but the worst of it was that I couldn't remember a thing."

"Nothing?" Jessica questioned.

His eyes seemed to darken as they locked with hers. "Nothing. I didn't know who I was or where I was from. I only knew the pain and misery of my condition. I couldn't even tell the police what had happened."

"But God was watching over you," Kate chimed in. "We've been praying for you. When you didn't turn up by Christmas, we all had a feeling something wasn't quite right."

"Especially given that you didn't even bother to send a telegram," Buck added.

Devon pulled a wrinkled piece of paper from his pocket. It was clearly a telegram, and he unfolded it and held it up. "I found this waiting at the telegraph office. I sent this as soon as I had my memory back. Seems you people have been impossible to get to because of the snow."

Buck laughed. "That we were, but you could have let us know sooner."

"I know. I should have, but I kept thinking that I'd be coming home any day. Then one week's delay turned into two and so on, and then they mugged me, and well, now you know the story."

"But what happened to help you regain your memory?" Jessica asked.

"A fellow from the hotel came around to see me. He'd heard about the mugging, and since I never returned for the money in the safe, he thought it might be me. He brought some of my things, and little bits of memory started coming back. Then one of the vendors with whom I'd set up a purchase order for chairs came to the hotel when I never came back around to see him. He learned about my situation and came to see me at the hospital, and he was able to help me put together the rest of the mystery."

"What an awful time, Devon," Kate said shaking her head. "I just don't know how a fellow could manage without his memories."

"It was hard. I knew there was so much waiting for me, but I just couldn't force it to come to mind."

Jessica shook her head. "How very awful."

"Well, it's behind us now. I have a bit of limp from a broken ankle, and my ribs still hurt me a bit, but my hard head kept them from doing me in."

Buck laughed. "As many times as you've been thrown from one green horse or another, I'd say that head of yours has held up pretty well."

They all laughed at this. All but Jessica. She pretended to busy herself with preparing Ryan's food. The boy was growing bored with bread, and it was clear he felt himself entitled to something more. She thanked God silently for bringing Devon home to them. She couldn't imagine why such a thing had been necessary to endure, yet Kate had assured her that all things happened for a purpose. As if reading her mind, Devon spoke up again.

"Being laid up like that made me realize just how much I still wanted to accomplish. It made me realize how important some things were and how unimportant other things were."

"How so, Devon?" Kate asked, ladling him a large portion of the beef stew he'd specifically requested for supper.

"I realized it doesn't much matter what direction we go with Windridge so long as we're happy and doing what God would have us do. What does matter is that we honor God and care for one another. Everything else is just icing on the cake."

"Cake. Wyan want cake!"

Devon laughed and rubbed the boy's head. "I do believe this boy grew some hair while I was gone." Ryan squealed and clapped his hands as if acknowledging his own accomplishments.

Jessica thought about what Devon had said long after the supper meal was over and Ryan had been put to bed. She had thought to just stay in her room, but at the sound of the bell ringing downstairs, she figured Kate had forgotten something and was using the signal to keep from having to trudge up a flight of steps to get her answer.

With a sigh, Jessica went down the back stairs to the kitchen and found Devon leaning casually against the wall at the bottom of the stairs—bell in hand, grin on his face.

"I wondered if this would really work. Kate said it would, but I just didn't believe her."

Jessica began to tremble. She froze on the step and waited to see what he would do or say next. His smile broadened as he set the bell aside. "I thought maybe you'd take a walk with me. Kate says she'll listen for Ryan, so why don't you grab up your coat and come out to the ridge with me?"

Jessica felt her mouth go dry. "I don't know if that's such a good idea."

Devon laughed and reached up to pull her down the last few steps. "Well, I do. The country air seems to have a remarkable effect on you."

Jessica's face grew hot. Was he implying what she thought he was? She didn't get a chance to ask because he moved her toward the back door with such speed that she had no time to protest.

He pulled her work coat from the peg and helped her on with it. Then he took up his own coat, which he'd draped haphazardly atop the butter churn. "Come on."

He half dragged her up the hill, not saying a word as they made their way to the top. Jessica felt the warmth of his fingers intertwined with her own. It felt wonderful to have him so near. But how could she ever explain her actions from earlier in the day? No doubt he wanted to discuss her boldness, and he probably wanted to upbraid her for it, given the fact that he was taking her away from the house and other listening ears.

She bit at her lower lip and tried to think of how she would justify herself. She'd simply tell him she was overcome with joy. Which was true. Then, she'd make it clear the kiss meant nothing. Which was not true.

Devon slowed down as they neared the top and nearly swung her in a circle as they came to stand atop the ridge. "Now," he said without wasting any time. "I'd like an explanation."

"An explanation?" Jessica questioned, barely able to look him in the eye. "For what?"

The full moon overhead revealed the amusement in his expression. "All the time you've been here at Windridge, Jessica Albright, you've either been putting me in my place, arguing with me about how things would be, or calling me the hired help. You've berated me for my interference with Ryan, refusing to let him get too close for fear I might steal him away from you, and you've hidden yourself away anytime things got too uncomfortable."

Jessica said nothing. Everything he'd related was true. It hardly seemed productive to deny it.

"Then," he said, his voice lowering, "I return home from an experience that nearly sent me to my maker, and you greet me like I'm your long lost husband. And that, my dear Jessica, is what I want an explanation for."

Jessica took a deep breath. Her moment of truth had come. But she couldn't tell him the truth, not given the way he'd reacted to her. Or could she? Maybe if she was honest, he'd realize the merit in accepting her love. Maybe he'd even come to love her the way Kate presumed he already did.

The air had grown chilly, and Jessica shivered. She refused to give in to her fears. Her entire life had been a pattern of running away from painful situations, and while she'd not instigated the first time when her father had sent her from Windridge, she had certainly allowed many of the other situations.

"Well?" Devon prodded.

His expression was unreadable. Where earlier Devon had smiled with amusement and seemed quite entertained by her nervousness, Jessica could find nothing in his face to reveal how he really felt. She would have to swallow her pride and admit her feelings or lie to him.

"I suppose you do deserve an explanation," she began slowly. "I can best explain by telling you some of the things that happened to me while you were gone. First, Gertrude Jenkins showed up."

"Yes, I remember passing her on the way down the drive."

"Well, she came and we were introduced, and your name came up." She paused and looked away. Why couldn't this just be simple? *Because you're making it harder than it has to be*, Jessica's heart told her.

She held up her hand. "None of that is important. The truth is, I love you." She turned to see what his reaction might be. "It terrifies me in a way I can't even begin to explain, but that's the truth, and I thought from something Kate had told me that you might be given to feeling the same way. Then when I saw you coming home, I just forgot myself and let my heart take over. I'm sorry."

"Truly?"

She shook her head in confusion. "Truly what?"

"You're truly sorry? Sorry you let your heart guide you? Sorry you threw yourself into my arms and kissed me?" He stepped closer and reached his hand up to touch her cheek.

Jessica felt her breath quicken. "No."

"No?" he questioned, the tiniest grin causing his mustache to rise.

Jessica lifted her chin ever so slightly. "No, I'm not sorry. I'm powerfully embarrassed, but I'm not sorry."

"Why are you embarrassed?"

"Because I made a fool of myself," Jessica replied. "Something I seem to do quite a bit when you're around."

This made Devon laugh. "If this is you being a fool, then I like it, and I wouldn't have you change a single thing. But I don't think this is foolish."

"No?" It was Jessica's turn to question.

He moved his face closer to hers, and she knew without a doubt he would kiss her. Could it be, her mind reeled, that he did return her feelings? Was it possible he loved her?

"You never gave me much of a chance to speak to you on the matter," he whispered, his breath warm on her face. "I don't think being in love is foolish. Especially when both people feel the same way."

She felt her eyes grow wide. "Truly?" She found herself repeating the very word he'd used earlier. "You love me?"

"I do," he murmured. "And I'd like to respond to your earlier greeting."

His lips closed upon hers, and his arms pulled her tightly into his embrace. Jessica's knees grew weak. She embraced the overwhelming joy that flooded her heart and soul. It seemed impossible that Devon was standing there, saying the things he was saying, kissing her as he was kissing her, but it also seemed so right. Jessica thought it felt perfect, as if they were meant for each other.

Devon kissed her lips, then let his kisses trail up her cheek to her eyebrow and then to her forehead. Jessica sighed and put her head against his shoulder.

"You know, you seem to make a habit of kissing men you aren't engaged to," he whispered.

Jessica laughed and pulled away. "Then maybe you'd better rectify the situation."

He smiled. "I'd be happy to." He pulled out a ring from his pocket. "This belonged to my grandmother. It's the same one I gave to Jane and the same one she brought back to me. But it's special to me, and I hope you'll overlook her involvement with it. This ring was worn by my grandmother for some fifty-seven years of marriage. She adored my grandfather, and he adored her. I want that kind of marriage, Jess. I want that for us. Will you accept this ring and my proposal of marriage?"

Tears coursed down Jessica's face. She took the ring and slipped it on her finger. It fit perfectly, the little carved gold band glittering in the moonlight. "The past is gone, but this ring will be a reminder to us both of what true love can endure and accomplish. I've prayed for this, asked God to send me the kind of man who could be a father to my son, as well as a husband to me." She looked up from the ring to meet Devon's passionate gaze. "Yes, I'll marry you."

Epilogue

June 1892

Ryan danced circles around his parents. Devon and Jessica Carter laughed to see the spectacle the small boy was creating.

"People comin' to see me," he said happily. "Dey comin' now."

"Yes, Son," Devon said, scooping the boy up into his arms. "Buck is bringing us a whole bunch of people." He rubbed the thick dark curls that covered Ryan's head.

"I hope we aren't making a mistake," Jessica said, nervously twisting her hands. She'd been married less than two months to Devon, and now they were opening Windridge as a resort ranch. "I mean, maybe you were right. Maybe we should never have let this thing get this far."

Devon eyed her with a raised brow and laughed. "Now you're willing to listen to me?"

Jessica shook her head. "Oh, Devon, did we make the wrong decision?" She could see the stage approaching and knew that within a few minutes, total strangers would descend on their steps.

"Remember why you thought to do this in the first place?"

Jessica nodded. "I thought it would make a quiet respite."

"Not only that, but you saw it as the perfect opportunity to share God with other folks."

"But what if they don't like it here?"

Devon shrugged. "What if they don't? We have the partnership intact with the Rocking W, and it'll only be another year or so before we're completely solvent."

"Maybe we shouldn't have taken on all those cattle," Jessica said. "I mean you had to hire all those hands, and now we've got these people coming and—"

Devon put his finger to her lips, and Ryan leaned over to follow suit by placing his pudgy hand against her mouth. "Mama, peoples comin' to see me."

Jessica pulled back and smiled. "All right. I get your point. We can't do anything about it now. The guests are already here."

"Exactly. Let's give it a try. We've got a full summer ahead of us with plenty of folks who want to see what a dude ranch is all about. Let's just wait and see what happens. We might both be so happy to be done with it by the end of summer that we'll never even want to consider doing this another year."

"I suppose you're right," Jessica replied.

"I've no doubt people will find this place a blessing," Devon said. "I know I have."

Jessica sighed. "So have I."

Buck approached with the stage-styled carriage and brought the horses to a stop not ten feet from the front walk.

"Well, they're here," Devon said, shifting Ryan in his arms.

"Peoples here, Mama!" Ryan called and clapped his hands.

Jessica laughed at his enthusiasm. Through the open windows of the carriage, Jessica could hear animated conversation between the passengers. She couldn't make out the words, but knew that soon enough she'd probably hear plenty from her guests. Just then, Buck scrambled down from the driver's seat and positioned the stepping platform for the passengers. The door opened, and to Jessica's surprise the passengers poured out arguing—bickering over something that Jessica couldn't quite make out.

"Well, here are your people," Devon said, leaning close to whisper. "Looks like they could use a good dose of peace and quiet."

She nodded. "I suppose we'd better welcome them before they kill each other."

She stepped forward and rang a triangular bell that hung at the edge of the porch. The metallic ring caused everyone to fall into silence and give her their full attention.

Jessica gave them what she hoped was her friendliest smile. "Good afternoon. I'm Jessica Carter, and this is my husband, Devon, and son, Ryan. We'd like to welcome you to the house on Windridge."

TRACIE PETERSON

Tracie Peterson, best-selling author of nearly fifty fiction titles and one nonfiction title, lives and works in Montana. As a Christian, wife, mother, and writer (in that order), Tracie finds her slate quite full.

First published as a columnist for the *Kansas Christian* newspaper, Tracie resigned that position to turn her attention to novels. After signing her first contract with Barbour Publishing in 1992, her first novel appeared in 1993 under the pen name of Janelle Jamison, and the rest is history. She has over twenty-three titles with Heartsong Presents' book club and stories in six separate anthologies from Barbour, including the best-selling *Alaska*. From Bethany House Publishing, Tracie has several historical series, as well as a variety of women's fiction titles.

Voted favorite author for 1995, 1996, and 1997 by the Heartsong Presents readership, Tracie enjoys the pleasure of spinning stories for readers and thanks God for the imagination He's given. "I find myself blessed to be able to work at a job I love. I get to travel, study history, spin yarns, spend time with my family, and hopefully glorify God. I can't imagine a more perfect arrangement."

Tracie also does acquisitions work for Barbour Publishing and teaches workshops at a variety of conferences, giving workshops on inspirational romance, historical research, and anything else that offers assistance to fellow writers.

See Tracie on the Internet at http://members.aol.com/tjpbooks/

THREADS OF LOVE

Judith McCoy Miller

Chapter 1

The sounds in the kitchen caused Delphinia to startle awake, and she immediately felt the dreadful taste of bile rise in her throat. Jumping from her bed, she ran to the washstand, removed the pitcher, and expelled the few remains of last night's supper into the chipped bowl. Looking into the small mirror that hung over the washstand, she was met by a ghostly likeness of herself. *I can't bear this; I just can't,* she thought as she rinsed her mouth and reached for a small linen towel to wipe her perspiring forehead. Making her way back to bed, she wrapped herself in a quilt and prayed that this was a bad dream.

"Oh please, dear Lord, let me go to sleep and wake up to my mama's laughter in the kitchen. Let this all be a horrible nightmare."

Instead, she heard her father's harsh command, "I hear ya awake in there, Delphinia. This ain't no day to be lazin' around. You get yourself dressed and do it *now*. You still got things to pack, and time's getting short."

"I know, Pa, but I'm feeling poorly. Maybe you'd better tell that man I won't be able to go with him. I'm sure he won't want some sickly girl," she replied in a feeble attempt to dissuade him.

She heard her father's heavy footsteps come across the kitchen floor toward her room, knowing that she had tested his patience too far. The bedroom door swung open, and he said in a strained voice, "Either you get yourself dressed, or you'll travel as you are."

"Yes, Pa," she answered, knowing her efforts to deter him had failed and that she would soon be leaving home.

Trying to keep her stomach in check, she donned a green gingham dress and quickly pinned her hair in place. Not giving much care to her appearance, she sat down on the bed and placed her remaining belongings into the old trunk. Her hands trembled as she picked up a frayed shawl, threw it around her shoulders, and lay back on the bed, willing herself to think of happier days.

The noise outside the house brought her back to the present. How long had she been lying there? The streaming rays of sunlight that patterned the room told her that it must be close to noon. Her heart began to pound, and immediately she began pressing down the gathers of her skirt in a slow, methodical motion. There was a loud knock at the heavy wooden door, followed by footsteps and the sound of voices. Minutes passed, and then she heard her father calling out her name. She picked up her bonnet and sat staring at it, unwilling to accept that the time of departure had arrived. Her father called out again, and she could hear the impatience in his voice. Knowing she dared not provoke him further, she compelled herself to rise from the bed and walk to the kitchen.

There, standing before her, was Jonathan Wilshire, the man who had bargained with Pa to take her away from the only home she had ever known. It was a certainty that she would dislike him. She had prayed and prayed about her predicament, but somehow God had not seen fit to eliminate this man from her life. She had begun praying that his horse would break a leg, and he would not arrive. But soon she was asking forgiveness for thinking in such an unkind manner. She briefly considered a plea to God that Mr. Wilshire get lost on the journey, but she knew that would not be a Christian prayer, for he had children at home that required his safe return. So, in desperation, she did as her mama had told her many times: "When you don't know for sure what to pray for, just turn it over to the Lord, for He knows your heart and will provide the best way." Fervent prayers had been uttered each night outlining the folly of the decision to send her west and requesting the Lord's assistance in finding a remedy. Although she was not sure what was best for her, she knew that leaving for Kansas with Mr. Wilshire would be a mistake. Given the amount of time she had spent in dissertation, she had been positive the Lord would agree and save her from this pending disaster.

Just look at what results that had produced! Here was Jonathan Wilshire, standing in her kitchen and looking fit as a fiddle, ready to take her to some farm in Kansas and turn her into a mama for his children. Where had her mother ever gotten the notion that praying like that would work?

Her heart had slowed down somewhat, and she began to feel outrage and frustration begin to take over. She stepped toward her father and had just begun to open her mouth and voice that anger when, sensing her wrath, he said, "Delphinia, this is Jonathan Wilshire, the gentlemen we have discussed."

Once again, her palms began pressing down the gathers in her skirt, and, looking directly at her father, she blurted out, "We never *discussed* Mr. Wilshire, Papa. You merely announced you were sending me away with him."

Delphinia could sense the discomfort she was causing for both men. Feeling she must press any advantage that could be gained, she continued with her tirade. "Papa, I've told you over and over that I don't want to leave you. It's been only a few months since Mama died, and I don't want to lose you, too. . . and my home, Papa. Must I leave my home?" Tears had begun to roll down her cheeks and onto the pale green bodice of her frock. Her father stared at her in disbelief. She had never, in all of her seventeen years, questioned his decisions. Now, here she was, humiliating him in front of a total stranger. Not knowing if it was caused by anger or embarrassment, she watched as his short, thick neck and unshaven face quickly began to turn from deep tan to purplish red, clear to his receding hairline. Given the choices, she was hoping for embarrassment because her papa was not easy to contend with when angry. But as soon as their eyes met, she knew he was not only angry but that he had reached the "boilin' stage," as Mama used to call it. Well, so be it. He was sending her away, and she was going to tell him how she felt. After all, she had given God a chance to get things in order, and He had certainly missed the mark!

"Delphinia," her father roared, "you will fetch the rest of your possessions immediately and place them in Mr. Wilshire's wagon. We've already loaded the other trunks. I'll hear no more of this nonsense. You know you're goin' along with Mr. Wilshire to look after his children. He's ready to pull out. Now mind your tongue, Girl, and do as you're told."

Eyes downcast and knowing that her fate was sealed, she quietly murmured, "Of course, Papa. I'll only be a minute."

Walking back to her room, Delphinia allowed herself one last look at the dwelling she had called home for all of her seventeen years. She entered her sparsely furnished bedroom for the last time, grabbed the handle on the side of her trunk, and pulled it into the kitchen.

Making her way toward the center of the kitchen, her father once again began with his issuance of instructions. "Now mind your manners, Sis. I've told Mr. Wilshire that you know your reading and writing and can teach his youngsters what schooling they need to know."

Turning to the stranger, he continued his diatribe, "She even knows how to work with her numbers, and so if there isn't a school nearby, she'll make a fine teacher for you."

He sounds like he's selling a bill of goods, Delphinia thought. Besides, all of her studies had been through her mama's efforts. Pa had always said it was a waste of time and had chided Ma for spending time on Delphinia's lessons. But her mother had stood firm and said it was important for both girls and boys to know how to read, write, and do their figures. When Pa would become too obstinate about the subject, Ma would smile sweetly and tell him that no child of hers would be raised not knowing how to read God's Word. Then Pa would continue. Now here he was, using that bit of education to get rid of her.

Her thoughts ran rampant, wondering what kind of bargain had been struck between her pa and this man. Delphinia was not told the particulars, and she knew her pa would never divulge all of the information to her. She knew he just wanted to be free of any responsibility. Ever since Mama had died, all he could talk about was his going to search for gold and how he would be rich and free of his worries. He had talked about it for years, but Mama had always managed to keep him levelheaded and made him realize that going in search of gold was not the way of life for a married man with a family.

Well, he was "free" now. Mama had died, and Delphinia was being shipped off with this stranger to some unknown place out West. Once again, she began to feel the tears well up in her eyes, but she made up her mind that she would not cry in front of her pa again. If he wanted to be rid of her, so be it. She had no choice in the matter.

Suddenly, she felt a hand reach across hers and heard Mr. Wilshire saying, "Here, I'll take that out to the wagon for you. You tell your pa good-bye, and we'll be on our way. I'll be waiting outside."

Delphinia glanced up. Her father's anger had diminished, and he looked as though he might feel a bit of remorse. "I'm sorry, Pa. I know I shouldn't have talked to you with such disrespect. Mama would be very unhappy with my behavior. But I don't think she'd be happy with yours either," she added. When he gave no response, she continued, "Don't you think she'd want us to be together, now that she's gone?"

"I suppose, Delphinia, your mama would think that. You gotta remember, though, your mama knew I was never one to stay in one place too long. I've been living in the same place for nigh onto twenty years now. I kept my bargain with your ma, and we never took off for the unknown lands farther west. But now I just have to go. There's nothing left here for me."

His words were like a knife in her heart. Was she really nothing to him? Could he think so little of her that it was more important to go searching for something he would probably never find?

"I've made proper arrangements for you, Girl, and I know you'll be well cared for. Mr. Wilshire has a nice homestead in Kansas and needs help. It's a good arrangement for all of us, and once I get settled, I'll let you know my whereabouts. It'll all work out for the best." He bent down, put an arm around her, and started leading her toward the door.

"What's to become of our home? Will I never see it again? You can't just go off and leave it." She pulled back and looked up at him. Her large, brown eyes were once again wet with tears.

"Now, never you mind; I've taken care of all of that. Mama and I had to borrow against this place when times was bad, and I'm just turning it back over to the bank. I got a little cash to get me going and what with. . . Well, I've got enough to get set up when I hit the goldfields." Once again, he was moving her toward the door.

"Oh, Pa, I just don't think I can bear it," she murmured, reaching up and throwing her arms about his neck.

"Now, now, Girl, come along. It's all gonna be just fine. . .you'll see," he said, drawing her toward the wagon.

With Mr. Wilshire's help, Delphinia made her way up onto the seat of the buckboard, and, without looking back, she raised her hand in a small, waving gesture to her pa.

Mr. Wilshire slapped the reins, and the horses moved out.

Chapter 2

A wave of panic began to take over Delphinia. Here she was, on her way to who knew where, with a man she did not even know, and her pa thought it was just fine. And to think she had prayed so fervently about this! God must have been extremely busy when she issued her petitions, because she was absolutely sure that this could not be His plan for her life. Anyone could see this was a mistake. After all, she was only seventeen, and she could see the folly of this situation. And God was. . . Well, nobody knew how old God was, but He was certainly well over seventeen. Surely He would get her out of this mess. There must be some rescue in store for her. That was it! God had already planned her deliverance from Jonathan Wilshire!

Feeling somewhat comforted by the thought, Delphinia realized she hadn't even gotten a good look at Mr. Wilshire since his arrival. She didn't want to talk to him just now, but she was curious. Cautiously she glanced over his way, only to be met by two of the bluest eyes she had ever seen, and they were staring directly into hers.

She was so startled that she blurted out the first thing that came to mind. "Why would you need to come all the way to Illinois to find someone to care for your children?"

He did not answer but let out the deepest laugh she had ever heard.

"Just why is that such a funny question?" she countered.

"Well," he slowly answered, "I've not had a line of ladies waiting at my front door whom I'd consider suitable to meet the needs of my homestead."

Delphinia was not quite sure what that meant, but she knew she did not want to pursue the matter further, at least for now. "Why are we traveling to Kansas with a wagon train? Wouldn't it be quicker and easier to travel by train?" she queried, not sure which would be worse: an arduous trip by wagon train or arriving in Kansas quickly.

"You're right. It would be faster by train, and that had been my intention. I arrived in Illinois a couple days before I was to fetch you, and I was staying in town, planning to secure you shortly before our train would depart for Kansas. But, the day I arrived in Cherryvale, a group of folks from the wagon train were also in town. Their wagon master had become ill and wasn't able to continue his duties. Of course, they need to keep moving, or the snows will stop them in the mountains," he explained.

"What does that have to do with us returning by train?" she interrupted, having expected a simple answer.

"They weren't able to find anyone to help them. The hotel owner heard of their plight and related it to me. I believe God puts us in certain places at certain times for a purpose," he continued. "The folks on this wagon train are good people with a need. I can fulfill that need by leading them as far as Kansas. I've talked with the wagon master, and he thinks he'll be able to take over by then. . .probably before."

"But what if the wagon master isn't well by the time we reach Kansas? What if he dies?" she asked. "Then what?"

"Well, I don't believe either of those things will happen. But if they should, I've talked with folks on the wagon train and explained I can go on no farther. They'll either have to winter in Kansas or find someone else to lead them the rest of the way. They're willing to put their trust in God that this will work, and so am I," he responded.

She was trusting in God also but not for the same things as Jonathan Wilshire.

"I'll be needing to pick up our supplies," he stated, pulling the horses to a halt in front of the general store, "so if there's anything you think you might be wanting for the journey, better get on down and come in with me."

"Oh, I'll just trust your judgment, Mr. Wilshire, as I've certainly never purchased supplies for a long journey and wouldn't have any idea what you might be needing," she stated rather smugly. He needn't think he was getting someone here in Illinois who was all that suitable either! Besides, she hadn't fibbed, for she didn't have the faintest idea what might be needed on such a journey.

Delphinia watched him jump down from the wagon, and she could not help but admire his strength and size. Her pa was not a small man, but Mr. Wilshire was quite tall, and his shoulders were remarkably broad. She had never seen a man quite so large. Now that she thought about it, he was somewhat intimidating in his size. *Why haven't I noticed that before?* She wondered. She was surprised she hadn't been frightened by him but then he had been sitting down in the wagon before she had actually taken notice of him. *Well,* she determined, *I'll not be afraid of anyone, and that includes this giant of a man.*

A loud voice roused her from her thoughts. "Phiney, Phiney, are you sleeping up there?" Delphinia looked down in horror at Mr. Wilshire standing beside the wagon.

"You weren't speaking to me, were you, Mr. Wilshire?" she inquired.

"Of course I was," he stated, wondering who else she thought he might be talking to. "I was asking if you'd be wanting to choose some cloth to make a few dresses and britches for the children. They have a good selection here. . .better than the general store back home. Besides, we'll probably not go into Council Grove going back."

She stared at him, dumbfounded. "No, wait. What was it you were calling me?"

"Well, your name of course. I was trying to get your attention. Seemed like you were off daydreaming."

"I mean, what name did you call me?" she persisted.

"Phiney. I called you Phiney. Why?" he questioned.

"Mr. Wilshire," she said with as much decorum as she could muster, "my name is *Delphinia.* Delphinia Elizabeth Hughes—not Phiney, not Delphie, and not Della. Why would you ever call me such a name?" she asked in disgust.

He looked up at her and grinned. "Seems a mite formal to me. And you feel free to call me Jonathan if you like. I been meaning to tell you that anyhow. Mr. Wilshire. . .well, that's kind of formal too. Besides, I always think people are addressing my pa when they call me that."

A frown was etched on Delphinia's face as she looked down at him, her brown eyes flashing fire. "Mr. Wilshire, I do not think my name is too formal. My mother took great care in choosing my name, and I am very proud of it."

Jonathan's eyes sparkled with humor as he watched her trying to restrain her temper. If he was any judge, she would soon be stomping her foot to make a point of this whole issue. He knew he should let it drop, but for some reason he was enjoying the display of emotion she was exhibiting for him.

"I'm mighty pleased you're proud of your name, Phiney. I've always thought it was nice if folks liked their names," he said with a benevolent grin. With that, he moved on toward the general store, while calling over his shoulder, "Better hop on down if we're gonna get some yard goods picked out."

It took all her forbearance not to scream after him, "Don't call me Phiney," but before she could give it further thought, he had disappeared into the store.

She was fairly bristling as she climbed down from the wagon, her bonnet askew and with tendrils of blond hair poking out in every direction. Jonathan stood behind some shelves of dry goods and, with wry amusement, watched her dramatic entry. He did not wish to continue upsetting her, but she really was quite a picture to behold, her cheeks turned rosy and skirt gathered up in her fists. Realizing she was looking for him, he stepped out from behind the shelves.

"Glad you decided to come in and have a look around," he grinned. Ignoring his barb, she made her way to the table of yard goods.

"You realize, of course, Mr. Wilshire, that I have no idea what anyone in your home may need. I don't even know who lives there," she proclaimed, wanting to be sure he realized she was not a willing participant in the future that her father had planned.

"Guess you've got a point," he commented, leaning against the table and causing it to almost topple with his weight. "There's surely no time for going into that now, so just pick some material you like for boys and girls and maybe some for new curtains. Oh, and Granny might like something for a new dress too."

Her mouth had formed a large oval by the time he had finished his remarks, but before she could even exclaim, he added, "And don't forget to get something for yourself too."

Not waiting for a reply, he immediately moved on to look at tools, and Delphinia found herself staring back at the clerk, an older woman she had never seen before, who was impatiently waiting to take Delphinia's order and get to other customers. Having never before had such a task placed before her, Delphinia smiled pleasantly and approached the expectant clerk. "I'll take some of each of these," she said, pointing to six different fabrics.

Delphinia straightened her shoulders, her arms crossed in front of her, and stood there waiting. When the clerk made no move to cut the yard goods, Delphinia, looking perplexed, urged her on, stating, "That's all I'll be needing. You can cut it now."

"Would you care to give me some idea just how much you'd like of each fabric?" the clerk questioned in a hushed voice and added a smile.

Sensing that she had the sympathy of this woman, Delphinia answered, "Just whatever you think I should have."

"I'll cut enough for curtains to cover four windows out of this cream color, and you'll be able to get a dress for your little girl and a skirt for you out of this blue calico. Let's see, we'll cut a measure of this heavy fabric for some britches for your little boys, and this brown print might make up into a nice dress for your grandmother."

Delphinia watched in absolute astonishment. Did this woman actually think she looked old enough to have a husband and houseful of children? Well, she was not about to explain her circumstances to a total stranger. She would just smile and take whatever help she could get. Of course, Mr. Wilshire was also going to need all the help he could get, for she was going to educate him to the fact that he had chosen the wrong person for his Kansas family.

"Will you be wanting any thread or lace to go along with this?"

Delphinia was so deep in thought that the question caused her to startle to attention. "Whatever you think. I'll just trust your judgment," she smiled.

The clerk finished quickly, wrapped the goods in brown paper, and tied it with heavy twine. Jonathan moved forward and requested the clerk to add the cost to his other purchases, which were being totaled, and he began to usher Delphinia out of the store.

Turning back, Delphinia walked to the clerk and whispered, "Thank you for your help. I'll be praying for you this evening and thanking the Lord for your help."

"Oh, my dear, thank you," the clerk replied. "It was a pleasure to assist you. It's a long trip you're making, but you're young and strong. With that able-bodied husband of yours, you'll do just fine."

"He's not my husband," Delphinia retorted before thinking.

"Oh, well, I'll certainly be praying for you too, my dear," the clerk replied.

Delphinia felt her cheeks turn a crimson red, and she began to stutter a reply, but the clerk had already turned and was helping another customer. Feeling totally humiliated, she briskly made her way out of the store and back to the wagon where Jonathan was waiting.

Without a glance in his direction, she made her way around the wagon and quickly climbed up onto the seat. Not knowing how many people had overheard their conversation, Delphinia was anxious to join the wagon train as soon as possible.

"I thought maybe you'd like to have dinner in town. There's a good restaurant down the street," Jonathan offered.

"I'm not hungry. Let's get going," she answered, her voice sounding somewhat shrill.

"What's wrong?" he questioned.

"Nothing. Let's just go," she replied.

"I'm not going anywhere until you tell me what's wrong," Jonathan said.

Delphinia knew from the set of his jaw that she was not going to have her way. Grudgingly she recounted the conversation, trying to keep as much composure as possible.

"Is that all?" he questioned. "I'll be right back after I explain our situation to the woman," and he started to make his way into the store.

"No, please," she countered. "I'd rather go no further with this. Let's just go. I'm honestly not hungry."

Sensing her discomfort and not wishing to cause her further embarrassment, Jonathan jumped up onto the seat, flicked the reins, and yelled, "Giddyup," to the team of brown mares.

Neither of them said anything, but as they grew closer to the wagon-train camp, Jonathan sensed an uneasiness come over Delphinia. She was moving restlessly on the wooden seat, and her hands began pressing the gathers in her skirt as he had seen her do on several earlier occasions.

In an attempt to make her feel more comfortable, he said, "You'll not be staying in my wagon at night. Mrs. Clauson has agreed you can stay with her."

Delphinia did not respond, but he noticed she was not fidgeting quite so much. This pleased him, though he was not sure why.

Slowing the team, he maneuvered the buckboard beside one of the covered wagons that had formed a circle for the night.

"Thought maybe you wasn't gonna make it back before supper," a voice called out.

"I'd have gotten word to you if we weren't coming back this evening," Jonathan replied as he jumped down from the wagon and held his arms up to assist Delphinia.

As she was making her descent from the wagon, Jonathan matter-of-factly said, "Mr. and Mrs. Clauson, I'd like you to meet Phiney. . .Phiney Hughes. It was *Hughes,* wasn't it?"

He watched her eyes once again take on that fiery look as she very formally stated, "Mr. and Mrs. Clauson, my name is Delphinia Elizabeth Hughes. Mr. Wilshire seems to find it a difficult name. I, however, prefer to be called *Delphinia*. . .not Phiney." Smiling sweetly at the Clausons, she added, "Pleased to meet you both."

Turning, she gave Jonathan a look meant to put him in his place. He grinned back at her but soon found himself trying to control a fit of laughter when Mr. Clauson replied, "We're real pleased to meet you too, Phiney."

Not wanting to give him further cause for laughter and certain that a woman would better understand the proper use of her name, Delphinia decided she would discuss the matter of her name privately with Mrs. Clauson.

Jonathan and Mr. Clauson began unloading the wagon, and the older woman, while placing her arm around Delphinia's shoulder, said, "Come on over here with me, Phiney. I'm just finishing up supper, and we can visit while the menfolk finish unloading."

So much for another woman's understanding, Delphinia decided, moving over toward the fire. Perhaps she should just let the issue of her name drop with the Clausons. After all, once they arrived in Kansas, she would probably never see them again. Mr. Wilshire, though, was another matter!

"Is there anything I can do to help?" Delphinia inquired.

"No, no. Just set a spell and tell me about yourself. You sure are a pretty thing, with all that blond hair and those big brown eyes. Jonathan figured you probably weren't a looker since your pa was willin' to let you go west with a stranger. Thought maybe you couldn't get a husband."

Noting the look of dismay that came over Delphinia's face and the effect her words had on the young woman, Mrs. Clauson hurried to add, "He didn't mean nothin' bad by that. It's just that most folks wouldn't let their daughter take off with a complete stranger, let alone be advertisin' in a paper to. . . Oh, I'm just jumblin' this all up and hurtin' you more. Mr. Clauson says

I need to think 'fore I open my mouth. I'm real sorry if I upset you, Phiney."

Lifting her rounded chin a little higher, Delphinia straightened her back and said, "There's no need for you to feel concern over what you've said. After all, I'm sure you've spoken the truth of the matter."

Chapter 3

Neither Delphinia nor Mrs. Clauson spoke for a time, each lost in her thoughts. Delphinia was not sure how long she had been reflecting on the older woman's words when she noticed that Mrs. Clauson was about to serve the evening meal.

"It looks like you've about got dinner ready. Shall I ladle up the stew?"

Mrs. Clauson turned toward the large pot hanging over a slow-burning fire and shook her head. "No, no, I'll do it. You just tell the menfolk we're ready. They should be about done unloading the buckboard and can finish up after supper."

Delphinia rose and, after locating the men and announcing dinner, slowly continued walking toward Jonathan's wagon. Jonathan pulled off his wide-brimmed hat, wiped his brow with a large, dark blue kerchief, and watched Delphinia as she continued toward his wagon. Her head lowered, her shoulders slumped, she was a picture of total dejection.

"Where are you going? You just told us dinner was ready."

Acting as though she did not hear, Delphinia continued along the outer edge of the circled wagons.

"Hey, wait a minute," Jonathan called as he quickened his step to catch up. When he came even with her, she glanced over and said, "I'm not hungry. You go on and eat. Mrs. Clauson's waiting on you."

Realizing something was amiss, Jonathan gently took hold of her shoulders and turned her to face him. "Phiney, you've got to eat. I know it's hard for you to leave your home, but please come have some dinner."

When there was no reaction to his use of "Phiney," he knew she was upset, but she turned and walked back to the campfire with him. She took the steaming plate of food offered by Mrs. Clauson who, Jonathan noted, seemed somewhat downcast.

Giving him a tentative smile, Mrs. Clauson asked, "Would you be so good as to lead us in prayer before we begin our meal, Jonathan?"

As they bowed their heads, Jonathan gave thanks for the food provided and asked God's protection over all the folks in the wagon train as they began the journey. Delphinia was surprised, however, when Jonathan proceeded to ask the Lord to give her strength as she left her father and all those she knew to make a new home in Kansas. She was pleased that he cared enough about her feelings to ask God to give her strength. As she looked up at Jonathan after he had pronounced "amen," he was smiling at her and remarked, "Well, eat up, Phiney." At that moment, she was not sure if she needed more strength to endure leaving home or to put up with his determination to call her Phiney!

As soon as the meal was over, Delphinia and Mrs. Clauson proceeded to wash the dishes while the men finished loading the covered wagon, and Jonathan returned the buckboard to town. By the time he got back to the campsite, folks were beginning to bed down for the night.

"Why don't you get the things you'll be needin' for tonight and bring them over to our wagon? We best turn in soon," Mrs. Clauson advised.

Nodding in agreement, Delphinia made her way to the wagon. Climbing in, she spotted the old brown trunk and slowly lifted the heavy lid. Pulling out her nightgown, she caught sight of her beloved quilt. Reaching in, she pulled it out of the trunk and hugged it close.

She was so caught up in her thoughts that Mrs. Clauson's "Do you need help, Phiney?" caused her to almost jump out of her skin.

"No, I'm coming," she replied, wrapping the quilt around her and closing the trunk. She made her way down, careful not to trip over the covering that surrounded her.

After preparing for the night, Delphinia and Mrs. Clauson made themselves as comfortable as possible on pallets in the wagon. "Jonathan's been having some Bible readin' for us since he came to our rescue, but since he was gone so late tonight, he said we'll double up on readin' tomorrow night. The mister and me, well, we don't know how to read much, so it surely has been a pleasure to have Jonathan read the Scriptures for us," she whispered almost ashamedly.

"Oh, Mrs. Clauson, I would have read for you tonight, if I had known," Delphinia replied.

"Why aren't you just the one. Such a pretty girl and bright too. That Jonathan surely did luck out," she exclaimed.

Delphinia could feel her cheeks grow hot at the remark and knew it was meant as a compliment. All the same, she wished Mrs. Clauson would quit making it sound like Jonathan had just secured himself a wife.

Bidding the older woman good night, Delphinia spent a great deal of her prayer time petitioning the Lord to execute His rescue plan for her as soon as possible. She did give thanks for the fact that Jonathan seemed a decent sort and that she would have Mrs. Clauson with her for the journey. Once she had finished her prayers, she reached down and pulled the quilt around her, not that she needed the warmth, for in fact, it was nearly summer. Instead, it was the security that the wonderful quilt gave her, almost like a cocoon surrounding her with her mama's presence and love.

Many hours of love and laughter had been shared in completing what had seemed to Delphinia an immense project. Now, she was somewhat in awe that her mother had given so much time and effort to teaching her how to sew those many blocks and make the tiny, intricate stitches required for the beautiful pattern she had chosen.

When Delphinia had announced she wanted to make a quilt, her mother had explained it would take many hours of tedious work. She was doggedly determined about the idea, however, and her mother had patiently shown her each step of the way, allowing Delphinia to make and repair her own mistakes on the beloved project. How they had laughed over some of those mistakes and, oh, the hours spent ripping out and restitching until it was just right. Mama had always said that anything worth doing was worth doing right. And when that last stitch had been sewn and the quilt was finally completed, Mama had abundantly praised her hard work and perseverance. She had even called for a celebration and, using the good teapot and china plates, served Delphinia some of her special mint tea and thick slices of homemade bread smeared with strawberry preserves.

Tears began to slide down Delphinia's cheeks as she thought of those wonderful memories. Had it been only three years since she had enjoyed that special celebration? It seemed an eternity. In fact, it seemed like Mama had been gone forever, yet she knew it wasn't even six months since she had died. Sometimes she had trouble remembering just what her mother looked like, and yet other times it seemed that Mama would walk in the door any minute and call her for supper or ask for help hanging a curtain. How she missed her and the stability she had brought to their home! It seemed to Delphinia that her life had been in constant change and turmoil since the day Mama died.

Delphinia closed her eyes, hoping that sleep would soon overtake her. Her mind wandered back to stories her mother had related of how she had come west to Illinois after she and Pa had married. Mama had tried to convince him it would be a better life for them back East, but he was bound and determined to see new lands. It had been a difficult trip for Mama. She had lived a life of relative ease. Having been born the only daughter in a family of six boys had been cause for much jubilation, and when she later contracted rheumatic fever as a child, it had made her family all the more determined to protect her. Delphinia remembered Mama talking about all those uncles and the grandparents she had never known. Mama had made certain that Delphinia knew that her grandfather had been a preacher and that he had held great stock in everyone's learning how to read—not just the boys. He had made sure that Delphinia's mama was taught the same lessons as the boys. In fact, she had gone to school longer than any of the boys so that she could receive a teaching certificate, just in case she did not get married. Her pa wanted to be sure she would have a respectable profession. But she did get married six months later. Less than two months after the ceremony, they made their trip west to Illinois.

They had settled in a small house a few miles from Cherryvale. Pa had gone to work for the blacksmith who owned the livery stable. Delphinia knew her mama had been lonely. They did not get to town often, and she had longed for the company of other people. Papa would give in and take them to church about once a month to keep Mama in better spirits, but he was usually anxious to get home afterward. Mama always loved it when there would be a picnic dinner after services in the summer, and everyone would gather under the big elms, spread out some lunch, and visit; or when the preacher would hold Bible study in the afternoon. Papa had always seemed uncomfortable and would stay to himself while Mama fluttered from person to person, savoring each moment. Papa was not much of a churchgoer and had never studied the Bible. His folks had not seen any reason for his learning to read or write. They felt children were needed to help with the chores and plow the fields. Delphinia remembered Mama telling her how much she wanted to teach Papa to read, but he had put her off saying he was too old to learn. Sometimes, when Mama would be teaching Delphinia, Papa would become almost angry and storm out of the house. Mama always said it was nothing to worry about, that Papa just needed a breath of fresh air. *Maybe,* Delphinia thought, *Papa was angry at himself because he hadn't let Mama teach him, and now his little girl knew how to read, and he didn't.* Strange she hadn't thought of that before tonight.

She reflected on the time shortly before Mama's death, when she had overheard their hushed talk about not having money. That must have been when Papa borrowed against the house and how they managed to make ends meet until Mama died. When she once questioned about money, her mother had told her there was time enough for that worry when she became an adult and that she should not concern herself. Her parents had never included her in any family business or, for that matter, anything of an unpleasant nature. She had always been protected. . .until now.

Burrowing farther under the quilt, Mrs. Clauson's remark about Pa advertising to send her west was the last thought that lingered in her mind as she drifted into a restless sleep.

Chapter 4

Delphinia bounced along on the hard wooden seat, the blistering sun causing rivulets of perspiration to trickle down the sides of her face. She could feel her hair turning damp under the bonnet she was forced to wear in order to keep the sun from scorching her face. It seemed she had been traveling forever, and yet in spite of the heat and dust, she found joy in the beauty of the wildflowers and rolling plains.

Except for the short period of training that Jonathan had given her on how to handle the wagon and team, or those times when it was necessary to cross high waters and climb steep terrain, Jonathan rode his chestnut mare and few words passed between them. She was somewhat surprised when today he had tied his horse to the back of the wagon and climbed up beside her. Taking the reins from her hands, he urged the team into motion, and with a slight jolt, they moved forward in the slow procession taking them farther west.

"Sorry we haven't had more opportunity to talk," Jonathan commented, "but it seems I'm needed more to help keep the train moving. Besides, you've been doing just fine on your own with the wagon."

Delphinia did not respond but smiled inwardly at his compliment. When Jonathan had told her she would be driving the team, she had nearly fainted dead away. She, who had never handled so much as her pa's mules, was now expected to maneuver a team of horses and a lumbering wagon. With Jonathan's patience and her determination, she had finally mastered it, at least well enough not to run into the wagon in front of her.

"We're getting close to home, and I thought we should talk a little beforehand about what you can expect," Jonathan stated.

Delphinia expelled a sigh of relief. Finally, he was going to acquaint her with what lay ahead. Nodding her encouragement that he continue, she gave a slight smile, folded her hands, and placed them on her lap.

"My brother, Jacob, and his wife, Sarah, died some four months ago. Since that time Granny, that would be Sarah's mother, has been staying in the big cabin with the children. She's become quite frail and isn't able to handle five children and do chores any longer. Tessie, she's the oldest, doesn't think she needs anyone else to help out. At twelve, she's sure she can raise the others and take care of everything on her own.

Delphinia's face registered confusion and alarm. "Are you telling me the children I'm to take care of aren't yours? They are your brother's children? That there are five of them under age twelve? And I will be caring for all of them as well as doing chores and nursing their ill grandmother?" she questioned in rapid succession.

"Whoa, wait a minute," he laughed. "How can I answer your questions if you throw so many my way I can't even keep them straight?"

"I'm glad you find this a matter to laugh about," she exclaimed, feeling tears close at hand and not wanting to cry, "but I'm not at all amused."

"I'm really sorry, Phiney. I guess because I know the situation, it doesn't seem all that bleak to me. You'll get used to it too. It's just a matter of adjustment and leaning on the Lord. The children are fine youngsters, and although the older ones are having a little trouble dealing with the deaths of their folks, they're a big help."

"Just what ages are the children?" she asked, almost afraid to hear the answer.

"Well, there's Tessie; she's twelve and the oldest. She has the prettiest mop of red ringlets hanging down her back, which, I might add, match her temper. She also has a bunch of freckles, which she detests, right across the bridge of her nose. She's not very happy that I'm bringing you home to help out. She thinks she's able to cope with the situation on her own, even though she knows her ma and pa wouldn't want it that way. They'd want her to have time to be a little girl and get more schooling before she starts raising a family and taking care of a household. She's had the most trouble dealing with the deaths of her parents. Then there's Joshua; we call him Josh. He's seven and all boy. A good helper, though, and minds real well. He misses his ma's cooking and cheerfulness. I've tried to fill some of the gaps left by his pa. Then there's Joseph. We call him Joey, and he just turned four. He follows Josh around and mimics everything his big brother does, or at least gives it a good try. He doesn't understand death, but we've told him his folks are with Jesus, and he'll see them again when he gets to heaven. I think he misses his ma most at bedtime. Then there are the twins, Nathan and Nettie. They're eight months old now and quite a handful. I guess that just about sums up the situation," he said, giving the horses a slap of the reins to move them up closer in line.

"Sums it up!" Delphinia retorted. "That doesn't even begin to *sum it up.*"

"Well," he drawled, "why don't you just ask me questions, and I'll try to answer them. . .but one at a time, *please.*"

"All right, number one," she began, with teeth clenched and eyes fixed straight ahead, "why did you tell my pa you needed someone to help with your children if they're your brother's children?"

"From the way you asked that question, Phiney, I'm sure you think I concocted a whole string of untruths, presented them to your pa, and he just swallowed it like a fish swallowing bait. Believe me, that's not the way it was. He knew the truth. He knew the children weren't mine. I wrote him a letter telling him of my need and explaining the urgency for a young woman to help out."

"My pa can't read," she interrupted, sure she had caught him in a lie.

Leaning forward and resting his arms across his thighs in order to gain a look at her, he answered, "I know, Phiney. He had a friend of his, a Mr. Potter, read the letter to him and write to me. Mr. Potter started out the letter by telling me your pa could neither read nor write, but he was corresponding on his behalf."

Delphinia knew what Jonathan said was probably the truth. After Mama had died, when there was anything he did not want her to know about, Pa would get Mr. Potter at the bank to help him.

Jonathan watched as Delphinia seemed to sift through what he had said. It was obvious her father had told her very little about the plan he had devised or the correspondence and agreement that had followed. Not one to keep secrets, Jonathan asked, "Is there anything else you want to know?"

"Yes," she responded quietly. "Did you pay my pa for me?"

"No. That wasn't the way of it. You're not a slave or some kind of bonded person. I don't own you."

"But you did give him money, didn't you?' she questioned.

"Well—"

"Did you or didn't you give my pa money, Mr. Wilshire?" she determinedly inquired.

"There was money that exchanged hands, but not like I was buying you. He needed some financial help to get started with his prospecting and said he'd pay it back when he had a strike. I told him it wasn't necessary. I guess if you had to liken it to something, it was more like a dowry. . .only in reverse." Noting the shock that registered on her face at that remark, he continued, " 'Course we're not getting married so maybe that's not a good way to explain."

Delphinia could feel herself shrinking down, total humiliation taking over her whole being. How could her pa have done this to her? How could he think so little of her he would sell her to a total stranger? She was his flesh and blood. . .his only child. She had never felt so unloved and unwanted in her life.

She did not know how far they had come when she finally said, "Mr. Wilshire, please, would you explain how all of this happened to me?"

The question confirmed his earlier belief that her father had intentionally kept her uninformed. Her voice was so soft and sad, he couldn't possibly deny the request.

"I'll tell you what I know. Please understand, I won't be speaking for your pa or why he made his decisions. Only the choices I made. . .and the reasons."

When she did not respond but merely nodded her head, he continued. "Well now, I've told you about the deaths of my brother and his wife. I had come out to Kansas a year or so after them because Jake thought if I homesteaded the acreage next to his, we could work the land together. You know, help each other. I wanted to move west, and he thought it would give us an advantage. Sarah and Jake built their house near the western boundary of their land so when I arrived, we constructed a cabin on the eastern boundary of my tract, allowing me to be nearby. We'd always been close, and we decided it would be good for both of us. And we were right. It has been good for all of us. . .or at least it was until now. Jake and Sarah brought Granny Dowd with them when they came west. Sarah's pa was dead, and she didn't want to leave her mother alone. Granny's been a real wonder to all of us. What a worker! She was just like a little whirlwind, even when I came out here. Then about a year ago, she took ill and just hasn't snapped back to her old self. She seems to rally for awhile, but then she has to take to her bed again. She was always a big help to Sarah. I'm sure you'll like her, Phiney. She loves the Lord, her grandchildren, and the West, in that order." He smiled and glanced over at the dejected looking figure jostling along beside him, hoping for some sort of response.

Finally, realizing he was not going to continue further, Delphinia looked over and was greeted by a slight smile and his blue eyes full of sympathy. "You needn't look at me like you're full of pity for me or my situation, Mr. Wilshire. After all, you're the cause of this," she criticized.

"I didn't cause this, Miss Hughes," he replied. "I merely responded to your pa's ad in the newspaper." *Why can't this woman understand it was her father who was at fault?*

"Ah yes, the newspaper advertisement. I'd like to hear about that," she retorted, her face flushed not only from the rising sun but the subject under discussion.

"Well," he fairly drawled, "it appears we're getting ready to stop for the noon meal. I think we better finish this discussion after dinner when you're not quite so hot under the collar. Besides, I don't plan on discussin' this in front of the Clausons," he said as he pulled the team to a stop and jumped down.

He watched in absolute astonishment as she pushed away the arms he extended to assist her, lost her footing, and almost turned a complete somersault at his feet.

Looking up at him, her bonnet all cockeyed and her skirt clear to her knees, she defiantly stated, "I meant to do that."

"I'm sure you did, Phiney. I'm sure you did," he laughed as he began to walk toward the rear of the wagon to untie his mare.

"You could at least help me up," she hollered after him.

Glancing over his shoulder, he grinned and remarked, "Why would you need my help? I thought you planned that whole performance!" She could hear him chuckling as he led his horse down to the small creek.

"Ooh, that man," she mused, as she gathered herself up and proceeded to brush the dust from her dress and straighten her bonnet. "The Lord has a lot of work to do with him yet!"

Delphinia and Mrs. Clauson had just finished preparing the noon meal when Jonathan strode up to the older woman. "Phiney's wanting to be alone and talk to me, Mrs. Clauson, so I thought we'd take our plates down by the creek and eat, if you don't mind. I understand we're going to be makin' camp here since the Johnsons have a wagon wheel that needs repairing before we continue. It's been agreed that this is a fine spot to spend the night. Besides, we've traveled a considerable ways, and the rest will do us all good."

"I don't mind at all. You two go on and have a chat. I can sure understand you wanting some time alone," she said with a knowing grin.

Delphinia was positively glaring at him as he said, "Come along, Phiney. Let's go down by the water." He smiled, noting her feet appeared to have become rooted to the spot where she was standing. "I thought you wanted some answers, Phiney. Better come along. I may not have time later."

She did not want to give in and let him have his way. It was childish of her to act peevish over such a little thing. Her mother had always told her to save her arguments for the important issues. Perhaps this was one of those times she should heed that advice. Besides, if she did not go, he might hold true to his word and not discuss the matter later. Picking up her plate and cup, she followed along, calling over her shoulder, "We'll not be long." Mrs. Clauson merely smiled and nodded.

Hurrying to catch up, Delphinia watched as her coffee sloshed out of the metal cup, dribbling onto her apron. "Don't walk so fast. Your legs are longer than mine, and I can't keep up," she chided, angry that he once again had the last word.

"I'm sure that haughty little temper of yours gives you enough strength to keep up with anyone," he retorted.

"You needn't make unkind remarks, Mr. Wilshire," she exclaimed.

"I needn't make unkind remarks?" he exploded. "I've been listening to your thoughtless insinuations and comments all morning, but when I point out that you've got quite a little temper, you call that an unkind remark. I'd find that funny if I weren't so aggravated with you right now." He plopped himself down in the shade and shoved a large forkful of beans into his mouth.

"You have control over my life, but don't expect me to be happy about it. I'm not one to apologize unless I feel it's in order, Mr. Wilshire. However, since I don't know all that occurred between you and my pa, I will, just this once, offer my apology. Of course, I may withdraw it after I've heard all you have to say about this odious matter," she informed him authoritatively.

"Odious? Well, that's extremely considerate of you, *Miss Hughes,*" he responded, trying to keep the sarcasm from his voice but missing the mark.

Settling on the grass not far from him, she arranged her skirt and commanded, "You may now continue with your account of what occurred between you and my father, Jonathan."

He was so startled she had called him Jonathan, that he didn't even mind the fact that he had been given a direct order to speak. "I believe we left off when you asked about the newspaper advertisement," he began.

She nodded in agreement, and he noticed she was again pressing the pleats in her skirt with the palm of her hand as he had observed on several other occasions. *Must be a nervous habit,* he decided to himself.

"I've been trying to find help ever since Sarah and Jake died, but the few unmarried young women around our area were either, shall we say, unwholesome or looking for a husband in the bargain. Granny Dowd wouldn't accept unwholesome, and I wouldn't accept a wife. . .not that I plan to stay a bachelor forever. I want to, you know, marry. . . ," he stammered. "It's just that I plan on being in love with the woman I marry and sharing the same beliefs and goals. I don't want it to be some sort of bargain—"

"Mr. Wilshire, I really am not interested in your marriage plans. I'm just trying to find out why I'm here," Delphinia interrupted.

"That's what I'm trying to explain, if you'll just quit breaking in! Now, like I said, we didn't seem to find anyone who was suitable. Granny and I kept praying we would find an answer. A few weeks later, I was in town to pick up supplies. While I was waiting for my order to be filled, I picked up an old St. Louis newspaper that someone had left in the store. I looked through the advertisements and noticed one that stated: 'Looking for good home and possible teaching position immediately for my daughter.' There were instructions to write a Mr. Potter at the Union National Bank in Cherryvale, Illinois. I was sure it was an answer to prayer, and so was Granny.

"That night, we composed a letter to your pa telling him about Jake and Sarah, the children, and Granny's failing health. We told him we were Christians who tried to live by God's Word and would do everything possible to give you a good home in return for your help with the children and the house. We also told him we would pay you a small stipend each month so you'd have some independence."

Jonathan got up and moved toward the creek. Rinsing off his plate, he continued, "We sent that letter off the very next day and waited anxiously for a reply. When it finally came, we were almost afraid to open it for fear it would be a rejection of our offer. Instead, it started out with Mr. Potter telling us your pa could neither read nor write and that he was acting as his intermediary. Mr. Potter said your pa was pleased with the idea of your coming out to Kansas and that I should make arrangements to come to Illinois because he wanted to meet with me personally."

"If that's supposed to impress me as loving, fatherly concern for my well-being, I'm afraid it doesn't persuade me," Delphinia remarked.

"I'm not trying to justify anything. I'm just telling you how it all happened."

"I know. I'm sorry. Please continue, and I'll try to keep quiet," she murmured.

"I left Kansas the next morning. When I arrived in town, I went straight to the bank and met with Mr. Potter. He sent for your pa, and we met the afternoon I arrived in Cherryvale. I presented him with letters I had secured from our minister and some folks in the community during the time we waited for your father's response. Granny said she was sure you were the Lord's answer, and we were going to be prepared."

Delphinia couldn't help but smile at that remark. It sounded just like something her ma would have said.

"Mr. Potter looked over the letters I had with me, read them to your pa, and he seemed satisfied that we were upstanding folks who would do right by you. He said he was wanting to go farther west in hopes of striking gold and that it would be no life for a young woman. I agreed with him. . .not just because we needed you, but because I felt what he said was true."

Jonathan paused, took a deep breath, and continued, "He told me he had fallen on hard times and mortgaged his house for just about all it was worth. Mr. Potter confirmed the bank held notes on the property and that your pa was going to deed it back over to the bank for a very small sum of money. Your father said he needed extra funds to get supplies and have enough to keep him going until he hit gold. I gave him some money to cover those expenses, but nobody considered it to be like I was buying you, Phiney. I was just so thankful we had found you, I didn't want anything like your pa needin' a little money to stand in the way. Then when the wagon train needed help, I was sure God's hand was at work in all that was happening."

"Phiney, your pa had made up his mind he was going to go west and search for gold. Nothing was going to stop him. He'd have taken you with him if he had to, I suppose, but he was right—it would have been a terrible life for you. But if you're determined this is not what you want, I'll not fight you. The next town we get close to, I'll put you on a train and send you back to Cherryvale."

"To what?" she asked. "My father's gone, and if he isn't, he won't want to see me back. The bank owns our land. I have no one to go to," she said dejectedly.

"Your pa loves you, Phiney. He just has a restlessness that needs to be filled. He was careful about the arrangements he made for you. Your father was very concerned about your safety and well-being."

"He cared as long as I was out of his way," she retorted.

"You know, we all get selfish at times, and your pa was looking out for what he wanted first. That doesn't mean he loves you any less. I guess we just have to learn to believe what the Bible tells us about all things working for good to those that love the Lord."

Delphinia picked up her cup and plate, slowly walked to the water's edge, and rinsed them off as Jonathan issued a silent prayer that God would help Delphinia forgive her father and find peace and happiness in her new home with them.

"We better get back. Mrs. Clauson said we should wash some clothes since we don't get many opportunities like this one," she remarked, walking past him.

Jonathan was still sitting and watching her as she moved toward the wagons when she turned and said, "I guess you weren't at fault, so my apology stands."

Chapter 5

For the remainder of the day Delphinia was completely absorbed in her own thoughts. She wandered from one chore to another without realizing when she had begun one thing and ended another. After the evening meal, Jonathan led them in devotions and the moment the final amen had been uttered, Delphinia excused herself, anxious for the solitude the wagon would provide, even if only for an hour or two.

As Delphinia lay there, she began to pray. This prayer was different, however. It was not a request that God rescue her or that anything terrible happen to Mr. Wilshire. Rather, this prayer was that God would give her the ability to forgive her father for deserting her and grant her peace. Almost as an afterthought, she added that she could also use a bit of joy in her life. She fell asleep with that prayer on her lips.

Their few remaining days with the wagon train had passed in rapid succession when Jonathan advised her that the next day they would break away on their own. "I think the wagon master will be happy to see me leave. I've noticed it seems to upset him when folks look to me for leadership now that he's well again," he said with a grin.

" I think you may be right about that. I don't think some of the folks will look to him unless you're gone. They take to you more. Maybe it's because they view you as an answer to prayer," she responded.

"I hope I have been. Maybe someday I can be an answer to your prayers too," he stated and then, noting her uneasiness, quickly changed the subject. "It's faster if we break off and head north on our own. We can make it home by evening without pushing too hard, and it's safe, since the Indians around our area are pretty friendly. Besides, I've been gone quite a spell, and I'm anxious to get home, if that's all right with you."

"Whatever you think is best," she replied, but suddenly a multitude of emotions began to envelop her. She was going to miss the Clausons and the other folks she had gotten to know on the train. She was frightened that Granny and the children would not accept her. And how, oh how, was she going to be able to take care of a houseful of children? The thought of such responsibility almost overwhelmed her. *Lord, please give me peace and joy and lots and lots of help,* she quietly prayed.

The next morning they joined the Clausons for breakfast, and Jonathan led them in a final prayer, while Delphinia attempted to remain calm. Mrs. Clauson hugged her close and whispered in her ear to be brave, which only served to heighten her level of anxiety. She forced a feeble smile, took up the reins, and bid the horses move out.

Delphinia found herself deep in thought as they made their way to the Wilshire homestead. Jonathan rode the mare, scouting ahead, then riding back to assure her all was well, not allowing much time for conversation. With each mile they traversed, she felt fear beginning to well up inside. As Jonathan came abreast of the wagon to tell her they would be home in about three hours, he noticed she was holding the reins with one hand and pressing down the pleats of her skirt in that slow, methodical motion he had come to recognize as a sign of uneasiness.

"This looks like it might be a good spot for us to stop for a short spell. I'm sure you could use a little rest, and the horses won't mind either," he remarked, hoping to give them a little time to talk and perhaps find out what was bothering her.

"I thought you wanted to keep moving. . .get home as early as possible. Isn't that what you've told me every time you rode back from scouting?" she asked, her voice sounding strained.

"You're right; I did say that," he commented as he reached across his mare and took hold of the reins, bringing the team and wagon to a halt. "But I think a short rest will do us both some good."

Climbing down from his horse, he tied it to the back of the wagon and then, walking to the side of the wagon, stretched his arms up to assist her down. As her feet touched the ground, Delphinia looked up, and Jonathan was met by two of the saddest brown eyes he had ever seen. Instead of releasing her, he gathered her into his arms and held her, trying his best to give her comfort. Standing there with her in his arms, he realized he truly cared for this young woman.

Pushing away from him, Delphinia retorted, "I'm not a child anymore, Mr. Wilshire, so you needn't feel you have to stop and coddle me. I'll be fine, just fine," she said. Not wanting to ever again experience the pain of losing someone she cared about, Delphinia knew she would have to hold herself aloof.

"Is that what you think? That I feel you're a child who needs to be coddled? Well, believe me, Phiney, I know you're not a child, but I also know there isn't a soul who doesn't need comforting from time to time. . .even you."

Immediately, she regretted her abruptness but was not about to let down her defenses. Turning, she saw Jonathan walking down toward the dry creek bed below. Not sure what else to do, she followed along behind, trying to keep herself upright by grabbing at tree branches as the rocks underfoot began to slide.

"You sure wouldn't do well sneaking up on a person," he remarked without looking back.

"I wasn't trying to sneak up on you. I wanted to apologize for acting so supercilious. You've probably noticed that I sometimes lack the art of tactfulness. At least that's what Mama used to tell me on occasion."

When he did not respond, she looked at their surroundings and asked, "Is there some reason why you've come down here?"

"I guess I just wanted to look around. About two miles up this creek bed is where Sarah and Jake died. It's hard to believe, looking at it now."

"What do you mean by that? You never mentioned how they died. I thought they probably contracted some type of illness. Was it Indians?" she asked with a tremor in her voice.

Sitting down on a small boulder, he pulled a long piece of grass and tucked it between his teeth. "No, it wasn't illness or Indians that caused their death. It was a much-needed rain."

"I don't understand," she commented, coming up behind where he sat and making her way around the rock to sit next to him.

"I wasn't with them. Granny and I had stayed back at the farm. She hadn't been feeling herself, and we needed supplies from town. Sarah hadn't been in town since the twins' birth, and she was wanting to get a change of scenery and see folks. The children wanted to go along too. Going to town is just about the next best thing to Christmas for the youngsters.

"So they got all loaded up, Sarah and Tessie each holding one of the twins and the boys all excited about showing off the babies and maybe getting a piece or two of candy. They packed a lunch thinking they'd stop on the way home and eat so Granny wouldn't have to prepare for them. We watched them pull out, and Granny said she was going to have a cup of tea and rest awhile, so I went out to the barn to do some chores. The morning passed by uneventfully. I noticed some clouds gathering but didn't think much of it. We needed rain badly, but every time storm clouds would appear, it seemed they'd pass us by, and we'd be lucky to get a drop or two out of all the thunder and darkness.

"Granny and I just had some biscuits and cold meat for lunch, and I told her I was going to move the livestock into the barn and pen up the chickens and hogs since it looked like a storm was headed our way. We always took precautions, figuring rain had to come behind some of those clouds one day.

"As it turned out, that was the day. It started with big, fat raindrops, and I thought it was going to be another false alarm. But shortly, the animals started getting real skittish, and it began to rain at a nice steady pace. I just stood there letting it wash over me; it felt so good. I ran back to the cabin, and Granny was standing on the porch, laughing and holding her hands out to feel that wonderful, much-needed rain. It must have been a full ten minutes we stood there in delight when all of a sudden, there was the loudest clap of thunder and a huge bolt of lightning. The skies appeared to just open up and pour water down so fast and hard I couldn't believe it.

"Granny and I got into the cabin as quick as we could when the downpour began, and as soon as we got our senses about us, we thought about Jake, Sarah, and the children, praying they hadn't begun the trip home before the rain started. I think it was probably the longest time of my life, just waiting there. I couldn't leave to go search for them, knowing I could never make it through that downpour. It seemed it would never stop.

"It was the next day before it let up enough so I could travel at all. I started out with a few supplies and had to go slowly with the horse, the ground was so soaked. I wasn't sure which way Jake would be coming back from town, so I told Granny to pray that if they'd left town I'd choose the right direction. There are two ways for us to make it to town, and we usually didn't come by way of this creek bed. I was hoping that Jake hadn't chosen this, of all days, to come the creek-bed route, but I felt led to start my search in this direction.

"The going was slow and rough, and I became more and more frightened as I continued my search. I stopped at the Aplingtons' homestead, but they hadn't seen anything of Jake and Sarah. After having a quick cup of coffee, I continued on toward the creek bed. . .or a least what had been a creek bed. It had turned into a virtual torrent of rushing water, limbs, and debris. As I looked down into that flood of water, I saw what I thought was one of the baskets Sarah used to carry the twins. I just stood there staring at the rushing water, completely out of its banks and roaring like a train engine, whipping that tiny basket back and forth.

"When I finally got my wits about me," he continued, "I knew I had to go farther upstream in hopes of finding the family. I tried to holler for them, but the roar of the water drowned out my voice. I stayed as close to the creek as I could, hoping I'd see something to give me a clue about where they might be; I wasn't giving in to the fact that anything could have happened to any of them. Finally, after hours of searching, I stopped to pray, and, as I finished my prayer, I looked up and spotted Tessie, waving a piece of Josh's shirt high in the air to get my attention. They were inside a small natural cave that had formed above the creek bed. I had no doubt the Lord had placed me in that spot so that when I looked up, the first thing I would see was those children.

"I made my way up to them. They were in sad condition, all of them. . .not just being without food and water but sick with worry and fear knowing their ma and pa were gone. That was a rough time I'd not like to go through again."

Delphinia stared fixedly at Jonathan as he related the story. It seemed he was almost in a trance as he recited the events. She reached over and placed her hand on his, but he didn't even seem to realize she was there. "What happened after you found them?"

"Even in the midst of all the sadness, the Lord provided. I had just managed to get two of the children down when Mr. Aplington and his older son arrived with a spring wagon. They worked with me until we had everyone down and loaded into the wagon.

"Tessie managed to tell us that Jake and Sarah were dead, but it was much later before she was able to tell us what had happened. It seems that when the thunder and lightning started, the horses began to get excited. Jake decided to locate shelter and couldn't find any place to put them, except in that small cave. He went back down to try and get the horses and wagon to higher ground when a bolt of lightning hit, causing the horses to rear up and go out of control. They knocked him over, and the wagon turned, landing on top of him. Sarah climbed back down, determined to get that wagon off of him, even though I'm sure he was already dead. Tessie said she screamed and screamed for her ma to come back up to them, but she stayed there pushing and pushing, trying to get the wagon off Jake. When the water started rising, she tried to hold his head up, determined he was going to live.

"I imagine by the time she realized the futility of her efforts, the current was so strong there was no way she could make her way back. We found both of their bodies a few days later." His shoulders sagged as he finished relating the event.

"Oh, how awful for all of you. How those poor children ever managed to make it is truly a miracle," she said, having difficulty holding back the hot tears that threatened to spill over at any minute.

"You're right. It was God guiding my steps that caused me to find the children. I must admit, though, that the whole incident left some pretty deep scars on Tessie. The younger ones seem to have done better. Those poor little twins were so bedraggled and hungry by the time we got them back to the Aplingtons', I didn't ever expect them to pull through. The Lord provided for them too, though. Mrs. Aplington had a goat she sent home with us, and those twins took to that goat milk just like it was their mama's. Granny had me take the goat back just before I left to come for you. The twins seem to get along pretty well now with milk from old Josie, one of our cows, and food from the table, even if they are awful messy," he chuckled.

"I guess it's about time we get back to the wagon if we're going to get home before dark. Give me your hand, and I'll help you back up the hill."

Several hours later, Delphinia spotted two cabins and looked questioningly at Jonathan who merely nodded his affirmance that they were home. Drawing closer, Delphinia could make out several children standing on the porch waving. Jonathan grinned widely at the sight of those familiar faces, and Delphinia felt a knot rise up in her stomach.

Chapter 6

Jonathan reached up in his familiar stance to help Delphinia down from the wagon, and as she lowered herself into his arms, three sets of eyes peered at her from the porch. They were such handsome children!

Tessie was all Jonathan had described and more. She had beautiful red hair and eyes of pale blue that seemed to flash with anger and then go dull. Josh and Joey were towheads with big blue eyes, like Jonathan. "Uncle Jon, Uncle Jon," called Joey. "Is this our new mama?"

"She's not our ma, Joey. Our ma is dead. No one can take Ma's place, and don't you ever forget that," Tessie seethed back at the child.

"Mind your manners, young lady," Jonathan said, reaching down to lift Joey and swing him high in the air. "Joey, this is Phiney, and she's come to help Granny and Tessie take care of you," he said, trying to soothe Tessie's outburst.

"And this is Joshua, the man of the house when I'm not around. You've already figured out who Tessie is," he said, giving an admonishing look to the redhead.

"Where are Granny and the twins?" he questioned the pouting girl.

"In the house. The twins are having supper early so we can enjoy the meal," Tessie remarked.

Jonathan laughed and grabbed Phiney's hand, pulling her through the doorway. "Granny, we've finally made it, let me introduce you to—"

"Delphinia Elizabeth Hughes," she interrupted.

Delphinia was met by a radiant smile, wisps of gray-white hair, and a sparkling set of eyes amid creases and lines on a well-weathered face. "Delphinia, my dear, I am so pleased to have you with us. I have prayed daily for you and Jonathan, that your journey would be safe. You can't imagine how pleased I am that the Lord has sent you to be part of our family," she beamed.

"Jonathan, we'll get dinner on the table soon. Hopefully the twins will have finished their mess before we're ready. Delphinia, let me show you where your room will be, and, Jon, bring her trunk in so she can get comfortable. Better get the horses put up too, and might as well have Josh help you unload the wagon before we sit down to eat," she continued.

"Granny, I don't know how we made it back home without you telling us what to do and when to do it," Jonathan laughingly chided.

"Oh posh, just get going and do as I say. By tomorrow I'll probably be bedfast again, and you can enjoy the peace and quiet."

Granny led Delphinia into a bedroom off the kitchen, and she immediately knew it had belonged to Sarah and Jake. Judging from Tessie's critical looks, she surmised the room was regarded as sacred ground by the eldest child. Hoping to defuse the situation, Delphinia requested a bed in the loft with the smaller children.

"The room is to be yours, and I'll hear no more about it," the older woman insisted.

Delphinia placed her clothes in the drawers of the ornately carved chest and hung her dresses in the matching wardrobe, which had been brought from Ohio when Sarah and Jake had moved west. The room had been cleaned until it nearly shone; there was nothing left as a reminder that it had ever belonged to anyone else. Delphinia spread her quilt on the bed in coverlet fashion and placed her brush, mirror, and a picture of her parents on the chest in an attempt to make the room feel more like home. She had just about completed her unpacking when she saw Tessie standing in the doorway, peering into the room.

"Why don't you come in and join me while I finish?" Delphinia offered.

"I like your quilt," Tessie ventured, slowly entering the room.

"Why, thank you. It's a precious treasure to me. My mama and I made this quilt before she died. I don't think my mother ever thought I'd get it finished. She spent lots of hours teaching me how to make the different stitches until they met her inspection. I wasn't much older than you when I started making the quilt. Mama told me quilts were sewn with threads of love. I thought it must have been threads of patience because they took so long to make. Especially the ones Mama supervised! She was a real stickler for perfect stitches," she laughed.

"I've found great comfort having it since my mother died; and through the journey here, it was like I was bringing a part of her with me, more than a picture or piece of jewelry, because her hands helped sew those threads that run through the quilt. I'm not near as good as she was, but if you'd like to make a quilt, perhaps we could find some old pieces of cloth, and I could help you," she offered.

Overhearing their conversation, Granny commented, "Why, Sarah had started a quilt top last winter, and I'll bet it's around here somewhere, Tessie. We'll see if we can find it, and you and Delphinia can finish it. Once winter sets in, it'll be a good project for the two of you."

"No, I'm not making any quilt, not this winter, not ever, and I don't want her touching Mama's quilt either," Tessie hastened to add, her voice full of anger.

Not wanting to upset the girl, Delphinia smiled and moved into the kitchen to assist with dinner. Shortly after, they were all around a table laden with wonderful food and conversation. Granny told them she had been sure they would arrive home that very day, which was why she and Tessie had prepared a special dinner of chicken and dumplings. Delphinia was quick to tell both women the meal was as good as anything she had ever tasted. The children tried to talk all at once, telling Jonathan of the happenings since his departure. All but Tessie. She remained sullen and aloof, speaking only when necessary.

After dinner while they sat visiting, Delphinia watched as Nettie crawled toward her with a big grin. Attempting to pull herself up, she looked at Delphinia and babbled, "Mama." No sooner had she uttered the word than Tessie became hysterical, screaming to the infant that her mama was dead. Startled, Nettie lost her balance and toppled backward, her head hitting the chair as she fell. Reaching down, Delphinia lifted the crying child into her arms, cooing and rocking in an attempt to soothe her.

"Give her to me! She's my sister," Tessie fumed.

"Leave her be. You march yourself outside right now," Jonathan instructed, his voice cold and hard.

Delphinia did not miss the expressions of hatred and enmity that crossed Tessie's face as she walked toward the door. They were embedded in her memory. When Jonathan and Tessie returned a short time later, she apologized, but Delphinia and Tessie both knew it came only from her lips, not her heart. The child's pain was obvious to everyone, including Delphinia, for she too knew the pain of losing parents.

Lying in bed that night and comparing her loss to Tessie's, she realized the Lord had answered her prayers. She no longer was harboring the resentment for her pa and feeling sorry for herself. It had happened so subtly she hadn't even discerned it, and the realization amazed her. She slipped out of bed and knelt down beside her bed, thanking God for an answer to her prayers and then petitioning Him to help Tessie as He had helped her.

Please, Lord, she prayed, *give me the knowledge to help this girl find some peace.* She crawled back into bed, and the next thing she heard were noises in the kitchen and the sound of the twins' babbling voices.

Jumping out of bed she quickly dressed, pulled her hair back, and tied it with a ribbon at the nape of her neck. *I'll put it up later when there's more time,* she decided. Rushing to the kitchen, she was met by Granny's smiling face and the twins' almost toothless grins.

"I'm so sorry. I must have overslept. I'm usually up quite early. You can ask Mr. Wilshire. Even on the wagon train, I was almost always up before the others," she blurted without pausing for breath.

"You needn't get so excited, Child. Jonathan said to let you sleep late. He knew you were tired, as did I. There's no need to be upset. When I'm feeling well enough, I always get up with the twins and fix Jonathan's breakfast. I usually let the others sleep until after he's gone to do his chores. That way we get to visit with a little peace and quiet. Jonathan and I both enjoy having a short devotion time in the morning before we start the day, and I hope you'll join us for that," she continued. "One other thing, Delphinia, *please* quit calling Jonathan *Mr. Wilshire.* Either call him Jonathan or Jon, I don't care which, but not Mr. Wilshire. We don't stand on formality around here, and you're a part of this family now. I want you to call me Granny just like every other member of this family and I'll call you Delphinia. Jonathan tells me your name is very important to you. Now then, let's wake up the rest of the family and get this day going," she said. "I'll let you have the honor of climbing to the loft and rousing the children," she said, moving to set the table.

Delphinia could not believe the way the day was flying by. Granny seemed to have enough energy for two people. Leaning over a tub of hot water, scrubbing a pair of work pants, Delphinia commented that she did not understand why anyone felt that the older woman needed help.

"Well, Child," Granny answered, "right now I'm doing just fine, and I have been this past week or so. But shortly after Jon left for Illinois, I had a real setback. 'Course this has been happening more and more lately. Jonathan made arrangements for Katy McVay to come stay if I had trouble. I sent Josh down to Aplingtons' place, and Ned Aplington went to town and fetched Katy for me. She's a nice girl. Not a whole lot of sense and doesn't know how to do as much as some around the house, but she's good with the young children. 'Course Tessie helped a lot too. Once I got to feeling better, I sent Katy back home. Her folks run the general store in town, and they need her there to help out, so I didn't want to keep her longer than necessary."

Tessie was hanging the clothes on a rope tied between two small trees, intently listening to the conversation of the older woman as they performed their chores.

"Katy's got her cap set for Uncle Jon. That's why she wanted to come over to help out," Tessie injected into the conversation, with a smirk on her face. "I think he's sweet on her too, 'cause Katy told me they were going to the basket dinner after church next week. He's probably going to ask her to marry him," she said, watching Delphinia for a reaction.

Delphinia wasn't sure why, but she felt a dull ache in the pit of her stomach.

"Tessie, I don't know where you get such notions," Granny scolded. "I sometimes think you must lie awake at night, dreamin' up some of these stories. If Jonathan was of a mind to marry Katy, I think someone besides you and Katy would know about it."

"Did I hear my name?" Jonathan asked as he came striding up from the barn, a bucket of milk in each large hand.

"Oh, Tessie's just going on about Katy having her cap set for you and telling us you two have plans to get married. How come you're carrying that milk up here? I thought Josh would have brought it up hours ago," Granny replied.

"Think he must have his mind on something besides his chores today. I told him he could go do some fishing at the pond when he finished milking since he worked so hard while I was gone. Seems he forgot that bringing the buckets up to the house is part of milking. Besides, I don't mind doing it, but I'm sure you women can find something better to talk about than my love life," he chuckled.

Not wanting to miss an opportunity to put Delphinia in her place, Tessie said in an almost syrupy voice, "But, Uncle Jon, Katy said you had asked her to the church picnic. Everyone knows you're sweet on each other."

"Well, Tessie, I don't think you've got the story quite right, which is what usually comes of idle gossip. In any event, Katy asked me if I'd escort her to the church dinner, and I told her I didn't know if I would be back in time. I feel sure she's made other arrangements by now, and I'm planning on all of us attending as a family. Why don't you get out to the chicken coop and see about collecting eggs instead of spreading gossip?" he ordered as he continued toward the house.

Chapter 7

The following days were filled with endless chores and wonderful conversations with Granny. Her love of the Lord caused her to nearly glow all the time. She could quote Scriptures for almost any situation, and then she would smile and say, "Praise God, I may not be as strong as when I was young, but I've still got my memory." That statement never ceased to make Delphinia grin.

Delphinia felt as if she had known Granny all her life, and a closeness emerged that she had not felt since her mama died. Kneeling at her bed each night, Delphinia thanked God for the older woman and all she was teaching her about life and survival in the West, but most of all, how to love God and find joy in any circumstances.

Sunday morning found Delphinia musing about mornings long ago when she would rise and have only herself to clothe and care for. How things had changed! Granny advised her to dress the twins last, since they always managed to get themselves dirty if given an opportunity. Jonathan had already loaded the baskets of food, and everyone was waiting in the wagon. With great care, she placed a tiny ribbon around Nettie's head, lifted her off the bed, and walked out to join them.

Jonathan jumped down to help her, a wide grin on his face. "I think Nettie's more prone to eating hair ribbons than wearing them," he laughed, pulling the ribbon out of the baby's chubby fist and handing it to Delphinia. Smiling, she gave a sigh and placed the ribbon into her pocket.

The twins slept through most of the church service with Jonathan holding Nathan and Nettie snuggled in Delphinia's arms. Tessie made sure she was seated between the two of them. Josh and Joey were on either side of Granny, who managed to keep their fidgeting to a minimum by simply patting a hand on occasion.

After services, Granny tugged Delphinia along, telling her she wanted to introduce the pastor before they unloaded the wagon. Granny presented her to Pastor Martin and continued with a recitation about all of her fine qualities until Delphinia was embarrassed to even look at him. She merely extended her hand and mumbled, "Pleased to meet you. I think I better change Nettie's diaper."

Turning to make her getaway, she nearly collided with Jonathan, who was visiting with a beautiful young woman.

"Delphinia, I'd like you to meet Katy McVay," he said as they walked along beside her to the wagon.

Just as they rounded the corner of the church, Tessie appeared. "Oh, Katy, please join us for lunch. It won't be any fun without you," she pleaded.

"Well, if you *all* want me to, I couldn't refuse," Katy responded, smiling demurely as she looped her arm through Jonathan's.

Jonathan wasn't quite sure how to handle the turn of events and looked from Katy to Delphinia. His eyes finally settled on Tessie who was beaming with her accomplishment but quickly looked away when she noted her uncle's glare.

Watching the unfolding events from her position just outside the church, Granny decided to invite the young pastor to join them and share their meal. Realizing Tessie was enjoying the uncomfortable situation she had created, Granny assigned her the task of caring for the twins and Joey after dinner. Josh was off playing games with the other young boys, while the adults visited with several other families. Delphinia was introduced to everyone as the newest member of the Wilshire household, and the afternoon passed all too quickly when Jonathan announced it was time to load up and head for home.

Delphinia took note that Katy was still following after Jonathan like a lost puppy. Smiling inwardly, she wondered if Katy would climb into the wagon with the rest of the family—not that she cared, of course. *Jonathan could spend his time with whomever he chose,* she thought to herself.

Granny organized the children in the back of the wagon, firmly plopped Nettie and Nate in Tessie's lap, and waited until Delphinia was seated. She then ordered Jonathan to help her to the front, telling him she wished to visit with Delphinia on the return trip. Delphinia slid to the middle of the seat and once Jonathan had hoisted himself into place, the three of them were sandwiched together in much closer proximity than Katy McVay would have preferred. With mounting displeasure the young woman stood watching the group but tried to keep her composure by saying, "Be sure and put that shawl around your shoulders, Granny. It's getting chilly."

"Not to worry, Katy," smiled the older woman, a twinkle in her eye. "We'll keep each other warm. You better run along before your folks miss you." The dismissal was apparent as Granny turned to Delphinia and began to chat.

"It sure was a fine day. I don't think I've gotten to visit with so many folks since Zeb and Ellie got married last year. I'm glad you got to meet everyone so soon after your arrival, Delphinia. You probably won't remember all their names, but the faces will be familiar, and it makes you feel more at home when you see a friendly face," Granny commented. "Pastor Martin seemed mighty impressed with you, I might add."

Jonathan let out a grunt to her last remark, and although Delphinia did not comment, Jonathan saw a slight blush rise in her cheeks and a smile form on her lips.

"It seemed to me you were pretty impressed with Pastor Martin yourself, Phiney," Jonathan bantered. "Every time I saw you, you were at his side."

Delphinia felt herself bristle at his remark. Why, he made it sound like she had been throwing herself at the pastor. She, with two tiny babies to diaper and feed, while he was off squiring Miss Katy McVay, fixing her a plate of food, carrying her parasol like it belonged to him, and making a total fool of himself. She all but bit her tongue off trying to remain in control.

"You might as well say what's on your mind 'fore you bust a button, Phiney. I can see you've got a whole lot of things you're just itching to say," he goaded.

Glancing over her shoulder, she observed the children were asleep. Looking at him with those same fiery eyes he had seen at the general store before he brought her west, he felt a strong urge to gather her into his arms and hold her close. Instead, he listened as she went into a tirade about how Katy McVay had been attached to him like another appendage and how foolish he had looked carrying her parasol.

"Well, I thank you for your insights, Miss Hughes," he responded as he lifted her down from the wagon and firmly placed her on the ground, "but I doubt I looked any more foolish than you did prancing behind Pastor Martin. I'm surprised you didn't ask to carry his Bible."

"How could I?" she retorted. "I was too busy carrying your nephew most of the time." With that said, she turned and carried Nathan into the cabin without so much as a good night. *I'm not going to let myself care for any man,* she thought to herself. *I've forgiven Pa for sending me away, but I've not forgotten. I don't need that kind of pain ever again.*

"My, my," Granny smiled as she gathered the other children and walked toward the cabin. "You two certainly have hit it off well. I'm so pleased."

Jonathan stood staring after her, wondering if she had lost her senses.

Life began to fit into a routine for the family, and although Delphinia still relied on Granny for many things, Granny had fewer and fewer days when she was up and about for any period of time. Jonathan made a bed for her to lie on in the living area so she could be in the midst of things. Granny still led them in devotions each morning and continued to be a stabilizing factor for Tessie, whose resentment of Delphinia seemed immeasurable. Everyone else was accepting Delphinia's presence and enjoying her company, particularly Pastor Martin.

It was a warm day, and Delphinia had risen early, hoping to get the bread baking done before the heat of the day made the cabin unbearable. Her back was to the door as she stood kneading the coarse dough, methodically punching and turning the mixture, her thoughts occasionally drifting to Pastor Martin's good looks and kind manner. This was the last batch of dough, and she was glad it would soon be done. She could feel droplets of perspiration forming across her forehead when she heard Granny say from the narrow cot, "Delphinia, don't be alarmed and don't scream. Just slowly turn around and smile like this is the happiest moment of your life."

Not knowing what to expect, the younger woman whirled around to be greeted by three Indians who were solemnly staring at her as her mouth fell open, and she began moving backward.

"Smile, Delphinia, smile," Granny commanded.

"I'm trying, Granny, I'm honestly trying, but I can't seem to get my lips to turn upward right now. What do they want? Is Jonathan anywhere nearby?"

"Oh, they're friendly enough, and they belong to the Kansa tribe. Just don't act like you're afraid. It offends them since they've come here from time to time and have never hurt anyone. They seem to know the days when I bake bread, and that's what they want. I thought they had moved to the reservation; it's been so long since they've been here. They used to come every week or two and expect a loaf of bread and maybe some cheese or a chicken. Then they just quit coming. They never knock, just walk in and stand there until they're noticed. Gives you quite a start the first time, though."

"You want bread?" Granny asked, pointing at the freshly baked loaves resting on the wooden table.

Nodding in the affirmative, they each reached out and grabbed a loaf of bread.

"Now just a minute," Delphinia chastened. "You can't each have a loaf. You'll have to settle for one loaf. I have children here to feed."

"Well, you lost your fear mighty fast, Child," Granny commented as she looked over to see both twins toddling into the kitchen.

"You papoose?" one of the Indians asked, pointing first at Delphinia and then the twins, seeming amazed at the sight of them.

"They haven't been here since the twins were born," Granny commented. "I don't know if they realize you're not Sarah, but just nod yes."

"Yes, my papoose," Delphinia said, pointing to herself and to each of the twins while the Indians walked toward the babies, looking at them curiously. Then, reaching down, the spokesman picked up Nettie in one arm and Nathan in the other. He began bouncing the babies as he talked and laughed with his companions. Both infants were enthralled with the attention and were busy stuffing the Indian's necklaces into their mouths.

Delphinia glanced at the older woman and knew she was becoming alarmed by the Indian's interest in the babies. Forgetting her fear, she walked to the Indian and said, "My papoose," and extended her arms. Grunting in agreement, the Indian passed the children to her, picked up a loaf of bread, held it in the air, and the three of them left the cabin without saying another word.

"Wow," said Josh, coming from behind the bedroom door. "You sure were brave."

"Yeah, brave," mimicked Joey.

"I don't know about brave," Delphinia answered, "but they were making me terribly nervous, and I was afraid they'd walk out with more than a loaf of bread."

Jonathan was just coming over from his cabin when he was met by Joey and Josh, both trying to give an account of everything that had happened, even though they had witnessed very little of the actual events.

"Slow down, you guys, or I'll never be able to understand. Better yet, why don't you let Granny or Phiney tell me what happened."

Joint "ahs" emitted from both boys at that suggestion, and they plopped down on the bed with Granny as she began to tell Jonathan what had occurred.

"Seems you finally put that temper of yours to good use, Phiney," Jonathan responded after hearing Granny's account of what had happened.

"I what? Well, of all the—"

"Now, now, Child," Granny interrupted, "he's just trying to get you riled up, and doing a mighty fine job of it too, I might add. Pay him no mind. He's as proud of you as the rest of us."

"She's right, Phiney. I should be thanking you instead of teasing. That was mighty brave of you, and we're grateful, although I can't say as I blame those Indians for wanting some of Granny's bread. Those are some fine-looking loaves."

"They're not mine, Jonathan. I couldn't begin to knead that bread the way I've been feeling. Delphinia's baked all the bread around here for weeks now."

"Well, I think Granny's bread is much better, and so was Mama's," came Tessie's response from the other side of the room. "I don't know why you're making such a big fuss. Those Indians weren't going to hurt anyone. They were just curious about the twins and wanted a handout. She's no big deal. We've had Indians in and out of this cabin before she ever came here."

"You're right, Tessie. I'm sure the Indians meant no harm, and I did nothing the rest of you wouldn't have done. So let's just forget it and get breakfast going. Tessie, if you'll start coffee, I believe I'll go to my room for a few minutes and freshen up."

Once inside her room, Delphinia willed herself to stop shaking. Leaning against the closed door, her ghostlike reflection greeted her in the bureau mirror. Aware the family was waiting breakfast and not wanting to appear fainthearted, she pinched her cheeks, forced a smile on her face, and walked back to the kitchen, realizing she had been thanking God from the instant the Indians left the cabin until this moment. Immediately, she felt herself quit shivering, and a peaceful calm took the place of her fear.

Granny's supplication at the morning meal was more eloquent than usual, and Jonathan was quick to add a hearty "amen" on several occasions throughout the prayer. Delphinia silently thanked God for the peace He had granted her. She was not aware until this day that some time ago she had quit praying for God to rescue her and had allowed laughter and joy to return to her life. It was not the same as when she had been at home with her parents, but a warmth and love of a new and special kind had slowly begun to grow in her heart.

Chapter 8

Autumn arrived, and the trees burst forth in glorious yellows, reds, and oranges. The rolling hills took on a new beauty, and Delphinia delighted in the changing season. The warm air belied the fact that winter would soon follow.

For several days Josh and Joey had been hard at work, gathering apples from the surrounding trees, stripping them of the tart, crisp fruit. An ample supply had been placed in the root cellar, and she and Granny had spent days drying the rest. Hoping she might find enough to make pies for dessert that evening, Delphinia had gone to the trees in the orchard behind the house. Once the basket was full, she started back toward the cabin, and when coming around the house, she noticed Pastor Martin riding toward her on his sorrel. Waving in recognition, he came directly to where she stood, dismounted, and joined her.

"I was hoping to catch you alone for a minute," he commented as he walked beside her, leading the horse. "I've come to ask if you'd accompany me to the social next Friday evening," he blurted, "unless you're going with Jonathan. . .or has someone else already asked you?"

Before she could answer, Tessie came around the side of the house, a twin at each hand. "You'd better take him up on the offer, Phiney. Jonathan will be taking Katy McVay, and I doubt *you'll* be getting any other invitations," she said, a malicious smile crossing her face.

"I don't know if I'll be attending at all, Pastor Martin. I had quite forgotten about the party, and I'm not sure I can leave the family. Granny hasn't been quite as good the last few days."

"Really, Phiney. We're not totally helpless, you know. We managed before you got here, and I'm sure we could manage for a few hours on Friday night," came Tessie's rebuttal.

Not sure whether she should thank Tessie for the offer to assist with the family or upbraid her for her rude intrusion, Delphinia invited the pastor to join her in the cabin where they could discuss the matter further and gain Granny's opinion.

Granny was always pleased to see Pastor Martin, and her face shone with immediate pleasure as he walked into the room. "I didn't know you made calls this early in the day," she called out in greeting.

Smiling, he sat in the chair beside the bed where she rested, and he took her hand. "Normally I don't and only for very special occasions. I've come to ask Delphinia if she'd allow me to escort her to the social Friday night," he answered, accepting the cup of coffee Delphinia offered.

"Well, I'd say that's a pretty special event. What kind of answer did you give this young man, Delphinia?" she asked the embarrassed young woman.

"I haven't answered him just yet, Granny. I didn't think I should leave the children with you for that long. Tessie overheard the conversation and said she could help, but I wanted to talk it over with you first."

"Why, we can manage long enough for you to have a little fun, Delphinia. Wouldn't want you away too long, though. I'd miss your company and sweet face."

Delphinia leaned down to place a light kiss on the older woman's wrinkled cheek. "I love you, Granny," she whispered.

"Does that mean you've accepted?" asked Tessie, coming from the doorway where she had been standing out of sight and listening.

"Well. . .yes. . .I suppose it does," she replied. "Pastor Martin, I'd be pleased to accompany you. What time should I be ready?"

"I'll be here about seven, if that's agreeable."

Glancing over at Granny for affirmation and seeing her nod, Delphinia voiced her agreement.

Downing the remains of coffee in the stoneware cup, the young parson bid them farewell, explaining he needed to stop by the Aplingtons' for a visit and get back to town before noon. Walking outside, Delphinia strolled along beside him until he had come even with his mare. "If you're going to attend the social with me, Delphinia, I think it would be appropriate for you to call me George," he stated and swung atop the animal, which was prancing, anxious to be allowed its rein.

"Fine, George," she answered modestly, stepping back from the horse.

Smiling, he lightly kicked the mare in the sides and took off, reaching full gallop before he hit the main road, his arm waving in farewell.

Delphinia was standing in the same spot when Jonathan came up behind her and eyed the cloud of billowing dust down the road. Unable to identify the rider, he asked, "Who was that just leaving?"

"Jonathan, you frightened me. I didn't hear you come up behind me," she said, not answering his question.

"I'm sorry if I startled you. Who did you say that was, or is it a secret?"

"I didn't say, but it's not a secret. It was George. . .I mean, Pastor Martin."

"Oh, *George,* is it? Since when are you and the parson on a first-name basis, Phiney?"

"Pastor Martin. . .George. . .has asked me to attend the social with him on Friday night," she responded.

"You didn't agree, did you?" His anger evident, the look on his face almost defied her to admit her acceptance.

"I checked with Granny. She found no fault in my going. I'll make sure the twins and Joey are ready for bed before leaving, if that's your concern." Irritated by the tone he was taking, Delphinia turned and headed back toward the house, leaving him to stare after her.

"Just you wait a minute. I'm not through discussin' this," he called after her.

"You needn't bellow. I didn't realize we were having a discussion. I thought it was an inquisition," she stated, continuing toward the house. *Why is he acting so hateful,* she wondered? *Jonathan knows George Martin is a good man. He should be pleased that such a nice man wants to keep company with me.*

"The problem is that I planned on taking you to the social, and here you've gone and promised to go with George," he retorted.

Stopping short, she whirled around almost colliding with him. "You planned on taking me? Well, just when were you going to tell me about it? This is the first time you've said one word about the social. Besides, Tessie said you were taking Katy McVay."

"Tessie said what?" he nearly yelled at her. "Since when do you listen to what Tessie has to say?"

"Why wouldn't I believe her? I've heard enough rumors that you and Katy are a match. She's got her cap set for you, and from what I've been told, the feeling is mutual," she retorted.

"Oh, really? Well I don't pay much heed to the gossip that's floating around. For your information, we are not a match. I've escorted Katy to a few functions, but that doesn't make us betrothed or anything near it. If Tessie told you I invited Katy, she spoke out of turn. I've not asked anyone to the social because I planned on taking you."

"I can't read your mind, Jonathan. If you want me to know what you're planning, next time you need to tell me," she answered, his comments making her more certain that men were not to be trusted.

The kitchen was filled with an air of tension throughout the noon meal until Granny finally questioned Jonathan. Hearing his explanation, she let out a whoop and sided with Delphinia. "Just because she lives here doesn't mean you can take her for granted," she chided.

Feeling frustration with Granny's lack of allegiance, Jonathan turned on Tessie, scolding her mightily for interfering.

"That's enough, Jon. I know you're upset, and the girl was wrong in telling an outright lie, but all your ranting and raving isn't going to change the fact that the preacher is calling on Delphinia Friday night," Granny resolutely stated.

Not willing to let the matter rest and hoping to aid Katy in her conquest, Tessie suggested Jonathan ride into town and invite her. "I'm sure she'll not accept an invitation from anyone else," she added as her final comment.

"Tessie, I would appreciate it if you would spend as much time performing chores as you do meddling in other people's affairs. If you'd do that, the rest of us wouldn't have to do a thing around here!" His face was reddened with anger as he pushed away from the table and left the house.

When Friday evening finally arrived, Granny made sure that Josh fetched water, and it was kept warm on the stove for Delphinia's bath. After dinner, she ordered Jonathan to carry the metal tub into Delphinia's room, then smiled to herself as Jonathan made a dash for his own cabin to prepare for the evening.

Scooting down in the tub, Delphinia let her head go completely underwater and, sliding back up, began to lather her hair. She rubbed in a small amount of the lavender oil that had belonged to her mother and finished washing herself. Never had she taken such care in preparing herself. She towel dried her hair and pinned it on top of her head. An ivory ribbon surrounded the mass of curls except for a few short tendrils that escaped, framing her oval face. Her mother's small, golden locket was at her neck, and she placed a tiny gold earring in each lobe.

She had decided upon wearing a deep blue dress that had belonged to her mother. Granny helped with the few necessary alterations, and it now fit beautifully. She slipped it over her head and fastened the tiny cover buttons that began at the scooped neckline and trailed to the waist. Slipping on her good shoes, she took one final look in the mirror and exited the bedroom.

Her entry into the living area was met with lusty approval from the boys. Granny beamed at the sight of her, and Tessie glared in distaste. Jonathan had gone to sit on the porch when he heard the raves from inside. Rising, he entered the house and was overcome by the sight he beheld. She was, without a doubt, the most glorious looking creature he had ever seen. Noting the look on his face, Tessie stepped toward him. "Aren't you leaving to pick up Katy, Uncle Jon?"

Gaining his attention with her question, he looked her straight in the eyes. "I told you earlier this week I was not escorting Katy. Have you forgotten, Tessie?"

"Oh, I thought maybe you'd asked her since then," she murmured. Gathering her wits about her, she quizzed, "Well, who are you taking?"

"No one," he responded, unable to take his eyes off the beautiful young woman in the blue dress. "I'm just going to ride along with George and Phiney."

"You're going to *what?*" stammered Delphinia.

"No need in getting my horse all lathered up riding into town when there's a buggy going anyway. Doesn't make good sense, Phiney. Besides, I'm sure the parson won't mind if I ride along."

No sooner had he uttered those words, when the sound of a buggy could be heard coming up the roadway. Jonathan stepped to the porch and called out, "Evenin', George. Good to see you. I was just telling Phiney I didn't think you'd have any objection to my riding into town with the two of you. Didn't see any need to saddle up my horse when I could ride along with you."

The pastor's face registered a look of surprise and then disappointment. "No, no, that's fine, Jon. Might be a little crowded—"

"Don't mind a bit," interrupted Jonathan. "You just stay put, and I'll fetch Phiney."

"I think perhaps I should fetch her myself, Jon," he said, his voice hinting of irritation.

Both men arrived at the door simultaneously, and for a moment Delphinia thought they were going to be permanently wedged in the doorway until the pastor turned slightly, allowing himself to advance into the room. "You look absolutely stunning, Delphinia," he complimented, watching her cheeks flush from the remark.

"She's a real sight to behold, that's for sure," responded Jonathan as every eye in the room turned to stare at him.

Nate and Nettie toddled to where she stood, their hands extended to grab at the flowing gown. "No, you don't, you two. Tessie, grab the twins, or they'll be drooling all over her before she can get out the door," ordered Jonathan.

"Seems to me you're already drooling all over her," Tessie muttered under her breath.

The evening passed in a succession of dances with Jonathan and George vying for each one, occasionally being bested by some other young man who would manage to whisk her off in the midst of their sparring over who should have the next dance. By the end of the social, Delphinia's feet ached, but the gaiety of the event far outweighed any complaint she might have. The only blemish of the evening had been overhearing some unkind remarks from Katy McVay at the refreshment table. When she noticed Delphinia standing close by, she had given her a syrupy smile and excused herself to "find more appealing company."

Although they were cramped close together on the seat of the buggy, the autumn air had cooled, and Delphinia felt herself shiver. "You're cold. Why didn't you say something? Let me help you with your shawl," Jonathan offered as the pastor kept his hands on the reins. Unfolding the wrap, he slipped it around her shoulders and allowed his arm to rest across her shoulders in a possessive manner. Much to George's irritation, he remained thus until the horses came to a halt in front of the house. Jumping down, George hurried to secure the horses in hopes of helping Delphinia from the buggy, but to no avail. Jonathan had already assisted her and was standing with his arm draped across her small shoulders. Delphinia attempted to shrug him off, but he only tightened his grip.

"It's getting late, Parson, and you've still got to make the trip back to town. Thanks for the ride and good night," Jonathan stated, attempting to dismiss the preacher before he could usher Delphinia to the house.

"Now, just a minute, Jonathan. I'm capable of saying thank you and good night for myself. You go on to your place. George and I will be just fine," Delphinia answered.

"Nah, that's okay. Want to make sure everything's okay here before I go over to my place, so I'll just wait here on the porch till George is on his way."

Knowing that Jonathan was not about to leave and not wanting to create a scene, the pastor thanked Delphinia for a lovely evening and bid them both good night.

"Of all the nerve," she shouted at the relaxed figure on the porch. "You are the most vexing man I have ever met. George Martin made a trip here especially to invite me to the social, made another trip to escort me and return me safely home, and you have the nerve to not only invite yourself along but won't even give him the opportunity to spend a moment alone with me!" The full moon shone on her face, and he could see her eyes flashing with anger.

"I'll not apologize for that, Phiney. After all, I have a responsibility to keep you safe. You're a part of this family," he said with a boyish grin.

Hands on her hips and chin jutted forward, she made her way to the porch where he stood, and she said, "I'll have you know, *Mr. Wilshire,* that I do not need your protection from George Martin, nor do I want it."

But, before she could move, he leaned down and kissed her full on the mouth. When he released her, she was so stunned that she stared at him in utter disbelief, unable to say a word, her heart pounding rapidly. A slow smile came across his lips as he once again gathered her into his arms, and his mouth slowly descended and captured her lips in a breathtaking kiss. She felt her legs grow limp, and as he leaned back, she lost her balance causing her to reach out and grab Jonathan's arm for support.

"Now, now, Phiney, don't go begging me to stay any longer. I've got to get over to my place and get some sleep," he said with an ornery glint in his eyes.

That remark caused Delphinia to immediately regain her composure. "Beg you to stay? Is that what you think I want? Why, you are the most conceited, arrogant, irritating, interfering—"

"You just keep on with your chattering, Phiney. Think I'll get some sleep," he interrupted, stepping off the porch and walking toward his cabin.

"Ooh, that man! I don't think the Lord is ever going to get around to straightening him out," she muttered under her breath as she turned and opened the cabin door.

Chapter 9

The beginning of the school year brought excitement to the household, and the children were anxious for the change in routine. Delphinia made sure that each of the youngsters looked their very best for the first day, especially Joey, since this marked the beginning of his career as a student. Although he was not yet five, the new schoolteacher had come to visit and, much to his delight, declared him bright enough to begin his formal education with the other children. Delphinia and Granny packed their tin pails with thick slices of bread and cheese, an apple, and a piece of dried peach pie. The two women stood at the cabin door watching as the young Wilshires made their way toward the dusty road, their happy chatter floating through the morning air.

With the older children gone to school each day, Delphinia and Granny were left at home with only the twins to care for. Although she loved all the children, even Tessie with her malicious ways, Delphinia cherished the additional time it allowed her to be alone with the older woman.

Granny took advantage of the newfound freedom and devoted most of the extra hours to teaching Delphinia all the things that would assist the young woman in running the household once she had only herself to rely upon. Shortly after her arrival, Delphinia confided that her mother had given her a wonderful education, insisting she spend her time studying, reading, and doing fancy stitching rather than household tasks. It was soon evident that she had much to learn. During the months since her arrival, she had proven herself a capable student of the older woman's tutelage. But there remained much to learn, and Granny spent hours carefully explaining how to use the children's clothing to make patterns for new garments; how to plant and tend a garden; how to preserve the meats, vegetables, and fruits that would provide for them throughout the winter and early spring; how to make tallow candles and lye soap, being sure to wrap each candle and bar in straw for storage; how to make big wheels of cheese, being sure to allow time for aging; and how to prepare meals for the large threshing crews that would hopefully be needed in early summer. Listening intently, she absorbed everything Granny taught her.

Delphinia's true pleasure came, however, when Granny would call for a quiet time during the twins' nap, and the two of them would read from the Bible and discuss the passages. Their sharing of God's Word caused a bond of love to flourish between the two women, just as the one that had grown between Delphinia and her mother when they stitched her cherished quilt. Both women were especially pleased when Pastor Martin would stop by, which was happening more frequently. He never failed to raise their spirits. Delphinia enjoyed his attentiveness and insights, while Granny hoped the visits would light a fire under Jonathan.

As winter began to settle on the prairie, Delphinia thought she would never see a blade of grass or a flower bloom again. The snow came in blizzard proportions, keeping the children, as well as the adults, inside most of the time. Although everyone made great effort to create harmony, boredom overcame the children, and tempers grew short.

After several days, Delphinia was sure something would have to be done to keep the children diverted. That evening as Jonathan prepared to go to the barn and milk Josie, their old brown-and-white cow, Delphinia began putting on her coat and hat. "Where do you think you're going?" he asked.

"I want to go to the barn and unpack some things from one of my trunks stored out there," she answered, falling in step behind him.

Barely able to see, the snow blowing in giant swirls with each new gust of wind, they made their way to the barn, and, while Jonathan milked, Delphinia began going through the items in one of her trunks. She found her old slate and schoolbooks, an old cloth ball, a rag doll from when she was a small child, and some marbles her father had bought for her one Christmas, much to her mother's chagrin. She bundled the items in a heavy shawl and sat down on top of the trunk to await Jonathan.

"Come sit over here and visit with me while I finish," he requested.

Picking up the parcel, she walked over and sat on one of the milking stools, watching intently as the milk pinged into the battered pail at a steady rhythm.

"Granny tells me George has been coming out to see you some."

"He's been here occasionally."

"I take it that makes you happy?" Jonathan questioned, noting the blush that had risen in her cheeks.

"George is a fine man. I enjoy his company. And what of Katy McVay? Do your visits with her make you happy?" she questioned.

"I haven't been visiting with Katy. I don't know how I've missed George when he's come calling," he replied, rising from the stool. "Guess I need to be a little more observant," he grumbled as the two of them headed back toward the house.

"From the looks of that bundle, it appears your trip was successful," Granny said, watching the children assemble around Delphinia who was struggling to remove her wet outer garments. "Perhaps more successful than the children will care for in a few days," she answered with a slight smile, pointing at the teaching materials she was removing from the shawl. Handing the rag doll to Nettie, she smiled as the baby hugged it close and toddled away, with Nate in close pursuit.

"Here Nathan, catch the ball," she called, just as he was reaching to pull the doll away from Nettie. Chortling in delight, he grabbed the ball with his chubby hands as it rolled across the floor in front of him.

"Where are our toys?" asked Josh, a frown crossing his face.

"I don't have a lot of toys, Josh," she replied. "I do have some marbles my pa gave me one Christmas that I'd be willing to let you boys earn by doing well with your lessons."

"Ah, that's not fair," they replied in unison. "The twins don't have to do no lessons."

"Any lessons," Delphinia corrected. "The twins are still babies. You boys are old enough to know you must work for rewards. . .in this case, marbles. Tessie already understands that the true reward of a student is the knowledge you receive," she explained, although Tessie's look of boredom belied a real zeal for knowledge, or anything else at the moment.

"I did, however, find this tortoiseshell comb, and if you'd like, Tessie, I would be willing to consider it a little something extra, over and above the reward of knowledge."

Tessie eyed the comb, trying to hide her excitement. It was the most beautiful hairpiece she had ever seen, and she desperately wanted it. As much as she wanted it, however, she would never concede that fact to Delphinia.

"I suppose it would make the boys try harder if they knew we were all working toward a reward," she responded.

Granny and Delphinia exchanged knowing smiles, and the lessons began. The children worked hard on their studies, and the days passed, some with more success than others. The boys finally were rewarded with all the marbles, and Tessie had become the proud owner of the tortoiseshell comb.

When at last the snows abated and the roads were clear enough for school to resume the first week in December, both women heaved a sigh of relief, along with a prayer of thanksgiving. They waved from the doorway as the three older children climbed up on the buckboard, and Jonathan drove off toward school, all of them agreeing the weather was still not fit to walk such a distance.

The children returned home that first day, each clutching a paper with their part for the Christmas pageant. Delphinia quickly realized the evenings would be spent with the children practicing elocution and memorization. Tessie was to portray Mary but had detailed instructions that her red hair was to be completely tucked under a scarf.

"Why'd they pick her if they didn't want a redhead? It's not like she's the prettiest girl in class," Josh commented, tiring of the discussion of how to best cover Tessie's hair.

"They picked me because I'm the best actress in the school," Tessie retorted.

"I must be one of the smartest since the teacher picked me to be one of the wise men," Josh bantered back.

By this time, Joey was totally confused. "How come they picked me to be a shepherd, Granny?" he inquired. "Does that mean I have to take a sheep with me to school?"

Everyone broke into gales of laughter at his remark as he stood there with a look of bewilderment on his face.

"No, sweet thing, you don't need any sheep," Granny replied. "But I think you all better get busy learning your lines instead of telling us how wise and talented you are."

After school the next day, Miss Sanders arrived to request that Nate or Nettie portray the baby Jesus in the pageant. Just as Delphinia was beginning to explain that neither of them would hold still long enough for a stage production, both twins came toddling into the room. Squealing in delight and their hands smeared with jelly, they headed directly for the visitor. Delphinia was unable to head off the attack, and Miss Sanders left soon after with jelly stains on the front of her dress and a withdrawal of her request for a baby Jesus from the Wilshire home.

Granny, Jonathan, and Delphinia had been making plans for months, hoping the upcoming holiday would be a special time, since this was the first Christmas the children, as well as Delphinia, would be without their parents.

"I want it to be a good Christmas, one we'll all remember fondly," Granny kept reminding them.

Jonathan made several trips to town for special purchases, and while the children were at school, gifts were ordered through the mail or made by the women. Oranges, a rare treat for all of them, were poked full of cloves, and tins of dried apricots and candied fruits arrived. Gingerbread men were baked with the distinctive spice Granny ordered from back East, and the children delighted in helping cut and bake them the Saturday before Christmas. Even Tessie seemed to enjoy the preparations, helping the younger children make decorations.

The day before Christmas Jonathan and the two older boys went in search of a tree with instructions from Granny that it not be too large. They came back with a somewhat scraggly cedar and placed it in the corner. The homemade garland and strings of popcorn were placed on the branches, and Delphinia hung ornaments and a star that she had brought from home. The tin candleholders were clipped onto the tree, with a promise that the candles would be lit Christmas morning.

The day went by in a stir of confusion, and soon everyone scurried to get ready for the Christmas pageant being held at the church. Jonathan worried the weather would be too hard on Granny, but she insisted on going. Dressed in her heaviest woolen dress and winter coat, Jonathan wrapped her frail figure in blankets, carried her to the wagon, and placing her on a mattress stuffed with corn husks, tucked a twin on either side. Finally, he covered all of them with a feather comforter. The rest of the children piled into the back, all snuggling together to gain warmth from each other. Jonathan helped Delphinia to the seat beside him. Starting down the road, he pulled her closer with the admonition she would certainly be too cold sitting so far away. She did not resist, nor did she respond, but his touch caused her cheeks to feel fiery in the frosty night air.

The program was enchanting with each of the children performing admirably. The audience gave its enthusiastic approval, and the evening ended with the group of delighted parents and relatives sharing cocoa and cookies. Miss Sanders proudly presented each of the children with a stick of peppermint candy as a gift for their hard work.

"I'm sorry I haven't been out to see you," George told Delphinia, offering her a cup of cocoa. "The weather has made it impossible, but I hope to come by again soon," he told her.

"We always look forward to your visits, George. I'm sorry I've missed you the last few times you've come to call," came Jonathan's reply from behind Delphinia. "You just come on out anytime. I'll make a point to be watching for you," he continued. "We're getting ready to leave, Phiney," he stated, holding out her coat and giving her a wink, sure that George would notice.

"Pastor Martin plans on coming out to visit soon," Delphinia informed Granny on the trip home.

"I think he's more interested in visiting Phiney than the rest of us, but I told him we'd be happy to have him anytime," Jonathan stated. "You two be sure and let me know when he comes calling so I don't miss another visit," he instructed and was disappointed when Delphinia did not give one of her quick retorts.

Once home, the children were soon tucked into bed, anxious for morning to arrive. Granny was quick to admit that she too needed her rest and apologetically requested that Delphinia complete the Christmas preparations. Before retiring, the older woman instructed Delphinia where everything had been hidden, fearful that a gift or two might be forgotten. Smiling and placing a kiss on her cheek, Delphinia reassured her that all would be ready by morning.

Christmas day was a joyous event of sparkling eyes and joyous laughter. The children were in good spirits, the tree was beautiful, and the gifts well received. Jonathan had gone hunting the morning before and returned with a wild turkey, which was the main attraction of the festive holiday meal. After dinner, Granny read the Christmas story from the Bible while the family sat in a circle around her listening intently, even the young twins. When she finished, Jonathan began to sing "Silent Night," and the others joined in. One by one, they sang all the Christmas carols they could remember until Jonathan declared it was bedtime for the children. Not long after, Granny bid them good night, thanking them both for all they had done to make it such a wonderful day. "Don't stay up too long," she admonished, always in charge.

"We won't, Granny," answered Jonathan, smiling back at her.

As the burning candles flickered, Jonathan reached into his pocket, pulled out a small package, and handed it to Delphinia. Her face registered surprise.

"What's this for?" she inquired.

"It's a Christmas gift from me to you. I didn't want to give it to you in front of the others."

"You shouldn't have, Jonathan," she chided as she slowly untied the ribbon and removed the wrapping to reveal a beautiful gold thimble on which the initials DEH had been engraved. Her face radiated as she examined it and placed it on her finger. "It's beautiful, Jonathan. I love it. How did you ever happen to choose a thimble?" she inquired.

"Granny told me about the quilt you and your mother stitched and how special it was to you. I figured sewing was important to you, and I'd never seen you using a thimble when you were sewing. Granny said she didn't think you had one. The initials were Granny's idea."

"I'm surprised you didn't have it engraved P-E-H instead of D-E-H."

"To tell the truth, I wanted to have it engraved with P-H-I-N-E-Y, but Granny wouldn't hear of it, and the engraver said it was too many letters for such a small piece," he laughed.

"I'd better be getting over to my place. It's getting late, and Granny will have my hide if I'm not out of here soon," he said, rising from his chair.

At the door he reached down and placed his hand alongside her face and lightly kissed her on the lips. "Merry Christmas, Phiney. I'll see you tomorrow," he said and headed toward his cabin.

Delphinia sat on the edge of her bed staring at the golden thimble and remembering Jonathan's kiss, still unsure she should trust any man again. *If I were to trust someone, George would probably be the safest choice,* she thought.

Chapter 10

Delphinia sat in the rocker, Nettie on one arm, Nathan on the other, watching their eyes slowly close in readiness for a nap. They had developed a real sense of independence, seldom wanting to be rocked anymore, except at bedtime. It was hard to believe that almost a year had passed since she left home. The birds were once again singing, and the aroma of blooming honeysuckle gave notice of spring's arrival. New life had begun to appear in everything except Granny. Her health fell in rapid decline throughout the winter, and she lost the will to battle her debilitating illness any longer. It had been only a few weeks since her death, but life had taken a turn for the worse since her departure. Delphinia's sense of loss was extraordinary. Tessie had grown more sullen and less helpful, the boys seemed rowdier, the twins fussier, and Jonathan tried to cheer all of them, with sadness showing in his own eyes.

Delphinia thought of Granny's final words the morning she lay dying. "Remember I love you like a daughter, and the Lord loves you even more. Never turn from Him, Delphinia. I can see the peace you've gained since coming here, and I don't want you to lose it. Nothing would make me sadder than to think my death would cause you to stumble in your faith.

"One more thing, my dear. Jonathan loves you, and you love him. I'm not sure either of you realizes it yet, but I'm sure God has wonderful plans for the two of you. You've learned well, and there's nothing to fear. Jonathan will be close at hand whenever you need him," the dying woman had said as she reached up and wiped the tears from Delphinia's cheeks.

Shortly thereafter, she summoned Jonathan, and, in hushed murmurs, they said their final good-byes.

The services were held at the church, and everyone in the surrounding area came to pay their tribute. Granny would have been pleased, not because they came to honor her, but because some of them hadn't been inside the church since it had been built!

Several days after the funeral, Pastor Martin came to visit and confided that the services had been planned by Granny. She had known it might be the only opportunity the minister would have to preach the plan of salvation to some of the homesteaders. Determined her death might provide eternal life for at least one of those settlers if they heard the message of God's love, she had ordered, "Don't talk about me, tell them about the precious Savior I've gone to join."

There had been no flowery eulogies, no words of praise about her many acts of charity, or sentimental stories about her life. Pastor Martin had given an eloquent sermon based on Romans 10:9-13 telling all those assembled that Granny's deepest desire had been consistent with that of her Lord. She wanted them to have the opportunity to receive Jesus Christ as their Savior. She wanted them to experience the joy of serving a Lord who would be with them in the times of happiness as well as sorrow. She wanted them to know the pure joy and peace that could be attained in service to the living God. Yes, he pointed out, there would still be sorrow, even while faithfully serving the Lord. He told them there was no promise made that their lives would be free of unhappiness and grief but, he added, the Word of God does say we will not be alone at those times. We have comfort through our Lord, Jesus Christ.

"That is what Jesus wanted you to know, and that is what Granny wanted you to know," he had said as he finished the message.

The service ended more like a revival meeting than a funeral. The pastor explained to those attending that if they had not received Jesus as their Savior, nothing would make Granny happier than to use this opportunity to take that step of commitment at her funeral. When two men and one young girl stepped forward, Delphinia was sure the angels in heaven were singing and that Granny was probably leading the chorus!

It had been a unique experience for all of them. The burial had taken place, followed by a baptism at the river, and everyone had then returned to the church for dinner and visiting afterward.

Granny would have loved it!

The twins stirred in Delphinia's arms, and carefully she placed them in bed, hoping they would not awaken. Hearing the sound of a horse coming toward the house, she walked to the porch and watched as George Martin approached, quickly returning his smile and wave. "It's good to see you, George," she welcomed as he climbed down from the horse. "Come in and I'll pour you some coffee."

"It's good to see you too. Coffee sounds good. I hope you have some time so we can visit privately," he stated as they walked into the house.

"It appears you're in luck. The twins are napping, Tessie's gone to pick berries, and the older boys are with Jonathan," she answered.

"I really don't know how to begin," he stammered, taking a sip of coffee, "so I guess I'll just get to the heart of the matter."

"That's usually best," she encouraged, leaning forward.

"Delphinia, I don't know if you realize that I've come to care for you a great deal. We don't know each other well. . . . I don't really think we could ever get to know each other very well as long as Jonathan's around. Anyway, I've been called to another church and must leave here by the end of the month. I'd like you to come with. . .as my wife, of course," he stated.

"George. . .I don't know what to say. You've taken me by surprise," she said, her voice faltering. "You're a wonderful man, but I don't think I could marry unless I was sure I loved you. I don't think a few weeks would assure us of that. Furthermore, I couldn't just leave the children. That's why I'm here—to care for them. I have an obligation to the bargain that was made, even if I wasn't a part of it," she stated, sadness evident in her voice.

"I'm not worried about the fact that you're not in love with me. I think our love for each other will grow once we're married. Your feeling of obligation to the Wilshires is admirable, and I certainly don't want to see the children left without someone to help, but I'm sure we can overcome that problem. That is, if you really want to," he said in a questioning manner.

"I'm not sure, George. I don't think I can give you an answer so quickly," she responded. *I'm just not ready to trust a man again,* she thought, *especially one I don't love.*

"Please don't think I'm placing pressure upon you, Delphinia, but I want to be absolutely honest. I've been calling on Katy McVay from time to time also. I would prefer to marry you, but if you're going to turn me down, I need to know now," he replied.

"You mean if I reject you, you're going to ask Katy to marry you?"

"I am. I think highly of Katy also. Unlike you, I believe love truly blossoms after marriage. You are my first choice, but I want to be married when I start my new assignment," he responded.

"Under the circumstances, I hope she will accept your offer and the two of you will be very happy," Delphinia answered. Rising from her chair, she held out her hand to him. "I have truly enjoyed our friendship, George. I wish you much happiness and thank you for all the kindness you've extended. I am honored you would ask me to marry you, but I think we both now realize our thoughts on love and marriage differ enough that your choice should be someone else."

"I'm sorry we can't make this work," he replied as they walked outside and he got on his horse.

"Good luck with Katy," she called out, watching him ride down the path. Slowly she walked into the house and sat down in the rocker, contemplating the consequences of her decision, wondering if she should change her mind and go after him.

Voices from outside brought her back to the present, and the twins began to stir in the bedroom. Jonathan, Josh, and Joey came rushing into the room, concern and excitement evident as they all tried to talk at once.

"I need your help, Phiney. The boys can watch the twins," Jonathan shouted above the boys' chatter.

"Let's find Tessie. I'd rather have her stay with them. What's going on?" she asked, not yet convinced it was necessary to leave the twins in the care of their overanxious brothers.

"She's gone to pick berries. I need you now. The cow's giving birth, and she's having a hard time. Come on," he shouted, rushing to the barn to grab some rope and then running for the pasture.

Soon after Delphinia left the cabin, she could hear the cow's deep bellowing, and she wondered what Jonathan could possibly expect her to do. She did not know anything about birthing children, let alone animals, and besides, couldn't a cow do that without help? she wondered.

Nellie, the small black heifer was lying down as Josie, the older brown-and-white cow, appeared to stand guard a short distance away. Jonathan was already at Nellie's side, motioning Delphinia to hurry. Not sure what to expect, her gait had grown slower and slower as she approached the laboring animal. Nothing could have prepared her for the experience. The cow's eyes were open wide, registering fear and pain. A low, bellowing moan came from deep in the animal's throat just as Delphinia walked up beside Jonathan.

"I don't know what to do. I think we should have Josh ride for Mr. Aplington. He'll be able to help," she offered, near panic.

"There's no time for that. If we don't get this calf out, we'll lose both of them. I don't want to lose the calf, but it's probably already dead. I'll hold onto Nellie while you reach up inside her and see if you can grab hold of the calf's legs. If you can, pull with all your might."

"I can't do that! You want me to reach up inside the cow? That is the most absurd thing I've ever heard. . .not to mention offensive. If it's so important, do it yourself," she retorted, her face registering disgust.

"*Delphinia,* this cow is going to die! I don't have time to listen to your nonsense. You can't hold onto Nellie. Now reach in there and pull!" he commanded as froth oozed from Nellie's mouth, and her tongue lolled to the side.

Going down on her knees, Delphinia closed her eyes and felt her hands begin to shake. "All right, I can do this," she told herself, peeking out of one eye. Taking in a gulp of air, she thrust her arm high inside the cow. The assault was met by Nellie's bellow and a flailing leg. "I thought you were going to hold her!" Delphinia screamed.

"I'm trying. Can you feel anything?"

"I think so. . .yes. Jonathan, hold her still! How do you expect me to take care of this when you're not doing your part?"

He looked at her in astonishment. "*You're taking care of it?*"

"I don't see you doing much of anything," she grunted, leaning back and pulling with all her might. "This isn't working. I think it moved a little, but I can't get a good hold."

Jonathan grabbed the piece of rope he had brought from the barn and tossed it to her. "Reach in and tie that around its legs. Be sure you get both legs."

"This isn't a quilting party, Jonathan," she rebutted. "Next, you'll be telling me to embroider a lazy-daisy stitch on its rump."

Her remark brought the hint of a smile to his face. "Make a loop in the rope, slide it around the legs, and tighten it. When you're sure the rope is tight, try pulling again. Once you feel it coming, don't let up. If you slack off, it might get hop-locked, and we'll lose both of them," he instructed.

All of a sudden, the heat was stifling, and Delphinia felt herself begin to retch. "Not now, Phiney. There isn't time for you to be sick," he commanded.

"I'll try to keep that in mind," she replied curtly, tying a slipknot into the rope.

"You need to hurry!" he yelled.

"Jonathan, you are not helping this predicament with your obtrusive behavior! How do you expect the cow to remain calm if you keep hollering all the time," she preached at him. "I have the rope ready, and if you will kindly hold Nellie still this time, I will begin. Everything is going to be fine."

His jaw went slack as she finished her short speech. Where had that come from? She seemed totally in command, and a calmness had taken the place of the near hysteria she had exhibited only minutes before. He kept his eyes on her and tightly gripped the heifer when she nodded she was ready to begin.

With almost expert ease, and over the vigorous protests of Nellie, she managed to secure both of the calf's front legs. Being careful not to let up, she worked arduously, pulling and tugging, her arms aching as the calf was finally pulled into the world. The calf's feeble bawl affirmed its birth. "It's alive," she said, tears streaming down her face.

"Let's hope it stays that way, and let's hope Nellie does the same," Jonathan answered.

"They're both going to be fine," she replied confidently.

"Take your apron and clean out its nose, while I check Nellie," he ordered.

"Yes, Sir! Any other commands?" she inquired, watching the new mother turn and begin lapping her tongue over the calf in a slow, deliberate manner.

"Not right now. It looks like Nellie's going to be a good mama. She's got her a nice lookin' little calf," he said, ignoring the barb she had given.

Delphinia sat back on her heels watching the two animals in wonderment. "There surely was a transformation in your attitude when you were helping me," Jonathan commented. "At first, I thought you were going to be less help than Josh. One minute you were retching, and the next you were ordering me around and taking charge," he laughed.

Turning to look at him, she quietly replied, "It was God who took charge, Jonathan. I merely prayed. But I knew that as soon as I finished that prayer for help, everything was going to be all right."

"You're quite a mystery, Phiney," he said, slowly shaking his head. "First, you're giving me the devil, and next, you're praising God."

"I'm not sure I'm such a mystery. I criticize you only when it's needed," she laughed. "I do know I fail to praise God enough for all He does. I sometimes forget we serve a mighty God and that much can be wrought through prayer. My mother taught me that when I was very young, and I watched Granny live it daily." She reached up from where she sat and grasped his extended hand.

"Thanks for your help, Phiney. I couldn't have done it without you. I'm sure if Nellie and her baby could thank you, they would." Almost as if on cue, the tiny calf let out a warbling cry, causing both of them to smile.

"By the way, was that George Martin I saw leaving awhile ago?" he questioned later, as they walked toward the house.

"Yes. He's been called to another church and will be leaving the end of the month," she answered.

"George is a fine preacher, but I can't say I'm sorry to see him leave," he responded.

"You may be. He's gone to ask for Katy McVay's hand in marriage," she told him, sure that that would take the smug grin from his face.

"Katy? Why would he be asking for Katy's hand? I know he's fond of you."

"He asked for my hand," she answered, saying nothing further.

"He what?" Jonathan pulled her to an abrupt stop. "What did you tell him?"

"I told him no."

"So now he's gone to ask Katy?"

"It appears so," she answered and then related enough of their conversation to hopefully stop his questions, while watching his face for reaction.

"I didn't know she had taken a shine to the preacher. They might make a good match," he replied. "The less competition the better, as far as I'm concerned," he mumbled under his breath.

"What did you say?" she asked, turning toward him.

"Nothing to concern yourself with," he replied and began whistling as they walked to the house.

Chapter 11

With the coming of early summer, the days grew longer, and the beauty of nature began to unfold. The twins were able to play outside as Delphinia, aided by Jonathan, prepared the ground for her garden. Surprisingly, she found herself anxious to begin the arduous task, wondering if she would remember all that Granny had taught her. She felt challenged to prove she had been a capable student, worthy of the older woman's confidence.

Jonathan assured her she would be an adept gardener, pointing to the fact that she had nagged him almost continuously until he had given in and tilled enough ground for an early planting of potatoes in late March. Besides, the strawberries were already beginning to blossom, thanks to her attentive care and the cooperative weather.

Nate and Nettie found enjoyment following behind and playing in the turned soil, occasionally spotting a worm or some other crawling creature that they would attempt to capture. In late afternoon, the older children would return from school and go about their chores, enjoying the freedom that the change of season allowed. All but Tessie. If she found enjoyment in anything, she hid it from Delphinia.

It seemed that no matter how earnestly Delphinia prayed, she had not been able to make any headway with Tessie. She tried everything from cajoling to ignoring her, but nothing seemed to work. The young girl was determined to do all in her power to make those around her miserable, particularly Delphinia. She was not unkind to the other children, yet she did not go out of her way to help them. She performed her chores, but if Delphinia requested additional help, she would become angry or sulk. When Jonathan was about, she was on her best behavior, although it was obvious that even at those times, she was unhappy.

Saturday arrived bright and sunny, and Jonathan declared it would be a wonderful day for fishing down at the creek. In return for preparation of a picnic lunch, he offered to take all of the children on the excursion and give Delphinia some much-needed time alone. She was overwhelmed by the offer and questioned whether he thought the twins would allow him to do any fishing. When he assured her he would be able to handle the twins, she began packing a lunch for their outing.

"I'm not going," Tessie announced in a voice that almost defied either of them to oppose her decision.

"I'd like you to come with us, Tessie," her uncle answered, sitting down at the kitchen table with a cup of coffee. "Delphinia has little time to herself. She's had to care for all of us without much opportunity for leisure. I hope you'll reconsider your decision."

"If she doesn't want me around, I'll stay out on the porch or in the orchard," she petulantly answered.

"No, I'd like to have you stay with me, Tessie. If you don't want to go fishing, we can enjoy the day together," Delphinia replied sweetly, looking over at Jonathan to let him know she would not mind.

The children were so excited that Delphinia finally sent them outdoors until she completed packing the lunch and Jonathan was prepared to leave. Following him to the porch, Delphinia noticed the questioning look in his eyes as he turned to bid her farewell.

"We'll be just fine," she assured him. "It's you who will be in for a day of it, believe me! I'm sure there will be no fish returning with you, so I'll have some beans and corn bread ready," she bantered.

"We'll see about that!" Jonathan responded, accepting her challenge. Lifting Nettie upon his shoulders, he grabbed Nate's chubby hand and cautioned Josh not to forget their lunch. Joey ran along carrying the fishing poles Jonathan had crafted, all of them full of eagerness to catch a fish for supper. Waving after the departing group, Delphinia wished them good luck and stood watching until they were out of sight.

Slowly returning to the kitchen, she began clearing the breakfast dishes from the table. "I think I'll make gooseberry pies for dessert tonight, Tessie. If you'll wash off the berries while I finish up the dishes, we can be done in no time. I thought I'd go out to the barn and go through my trunks. I have some things stored out there I'd like to use."

Although there was no response, Tessie picked up the pail of berries and headed toward the well to fetch water. Delphinia noticed that instead of returning to the kitchen to visit, she sat isolated on the porch until her task was completed and then reappeared.

As Delphinia mixed the pie dough and began to roll it, she asked if Tessie would like to accompany her to the barn.

"I suppose. There's nothing else to do," came the girl's curt reply. Nothing further passed between them, and once the gooseberries had been sweetened and poured into the pie shells, Delphinia placed them in the oven.

"I think these will be fine while we're down at the barn. You remind me they're in the oven if I get forgetful. Once I get going through those trunks, I may get absentminded," she smiled, removing her apron and throwing it over the back of a wooden chair.

Tessie followed her, giving no acknowledgment that any words had been spoken.

The barn was warm, and the smell of hay wafted through the air as Delphinia proceeded to the far stall to see the calf she had pulled into the world only a few weeks ago. How he was growing! Josh had named him "Lucky," and they had agreed it was a good choice.

Tessie stood by waiting, a look of boredom evident on her face, but Delphinia pretended not to notice. They made their way toward the rear of the barn and, after brushing off the dirt, unlatched the hasp and opened the trunk. Lifting the items out one by one, Delphinia began sorting into piles those belongings she wished to take into the house and the ones she would leave packed. From time to time, Tessie would show a spark of interest in an item but would not allow herself to inquire. Near the bottom of the trunk, wrapped in a woolen blanket, Delphinia found her mother's china teapot. She carefully unwrapped it and stared at it as if she expected it to come to life.

"We've already got a teapot," Tessie exclaimed, wanting her to hurry up.

"Yes, I know. But this was my mother's teapot and her mother's before her. It is very special to me. In fact, I remember the last time it was used," she continued, not particularly caring if the girl listened. She needed to recall the memory, just to validate who she had been, even if no one else cared.

"You may remember I told you about the quilt that's on my bed. My mother and I spent many hours making that quilt. It's probably my most precious possession. When I had finally completed the final stitches and it had passed Mama's inspection, we had a celebration. My mother seldom used this china teapot. It sat on a shelf in the cabinet because she feared it might get broken. It was one of the few possessions her mother had passed on to her when she married and moved to Illinois," Delphinia related as Tessie stared toward the barn door.

"Anyway, that day my mother had baked bread, and she said we were going to have a tea party to commemorate the completion of my first quilt. She brewed a special mint tea in this teapot and cut slices of warm bread for us. She opened one of her jars of preserves, and we had such a gay time," she reminisced.

"Do you think the pies are done yet?" was Tessie's only remark to the account Delphinia had just given.

"What? Oh yes, I suppose they'll soon be ready," answered Delphinia, coming back to the present. Lovingly she wrapped the teapot back in the woolen blanket and placed it in the trunk, knowing this was not the time to move it into the cabin. *Perhaps, one day it will sit on a shelf in my home,* she hoped.

Swiftly, she placed one pile of her belongings back into the trunk and bundled the rest in a tablecloth. Walking back to the house with her collection, she could smell the pies and quickened her step.

"Tessie, check those pies while I put this in my room, please," she requested as she stepped into her bedroom, coming face-to-face with a large Indian bouncing on the edge of her bed.

Stifling the scream that was caught in her throat, she attempted to smile and remain calm. "Tessie, there's an Indian sitting on my bed," she said, staring directly at the warrior. "Try and quietly leave the cabin. I'm hopeful he thinks I'm talking to him, so don't say anything, just leave. He doesn't look like the other Indians that have been to the house. Go to the Aplingtons' for help."

The Indian continued to bounce on the mattress until she quit speaking; and then, with alarming speed, he jumped up, pushed his way by her, and ran into the kitchen. Delphinia turned to see him holding Tessie by the arm, pulling her back inside the house. He slammed the door shut and, standing in front of the barrier, motioned they should not attempt to leave.

Slowly he walked toward Tessie and began circling her, occasionally stopping and staring. Tears began to trickle down the girl's face, and Delphinia moved closer to place an arm around her, only to have it slapped away by the intruder.

"Stay," he commanded Delphinia, pointing to the spot where she was standing. He moved closer to Tessie and grabbed a handful of her hair back and forth between his fingers, occasionally making some sound.

Tessie, overcome by fear and sure he was planning to scalp her, could stand it no longer and lunged toward Delphinia for protection.

"You, sit," he commanded, pushing the young girl into a chair.

"Obviously, he understands some English, Tessie. Just try to remain calm, and I'll see if we can communicate," Delphinia said as soothingly as possible.

Issuing a prayer for help, Delphinia smiled at the uninvited visitor and, while making hand motions, asked, "You, hungry? Want to eat?"

She walked toward one of the pies cooling on the table and lifted it toward him as an offering. Lowering and raising his head in affirmation, he reached across the table and, forming his hand into a scoop, dug into the pie and brought out a handful of steaming gooseberries. Letting out a howl, he flung his arm, causing the berries to fly in all directions about the room. Tessie was close to hysteria, unable to control her high-pitched laughter, which further angered the injured warrior.

Dear God, Delphinia prayed silently, *I'm relying on Mark 11:24. You promise that if we believe we've already received what we're praying for, it will be ours. Well, Lord, I believe this Indian is going to leave our house and not harm either of us. The problem is, I'm afraid things have gotten out of control, what with his burned hand and Tessie's continual outbursts. So I'd be real thankful if I could claim that promise right now.*

Assured the matter was safely in God's hands and would be favorably resolved, Delphinia confidently offered the glowering trespasser a wet towel for his hand. He grunted and wrapped the moist cloth around the burn. Tessie became silent until the Indian once again walked to where she sat and began caressing her hair.

"Please, Tessie, try to remain composed. The Lord is going to see us through this, but you must act rationally. I'm going to try and find out what he wants," Delphinia quietly advised. The blue eyes that looked back at her were apprehensive, but Tessie did not cry.

Considering the pie disaster, Delphinia thought it best she try to distract the Indian with something other than food. Eyeing a small mirror, she tentatively offered it. Although somewhat suspicious, curiosity won out, and he took the object from her hand. At first, his reflection startled him, but then, as he made faces at himself in the glass, he seemed pleased. Soon, he was walking around the room holding it up to objects and peeking to see what had been reproduced for him. Standing behind Tessie, he held the mirror in front of her, producing an image of both their faces that, from the sounds he was making, he found highly amusing.

While the Indian continued his antics with the mirror, Delphinia tried to assemble her thoughts. It was obvious he was quite fascinated with Tessie's red hair. If only she knew what he was planning. No sooner had that thought rushed through her head than the Indian grabbed Tessie's arm and started toward the door.

"We go," he pronounced in a commanding voice.

Once again, Tessie broke into wails, and Delphinia's heart began pounding as she screamed, "No, stop!" and motioned him into her bedroom. Dragging Tessie along, he followed and was met by Delphinia's display of belongings she had just carried from the barn.

"Take these things," she said, pointing to the array on her bed. "She stays here," she continued, trying to pull Tessie beside her.

A deep grunt emitted while he sorted through the items. He was smiling, which pleased Delphinia, and she whispered to Tessie she should move behind her. He did not seem to notice the movement, or so they thought, as he pulled the tablecloth around the items and tied a large knot.

"I take," he said, placing the bundle on the floor and pointing to himself. "Her too," he said, indicating Tessie.

Well, this is really beginning to try my patience, Delphinia thought. *Not only is he going to take all my treasures, but he wants Tessie to boot. I just won't tolerate that kind of behavior. After all, fair is fair!*

Moving a step toward him and placing both hands on her hips, Delphinia looked him full in the eyes and vehemently retorted, "No. Not her." She shook her head negatively and pointed to Tessie. "She's mine," and placed an arm around the girl to indicate possession.

Somewhat taken aback by Delphinia's aggressive behavior, the Indian stood observing the two young women. Raising an arm to his head and lifting a bit of hair, he pointed toward Tessie.

"Oh, no! He wants to scalp me!" the child screamed.

"I don't think he's ever seen red hair before, Tessie. Perhaps if we would just cut a lock or two and give it to him. What do you think?" asked Delphinia, not sure of what the Indian wanted.

Tessie merely nodded her head, and Delphinia walked to her bureau, removed her sewing scissors, and walked toward Tessie, all under the close observation of the man. Reaching toward the mass of red ringlets, Delphinia snipped a thick lock of hair and handed it to the warrior. He smiled and seemed in agreement.

"You, go now," Delphinia ordered.

Stooping to pick up the bundle, he reached across the bed and in one sweeping motion pulled the quilt from Delphinia's bed and wrapped it around himself.

"Oh no, you don't," yelled Delphinia. "Not my quilt. That's mine, and you can't have it," she screamed, attempting to pull it from his shoulders.

Angered by her actions, the Indian threw down the quilt and reached to grab Tessie.

Realizing she had provoked him and was about to lose her advantage, she tried to calm herself. "No, not her. Take me," she said, throwing herself in front of the girl.

The intruder backed up slightly, and Delphinia, with tears in her eyes, pleaded, "You can have my quilt; you can have me and all of my belongings. Just don't take this child. She needs to be here with her family. I'll go with you willingly, and I'll give you anything from this house you want. . .just not the girl. Please, not her," she begged.

She did not know how much he understood, or what he would do, but she lifted the quilt back around his shoulders and then held out the bundle that had been resting on the floor. Looking directly in her eyes, he took the bundle and, wearing her quilt across his shoulders, slowly walked from the room and out of the house.

Chapter 12

Hearing the door close, Delphinia rushed into the kitchen and lowered the wooden bar they used as a lock. Returning to the bedroom, she found Tessie huddled in the far corner of the bedroom, legs drawn to her chest and with her head buried low, resting on her knees. Going to her, Delphinia enveloped the child with both her arms and began talking to her in a soothing, melodic voice. Tessie did not respond, and Delphinia began to worry that she had slipped away into the recesses of her own mind, like those people she had heard about, who were sent off to insane asylums.

"Tessie," she said quietly, "this isn't going to do at all. The Lord has kept His promise, and we're safe from harm. Now, you're going to have to do your part." Moving back slightly and cupping her hands under the girl's chin, she lifted the beautiful crown of red hair until Tessie was eye to eye with her.

Her eyes are vacant, and she's not going to respond, Delphinia thought.

"Tessie, I know you may not hear me, but in case you do, I apologize," and then Delphinia landed a resounding slap across the girl's cheek.

"What are you doing?" Tessie asked, dismayed by the act.

Overjoyed with the results, Delphinia hugged her close, laughing and crying simultaneously. "Oh, Tessie, I was so worried you weren't going to respond. I tried to arouse you, but to no avail. I'm so sorry, but I didn't know what else to do but give you a good whack."

"Are you sure he's gone?" the girl sobbed, tightly embracing Delphinia.

"Yes, he's gone, and everything is fine," she reassured, returning the embrace.

Tessie's body trembled, and once again she broke into racking sobs. "Why did he try to take me? What if he comes back? What are we going to do?" she wailed between sobs and gulps of breath, her body heaving in distress.

"Tessie, calm yourself. Everything is fine. He won't come back. He's probably miles away by now," she crooned, wiping the girl's tears.

"But what if he isn't? What if he's outside lurking about, just waiting for one of us?" she questioned, faltering in her attempt to gain composure.

"If he wanted one of us, he wouldn't have left the cabin," Delphinia answered, holding the girl and stroking her hair. "We're fine, Tessie, just fine," she assured for what seemed like the hundredth time.

Slowly Tessie's body began to relax, and finally she gave Delphinia a half-hearted smile. "Perhaps we should go sit in the kitchen where it's a bit more comfortable," she suggested.

"That's a wonderful idea," Delphinia responded, her cramped body needing to stretch. "I'll put the kettle on for tea."

"We need to talk," Tessie whispered.

"I'd like that very much," came Delphinia's response.

Making their way into the kitchen, Tessie wearily dropped onto one of the wooden chairs. "I know I've been spiteful to you for no apparent reason. You didn't do anything but try to be nice to me. I've treated you horribly, and in return you offered yourself to that savage. You allowed him to take your beautiful quilt and other belongings. I know that quilt was very special, and yet you gave it willingly for me. Why did you do it?" she coaxed, tears slipping down her face.

Delphinia poured two cups of steaming tea and sat down beside her. "When I first came here, I anticipated you would resent me. Your Uncle Jonathan had forewarned me you had not accepted the deaths of your parents. I must add, however, that I didn't expect your bitterness to last this long! Granny and I prayed for you every day, Tessie, and I have continued since her death. We both realized you were in torment, and, although it has been difficult at times, I have tried to remember your pain when you've treated me impertinently." She smiled, pausing to take a sip of tea.

"Yes, but *why* did you do it?" she implored.

"This is going to take a few minutes of explanation, Tessie. Please try to be patient. I've been waiting for a very long time for this moment to arrive."

Tessie smiled, and Delphinia continued. "You're right about the quilt. It was my pride and joy. But it is merely an object, not a living, breathing child of God, like you. In my prayers, I have consistently asked God to show me a way to give you peace from your anger and turmoil. That Indian's appearance while we were here alone was God's answer to my prayers. Had I not offered myself and those possessions that were important to me, you might never have believed that anybody loved you. I'm sure you know the verse in the Bible that says, 'Greater love hath no man than this—' "

" 'That a man lay down his life for his friends.' John 15:13," interrupted Tessie. "Granny taught me that verse long ago."

"I love you that much, Tessie, and Jesus loves you that much too. He sacrificed His life for you, so that you could live. . .not be consumed by hate and anger," she said, watching the play of emotions that crossed the girl's face.

"I'm not just angry because Ma and Pa died, Phiney," she began. "Nobody knows everything that happened that day, except me."

"Perhaps you'd feel better if you confided in someone. I know Jonathan would sympathize with anything you told him," Delphinia encouraged.

"No, I think perhaps I should tell you. Uncle Jonathan might not be so understanding. You see, it's my fault. I killed my parents. *Do you still love me now?*" she asked, her voice trembling.

"Yes, Tessie, I still love you. But since you've taken me into your confidence, would you consider telling me what part you played in their deaths?" she asked in a kindly manner.

Her eyes seemed to glaze over as she recounted the events of that day. Delphinia noted the story was almost identical to what Jonathan had previously related to her on the wagon train. "So now, you can see how I am the cause of their deaths," she said, ending the narrative.

Delphinia stared at her, dumbfounded. "No, Tessie, I don't. Jonathan related that exact account to me before my arrival. Please explain what was your fault," she queried.

"Don't you see? I was the one who wanted to go the creek-bed route. If we had gone the other way, we would have been safe," she wailed.

"Oh, Tessie," Delphinia whispered, embracing the child, "there is no way we can possibly guess what would have happened if you'd taken the other route. Perhaps the wagon would have been struck by lightning, causing it to go up in flames. Perhaps one of the horses would have broken a leg in a chuckhole causing the wagon to overturn and crush all of you. Any number of things could have happened. We'll never know. What we do know is that the lives of you children were saved. You're not guilty of anything. You asked your father to travel a different road. He knew the dangers that route held, and he made a decision to go that direction. His choice was based on knowledge he had available to him. It didn't appear it was going to rain, and there were no more hazards than the other road might have had in store for his family. You have no fault in their deaths and no reason to condemn yourself. Somehow you must accept that fact. Don't die with your parents, Tessie. Let them live through you. If you'll only allow it, others will see the love and gentleness of Sarah and Jake Wilshire shining in your eyes. That's what they would have wanted, and I think if you'll search your heart, you know that already."

"I know you're right, but it hurts so much, and I don't want them to be forgotten," she confided.

Clasping her hands around Tessie's, Delphinia looked at her with a sense of understanding and said, "How could they ever be forgotten with five such wonderful children? You're a testimony to their lives. It's not easy to lose your parents, but God will help fill that emptiness, if you'll allow it. It's up to you, but I don't think you want a life full of unhappiness and brooding any more than I do. Pray for peace and joy, Tessie, and it will come to you when you least expect it."

The girl gave a half-hearted smile through her tears and whispered, "I'll try."

"I know you will, and I'll be praying right along with you."

Jonathan had never been so exhausted. *I don't know how Phiney keeps up with these children all day long, day after day,* he thought.

He lost count of the times he had chased after the twins, both of them determined to wander off and pick a flower or run after a squirrel. When they weren't trying to explore, they were playing at the edge of the water, caking mud in their hair and all over their clothes. With no soap or washcloth available, he decided the only way to get them presentable was to dunk them in the creek before starting home. Josh and Joey thought it was hilarious watching their Uncle Jonathan put a twin under each arm and wade into the cool water. Their squeals of protest only added to the boys' enjoyment of the event.

"You guys quit your laughin' and get our gear picked up. It's time we headed back to the house. They'll be expecting some fish for supper, so get a move on."

The air was warm as they made their way through the orchard, and, as they approached the cabin, the boys were still chattering about who caught the biggest fish and who tangled the fishing lines. On and on it went, Jonathan ignoring them for the most part and hoping the twins were "dried out" before Phiney got hold of them.

"Wonder why they got the door closed, Uncle Jonathan. You suppose they went visiting somewhere, and you'll have to cook the fish?" Josh questioned.

"I don't know, Josh. But if they're gone, you can forget the fish. I'm not cooking. I've about had all the women's work I can stand for one day."

"Ahhh, Uncle Jon, please," came from both boys in unison.

"Let's just wait and see if they're home. Run ahead and check the door, Josh."

"I can't get in, Uncle Jon. It's locked," he yelled back to them.

Terror ran through Jonathan. Why would Phiney have the door barred? There had been no rumors of problems with the Indians, and it did not appear that anyone else was at the cabin. Placing the twins on the ground, he took off at full speed toward the cabin, calling back to Joey to remain with the smaller children until he was sure all was safe.

"Phiney, Phiney!" he yelled as he reached the entry and began pounding on the door.

"I'm coming, Jonathan. You need not yell," she answered, allowing him entry.

His eyes immediately fixed on Tessie. Bedraggled, a red handprint across her cheek, her face wet from tears, and her eyes puffy from crying, he went racing to her, swooping her into his arms.

"What's happened here?" he asked in an accusatory tone, looking directly at Delphinia.

She could feel the hair on the back of her neck begin to bristle at this tone. "Why, I've just finished beating her, Jonathan. Why do you ask?" she quietly responded with an angelic smile.

Both women began to laugh, causing Tessie to erupt into loud hiccups. Jonathan stared at the two of them as if they had gone mad. "If you'll quit acting so preposterous, we'll explain what happened. Where are the twins?" Delphinia inquired, "I hope you haven't forgotten them," she smirked.

"That's enough," he answered, calming somewhat. "Joey, you can bring the twins up now," he called out the door.

"Josh, go help him and bring the fish. I'm sure Phiney is ready to eat crow while we eat fish," he said, tilting his head to one side and giving her a crooked grin.

As Josh came in, carrying a string of fish and pulling Nettie along under protest, Jonathan said, "I'd be happy to sit here and listen to the events of the afternoon, ladies, while you fry that fish." But he was not prepared for the story he heard and continually interrupted them, pacing back and forth while they related the tale. Tessie completed the narrative by telling how the Indian finally left the cabin with Delphinia's possessions and her quilt wrapped around him.

"There's an even more important part, but I'll tell you that when we're alone, Uncle Jon," Tessie remarked.

Delphinia smiled and nodded toward the door. "Why don't the two of you take a short walk while I finish supper? We'll be fine in here."

When they returned, Jonathan immediately went to Delphinia and, placing his arms around her, whispered, "How can I ever thank you? She's finally come back to us."

"It wasn't me that did it, Jonathan. It was answered prayer," she responded. "However, if you're determined to find a way to thank me, you can fry this fish for supper," she said, laughing at the look of disdain he displayed with that request.

Grinning, he released her and said, "I should have known you'd be quick with an answer."

Chapter 13

The morning dawned glorious with puffy white clouds that appeared to almost touch the earth. A pale orange sun shone through, causing a profusion of magnificent colors and the promise of a gorgeous day. Looking out the front door of the place she now called home, Delphinia wondered how anything could be more beautiful. The view nearly took her breath away.

She waved her arm in welcome to Jonathan who was coming from the barn, apparently already through with some of his morning chores. "Breakfast is just about ready. Isn't it a splendid morning?" she called out.

"That it is. We couldn't have planned a better day for going to town," he responded.

Delphinia watched as he continued toward her, knowing Granny had been right. She did love this giant of a man who had turned her world upside down. Her day became joyful just watching him walk into a room. Her feelings were undeniably true, and they had been for quite some time, although she did not want to admit it. She had given this thing called "love" a considerable amount of thought. Late at night lying in bed, she had gone through the diverse emotions she had felt for Jonathan since that first day when they had met back in Illinois. They seemed to range from dread and dislike to admiration and caring. For some time she had had difficulty keeping herself from staring at him all the time. Even Tessie had mentioned it and knowingly grinned. When she considered how Jonathan might feel toward her, she was not so sure her feelings were fully returned. He treated her well, was kind and considerate, and listened to her before making decisions. But that was not love. Also, he treated everyone that way. He had kissed her on a few occasions, but it seemed that each of those times had either ended in a quarrel or could be interpreted as pity. She realized he had tried to make the preacher jealous with his attention, but she was sure that was so he would not have to go looking for someone else to care for the children. On several occasions he had mentioned he could not get along without her, but she reasoned that that was because he needed help with the children, not because of love.

"Are those the biscuits I smell burning?" Jonathan asked, bringing her back to the present. "That's just about once a day now you're scorching something, isn't it?" He sat down at the table with a cup of freshly poured coffee.

"Is there something wrong with the stove, or have you just forgotten how to cook these days?" he joked.

"I think she's in love," Tessie teased.

"That will be enough out of you, Tessie. Get busy and dress the twins so we can get started for town," Delphinia responded angrily, knowing the girl had spoken the truth.

"She's only having fun, Phiney. You don't need to bite her head off," Jonathan responded, giving Tessie a quick hug and nodding for her to get the twins ready.

Irritated with herself for scolding the girl, Delphinia walked into the other room and sat down on the bed. "I'm sorry, Tessie. My remark was uncalled for. Perhaps it made me uncomfortable."

"Why, because it's the truth? Anyone can see you're in love with Uncle Jon. You look like a lovesick calf when he comes into a room, so it's hard not to notice." They both burst out laughing at her remark; and Jonathan, hearing the giggles from the bedroom, smiled in relief, pleased that this had not caused discord between the two now that they had become friends.

"How 'bout we get this burned breakfast eaten and get started toward town before nightfall, unless you two would rather stay here and do chores all day," Jonathan called from the kitchen.

That statement brought everyone clamoring for the table, and they all agreed the biscuits weren't too bad if you put lots of gravy on them. Delphinia good-naturedly took their bantering, and soon, they were loaded into the wagon and on their way. Tessie offered to sit in back with both of the twins, allowing Jonathan and Delphinia a small amount of privacy.

"How many supplies do you plan on buying today?" Jonathan queried.

"Just the usual, except Tessie and I want to spend a little time looking about for some thread and fabric. In fact, if you could keep an eye on the younger ones while we do that, I'd be thankful," she responded.

"What are the two of you planning now?" he asked with a grin.

"Tessie's asked me to help her finish the quilt that Sarah started before her death. She wants to use it for her bed. We decided to purchase the items needed to finish it today, and as soon as harvest is over, we'll get started with our sewing."

"You hadn't told me about that. I can't tell you how pleased it makes me that Tessie has finally accepted your friendship. I know Sarah and Granny would be mighty happy," he smiled.

"I think they would be too, Jonathan. She's a sweet girl, and I hope completing the quilt with her will be good for both of us. Somehow, quilting with my mother gave me a feeling of closeness. We would visit and laugh together as we sewed the stitches, knowing each one helped hold the quilt together and made it more beautiful. It's much like the threads of love that tie folks' hearts together. There are the small, tightly sewn stitches, close together, like a family. Then there are the larger, scattered stitches, like the friends we make in our lifetime. I believe God weaves all those threads together in a beautiful pattern to join our hearts and make us who we are, don't you think?"

He looked down at her, and a slow smile crossed his face. "You, know, you never cease to amaze me with your ideas. That's a beautiful thought, and I agree," he answered, placing his hand on top of Delphinia's.

She glanced toward him, and he was staring down at their two hands. She watched as he enveloped hers and gave a gentle squeeze. Slowly, he looked up and met her watchful eyes as Delphinia felt her cheeks flush and a quiver of emotions run through her entire being. The question in her eyes was evident.

"Yes," he said, looking deep into the two, dark brown liquid pools.

"Yes, what?" she inquired. "I didn't ask you anything."

"Yes, you did, Phiney, and the answer is yes. I love you very much."

Leaning over toward him, she said, "I can't hear you above the children's singing."

"I said I love you, Delphinia Elizabeth Hughes," he said and leaned down to gently place a kiss on her lips.

The children burst forth with hoots of laughter and loud clapping at the scene unfolding in front of them. Jonathan joined in their laughter and then lifted Delphinia's hand to his lips for a kiss, just as they arrived at the general store.

"Jonathan, there's some mail over here for ya," called Mr. McVay from the rear of the store. "Think there's one in there for Phiney too."

"For me?" she questioned, looking at Jonathan. "Who would be writing me?"

"Only one way to find out. Let's take a look," he answered as they headed toward the voice.

Jonathan quickly perused the mail and handed over the envelope bearing Delphinia's name. He could see from the return address that it was from her father.

"It's from my pa," she commented. "From the looks of the envelope, he's in Colorado. I think I'll wait until I get home to read it," she said, folding the letter in half and placing it in her skirt pocket.

"I'll go give my order to Mrs. McVay, and as soon as she's finished, Tessie and I can look at fabric. I better get back to the children. It looks like the twins are going to try and get into the cracker barrel head first," she exclaimed, moving toward the front of the store at a quick pace.

Jonathan smiled after her but could not shake the feeling of foreboding that had come over him ever since he had seen the letter.

Why now? He thought. *What does he want after all this time?* He did not know how long he had been wandering through the store, aimlessly looking at a variety of tools and dry goods when Tessie's voice brought him to attention.

"Uncle Jon, come on, we've got the order filled except for the thread and fabric. It's your turn to look after the twins."

"Sure, be right there. You women go pick out your sewing things," he smiled back at her.

He could hear them murmuring about the different thread and what color would look good with the quilt top while he helped the younger children pick out their candy.

"Oh, Jonathan, not so much," he heard Delphinia exclaim. She was looking over her shoulder at the twins who had their hands stuffed full of candy.

His attempts to extract the candy from their clenched fists resulted in wails that could be heard throughout the store. Grabbing one under each arm, Jonathan looked over at Delphinia and with a weak smile replied, "Guess I'm not doing my job very well. Think we better get out of here."

"We'll be along in just a few minutes," she called after him.

"Tessie, I think we'd better make our choices soon. Otherwise, your Uncle Jon may be forced to leave without us. I don't think he's feeling particularly patient today," she said as the two women gave each other a knowing smile.

Shortly out of town Jonathan spotted a small grove of trees and pulled over so they could have their picnic. Dinner finished, the twins romped with Joey and Josh while the women discussed getting started on the quilt and the preparations they would need to do for the harvest crew. Jonathan seemed distracted and paid little attention to anyone or the activity surrounding him, appearing lost in his own thoughts until quite suddenly he said, "Tessie, I'd like to visit with Phiney for a few minutes. Would you mind looking after the children?"

"No, of course not, Uncle Jon," she answered, rising from the blanket where she had been sitting.

As soon as Tessie was out of earshot, Jonathan took Delphinia's hands in his, looked directly in her eyes, and asked, "Have you read your pa's letter yet?"

"No, I'd almost forgotten about it. I planned to read it when we got back home. I thought I had mentioned I was going to wait," she answered with a questioning look as she patted the pocket where she had placed the letter.

"You did. I just thought perhaps you had glanced through it and had an idea of what he wanted. I'm concerned why he's writing after all this time," Jonathan remarked.

"Do you want me to read it now? In case it's bad news, I didn't want to spoil our trip, but I'll open it if you prefer," she responded.

"No, you wait like you planned. I suppose we really ought to be getting packed up before it gets much later," he answered, starting to gather their belongings and placing them in the wagon.

"You're right," she said, forcing a smile. "Tessie, would you get the children together while I finish packing the food and dishes? We need to be getting started," Delphinia called to the younger woman.

Noting Jonathan's solemn disposition, Delphinia made every attempt to pull him out of his mood. She sang, made jokes with the children, and even tried to get him to join in their word games, but her attempts were fruitless, and finally, she ceased trying.

As they neared home, a light breeze began to blow across the fields of wheat, causing the grain to bend and rise in gentle waves. "Isn't it beautiful, Jonathan? I've never seen the ocean, but my guess would be it looks a lot like that field of wheat, moving in a contented motion to greet the shore," she smiled.

A smile crossed his face as he looked at her. "I never heard anybody get quite so poetic about it, but you're right. It's downright pretty. Almost as pretty as you!"

"Why, Jonathan Wilshire! You keep up that kind of talk, and you'll have me blushing."

"Looks to me like you already are," laughed Tessie from the wagon bed as they pulled up in front of the house.

"Tessie, Josh, let's get this wagon unloaded while Phiney gets Joey and the twins ready for bed," Jonathan instructed as he lifted Delphinia down.

With one of the twins on either side and Joey in the lead, they made their way into the house, and, without any difficulty, the younger children were in bed and fast asleep.

"I've got to get a few chores done, so I'll be back in shortly," Jonathan advised Delphinia from the doorway.

"Fine," she smiled. "I'll just put a pot of coffee on, and it should be ready by the time you're finished."

After Tessie and Josh had gone to bed, Delphinia sat down in the kitchen. She slid her hand into the pocket of her skirt, pulled out the letter, and slowly opened the envelope.

Chapter 14

Dearest daughter,

I have asked an acquaintance to pen my letter. I hope this finds you well and happy in Kansas. First, I must say I am sorry for not writing you sooner. I know it was thoughtless of me, and in these almost two years, I should have acted more fatherly. However, I can't change what's in the past, and I'm hopeful you don't hold my unkind actions against me.

I wanted you to know I am in Denver City, Colorado, which is not so very far by train. As you know, I had planned on going to California in search of gold, but I stopped in Colorado and never got farther. I don't expect I will either.

Delphinia, I am dying. The doctor tells me there is no cure for this disease of consumption, but. . .

Reading that dreaded word caused Delphinia's hand to begin shaking, and the sound of Jonathan coming through the door captured her attention.

"What is it?" he asked, seeing the look of horror written on her face.

"It's Pa. He's got consumption," she quietly answered.

"How bad is he?"

"I'm not sure. I haven't finished the letter yet. Here, let me get you some coffee," she said, starting to rise from her chair.

Gently placing his hand on her shoulder, he said, "No, you finish the letter. I'll get us coffee."

Nodding her assent, she lifted the letter back into sight and read aloud.

. . .I have implored him to keep me alive so that I may see the face of my darling daughter before I die. He is doing all in his power, practicing his painful bleeding and purging remedies upon me. I am a cooperative patient, although at times I feel it would be easier to tell him: No more, I shall die now. If it were not for the fact that I must see you and know you've forgiven me, I would give it up.

My dearest, darling daughter, I implore you to come to Denver City with all haste so that I may see you before the end comes to me. I have taken the liberty of having a ticket purchased for your departure on the eight o'clock morning train out of Council Grove. You will go north to Junction City and board the Kansas Pacific, which will depart at four-twenty in the evening and arrive in Sheridan at ten the next morning. It will then be necessary for you to embark by stage into Denver City on the United States Express Company Overland Mail and Express Coach. My acquaintance has made all arrangements for your departure on the tenth of July. Your boarding passes will await you at each stop.

I beg you. Please do not disappoint me.

Your loving father

They stared silently at each other, the lack of noise deafening in their ears. Finally, Delphinia gave a forced smile and commented, "I wonder who penned that letter for Pa. It certainly was eloquent."

"Somebody else may have thought up the proper words for him, but it's his command. He wants you there. What are you going to do?"

"I don't know. It's just so. . .so sudden. I don't know what to think or what to do. How could I leave now? We've got the harvest crew due here in a week, and if I went I don't know how long I'd need to be gone. Who would do all the cooking during harvest? Who would take care of the children? Who would look after everything. It's too much of a burden for Tessie, and yet. . ."

"And yet you're going, isn't that right?" Jonathan queried, knowing his voice sounded harsh.

"He's my father, Jonathan. My only living relative."

"Right. So where was your only living relative when you wanted to stay in Illinois? He was selling you off so he could go live his own dreams. He didn't care about you," he rebutted.

But as soon as the words had been spoken, Jonathan wished he could pull them back into his mouth, for he saw the pain they had caused her.

"Oh, Phiney, I'm so very sorry," he said, pulling her into his arms as she burst forth into sobs that racked her body. "I'm criticizing your pa for being selfish and unfeeling, and here I am doing the same thing to you."

She buried her head in his shoulder, his shirt turning damp from the deluge of tears. "Please don't cry any more. You must go to your father. I know that as well as you. I'm just full of regret for waiting so long to declare my love and afraid of losing you just when I felt our lives were beginning."

"You're not losing me. I would be gone for only a short time, and then I'd return," she replied.

"I know that's what you think now, but once you get to Colorado, who knows what will happen. I realize your intentions are to return, but if your father's health is restored and he wants you to stay, or if you meet someone else. . . It's better you leave and make no promises to return."

"That's unfair, Jonathan. You make it sound as though I have no allegiance to my word and that I could not honor an engagement—if you ever asked me to marry," she haughtily answered.

He looked down into her face, feeling such a deep love rise up in him, he thought he would die from the thought of losing her. "Phiney, I would be honored to have you as my wife, but I'll not ask you for your hand in marriage until you return to Kansas. You're an honest, courageous woman, and I know you would make every effort to honor your word, but I'll not try to hamper you in that way. It would be unfair. We'll talk marriage if you return. Right now, we need to talk about getting you ready to leave."

"If that's what you truly want, Jonathan. But we will talk marriage when I return," she answered adamantly.

They talked until late deciding how to accomplish all that needed to be done before Jonathan could take her to Council Grove to meet the train. By the time they had completed their plans, both of them were exhausted. Delphinia bid Jonathan good night from the front porch, and, as she watched him walk toward his cabin, her heart was heavy with the thought of leaving this family she had grown to love. Yet deep inside, she ached to once again see her father and knew she must go.

Morning arrived all too soon, and both Delphinia and Jonathan were weary, not only from their lack of sleep but from the tasks that lay ahead. The older children uttered their disbelief that Delphinia would even consider leaving, sure they could not exist without her. Amidst flaring tempers and flowing tears, preparations for her departure continued.

Mrs. Aplington agreed to make arrangements with the neighboring farm women to feed the harvest crew, and she talked to Jennie O'Laughlin who knew a widow who agreed to come and help care for the children. Delphinia packed her smallest trunk in an effort to assure Jonathan she would not be gone long, and the next morning, after many tears and promises to write, they were on their way to meet the train.

It was a trip filled with a profusion of emotions. Fear of riding the train and meeting a stage by herself, traveling such a great distance, leaving the farm, the children, and man she now loved so dearly, all mixed with the anticipation of seeing her father.

"We've got time to spare. Let's go over to the hotel restaurant and get a hot meal," Jonathan suggested, trying to keep things seeming normal.

The meal smelled delicious, but somehow the food would not pass over the lump in her throat, and she finally ceased trying. The two of them made small talk, neither saying the things that were uppermost in their minds.

"Better finish up. The train is about ready to pull out. They're loading the baggage," Jonathan remarked.

"I guess I wasn't as hungry as I thought. Let's go ahead and leave," she answered, pushing back the wooden chair, causing it to scrape across the floor.

She waited as Jonathan paid for their meal and slowly they trod toward the waiting train.

"Looks like there's not many passengers, so you should be able to stretch out and relax a little," Jonathan stated, trying to keep from pulling her into his arms and carrying her back to his wagon.

She smiled and nodded, knowing that if she spoke at this moment, her voice would give way to tears, and she did not want to cry in front of these strangers.

"Them that's goin', let's get on board," the conductor yelled out.

Jonathan pulled her close, and Delphinia felt as though his embrace would crush the life out of her. She tilted her head back and was met by his beautiful blue eyes as he lowered his head and covered her mouth with a tender kiss.

"I love you, Delphinia Elizabeth Hughes, and the day you return, I'll ask you to be my wife," he said as he lifted his head.

"I love you also, Jonathan, and I shall answer 'yes' when you ask for my hand in marriage," she responded, smiling up at him.

He leaned down, kissed her soundly, and then turned her toward the train. "You need to board now. You'll be in our thoughts and prayers," he said as he took hold of her elbow and assisted her up the step and onto the train.

Standing on the platform, he watched as she made her way to one of the wooden seats, trying to memorize every detail of her face for fear he would never see her again.

Peering out the small window, trying to smile as a tear overflowed each eye, she waved her farewell while the train slowly clanked and chugged out of the station, leaving nothing but a billow of dark smoke hanging in the air.

Exhausted from the days of preparation for her trip, Delphinia leaned her head against the window frame and was quickly lulled to sleep by the clacking sounds of the train. She startled awake as the train jerked to a stop, and the conductor announced their arrival in Junction City. Gingerly stepping onto the platform, she made her way into the neat, limestone train depot and inquired about her ticket to Sheridan, half expecting to be told they had never heard of her. Instead, the gentleman handed her a ticket, instructed her as to the whereabouts of a nearby restaurant, and advised her the train would leave promptly at 4:20 P.M. and that she best not be late.

The information she received was correct. As they pulled out of the station,

Delphinia noted it was exactly 4:20 P.M. She found pleasure in the sights as they made their way farther west, but as nightfall arrived, she longed to be back at the cabin, getting the children ready for bed and listening to their prayers. They were due to arrive in Sheridan the next morning at ten o'clock, but the train was running late, causing Delphinia concern she might miss her stage although the conductor assured her they would arrive in ample time.

Once again, she found her ticket as promised when she arrived at the stage line, although the conductor had been wrong. She had missed the last stage and would have to wait until the next morning. That proved to be a blessing. She was able to make accommodations at the small hotel and even arranged to have a bath in her room. It was heavenly! In fact, later she tried to remember just how heavenly that bath had been, sitting cramped on the stage between two men who smelled as though they hadn't been near water in months. The dust and dirt billowed in the windows of the stage, making her even more uncomfortable, but at least she hadn't been forced to eat at the filthy way stations along the route. The hotel owner's wife had warned her of the squalid conditions she would encounter on the trip, counseling Delphinia to take along her own food and water, which had proved to be sound advice.

The trip was long and arduous, and when the man beside her said they would soon be arriving in Denver City, she heaved a sigh of relief. The stage rolled into town with the horses at full gallop and then snapped to a stop. Delphinia's head bobbed forward and then lurched back, causing her to feel as though her stomach had risen to her throat and then quickly plummeted to her feet. Not to be denied refreshment at the first saloon, her traveling companions disembarked while the coach was still moving down the dusty street. She almost laughed when the stage driver looked in the door and said, "You plannin' on jest sittin' in there, or you gonna get out, Ma'am?"

"I thought I'd wait until we came to a full stop," she answered with a slight smile.

"Well, this is about as stopped as we'll be getting, so better let me give ya a hand," he replied as he reached to assist her down.

"Thank you," she answered, just in time to see the other driver throw her trunk to the ground with a resounding thud.

"You got someone meetin' ya?" he inquired.

"I'm not sure. Perhaps it would be best if you'd move my trunk from the middle of the street into the stage office. I would be most appreciative," she said.

Delphinia was on her way to the office to inquire if her father had left a message when she heard a voice calling her name. Turning, she came face-to-face with the man who had called out to her.

"Miss Hughes, I'm sorry I'm late. We expected you on the last stage. Your father was so upset when you didn't arrive, that I've had to stay with him constantly. He went to sleep just a little while ago, and I didn't notice the time. Please forgive me. The time got away before I realized. I hope you've not been waiting long."

"No, I just arrived," she responded. "But how did you know who I was?"

"Your father told me to look for a beautiful blond with big brown eyes. You fit his description," he answered with a grin.

"I find it hard to believe my father would say I'm beautiful, Mister. . .I'm sorry, but I don't know your name."

"It's Doctor. . .Dr. Samuel Finley, at your service, Ma'am. And your father did say you are beautiful; you may ask him," he replied.

"You're the doctor my father wrote about? The one that diagnosed and has been treating him for consumption?" she questioned.

"One and the same. I'm also the acquaintance that penned the letter to you and made arrangements for your trip," he advised.

"Well, I suppose my thanks are in order, Dr. Finley. I'm sure my father appreciates your assistance as much as I do. Will you be taking me to my father now?"

"Since he's resting, perhaps you'd like to get settled and refresh yourself."

"If you're sure there's time before he awakens, that would be wonderful," she answered.

Having loaded her trunk, he assisted her into his buggy, and after traveling a short distance, they stopped in front of a white frame house with an iron fence surrounding the neatly trimmed yard. Small pink roses were climbing through latticework on each end of the front porch, and neatly trimmed shrubs lined both sides of the brick sidewalk.

"Is this my father's house?" she asked with an astonished look on her face.

"No," he replied. "This is my house. Your father needs almost constant care, and since he had no one here to stay with and I'm alone, we agreed this arrangement would be best."

When she did not respond but gave him a questioning look, he continued by adding, "It's really easier for me. I don't have to get out to make house calls since he's right here with me."

"I understand," she answered as he led her into the fashionably appointed parlor, although she was not quite sure she understood anything.

"You just sit down and make yourself at home while I fetch your trunk, and then you can get settled," he advised, exiting the front door.

Delphinia watched out the front window as Dr. Finley walked toward the buggy. He was tall, although not as tall as Jonathan, perhaps an inch or two shorter. He had hair that was almost coal black with just a touch of gray at the temples and a slight wave on either side, gray eyes, and the complexion of a man who worked outdoors rather than practiced medicine. His broad shoulders allowed him to carry her trunk with apparent ease, and he carried himself with an air of assurance, perhaps bordering on arrogance, Delphinia thought.

She moved away from the window as he entered the house, and when he beckoned for her to follow him, she did so without question.

"This is to be your room; I hope you will find it adequate. But if there is anything you need, please let me know. You go ahead and freshen up, and I'll check on your father. I promise to let you know as soon as he's awake," he said as he left the room, pulling the door closed behind him.

After washing herself, she unpinned her hair and began to methodically pull the short-bristled brush through the long blond tresses. Leaning back on the tapestry-covered chair, she took note of her surroundings. The walnut dressing table at which she sat was ornately carved with a large oval mirror attached. The bed and bureau were both made of matching walnut and boasted the same ornate carving. All of the windows were adorned with a frilly blue-and-white sheer fabric, the coverlet on the bed matching the blue in the curtains. A beautiful carpet in shades of blue and ivory covered the floor, complementing the other furnishings. It looked opulent and was a startling contrast to the rudimentary conveniences on her journey. She found herself wondering why a doctor would have such a feminine room in his house. Everything, she noted, including the blue-and-white embroidered scarves on the dressing table, emphasized a woman's touch. A knock on the door and Dr. Finley's announcement that her father was awake brought Delphinia's wandering thoughts to an abrupt halt.

Chapter 15

When Delphinia finally opened the door, Samuel Finley came eye to eye with a beautiful young woman. Her hair, golden and wavy, hung loose to her shoulders, making a wreath around her oval face. The paleness of her skin was accentuated by her deep brown eyes that held just a glint of copper, and her lips seemed to have a tiny upward curve with a very slight dimple just above each end of her mouth.

He stood staring at her until Delphinia, not sure what he was thinking, reached toward her hair and remarked, "I guess I was daydreaming. I didn't get my hair pinned up just yet."

"You look absolutely radiant," he replied and smiled as a deep blush colored her cheeks.

"I'll take you to your father now," he said, breaking the silence that followed his compliment.

"Does my father know I've arrived?" she asked, following him down the hallway.

"He does, but try not to look surprised by his appearance when you see him. He's lost weight, and his general health is very poor," he responded.

Opening the door for her, he stood back as she brushed by him to enter the room, a distinct scent of lilac filling his nostrils.

"Papa," she almost cried as she made her way to the emaciated figure that lay on the bed, his thin arms outstretched to embrace her.

"Ah, Delphinia, you've let your hair down the way I like it. Come give your papa a hug," he responded in a weakened voice she almost did not recognize. Dr. Finley momentarily watched the unfolding reunion and then quietly backed out the doorway, pulling the door closed behind him.

Her heart ached as she held him, but she forced a bright smile and then said, "I'm not a child anymore, Pa."

"You'll always be my child," he said, reaching up to lay his hand alongside her face. "I know I've done wrong by you, and before I die I need your forgiveness for sending you off the way I did. I know now it was selfish and wrong. Say you'll forgive me, Delphinia," he requested in a pleading voice.

"I forgave you long ago, Pa. I was angry when you sent me away and then when I found out you'd gone so far as to advertise in a newspaper to find someplace to send me, I was horrified—"

"I just wasn't—" he interrupted.

"No, Pa. Let me finish. I was shocked and devastated you would do that. Later, though, after some time had passed and I had prayed steadfastly for understanding, I no longer resented your actions. It caused me a lot of pain, but that's behind me now. I've missed you, but my life with the Wilshires has been good. You must now concentrate on making yourself well and quit worrying about my forgiveness," she finished.

Tears brimmed his sunken eyes as her father gave a feeble smile. "I don't deserve your forgiveness or love, but I am thankful for both. As for concentrating on getting well, I'm afraid that's not possible. This illness seldom allows its victims to regain their health. Besides, your forgiveness is all I want. Now I don't care when I die," he said, caressing her hand.

"Papa, my forgiveness is not most important," she said. "It's God's forgiveness we must always seek. It is important to ask those we offend to forgive us, but most importantly we must repent and ask God's forgiveness for our sins. I know you used to go to church, but did you accept Jesus as your Savior and invite Him into your heart? Did you repent and ask God's forgiveness of your sins? Have you tried to live a life that would be pleasing to God? If not, Papa, you're not ready to die, and I won't get to see you in heaven. I want us to be together again one day. Just think, you and Mama and me, together in heaven," she said, not sure how he would react to her intonation.

"You're a lot like your mama, young lady," he said. "Maybe you're right, and I have been looking in the wrong direction for my forgiveness. You continue to pray for me, and I'll ask for some forgiveness. It probably wouldn't hurt for me to have a talk with the preacher," he said and then broke into a spasm of racking coughs.

Hearing the sound, Dr. Finley entered the room just as Delphinia rose from her chair to fetch him.

"Don't worry. This is common with his illness. Why don't you let him rest awhile? Sometimes talking causes these bouts to come on, but it will cease shortly," he reassured her. "Why don't you take a few minutes and relax outside? We'll be having dinner soon."

Sitting on one of the two rockers that faced each other on the front porch, Delphinia uttered a prayer of thankfulness for her father's receptive attitude to their conversation about God. As she finished her prayer, Dr. Finley walked out the door and sat down in the chair opposite her.

"He's doing fine," he said in answer to the questioning look she gave him.

"Is there anything I can do to assist? I'm a decent cook and would be happy to help," she offered.

"Well, I thank you kindly, but I'm afraid my neighbor, Mrs. O'Mallie, might take offense. She's been cooking for me ever since my wife passed away.

She likes making the extra money, and I like having a warm meal. She looks after your pa when I have to be gone on calls, and she even does my laundry. Her husband passed away a week after my wife, Lydia, so we've been a help to each other," he responded.

"I'm sorry about your wife," she said, not sure how to react to his casual declaration of her death.

"Don't be. She suffered from severe mental depression after the death of our baby and never got over it. Several months after the baby died, she contracted typhoid and was actually happy about it. She wanted to die. It's been eight years now, and I've made my peace with the situation," he responded, giving her a slight smile.

"And you never remarried?" Delphinia asked, realizing too late that her question was intrusive and wishing she could take it back.

Dr. Finley burst into laughter as he watched how uncomfortable the young woman had become once she issued her question.

"No," he replied. "I've never met the right woman, although I believe that may have changed several hours ago. Your father told me what a beautiful, high-spirited daughter he had, but I thought it was the usual boasting of a proud parent. I find he spoke the truth, and I couldn't be more delighted."

Disconcerted by the doctor's remarks, Delphinia began pressing down the pleats in her skirt with the palm of her hand in a slow, methodical motion. "I'm sure my pa told you of my temper and feisty behavior also," she replied, trying to make light of the compliments.

"I believe he did, at that," he answered and gave a chuckle. "Looks like Mrs. O'Mallie is on her way to the back door with dinner. I better go meet her," he said as he bounded out of the chair and into the house.

Later, lying in bed, Delphinia reflected upon the events of the day. Exhausted, she had unpacked only what was necessary for the night and then had fallen into bed, sure she would be asleep before finishing her prayers. But instead of sleep, her mind kept wandering back to the conversation on the front porch with Dr. Finley. During dinner, he had insisted that she call him Sam, and he had certainly made her feel at home. Yet she was not sure how to take some of the remarks he made, nor how much her pa had told him about why she lived in Kansas.

The next week passed quickly. Sam was always there, willing to help in any way she asked. He arranged for the preacher to visit with her father, posted her letters, insisted on showing her around town, and still maintained a thriving medical practice. Most of the time she spent with her father, and when she would mention returning to Kansas, he would beg her to remain until his death.

Toward the beginning of the second week, she confided in Sam that she planned to leave within the next few days.

"I'd rethink that decision. If you leave, I'm sure it will break your father's heart," he said, knowing he was arguing as much for himself as he was for her father.

"But you've told me he may live for a month or longer. I couldn't possibly wait that long." She argued, feeling selfish. "Besides, I told the Wilshires I would be gone for only a few weeks at the most," she continued, trying to defend her position, his statements adding to her guilt.

She was torn by uncertainty, feeling that she would fail someone, no matter what. Her prayers had been fervent about where she belonged, but no answer had been forthcoming, at least none that she could discern. She hadn't even unpacked all her clothing, fearing she would begin to feel settled.

As the days passed and her indecision continued, Sam and her father felt assured that she would remain in Denver City. She accompanied Sam to several socials at the church, and he proved to be an enjoyable companion, making her realize that city life held a certain appeal. But she found herself missing Jonathan and the children. The letters she received from them were cheerful and told of missing her, but not to worry about them. They did not ask when she would return, and she did not mention it in her letters to them.

Delphinia's father watched out the window by his bed as she and Sam came up the sidewalk returning from an evening stroll, her arm laced through his. Her father gave a slight smile as they stepped out of his sight and onto the porch.

"Let's sit here on the porch and visit awhile, if you're not too tired," Sam invited.

"How could I be tired?" she bantered. "I do nothing but sit all day."

"You're growing restless, aren't you? I could sense it all day," he responded.

"Sam, I'm used to hard work and keeping busy. I've been caring for five children and a homestead out on the Kansas prairie. I miss the children, and I guess I miss the work too," she admitted.

"You're far too beautiful to work on a farm. There's no need for you to return to that kind of life. You should be living in a city, married, and having children of your own. Don't you want to have your own children?" he asked.

"Of course, I want to have my own children, but that doesn't cause me to love or miss the Wilshires any the less. You say there's no need to return to that kind of life. My father doesn't have much longer to live by your calculations, and once he's gone, I'll have no one but my substitute family in Kansas. I think that is where I belong," she stated.

Reaching toward her he took hold of her hand and lifted it to his lips, gently placing a kiss in the center of her palm. "No, Delphinia, you belong here with me. I care for you more than you can imagine. I have from the first day you arrived."

"Oh, Jonathan. . .I. . .I mean, Samuel," she stammered. "I think I had better retire," she said, rising from the chair and moving toward the front door.

"So, I do have competition. It's not just the children you miss. Are you in love with this Kansas farmer?" he asked, blocking her entry to the house.

"I. . .well, I think so," she finally answered.

The last word had barely passed her lips when he drew her into his arms and kissed her with an impatient fervor that almost frightened her.

"Please, don't. I must check on my father," she said, entering the house and leaving him on the front porch.

"I wasn't sure if you'd still be awake, Pa," Delphinia said, approaching his bedside.

"You two have a nice walk?"

"Why, uh, I guess so. Yes, it's a pleasant evening. I wish you could be outdoors awhile and enjoy it with me," she answered, trying to hide her emotions over the recent incident with Sam.

"I get a nice breeze through the window. Sometimes I even hear people talkin' on the porch," he said with a grin.

She did not respond but began to tidy the room and straighten his sheets.

"He's a good man, Delphinia. You couldn't ask for a better catch to marry up with. I know he's thinkin' hard on the prospect of asking you 'cause he asked if I'd have any objection," her father continued.

Her head jerked to attention at his remark. "What did you tell him?" she asked, her voice sounding harsh to her ears.

"I didn't mean to upset you. I thought you'd be happy to know he was interested in you. I told him I didn't know anyone I'd be more pleased to have marry my daughter, but he'd have to take it up with you," he answered, seeing that she was disturbed by the conversation.

"Pa, I'm not looking for a prize catch. I'm not even looking for a husband. The only reason I came to Denver City was to see you, and then I'll be returning to Kansas. In fact, I should have returned a week ago," she responded.

"Now, I've gone and made you unhappy, and you're gonna run off and leave me here to die alone, aren't ya?" he asked, hoping her tender heart would not allow her to rush off in anger.

"You've not made me unhappy, Pa. I know you're thinking about my future, but I've been on my own for some time now, and I don't need anyone making marriage plans for me. Besides, Jonathan Wilshire has pledged his love and intent to marry me once I return to Kansas," she told him as she rearranged the small bottles on a nearby table for the third time.

"Those bottles look fine; you've straightened them enough. Now come and sit down here," he said, indicating the chair beside him.

"Delphinia, I'll not try and push you into any marriage. Folks need to marry those they love. I know that. I loved your ma like I could never love anyone else. But there's a lot to be said for finding the person you're suited to. It makes things run smoother."

"I know that. But I think Jonathan and I are suited," she answered.

"Maybe so. I thought your ma and I were too. I tried to make her happy, but she longed for city life, and even though I helped her as much as I could, it was a hard life. She always wanted the kind of life she'd had as a child, but she gave in to my dreams and left it behind. I'm not sure she ever got over leaving her family," he continued.

"She wasn't unhappy, and you know it, Pa. We both know she would have preferred living in the East, close to her family, but she understood."

"I was married to her, Child. You saw what she wanted you to see. But many's the night I listened to her cry about life out in the middle of nowhere and longin' to see her family and lead a city life. I'm real sorry I did that to her," he said, a distant look in his eyes.

"You did the best you could," Delphinia answered, not knowing what to say that would relieve some of his pain.

"That's true. I did. The only thing I could have done different would have been to stay in the city. You got that chance to stay now. It's what your ma would have wanted for you, and here you are with this wonderful opportunity. Denver's not like those big eastern cities, but it's an up-and-coming kind of town. One day it's gonna be grand, for sure," he boasted.

"That was Ma who wanted the big city. I've never said that."

"Perhaps, but you could have a good life here. You're too young to be tied down to somebody else's children. Doc Finley's a fine man, and he could take care of you. You'd never want for anything, and you could eventually have children of your own. You'd be able to give them what they needed without worrying about money," he said, beginning to cough from the exertion of talking so much.

"That's enough for tonight, Pa. You're getting excited, and you're going to make yourself worse. I'm going to get your medicine ready, and then I want you to get some rest," she said as she moved toward the bottles and poured out a spoonful of the yellow liquid.

"I'll take the medicine and go to sleep if you promise to think on what we've talked about," he responded and then clenched his mouth together like a small child.

Looking at his face, she was unable to hold back her laughter. "It's a deal. Now, open up," she said as she cradled his head and lifted him to take the spoon.

She leaned down and placed a kiss on his cheek. "Good night, Papa. I love you."

Smiling, he bid her good night with the admonition she think hard on his words. She smiled and nodded her assent as she left the room and pulled the door closed behind her.

"How is he?" Sam asked.

Delphinia jumped at the sound of his voice. "You startled me. I thought you'd gone to bed," she said, turning to find him sitting on the stairway outside her father's bedroom. "He's doing pretty well. He got a bit excited and talked too much, which caused his cough to start up. I just gave him his medicine, and hopefully, he'll get a good night's rest," she answered.

"I want to apologize for my behavior this evening. I didn't mean to offend you. I care for you very much, and it's been difficult for me not to kiss you before now," he stated.

"Perhaps this is something we should talk about another time. I'm really very tired," she answered and moved toward her bedroom.

"Whenever you're ready, my love," he said, going up the stairway.

Quickly, she made her way down the hallway to her bedroom but could not deny the small flutter she felt when he used the term of endearment.

She lay in bed thinking of the things both her pa and Sam had said. *I do want children of my own, and I wonder if I'll grow weary of raising my Kansas family and never really have time for my own,* she thought.

Tossing restlessly, she questioned the excitement she felt when Dr. Finley had called her by a term of endearment.

"Can I be in love with Jonathan and still feel something for another man?" she whispered to herself.

That night her prayers were fervent for God's direction.

Chapter 16

Delphinia awakened to a day that had dawned bright and sunny with a crispness to the air, giving notice that summer was over. Just as she finished making her bed, she heard the back door slam and Mrs. O'Mallie enter the kitchen.

"I'll be right there to help you, Mrs. O'Mallie," she called out.

"Take your time. I'm in no hurry," the older woman answered.

"Here, let me take that tray," she offered, reaching toward the huge silver platter and placing it on the kitchen table.

"It's a beauty of a day out there, and I've been thankin' the Lord for that. Don't want anything to spoil our meeting tonight," she said.

"You have special plans for today?" Delphinia inquired hospitably.

"Why, sure. It's the autumn revival. Thought maybe Doc Finley might have mentioned it. All the churches get together and have one big revival each fall. It's going to be wonderful. There's a service every night this week, so if your pa is doing all right, I hope you'll come," she invited.

"I'd love to, but I'll have to see how he's feeling later this afternoon. Thank you for telling me about it," Delphinia answered.

"Well, guess I better be getting back home. You give thought to coming tonight," Mrs. O'Mallie said, leaving by the back door.

"Looks like Mrs. O'Mallie's already been here and gone," Sam said as he entered the kitchen.

"She just left. I'll take Pa's tray to him. You go ahead and eat," she responded.

"I'll wait for you," he answered as she left the room.

"There's no need to do that," she answered, walking out of the kitchen before he could respond.

"Good morning, Pa. How are you feeling today?" she inquired, thinking he looked thinner each day.

"Not too bad, but I'm not hungry. You go eat. I'll try and eat later," he responded. But seeing the look of determination on his daughter's face, he shook his head and said, "I'm not going to eat now, so you needn't argue with me. Go!"

"All right, all right," she answered with a smile. "I'm going."

"He's not hungry," she announced, walking into the kitchen and sitting down opposite Sam at the wooden table.

"Don't look so downcast. That doesn't necessarily mean anything bad. We all have times when we're not hungry. Looks to me like you'd better quit worrying about your pa's eating and take a nap this afternoon. Those dark circles under your eyes tell me you didn't get much sleep last night."

"You're right; I didn't. I'll think about the nap if you'll tell me about the revival," she said.

"Revival? How'd you hear about that?" he questioned.

"Mrs. O'Mallie told me. I'd love to go if Pa is all right. Do you think that would be possible?" she asked.

He smiled as he watched her face become animated and bright, like a child seeing a jar of peppermint sticks.

"There's really nothing to tell. Several years ago the churches here in Denver City decided to have one big revival each autumn. They all get together and select a preacher to come, and they hold services outdoors every night. If the weather doesn't cooperate, they go over to the Methodist Church since it's the biggest. I don't see any reason why you couldn't go, but not unescorted since it's held during the evening," he responded.

"Perhaps I could go with Mrs. O'Mallie," she suggested.

"If your pa's doing all right, I'll escort you," he said, "at least this one evening, but you must promise to rest this afternoon."

"I will," she answered delightedly. "Our breakfast is probably cold. Do you want to give thanks?" she asked.

"You go ahead and do it for us," he answered.

"Mrs. O'Mallie certainly knows how to start off the day with a hearty breakfast," he said, having devoured all that was on his plate and wiping his hands with the large cloth napkin. "I'd better get busy on my house calls. Don't forget your pa's medicine this morning, and I expect you to be taking a nap when I return," he admonished.

"Oh, I will be," she answered, excited by the prospect of the evening.

"Guess what, Papa," she exclaimed, almost skipping into his room.

"I don't know what to guess except that something has made you happy," he ventured.

"There's a revival beginning tonight, and Sam said that if you're doing all right this evening and if I take a nap this afternoon, he'll escort me. Isn't that wonderful?"

"Well, it certainly is wonderful, and I'll be doing just fine. You just be sure and get that nap and find yourself something to wear," he said, pleased to see her so happy about going out with Sam.

"Something to wear. Oh, yes. I'd not even thought of that. I'll need to look in my trunk and see if I can find something extra special. Oh, and then

I'll need to get it pressed. I'd better get that done, or I'll not have my nap taken before Sam returns," she said.

"You get a move on then. I'm feeling fine, and I'll ring the bell if I need anything," he said.

He waved her out of the room as she blew him a kiss and headed toward the doorway. *Perhaps she's decided that Sam would be the right man for her after all,* he thought, pleased by the prospect.

Delphinia lifted the lid on the partially empty trunk. She still hadn't completely unpacked the contents. *I hope I packed something warmer in the bottom of this trunk,* she thought, methodically removing each item. Lifting a dark gold dress, her eyes flew open at the sight of fabric tucked within the folds of the dress. It was Sarah's quilt top! And there, underneath the dress was a neatly folded piece of paper. She sat down on the edge of the bed and slowly opened the page.

Dear Phiney,

While you were busy with the twins, I packed Mama's quilt top in with your dress. I want you to come back to Kansas. I didn't know how else to be sure of your return. I'm hoping the threads of love in this quilt are strong enough to bring you home to us.

Love,
Tessie

Tears rolled down her cheeks as she read the letter a second time. The words tugged at her heart and made her even lonelier for Kansas and the family she had left behind. *I've got to make a decision soon,* she thought, folding the letter and placing it with the quilt top in her trunk. *Surely God will give me an answer soon.*

She carried her dress into the kitchen, searching until she found a pressing board and then heated the iron. Carefully, she pressed the gown, watchful not to burn the silk fabric. Certain all the wrinkles had been removed, she draped it over a chair in her bedroom and took the promised nap.

Later, she could hardly wait for dinner to be over in order to clear off the dishes and get ready. Sam had declared her father was doing fine, and they would leave in an hour. She took her time getting ready, pinning her hair up on top of her head and securing it with a thin black-and-gold ribbon. A white lace collar surrounded the neckline of her dress, and she placed a gold earring in each lobe. Looking at her reflection in the mirror above the walnut bureau, she remembered that the last time she had worn the earrings had been when Pastor Martin escorted her to the dance. She smiled thinking about that night when Jonathan had become their uninvited guest. It seemed so long ago, almost a different world, she mused.

"You about ready? Your pa wants to see you before we leave. I'll wait in his room," Sam said, knocking on the door.

"Be right there," she answered. Taking one last look in the mirror, she pinned a wisp of hair and then went to her father's room.

Her entry brought raves from her father who insisted that she twirl around several times so he could see her from all angles. Sam was silent, although she could feel his eyes on her from the moment she entered the room.

"We'd better leave, or we'll be late," he said, rising from the chair.

"Are you sure you'll be okay, Pa?"

"I'm sure. Now you two go on and have a nice time," he instructed.

Sam had drawn his carriage to the front of the house and carefully assisted her into the buggy, his two black horses appearing sleek in the semidarkness.

"You look quite beautiful. I didn't want to tell you in front of your father for fear of causing you embarrassment. Besides, it would have been difficult to get a word in," he said, smiling down at her.

"Fathers tend to think their daughters are beautiful, no matter what," she responded.

"Perhaps. But in your case it's true," he answered as he pulled himself into the buggy and flicked the reins.

"How far is it to the meeting place?" she asked, wanting to change the subject.

"Not far, just south of town. There's a large grove, and they set up benches and chairs, whatever they can move from the churches. There's been ample seating when I've been there," he commented.

The crowd had already begun to gather by the time they arrived. Mrs. O'Mallie had saved seats, hopeful they would attend. She was in the third row, waving them forward with unbridled enthusiasm.

"Oh, there's Mrs. O'Mallie. Come on, Sam, we can sit up front, She's saved seats," Delphinia pointed out, tugging his arm.

"I'd rather sit farther back, if it's all the same to you," he answered, holding back.

"Oh," she said, somewhat surprised, "that's fine. I'll just go tell Mrs. O'Mallie. Why don't you see if you can find a spot for us."

The older woman was disappointed, and Delphinia would have much preferred to sit up front but deferred to Sam's choice since he had been kind enough to escort her.

The services were all that Delphinia had hoped for. The preacher was dynamic, and the crowd was receptive to his message. They sang songs, read Scripture, and heard the Word preached; and when the service was over, Delphinia could hardly wait to return for the next evening.

"Wasn't it wonderful?" she asked Sam as they made their way to the buggy.

"It was interesting," he responded, saying nothing further.

Delphinia was so excited about the meeting, she did not note how quiet Sam had been, nor the fact that he had little to say the whole way home.

When they finally reached the porch, she said, "Do you think we could go tomorrow?" She sounded so full of anticipation. He thought once again of a child being offered candy.

"I don't think so," he answered, watching as her face became void of the animation it had held just minutes before.

"Why? Do you think it unwise to leave Pa again?" she asked.

"No, that's not why. I think one night of observation is sufficient," he answered.

"Observation? What an odd thing to say. Attending church or revival is not something one observes. It's something you do. It's worshipping God," she said, looking at him through a haze of confusion.

"Not for me," he responded.

"Whatever do you mean, Sam? You believe in God. You've accepted Jesus as your Savior. . .haven't you?" she asked, doubt beginning to creep into her thoughts.

"I attend church because it's the respectable thing to do, and people expect it of a doctor. As for your question, however, the answer is no, I don't believe in God."

With that pronouncement, Delphinia almost fell onto the chair just behind her and stared at him in openmouthed disbelief.

"I'm sure that comes as a shock to you, but I consider myself an educated man. I believe in science and have studied in some of the best schools in this country and Europe. There is absolutely nothing to support the theory of your God, Delphinia. I realize most people have a need to believe in some higher being and so they cling to this God and Jesus ideology. I don't need it. I believe in myself and when life is over, it's over," he said, sitting down opposite her.

"But, but, you've acted as though you believe. You went and got the pastor for my father, and you attend church, and you talk to Mrs. O'Mallie about God, and you pray—"

"No," he interrupted, "I do not pray. I allow others to pray over their food, and I discuss God with Mrs. O'Mallie because she enjoys talking about such things. You have never heard me pray, and you won't. When a dying patient wants a preacher, I see to it. That doesn't mean I think it's needed," he answered.

"I don't know what to say. I just can't believe you're saying this," she said, rising from the chair and pacing back and forth. "I know you place great value on your education, but I hope you'll heed the words of 1 Corinthians 3:18 where it tells us that if any man seems to be wise in this world, let him become a fool so he may become wise," she said, hoping he would listen, but realizing from his vacant stare that he did not care to hear.

"I've heard that rhetoric preached all my life. My parents took me to church every Sunday. My mother was devout, although my father confided to me in later years that he never believed; but for my mother's sake, he acted like he believed," he said.

When she did not respond, he continued, "I wanted you to know how I felt before we marry. I'll not stop you from attending church, and on occasion I'll escort you. But I'll not want you there all the time, nor would I want our children indoctrinated with such nonsense," he added.

"Before we marry? I never said I would marry you. I never even gave you cause to think that," she fired back at him.

"I never doubted you would accept. I realize how much I have to offer a woman. A nice home, security. I'm kind and, I've been told, good-looking," he said with a smile.

"I'm sure to many women those would be the most important qualities, but your confidence in my acceptance is unfounded. I would never marry a man who didn't believe in Jesus Christ as his Savior. I feel sorry for you, Sam, if you've hardened your heart against the Lord, but I want you to know I'll be praying for you," she said, walking toward her father's room.

"I think I'd better check on my father and get ready for bed. Good night, Sam."

"Good night, Delphinia. I've not accepted what you said as your final word however. We'll discuss this further tomorrow," he answered, not moving from the chair.

Her father was fast asleep when she stepped into his room. She backed out quietly and made her way down the hall to prepare for bed.

Sitting at the dressing table, she gazed at the reflection of herself. *How could I have been so blind?* She forced herself to think back over the weeks she had lived in this house. It was true; she had never seen Sam pray. At meals he always deferred to someone else, and now that she thought about it, whenever she would pray with her father, he would leave the room. When she had tried to discuss the sermons they had heard on Sundays or ask his opinion about a verse of Scripture, he would always change the subject.

She slipped into her nightgown and dropped to her knees beside the bed and earnestly thanked God for answered prayer, certain His intent was for her to return to Kansas and be joined with a godly man. She prayed regularly for those she loved, and tonight she added a prayer for the salvation of Dr. Samuel Finley, an educated man, walking in darkness.

Arising the next morning, Delphinia hastened to get herself dressed, wanting to talk with her father. Sam was waiting in the kitchen when she entered and requested she join him for breakfast.

"I'd rather not this morning. I'm not very hungry, and I'd like to visit with my father. I didn't spend much time with him yesterday, and we need to talk," she said, lifting the tray of food and moving toward the door.

"We will talk later," he said tersely.

"There is no doubt about that," she answered emphatically, without looking back.

Who does he think he is? she thought, marching down the hallway to her father's room. She stopped before entering, knowing she must change her attitude before seeing him and took a moment to issue a short prayer that God would assist her in this discussion.

"Good morning, Papa," she greeted, smiling brightly.

"Good morning to you," he said, indicating the chair by his bed. "Sit and tell me all about your evening."

"I plan to do just that, but first, you must eat," she told him, lifting a napkin off the tray and placing an extra pillow behind him.

"I'll eat while you talk. Have we got a deal?" he asked.

"As long as you eat, I'll talk," she said, glad to see a little more color in his cheeks.

He lifted a small forkful of food to his mouth and nodded at her to begin.

"Papa, I know you have a desire for me to marry Sam, and he has asked for my hand."

"I'm glad to hear that, Delphinia. When's the weddin' to be? Maybe, I'll be well enough to attend," he said excitedly.

"There won't be a wedding. At least not a wedding between Sam and me," she answered.

"What do you mean? You're confusing me," he said, slapping the fork on his tray.

"There's no need to get upset. I'm going to explain, if you'll just eat and let me talk," she admonished. "Sam has asked for my hand, but I could never marry a man unless he's a Christian. Sam doesn't believe in God. Besides, Papa, I don't love Sam. I love Jonathan Wilshire. I have to admit that I was swayed by Sam's good looks and kind ways and that it was nice to be escorted about the city and have his attention. But that's not love. A marriage between us would be doomed for failure."

"You can't be sure of that. You just said he's good and kind, and you enjoy his company. I don't want you livin' out your days workin' like your mama, always unhappy and wishin' for more," he said.

"Just because Mama was unhappy some of the time doesn't mean she would have changed things. She loved you, Pa, and that's where a woman belongs. With the man she loves. You've got to understand that I could never love Sam. Not unless he turned to the Lord, and then I'm not sure. He's hardened his heart against God. Why, he told me he wouldn't even allow his children to be brought up as Christians. You know I couldn't turn my back on God like that," she responded adamantly.

"I understand what you're saying, and I know you're right. I guess I'm just being selfish again. I want you to have all the things I could never give your mother, even if you don't want them."

"Don't you see, she had the most important things: a family that loved her and the love of our Savior. That's all any of us really need to be happy," she said, leaning down and placing a kiss on his cheek.

Chapter 17

When Sam returned later in the afternoon, Delphinia was sitting on the front porch, enjoying the cool breeze and silently thanking God for the afternoon discussion with her father and his agreement that she return to Kansas.

"I thought you'd be in tending to your father," Sam said with no other greeting.

"I just came out. He's asleep, and I wanted some fresh air," she answered defensively.

"Good, then we can have our talk," he rebutted, sitting down and moving the chair closer.

"There's really nothing further to say, Sam. I can't marry you. I've explained that I could never marry a non-Christian, and besides, I'm in love with Jonathan Wilshire," she said, leaning back in her chair in an effort to place a little more distance between them.

"As I recall, you weren't quite so sure of your love for that Wilshire fellow when I kissed you on this very porch."

"I'm not going to defend myself or my actions to you, but I hope you'll believe and accept my decision in this matter. It will make life easier for all three of us," she responded, hoping to ease the tension between them.

"I think your pa will have something to say about this. I've already asked for your hand, and he as much as promised it. So you see, the decision really hasn't been made yet," he answered with a smug look on his face.

"I've discussed the matter fully with my father, Sam. He is in agreement that I should follow my heart and return to Kansas. He was unaware of your disbelief in God, as much as I was. There is no doubt in my mind that I could not be happily married to a non-Christian. The Bible warns Christians about being unequally yoked."

"Don't start quoting Scripture to me. That's the last thing I want to hear. What I want to know is how you talked your father into allowing you to return to Kansas," he interrupted.

"I've already explained, and he realizes the folly of my marrying someone like you. He may have discussed the fact that he thought a marriage between us would be good, but you deceived him too. I'm not sure it was intentional, since you find faith in God so unimportant. I would rather believe you did not set out to mislead either of us. I'd prefer you didn't upset my father by discussing this further, but you're the doctor. Do as you see fit," she said, hearing the small bell at her father's bedside and rising to go to his room.

"Stay here. I'll see to him," Sam said, standing and picking up his bag.

She did not move from the chair, but it was not long before Sam returned. Leaning against the thick rail that surrounded the porch, he looked down at her, his eyes filled with sadness.

"We could be happy, you know. If I'm willing to overlook your foolish beliefs and allow you to practice your Christian rituals, why is it so difficult for you to think our marriage wouldn't work?" he asked.

"That's exactly why—because you don't believe. It would always be a struggle between us. I want to be able to share my love of the Lord with my husband and raise my children to know God. I want God to be the head of our house, and that could never happen if I were married to you," she answered.

"You've done a good job of convincing your father. I found no allegiance from him when we talked. I guess there's nothing more to say, except that I love you, and if you change your mind, we can forget this conversation ever took place," he said and walked into the house.

Delphinia remained, not wanting to discuss the matter further. When she was sure Sam had gone upstairs, she went to her father's room.

"I wondered if you'd gone to bed without a good-night kiss for me," he said, watching her enter the room.

"No, I'd not do that," she replied, straightening the sheet and pulling the woolen blanket up around his chest. "How are you feeling this evening?"

"Not too bad," he answered. "I talked with Sam."

"I know. He told me," she said, sitting down beside him.

"He's not happy with either of us. Maybe one day he'll open his heart to the Lord. If not, I suppose someday he may find a woman who thinks as he does. I have something I'd like for you to do tomorrow," he said, taking her hand.

"I'll try," she answered.

"I want you to go to town," he instructed, pulling a small leather pouch from beneath his pillow. "I'd like for you to purchase your wedding gown here in Denver City. I know I can't attend the ceremony, but it would give me great pleasure to see you in your wedding dress. Would you consider doing that?"

"You don't need to spend your money on a wedding gown, Pa. I have a dress that will do," she answered.

"Always trying to look out for everyone else, aren't ya? I can afford to buy you a dress, and it would give me great pleasure. Now, will you do that for me? Mrs. O'Mallie has agreed to go with you. Quite enthusiastically, I might add," he said with a smile.

"If it would please you, I'll go shopping with Mrs. O'Mallie. Did you and Mrs. O'Mallie decide when this shopping trip is to take place?" she inquired, plumping his pillow.

"Tomorrow morning, just as soon as the shops are open. She said she'd come over for you, and I told her you'd be ready," he answered.

"Pretty sure of yourself, weren't you?" she asked, letting out a chuckle.

"I know you pretty well, Girl. You wouldn't deny an old man his dying wish."

"Don't talk like that, please," she said, shaking her head.

"It's better to face the facts. We both know I've not long for this world. You mustn't get sad on me. After all, it's you who gave me hope, knowing I'd be seeing you and your mother again one day. You just keep thinking on that and forget this dying business," he said and then waved his hand, gesturing her to leave the room. "You get off to bed now. You need your rest for all that shopping you're going to do tomorrow, and I need my sleep."

She leaned down and placed a kiss on his cheek. "I'll stop in before I go tomorrow. You sleep well," she said, departing for her own room.

Delphinia took care in dressing, wanting to look her best when she visited the shops in Denver City. Just as she was tying on her bonnet, Frances O'Mallie arrived. The older woman was so excited at the prospect of purchasing a wedding dress, she talked nonstop from the time she entered the house until they reached the door of the first small shop.

The store owner was a lovely woman, delighted to see her first customers of the day. It was immediately obvious to her that these women were going to make purchases, and she needed the business. Mrs. O'Mallie instantly took charge, asking to see what fabrics and laces the woman had in stock, fingering each item with a knowledge that surprised Delphinia. Taking her assignment seriously, the older woman inquired about how long it would take to make the dress, how many yards of fabric for each of the patterns they had viewed, and the exact cost for everything from the tiny buttons to the lace trimming. Just when the clerk was sure the women were ready to make their decision, Mrs. O'Mallie took Delphinia by the elbow and said, "Come, my dear, we must check the other stores."

Opening the door to exit, she informed the store owner, "We'll be back unless we find something more to our liking."

Delphinia, somewhat stunned by Mrs. O'Mallie's actions, was quick to tell her she particularly liked one of the patterns and wanted to discuss it further.

"Tut, tut, don't you worry. These merchants always need business, and it's good to know what the competition has to offer," she said, ushering Delphinia into a shop with beautiful gold lettering on the windows proclaiming the finest needlework west of the Mississippi.

"Lucy Blodgett owns this place," Mrs. O'Mallie whispered. "She can be real hard to deal with, but her sign on the window is true. She does the finest needlework I've ever seen. Just let me do the talking," she instructed.

The brass bell over the front door announced their entry, and the women observed Lucy Blodgett making her way from the back room of the shop.

"Mornin', Lucy. This is Delphinia Hughes. She's out here from Kansas looking for a wedding dress, and I told her you do the handsomest needlework in these parts," Mrs. O'Mallie praised.

"Good morning to you, Frances. Nice to make your acquaintance, Miss Hughes. Why don't you ladies come back and have a seat. I find it much more expeditious to discuss just what my customer is here for and then proceed to show you my line of goods," she smiled, leading them toward four elegant walnut chairs that encircled a matching table.

Flitting through patterns that were neatly stacked on a shelf, she produced five different styles. "Why don't you look at these while I get us some tea?" she offered.

"She knows how to run a business, wouldn't you say?" Mrs. O'Mallie asked, thoroughly enjoying the opulent surroundings.

"It would appear that way, but are you sure this shop isn't too expensive?" Delphinia questioned.

"We'll see, we'll see," the older woman replied, pushing the patterns toward the younger woman. "I rather like this one."

"Here we are, tea and some biscuits," Miss Blodgett said, placing a tray in the middle of the table. "Why don't you pour for us, Frances, and I'll visit with Miss Hughes."

Mrs. O'Mallie was glad to oblige. The silver tea service and china cups seemed exactly what should be used while discussing wedding gowns with Miss Lucy Blodgett. Delphinia's escort sat back and had her tea and biscuits, not missing a word that passed between the other women.

"How long would it take for you to complete the gown?" Delphinia asked, having finally settled on one of the patterns.

"At a minimum, three weeks. I have many orders to fill, and once I give my word that a purchase will be ready, I am never late. Isn't that right, Frances?"

"Absolutely," said Mrs. O'Mallie, wiping the crumbs from her mouth and taking a swallow of tea.

"Well, I'm sorry to have taken your time, Miss Blodgett, but I must leave for Kansas within the week. My father wanted me to purchase a gown here in Denver City so he might see it before I depart. It appears that isn't going to be possible," Delphinia said, rising from the chair.

"I'm sorry too, Miss Hughes. You're a lovely young woman, and I could make you into a beautiful bride," Miss Blodgett replied.

"You'll not find a seamstress in this city who can make you a wedding gown within the week, I'm sorry to say," she continued as Mrs. O'Mallie and Delphinia tied their bonnets, preparing to leave.

"We appreciate your time, Lucy," Mrs. O'Mallie said as they walked out of the store and walked toward another shop down the street.

The two women had walked as far as the livery stable when they heard Lucy Blodgett calling and observed her motioning them to return.

"Lucy Blodgett, I've never seen you make such a spectacle of yourself," Mrs. O'Mallie said, feigning surprise.

"I've been making a fool of myself for years, Frances. At least whenever I felt there was cause to do so," she answered with a smile.

"Come back into the shop. I just may be able to solve your problem, Miss Hughes," she said, leading Delphinia to the rear of the store and into her workroom.

"Stand right here," she said, placing Delphinia along the wall opposite her cutting table. Moving across the room, Miss Blodgett walked to a closet and removed a hanger that was draped with a sheet. In one dramatic swoop, she pulled off the sheet revealing a beautiful white gown that absolutely took Delphinia's breath away.

"Oh, Miss Blodgett, it's beautiful. . .truly beautiful," Delphinia said, staring at the creation. Walking toward the dress, she reached out and touched the tiny beads that had been sewn in an intricate pattern on the bodice. The long sleeves were made of a delicate lace that matched the overlay of the floor-length skirt, flowing into a short train.

"It appears to be just about your size, I would guess," Miss Blodgett replied, ignoring the compliment.

"Perhaps a mite big," Mrs. O'Mallie responded.

"Well, certainly nothing a good seamstress couldn't remedy in short order," the shop owner replied rather curtly.

"What difference does it make?" Delphinia interrupted, exasperated that the two women were arguing over alterations on a wedding dress that had been made for another bride.

"That's why I called you back to the shop," Miss Blodgett responded, looking at Delphinia as if she were dimwitted. "This dress is available."

"Available? How could it be available?" she asked, stunned by the remark.

"I hesitate to tell you why for fear you'll not want the dress, but with all the folks Mrs. O'Mallie knows, I'm sure she'd find out soon enough anyway. This is the dress I made for Mary Sullivan's daughter, Estelle," Miss Blodgett began.

"Ah yes," Mrs. O'Mallie said, nodding her head in recognition.

"Estelle Sullivan was to be married last Sunday afternoon. Her intended made a little money mining for gold, but his claim went dry. They decided to settle in California so he went out in June to look at some possible investments. Two weeks before the wedding, she got a letter saying that he had married a California woman and wouldn't be returning. Her dress had been ready for two months. Her future husband even picked the pattern," she commented in disgust.

"Would it bother you to wear a dress that had been made for another who met with misfortune?" Mrs. O'Mallie asked.

"I don't think so," Delphinia answered. "It's so pretty, and it's never been worn. Would they be willing to sell it, do you think?"

"It's mine," Miss Blodgett said. "Estelle was so devastated, and Mary doesn't have the money to pay for a dress her daughter will never wear. I told them I'd take it apart and use the pieces for another gown. Would you like to try it on, Miss Hughes?"

"Oh yes, I'd love to," she said, the excitement evident in her voice. "Unless you think it would make Estelle and her mother unhappy."

"I don't think they would mind a bit under the circumstances. Besides, your marriage won't even take place in Denver City," she responded.

"Then I'd like very much to see how it fits."

By the time they left the shop, Delphinia had purchased a properly fitted wedding dress, a matching veil, and a pair of shoes. Miss Blodgett was good to her word. She was able to stitch a few well-hidden tucks, and the dress fit like it had been made for Delphinia. Mrs. O'Mallie was pleased because she had been able to convince Lucy to lower the price on the premise she was selling "previously purchased goods." That statement had caused a bit of a riff between the two older women, but eventually they came to terms. Delphinia, however, thought the dress was worth every cent of the original asking price.

The older women agreed that Delphinia made quite a spectacle in her finery, both feeling like they had championed a special cause.

Mrs. O'Mallie helped carry the purchases into the house and then bid Delphinia a quick farewell, knowing she would need to hurry with dinner preparations.

"Thank you again for all your assistance," Delphinia called after her as the older woman bustled out the back door.

Delphinia heard the jingle of her father's bedside bell and quickly hastened to his bedroom. "I thought I heard voices," he said, holding out his hand to beckon her forward. "Did you and Mrs. O'Mallie have success with your shopping?"

"Oh, Pa, we did! I purchased the most beautiful gown you could ever imagine. I know that God led me to it," she said smiling, as she proceeded to give him a detailed report of their shopping excursion.

"I'm looking forward to having you model it for me after dinner this evening," he said. "I wonder if Mrs. O'Mallie thinks she or God should have credit for leading you to that gown," he said with a small chuckle.

"I don't think she'd mind giving God some praise as long as she gets credit for Miss Blodgett's lowering the price," she answered, which caused them both to smile in appreciation of their neighbor's love of a bargain.

"I think I'll take a nap. I've been tired today," her father said, shifting in the bed to try and become more comfortable.

"How thoughtless of me. Here I've been rambling on while you need your rest. How's that?" she asked, adjusting his sheets.

"Fine, and you've not been rambling. It's given me more pleasure than you can imagine to hear you relate the events of today, and I'm looking forward to seeing that dress on you a little later," he said, closing his eyes.

Sam arrived home for dinner, and although somewhat subdued, he remained cordial during their meal. The minute they finished, he rose from the table, informing Delphinia that he would be making house calls for the next several hours. As soon as he had departed, she ran next door to Mrs. O'Mallie's, requesting assistance buttoning her gown.

"I'll be over shortly," the older woman told her. "You get your hair fixed, and by then I should be done in the kitchen."

Thirty minutes later, Mrs. O'Mallie came scurrying in the back doorway, proceeded to Delphinia's room, and her nimble fingers went to work closing the tiny pearl buttons that trailed down the back of the dress. "Now, let's put your veil on," she said after Delphinia had slipped her feet into the new white slippers. Carefully, Mrs. O'Mallie pulled curly tendrils of hair from behind the veil to frame either side of Delphinia's face.

"There! God never made a more beautiful bride," she said, stepping back and taking full view of the young woman. "Let's get you down the hall to your pa. You wait here in the hallway, and I'll see if he's awake," Mrs. O'Mallie instructed.

Delphinia could hear Mrs. O'Mallie talking with her father, propping him up to permit a good view as she entered the room.

"All right. You can come in now," Mrs. O'Mallie called out.

Delphinia watched her father as she walked into the room. He appeared awestruck after she pivoted in a full circle allowing him to see the entire dress. Turning back to face him, she watched a small tear slide down each of his sunken cheeks.

"I wish your mama could see you," he said, his voice cracking with emotion. "I know I've never seen such a pretty picture as you in that dress. Hasn't God been good to allow me such joy?"

"I'm glad you're pleased with my choice," Delphinia said, walking to the bed and placing a kiss on his damp cheek. "Thank you for accepting my decision to marry Jonathan, Papa, and thank you for this lovely wedding gift. I just wish you could be there for the wedding," she said.

"Your mama and I may not be with you in person, but we'll be there. You just remember that," he answered, trying to force his quivering lips into a smile.

"I know you will, I know," she answered.

"I think we better get this young lady out of her gown before she has it worn out," Mrs. O'Mallie said, trying to brighten the spirits of both father and daughter.

"We wouldn't want that," her father answered, "at least not until she's said her vows. You go ahead and change. We can visit again before you go to bed."

Delphinia returned once Mrs. O'Mallie had gone home. She sat by her father's bedside, visiting when he was awake and holding his hand as he slept, aware he was now in constant pain.

Later that night, a knock on her bedroom door awakened Delphinia from a sound sleep. Thinking she had overslept, her feet hit the floor before she realized it was still dark outside. Quickly, she pulled on her robe and rushed to open the door. Sam's eyes told it all.

"He's gone, isn't he?" she asked.

He nodded his head in affirmation. "I got home a few minutes ago and went in to check on him. He was dead. I'm sure he slipped away in his sleep," he said, watching her reaction, not sure how she would handle the news.

"He was ready," she said. "I know the pain had worn him down. What time is it?" she asked.

"Around five-thirty," he answered sheepishly. "I was gone longer than expected."

She did not respond to his comment but knew from the odor of his breath that he had been drinking.

"I think I'll put on a pot of coffee. Mrs. O'Mallie will be up and about soon. She'll want to know. Why don't you get some sleep? There's nothing that needs to be done right now," she said, hoping he would take her suggestion.

"If you're all right, I'll do that. I have several calls to make later this morning, and I'm going to need some rest," he responded.

"I'm fine. You go ahead," she answered, already lost in her own thoughts.

When Mrs. O'Mallie arrived, Delphinia was dressed and sitting at the kitchen table, sipping her third cup of coffee.

"Aren't you the early bird? Coffee made and gone already," she said brightly.

Taking a closer look at the young woman, she saw her eyes were red and puffy. "Come here, Child," she said, her arms outstretched to enfold and give comfort, her instincts telling her that death had come.

"Does Sam know?" Mrs. O'Mallie inquired.

"Yes, he went up to get some rest a little while ago. He didn't get much sleep last night," she answered without further explanation. "I was hoping you would help me with arrangements," Delphinia said, a sense of foreboding in her voice.

"Of course, I will. In fact, I'll take care of as much or as little as you'd like. You just tell me how much help you want," Mrs. O'Mallie answered, patting the younger woman's hand.

"Perhaps if you would go with me?" Delphinia asked. "Oh, and, Mrs. O'Mallie, I was wondering. . ." She paused, not sure how to proceed.

"Yes? Come now, Delphinia, you can ask me anything," the older woman urged.

"I don't think it would be proper for me to remain in Dr. Finley's house. Would you mind very much if I stayed with you until after the funeral? I'll leave just as soon as I can make travel arrangements," she said apologetically.

"I would love to have you come stay with me. If I would have been thinking straight, I would have already offered. Why don't you pack your things while I get myself ready?" she replied, already heading for the door.

Two days later, Mrs. O'Mallie and Sam Finley took Delphinia to meet the stage heading east out of Denver City.

Chapter 18

The journey by stage was tiring, but the air was cool, and Delphinia felt exhilarated to be on her way home. The stage was on schedule, allowing her to make the train connections, and the trip home, although long, went smoothly. Her body ached for rest, however, and she wished she had been able to notify Jonathan of her arrival.

The train lurched to a stop, and the conductor walked the aisle of the coach calling out, "Council Grove." Wearily, Delphinia made her way to the end of the coach where the conductor assisted her to the platform. "We'll have your trunk unloaded in just a few minutes, Ma'am. You can wait in the station," he said politely.

She nodded and thanked him, too tired to be concerned about her trunk. The station was empty of customers, and Delphinia sat on one of the two long wooden benches, waiting as instructed.

Her eyes fluttered open when she heard a voice asking, "Do you often sleep in train stations, Phiney?"

Looking down at her were those two beautiful blue eyes that belonged to the man she loved. "Jonathan, how did you. . .? Why are you. . .? What. . .?" she stammered.

"I don't believe you're quite awake. Seems like you can't get your words out," he said with a smile, lifting her into his arms and lightly kissing her lips.

"I don't. . . We ought not. . ."

"Seems my kiss wasn't quite enough to waken you. You're still stammering. I must be out of practice," he said and once again covered her mouth, enjoying the sweetness of her.

"Oh, Jonathan, I've missed you so. It's even good to be called Phiney," she said when he finally released her. "It seems I've been gone forever, and so much has happened. How did you know I would be here?"

"I didn't know for sure, but I got a letter from your pa yesterday saying if things went as planned, he expected you'd be back today. I decided I wasn't going to miss the opportunity to meet your train. I checked the schedules and knew you couldn't make connections for another three days if you didn't get here today," he answered.

"You got a letter from Pa? Isn't that amazing?" she said, wonderment on her face.

"Well, Mrs. O'Mallie had written it for him."

"Oh, I realize he didn't write it," she said. "I'm amazed because he wrote a letter telling you when I'd be home before he took a turn for the worse and died. It's almost as if he planned just what he wanted to accomplish and then died," she responded.

"I didn't know. . . . I'm so sorry," he began.

"I know. It's all right," she answered. "Papa was ready to meet the Lord, and I know he and Mama are enjoying their reunion," she said with a smile.

"Where are the children?" she asked, finally looking around to see if they were outside the station.

"Guess I was selfish. I left them at home with Maggie," he answered.

"Maggie?" she questioned.

"Maggie Landry, the widow who's been helping while you were gone," he responded.

"I guess I left in such a rush, I never knew her name. I only remembered that Jennie O'Laughlin knew of a widow. How has she worked out? Do the children like her? Is she a good cook? You and Tessie never mentioned her when you wrote, and I guess I didn't think to ask," she said, her voice suddenly full of concern.

"I didn't worry too much about her cooking and cleaning or whether the children liked her," he answered, his voice serious. "She's such a beauty, I didn't care about her homemaking abilities," he said and then seeing the look on her face, broke into gales of laughter.

"She's probably close to sixty years old, Phiney!" His laughter continued until Delphinia stomped her foot in agitation and insisted he quiet down.

"Jonathan Wilshire, I was merely inquiring about the woman's expertise. You make it sound as though I were jealous," she said with an air of indignation.

"Weren't you? Now, don't answer too quickly, Phiney. I don't want you to have to ask forgiveness for telling a lie," he said with a grin.

He watched her face as she tried to think of just the right answer. "Perhaps, just a little, but then my jealousy was quickly replaced by pity for the poor woman, since she'd have to put up with you and your antics if you took a fancy to her," she answered smugly.

"Is that so?" he asked, once again kissing her soundly as he lifted her onto the seat of the wagon. "You stay put until I get your trunk loaded. If I don't get you home soon, I know five little Wilshires that are going to have my hide."

"I'm not planning on going anywhere without you again," she said, smiling down at him.

The reunion with the children was full of chaos. The twins greeted her with sounds of "Mama" and clung to her skirt while the boys tried to shout over each other to be heard. In the midst of the confusion, Tessie and Mrs. Landry tried to get dinner on the table.

The meal reminded Delphinia of the day she and Jonathan had first come to Kansas. It seemed like yesterday, and yet, in other ways, it was a lifetime ago. This was her home now. This was where she belonged.

After dinner Jonathan hitched the horses to the buggy and delivered Mrs. Landry back home for a much-needed rest, leaving Tessie and Delphinia to visit while cleaning the kitchen. They had talked of the children's antics while she had been gone and news of neighbors, school, and church, when Delphinia mentioned her surprise at finding the quilt top in her trunk.

"I was pleased you sent your quilt top with me," Delphinia said. "I didn't find it until I had been in Denver City for over a week. I didn't unpack my trunk right away, thinking I'd be able to return sooner," she confided.

"I was afraid you wouldn't come back to us. I'm sure Denver City is wonderful and full of excitement. I guess I thought if I sent the quilt along, you'd be sure and return," Tessie said sheepishly.

"It was more special for me to find that quilt top than almost anything you can imagine, Tessie, and we're going to begin work on it right away," she said just as Jonathan came into the room.

"I don't think so," he said, interrupting their conversation.

"Why not?" they asked in unison.

"Because I plan on keeping you occupied for the next week or so," he said sternly.

"Is that so?" she responded, rising to the challenge in his voice.

"I've sure missed being able to spar with you, Gal," he said with a laugh. "But the fact is, I intend to have a wedding right away and spend a few days with you all to myself. What have you got to say to that?" he asked.

"I'd say it sounds wonderful," she answered. "I'm sure Tessie would allow us a little time before we start our project. Especially if she knows I've found something special for the binding on her quilt," she remarked, watching Tessie's eyes light up with anticipation.

"What did you get? Please show me, and then I promise I'll be off to bed," she begged.

"I think she's convinced me," said Jonathan.

Delphinia opened the trunk that Jonathan had placed just inside the door, and, reaching down along one side with her hand, she pulled out a roll of soft fabric. With a smile that showed her pleasure, she placed the coil of lustrous ivory fabric in Tessie's hands.

"Oh, it's so elegant. Where did you ever find it?" Tessie asked.

"It's the same material that my wedding dress is made from. When I was being fitted for my gown, I told the shopkeeper about the quilt we were going to finish when I returned to Kansas. She suggested we might like to use the leftover fabric from my gown. I hoped you would like the idea," she answered.

"How could I not like it?" she asked, giving Delphinia a hug.

"And now, young lady, off to bed," Jonathan said. "I'd like to visit with Phiney a little while before I go over to my cabin. It's not too cool outside. Why don't we sit on the porch?" Jonathan said, moving toward the door.

Once they were seated, he continued, "I know you're tired, and I don't plan to keep you up long, but I hope you'll consent to our being married a week from Saturday. Mrs. Aplington and the other women at church have already begun planning the festivities for afterward, and I announced in church we'd be getting married on your return. The preacher says he'll keep the date open, and I've got some ideas about a wedding trip. You've got your wedding dress, so there's nothing to hold us back," he said convincingly.

"I think that sounds fine, except I don't want to go on a wedding trip. I've just gotten home," she answered.

"Don't you think we need a little time alone, without the children around?" he asked, not wanting to sound selfish but sure he did not want to marry and return home to the five children on their wedding day.

"What would you think about our staying at your cabin for a week or so after we're married? Just the two of us. We could see if Maggie would stay with the children, but we'd still be close by."

"I think that would be just fine," he answered, giving her a hug. "It's so good to have you home. You can't imagine how much I've missed you. Now, I think I'd better let you get some rest. I'll see you in the morning," he said and gave her a kiss.

She stood on the porch watching as he made his way toward the smaller cabin. He was almost to his cabin when he turned and shouted loudly, "I love you, Phiney."

Smiling, she turned and walked into the house, savoring the pure joy of being back home with her Kansas family.

A light tap on the door awakened Delphinia from a sound sleep, and she was surprised to see the sun already beginning its ascent. A cool autumn breeze drifted through the small bedroom window as she called out, "Who is it?"

"Just me," came Tessie's voice. "May I come in?" she asked.

"Of course, you can," Delphinia answered and watched as the young redhead walked into the room and plopped herself at the foot of the bed.

"How can you be sleeping like this? You're always first up, and here it is your wedding day when you should be all fluttery or something, and you're sleeping like a baby," Tessie exclaimed, full of frustration that she was the only one awake on a day she considered should be full of excitement from dawn until dark.

"I'm not sure why I'm still asleep," Delphinia answered. "Perhaps because I wasn't able to doze off until a short time ago," she admitted.

"Well, now that you're awake, what do we do first?" Tessie questioned, beginning to bounce on the side of the bed, unable to control her anticipation.

"For starters, you can quit jostling the bed," Delphinia answered with a smile. "If you really want to help, you can get breakfast started. Jonathan will be through with chores before I get out of bed, at this rate," she said, throwing back the covers and swinging her feet over the side of the bed.

"Aw, that's not what I meant. I want to really do something. You know, for the wedding," Tessie replied.

"Wedding or not, we still have to eat breakfast, Tessie. The wedding isn't until this afternoon, and we've got to finish our regular work before we can get ready," Delphinia prodded.

"Okay, I'll get breakfast started," she answered, somewhat disheartened.

Delphinia smiled inwardly at the girl's excitement over the wedding. *Seems like only yesterday, she didn't even want me on this homestead, and now you'd think this wedding was the greatest event of her life,* Delphinia mused, thankful that God had been so good to all of them.

By three o'clock, the appointed time to leave the cabin, Delphinia wasn't sure anything was ready. If Maggie Landry hadn't shown up early to help, they wouldn't have been to the church until dusk. Insistent that Jonathan not see her before the wedding, the Aplingtons agreed Delphinia would go to the church with them, and Jonathan could bring the rest of the family in the buckboard. The twins protested vehemently when Delphinia began to leave, Nate tugged on her gown, while Nettie kept calling after her in a tearful voice, trying to suck her thumb and cry at the same time.

Mrs. Aplington and some of the other women had been to the church earlier that day, carrying in food and bringing fall flowers from their gardens to decorate the church. Their handiwork was beautiful, and Delphinia was touched by all they had done, but even more by their love and acceptance.

As she began her slow walk down the aisle to meet her future husband, Jonathan smiled broadly, noting she was pressing down the gathers in the skirt of her wedding dress as she walked to meet him. When she reached his side, Jonathan leaned down and whispered, "There's nothing to be nervous about, Phiney."

"I'm not nervous. I'm very calm," she replied, her quivering voice belying that statement.

"Now, Phiney, we're in the house of God and there you go, trying to fib to me," he muttered back.

"Why are you trying to upset me, Jonathan?" she questioned, her voice louder than she intended, causing the guests to wonder just what was taking place.

The pastor loudly cleared his throat and whispered to both of them, "May we begin?"

"Well, I wish you would. We're in our places," came Delphinia's feisty response.

"She's something, isn't she?" Jonathan remarked to the preacher with a broad smile. "Sorry for the delay, but I wanted her to relax and enjoy the wedding. She needs to get a little fired up before she can calm down," he said to the pastor who merely shook his head, not sure he even wanted to try and understand that explanation.

As they exchanged their vows and pledged their love, Delphinia knew her parents and Granny were with them. In fact, if the truth were known, Granny was probably up in heaven impatiently tapping her foot and saying, "It's about time!"

The festivities were still in full swing at the church when the young couple made their way back to Jonathan's house.

"Tessie said she put something in the back of the buggy for us," Delphinia advised Jonathan when they arrived at his cabin.

Reaching behind him, he pulled out a wicker basket. The handle was wrapped with white ribbon and topped with two large bows. Entering the house, he placed it on a small wooden table and then returned to the buggy, lifted Delphinia into his arms, and carried her into the cabin.

Placing her on the floor in front of him, he gathered her into his arms and kissed her with such passion, she felt her body go limp as she leaned against him. "That, Mrs. Wilshire, is how I intend to be kissed every morning, noon, and evening from now on," he announced, being careful to hold her upright.

"I'm not sure how much work I'll get done if you kiss me like that all day long," she answered with a smile.

"Let's see what Tessie sent along for us," he said, keeping her by his side as he lifted the covering from the basket.

"Looks like she didn't want you to spend your first day of married life having to cook for me," he told her. She peeked around him and saw fried chicken, a jar of homemade preserves, two loaves of bread, pickles, and sandwiches that had been cut into heart shapes, causing both of them to smile.

"There's a note in here too. I'll let you open it," he said.

The note was written on a heart-shaped piece of paper and on the outside it said, *Before you open this, walk into the bedroom.*

Jonathan took her hand, guiding her into the small bedroom, and watched as Delphinia's face shone with absolute joy. "Oh, Jonathan, it's my quilt. How did you ever get my quilt back?"

"I didn't," he said. "The last time we were in town Tessie saw the Indian who had been to the cabin. He was carrying your quilt over his arm. There was no holding her back. She went straight to him, and the next thing I knew, she had his knife and was cutting off some more of her hair. I sat watching to make sure nothing would happen. A short time later she returned to the wagon with your quilt," he answered.

"What does her note say?" he asked.

She opened it and read out loud,

Dearest Delphinia and Jonathan,

May the threads of love that hold this quilt tie your hearts with love and joy forever.

Love,
Tessie

WOVEN THREADS

Judith McCoy Miller

Dedicated to my husband, Jim,
for giving me the wonderful opportunity to become
one of the threads woven into the fabric of his life,
and in memory of our daughter, Michelle,
with whom we shall be rewoven in heaven.

Chapter 1

Charlie Banion stared down at the list of names scribbled on his calendar; Mary had scheduled five interviews starting at one o'clock. Allowing a half-hour for each, he could still catch the four o'clock train and be in Florence for dinner. Hopefully this group would be better than the last. He had been at this three days now and still hadn't met the quota he needed for the remaining railroad jobs. No doubt the boss was going to be unhappy with his lack of success.

Might as well get a bite to eat before I start again, he thought, wishing the afternoon was already behind him. Tapping his pencil on the large wooden desk, he leaned back in his chair and wondered why it had been so difficult to find the employees he was looking for this time. It was easy enough locating general laborers to lay track, but now they needed some good, reliable men with mechanical skills to keep the trains running. His attempt to find the caliber of employees they were looking for had failed, especially when the applicants were told they would have to relocate to smaller towns.

"Sitting here thinking about it isn't going to accomplish anything," he mumbled to himself, walking toward the office door.

"I'll be back in time for my one o'clock appointment, Mary," he said, striding past the secretary's desk.

"Yes, Sir. I'll put the file on your desk," she answered. He didn't even glance her way as he nodded his head up and down in affirmation.

"Isn't he the most handsome thing you've ever seen?" Mary inquired of the short, round brunette sitting at the desk across the room.

"I guess. That is, if you like single men who are six feet tall with broad shoulders, wavy black hair, and slate gray eyes," she answered, both of them giggling at her response.

"He doesn't seem to notice me at all," Mary complained, "even though I take forever primping for work when I know he'll be around."

"Maybe he's got a gal at one of the other stations or back East somewhere," Cora volunteered, aware that most men found it difficult to overlook Mary Wilson, even when she didn't primp for hours.

"I'd even be willing to share him with one of those eastern society women. At least until I get him hooked," Mary responded, pushing back from her desk. "Guess I'll go to lunch too. Maybe I can find a seat next to Mr. Banion. Keep an eye on things until I get back," she ordered Cora, who sat looking after her with a look of envy and admiration etched on her face.

Tessie Wilshire stared out the window of the clacking train, unable to keep her mind from racing. The newly bloomed columbine and wild flax were poking their blossoms toward the sun after a long cold winter. Fields of winter wheat appeared in shades of bright green, giving the countryside the appearance of a huge well-manicured lawn.

In about three months this will be a sea of golden yellow ready for the threshers and harvest crews, she thought. She had forgotten the beauty of these wheat fields and the Kansas prairie. It was hard to believe that she had been gone so long, and yet, things hadn't changed so very much. *I've missed it more than I realized,* she mused, trying to keep herself from thinking about the upcoming interview.

Always a pretty child, Tessie's age had enhanced her beauty even more. The red hair of her youth had turned a deep coppery shade, and the freckles of her childhood had finally given way to a flawless creamy complexion. Her bright blue eyes were accented by long golden lashes, and her full lips turned slightly upward, punctuated by a small dimple at each side.

"Topeka. Next stop Topeka," came the conductor's call as he made his way down the narrow aisle between the seated passengers.

Tessie felt herself stiffen at the announcement. In an effort to relax, she took a deep breath and said softly, "I'm going to be fine. I know this is where God wants me."

"Watch your step, Miss," the conductor instructed, extending his hand to assist Tessie as she stepped down from the train.

"Thank you. Could you tell me where I might find Mr. Banion's office?" she inquired, pulling on her gloves.

"He would be in the stationmaster's office, Miss. Just go in the main door and turn to your right," he replied, thinking it had been a long time since he had seen such a beauty.

Tessie clicked open the small brooch pinned to her lapel. The timepiece hidden inside revealed the fact that she had only a few moments to spare. Quickening her step, she turned and walked toward the office identified by the conductor.

"Is the last one here yet, Mary?" Charlie Banion called from the stationmaster's office.

"Haven't seen anyone. You want me to show him in when he gets here?" she asked, posing against the doorway to his office in an effort to gain his attention.

"That'll be fine," he answered, not looking in her direction. O*nly one more left,* he thought, *and I'll be out of here.* At least the afternoon hadn't been a total waste. He had hired three of the last four applicants. If they didn't need a doctor so badly at the Florence train yard, he would be tempted to call it a day.

Seeing the look of frustration on Mary's face as she returned to her desk, Cora shrugged her shoulders at the other woman. "Maybe he's not feeling well," she offered.

"Right!" came Mary's sarcastic response as she plopped down in her chair and watched a beautiful redhead walking toward the door.

"Good afternoon. I'm Tessie Wilshire. I believe Mr. Banion is expecting me at three o'clock," she announced, glancing from Mary to Cora, not sure which one was in charge.

"Don't think so. The Harvey Girls are interviewed next door in the restaurant office," Mary answered in an aloof tone.

"I'm not sure what a Harvey Girl is, but my appointment is with Mr. Charles Banion for three o'clock. I received a letter over a month ago scheduling this appointment," Tessie replied, fearing there had been a mix-up and she had traveled to Topeka for nothing.

"Mr. Banion doesn't interview for Mr. Harvey. I don't think they're even taking applications right now. The new women finished training yesterday, and they're leaving on the next train," Mary advised haughtily, irritated by the woman's persistence.

"I'm trying to explain to you that my appointment is with Mr. Banion. I have never heard of Mr. Harvey," Tessie said, trying to hold her temper but wishing she could shake some sense into the secretary's head.

Hearing the commotion in the outer office, Charlie walked to the doorway. "What seems to be the problem, Mary?" he asked, locking eyes with the gorgeous redhead standing in front of the secretary's desk.

"She says she has an appointment with you, Mr. Banion. I told her the Harvey Girls are interviewed next door, but she won't listen. Keeps insisting she's to meet with you," his secretary answered, her exasperation obvious.

"Mr. Banion," Tessie said, extending her hand, "I am Dr. Wilshire, and I believe we have a three o'clock appointment."

"Indeed we do, Miss. . .uh, Dr. Wilshire. Please come in," he replied, ushering her into his office and then turning to give Mary a glare.

"I didn't know. . . ," came the secretary's feeble reply as the door closed behind them. She slowly slid down into her chair, her jaw gone slack in astonishment at the turn of events.

"How was I supposed to know?" she hissed at Cora.

"It'll be all right. He'll understand. Anybody could have made the same mistake," Cora replied, attempting to cheer her friend.

"Have a seat, Dr. Wilshire," Charlie offered, moving to the other side of the desk. "I must admit that I'm as surprised as my secretary. I didn't realize you were a woman. . .well, I mean I realize you're a woman, but I didn't know. . .," he stammered.

"It's quite all right, Mr. Banion. I gather you've not studied my application," she said, giving him a bright smile that caused his heart to skip a beat.

"To be honest, I've been conducting interviews for several days now, and I must admit I didn't look at any of the files for today's interviews," he responded, somewhat embarrassed by his lack of preparation. "I usually don't take such a lackadaisical attitude, but interviewing is not a job I particularly enjoy. After several days, it loses absolutely all appeal," he continued in an attempt to redeem himself.

"I'm sure it can become quite tiring," she stated. "Of course, for those of us being interviewed, it's a very important appointment," she said, a hint of criticism edging through her soft tone.

"I realize that, and I do apologize. If I'd done my homework, it would have saved everyone needless discomfort," he answered, flipping open her application file.

"I can assure you that Mr. Vance is aware I'm not a man. I met him on one of his visits to Chicago, and we've written on several occasions. When he discovered I was from Kansas, he encouraged me to apply for this position," she responded, realizing Mr. Banion was flustered and somewhat embarrassed by the whole scenario.

"So you've already met the president of the Santa Fe. He's always on the lookout for capable employees," Charlie replied.

Watching as he hastily read through her file, Tessie settled back in the overstuffed chair. Although the office décor was masculine, it was an inviting room. The large desk was of a rich mahogany with matching chair. A table along the north wall was ornately carved from the same wood and held several stacks of papers and files, the only site of disarray throughout the office. Oil paintings in ornate gilded frames were tastefully displayed on several walls. Tessie noticed a picture of Mr. Vance and several austere looking gentlemen standing in front of a locomotive. In the picture, Mr. Vance appeared somewhat younger and much more pompous than the man she had met in Chicago.

"It seems your application is in order, and I have only a few questions, Dr. Wilshire," Charlie commented, startling Tessie, who had become absorbed in her surroundings. "Sorry. I didn't mean to alarm you," he said, noting she had jumped at the sound of his voice.

"I must have been daydreaming. The trip was more tiring than I anticipated," she responded, bringing her eyes directly forward to meet his. "What questions did you wish to ask me?" she inquired with great formality.

"I have a list of specific questions I ask the men applying for positions with the railroad, but I don't think those would apply to you," he said with a smile, hoping to ease the procedure. "Why are you interested in working for the railroad?" he asked.

"I believe it's where God wants me to practice medicine," she quickly responded, sitting so straight that she appeared to have a rod down her back.

"Well, that's one I've not heard before. I've been told it's where someone's wife or mother wants him to work, but I've never heard the railroad being where God wanted anyone," he said with a chuckle.

"You needn't laugh at me, Mr. Banion," Tessie retorted, her cheeks turning flush and her back becoming even more rigid.

"I'm not laughing at you, Dr. Wilshire, and I'm not doubting the honesty of your statement. If you say God wants you with the Santa Fe Railroad, who am I to argue? Besides, your file reflects the necessary credentials and a letter of recommendation from Mr. Vance. There's really nothing for me to do except tell you the job is yours if you want it," he said, hoping to complete the interview without making her an enemy.

"Since you've offered the position, I have a few questions for you, Mr. Banion," she responded, her voice lacking much warmth.

"Please, call me Charlie," he requested. "I'll be glad to answer any questions if you'll grant that one concession," he said while giving her a beseeching look.

"Fine," she responded. "I need to know when I am to report for the position, what the living accommodations are in the community, and of course, what my salary will be," she answered without using his name in any form.

"Well, Tessie—may I call you Tessie since you've agreed to call me Charlie?" he asked, watching for her reaction.

"That will be fine," she replied, though not meeting his eyes.

"Good, because we'll probably be seeing quite a bit of each other, and I much prefer being on a first-name basis with people. I don't hold much stock in. . ."

"Mr. Banion. . .Charlie, I've agreed we'll be on a first-name basis if I accept the position. If you'll answer my questions, I'll be able to decide if I want to accept the offer," she interrupted.

"You told me God wants you working for the Santa Fe, Tessie, and I've offered you that opportunity. You can hardly turn it down, can you?" he said with a grin. "Oh, all right. I'll answer your questions," he continued, seeing that she was becoming exasperated with him. "The position begins immediately. You can catch the four o'clock train if I'm through answering your questions by then. If not, you'll have to catch the ten o'clock. The salary is $150 a month, and the railroad furnishes your house. No choice on the house; it belongs to the railroad."

"You don't really expect me to begin today, do you?" she queried, her eyes wide in disbelief.

"Yes, I thought you understood that when a position was offered, employment was immediate. Isn't that what your letter stated?"

"Well, yes, but I didn't think it—I suppose I should have made arrangements," she stated, her voice full of hesitation.

"Are you accepting the position, Dr. Wilshire?" Charlie inquired with some of the formality she had exhibited earlier.

"Yes, but I'll need to make arrangements to have my belongings sent if I must start immediately," she answered, hoping he would grant some leniency.

"It's not my rule. I'd allow you as much time as you need, but it's a rule enforced for all new employees. There's no problem about your belongings, though. The railroad will ship them for you free of charge. Just a little added benefit," he remarked, not sure she was convinced he couldn't bend the rule.

"We have about thirty minutes before the train leaves. Have you had a chance to eat?" he asked.

"No, but I'm not hungry," she answered. "I'll wait until I get to Florence."

"Well, in that case, perhaps you'll join me for dinner?"

"You're going to Florence?" she queried.

"Sure am. I'm the operations manager, which means I spend a lot of time there keeping things on schedule, so you'll be seeing a lot of me," he responded with a grin, hoping she would be pleased.

"I'll need to purchase a ticket and send word to my family that I've accepted the position. Since you're going to Florence, I suppose you'll be available to answer any other inquiry I might have," she said with a question in her voice.

"You can be assured that I will make myself available to you whenever and wherever you request," he answered, his gray eyes twinkling.

She wasn't sure if he was making fun of her but decided it wasn't important enough to bother with. "If the interview is over, Mr. Banion," she began, rising from the chair.

"Charlie. Remember you said you'd call me Charlie," he reminded, coming around the side of the desk. "As far as I'm concerned, the interview is over, but you need not rush to buy a ticket. Your travel on the railroad is free. Another benefit of the job," he said, escorting her to the door.

"May I at least buy you a cup of coffee after you've sent your message home?" he invited as they walked through the outer office.

"I suppose that would be acceptable," she replied, though her voice lacked much enthusiasm at the prospect.

"I'll meet you next door at the Harvey House when you've finished," he responded.

Had he not been looking at her back and observed the slight nod of her head, he wouldn't have known she even heard him speak. Staring after her as she walked across the room, he was unable to remember when he had been quite so impressed with a young woman.

"Did you have any letters you needed me to take care of?" Mary asked, attempting to regain Charlie's attention.

"What? Oh, yes, I need to get a letter written to Mr. Vance advising him of the new employees I've hired," he responded.

When he had finished dictating the letter, Mary's worst fears were confirmed. He had hired the stunning redhead, and the possibility of snagging a marriage proposal out of Charlie Banion was going to be more difficult than she had anticipated.

"I'd like that letter ready for my signature before the train leaves. I'm going to the restaurant, but I'll return to sign it shortly," he instructed Mary and hurried toward the lunch counter, anxious to once again be in the company of the newest employee of the Santa Fe Railroad.

Chapter 2

Tessie had just finished a cup of tea when Charlie arrived in the restaurant and seated himself opposite her. "Sorry to have taken so long. I had to get a letter dictated to Mr. Vance," he explained, feeling like a schoolboy on a first date.

"No need to apologize. I'm quite used to taking care of myself," she told him as the waitress brought Charlie a cup of coffee. "Living alone while in college and medical school has tended to make me quite independent. I've learned to use my time alone quite constructively."

Before Charlie could decide if she had dubbed him a welcome intrusion or a pesky annoyance, the conductor's shout rang out, "All aboard!"

"I've got to go back to the office for a few minutes. I'll see you on board," he said, getting up from his seat.

"Fine," Tessie answered nonchalantly, more interested in the group of chattering young women anxiously waiting on the platform. She wondered who they were and why they were all boarding a train to some tiny town seventy-five miles to the southwest. Picking up her black medical bag, she mentally gave thanks that Uncle Jon had insisted she carry it. "Never know when you might happen upon an emergency. If you're a doctor, you ought to be prepared. Preachers carry a Bible, and doctors ought to carry the tools of their trade too," he had counseled.

He and Aunt Phiney had given her sound advice thus far. They had warned that she should pack a few personal belongings in case the train was delayed or the interview postponed, requiring her to be away more than one day. Because of their foresight, she would at least have a few clothes until her trunks arrived.

The young women were already seated on the train by the time Tessie boarded. Picking her way down the aisle, she found an empty seat, settled herself, and placed her bag on the floor. Just as the train began its lumbering exit from the station, Charlie bounded down the aisle and slid onto the seat across the aisle from her.

"Were you worried I wouldn't make it?" he inquired, a smile spread across his face.

"To be honest, my thoughts were occupied with all these young women, wondering where they come from and why they left their homes," she responded, not realizing that such a remark was a rarity to a man of Charlie Banion's looks and position.

"You sure know how to keep a man from feeling sure of himself, don't you?" he asked jokingly.

"What? Oh, I'm sorry. What were you saying? Isn't she a beautiful child?" Tessie inquired, nodding toward the little girl sitting on the seat in front of her.

Charlie broke forth in a laugh, aware that he would not engage this lovely woman in any meaningful conversation until she had surveyed all the passengers. "She *is* a pretty child," he answered, looking at the youngster and smiling into the small dark brown eyes that were staring back at him. The child's eyes quickly darted back toward Tessie.

"Hello. My name is Tessie," she said to the young girl. "What's your name?"

The child smiled and turned around facing them. She perched on her knees while resting her arms across the back of the seat. "Hi, I'm Addie Baker. That's my sister, Lydia," she answered, pointing across the aisle toward the front of the train, her words slightly garbled. The gesture caught her sister's eye.

"Addie, turn around and mind your business," Lydia reprimanded the youngster, her lips mouthing the words in exaggerated fashion, although her voice was but a whisper. The child nodded, immediately turned, and stared out the window, only to be met by her own forlorn reflection in the glass.

Tessie leaned forward and whispered, "I'm pleased to meet you, Addie," but the child gave no response, and Tessie received a sharp look from the older sister.

Charlie turned his legs toward the aisle and leaned forward, resting his arms on his thighs. "I'd be happy to visit with you."

Tessie was tempted to ignore his forward behavior but allowed her interest in the young women to take precedence over Charlie's obvious lack of manners.

"Tell me about these young women. I believe you called them Harvey Girls," she requested, pulling off her gloves and reaching to remove a pearl hat pin from the navy blue adornment perched on her head.

He didn't answer for a moment but watched her movements, totally entranced by the feminine display. When she finally looked at him to see if he had heard the question, he smiled. "I'd rather talk about you, but if that's not your choice of subject, I'll tell you a little about the Harvey Girls."

He remained seated with his legs in the aisle, which allowed him closer proximity to her. "These women have just completed their training as Harvey Girls and are going to work at the Harvey House in Florence. It's a hotel and restaurant, close to the train station. Fred Harvey has a contract with the Santa Fe Railroad to place restaurants near some of the train stations. The one in Topeka is merely a restaurant—a very good one I might add—but Fred decided that a hotel and restaurant would be even better at some of the stations."

"Are these women hired as maids for the hotel?" she interrupted, her interest piqued.

"Some of them may end up doing that part of the time," he responded, "but primarily they are hired and trained to work as waitresses in the restaurants. Fred has extremely high standards, and the women must live in the establishment. Even in Topeka, those who work for him must reside in the accommodations he provides."

"Even if their parents live in the same town?" she asked, entranced with the idea.

"Yes, even then. It's one of the hard-and-fast rules of the Harvey Houses, just like our hard-and-fast rule that you begin work immediately," he replied, hoping she would indicate her forgiveness.

"From the size of the group, it looks as if there are plenty of women interested in the jobs," she observed, once again scrutinizing the young women clustered at the front of the coach and ignoring his remark about the rules.

"Fred pays a decent wage, and for many of these women, it's the only opportunity they'll have to see a bit of the country. It's exciting for many of them, and they're hoping for a better life than they've come from. That would be my guess," he stated, staring at her long graceful fingers.

"What's the conductor doing up there?" Tessie asked, watching the man move from passenger to passenger while taking down information.

"Dinner orders," Charlie replied. Tessie's eyebrows furrowed together at his answer as if he might be joking.

"Really?" she questioned.

"Yes, really. The conductor takes down orders, and then they're sent ahead to the Harvey House. That way the chef knows in advance how many meals to prepare, and the staff can be ready to serve the passengers immediately upon their arrival."

"Mr. Banion, good to see you. Will you be dining at the Harvey House this evening?" the conductor inquired, his friendliness making it obvious that he and Charlie had known each other for some period of time.

"I certainly will, and Dr. Wilshire will be joining me," he answered, indicating his traveling companion across the aisle.

"Doctor, huh? Well, good to have you aboard, Dr. Wilshire," he said with a nod and looked back toward Charlie.

"You folks going to be eating in the dining room or the lunchroom?"

"The dining room," Charlie answered for both of them.

"In that case, I need to know if you'd prefer the baked veal pie, pork with applesauce, or the roast sirloin of beef au jus," he inquired, his pencil poised to take their order.

"Tessie? What sounds good to you?" Charlie inquired.

"I believe I'll have the baked veal pie," she responded.

"Make mine the same," Charlie told the conductor.

"That's two baked veal pies," the conductor repeated. "That comes with asparagus in cream sauce, lobster salad, and your choice of dessert," he proudly announced. "Coffee, tea, or milk?"

Charlie looked over toward Tessie, who replied that she would like tea. Charlie requested coffee. Having completed their order, the conductor continued down the aisle.

"Look, Addie, see the deer and her baby," Tessie said, pointing out the window toward the graceful animals. When no response came from the child, she reached over the seat and touched Addie's shoulder to gain the child's attention. Once again she pointed toward the deer and watched Addie smile in delight when she sighted them.

"Pretty, aren't they?" Tessie asked the child.

Addie's face was still pressed against the train window when Lydia came down the aisle and plopped in the seat beside her little sister.

"She won't answer you. She doesn't know you're talking to her—she's deaf," Lydia remarked to Tessie, her voice void of emotion.

"She talked to me earlier," Tessie replied, sure the statement was untrue.

"Probably read your lips. She wouldn't hear a gunshot if it went off right next to her," Lydia stated coldly.

"I didn't realize. I'm very sorry," Tessie said, saddened by the revelation.

"She gets by all right most of the time. I'm the one who gets stuck with all the worries, and she gets all the sympathy," the young woman replied, her resentment toward the child evident. "It's a real pain having to look after her all the time. I'm just hoping I get to keep my job once they find out I brought the brat along. Be just my luck to get fired after doing so well in my training, but maybe they'll have some kind of work for her," she told the captive audience seated behind her.

"I don't know if Fred has anyone that young working for him," Charlie stated, eyeing the girl with a look she interpreted as disapproval.

"Oh no! Don't tell me you work for Mr. Harvey," Lydia wailed. "I have the worst luck in the world. Who else but me would sit down and pour out her heart to the one person who could ruin everything."

"I don't work for Mr. Harvey," Charlie interrupted. "I work for the Santa Fe Railroad, but I do know Fred. He's a good man, but I don't believe he would want a child of Addie's age employed in one of his establishments."

"Whew, that was a close call!" Lydia exclaimed. "I can't tell you how relieved I am. You won't tell Mr. Harvey about Addie, will you?"

Charlie met her eyes. "I don't want to see you and your little sister in dire circumstances, but I'll not lie for you either," he answered.

Lydia glowered at him and began to rise from the seat.

"Why don't you sit back down and tell us why you brought Addie with you? It might make it easier for us to help you," Tessie cajoled, hoping to placate the older girl.

Quickly realizing that it would be more advantageous to have these folks as friends, Lydia reclaimed her seat and, gazing at some unknown object just behind Tessie's shoulder, launched into her account.

"My parents got divorced about three years ago," she began. "Ma got word about a year later that Pa had died. Not that it mattered too much. He never sent any money to help out when he was alive. Ma went to work as a housekeeper and cook for some rich folks in town. They didn't want us living in their fancy house, so Ma rented a small place outside of town. She had to walk over three miles every morning and evening, no matter what the weather was like. Not once did they so much as offer to give her a ride in their buggy, even when it was pouring rain or the snow was a foot deep. Ma never did complain, though," she continued, shaking her head in dismay.

"I know that must have been difficult for all three of you," Tessie responded, her heart going out to the two young women.

Lydia didn't respond but continued in a hollow voice. "About a year ago Ma got sick with influenza. We couldn't afford a doctor, so she just kept getting worse until finally she died."

"Sounds like your mother tried real hard to take care of things on her own," Charlie commented.

"She did, but she needed help, and there was never anyone around to give her a hand. It was all she could do to make enough money to pay the rent and buy food. Even when she was hot with fever, she would drag herself out of bed and go to work," Lydia stated. "After she died, I knew I had to find some way to take care of myself. I had just finished high school, and Ma was so proud. She always wanted me to have a better life, but I was left trying to find a place to live and a job that would pay decent wages. A friend told me about an advertisement she had seen for the Harvey Houses. She said it paid good money, and you got a place to live. It didn't take me long to make my decision. 'Course Addie has been my biggest problem as usual," she said, giving the child a look of disdain.

"I'm sure Addie's had her share of difficulty dealing with your mother's death," Tessie stated, disquieted by the older girl's attitude.

"Oh sure, poor little deaf Addie. Let's all feel sorry for Addie," Lydia spat mockingly, while twisting the ties of her bonnet.

Tessie glanced over and saw the look of sadness on Addie's face. The child had been watching her sister's performance and appeared to have a clear understanding of Lydia's truculent attitude.

"I didn't mean to discount the problems you've had to deal with, Lydia," Tessie responded soothingly. "I doubt there are many young women your age who could have handled themselves as admirably under the circumstances. Tell me—where did Addie stay while you took your training as a Harvey Girl?" Tessie inquired, hoping to gain further information about their situation.

"She lived with some folks from the church. They said they could keep her while I took my training, but they've got ten kids of their own. There's no way they could afford another one. I probably could have found some place for her if she could hear, but nobody wants an extra kid around if she has problems," Lydia expounded.

"Was Addie born deaf?" Tessie questioned.

"No, she could hear up until a year ago. I don't know what happened. She just couldn't hear anymore," Lydia answered.

"Did she slowly lose her ability to hear? Was she sick, and did she run a high temperature? Did she fall down and hit her head?" Tessie questioned in rapid succession.

"I don't know," Lydia responded, irritated that all of Tessie's interest seemed directed at her sister. "What do you care anyway? It doesn't make any difference *when* she quit hearing. She can't hear now, and she's a pain in the neck!"

"I'm sorry. I certainly didn't mean to upset you," Tessie quickly apologized.

"This woman is a doctor, Lydia. I'm sure that's why she's showing such interest in your sister's ailment," Charlie offered in an attempt to smooth the discussion between the two women.

"A doctor? I don't believe it. A woman doctor! If that don't beat all. Wish you'd have been around when my Ma was so sick," the young woman replied, shaking her head in disbelief. "Where you headed?" she asked Tessie.

"She's going to Florence, same as you," Charlie answered. "Dr. Wilshire's going to be the new physician for the Santa Fe employees," Charlie proudly announced to the young woman.

Tessie sat staring at him, wondering why he felt compelled to answer on her behalf.

"You been a doctor very long?" Lydia inquired.

"No," Tessie and Charlie replied in unison.

"I believe that Mr. Banion feels qualified to speak on my behalf since he hastily read my resumé a few hours ago," Tessie continued, with a grin on her face.

"I'm sorry. That was very rude of me, wasn't it?"

"That's all right. It's just that I've been used to answering for myself the last several years," Tessie remarked, causing all three of them to laugh and relieving some of the mounting tension.

"Your folks must have lots of money if they could send you for schooling to be a doctor," Lydia stated, the sound of envy obvious in her voice.

"My parents died when I was twelve years old, Lydia," Tessie answered. "I was very fortunate, however. My Uncle Jon lived on the adjoining farm, and our grandmother lived with us also. Then a couple years after my parents died, Uncle Jon married a wonderful woman. Nobody could have asked for a better substitute mother than Aunt Phiney. She encouraged me to use all of my God-given talents."

"Yeah, well, my mother didn't have a good job or good luck, so I'm stuck taking care of Addie. But it's *my* turn now, and I'm not going to let her get in my way. I'm going to work at the Harvey House and meet me a man to take care of me," Lydia retorted, flinging her head in a decisive nod.

Tessie thought the young woman looked almost triumphant—as though she had discovered the secret to a guaranteed happy life. It was obvious that Lydia thought the solution to her unhappiness was a husband to take over the burdens and responsibilities that had been thrust upon her. For now, however, she was mistakenly directing her resentment at what she considered the source of her problems—Addie.

"I hope everything will work out for both you and Addie," Tessie stated. "If there is anything I can do to help, I hope you won't hesitate to let me know," Tessie offered. She didn't know what she could do, but certainly both of these sisters needed a friend.

"Thanks," Lydia answered. "Maybe you or your gentleman friend can help me find a way to keep Addie at the Harvey House," she ventured.

"Do you think you could help, Charlie?" Tessie asked with a look of hopefulness.

"I'll see what I can do," Charlie answered, not certain he could be of much assistance but wanting to please Tessie. He watched her small smile develop more broadly and her cheeks take on a slight blush, her happiness evident at his remark. "I'm not promising anything," he quickly continued, the remark directed more at Tessie than the two sisters.

"I understand," Tessie interrupted. "I appreciate the fact that you are willing at least to make an attempt."

"Well, don't expect a miracle," he responded.

"Why not? I'm sure that God is quite capable of a miracle for these two girls, and that may be the very reason you're on this train," Tessie answered in an authoritative manner.

"That may be so," Charlie remarked, "but I had rather hoped it was because we were destined to meet and fall in love," he said quickly before moving across the aisle and firmly squeezing her into the corner of the seat.

"Mr. Banion, just because you have agreed to assist these women does not mean I am giving you permission to make advances toward me," Tessie retorted, attempting to put this brash man in his place.

"Now, Tessie, remember that you agreed to call me Charlie," he replied, the humor in his voice causing Lydia to giggle.

"Looks like you've already got you a man," Lydia teased. "I'll go back up with the other women so you two lovebirds can be alone," she said, giving them an exaggerated wink before she turned to move forward with her friends.

"Now, look what ideas you've put in her head," Tessie reprimanded, giving a sharp jab with her elbow that landed in Charlie's right side.

"Ouch! I thought you took an oath to heal, not do bodily harm to people," Charlie complained, rubbing the spot where she had inflicted the blow.

"Oh, don't be such a big baby," she chided. "If that's all it takes to turn you into a whimpering soul, you'd better never come to my office for treatment."

He watched her give Addie a quick smile when she noticed the little girl observing their sparring match.

The train whistle exploded in two long blasts, signaling that they would soon be arriving at their destination. Tessie watched Addie as another shrill whistle sounded out into the late afternoon dusk, but there was no indication the child heard a sound.

Chapter 3

Amid clouds of billowing gray smoke, the train came to a hissing, belching stop, allowing the passengers to disembark onto a wooden platform. The sturdy brick station stoically guarded the rails while passengers entered and exited the trains in a flurry of activity.

"Harvey House is just this way," Charlie stated, taking her arm as she stepped down from the train.

The establishment still carried the name Clifton Hotel, although Charlie was quick to tell her that it bore little resemblance to the old hostelry. Most folks now referred to it as the Harvey House.

The waitresses were dressed just like those Tessie had seen in Topeka. The black-and-white uniforms, with Elsie collars, black stockings, black shoes, and white ribbons tying back their hair did little to accentuate the femininity of the young women. The waitresses seemed to weave in and out among the tables with an ease and familiarity that belied the fact that most of them had been working for Fred Harvey only a short time. It was a superb testimonial to their training.

Charlie and Tessie were seated at a small table by themselves, although most of the passengers were at larger tables visiting and enjoying the attention being lavished upon them the minute they entered the establishment.

"What do you think of your new community so far?" Charlie asked, pleased that his companion appeared impressed by the surroundings.

"I must say, I am surprised," she exclaimed delightedly. "My expectations didn't include dining in such elegance. Who would have expected to find English china and Irish linen on the tables of a restaurant in Florence, Kansas?"

"Not many folks, I suppose," Charlie agreed, "but more and more people will come to expect elegance at all of the stops along the Santa Fe."

Tessie was sure that he was right, especially if they all measured up to the bill of fare presented at the Harvey House. "Would you like another cup of tea?" Charlie inquired, hoping she would be willing to linger a few minutes longer.

"If you don't mind, I'd rather get myself settled. It's been a long day, and I don't think I could hold another ounce of food or drink," she replied with a smile.

"I guess I'm just trying to keep you with me as long as possible," Charlie admitted. "However, I'm sure you're tired and would like to see your new home.

Let me introduce you to the chef before we leave," he said, directing her toward the kitchen doorway.

As they approached, Tessie could hear the sound of Lydia's voice coming from the kitchen. It was evident that an argument had ensued, and from the sound of things, Lydia had met her match. Just as Charlie opened the kitchen door, Tessie heard someone yelling at Lydia to get her brat out of the kitchen.

"What's the problem, John?" Charlie asked, walking into the kitchen with an air of authority.

"I'm not real sure. From the sound of things, one of the new waitresses has a little sister with her. Guess she thinks Mrs. Winter should allow the kid to stay in the dormitory," replied the chef. "You know that's not gonna happen. Mrs. Winter won't let anyone sleep in those rooms unless they work here. Me?—I'm just trying to stay clear of the ruckus," he stated, shrugging his shoulders and shaking his head in disgust.

"Say, John, would you consider hiring the little girl as a pearl diver?" Charlie asked, hoping the chef's agreement would cancel out Mrs. Winter's objection to Addie's living with her sister.

"I don't know. That little tyke couldn't even reach the sinks," he replied.

"What's a pearl diver?" Tessie inquired, wondering if Charlie had lost his senses.

"Oh, that's just a nickname we give the dishwashers," the chef replied, his wide grin revealing a set of uneven white teeth sitting under an inky black moustache.

"Come on, Johnny. She could do it! The kid's probably worked harder in the last year than most of the guys we've got laying track," Charlie exaggerated, hoping to make good on his promise to Tessie and Lydia.

"I suppose we could turn one of those big tubs upside down and let her stand on it," he replied.

It would be good just once to get the upper hand with old Mrs. Winter, decided John. She didn't seem to have much of a heart, and John knew that she liked the power of her position. If the little girl had a job and was related to one of the Harvey Girls, Mrs. Winter would have to let her stay in the hotel with the rest of the hired help, he reasoned to himself. Maybe it would bring her down a peg or two if she realized the employees were going to stick together. Besides, he could use another dishwasher.

"Thanks, John. I owe you one," Charlie responded, giving the chef a slap on the back and extending his hand.

"That's okay, Charlie. She's a cute little kid, and we can find something to keep her busy."

The men had just finished their conversation when Mrs. Winter came bustling through the kitchen, obviously a woman intent on getting things settled.

"Ah, Mrs. Winter, you appear to be a bit frazzled this evening," Charlie crooned. "I would think you'd be in good spirits with all this new help arriving," he added.

"I'm glad to have the additional help, Mr. Banion, but not the additional problems! You can't imagine the difficulties some of these women can create," she stated, grabbing a dishcloth and vehemently rubbing a nonexistent spot on one of the counters.

"Perhaps I could be of assistance," Charlie offered, hoping to entice her into a conversation regarding young Addie.

"I doubt that—not that you're not capable, mind you. It's just one of these new women brought a younger sister with her, expecting I'd allow her to live with the rest of us. There are rules, Mr. Banion. Some of these women, especially the new ones, just do not understand rules," she stated, sure she had found a comrade in the personnel manager for the railroad.

"Yes, rules need to be followed. I agree," he stated. "Isn't it a rule that if you work in a Harvey House, you live there?"

"Of course," she replied smugly, not realizing she had just been caught in his snare.

"Well then, you have no problem. That little girl is an employee of the House," he retorted, watching as deep lines formed across her forehead.

"How can that be?" she asked, sure there had to be a misunderstanding.

"I hired her. She's gonna be a pearl diver," John answered.

"Whaaat? I don't believe it. She's too little to wash dishes, and you know it, Johnny," she retorted, angry at the turn of events. The entire staff was now gathered in the kitchen listening to Mrs. Winter receive her comeuppance from the chef. They all knew that Johnny was the one person she wouldn't upset. After all, he was one of the country's finest chefs, and Mr. Harvey had brought him all the way from Chicago. Mrs. Winter didn't dare cause a problem that would make Johnny unhappy. She turned on her heel and caught Lydia's wide-eyed stare.

"She'll have to sleep in the same bed with you," she directed, her teeth clenched and jaw set.

"I bet you could find a cot somewhere if you tried real hard. After all, we run a hotel," John called after the retreating matron.

"I'll see what I can do," she retorted and marched from the room, trying to maintain an iota of dignity as her staff smiled at the back of the rigid form departing the room.

"I think I may have made an enemy," John stated to no one in particular.

"She'll get over it. Think she needs a few lessons in how to deal with employees," Charlie stated.

Lydia was irritated that Addie had once again caused her trouble but realized she owed a thank-you to Mr. Banion and the chef. Not wanting to make a spectacle of herself in front of the other employees, she waited until most of them had left the room and then made her way to where John, Charlie, and Tessie were talking. As she approached the trio, she noticed Addie standing close by, Tessie's hand resting protectively on the child's shoulder.

"I want to thank you both," Lydia stated, extending her hand first to Charlie and then to John. "It's very kind of you to give my sister a job," she said to the chef.

Pulling Addie beside her and looking directly into her eyes, she stated, "You'll do a good job, won't you, Addie?"

The child nodded in agreement and immediately tried to navigate back to her previous position beside Tessie. Lydia firmly gripped her arm, causing the child to grimace, but she made no sound. Tessie felt anger begin to well up inside but knew it would serve no purpose to confront Lydia. It would only make matters worse for Addie, and she certainly didn't want that to occur.

"I guess it's about time I get you over to your new home," Charlie stated. "It's been a long day, and I'm sure you're tired."

"I'm sure we all are. Nice to meet you, John. Good night, Lydia—Addie," Tessie said, her smile directed at the child.

The little girl looked totally bewildered by the events that had taken place in her midst. *I wonder just how much she understood of all that occurred,* Tessie thought as they left the restaurant and walked down the brick sidewalk.

"Your house is nearby. Makes it convenient for you to be close to the station, although it's a little noisy when the trains are coming through," Charlie commented.

"I'm sure I'll get used to it. I may have to bury my head under a pillow for the first few nights," she joked.

The night air was warm, and they sauntered down the street until Charlie stopped in front of a white frame house with a picket fence and large porch. There were rosebushes on either side of the gate, and the honeysuckle was in full bloom, its sweet fragrance wafting in the breeze.

"This is it!" Charlie announced, pushing open the gate for his companion.

He watched closely for her reaction, not sure why it was so important to him that she like the dwelling. Her shoulders held erect, he couldn't detect a single wrinkle in her navy traveling suit as she walked toward the house. Tiny wisps of coppery hair escaped the blue wool hat that she had carefully secured when they disembarked the train. He continued his observation as she peeked around the side of the house and turned to him with a look of delighted expectation.

"It's wonderful, Charlie. If it's only half as splendid inside, I'm going to be extremely pleased," she stated, walking up the front steps, her hips swaying slightly beneath the wool skirt.

"Let me unlock the door for you," he offered, withdrawing a silver skeleton key from his pocket. With a click, the door unlatched, and bowing in a grand sweep, Charlie stepped aside to allow her entrance.

"It's completely furnished, but if you want to bring your own things, we can remove any of the furniture," he said in a rush, not sure she would be pleased with the décor.

Charlie bent down and ignited the lamp just inside the front door. The illumination from the frosted globe mingled with the etched mirror hanging in the hallway, giving the room a scintillating luminescence. Everything from the overstuffed floral divan to the cream-colored armchairs were to her taste. The large oak mirror hanging over the fireplace was flanked on either side by wood-framed paintings of the countryside. The kitchen was large enough for a small table and two chairs. There were more shelves than she would ever be able to fill, and the pump over the kitchen sink gave her an unimaginable thrill. A home where she wouldn't have to fetch water from the well. *What more could anyone wish for,* she thought, until Charlie escorted her into the fully equipped treatment room and office! It was grand beyond her expectations. There were doctors who had been in practice for years but had not enjoyed an office the likes of this.

"Well, what do you think? Sorry you signed that contract?" Charlie asked, feeling assured of her answer.

Not even aware that he remained in the room, Tessie moved through the office in a calculated manner, touching and checking each drawer and cabinet, running her fingers over the instruments while taking a mental inventory. Occasionally she would stop and examine some particular item more closely and then continue. Reaching the bookcase, she opened the oak-and-glass door and removed the books one by one, almost caressing them as she turned the pages.

"It would appear that someone knows how to equip a doctor's office," Tessie commented when she had concluded surveying the rooms.

"I was beginning to think you had forgotten I exist," Charlie replied. "I take it you're willing to remain an employee of the Santa Fe, and you're not going to beg me to tear up your contract?" he teased.

"I think I just may be able to force myself to practice medicine here," she answered with a grin that made her appear much younger than her twenty-eight years.

"If you think you know your way around the place well enough, I'd better get back to the train station. I've got some paperwork to take care of before going back to the hotel," he told her, not wanting to leave but realizing that she was weary.

"I'll be just fine. I plan to make an early night of it," she said while she walked with him toward the front door.

"Please say you'll have breakfast with me," he requested as they reached the porch, not wanting to leave her until he was sure when he would see her again.

"Since I've nothing here to eat, how could I turn down such an invitation?" she answered, though regretting immediately how coquettish she sounded.

Taking her hand, he lifted it to his lips and gently placed a kiss on her palm. "Until morning," he said, smiling.

Tessie watched after him as Charlie walked down the sidewalk toward the train station, and then she sat down on the porch step. The air was warm, and she leaned back, looking up at the darkening sky, where a few twinkling stars were beginning their nightly vigil.

"Thank You, Lord. I don't know what plans You have for me in this place, but thank You for sending me here," she whispered.

Chapter 4

The morning dawned clear and crisp, a beautiful spring day. Tessie walked out the front door just as Charlie was approaching her new home.

"Beautiful day, wouldn't you say?" Charlie called as he climbed from his small horse-drawn buggy.

"Oh, indeed it is! I was going to sit on the porch and enjoy listening to the birds sing until you arrived," she responded.

"Well, I may allow you to do just that," he replied with a grin. "I thought it would be a splendid morning to eat outdoors. I hope you won't think me too forward, but I stopped at the Harvey House and had them pack breakfast for two," he said, producing a wicker basket covered by a large linen napkin.

"What a wonderful idea," she proclaimed, thrilled at his innovative proposal. "Shall we eat here on the porch?" she inquired.

"I think that's an excellent choice, Dr. Wilshire," he responded with a mock formality, causing her to giggle.

Tessie moved a plant from the small table sitting on the porch and covered it with a blue and white checkered tablecloth she found in the kitchen. From the contents of the basket, it appeared the Harvey House took as much care in preparing breakfast as it did the evening bill of fare. The croissants were light as a feather and the apricot preserves divine. Tessie was amazed at the cup of fresh fruit, knowing most of what she was eating would not be ready for harvest in Kansas for months. She savored every bite, and Charlie was pleased that he had been the one responsible for providing her with such enjoyment.

"That was a delightful surprise, Charlie. Thank you for your thoughtfulness," she said, wiping the corners of her mouth with one of the cloth napkins.

"It was my pleasure. I wish I could extend an invitation for tomorrow morning, but unfortunately, I must get back to Topeka for a few days," he told her.

Tessie was surprised at the sense of disappointment she felt upon hearing those words. "Will you be back soon?" she asked then chided herself for being so forward.

"Probably a week to ten days," he answered, "but it's good to know I'll be missed."

"It's just that I assumed you would be here to introduce me to some of the employees, but you needn't give it another thought. I've been on my own in much more foreign environments than Florence, Kansas, and I'm sure things will go splendidly," she responded hastily, not wanting to appear overly interested in Charlie's companionship.

"I don't think you'll need much introduction. The railroaders and their families have been anticipating the arrival of a doctor for several months now. I doubt there's much of anybody in town who doesn't know you moved in last evening. Course, I'm still hoping you're going to miss me just a little," he said with a crooked grin on his face.

"I'm not sure I'd classify myself as moved in just yet. I think I'll need a few more of my belongings before I feel settled," she responded, avoiding his last remark.

"I can understand that," he answered, beginning to place the dishes back into the basket. "I'm afraid I must get back to the station. There are a few things I need to complete before the train arrives, but I hope you'll agree to see me when I'm back in town," he said, looking up from the table and meeting her eyes.

"Well, of course, I'll see you. You're a Santa Fe employee," she answered, wanting to avoid a personal commitment. Charlie was a nice man, but things seemed to be moving a little too fast. She had a lot of adjustments to make, and Charlie might cloud her judgment. *I'll just have to keep him at arms' length,* she decided.

Charlie smiled and merely nodded at her answer. "I'll see you when I get back to town, Tessie. Don't you let any of those single ruffians from town come calling on you while I'm gone," he added as he pulled himself up into the buggy and waved to her.

He seems mighty pleased with himself, Tessie thought as she watched the buggy turn and head toward the train station.

Ten days later, a strange voice and loud banging on the front door brought Tessie running from the office, where she had been making notations in a patient's medical folder.

"Morning, Doc. Hope we ain't disturbing you, but Mr. Banion gave strict instructions that we were to get these trunks over to you as soon as we got the freight unloaded," Howard Malone, one of the new employees, explained.

"You're not disturbing me, Mr. Malone; you are making me immeasurably happy," she answered, delighted to finally have more than two changes of clothing.

"Where you want 'em?"

"If you'll just put the two larger ones here in the parlor and those two smaller ones in my bedroom, I'd be very appreciative," she responded, pointing toward the bedroom doorway.

"Mr. Banion said he would bring over the rest after a bit," Howard called over his shoulder as he carried the last of the two smaller trunks into her bedroom.

"Rest of it? What else was there?" she questioned when he had returned to the parlor.

"I don't know, Ma'am. He just told us to get these trunks over here, and he would bring the rest," he repeated. "You need us to do anything else 'fore we get back to work?"

"No, you've been a great help. Thank you again, and please tell Mr. Banion that I appreciate his kindness."

"Will do, Ma'am," he replied, ambling out the door and back toward the train station.

As soon as the door had closed, Tessie raced toward the bedroom and unlocked both of the smaller trunks. It was like Christmas morning with four wonderful gifts to open.

"This is silly. I know what's in all of these trunks," she reprimanded herself aloud, but that didn't squelch the excitement of finally receiving her belongings. Aunt Phiney and Uncle Jon had carefully packed all of her clothing and personal items in the smaller trunks. The two larger ones had not been unpacked since her return home from Chicago after completing medical school.

"I'm glad they had to pack only these two smaller trunks," she mused, digging deeper into the second one. Slowly she pulled out the beautiful quilt that she and Aunt Phiney had sewn and lovingly placed it on her bed. It was like greeting an old friend.

"Now I feel like I'm home," she murmured.

It was almost noon when she finished unpacking the trunks. Undoubtedly she would need to rearrange some of the items, but for the present, she was satisfied. Several times throughout the morning, her thoughts wandered to what other items could have arrived on the train. It appeared everything was accounted for, including her medical books and a few of her childhood toys that had always given her a sense of comfort. A knock at the door sounded just as she was carrying a small stuffed doll to the bedroom. Giving no heed to her appearance, she opened the door and was met by Charlie's broad smile and an invitation for lunch.

"I couldn't possibly go anywhere looking like this," she stated, catching a glimpse of herself in the hall mirror. "I'd frighten off the rest of the customers!"

"You look beautiful," he retorted, loving the look of her somewhat disheveled hair.

"Why are you standing there like you're hiding something?" she inquired.

"I've brought the rest of your belongings," he said. "Would you care to come out here and take a look?" he asked, grinning at her.

Walking onto the porch, she peeked behind him and spotted a brand-new bicycle with a bright red ribbon attached to the seat. Reading the letter that had been tied to the handlebars, she burst forth in gales of laughter. Tears began to stream down her face, and she doubled over, unable to control the fit of laughter.

"I know this must be as much a surprise to you as it was to me, but I didn't think you'd find it quite so humorous," he stated when she had finally begun to regain her composure. Hoping she would enlighten him about the gift, Charlie attempted to hide his disappointment when, without a word, she tucked the letter into her pocket.

"Don't I deserve to know the origin of your gift since I served as the delivery boy?" he inquired.

"Certainly," she replied with a smile. "Why don't you come in and have a cup of tea, and I'll explain," she offered.

"What about my lunch invitation?" he asked, still hopeful she would accept.

"I really can't leave, Charlie. I have two appointments later this afternoon and need to finish a few things before then. I am a working woman, you remember," she chided.

"Tell you what. I'll leave now and let you get your work finished if you'll agree to have dinner and spend the evening with me," he bargained.

"Oh, I don't know if I could give you a whole evening," she teased. Charlie's face took on a mock scowl which caused her to laugh again. "Okay, it's a deal," she answered. "Now, move along, and let me get my work completed."

"You sure drive a hard bargain, Dr. Wilshire," he replied, walking out the front door. "I'll be anxious to hear all about this bicycle tonight. Pick you up at six-thirty," he advised, giving her a jaunty salute.

She had to admit it was good to see Charlie. Since their breakfast the morning after her arrival, she hadn't had the pleasure of his company. Now, ten days later, he seemed a familiar face in this new locale. *Be careful,* she thought to herself. *Remember, you're not going to let things move too quickly.*

It had been a busy and enjoyable time getting her practice set up, although it hadn't been enjoyable making do with only two changes of clothing. She had spent a good deal of time washing and pressing in the last ten days!

By five o'clock Tessie completed her last appointment, cleaned the office, made her notations to the files, and rushed to her room, anxious to decide which of her newly arrived dresses she would wear this evening. She finally chose the lavender one with a striped, soft silk bodice and skirt. After a quick search, she located her straw hat, adorned with a deep lilac bow. A knock at the door sounded just as she pulled her white gloves from the drawer.

She smiled at Charlie's look of appreciation. "You look like a breath of spring. Shall we enjoy a stroll, or would you prefer riding in the carriage?"

"I'd much prefer the walk after being indoors all day," she answered, slipping her hand through the extended crook of his arm.

"Did you by any chance issue any threats to your employees after my arrival?" she inquired as they proceeded down the sidewalk.

"Of course not. What are you talking about?" he inquired.

"I guess I've been surprised how easily the employees and community have accepted a female doctor. It's one of the things my professors drilled into me during medical school—the fact that people did not approve of women doctors, and I would never gain their trust," she explained.

Charlie laughed at her answer. "I don't mean to make light of what you've said. I'm sure there are a lot of folks, especially men, who wouldn't take a shine to female doctors. With the additional employees here, folks have been making due with the midwives or no medical care at all, unless they can force Doc Rayburn out of retirement long enough to treat someone. There wasn't any need for me to issue threats; your training and ability speak for themselves. I had no doubt folks would be pleased to have you as their physician," he stated.

By the time they arrived, the dinner train and its host of travelers had departed, allowing townspeople a quiet enjoyment of the restaurant. Charlie noted the turned heads and stares of admiration as they walked through the restaurant and were seated, although Tessie seemed oblivious. Reaching their table, she scanned the room, hoping to catch a glimpse of Lydia.

"Anything look particularly inviting?" Charlie asked, trying to draw Tessie's attention back to the table.

"Oh, I'm sorry. I haven't even looked at the menu," she apologized, a small smile tracing her lips. "I was hoping Lydia would be working. What are you going to order?"

"Think I'll have the steak, but I understand the Chicken Maciel is one of the favorites around here," he replied.

"In that case, I'll try it," she answered, just as Lydia appeared at their table.

"Evening, Dr. Wilshire, Mr. Banion. Had time to decide on what you'd like?" she asked.

"Sure have," Charlie answered and gave her their order. She poured coffee for each of them and was off in a flurry, taking orders, pouring drinks, and serving meals, the pace never seeming to lose momentum.

When Lydia returned with their meals, Tessie decided she needed to speak quickly or lose the opportunity. "Lydia, would you and Addie like to come for tea next Wednesday afternoon?"

"Me?" the girl asked, seeming amazed at the invitation. Tessie nodded her head, assuring Lydia she had heard correctly.

"What time? I only have a couple hours off in the afternoon, between two and four," she hesitantly answered.

"That would be fine. I don't schedule office visits on Wednesday afternoons, so whenever it's convenient for you and Addie, just stop by," Tessie proposed.

"Right. We'll do that," she responded. She had only taken a few steps when she quickly returned and whispered, "I don't know where you live."

Before Tessie could answer, Charlie spoke up and gave the young woman detailed instructions. Tessie merely shook her head at his obvious need to speak for her.

"I haven't heard about your bicycle as yet," Charlie mentioned as Lydia hastened off to secure two apple dumplings with caramel sauce for their dessert.

"When I first arrived at medical school, I met one of the students who had recently graduated and was returning home. He convinced me to purchase his bicycle, expounding upon what a convenience it had proved for him, cycling from his boardinghouse to classes. I liked the idea of saving time and the fact there would be no additional care and expense with a bicycle. She stopped to taste a forkful of the warm apple dumpling.

"That is simply delicious," she stated, pointing her fork at the dessert.

"It is certainly that," Charlie replied. "But, please, back to the bicycle," he prodded.

"Well, never having ridden a bicycle, I had no idea one needed balance or that a woman's full skirt would cause additional problems. Feeling proud of my frugality, I paid for the bicycle, which he delivered to my boardinghouse. The next morning after breakfast, I tossed my books into the basket and began the ride of my life!"

An enormous, knowing smile sprawled across Charlie's face. "That must have been quite a sight," he exclaimed, bursting into laughter, the surrounding dinner guests eyeing him as if he had lost his senses.

"It's obvious you have a good idea just how graceful I appeared," Tessie commented. "I'm not sure what was injured most, my knees or my pride—not to mention the new skirt and stockings I ruined," she continued, now joining him in laughter, tears beginning to collect in the corner of each eye. Intermittently interrupted by spurts of laughter, she confessed that she began wearing bloomers when cycling, although it was frowned upon by her instructors. "I was required to change into a skirt as soon as I arrived at school, but it was decidedly worth that concession since once I learned to stay astraddle the contraption, I did save immeasurable time."

"Why did your aunt and uncle think you would want another bicycle?" he questioned.

"Both of them are open-minded enough to think that wearing bloomers is appropriate attire for riding a bicycle, and they are frugal enough to realize a bicycle is more economical than feeding and caring for a horse. Besides, they knew I enjoyed bicycling once I had conquered the metal beast. I traded mine for a medical book before leaving Chicago and had mentioned on several occasions that I missed the exercise and freedom it afforded me," she replied.

"In that case, I would say they've given you a fine gift," he responded as they rose to leave the restaurant.

Catching Lydia's eye, Tessie raised her hand and called out, "See you and Addie on Wednesday."

Lydia nodded and smiled as she continued jotting down another customer's order.

"Why the persistence about Lydia coming to visit?" Charlie inquired.

"I'm concerned about Addie and how she's managing with all the changes in her life. Lydia seems to resent being thrust into the role of provider. Perhaps if I can ease the burden a bit for Lydia, it will make things better for both of them," she declared, not wanting to discuss the topic further.

"You need to be careful about overinvolvement. I'm sure Lydia is the type to take advantage," he counseled.

"I think I'm quite capable of deciding my level of involvement with people," she responded, irritated with his condescending manner.

"I didn't mean to interfere," he apologized. "It's just my nature, I guess."

Tessie didn't respond but tucked his words away for future reference. *If it's his nature to interfere,* she thought to herself, *I'm not sure he's the man for me.*

"I'll be leaving in the morning, but I'll be back late Wednesday afternoon," Charlie said, bringing her back to the present. "How about dinner?" he asked.

"I suppose that would be fine," she answered without much fervor. She was thinking about the upcoming visit with Addie and Lydia rather than her handsome escort.

"Here we are," Charlie announced as he leaned down and unlatched the gate, hoping for an invitation to sit on the porch and visit awhile longer.

"So, we are. Thank you for dinner, Charlie. I hope you have a good trip tomorrow. See you next week," she stated without any hint of wanting to prolong the evening.

"Good night," Charlie called back as she entered the front doorway, hopeful she would forget his transgression by the time he returned.

Wednesday afternoon finally arrived, and Tessie found herself peeking out the lace curtains in the parlor every five minutes, hoping to glimpse her expected visitors. She had almost decided they wouldn't arrive when a light knock sounded at the front door.

"I had almost given up," she said, smiling at the two girls as she led them into the parlor.

"We can't stay long 'cause I have to be back in half an hour," Lydia replied. "A friend of mine came through on the train, and I wanted to visit with him. That's why we're late," she explained.

"How wonderful! Is it someone from back home?" Tessie asked, excited the girls had a friend that was interested in their welfare.

"No, he's a salesman I met since working at the restaurant. We've gone on a couple outings when he's stayed over a few days. We're going out after work tonight," Lydia answered, obviously pleased with her suitor.

"That's nice, Lydia. Does he sell his goods to Mr. Alexander at the general store?"

"Oh, no. He sells at the Harvey House. There's a room where the salesmen set up their merchandise when they're traveling through, and townspeople can stop by and do their shopping. You ought to come over and see all the things they have for sale. There's almost always someone set up there," she stated, all the while her eyes were darting about the house, clearly impressed with the furnishings.

Tessie placed a cool glass of lemonade in front of Addie and poured cups of tea for Lydia and herself. A large plate of freshly baked cookies sat in front of them, although neither of the young women reached for one until they'd been offered.

"What have you and Addie been doing in your spare time?" Tessie asked, watching the younger girl devour her cookie.

"I'm so tired by the time I get off my shift, I just about fall into bed at night," Lydia exclaimed. "I'm off a couple hours in the afternoon, and that's it except for my one day off. Even when we don't have customers, we've got to polish silver, set tables, scrub counters, and change linens. Course if Floyd's in town, I squeeze in a little time for fun where I can," she said, flipping her head to one side. "When I get married, I'll have a house as nice as this," she proclaimed.

"I'm sure you will," Tessie responded. "And what about Addie? Is she working all the time also?"

"No, I told 'em she could, but John, the chef, said she was too little for long hours. He's got her washing dishes for the first two trains each day; then she's done. I should have it so good!"

"What's she do then?" asked Tessie.

"That's exactly my point. She's not doing anything. She could be making extra money if that silly chef would just let her work the same hours as everyone else. I get off work all worn out, and she's been lolling around and thinks I should entertain her. On my day off she thinks she should come along with me, even if I'm with Floyd," Lydia replied, giving the smaller girl an accusatory look.

"Perhaps I could help out, Lydia. You could send Addie over here when she gets through in the morning and on her day off. She could play outdoors and keep more active here. Then perhaps she would be ready for bed when you get off work," Tessie offered.

The young woman looked at her suspiciously, not sure why she would make such a generous offer. "I don't know. She gets Sundays off—wouldn't you know she would get Sundays off? Me—I get Tuesday," she responded, not giving a definite answer. "Why do you want her around?" she asked, with a hint of jealousy creeping into her voice.

"I'm just trying to think how I could help out, Lydia. You're more than welcome to visit anytime too," she responded, trying to relieve any hostility the offer might have induced.

"Guess it wouldn't hurt to give it a try. She would be out of my way. I'll send her over tomorrow afternoon," she stated.

"Why don't we ask Addie if she would like to spend some of her time here? She may be unwilling," Tessie suggested.

"She does what she's told," Lydia replied emphatically, giving the child a quick glare.

Ignoring Lydia's reply Tessie turned toward Addie, making sure the child could read her lips. "Would you like to come to my house each day after work?"

Addie immediately looked toward her sister for the correct answer. From the corner of her eye, Tessie watched Lydia mouth the word "yes," and that was followed by Addie nodding her head up and down.

"We gotta go. I'm going to be late for work if I don't get moving," Lydia pronounced, jumping up from her chair and grabbing Addie's arm.

"I'll send her over tomorrow. Thanks for the tea and cookies," she stated, all the while walking toward the door with her sister in tow.

"Thank you both for coming," Tessie responded, watching as the two sisters went running down the sidewalk toward the Harvey House.

Walking back into her house, Tessie looked at the large clock sitting on the mantel. She had several hours before Charlie would arrive for their dinner engagement. Plenty of time to get a few chores done and catch up on some reading, she determined, picking up the teacups and plates.

If nothing else, he's certainly punctual, Tessie decided when Charlie knocked on the front door at exactly 6:30 P.M. *I shouldn't be angry with him for being on time.*

It's not his fault that I read too long, and now I'm rushing around like a chicken with its head cut off, she mused.

The second loud knock did nothing toward helping her gain a modicum of composure. She rushed to the door, still struggling with the small pearl buttons on the sleeve of her champagne silk shirtwaist.

"I was beginning to think you'd found a better offer," Charlie greeted, holding out a small bouquet of spring flowers. "I hope I didn't rush you," he continued, noting that she appeared somewhat disconcerted.

"What? Oh, no—it's my fault. I lost all sense of time when I began reading an article in the medical journal. Why don't you come in while I get my hat and gloves, and we can be on our way," she offered.

"What is it you were reading about?" Charlie inquired as they sauntered toward the restaurant.

Immediately, Tessie's face lit up. "I've found the most interesting commentary about deafness. It's written by a highly respected Chicago physician who has been studying deaf patients for a number of years. He and several of his colleagues collaborated on the article," she related with great enthusiasm.

"I see," Charlie replied, squelching his desire to once again admonish her about becoming overly involved with Lydia and Addie.

Tessie didn't fail to notice his lack of excitement about the subject matter. When Lydia came to their table shortly thereafter and whispered that she would send Addie over after lunch the next day, his jaw visibly tightened.

"What else have you been up to aside from mothering the Baker sisters?" he inquired with more sarcasm than he had intended. As soon as the words were spoken, he wanted to retract them.

Tessie stiffened and stared directly into Charlie's gray eyes. "I think there needs to be some clarification about our relationship if we're to continue seeing each other on a social basis, Mr. Banion," Tessie stated quite formally.

"I'm sorry—" Charlie began.

"No, please don't interrupt me. You need to understand that I am open to listening to your opinions. I will then evaluate that information based on my education and beliefs. I am not, however, willing to allow you or any other person to impose ideas and beliefs upon me."

Holding up her hand to ward off his attempt to speak, she continued, "I won't allow you to make me feel foolish or imprudent because I want to befriend two young women. If that makes you uncomfortable, I don't think we should see each other again," she finished.

Charlie leaned back in his chair, now certain the tales he had heard about redheads and their tempers had some validity. "I truly am sorry," he declared. "You are absolutely correct that I have no right to impose my opinions upon you, and perhaps that is what I've been doing. For that I apologize. You, however, have been extremely defensive when I've attempted to discuss Addie and Lydia. I merely wanted to point out that sometimes it is wise to move forward cautiously in order to prevent being hurt or exploited by others."

"Does that apply to you as well as Lydia and Addie?" she inquired.

"Well, no, of course not. I. . .I," he stammered and then looked up when he heard her giggle.

"You see, Charlie," she said, "I don't know any more about you than I do of Lydia and Addie. If you're willing to trust my judgment of people in befriending *you,* I hope you will extend that trust to my companionship with Lydia and Addie."

"I guess you've got me," he answered with a grin. "Tell you what, I'll try to keep my mind open if you'll promise to keep your eyes open. How about it?"

"I think that will work," she replied.

I truly hope so, Charlie thought to himself, sure that Lydia Baker was interested in more than Tessie's friendship.

Chapter 5

Shortly after lunch the next day, Addie appeared at Tessie's front door in a tattered, brown-print dress, her hair damp from leaning over steamy dishwater all morning.

"Good afternoon, Addie," Tessie greeted as she swung open the front door.

"Hi," Addie responded hesitantly. "How come you want me to come here?" she bluntly asked before entering the house.

"Because we're both new in town, and I know I could use a friend. How about you?" Tessie answered, extending her hand to the child.

"I guess we could try, but I've never had a friend as old as you," the child innocently replied, causing Tessie to laugh. Addie wasn't sure what was so humorous, but she smiled and entered the house.

"Is there something special you'd like to do this afternoon?" Tessie asked, but when Addie didn't answer, she realized she had not been heard. *I must remember to gain her attention before speaking,* Tessie reminded herself and then touched the child's arm.

"What would you like to do today?" she repeated, looking directly into the small brown eyes.

Addie merely shrugged her shoulders in response, leaving the decision to Tessie.

"I have several patients I'll need to see in my office a little later," she told the youngster, "but I do have a few playthings from when I was a little girl."

"Do you have a ball?" Addie asked. "I like to play outside when it's nice, but Lydia always makes me go upstairs and take a nap," she said, beginning to loosen up with her new friend.

"I think I may have one," Tessie answered, pulling a cloth bag out of the hallway closet. "Why don't you look through here and find what you'd like to play with? I have a patient arriving, but if you need me, just come through that door to the office," she said, pointing toward the office entrance.

"Okay," Addie responded. Obviously, her thoughts were on the toys and nothing else.

Tessie checked on Addie several times throughout the day, and the two of them enjoyed lemonade on the front porch between appointments. Addie seemed content, and Tessie was savoring their brief visits between patients.

"What's that you're doing there?" Charlie called out, forgetting for the moment Addie could not hear him. Tessie looked up from her desk at the sound of his voice and watched as Charlie walked over toward a spot in the yard where Addie was sitting. The child noticed him as he drew closer and waved her hand in recognition.

"I'll play you a game," Charlie said, kneeling down beside her. Having found a small bag of marbles among Tessie's old toys, Addie located a spot alongside the house where there were a few weeds, but the grass had failed to grow. Meticulously she pulled the weeds, and now sat shooting the round balls, thoroughly enjoying the sunshine and newfound entertainment.

"Okay," she told Charlie and watched as he drew a circle in the dirt.

"Let me show you how this is done," he said, patiently explaining the finer points of how to shoot a good game of marbles.

Tessie sat listening through the open window in her office. When she had completed writing notes in a file, she walked out to join them. "Good afternoon, Charlie," she welcomed. "What caused this unexpected visit?" she inquired, pleased to see Addie enjoying the game.

"No frivolous chitchat while I'm concentrating on my game," he admonished, giving her a winsome grin. Addie fervently watched as he made the shot.

"You lose," she said, clapping her hands together.

"That's because I taught you too well," he said, gathering her into his arms and giving her a spontaneous hug. Tessie stood watching as the small child clung to his neck, hungry for the love and attention she had been denied since her mother's death.

"I assume it's been a good first-day visit," Charlie questioned, Addie still clinging to him.

"It has gone very well. Thank you for being so kind," Tessie responded, looking down at the small figure tightly clutching him.

"I'm going to be leaving for Topeka in an hour, but I'll be back this weekend. I know that Addie will be with you all day on Sunday, so I was wondering if I might accompany the two of you to church. Then we could go on a picnic," he ventured, hopeful she would think it was a good idea.

"That would be wonderful," she exclaimed. "If, by chance, the weather doesn't cooperate with a picnic, we can eat here," she suggested.

"Great. I'll come by for you at ten o'clock, but don't you cook, even if the weather is bad. I'll make arrangements with John over at the Harvey House to fix up a basket lunch, and if it rains, we'll have our picnic indoors," he told her. "I'd better get going, or I'll not be ready to leave when the train pulls out," he advised with a smile. "I'll see you both on Sunday," he told her and then leaned down and said, "I'll be by to pick you up for church on Sunday, Addie," and gave the child a hug.

"I don't want to go to church," the child informed Tessie shortly after Charlie's departure.

"Why not?" Tessie questioned.

"Lydia makes me go by myself, and the kids make fun of my clothes and call me a dummy," she replied honestly, the pain evident in her eyes.

"Sometimes people don't realize how much they hurt us with their words," Tessie told the child. "You must always remember that you are special. God made only one Addie Baker, and He loves her very much. Even though other people hurt your feelings, you can always depend on God and know He loves you just the way you are," she counseled the child.

"Does He love those kids that were mean to me?" Addie asked.

"Yes, Addie, He loves them too. He doesn't love the sinful things any of us do, but He never stops loving us. God will forgive us for doing wrong if we just ask Him, but He does expect us to try and do better the next time," she instructed.

"Well, I don't love them. I don't even like those naughty kids, and I don't want to go to church and be around them," Addie said, a tear sliding down her cheek.

"I know, Addie. It's harder for us to forgive people. God does a much better job, but He would want you to try and forgive the mean actions of those children. He certainly wouldn't want the actions of others to keep you from worshipping Him. Besides, Charlie and I will be with you this time. Will you try it just this once?" Tessie cajoled.

"If you promise I can sit between you and Charlie, so they won't see me," Addie bargained.

"Absolutely," Tessie agreed. "And after church we'll go on a picnic. Would you like that?"

"Oh, yes!" the child exclaimed, jumping up and down. "Oh, yes, yes."

Bright and early Saturday morning, Tessie paid a visit to the general store. She found a Liberty-print cotton dress with a contrasting blue silk sash that looked as though it would be a perfect fit for Addie. At the end of the aisle, she spotted a straw cartwheel hat with a ribbon in the same shade of blue. Without a moment's hesitation, she purchased both items, along with a pair of child-sized black cotton stockings and a white muslin petticoat.

"Is there anything else I can help you find, Dr. Wilshire?" Mr. Alexander, the owner of the general store, offered.

"No, I think that will be all," she responded, pleased with her purchases.

While Mr. Alexander was wrapping the items, Mrs. Alexander stepped behind him, peering over his shoulder.

"I didn't know you had anyone that small living with you, Doctor," the woman remarked, the curiosity noticeable in her voice.

"I don't have anyone of *any* size living with me, Mrs. Alexander," Tessie responded, irritated by the woman's intrusive manner. Mrs. Alexander was known for collecting gossip while working in her husband's store and passing it along to anyone who would lend an ear. Tessie did not intend for her business to become grist for the town rumormongers.

Mr. Alexander handed her the purchases and gave his wife a stern look of disapproval. *At least he doesn't condone her meddling behavior,* Tessie thought as she turned and exited the store.

A light knock at her door Sunday morning made Tessie wonder if someone other than Addie had come calling. Although she had been coming to the house for only a few days, Tessie had instructed her that there was no need to knock.

"Come in, Addie," she offered. Addie stood looking up at her in the same brown dress she had worn for several days, having made a valiant effort to adorn herself by placing a small ribbon around her head.

"You look very nice," Tessie told her. "I hope you won't mind, but I was in the general store yesterday and saw a dress I thought might fit you. It was so pretty, I couldn't resist," she told the youngster. "Would you like to see if you like it? If it fits, you could wear it to church. That is, if you want to," Tessie continued, leading her into the spare bedroom where the dress, hat, and undergarments lay on the bed.

Nothing could have prepared Addie for the thrill of receiving that beautiful new dress and hat. Once Tessie had tied the blue silk sash and placed the straw hat upon the girl's curly chestnut tresses, she took the child and stood her before the mirror. Leaning down and placing her head behind Addie's shoulder, they looked at their reflections staring back at them.

"You look lovely," Tessie told her.

"Almost as pretty as you?" the child questioned, tipping her head back to look into Tessie's eyes.

"Much prettier," Tessie answered. "Now, come along," she said, extending her hand toward the child's just as Charlie came bounding up the front steps.

"I have to be the luckiest man in all of Kansas," he exclaimed to the pair. "There's no other man who has the good fortune to escort such beautiful women. Turn around for me, Addie," he instructed, twirling the child in front of him.

"Tessie got me these new clothes," she proudly announced.

"And you look magnificent in them," he responded, catching Tessie's eye and giving her a smile.

His reaction pleased Tessie, who had expected him to give her a reproachful look or once again caution her about the "Baker sisters."

The day flew by quickly. Tessie had been true to her word and allowed Addie to sit between the two adults. Although it wasn't Charlie's choice of seating arrangement, he did, however, bow to Tessie's wishes once again. While at the park, he was attentive to Tessie but included Addie in the conversation and even took her down to a small stream to wade for a short time. Although he didn't know it, his tolerance and thoughtfulness did not go unnoticed. Tessie knew she was beginning to care more deeply about him than she had anyone for many years.

"I think perhaps we should be heading home," she told the pair as they returned from the stream. "I packed up the picnic basket while you two were off exploring. It's almost time for you to catch your train, isn't it?" she asked Charlie.

"I'm afraid so. I'll be glad when I can quit traveling quite so much," he acknowledged as they walked toward the carriage.

"That will be nice," she answered, squeezing his arm and giving him an inviting smile.

Addie had been particularly careful not to soil her new dress, and as soon as they arrived at the house, she announced that she was going to change into her old dress and went running off to the bedroom.

"I had a wonderful time today, Tessie, and I hope there will be many more in store for us," Charlie said, cupping her face in his large hands and placing a tender kiss on her lips. "You're very special," he told her, gathering her into his arms.

Tessie felt as though she could stay wrapped in his protection forever, and although she enjoyed the sensation, it confused her. She had always been so independent, never allowing herself to become overly involved with a man, and now, here she was not wanting Charlie to leave. It made no sense. *I hardly know him,* she thought to herself as Addie came bounding out of the bedroom.

"I'd like a hug too," she told the pair.

"Well, of course," Charlie answered with a smile, opening his arms as she came running across the room toward him.

"Would you like something to eat?" Tessie inquired shortly after Charlie left.

"I'm not hungry," Addie responded, walking through the room, running her hand across different pieces of furniture, then wandering into Tessie's bedroom. She stared at the quilt that covered the four-poster bed and traced her fingers over the intricate design.

"This is very pretty," she told Tessie. "I've never seen anything this pretty on anyone's bed."

Turning to face Addie, Tessie said, "My mother and my Aunt Phiney and I all worked on this quilt, and it is very special because lots and lots of love went into it. If you like to sew, perhaps you and I could make a quilt. What do you think about that idea?" she asked the child.

"I only know how to sew a little. Mama didn't have much time to show me, but I learn quick," Addie responded expectantly.

"I didn't know a lot about sewing when I started on this quilt either," she told Addie. "I think you'll do a wonderful job. Tell you what, I'll find some fabric, and we'll get started next week. Would that be all right?"

"Oh yes," Addie answered, clapping her hands in delight. "I promise I'll work hard on it."

"I'm sure you will," Tessie answered, just as a knock sounded at the front door.

"There's someone at the door. I'll be right back," she told the child and quickly walked to the parlor and opened the door.

"Evening, Dr. Wilshire," Lydia said, "hope you weren't real busy. This is Floyd—I told you about him—the salesman I met at the Harvey House. We're going to town for awhile, so would you mind just taking Addie back over to the hotel when you get tired of her?" Lydia pressed herself close to Floyd and gave him a sensual smile. Tessie noticed the young man seemed embarrassed by Lydia's advances, but his embarrassment didn't deter her seductive behavior.

"I'll be happy to walk her back, but I thought you had to work this evening," Tessie inquired after hearing Lydia's plans.

"I traded with Lucy," she answered. "Floyd has to leave at ten o'clock, and Lucy owed me a favor."

"You two have a nice time," Tessie replied and watched as they walked down the steps, with Lydia clearly attempting to captivate the young man.

Addie was peeking around the doorway, pleased that Lydia hadn't come to escort her back to the hotel. "Where's my sister going?" the youngster inquired.

"She and Floyd are going into town for awhile, so I'll walk you back to the hotel a little later. Will that be all right with you?"

Addie nodded her head up and down and sat down in the parlor, facing Tessie. "Tell me about making your quilt," she requested.

"Well, let's see. I'm not sure how to begin," Tessie remarked.

"At the beginning," Addie responded laughingly.

"You're right. I'll do just that," Tessie replied. "When I was a little older than you, my mother began making the quilt that's on my bed, but she died before it was completed."

"Just like my mama?" Addie asked, the tearful sound of her voice making Tessie's heart ache.

"Yes, Addie, just like your mama."

"Did your papa run off and leave you too?" the child inquired.

"No, I had a wonderful papa, but he died at the same time as my mother. They were in an accident," she answered.

"Oh, that was hard for you, wasn't it?" Addie asked, her perception surprising Tessie.

"Yes, it was very difficult. There were five of us children, and I was the oldest. My grandmother lived with us, and Uncle Jon had a small house on the land adjoining ours. He and Granny were left to raise all five of us, and Granny's health wasn't good. So Uncle Jon decided to advertise in the newspaper looking for a young woman to come and help Granny with the chores and all of us children."

Addie sat in front of her, eyes held wide open, not wanting to miss anything that Tessie related. "Then what happened?" she asked anxiously.

"Uncle Jon finally got a letter about a young woman who he and Granny thought would be suitable. So he left and went to Illinois to fetch her. Well, I didn't want any other woman coming into our house trying to take the place of my mother, so when Uncle Jon returned, I was very hateful to the young woman. No matter what she did, I wouldn't let her become my friend, but she did have a beautiful quilt on her bed that I truly admired," Tessie related.

"Was it as pretty as yours?" the child inquired, sure that would be impossible.

"I don't think so," Tessie answered. "But I'm sure Aunt Phiney thinks *her* quilt is prettiest, because it's special to her. One day I told Granny I thought Aunt Phiney's quilt was beautiful. After I'd told her that, my grandmother showed me the quilt my mother had begun and suggested that Aunt Phiney and I complete it for my bed. Well, I wouldn't hear of it. I said I didn't want Aunt Phiney touching anything that had belonged to my mother."

"That wasn't very nice, was it?" Addie inquired, shaking her head negatively.

"No. But it wasn't until Aunt Phiney showed me she was willing to die in my place that I finally believed she truly cared for me. It was after that the two of us set to work on the quilt. Aunt Phiney said it was sewn with threads of love because the two of us really learned to love each other while making that quilt. It took us awhile, but we finally finished, and it's been my constant companion ever since," Tessie concluded.

"I'd like to have something like that to keep with me always," Addie quietly commented.

"You will. It may take some time, but you will. I promise," Tessie answered. "I'd better get you back to the hotel, or you're going to miss curfew, young woman!"

In the weeks that followed, Addie proved herself a quick study, and Tessie was constantly amazed at the child's proficiency with a needle and thread. She would sit quietly watching Tessie and then take up her needle and thread with the expertise of an age-old quilter. Although most of the quilts Tessie had worked on were made from scraps, she had carefully chosen the colors and fabrics for Addie's, wanting it to be very special. She had finally settled on cotton prints of lavender, pale blue, and shades of pink. Tessie convinced herself they could conquer the double-wedding-ring pattern, and so far she was right.

"Are you going to make me hear again?" Addie asked one crisp fall afternoon as the two of them sat in Tessie's parlor.

The question startled Tessie, for although she had extensively examined Addie on several occasions, the child had never hinted at such an expectation.

"I don't know if I can do that," she responded, wishing she could give the answer Addie longed for.

"You make everyone else well," came Addie's quick rebuttal.

"Not quite everyone. There are some things I can't heal, but I promise you, Addie, that I will do all I can," Tessie concluded, hoping God would provide the answer her medical journals had failed to give her.

Chapter 6

Doc, come quick! Levi Wilson is mighty sick, and he needs a doctor now!" shouted Joe Carlin, the local blacksmith, as he came racing toward the house in a buggy drawn by a sleek black horse. The smithy pulled the animal to a rapid halt in front of the house, where it immediately began snorting and pawing at the dirt, anxious to again run at full speed.

"Let me get my bag. Addie, get in the buggy," Tessie mouthed to the child who had arrived only minutes earlier. Rushing into the house, she grabbed her bag and some additional medical supplies. Running toward the carriage, she lost no time issuing orders to the blacksmith.

"What do you know about his problem?" she asked as the buggy sped out of town.

"Can't breathe. I hear tell he's had breathing problems for quite a spell now," the blacksmith advised.

Tessie merely nodded, not sure what to expect but hoping her skills would serve her well. Once the carriage had drawn to a halt in front of a wooden shanty that appeared to be no bigger than one room, she didn't have long to contemplate her abilities. Jumping down, all three of them made their way inside and found the patient sitting up and battling for breath. A hasty examination revealed a goiter, which was almost concealed in the chest cavity. The room certainly was not appropriate for an operating room, but Tessie knew that if something wasn't done quickly, her patient would die. Issuing a hasty prayer for direction, she turned to the blacksmith and ordered him to remove the door from its hinges and motioned Addie to carry out several wooden boxes. Tessie placed water on the stove to boil and found two barrels, which she then moved outdoors.

"Place the door across these two barrels," she instructed, as she pulled a sheet from the items she had gathered from home. With a snap of her wrists she watched it flutter across the makeshift operating table. Placing her instruments on the boxes Addie had carried outdoors, she watched as the smithy helped Mr. Wilson onto the hastily constructed table.

"Mr. Wilson, I'll be back shortly. I need to scrub my hands before proceeding. Addie, come along. You'll need to scrub also. Stay with him," she instructed the blacksmith, walking toward the dilapidated house.

"Addie, stand by the instruments; I'll need your help. You too," she instructed the blacksmith, who was heading back toward the house, not sure if he wanted to be a part of the unfolding events.

After administering ether, Tessie made an incision to expose the goiter, which was resting on his windpipe. The mass appeared to be about the size of an apple, and with only small artery forceps, she realized it would be impossible to grasp and remove it. She stood staring at the object, unsure how to proceed.

Lord, I don't know what to do. Show me how to help this man, she silently prayed.

No sooner had her prayer been uttered than a tiny feather floated down directly under Mr. Wilson's nose. The incision that Tessie made permitted her patient to breathe in enough air so that when the feather tickled his nose, Levi Wilson burst forth with a stupendous sneeze. As his large chest contracted, the goiter shot so far out that it lay fully exposed in the wound. Tessie quickly seized it with one hand, grabbed her instruments to clamp the lower vessels with her other hand, and completed the remainder of the surgery uneventfully.

"I believe we've had a successful surgery," she announced to the blacksmith, who had turned ashen. "There's no reason you need to remain close by if you'd like to check on your horse, Mr. Carlin," was all the encouragement the smithy needed to get away from the makeshift operating room.

"I'll help you clean up, if you tell me what to do," Addie offered, never wavering from her duty station.

"Thank you, Addie. You can wrap those instruments and put them back into my bag. We'll clean and sterilize them at home," she instructed, finishing the sutures on Mr. Wilson's incision.

"Anything I need to be doing?" the blacksmith called out from in front of the shanty.

"Why don't you see if you can find a neighbor who can come over? He should have someone stay with him unless you'd like the job," Tessie answered.

"Think I'd better try and locate a neighbor. I'm not too good with sick folks," he responded.

"Really? I hadn't noticed," Tessie answered, giving him a quick grin.

Mr. Wilson had regained consciousness when his neighbors, the Madisons, arrived with the blacksmith. Mr. Madison and Joe supported and half-carried the patient into the house and placed him on the bed, which Mrs. Madison had quickly covered with clean linens. Tessie gave her a grateful smile.

"If you two men will dismantle my outdoor operating room, I'll go over the patient-care instructions with Mrs. Madison," she directed.

It was obvious that Mrs. Madison had taken care of more than a few medical emergencies, and Tessie knew Mr. Wilson would be in good hands.

"I don't think I'll need to see you again, Mr. Wilson. Mrs. Madison has assured me she's removed many stitches, and she lives much closer than I, so I'll leave you to her care."

He nodded his head and whispered his thanks for her good care.

"I think you owe your thanks to the Lord," Tessie advised. "He's the One who deserves credit for the success. Someday when you're in town, I'll explain," she told him, as he drifted back to sleep.

It was supper time when the trio finally loaded back into the buggy and headed for town.

"That was quite a spectacle," the smithy said admiringly.

"Well, thank you, Mr. Carlin. I appreciate your assistance," Tessie replied, realizing the blacksmith was genuinely surprised at her ability.

"Thank you too, Addie," she said, placing her arm around the child and hugging her close. Addie merely nodded, but her eyes were full of adoration.

The buggy pulled to a stop in front of the house, and the blacksmith quickly jumped down, lifted Addie to the ground, and assisted Tessie. "It's been a real pleasure, Ma'am. If I'm ever in need of a doctor, I sure hope you're the one I get," he stated.

"Well, I hope you won't be needing my services, but I sincerely thank you for the compliment," she replied, feeling embarrassed by his continued adulation. "Come along, Addie. Let's make some dinner; you must be starved," she said to the child, taking her hand and walking toward the house.

Addie proved an able assistant in the kitchen, and within a short time they had prepared a fine meal. "You are such a good helper. I don't know what I would have done without you today," she praised the child.

"I like helping you," Addie answered, beginning to clear the table.

"Let's leave the dishes, Addie. I can do them after you go home. Why don't we just sit on the porch and enjoy the evening breeze? There hasn't been much time to visit and enjoy each other today," she said as they walked outdoors.

"Could I be a doctor someday?" Addie asked as they settled on the swing.

Tessie's mind reeled. Without the ability to hear, how could anyone be a doctor, let alone make it through college and medical school? How should she answer without destroying a young girl's dreams? *Help me, Lord,* she silently prayed.

"I believe that with God's help we can do anything. You must remember that sometimes God has very special plans for us, and even though we don't understand them, He knows best," she answered.

"I think God wants me to be a doctor, and that's why we've become friends," the child answered, obviously pleased with her deduction.

"You could be right," Tessie answered, hoping the child would not be disappointed, while at the same time, Tessie mentally chastised herself for not doing further research into the article on deafness she had read in the medical journal.

"I have an idea for some fun this afternoon," Tessie told her young visitor several days later as they finished a glass of lemonade.

"What?" Addie inquired, her interest piqued.

"Come outside, and I'll show you," Tessie responded.

Striding toward the house, Charlie smiled as he watched Addie attempting to gain her balance on Tessie's bicycle. Tessie was running alongside holding onto the handlebars and back of the seat. From the look of things, he wasn't sure if they were having fun or punishing themselves.

"Let me help," he offered, coming upon them and grabbing the handlebars just in time to prevent a collision with a large elm tree.

"That would be wonderful," Tessie admitted, gasping for breath.

When Addie finally arrived at a point at which she was able to stay astride the bicycle for a short period of time without teetering to one side or the other, they decided to rest and hoped she wouldn't want another lesson until sometime in the future.

"Addie tells me this was your idea," Charlie said, plopping down on a chair in the parlor, still short of breath.

"Yes, I thought it would be something special for her. Obviously, I didn't think it out very well," she admitted sheepishly.

"It will be wonderful for her, but I believe either she needs to be a bit taller or the bicycle a bit smaller. It seems to me her legs aren't quite long enough, but she doesn't want to give up."

"Perhaps I can temporarily delay future rides until she's grown a bit," Tessie responded.

"By the way, I heard quite a story about you two shortly after my arrival this morning," he said, changing the subject.

"What about?" she inquired, not sure if she liked the idea of folks telling stories regarding her or Addie.

"Seems you've garnered quite a reputation for yourself. Joe Carlin, the blacksmith, is telling everyone he meets what a miracle worker you are—how you saved Levi Wilson's life operating on him out in the backyard," he related.

"Well, it's very kind of Joe to give me the credit, but I told Mr. Wilson and Mr. Carlin that if it hadn't been for God's help, I'd have never successfully completed that operation," she told Charlie.

He listened intently as she related the events surrounding Levi Wilson's ailment and the ensuing surgery. "Sounds to me like you, a bird with a loose feather, and the good Lord worked hand in hand on that one," he responded as she finished the tale.

"I was fortunate to have Addie with me also," she told Charlie. "She became quite an assistant," Tessie praised, giving Addie a smile.

"I must say that I am surprised to see you today. I don't recall your mentioning a trip to Florence this week," Tessie stated inquiringly.

"It wasn't planned in advance, but there were some things that needed attention. Besides, it meant an opportunity to visit with you," he said. "I hope you're pleased by the surprise."

"I'm always pleased to see you, Charlie," she responded, a tinge of color rising in her cheeks.

"Well, that's good to hear because I was hoping we could go to dinner and then work off our meal at the skating rink. Of course, that plan was made before I'd spent an hour running behind a bicycle," he confessed.

"Oh, I am sorry, but that won't be possible this evening," she answered.

"May I inquire why not?"

"Certainly," she said with a smile. "I promised Lydia that Addie could spend the night with me. It will be the first time she's stayed over with me, but since tomorrow is Sunday and she doesn't have to go to work in the morning, I thought it a splendid plan," she advised.

"Why does Lydia want Addie to spend the night?" he inquired, confused by the turn of events.

"She has a date with Floyd, a salesman she's been keeping company with for some time now. I didn't ask, but I got the impression that she may be planning on staying out after the curfew and didn't want to take a chance that Addie would give her away. I'm not sure, but she acted as if she were hiding something when she asked me," Tessie explained.

"Do you really think you should be a part of this?" Charlie asked.

"Charlie, I thought we had an agreement," she stated firmly.

"We do, and I think I've been keeping my part of the bargain. I'm not quite so sure you're keeping your eyes open, however," he answered.

"I like having Addie with me. If I felt Lydia were taking advantage of me, I'd call her on it. You know I have no trouble speaking my mind."

"That's a fact, but I can't help thinking there's more going on here than either one of us realizes," he answered.

"How would you feel about having dinner here with Addie and me?" she inquired.

"I couldn't refuse that offer," he told her. "I'll expect the two of you to accompany me to the skating rink afterward."

"We'll see," she responded, not sure if she was quite up to an evening of skating.

Once dinner was over and the kitchen duties completed by the trio, Charlie knelt down in front of Addie. "How would you like an evening at the skating rink?" he asked the child.

Addie wasn't sure what Charlie was asking since she had never seen a skating rink but agreed that she would be happy to go along. "It's two to one for the skating rink," Charlie told Tessie, pleased he had gotten the upper hand at least once.

"Charlie, I'm not sure I can even stay upright on roller skates. It's been ages since I've tried," she admitted.

"I'll be right at your side, more than happy to hold you up," he bantered, not willing to take no for an answer.

"Get your coat, Addie," he said, motioning toward the hall closet. "You too, Tessie. It will be chilly by the time we return," he informed her.

Addie skipped ahead as the two of them walked toward Charlie's carriage. "I think we'd better take the buggy. By the time we get through skating, we may be too tired to walk home," Charlie advised laughingly, although Tessie was almost positive that he was correct.

Tessie was glad there weren't many people at the skating rink to observe her uncoordinated attempts at roller skating. Charlie was busy trying to keep Addie upright while Tessie spent the first hour slowly circling as she held onto the railing whenever possible. Soon, Addie was making her way around the rink on her own, and Charlie took the opportunity to glide over toward Tessie just as she let go of the railing. His attempt to stabilize her proved an effort in futility. Instead, they both landed on the floor while Addie skated in a circle around them.

"Maybe I should give you lessons," the child laughed, gazing down at the couple sprawled on the floor.

Charlie gave her a look of mock indignation as he returned to an upright position and held a hand toward Tessie. "Please, don't pull me down," he chided, placing his arm around her waist. After several trips around the rink with Charlie at her side, Tessie decided that the skating rink had been an excellent idea.

"Thank you for a wonderful evening, Charlie," Tessie said, bidding him good night at the front door.

"You are more than welcome," he said. Before she knew it, Charlie had gathered her to him, his breath now on her cheek. "I think I love you," he said, leaning down and kissing her softly on the lips.

"Charlie, Addie will see you," she reprimanded, avoiding his declaration.

"There's nothing wrong with a young girl seeing two people who care about each other kissing good night," he defended.

"Perhaps not, but it's getting late, and I need to get Addie into bed," she told him.

"I'm planning on escorting you to church in the morning, if that's all right?" he asked.

"That will be fine," she answered, closing the door. *He loves me,* she thought to herself, walking toward the spare bedroom in a daze.

A noise on the front porch shortly after she had gone to bed startled Tessie awake. *Probably just a cat knocking over a flowerpot,* she decided and drifted back to sleep.

The next morning Charlie arrived at ten-thirty and was instructed to wait in the parlor while Tessie struggled with the ribbon in Addie's hair.

"I don't know what's wrong this morning," she said aloud. "Nothing seems to be getting completed on schedule. We'd better get going, or we'll be late," she told Charlie. "Just let me get our coats."

"This letter was in the door when I arrived," Charlie told her as she and Addie passed through the parlor on their way to the hall closet.

"Just leave it on the table. I'll read it after church," she replied, pinning her hat in place.

"Would you like to eat at the Harvey House?" Charlie invited as they walked toward church.

"I'd love to, but I'd like to stop off at the house first and read that letter you discovered, if you don't mind. My curiosity's beginning to get the best of me."

"Not at all," he said, each of them grasping one of Addie's hands as she skipped along between them.

Tessie and Addie had become regulars at church, and Charlie was always with them on the Sundays he was in Florence. Addie made a few friends, but remained most comfortable sitting between the two of them, leaning her head on Charlie's arm.

"Where did summer go, Charlie?" Tessie asked as they returned to the house. "It seems only yesterday that I was tending my roses, and now winter is almost upon us," she said, pulling her collar tighter.

"They say that's what happens when you get older. You lose all sense of time," he teased, opening the front door.

"We're going out to dinner shortly, Addie, so please stay neat," Tessie told the youngster, who nodded in agreement.

Tessie sat down on the sofa and tore open the envelope, quickly scanning the letter. Automatically her eyes looked toward Addie, who was sitting in the rocking chair stitching on her quilt. She handed the letter to Charlie, who slowly read the contents.

Dear Dr. Wilshire,

Floyd and me ran away and are getting married. Floyd says we can't afford to take Addie 'cause I won't be working since I'm going to have a baby. Anyways, I didn't know what to do about Addie, and since she spends most of her spare time with you, I decided you could just have her. I left all her things at the hotel, and maybe she could just keep working there like usual. It would keep her out of your way in the mornings most days. In case you don't want her around, maybe you could find some orphanage or something. Hope you don't get too angry about this, but I got my own life to live.

Yours truly,
Lydia

"How are you going to tell her?" he asked sympathetically.

"I'm not sure," Tessie answered, glad that he didn't say "I told you so." Lydia hadn't fooled Charlie, not for a minute.

"Do you want to be alone with Addie while you tell her, or would you like me to stay?" he asked.

"Please don't leave. I need all the help I can get with this," she answered, feeling desperately inadequate.

"I'm hungry. Are we going to eat now?" Addie called.

"Come here, Addie. I need to talk to you," Tessie responded, holding her hand out toward the youngster.

Addie slid onto Tessie's lap. "What?" she inquired when Tessie said nothing.

"When Charlie arrived this morning, he found a letter in the door. It's from Lydia," she began.

"Why did Lydia write you a letter? She can just walk over and talk to you. That was silly, wasn't it?"

"She wrote the letter because it was easier than talking to us. Last night Lydia and Floyd went away to get married," Tessie explained.

"When is she coming back?" the child asked, her eyes wide with surprise.

"She's not planning on coming back right away. She and Floyd are going to live in another town, but Lydia has agreed that you can stay with me. It makes me very happy that she's going to allow you to live here," Tessie concluded as enthusiastically as possible, hoping to soften the message.

"I guess she must love Floyd more than me," Addie responded. "Do you think she'll ever want to see me again?" she asked, her voice quivering.

"Lydia loves you very much, and I'm sure she'll be back one day to see you. It's just that she's ready to start a new life with Floyd and thought you'd be better off here," Tessie replied, pulling the child closer and issuing a silent prayer for guidance.

Suddenly, Addie pushed herself away. "When you and Charlie get married, who are you going to leave me with?" the child asked, looking back and forth between the couple.

"You would live with us, wouldn't she, Tess?" Charlie quickly responded, ignoring Tessie's reproving look.

"Charlie and I don't have plans to get married," she explained.

"But when we do, we'll tell you right away. We would want you to live with us when that happens," Charlie stated.

"We'll discuss this later," Tessie told him when Addie was looking away.

Disregarding her comment, he gained Addie's attention. "Are you still hungry?"

"Yes," she responded dejectedly.

"Well then, I think we should be on our way to the Harvey House. Maybe, we'll have some chocolate layer cake for dessert," he added, watching as Addie gave him a fleeting smile.

"She'll be all right," Charlie informed Tessie. "With our love and God's help, things will work out."

"I know. . . 'All things work together for good to them that love God.' I'm just not sure Addie knows that."

Chapter 7

November arrived, bringing several inches of snow and frigid temperatures. Charlie, Tessie, and Addie were well bundled as they left the opera house, their stomachs overly full. It had been a splendid Thanksgiving dinner, and the opera house had served as an excellent community dining room for the annual feast.

"Mr. Banion. . .Dr. Wilshire, come quick! There's a fire at the depot, and a couple of people are hurt pretty bad," came the cry of Lawrence MacAfee, racing toward them on his large stallion.

"Let me take your horse," Charlie ordered. "Take Dr. Wilshire to her house. She'll need to get her medical bag. Check to see if your wife is willing to come over to Dr. Wilshire's and look after Addie. We may be awhile."

After the instructions were issued, Charlie urged the horse into full gallop toward the railroad yard.

Tessie rapidly checked her black bag, adding several salves, clean sheets, and bandages. Confident she had those items that she might need to aid any victims, she hurried back to the carriage. Lawrence and Addie sat patiently waiting, their eyes riveted toward the heavy smoke spiraling ever upward, casting a smoggy glow over the surrounding area.

Tessie had barely made it into the carriage when Mr. MacAfee snapped the reins, commanding the horses into action and throwing both passengers backward against the seat. The horses scarcely had an opportunity to reach their speed when Lawrence pulled back on the reins, bringing them to an abrupt halt not far from the station.

"I'd better not get the horses any closer to the fire, or they'll spook on us, Doc. I'll take the little gal home and be back to help just as quick as a wink," he said, giving Addie a reassuring grin.

Tessie didn't bother to reply, her mind now fully focused toward the task at hand. It appeared that total chaos reigned throughout the area until she made her way a bit closer. Charlie had strategically placed himself in the midst of activity, shouting orders and assembling men in bucket brigades to douse the flames from every possible angle and as quickly as humanly possible. Spotting Tessie, he motioned her toward him while continuing his command post, mindful of each new sputter of flames threatening to ignite out of control.

"We've moved the injured to the depot. The fire broke out in one of the passenger cars. I'm not sure what happened, but it looks like there are only a few people needing medical care."

"If you keep pushing your men at this rate, you'll have me caring for a lot more," Tessie reprimanded him. "They need to trade off. Move some of the men that are closest to the fire farther back down the line and switch them about frequently. Otherwise, they'll drop from heat exhaustion," she ordered.

He smiled at the brusqueness of her order but knew she was right. He should have thought about that himself. Immediately, he ordered the last ten men to exchange places with the first ten, while he watched Tessie hurry off toward the train station. He smiled as she stopped momentarily to check the hand of a firefighter before motioning him to follow her into the depot. *That's quite a woman,* he thought and then quickly forced his mind back to the conflagration, knowing that any stir of wind could impede their progress.

Tessie entered the station and found there were only three patients awaiting her, not counting the unwilling young man she had forced from duty.

"It appears you're all doing fairly well without my assistance," she said, giving them a bright smile, which quickly faded upon hearing the muffled groans from the other side of the room.

Her eyes darted toward the sound, just as one of the men offered, "That one over there, he's hurt pretty bad. I'm not sure how it happened, but it looks like he's got a few broken bones."

"Do you know who he is?" she inquired, walking around the wooden benches toward the injured man.

"He was a passenger that came into town on the train earlier. One of our men went over to the Harvey House looking for volunteers for the bucket brigade—don't think he had been on the fire line long before collapsing. Charlie had him down the line quite a ways since he wasn't a railroader. Besides, he was dressed in those fancy duds."

"Are the rest of you all right for now?" she inquired, kneeling beside the man.

"Sure thing, Doc. We would have stayed out there, but Charlie wouldn't hear of it. Heat got to us, but we ain't burnt or nothing. Okay with you if we head back out?"

"Stick around a little longer. At least until I get a good look at this gentleman. I may need some help. Besides, I think they can do without you a little longer," she responded, knowing that wasn't the answer they wanted to hear.

It didn't take more than a quick glance to know she was going to need help. "Put some water on to boil, and if there's no water, melt some snow, lots of it. I'm going to need all of you to help in just a little while, so don't take off," she ordered, taking command of the situation.

Coming back toward the patient, she noted the pain reflected in his dark brown eyes. His lips were in a tight, straight line, which made them almost nonexistent, and he had turned ashen gray. As Tessie surveyed the situation, she was grateful to see that someone had placed a makeshift tourniquet around the upper leg to stop any excessive bleeding. It had done the job. A brief hand to his forehead proved there was little or no fever.

"I'm Dr. Wilshire, and hopefully, we're going to have you fixed up in a short while," she said, giving him her best smile.

"I'd be thankful if you could do that," he responded through clenched teeth, watching as she walked toward the stove at the end of the room.

Quickly, she surveyed the men and, finding the most muscular appearing of the group, quietly inquired, "Have you got a strong stomach, or are you given to fainting at the sight of blood and pain?"

"I can hold out with the best of 'em," he stated proudly, not sure what he was getting himself into.

"Ever seen your wife give birth or helped set a bone? Ever watched while someone had a cut sewn?" she fired at him.

"Been there to help when all my young 'uns was born—my wife does the hard part. I just pray and help the babe along when it gets time. Don't know that I've ever seen much else, but I grew up on the farm and helped with the sick animals a lot," he answered, not sure what she was wanting him to do.

"Have you ever fainted?" she asked, beginning to scrub her hands and arms in the hot water.

"No, Ma'am. Ain't never fainted."

"Good. Scrub yourself," she commanded.

"Excuse me, Ma'am, did you say scrub?"

"That's right. Get a bucket of that hot water and begin scrubbing. Watch how I do it. I want your hands clean as the day you were born, so you'd better get busy. By the way, what's your name?" she asked, giving him a quick smile.

"It's Alexander Thurston. Call me Alex," he responded.

"Pleased to meet you, Alex, and I appreciate your willingness to become my assistant," she replied, grinning at the look of dismay that passed across the man's face at that remark.

"As soon as we get through washing, I want you other men to throw out the water and pour some for yourselves. Each one of you scrub yourselves the same way we have. Make sure you take your time and get good and clean," she ordered.

None of them even thought to defy her command, each nodding in agreement as though it were commonplace for this young woman doctor to give them directives. They stood staring after her as she turned and walked back to the grimacing man on the floor.

Pulling one of the sterilized and carefully wrapped packets from her bag,

Tessie produced a pair of scissors and began cutting away the remainder of the pant leg at an unwieldy angle to his body. Nerves, bone, skin, and other debris protruded from the wound, banishing Tessie's hope the repair would be easy.

"I need to clean the wound; then we'll begin to get you put back together," Tessie told the man.

"I don't believe anybody here knows your name. You feel up to talking just a little?" she asked, hoping to keep his mind otherwise occupied while she probed the gash.

"Name's Edward Buford. I'm here visiting from England. My sister lives in Chicago, and I had been there to visit with her. Thought I'd see a bit more of the country before returning home," he told her, attempting to keep from yelping in pain as she carefully continued cleaning the leg.

"I thought I detected an English accent earlier," she remarked. "I am sorry you've met with an accident in our country. Especially at a time when you were acting as a goodwill ambassador, helping put out the fire," she continued. "How did this happen? The men tell me you were at the end of the line, and apparently no one saw the accident occur."

"It was a bizarre accident. A runaway team of horses pulling a loaded wagon went out of control and was headed right for me. I tried to jump out of the way and twisted my leg as I fell," he began.

"That couldn't have caused an injury this severe," she interrupted.

"No. I was unable to move quickly enough, and the wagon ran over my leg. Then, as if to add insult to injury, the horses reared, which caused the wagon to tip over. I was fortunate enough to have the wagon land elsewhere, but a large barrel landed on top of my injured leg. That would account for any cornmeal you may find hidden away in that leg," he advised, trying to make light of his condition.

"I appreciate that bit of information, Mr. Buford," she responded with a smile. "I'm going to wash out the wound. The water may be a little warm, but we need to get this leg cleansed."

"Alex, I'd appreciate it if you would keep the basin emptied and bring me hot water as needed," she instructed, noting the fact that the recently initiated assistant seemed to be bearing up throughout the ministrations thus far.

Tessie repeatedly poured hot water over the wound, irrigating it into a basin positioned beneath the leg, with Alex assisting her as they turned Mr. Buford to permit access from all angles. Her patient's lips once again formed a tight line, and his eyes closed securely with each new movement or the rush of water. A low groan emitted when she gave a final dousing of the area with iodine.

Looking toward the three men who had been busy scrubbing themselves, she noted all of them, with the exception of one, seemed up to the job at hand.

Gathering them around, she dismissed the young man who looked as though he would pass out at any moment and explained to the remainder how she was going to pull the bone back into Mr. Buford's leg and then position it to join together. They needed to retract the bone far enough to ease it into position, which would require all of them working together. Carefully, she explained where each of them should stand and exactly what they were to do when she issued the orders, making them individually repeat the instructions and wanting to feel assured that each knew his duty.

Returning to Mr. Buford, she leaned over him and took his hand. "Sir, I need to set your leg. Since it will be a rather painful procedure, unless you object, I am going to give you some anesthetic to knock you out for a short period of time," she explained.

"Dr. Wilshire, had I known you had ether with you, I would have requested it an hour ago and foregone the pain of your cleansing my wound," he said, giving her a weak smile.

"I take that to mean that we may proceed, Mr. Buford."

"As quickly as possible, my dear woman, and feel free to knock me out for more than just a few minutes," he replied as she placed a pad with the drops of ether over his nose.

"Quickly, gentlemen—let's take our positions and get to work," she called out as soon as the anesthetic had taken effect.

Uttering a fleeting prayer that God would guide them, Tessie called out the orders, "Pull, twist right, relax, pull, twist left, relax." Finally, they had the leg aligned to her exacting specifications and sat watching while she carefully sewed the wound—with the exception of Alex. He continued to anticipate her needs and fetch items until she completed the operation.

"You've been a very able assistant, Alex. I appreciate all you've done to help, and if ever there's anything I can do for you or your family, I hope you'll call upon me."

"Was my pleasure, Ma'am. Wait 'til I tell the missus I helped with a real operation. She'll never believe it."

"Well, if she doesn't, you have her come and see me the next time she's in town, and I'll tell her just what a wonderful job you did," she assured him.

Just as Mr. Buford was beginning to regain consciousness, Charlie walked into the station. "We've finally got the fire out," he announced, taking in the scene of men with rolled-up sleeves who were gathered around Tessie and her patient.

"How are things going in here?" he inquired.

"We're making progress," she answered. "Mr. Buford's leg has been set, and as soon as we get some splints on it, I believe we'll be finished."

"I'll take care of that, Doc. I know where there's some pieces of wood that would work real good," responded one of the men who had assisted in setting the leg.

"Thank you," she called after the disappearing young man. "You look as though you could use a basin of water and a little rest yourself, Charlie."

"That's an understatement," he confided, settling onto one of the wooden benches close at hand. "Tell me about your patient," he requested, indicating the groggy form of Mr. Buford.

Sitting down beside him, she wrung out a clean cloth in the basin of water Alex had brought to her. Reaching toward him, she sponged the soot and ash off his face and dipped the cloth back into the water once again and began rinsing.

"Thought I'd better get a few layers of that soot off and make sure it was really you I was talking to," she joked. "My patient is Edward Buford. He's here visiting from England. He tells me he had been to Chicago visiting his sister and, before departing, decided to see a little more of America. I gather he knows no one in the area. Since he must stay off that leg, I'll need to find some accommodations for him."

"I think Mr. Vance would agree the railroad should provide him a room at the Harvey House since he was helping with the fire. I'll see if I can get one on the first floor. Otherwise, I'll make other arrangements," he assured her.

"Will these work for splints, Doc?" the young man inquired, walking through the front door, proud of his find.

"Those will be wonderful," she beamed at him. "Bring them over, and we'll finish this job."

"I'll go check about a room at the Harvey House while you finish," Charlie told her.

"Good," she replied and moved toward her patient. "Alex, give us a hand, would you?" Together they placed the wooden splints on either side of the leg and bound them in place.

"That's about all we can do," she told the men. "I'd appreciate it if several of you would remain to help move Mr. Buford. Charlie should be back shortly," she advised.

Checking his vital signs, she was pleased to find they were normal. "Mr. Buford, I'm afraid you're going to be required to remain in our fair city for a period of time. I'm hopeful you'll walk without a limp if you follow instructions and remain off the leg as long as I deem necessary," she told him, not sure what his reactions would be to this change of plans.

"After you've worked so diligently to make me whole again, how could I fail to follow your prescribed instructions?" he asked, a woozy smile on his face.

"Everything's arranged at the Harvey House," Charlie announced, coming through the front door of the station. "I've explained he's had an injury, and they're expecting him."

"Thank you, Charlie. Men, if you'd carefully lift Mr. Buford onto one of the benches, I believe we can carry him over to the Harvey House," she instructed.

"Don't worry, Ma'am. We'll carry him as if he were a babe," Alex assured her as they gently lifted Mr. Buford onto the bench. "You just walk alongside and give a holler if we're doing anything to cause him pain," he instructed the young doctor.

Upon their arrival at the Harvey House, the entourage was met by Mrs. Winter. Resembling a drum major in a Fourth of July parade, she led the procession down the hall to the designated room. Tessie stood back and allowed the matron to remain in charge until it was time to move Mr. Buford onto the bed. Mrs. Winter's cheeks visibly colored at the praise Tessie heaped upon her.

"I believe you've won Mrs. Winter's allegiance," Charlie whispered to Tessie as the men carefully placed Mr. Buford on the bed.

"That was my intent. I want my patient to receive excellent care while he's residing here. The best way to ensure that is through Mrs. Winter. Don't you agree?" she whispered back.

Charlie leaned his head back and laughed delightedly at her response.

"Mr. Banion! You're going to have to keep your voice down if you want to remain in this room. Just think what damage could have occurred if your rowdiness startled Mr. Buford and caused him to twist that leg," Mrs. Winter reprimanded, with hands on hips and eyes shooting looks of disapproval.

"Yes, Ma'am," Charlie replied, giving her a salute while backing from the room and trying to keep from doubling over in laughter. "I'll meet you outside," Charlie loudly whispered to Tessie, peeking his head around the doorjamb and then quickly receding when Mrs. Winter started toward him.

"Thank you all for your able assistance. Now, if I could have a few moments alone with my patient, I believe he'll soon be ready for a good night of sleep," Tessie said to the gathered assistants.

As they filed out of the room, Tessie stopped Mrs. Winter. "I'd appreciate it if you'd remain, Mrs. Winter. Since you'll be in charge of the day-to-day care of Mr. Buford, I'd like you to hear my instructions." Mrs. Winter once again took on the cloak of self-importance as she ushered the delegation from the room and then returned to Mr. Buford's bedside, hands folded in front of her, prepared for instruction.

"You'll be pleased to know, Dr. Wilshire, that I've had previous experience nursing the infirm," Mrs. Winter offered.

"That does please me," Tessie responded, smiling at the woman and then her patient. "Mr. Buford is visiting from England, and I am hopeful that we can show him not only the best of medical care but the fine hospitality of our country while he's required to be bedfast. Mr. Banion located his trunk, and I feel certain he has all necessary items with him. Mr. Banion has requested that if Mr. Buford needs anything, the purchases be placed on his bill and presented to the railroad," she explained.

"I'm hopeful there is a strong young man working for you that is able to follow instructions and can assist Mr. Buford daily with bathing and dressing. With his leg splinted, it will present some special problems, and I certainly don't want him to bear weight on that leg for a period of time," Tessie continued.

"I know just the young man," Mrs. Winter declared. "I'll go and get him right now," and off she bustled, ready to fulfill the first order of her mission.

Once Mrs. Winter was out of earshot, Mr. Buford looked at Tessie and inquired with a slight twinkle in his eyes, "How long am I to be held hostage?"

"I'm not sure how long it will take you to heal. You've had a serious injury. If you do well, perhaps after a short period we can put you on a train back to Chicago, and you can finish recuperating with your sister and her family. Would that bolster your spirits a bit?"

"I suppose so, but it would appear that the time I envisioned seeing the country shall be spent looking out a window," he replied, trying to keep a pleasant frame of mind. "Don't misunderstand—I am truly grateful for your excellent medical attention, Doctor, and if you'll agree to continue treating me, I'll attempt to be a good patient."

"I can't ask for much more than that, Mr. Buford," Tessie responded as Mrs. Winter and a muscular young man of about eighteen entered the room.

Tessie carefully instructed both the young man and Mrs. Winter in the necessary care of Mr. Buford's injury. Bidding the three of them good night, she assured Mr. Buford that she would check on him in the morning.

Wearily she exited the front door and found Charlie leaning against the porch railing. "Did you get Mrs. Winter organized?" he inquired.

"I believe she'll do just fine," Tessie answered as they walked down the front steps.

"You look exhausted," Charlie remarked, lifting a wisp of hair that had worked its way out of her ribbon, carefully tucking it behind her ear.

"It's been a long evening," she replied. "I feel as though I could sleep for a week," she admitted.

When they had completed the short walk to her front door, Charlie leaned forward and enveloped her in his arms, allowing her head to rest upon his chest. He stroked her hair and held her close for just a few moments and then lifted her face toward his, placing a soft kiss upon her lips.

"I'm glad you've come into my life, Dr. Tessie Wilshire," he whispered to her and then pulled her in a tight embrace and kissed her thoroughly.

"I'm glad too," she answered, smiling up at him, "but I think we'd both better get some rest," she added.

"That's the doctor in you—always being practical," he said, giving her a broad smile. "I'll leave you now if you'll promise to stop at the station in the morning so we can have breakfast. Do you want me to check on Addie for you?" he inquired.

"Oh good heavens, how could I forget Addie?" she exclaimed sheepishly. "I'd better get her," she continued.

"Why don't I just stop over at the MacAfees'? She's probably already asleep. They'll enjoy having her, and you need to get to bed," he ordered.

"If you think they won't mind," she conceded.

Placing one last kiss on her cheek, Charlie bounded off the porch and back toward the station to get his horse and ride to the MacAfees'.

In the days that followed, Tessie diligently visited her new patient, pleased with his progress. She had begun making her visits to Mr. Buford in the late afternoon after completing office hours. Tessie enjoyed the daily visits, not only because her medical treatment was proving effective, but because Mr. Buford was an entertaining and knowledgeable companion. Addie would walk with her to the hotel and then head for the kitchen, anxious to see the chef and taste his inventive recipes. On this particular day, Tessie knew John would not be in the kitchen until later since he had gone to make a special purchase of oysters.

"Come along, Addie. You can meet Mr. Buford," Tessie instructed, helping Addie remove her new winter hat and coat.

Addie nodded agreement, although it was evident she would be off and running the minute John returned.

"Now who might this fine young woman be?" Mr. Buford inquired as Addie followed Tessie into the room.

"This is Addie Baker. She lives with me, and if you care to converse with her, you'll need to be sure she is looking directly at you. She's deaf," Tessie explained.

"Come here, young woman," Mr. Buford instructed while patting the side of the bed. "Come close so we can talk."

Tessie sat down in the rocking chair and nodded to Addie as the child cautiously approached Edward's bedside. Amazed at his ability to charm the young girl, Tessie sat mesmerized for almost an hour while he entertained the youngster. Several times Tessie was sure that he had attempted to sign with Addie, but not wanting to disrupt the developing rapport, she remained silent throughout their conversation, surprised that he had little difficulty understanding the child's occasional distorted words.

John's appearance outside the hotel snapped Addie out of her reverie, and with a hasty wave of her arm, she was off the edge of the bed and out of the room.

"I apologize, Mr. Buford. I'm afraid Addie's first love is being in the kitchen with John," Tessie stated. "That's not meant as an excuse for her rudeness but rather an explanation," she continued, shaking her head in mock exasperation.

"No explanations or excuses necessary," he responded laughingly. "She's a delightful child. By the way, do you recall that you've promised to call me Edward on several occasions?"

"Now that you mention it, I do remember. I'll try and do better in the future," she answered, picking up her medical bag and moving closer to the bedside.

"Would you be offended if I asked a few questions?"

"About Addie? Not at all," she answered.

"Well, about Addie and you," he countered.

"I suppose you can ask so long as I may retain the right not to answer," she offered.

"Fair enough! How did Addie come to live with you? Is she a relative?"

"No, we're not related," she stated and then, reminiscing, explained how she had met Addie and Lydia, along with the subsequent chain of events that had bonded them together.

"My heartfelt desire is that I can provide Addie with the necessary tools to prepare her for the future. I've prayed earnestly about her deafness for I'm sure life will be difficult unless she is equipped to meet many challenges."

"Do you know what caused her deafness?" he inquired.

"Her sister told me she was able to hear up until about a year ago. That was as much information as I was able to glean from her. Lydia, Addie's sister, was extremely jealous of any attention the child received, and when I questioned about Addie, she became infuriated. Consequently, I have very limited knowledge. I noticed you attempting to sign with her, didn't I?" Tessie asked as she finished checking her patient's vital signs and began to unwrap his leg to inspect the stitches.

"Yes, you did. My niece was deaf, and I learned to sign in order to better communicate with her several years ago when my sister brought her to England," he told her, watching as she carefully removed the bandages from his wound.

"You say she was deaf. Is she deceased?"

"Oh no, not at all. I've just come from visiting her at my sister's home in Chicago. She's had surgery and is now able to hear. That's why I inquired about Addie's loss of hearing," he explained.

A chill of excitement traveled up Tessie's spine at hearing his words. Her fingers ceased their movement, and she looked directly into his eyes. "I want to know everything about this surgery. How much can you tell me?" she asked, obviously impatient for answers.

"Not any of the technicalities, I'm afraid. My brother-in-law performed the surgery. While he and Juliette, my sister, were in England two years ago, he heard of a surgeon in Germany who was performing surgery to correct deafness with some success. He left Juliette and Genevive with our family in England and traveled to meet with the doctor in Germany. He remained in Germany for almost a year, studying and developing the technique. The success rate had been very limited, but for some, like Genevive, hearing is fully restored," he explained.

Tessie's mind whirled with the information she was receiving. Perhaps there was hope for Addie to hear again. Perhaps this surgery was the answer!

Carefully, she removed the sutures, then wrapped the splints back in place. "How can I find out more?" she asked, closing her medical bag and pulling the rocking chair close to his bedside.

"You could send an inquiry to my brother-in-law. I'd be happy to write a letter of introduction that you could enclose with it. I should have informed them of my whereabouts before now anyway. This will force me to take up my pen," he told her.

"Oh, Edward, would you do that? I'd be so grateful," she replied, clasping his hand between both of hers.

Lifting her hand, he lightly kissed it before she could pull away. "It will be my pleasure," he answered, holding onto her hand for a brief moment longer.

Tessie felt her face flush and hoped Edward would think it was from her excitement over the surgical prospects rather than from his kiss.

"I really must be leaving," she announced. "I'm going to write a letter to your brother-in-law this evening, Edward. I'd appreciate it if you wouldn't mention this to anyone yet. If it turns out that Addie isn't able to have the surgery, it will mean less explaining."

"I understand," he replied, "and I'll honor your wishes, but I have a good feeling about this."

"So do I. I'll see you tomorrow," she answered, slipping into her gray double-breasted wool coat before heading off in search of Addie.

Chapter 8

Although writing a letter to Edward's brother-in-law immediately after dinner was Tessie's intent, her resolve melted at the beckoning look of the young child holding out a needle and thread. Addie was determined to have her quilt completed before Christmas, notwithstanding the fact that everyone told her she had set an unobtainable goal.

"I'll sew for a little while, but then I must write a letter," Tessie said, reaching out to take the already-threaded needle Addie offered. "I wrote and told Aunt Phiney you were making a quilt. I even sent some little pieces of the fabric for her to see."

"Did she like it?" Addie inquired.

"Very much. In fact, when I received her letter the other day, she said she was sending you colored thread to match the cloth. She suggested perhaps you could weave the thread together to sew the binding, and it would be very pretty. What do you think?"

"Three colors woven together would be beautiful," Addie answered, as Tessie began sewing. Stitching effortlessly, Tessie found herself watching Addie, thinking that perhaps one day soon the young girl would be able to hear.

Addie looked up and smiled as she pulled her needle through the layers of fabric. "You're not sewing; you're daydreaming," Addie chided.

"Addie, what would you think if I told you that maybe, just maybe, there's an operation that would restore your hearing?" Tessie asked, leaning forward, her eyes riveted on the youngster.

"You know I want to be a doctor like you, so that would be wonderful," the child responded. "Would the operation hurt a lot?"

"It would probably hurt some. I'm not sure just how much. I shouldn't have even brought this up. I don't even know if it's possible, but Edward told me about his niece. She had this operation, and now she can hear. So, you see, I'd like to find out more about it—to see if you could get that same kind of help," she concluded.

"We shouldn't get too hopeful," Addie responded, taking over in an adult fashion, while Tessie seemed more the excited child.

"You're right," Tessie said, smiling. "We'll not talk about it any further until I have more information, but I'll be praying about it, and you do the same," she counseled Addie.

Praying that evening, Tessie felt a surge of excitement. She knew this was God's plan to restore Addie's hearing, and she was going to see it to fruition. The added medical expertise she might glean would be a bonus. Leaning down, she placed a kiss on Addie's cheek, tucked her into bed for the night, and carefully penned a letter to Dr. Byron Lundstrom. "No wonder I'm so tired," she mused, clicking open the watch pinned to her bodice. It was near midnight.

While working through her schedule the next morning, Tessie's thoughts wandered, delighting in the possibilities that lay ahead. She was anxious for noon to arrive, her concentration waning as the morning slowly progressed.

I hope Edward has his letter written, she thought, just as her last patient was leaving.

"Do you know of a doctor and little girl who might be interested in lunch at the Harvey House?" Charlie asked as he sauntered into the office, admiring how fresh and lovely she could look after a morning of seeing ill patients.

"Oh, I don't think I can today, Charlie. I need to see Edward before my first appointment this afternoon," she responded apologetically, continuing to bustle around the office to assure everything was in order for her next patient.

"Edward? Would that be Mr. Buford?"

"Yes," she responded without further explanation.

"The last I knew, you were addressing him as Mr. Buford. When did you and Mr. Buford begin addressing each other on a first-name basis?" he inquired, his thick eyebrows raised in speculation.

"Why, he requested that I call him by his first name shortly after I began treating him," she answered, surprised at the tone Charlie had taken.

"Are you now on a first-name basis with all your patients?" he countered, irritated at the fact she felt comfortable enough with this stranger to be so familiar.

"You're acting childish," she retorted. "I don't have time to stand and bicker over such a petty matter. I really must get to the Harvey House," she stated, tucking the letter into her handbag. "I need to get Addie, so, if you'll excuse me, I'll be on my way," she said, moving toward his tall figure which was blocking the doorway.

"Let's get Addie. We can all go to the Harvey House, see Mr. Buford, and then have lunch," he suggested, sure he had found a solution that would force her to accept his invitation.

"You're welcome to walk along with us, but once I see Edward, there are other errands I need to complete," she responded, pushing past him into the parlor where the child sat playing with a dollhouse Uncle Jon had constructed and sent to her.

"You have to eat lunch sometime, so I'll just tag along until the two of you are ready; then I'll join you," he replied with a grin, feeling sure she would succumb to his offer.

Handing Addie her white fur muff, they walked the short distance to the Harvey House. "I'll take Addie to the kitchen," Charlie offered upon their arrival.

"No, it's better if she comes with me. The kitchen will be in chaos with the noon rush, and she'll be in the way," she answered, placing an arm around Addie's shoulder and maneuvering her down the hallway.

"Sounds as if you're in charge," Charlie said, watching while Addie and Tessie went directly to Edward's room.

"This is a pleasant surprise," Edward stated as the two of them entered his room. "I was expecting Mrs. Winter with a lunch tray, and instead I see the two prettiest women in all of Kansas," he complimented with a large smile.

"Thank you for your kind words," Tessie replied. "I was wondering if possibly you'd had an opportunity to write your brother-in-law," she inquired meekly.

"Ah, so it's not me you're interested in but rather my brother-in-law. He's a happily married man, and you'd be much better off with me. I'm of a better temperament and considerably more lovable," he teased.

Tessie felt her face flush and was glad that Addie was looking out the window and hadn't been privy to Edward's words.

"I wanted to. . .I mean I was hoping. . .I thought perhaps. . . ," she stammered.

"Out with it, Woman—just what is it you want? Love, money, my family name? Don't hesitate—it's yours for the asking," he jested, causing her embarrassment but enjoying it too much to stop.

"Edward! Someone will hear you and take your words seriously," she reprimanded. "I came early to inquire if you'd written to your brother-in-law because I wanted to post the letters before the mail leaves on the afternoon train," she advised, her decorum now fully intact.

"I see," he responded somberly, stroking his chin. "So you thought I'd have a letter written to Byron by noon today, knowing I haven't written since I departed their home?" he asked, eyeing her in mock seriousness.

"I was hopeful," she responded plaintively, suddenly realizing his zeal would not be the same caliber as hers. After all, he had only met Addie yesterday!

Seeing the dejected look in her eyes, he quit bantering, reached under his pillow, and pulled out a sheet of paper, holding it up for her to see.

"Do you suppose this would do?" he asked.

"Oh, Edward, thank you," she replied.

"There's only one requirement," he told her stoically.

"What's that?" she asked, her tone serious.

"You'll have to come over here and get it," he answered with a grin.

As she approached the bed, he quickly moved the letter into his left hand. Just as she leaned forward to retrieve the epistle, he raised up, meeting her lips with a soft, gentle kiss.

"I know I shouldn't have done that," he said, lying back on his pillows.

"You're right! You shouldn't have, and if you weren't in that bed, I'd have your hide!" Charlie bellowed from the doorway.

"Charlie, please! There's no need for that kind of talk, and I'd appreciate it if you'd keep your voice down. We don't need to alert everyone in the hotel that you're unhappy," Tessie scolded in a hushed voice.

"I don't know why you're upset with *me!* You should be putting him in his place," he replied angrily.

"Why don't you take Addie and wait outside? We can discuss this privately when you've calmed down," she suggested, hopeful he wouldn't cause a further scene.

"Fine. Addie and I will wait outside—outside his door, not outside the hotel," he responded, giving Edward a final glare as he took Addie's hand.

"I'm sorry. I didn't realize you were promised to Mr. Banion," he stated apologetically.

"You need not apologize in that regard. Mr. Banion and I are not promised. We've been enjoying each other's company since I arrived in Florence. I do not, however, belong to anyone," she responded, angry at Charlie for his possessive attitude. "I would, however, be willing to accept your apology for kissing me without permission," she added.

"I'm afraid I could never apologize for kissing you. It gave me too much pleasure," he stated emphatically, a smile playing on his lips as he handed her the letter.

"Thank you for this," she stated, looking at the letter in her hand.

"My pleasure. I hope it will bring happiness to you. I'm afraid it's already brought unhappiness to Mr. Banion," he replied.

"I'd better leave now. I'll be back to check your leg around four o'clock," she told him, placing his letter in her handbag with the one she had written.

He lifted his hand in a wave as she left the room, pleased she would be returning later in the day.

Walking into the hallway, Tessie quickly retrieved Addie's hand and walked directly past Charlie and out of the hotel without uttering a word. She was acutely aware of Charlie's footsteps directly behind her as she marched toward the post office. She had almost reached the door when he took hold of her arm.

"Are you planning on walking all over town to avoid discussing this matter with me?" he questioned.

"I have a letter to mail immediately. After that, I will talk with you, but please, don't assume that I have an obligation to discuss my personal life with you, Charlie," she responded.

He felt as though he had been slapped in the face. She was actually angry with him when he felt that that presumptuous foreigner should be the one receiving her wrath. He didn't understand her attitude, but wanting some form of explanation, he waited outside the post office while she posted her letters and then moved alongside Addie when they exited the building.

Addie slipped her small gloved hand into Charlie's larger one. She didn't know all the words that had been spoken, but it was obvious Charlie and Tessie were arguing. The air crackled with animosity. Peeking up at Charlie from under the brim of her small hat, she felt a hint of reassurance when he gave her a quick wink and squeezed her hand. Tessie wasn't looking anywhere but straight ahead, and Charlie noted her face remained etched in a frown.

"I'm going to my room," Addie announced, shedding her coat as they walked in the front door, wanting no part of the dissension.

"Addie needs to eat lunch, and I have only a short time before my next patient arrives," Tessie remarked, avoiding his eyes.

"I'm not going to be the cause of Addie missing her lunch. Can you reschedule your next patient?" he cautiously inquired.

"No, I can't. I don't expect a patient to be inconvenienced by my personal problems," she replied, moving toward the kitchen.

"Perhaps it would be best if I came back later in the day when we've both had time to give this matter some thought. I could be back about four o'clock if that would be acceptable to you," Charlie offered.

"I must return to check Edward's leg at four o'clock," she answered, continuing to prepare lunch.

Charlie felt the blood begin to rise in his neck and then up his face. Edward again! He was glad Tessie wasn't looking at him. Attempting to gain control before speaking, he turned his back and took several deep breaths. A further outburst might cause irreconcilable differences, and he didn't want that to occur.

"Do you know what time you'll return? I could come by after your visit—or after dinner if you prefer," he asked, his words now spoken in a soft, precise manner.

"After dinner would be better, I believe," Tessie responded, setting two places at the table.

"Since it appears I'm not invited to lunch, I'll be back at seven o'clock," he stated, trying to lighten the mood.

When she didn't answer, he backed out the doorway and left the house, not sure how a simple invitation to lunch had turned into such a disaster.

For Tessie, the day quickly passed. She had several physicals for new railroad employees, as well as ailing townsfolk with a variety of complaints. By four o'clock she had seen her last patient, and she and Addie were on their way back to the Harvey House, both bundled against the declining temperature and cold winds.

"Could I go see John in the kitchen?" Addie requested as they drew closer to the hotel. Tessie smiled and gave her permission, aware the day's events had been stressful not only for her and Charlie but for Addie as well.

"Looks like my patient has taken on his own course of treatment," she stated, seeing Edward sitting in a chair with his leg propped on a stool.

"I promise I didn't place any weight on the leg. John and one of the other cooks helped move me. Mrs. Winter took pity on me when I complained of lying in bed all day and came back with the two men to help me into the chair. However, if it means you'll cease being my physician, I'll return to bed and not move an inch until ordered," he answered, giving her a charming smile.

"I'm sure it will do no harm. I had planned to make arrangements for you to be up in a chair by tomorrow anyway. I must say, you certainly seem to have captivated Mrs. Winter. She's generally not so accommodating," Tessie advised as she began unwrapping the leg.

"So I've been told by any number of people. Perhaps it's my accent," he offered.

"Perhaps, but most likely it's your flattery that's turned her head," she surmised.

"Flattery? And here I thought it was my perfect English and extraordinary good looks," he teased.

"I'm sure that's helped also," she affirmed, noting his well-chiseled features, sandy hair, and twinkling blue eyes, which seemed to laugh at her.

"And have I turned your head, Dr. Tessie Wilshire?" he asked, lifting her chin so their eyes would meet.

Tessie felt her face becoming warm and quickly looked down. "I've very much enjoyed making your acquaintance," she responded, keeping her hands busy unwrapping the bandage and hoping he wouldn't notice her fingers tremble.

"That's not much encouragement for a man who sits waiting for your visits each day, but I'll not ask for more right now. Be prepared, however. Once I'm up and about, I plan to pursue you with vigor, Doctor," he said, his words carrying a fervor of determination.

"Let's just concentrate on getting you well for now," she replied, completing her ministrations and closing her black bag.

"If that's what the doctor orders, I'll agree for now," he responded, quickly placing a kiss on her fingertips before she could object.

"Edward!"

"Sorry. I'll try to keep myself under control," he replied with an unmistakable twinkle in his eyes.

"I must be going. I'll see you tomorrow afternoon. You may tell Mrs. Winter you have permission to be up in a chair for two hours each morning and afternoon and one hour in the evening if she can make arrangements to have you moved about," Tessie formally instructed.

"Yes, Ma'am!" he replied, mimicking her formality.

"Have a good evening, Edward," she replied, unable to keep from smiling at his antics.

"It would be better if you'd return and read to me, but I suppose I'll have to make do with Mrs. Winter," he announced.

"You've convinced her to read to you?" Tessie asked, astounded by the remark.

"Of course. Since the first night I arrived," he told his incredulous visitor. "If you'd spend more time with me, you too would come to know just what a charming fellow I am."

"I don't doubt your charm, Edward. It's caused me enough problems already," she remarked, pulling on her gloves.

"Speaking of problems, you might put Mr. Banion on notice that unless he's managed to put a ring on your left finger by the time I'm out of this room, he's going to have some stiff competition for your affection," he stated, giving her a knowing wink.

"We'll see, Edward, we'll see," she replied, picking up her bag and leaving the room.

"Don't hesitate to come back after dinner," he called after her as she walked down the hallway, a smile on her face.

She nearly collided with Mrs. Winter, who was turning the corner and carrying a huge dinner tray.

"Just taking Mr. Buford his meal," she told Tessie. "Isn't he the most delightful gentleman? If I were thirty years younger, I'd set my cap for him," she announced.

"Mrs. Winter, you're a married woman," Tessie chastened.

"Nope. My husband's been dead over thirty years. He died a year after we were married. I wouldn't be working at this job if I had a husband, Dr. Wilshire, and if you're smart, you'll find a husband before you're too old! I thought I had time before I married again and decided I'd work awhile, spread my wings, but time got away from me. Before I knew it, I was too old and set in my ways to think about marrying again. Mark my words, you'll be sorry. Doctor or not, you'd better think about a husband," she earnestly counseled.

"Thank you for those words of concern, Mrs. Winter. I've given Mr. Buford instructions regarding his care, and he'll relate those to you," Tessie stated, changing the subject. "If you can make arrangements for men to assist with moving him, I know he will be most appreciative. I must be going now," she continued, making a quick turn toward the kitchen to find Addie.

The two of them hurried home, and Tessie had just finished washing the dinner dishes when Charlie knocked on the front door. Fatigued, Tessie had hoped he wouldn't return this evening and felt guilty when she opened the door only to be greeted by a huge bouquet of flowers.

"I hope you'll accept these with my deepest apologies," Charlie said as he extended the bouquet to her and entered the house.

"Thank you, but flowers weren't necessary. Let me take your coat," she offered as Addie came running across the room and wrapped her arms around his legs in a hug.

Charlie dropped to one knee and placed a kiss on her cheek. "Thank you for such a wonderful welcome," he said, squeezing her in return.

Tessie placed the flowers in a cut glass vase and turned toward Charlie. "Exactly what are you apologizing for?" she inquired.

"Whatever it is that made you angry," he responded.

"There! You see, Charlie, you don't even know what you've done to upset me. How can you apologize when you don't even recognize the problem?" she asked, her voice becoming incensed.

"I didn't come here to argue, Tessie. I came to apologize and try to forget what happened earlier today," he answered, not sure why she was becoming indignant.

Sensing things were not going well, and making a childlike effort to calm the two adults, Addie pulled on Charlie's hand. "Tessie's going to get me operated on so I can hear again."

Charlie's mouth dropped open as he stared down at the child. "What? What is she talking about, Tessie? Did she say you're going to operate on her so she can hear again?"

"No. I'm not going to perform the surgery. We're not even sure about this yet, so it's probably not worth discussing at this time. Why don't you sit down, and I'll make some coffee," Tessie answered, not wanting to discuss the surgical plans.

"Don't bother with the coffee; I had some before I came. Why don't we all sit down," he said, his voice taking a note of authority. Clasping Addie's hand, Charlie led her to the couch, where the child snuggled close beside him.

Tessie would have preferred that Addie to go back to her sewing, but the child now seemed determined to insert herself in the middle of the discussion.

"About the flowers," Tessie began as she seated herself in the chair across from Charlie and Addie.

"Forget the flowers! What's this about Addie having an operation? When did all of this come about, and why have I not heard anything? You'd think I was a stranger rather than a friend," Charlie stated, the hurt coming through in his voice.

Addie moved away from his side and was intently watching as he spoke, not wanting to miss anything he said. Her eyes darted toward Tessie, and she realized her attempt to distract the couple from their earlier argument had been a failure. It appeared they were going to quarrel about the operation. Disconsolate, she settled back on the couch as Tessie leaned forward in her chair.

"Don't try to make me feel guilty because I'm attempting to find help for Addie. It's not as though I've been planning this for a long time. I was given information just yesterday regarding surgery that could possibly restore her hearing. The details are unknown to me as yet, and I shouldn't have mentioned it to Addie until I knew more. I was so excited I couldn't help myself," she explained.

"You didn't seem to have any trouble keeping it from me," he bantered.

"I believe the majority of the time we've been together since you came to call at noon has been consumed with arguing," she retorted.

"Or the silent treatment," he shot back. "I'm sorry. That was uncalled for. I don't want to ruin the rest of the evening. Please tell me about this surgery. How did you find out about it?" he inquired, hoping the discussion about Addie would calm their nerves.

Tessie hesitated momentarily and then burst forth, "Edward's brother-in-law is a surgeon in Chicago. He went to Europe to study the technique and has successfully performed the surgery several times. His daughter is deaf, or she was before the surgery," Tessie hastily explained.

"Edward. I should have known," he said quietly. He felt as though his world was crashing in around him. Everything revolved around Edward.

Nobody said a word. Addie leaned her head against Charlie's arm. "I love you, Charlie," the child said, looking up at him.

"And I love you, sweet Addie," he said, giving her a hug. He could see the pain in Addie's eyes and resolved not to make matters worse.

"So what do you know of this surgery and this surgeon except that he's Edward's brother-in-law?" he inquired.

"Not too much. I've sent a letter to him today requesting additional information. I don't know if he'll even agree to see Addie or if she would be a candidate for the operation. I'm hopeful that I'll hear from him soon," she responded.

"So that was the rush to see Edward at noon and get to the post office," he surmised.

"Yes. He told me last evening about his brother-in-law and the fact that his niece had been totally deaf prior to the surgery. He agreed to send a letter of introduction along with my inquiry to his brother-in-law. I wanted to get the letter posted as soon as possible," she stated.

"And what do you think about all of this, Addie? Are you excited about having an operation and perhaps being able to hear again?" he asked.

She shrugged her shoulders, a sorrowful look on her face. "I'd rather have you and Tessie be happy," she responded, causing the two adults to feel ashamed of their behavior.

"Perhaps we can do that," Charlie answered. "If we try real hard, maybe we can convince Tessie to go bowling and then get some hot chocolate. What do you think?" he asked.

"Oh yes," she said, clapping her hands and looking at Tessie expectantly.

There was no way Tessie could refuse, and Charlie knew it. It appeared that he was going to have to use every tool at his disposal if he was going to outmaneuver Edward Buford—and he certainly planned to do that!

With each passing day, Tessie would vacillate while walking to the post office. She wanted to receive a letter from Dr. Lundstrom, yet she feared what the contents would say. It was apparent he had received her letter because a wheelchair had arrived by train for Edward last week. As she and Addie made their way down the snow-covered sidewalk, she convinced herself that Dr. Lundstrom did not want to see them, and rather than write a letter of rejection, he was not going to respond.

Entering the post office, Jed Smith called out that she had some mail from Chicago, and she felt her heart begin to race. Grasping Addie's hand, she quickly moved to where he stood and extended her hand.

"It's here someplace—saw it just a minute ago," he told her as he slowly checked through a stack of mail.

Attempting to keep her patience, she watched him slowly go through the pile, letter by letter, all the while wanting to grab it from him and find the dispatch for herself. *Be patient,* she kept telling herself as she waited, her exasperation building with each moment.

"Ah, here it is," he finally stated, pulling out a cream-colored envelope. "Looks like it's from a Dr. Lundstrom," he said, reading the envelope before handing it to her.

Once home, she quickly pulled off her wraps and sat down in a chair close to the fire. Finishing the letter, she glanced toward Addie, who stood staring at her, still bundled in her coat and muff.

"He wants to meet with us, Addie," she said, holding her arms out to the child.

"Does that mean I'm going to have the operation?" Addie asked.

"Dr. Lundstrom said if we will come to Chicago, he will examine you to see if the surgery would be helpful. If so, he is willing to operate," she told the child. "It will be wonderful, Addie. We'll have a nice trip, and maybe you'll come back to Kansas able to hear again," she said, her voice full of encouragement.

"But what about Christmas? Will we have to leave before Christmas?" Addie asked. "Charlie promised that we would all go to Christmas Eve services at church, and he would spend Christmas with us," she reminded.

"No, we won't go before Christmas. We'll wait until after the holidays," Tessie promised the child but inwardly wished they could leave tomorrow.

Her last patient seen, Tessie bundled Addie in her warmest coat and the two of them made their way to the Harvey House. Addie was off to the kitchen for John's beloved company, and Tessie rushed to Edward's room, anxious for his magnanimous encouragement.

"I've wonderful news," she burst out upon entering the room. Edward sat in the wheelchair staring out the window at a group of young boys playing in the snow. Her appearance brought an immediate smile to his face.

"You've heard from Byron?" he asked.

"How did you know?"

"Just a guess. I don't know too many other things that would cause you to burst into my room without a knock," he said, his voice filled with laughter.

"Oh, I'm sorry, Edward. I didn't knock, did I?" Her cheeks were now flushed with her own embarrassment as well as the chill winds.

"I was only jesting with you, dear Tessie. You needn't become unduly distressed with your behavior," he advised, holding out his hand to her.

"Are you going to permit me to read the letter?" he inquired when she merely looked at his extended arm.

"Of course; I'm sorry," she apologized, flustered that she hadn't immediately realized he wanted to read the correspondence.

"Tessie, you've done nothing but apologize to me since you entered the room. I must bring out your most conciliatory behavior," he stated with a smile as she pulled the letter from her handbag.

While Edward began to read, she removed her coat and hat, pulled off her gloves, and sat down in the rocker, watching his reaction as he read the letter.

"Well, it sounds very promising, don't you think?" he asked.

"Oh yes. I'm delighted with the prospects," she told him, leaning forward in the chair.

Grasping both of her hands in his, he looked deep into her eyes. "This is going to work out wonderfully, my dear. When are you planning on going to Chicago?"

"I'm not sure exactly," she stammered. "It's not that I wouldn't prefer to leave immediately, but Addie is looking forward to Christmas. I don't think we could possibly leave until after the holidays," she stated, careful not to explain Addie's desire to spend Christmas with Charlie.

"Oh," he responded in a disheartened tone.

"Why? What's the matter, Edward?"

"My sister and Byron would like for me to return to Chicago until I'm able to travel back to England. With the wheelchair, there's no reason why I can't take the train without fear of injuring my leg. I've told them I'd return," he explained.

"I see. Well, that certainly makes sense. There's no reason you should be sitting around in this hotel when you could be enjoying the company of your family while you recuperate," she concurred, when what she really wanted to tell him was not to leave, that she would miss him and needed him to stay and be her ally.

"So you want me to go?" he asked, hoping she would reject the idea.

"I didn't say I wanted you to go. I said it was a sensible plan," she responded.

"Do you want me to stay?" he asked, hopeful she would give the answer he wanted to hear.

"Your decision should not be based upon what I want. If you wish to travel to Chicago, it will not have an ill effect upon your recovery, and you would most likely be more comfortable with your family. If, however, you desire to remain in Kansas until you've further recuperated, that would be wonderful. . .medically sound, that is," she stammered.

"I see. Well, then, how medically sound would it be if I remained in Kansas until you and Addie leave for Chicago, and we make the trip together?" he questioned, a glint in his eye.

"I would say that would be very, very medically sound," she answered, thrilled that he would remain and travel with her, rather than enjoying the festivities with his family.

"Then that's what we'll do," he quickly responded, not wanting her to change her mind.

Suddenly, she felt ashamed of herself. Here was Edward, cooped up in his room except for his trips to the dining room and occasional visits with other visitors in the hotel, and she was encouraging him to miss the warmth and love of his family during their holiday celebration.

"I'm sorry, Edward. I'm acting very selfish. We both know the best thing for you would be to return to Chicago now so that you may be with your family. If you stay here, they'll miss the pleasure of your company through the holidays, and you'll be stuck away in this room for Christmas, wishing you were there," she told him.

"They've done without the pleasure of my company for the holidays in years past, so I believe they'll survive without me again. As for being stuck away in my room, I'm sure we can find a couple of fellows who would be willing to transport me to the home of one Dr. Tessie Wilshire for Christmas Day festivities," he responded.

"Yes. . .of course. . .that could be arranged," she hesitantly replied.

"You could put a little more enthusiasm into that," he encouraged, giving her a bright smile.

"Oh, I'm sorry. Of course, you're welcome to come and spend the day with us," she stated, attempting to sound more zealous.

"That's more like it! We'll have a wonderful time," he told her.

"Well, well. Look at the time. I need to be getting home," she said, gathering her belongings.

"I'm so pleased this is going to work out, Tessie. We'll have a wonderful Christmas, and the trip will be a grand adventure for the three of us," he concluded.

"Yes, I'm sure it will be a grand adventure," she said, forcing a smile. "I'll be by to check on you tomorrow. Good night, Edward."

"Good night, Tessie. I'll be busy making plans for Christmas," he said, giving her a cheerful wave.

Her head was whirring as she stopped by the kitchen for Addie. She didn't even hear John talking to her until he walked over and asked if she was ill.

"No, no, I'm fine. We just need to be getting home," she told the chef as she hurried Addie along.

The walk home was a blur. Neither of them spoke, but Addie sensed something was very wrong. Tessie had been with Mr. Buford, and now she was unhappy. It seemed to Addie that Mr. Buford was the center of the difficulty. She was beginning to dislike him and the problems he seemed to create.

"What's the matter?" the child asked while they were sitting at the dinner table. She had watched Tessie pushing her food around, not eating or talking.

"Nothing for you to be concerned about. I'm just trying to figure out a few things," she answered, realizing that Addie had sensed her distress. "Everything's going to be fine," she stated, a little too brightly.

Addie protested going to bed, but Tessie held firm. She needed time to think clearly and make some decisions about the approaching holiday. How was she going to handle both Charlie and Edward? There had been no way to avoid Edward's request to spend Christmas with them, and yet Charlie had been invited weeks ago. Addie would never forgive her if she tried to exclude Charlie at this late date. She knew the day would be a disaster with both of them in the house and was sure that nothing short of a miracle was going to prevent the day from turning into a donnybrook.

What have I done? she thought, drifting into a restless sleep fraught with bad dreams.

Chapter 9

Tessie eyed the letter on her bedside table. Slowly she removed the pages and began to once again read the latest missive from Dr. Lundstrom. He had solidified their travel plans and forwarded a plethora of information relating to the possible surgery. Additionally, he expressed his gratitude for her continued medical treatment of his brother-in-law, causing her a twinge of guilt.

"If it weren't for Edward, I'd probably have foregone this whole idea," she mused, certain she would have succumbed to Charlie's objections to the surgery. His negative responses and continual efforts to dissuade her had been the cause of many arguments. Edward, however, continued to encourage and bolster her pursuit, winning allegiance at every opportunity and becoming her sole confidant.

Tessie thought about the closeness that she and Charlie once enjoyed, feeling the void of his lost companionship. She missed the ability to share things with him but now was careful to tell him nothing of consequence. If he questioned, she adroitly changed the subject. Though she hadn't told an out-and-out lie, it was becoming increasingly difficult to feel at peace with this new behavior.

Guilt invaded her thoughts as she remembered her conversation with Edward earlier that day. Charlie would be furious if he knew the substance of that discussion, but she could think of no other solution to ensure that Christmas wouldn't end in total disaster. Divulging her fear that the two men would misbehave, Tessie was aghast when Edward admitted that such a prospect appeared uproariously inviting. It wasn't until she was reduced to tears, he understood the depth of her anxiety over the ensuing holiday. Quickly, he realized the situation could be used to his advantage. If he behaved according to her wishes, she would be eternally grateful—especially if Charlie's behavior was dreadful—and he would certainly do all he could to help in that regard!

Miraculously, Tessie had convinced Uncle Jon and Aunt Phiney to bring the twins and spend the holiday in Florence with them. It had taken a good deal of persuasion since they were just as determined she and Addie should travel to Council Grove for the holidays. They finally conceded when she wrote explaining the possibility of traveling to Chicago for Addie's surgery immediately after Christmas.

It would be wonderful to have them visit, and Tessie was sure they would help buffer the situation between Charlie and Edward. Addie's excitement that the twins would be coming with Uncle Jon and Aunt Phiney was evident. Tessie continued to remind her that the twins were fourteen, but Addie was sure age didn't matter much on Christmas. It would be fun having other young people for the holiday.

Charlie rushed to complete the last of his paperwork, anxious to be on the train headed for Florence and a week of vacation. The train pulled into the station just as he was putting on his woolen overcoat. Boarding the train, he leaned back and unbuttoned his coat, finally able to relax a bit. Surrounding him were gaily wrapped packages tucked into large brown bags, evidence of his shopping trip to Kansas City earlier in the month. Smiling, he realized it had been many years since the excitement of the holidays had affected him. It would be wonderful to see "his women" and share a magnificent holiday, certain they would be delighted with the many plans he had made for them.

The train pulled into the station exactly on time. Charlie quickly gathered the packages and swung down from the train, impatient to check into the Harvey House. It had been several weeks since he had seen Tessie, and although she had seemed distant during his last visit, he was sure it was because they both had been so busy. Now they would have a full week to regain what seemed to be slipping away.

"Looks like Santa's already arrived," said Mrs. Winter as she walked to the front desk of the hotel and surveyed the profusion of packages.

"Not quite, but he's got a good start on things," Charlie stated with a laugh, pulling his arms out of his overcoat.

"I've got your room ready, just like you asked," she told him. "Just sign the register. You know the way," she told him, pleased to have Charlie as a guest. "John asked if you'd be having dinner with us tonight," she stated with a question in her voice.

"Not sure, yet. Need to check with Tessie, and see what she's got on her agenda," he responded.

"You just missed her. She was in checking on Mr. Buford," the matron informed him.

The comment hit like a jab in the stomach. *Why does she still need to visit Edward so frequently?* he wondered. *Doctor or not, surely her daily presence wasn't still necessary. Stop,* he thought, *or you're going to ruin everything before you even see her.* Picking up the packages, he went to his room, dropped off his belongings, and immediately left the hotel. Abandoning all thoughts of Edward, he attempted to regain the happy spirit he had felt before Mrs.

Winter mentioned Tessie's earlier visit.

The walk to the house was invigorating. The cold air and dusting of snow gave the whole countryside a Christmas card appearance. Knocking on the door, Charlie stood patiently waiting, his breath puffing small billowy clouds of air in front of him.

"Charlie!" Tessie greeted, standing and staring from the doorway, her surprise unmistakable.

"Are you going to invite me in?" he asked when she neither moved nor said anything further.

"Oh yes, of course. I'm sorry," she responded, moving aside. "Come in."

"Charlie, Charlie!" Addie called, running toward him at full tilt, throwing her arms open for a hug.

"Hi, sweet Addie," he responded, picking her up into his arms and giving her a kiss.

"I've missed you, Charlie," she told him as he placed her back on her feet.

"I've missed you too, Addie, both of you," he said, glancing up toward Tessie, who appeared much less enthusiastic about his appearance.

"How about dinner with my two favorite gals at the Harvey House?" he asked.

"Oh, I've already begun dinner," Tessie quickly answered.

"Stay and eat with us, Charlie. Pleeease!" Addie begged, looking back and forth between the two adults.

"If it's okay with Tessie," he told her, wanting to stay yet unsure from Tessie's behavior if she would extend the invitation.

"What can I say? Of course, please have dinner with us," she responded, walking back toward the kitchen.

"If I didn't know better, I'd think you weren't expecting me," he called after her.

The remark brought her back into the parlor. "I wasn't expecting you," she stated, looking at him as if he had lost his senses.

"Didn't you get my letter?"

"No, Charlie, I didn't receive a letter, and I've been to pick up my mail regularly," she replied.

"I sent a letter with Harry Oglesby. We were both in Kansas City to meet with Mr. Vance. When I mentioned I needed to send you a letter, he said he would deliver it since he was passing through Florence. We agreed he would pass it along to Mary, my secretary, with instructions to deliver it to you right away. That was four days ago," he explained.

"I've never seen the letter, so perhaps you can enlighten me as to the contents while I finish preparing dinner," she requested.

Following her into the kitchen, he divulged the contents of his letter, wondering if Mary had received the letter from Oglesby. Tessie stood with her back to him as he excitedly related his plan to spend a full week in Florence.

"You're going to be here seven days?" she asked incredulously.

"Yes, isn't it wonderful? Wait 'til I tell you and Addie all the things I've got planned. I know a place not far from here where we can find a wonderful Christmas tree. We'll make it a real adventure for Addie. You know, find the perfect tree to cut down and decorate. Do you have any ornaments, or shall we make some?" he asked, his enthusiasm overflowing.

"I have some ornaments, but I hadn't intended for you to plan our Christmas," she replied, watching her words immediately deflate his mood.

"I'm sorry. It's just that I've been going over all these ideas, and my excitement has grown with each passing day. I thought it might be difficult for Addie since it will be her first Christmas without her mother and not having any word from Lydia. Anyway, I guess I got carried away thinking about how to make it special—for all of us," he finished, the enthusiasm gone from his voice.

Perceiving the obvious sadness caused by her biting remarks, Tessie felt a stab of remorse. If she didn't quit acting like such a shrew, Christmas would be spoiled for all of them.

"I'm sorry, Charlie, but you've caught me by surprise. It was extremely kind of you to think of Addie, but please understand that I've made plans too. When I didn't hear from you, I wasn't sure if you'd be here any longer than Christmas Day if that," she told him.

"I promised Addie I would be here. Surely you knew I wouldn't break that promise," he said, wondering how they could have drifted so far apart in such a short time.

"Yes, I knew you'd do everything in your power to keep your promise," she agreed, placing dinner on the table.

"You say grace, Charlie," Addie instructed as they scooted their chairs under the table.

"I'd be happy to," he replied, looking at Tessie for an indication that she was in agreement.

When she nodded her head, he reached out and grasped Tessie's hand in one of his and Addie's in the other. He smiled as Addie quickly extended her other hand toward Tessie. With hands joined and heads bowed, Charlie gave thanks for their meal and asked God to direct them as they sought the best way to honor Him during the upcoming holiday celebrating the birth of His Son.

Charlie's simple request confronted Tessie with the fact that she hadn't been seeking God's guidance lately, but just as quickly she brushed away the thought and began worrying how much she should tell Charlie about her plans.

"Guess what!" Addie exclaimed before she had eaten her first bite.

"What?" Charlie asked, pleased with the child's exuberance.

Tessie moved to the edge of her chair, not sure what morsel of information Addie was going to offer.

"Uncle Jon, Aunt Phiney, and the twins are coming to see us. They're coming on the train the day before Christmas," she excitedly informed him. "Won't that be fun?"

"That's wonderful. It's nice to have lots of family with you for the holidays," he agreed, looking toward Tessie for confirmation that her family would be arriving.

"It took a bit of coaxing, but Uncle Jon finally relented. He was holding out, sure I'd come home for Christmas," she told Charlie.

"How did you convince them?" Charlie inquired.

Addie, who had been intently watching their conversation, answered before Tessie had a chance. "She told them I was going to Chicago for my operation right after Christmas so they said they'd come here," she informed Charlie, proud that she had been able to follow their conversation and now interject a meaningful piece of information.

Charlie's fork fell and struck the edge of his plate, a small chip of blue china breaking off and landing near the edge of the table. His head jerked up, a startled look on his face.

"What's she talking about? You haven't made definite plans, have you?" he asked.

"Yes, but I'd rather not discuss them right now. I know you don't agree with me about the surgery, but a discussion right now will only result in an argument. Let's try to avoid that if we can," she requested.

"That makes it convenient for you, doesn't it? You tell yourself that keeping secrets and telling me half-truths is acceptable because you want harmony," he said, his voice calm and his face showing no evidence of anger.

"I want to spend a peaceful holiday. Is that so wrong?" she shot back.

"No, it's wonderful, but your actions belie what you say," he answered.

"And just what is that supposed to mean?" she asked, an edge to her voice.

"If you truly wanted a peaceful holiday, it seems you would have been open and honest in your actions. Instead, it appears you've been less than forthright and now plan to continue on that path using harmony as an excuse for your behavior. I don't plan to argue with you, and I won't spoil this holiday. I may not always agree with you, but I've always treated you honorably. I wish you'd do the same for me. If you've been seeking God's will and He has given you direction, then I must believe your decision is for the best. As I continue praying about Addie's surgery, perhaps I'll develop a little of your assurance," he told her quietly.

Addie had been watching the exchange between the two people she loved most. She had understood most of what Charlie had told Tessie. She was glad he wasn't angry, but neither of them seemed happy either. She moved from her chair, took hold of Charlie's hand, and joined it with Tessie's.

"There!" she said. "That's better." Addie gave them a big smile.

How could they resist her simple solution? "We'll talk tomorrow," Tessie told Charlie. "Let's finish dinner."

When Charlie arrived the next day, Tessie kept herself busy with patients while Charlie entertained Addie. He'd brought a gift for them—one for before Christmas, he declared—and insisted that Addie open it immediately. It was a beautiful Nativity scene he had found at a tiny shop in Kansas City. They'd spent their time arranging the figures, and later when Tessie peeked into the parlor, she had heard Charlie telling Addie the story of Christ's birth. Addie watched his lips, intent on each word. As he explained about each of the characters, Addie would point to a figure, watching for his confirmation that she had understood. Tessie forced herself to move back into her office. Leaning against the side of her desk, she reminded herself that she needed to remember Charlie was her adversary when it came to Addie's surgery.

After lunch he asked if they could go looking for a tree. He explained that he had made arrangements for a wagon, and since her relatives would be arriving the next day, it would be the perfect time. She conceded that Addie could go along, but no amount of cajoling from either of them could cause her to give in and join them. Charlie was disappointed, and Addie was confused by Tessie's attitude, but the two of them bundled up and had a wonderful time. They returned with one beautiful tree and four very cold feet several hours later.

Their discussion after dinner lasted much longer than either of them planned. Addie sat quilting, ignoring their conversation, and finally went to her room as one question led to another. Although Charlie was as good as his word and didn't start an argument, he voiced his disagreement and unhappiness at some of Tessie's conclusions. He was hurt to find that Edward had become her confidant. She immediately became defensive and wary during his questioning regarding the amount of time she had consumed seeking God's will for Addie.

"I've not been on my knees consistently, if that's what you're asking," she answered cautiously. "I did pray faithfully about Addie's hearing loss until Edward's appearance in Florence with news of the surgery. I feel that is God's answer," she replied, annoyed at herself for feeling so sensitive about the decision.

"God's answer for Addie, or an opportunity for you?" he asked quietly.

"That's unfair, Charlie. You think my primary interest is medical erudition for me and not Addie's welfare, don't you?"

"To be honest, I'm not sure about your priorities, but I do want you to know I've been praying steadfastly about Addie and the surgery since the day

I learned you were considering it," Charlie told her as he got up from his chair and moved toward the closet where his coat hung. "I can't say that God has given me an answer, but I can tell you I feel very uneasy about the situation. I know it's not my decision to make, but I hope you'll take time to talk to God before you go any further."

"Edward's appearance and the fact that his brother-in-law performs such specialized surgery is surely a sign that Addie is meant to have the operation," she stated, quickly defending her stance. "I've been praying about Addie's hearing since she came to live with me, and I have every confidence that the surgery will be a success. The difference between us is that I'm not afraid to put my trust in medical science," she retorted, as Charlie buttoned his overcoat.

"Be careful where you place your trust, Tessie. There are a couple of verses in Proverbs—Proverbs 3:5-6, if I remember correctly—that say, 'Trust in the LORD with all thine heart; and lean not unto thine own understanding. In all thy ways acknowledge him, and he shall direct thy paths.' You might want to spend a little time with God and see if He's the one directing your path to Chicago," he said, walking back to where she sat.

Even though she knew that he was standing directly in front of her, Tessie didn't lift her eyes from the floor. She sat staring down at his black leather shoes, wanting to lash out in anger. She knew Charlie spoke the truth, but she wanted the surgery to be God's answer for Addie. She wanted it so much that she was afraid to pray, fearful God would send an answer she didn't want to hear.

Charlie knelt down and took hold of her hands. When she still didn't meet his eyes, he placed a finger under her chin and lifted her head. When her eyes were level with his, he smiled gently and tucked a falling wisp of hair behind her ear. "I've loved you since that first day in the train station when you came for your interview. Did you know that?" he asked her.

"Don't, Charlie! It will only make matters worse," she replied, dropping her gaze back to the floor.

"I don't want you to think anything that has been said here tonight alters my love for you. I've come to think of you and Addie as my women, and I want the very best for both of you. If you decide it's best to go to Chicago, I'll support you in that decision, but please don't hide things from me," he requested.

"You've been very good to Addie—and to me, Charlie. I appreciate your concerns, and since you've asked that I not hide anything, you should know that we'll be leaving for Chicago the day after Christmas. Edward will be traveling with Addie and me. His sister requested that he return to Chicago until he's fully recuperated. Since we were making the trip so soon after Christmas, Edward decided that he would wait and travel with us," she stated, never once meeting his intent gray eyes.

"It appears that nothing I've said has meant much to you. I've declared my love and offered my support. I had hoped you would at least give my request to seek God's guidance some consideration, but it seems you're determined to follow your own path. It doesn't appear you need me for anything. I'm sure that Edward will provide delightful company on the trip. I hope you'll forgive me, but I don't think I'll stick around for Christmas. Seems to me I make you uncomfortable, and just between the two of us, Edward makes me uncomfortable," he said, rising and walking to the front door.

"Addie will be disappointed if you're not here for Christmas. She's planning on Christmas Eve services at church," she told him.

"I'm sure you can explain my absence to Addie. You and Edward can take her to church on Christmas Eve," he responded, turning the knob on the front door.

"You really are welcome to spend Christmas with us," she said, walking toward him.

"I don't think it would be wise. I have some gifts for Addie. I'll have John bring them by the house," he replied, shoving his hand into his coat pocket, his fingers wrapping around the small square box nestled deep inside.

"That would be fine," she answered, not sure what else to say.

"I'll be praying for Addie—and for you," he told her, walking into the cold night air.

"Merry Christmas," she murmured, watching his tall figure disappear into the darkness.

Chapter 10

The train slowly hissed and belched its way out of the station, with Addie and Tessie seated across the aisle from Edward. Addie carefully positioned herself near the window. Having concluded that Edward was the cause of Charlie's disappearance, she decided to show her displeasure by avoiding contact with him. Edward was delighted with the seating arrangement, entertaining Tessie with animated conversation, intent on keeping her from having any regrets about the trip. Tessie dutifully assisted Edward as they changed trains, with Addie scurrying along behind, resenting the object of Tessie's attention.

As they boarded their connecting train, Edward quickly showed his displeasure at being forced to sit several rows behind his traveling companions. The moment a gentleman riding behind them left his seat, Edward hobbled up the aisle on his crutches and dropped into the seat directly behind them for the remainder of their journey. It was a long, tiresome trip for Addie, who was meticulously endeavoring to hide her fears from Tessie.

As they disembarked the train, Edward immediately spotted his brother-in-law. Waving to gain his attention, Dr. Lundstrom hastened toward them, explaining he had already made the necessary arrangements for Addie's admittance as a surgical patient pending his examination the next morning.

"My wife and I would like for you to stay with us during your stay in Chicago," he stated to Tessie.

"It's lovely of you to invite me, Dr. Lundstrom, but I feel it would be best if I remained with Addie. She's going to be frightened, and I don't want to cause her further distress by being unavailable," she explained.

"We have an excellent nursing staff, and I'm sure her every need will be met," Dr. Lundstrom assured his visiting colleague.

"I don't doubt the staff's competency, but I won't change my mind about remaining at the hospital with Addie," she responded.

"As you wish. We'll make arrangements for another bed to be moved into her room," he conceded.

"I won't be long, Edward. If you think you'll be warm enough, why don't you just wait for me?" Dr. Lundstrom suggested.

"I'll be fine," he answered, pulling Tessie toward him and kissing her thoroughly. "Byron will keep me informed of your progress, and I'll see you soon," he told her as Dr. Lundstrom removed their luggage and came alongside to assist them from the carriage.

Addie attempted to digest the scene she had witnessed. What was that awful Edward doing kissing Tessie? Charlie wouldn't like it, and she didn't either. She hoped Johnny would remember to give her letter to Charlie. Her shoes felt as though they were weighted with lead as they reached the front door of the building looming in front of them. It was bigger than any place she had ever been and reminded her of stories she had heard about dark, ugly places where they kept children who had no parents. Walking through the door and down the shiny hallway toward a large oak desk, they stopped while Tessie signed papers, and then the nurse escorted them into a sparsely furnished room.

After bidding Dr. Lundstrom farewell, the two of them unpacked some of their belongings, grateful for something to pass the time.

"Do you think it would be all right if I put it on the bed? Will they get angry?" Addie asked, pulling her recently completed quilt from one of their bags.

"I don't think anyone will mind, but if they do, they'll have to take it up with me," Tessie responded, posing with fists doubled and arms lifted in a boxing position. Addie laughed at the sight, and the two of them placed her beautiful quilt over the starched white hospital linens.

Settled in her room several hours later, Addie watched as Tessie sat writing a letter. "Are you writing to Charlie?" she inquired, carefully tucking the quilt around her legs.

"No, I'm writing to Uncle Jon and Aunt Phiney. I promised to let them know we arrived safely," she replied, noting Addie's look of disappointment to the response. "I'm not going to send it until after Dr. Lundstrom's examination in the morning. That way I can tell them what he has to say about your operation."

"I think I'll go to sleep. Want to say prayers with me?"

"I would love to pray with you, Addie," Tessie replied, moving to sit on the edge of the bed.

Addie's prayer was simple. She thanked God for everything, requested that she not die in surgery because she wanted to be at Charlie and Tessie's wedding, and told Him it would be okay if she couldn't hear after the operation since she was doing all right since she had been living with Tessie.

Tessie leaned down to kiss her good night, hoping Addie couldn't see the tears she was holding back. She sat watching the child long after she had gone to sleep, wondering if she really didn't care if the operation was successful. *Is she subjecting herself to this ordeal merely to please me?* she mused and then pushed the thought aside, sure that the statement was merely a protection mechanism the child was using in case the surgery failed.

Morning dawned, and the sun shone through the frost on the window, casting prisms of light on the shiny hospital floor. Dr. Lundstrom strolled into the room, his shadow breaking the fragile pattern. A nurse in a crisp uniform followed close at his heels.

"Good morning. I trust you two women slept well," he greeted.

"As well as can be expected in a hospital room far from home," Tessie replied, giving him a bright smile and taking hold of Addie's hand in an attempt to relieve any developing fear.

Looking Addie squarely in the eyes, his lips carefully forming each word, he smiled and said, "I have a daughter two years older than you. She was deaf also, but now she can hear. I hope I will be able to do the same thing for you. If we can't perform the surgery, or if it isn't successful, I hope you will learn to sign. It will make it much easier for you, especially to receive an education. Now, let's get started with the examination."

Tessie realized his words were meant for everyone and without further encouragement moved away from the bed. Quickly, the nurse moved into position, anticipating Dr. Lundstrom's every request. Addie remained calm and cooperative throughout the probing and discussion, keeping her eyes fixed on an unknown object each time the doctor turned her head in yet another position.

"Thank you, Addie, for being such a good girl," Dr. Lundstrom told the child as he finished the examination. "I'm going to talk with Dr. Wilshire; then we will decide what's to be done."

As if on cue, the nurse left the room as quickly as if she had been ordered. "Would you prefer to talk here or in an office down the hall?" Dr. Lundstrom inquired.

"Right here would be fine. I don't want to leave Addie," she explained, turning to face him as he pulled a chair alongside her.

"I hope you don't feel I was rude by not including you in the examination. Being emotionally involved with a patient can sometimes cloud our vision. I speak from experience. If you elect to move forward with Addie's surgery, I will include you completely if that's your desire."

"Does that mean she's a good candidate for surgery?" Tessie inquired, unable to contain her excitement.

"It means I will consider surgery. It's difficult to know what caused Addie's deafness. I'm guessing from what you told me in your letters that she was slowly losing her hearing. Being a child, she probably didn't realize it was happening and that she should be hearing more competently. I imagine it went unnoticed by her mother and sister until she was nearly deaf. The procedure I perform, if successful, would restore her hearing by probing the cochlea and allowing sound to pass directly into the inner ear."

"Your diagnosis is that the stapes has become immobile, is that correct?"

"I'm impressed, Dr. Wilshire. You've either been doing extensive research on your own or had excellent medical training."

"Both," Tessie replied. "As a matter of fact, I took my medical training right here in Chicago, but I've been reading everything I could obtain since Edward told me of your surgical procedure."

"You must understand that even if the surgery is successful, Addie's hearing won't be completely normal, and there will most likely be some hearing loss after the operation. With the sound bypassing the entire chain of bones in the middle ear, it is impossible for hearing to be completely normal. You must also be aware that for several days, sometimes even weeks, a patient can suffer from severe vertigo. I need not tell you what a dreadful experience that can be. After three days of suffering with dizziness and nausea, my daughter wasn't sure the cure was worse than the affliction."

"She has no regrets now, does she?" Tessie asked, certain of what the answer would be.

"No, she has no regrets. Nor do we. You can't, however, base your decision on our circumstances. I don't envy you in your decision. It's a difficult decision when all the facts and circumstances are known. In Addie's case, we're groping for background information and merely able to make an educated guess. Even though you're a physician and have researched hearing impairments, I'm obligated to advise you there are other risks with the surgery."

"Yes, I realize there are risks," Tessie interrupted, "but if there's any possibility for Addie to regain her hearing, I think we should proceed with the surgery."

"Please let me finish, Doctor."

"I'm sorry," Tessie apologized, feeling the heat rise in her cheeks.

"As I was saying, along with the normal risks related to surgery, there is the possibility of infectious bacteria infiltrating the inner ear, which can be deadly. I've already advised you of the probability of vertigo. Additionally, it can be psychologically devastating for patients when they awaken and can hear the sounds around them and, after a few hours, they are once again deaf. Although it hasn't happened in any of my surgeries, there is the possibility the operation will be a complete failure, and she might not have the opportunity to hear even for a few hours. This is not a decision to be made lightly, but should you decide upon surgery, I would be willing to perform the operation. Why don't you and Addie take the rest of the day to decide, and I'll stop back this evening."

"When would you perform the operation—if we decide to go ahead?" Tessie inquired.

"I think it would be best to wait a few days. You are both tired, and I'll want additional time to examine and observe Addie," Dr. Lundstrom replied, sure the young doctor had made up her mind to proceed with surgery before ever setting foot on the train from Kansas. "Would you like to assist, or at least observe—if you decide to go ahead?"

"Oh yes," Tessie responded, her heart racing with excitement over the thought of assisting in such an innovative operation.

"Which?" he inquired.

"Assist, by all means, assist," she stated emphatically, giving him the answer he expected before he had ever posed the question.

"I'll leave the two of you to make your decision," he replied, walking to Addie's bedside. Taking her hand in his, he looked into the deep brown eyes that stared back at him. "It's been nice to meet you, Addie, and if you decide to have the operation, I hope I'll be able to help you hear again."

"I'll have the operation. That's what Tessie wants," she candidly responded in a soft voice.

"What about you? Don't you want to hear again?"

"I suppose, but it doesn't seem as important as it used to."

"Why is that?" he asked, sitting on the edge of her bed.

"I wanted to hear again because I thought I wanted to be a doctor like Tessie."

"Has something changed your mind about wanting to be a doctor?" he inquired, encouraging her to continue with her thoughts.

"I'd still like to be a doctor, but this trip to Chicago and the operation made Charlie unhappy. Now he and Tessie are angry. I miss Charlie and want things back the way they were—even if I can't hear," she responded in a sorrowful voice.

Glancing over at Tessie, he wondered if the child's words would cause her to have seconds thoughts but quickly realized they would not. Her resolve was obvious; she had decided Addie needed the surgery, and surgery she would have.

He smiled down at the child, remembering the turmoil of making the same decision for his daughter. He hoped things would turn out as well for this little girl with a pretty quilt tucked under her chin.

"Just where did you get that beautiful quilt?" he asked. "I know that's not hospital fare."

"Tessie and I made it," the child proudly responded.

"She did most of the work," Tessie quickly interjected, "and has become quite a little seamstress in the process."

"Tessie has her own quilt that she made. It's bigger than mine," Addie continued. "Tessie told me her quilt was sewn with threads of love. Mine has woven threads, three of them, to sew the binding, see?" she told the doctor, holding the quilt up for his inspection.

"That's very pretty. Was it your idea?"

"No, Aunt Phiney suggested it. When she was with us for Christmas, she told me quilts are special in our family. She said the woven thread I used weaves me into the family," the child proudly related.

"What an exceptional idea," the doctor responded, touched by the child's seriousness.

"She's a wonderful child, isn't she?" Tessie queried, noting the doctor's look of amazement at Addie's answer.

"That she is, and then some. . . ," he replied.

"Charlie! Hold up, Charlie, I've got a letter for you," John Willoughby called out to the figure rushing into the train station.

"What are you doing in Topeka, John?" Charlie inquired, startled to see the chef from the Florence Harvey House running toward him.

"Keeping a promise to a little girl," he responded, bending forward against the cold blast of air that whipped toward him. "Let's get inside before we both freeze to death," he said, pushing Charlie inside the door. "I don't know about you, but I'm heading straight for a hot cup of coffee. Care to join me?"

"I guess if I'm going to find out what you're talking about, I'd better," Charlie answered, tagging along behind. "What's this all about?" he asked after they'd removed their coats and settled at the lunch counter.

Reaching into his jacket pocket, John retrieved an envelope and handed it to his friend. "Addie made me promise I'd get this letter to you. I could have taken a chance on mailing it or having someone else bring it, but I promised Addie I'd deliver it by today. So, here I am. Don't let me stop you. Go ahead and read it," he encouraged.

Charlie stared down at the sealed envelope, his name printed in childish scrawl across the front. A tiny heart drawn in each corner. He tore open the envelope, unfolded the letter, and began to read. When he had finished, he carefully folded the letter, returned it to the envelope, and took a sip of the steaming coffee sitting on the counter.

"I don't know what to do, John," he said, looking down into his cup. "Addie's asked that I come to Chicago to be with them. I feel terrible; she's almost begging."

"Well, what's stopping you? Catch the next train and go be with them," John responded, wondering why someone as bright as Charlie Banion couldn't figure that out on his own.

"You don't understand. Tessie and I had quite a disagreement about the trip to Chicago. I'm not convinced she should be rushing Addie into this operation, and I told her so. Needless to say, that didn't sit too well with her."

"Hmm. I suppose that does muddy up the waters a bit, but I think that little gal needs you there right about now. Maybe you two adults need to put aside your own feelings for the time being and concentrate on Addie," he said, rising from the counter and slipping his arms into the wool overcoat. "I'm going to get me a room and then head back to Florence in the morning. I know you'll do what's right, Charlie."

"Thanks for bringing the letter so quickly, Johnny," Charlie called to the bundled-up figure.

John turned and looked at Charlie, saying nothing for a brief moment. Slowly he walked back to the lunch counter. "I think a lot of that child too, Charlie. I felt honored that she trusted me enough to ask for my help. I'm just praying everything turns out okay for her. Gotta go," he said, his voice beginning to falter.

Charlie watched the door close and soon felt the blast of cold air that had been permitted entry. A quick chill ran up his spine. *I'll accomplish nothing sitting here,* he thought, pulling on his coat. Heading toward the station to check train departures and connections that would get him to Chicago, he jotted down the information and then began the chilling walk to the boardinghouse he called home when he was in Topeka.

After what seemed like hours of prayer, Charlie fell into a restless sleep. He awoke the next morning feeling as though he had never been to bed, still not sure what he should do. "Lord, I hope there's an answer coming soon because that little girl's going to have her operation soon, and I don't know what to do," he said, looking into the mirror as he shaved his face.

"There's a telegram from Mr. Vance on your desk," Mary called to him as he brushed by her desk and into his office. Charlie didn't acknowledge her remark, but she knew he had heard.

"He's sure been in a foul mood lately," Mary whispered to Cora. "He pays even less attention to me now than he used to. One of the waitresses over at the Harvey House told me he had his cap set for that redheaded doctor. You know, the snooty one that came here and interviewed," she explained as Cora took a bite out of a biscuit smeared with apple butter.

"I know who you're talking about, Mary. I was here when all that happened!"

"I know, I'm sorry, but it's hard for me to understand. The waitress said Dr. Wilshire had given him the glove, so you'd think he would show a little more interest in me now. Wouldn't you?" she asked imploringly.

"Who knows what men want?" Cora answered. "I'm sure no authority, but it's not as if you don't have plenty of fellows interested in you. Why don't you just give it up, Mary? Sometimes I think you like the chase.

Once you've snagged someone, you're not interested anymore," her friend remarked, wiping her lips.

"I suppose there is some truth in that," Mary sheepishly replied. "I'll just ignore him; maybe that will get his attention!"

Cora shook her head at the remark. Mary hadn't listened to a word she had said.

"Mary, bring your notebook in; I have a few things that need to be completed before I leave for Chicago," Charlie called.

Giving Cora a wink, Mary seated herself across from Charlie without uttering a word.

"I'll be leaving for Chicago later this morning, Mary. Mr. Vance has called a meeting of company officials, and since he is in Chicago at the present time, he's requested I come there. I'll wire you information once I'm sure of a date. Now, let's get some letters taken care of as quickly as possible. I need to be ready to leave on the eleven o'clock train, and I'll need to get home and pack my things," he advised and quickly began dictating the first of several letters.

Rushing to board the train, Charlie knew his answer had come. Mr. Vance wanted him in Chicago, Addie wanted him in Chicago, he wanted to be in Chicago, and he now felt certain that God wanted him in Chicago. He wasn't quite so sure about Tessie, but he was positive Edward wanted him anywhere but Chicago. Leaning back in his seat, he hoped the trip would pass quickly, and he would reach the hospital in time to be of comfort to Addie.

Chapter 11

Hearing Dr. Lundstrom's voice in the hallway, Tessie looked up to see the doctor walking toward their room with an attractive young woman at his side. "Tessie, Addie, this is Marie. She works at our house and very much enjoys being with children. She spends a good deal of time with Genevive, our daughter, and would like to stay with Addie so that you can join us for dinner this evening. I will not take no for an answer. Marie understands deaf children. Addie will be in very competent hands. Marie will not leave her side, and you need to have some time away from here. It's going to be a couple of days before surgery and then the recuperation period afterward. It's necessary for you to get out of the hospital at every opportunity to revitalize yourself," he said, walking to the small closet and removing Tessie's coat.

"I don't think it would be a good idea to leave," she stammered, looking at Addie, who was already being entertained by Marie.

Tessie walked over to Addie. "Do you mind if I leave for awhile?" she asked. Addie shook her head, giving permission, then quickly returned to the game she and Marie were playing.

"I guess I've been dismissed," she said to Dr. Lundstrom, slipping her arms into the wool coat he held out for her.

"You'd better get your scarf and gloves. It's very cold," he instructed, as the two of them waved to Addie and Marie.

"We met Marie on one of our trips to Europe. She was employed at one of the hotels where we stayed. None of her family is alive. Genevive took a shine to her, and Marie was able to communicate with and entertain her like no one else except my wife. Since she needed a home and we needed assistance with Genevive, it turned out to be an excellent arrangement for all of us. She quickly became part of the family. Genevive adores her, thinks of her as an older sister, I believe. When Marie discovered you were here alone, she offered to make herself available so that you could have some respite during Addie's hospitalization. We've agreed it would be a wonderful arrangement for all of you. Now that Genevive can hear again, she's not nearly as dependent upon Marie. Nowadays, Marie has turned into my wife's social secretary and confidant. I don't think she enjoys it nearly as much as being with children," he said, a smile breaking across his face.

"That is a most generous offer, Dr. Lundstrom. I don't know how frequently I will feel comfortable to leave Addie, but I assure you I am indebted to you and your family for the many kindnesses you've extended us," she responded as their carriage turned into an oval driveway and stopped in front of an exquisite brick mansion.

"We're here," he said, assisting her from the carriage. "Edward will be so delighted. He has been after me to bring him to the hospital, but with this cold, snowy weather, I thought it better that he stay indoors. If I hadn't returned with you, I think he would have walked to the hospital. He is quite taken with you, but I'm sure you know that," he told her, as they entered the front door.

"Tessie, I can't tell you how grand it is to see you," Edward said, swinging toward her on his crutches and quickly placing a kiss on her cheek.

"Edward, please don't be so forward," she rebuked.

"We're all family here, Tessie. They don't mind a bit. No one would know how to behave if I acted in a refined manner all the time," he said, grabbing her hand and placing a kiss on her palm.

"You must be the incredible Dr. Tessie Wilshire I've been hearing so much about. I'm Juliette Lundstrom, Edward's sister," said the striking brunette who came gliding toward Tessie, her hands outstretched in welcome. "We are so pleased to have you join us. I hope it will be the first of many visits," she continued, leading the group into the dining room.

Hours later, Tessie was startled when she glanced at the hand-carved clock sitting on the mantel. "I didn't realize it was so late. I must get back immediately," she said, quickly rising from her chair. "Addie probably thinks I've deserted her. Juliette, may I have my coat, please," she requested.

"If I know Marie, Addie is probably fast asleep, having had a most enjoyable time this evening," Juliette responded. "I do understand your concern, however. I'll only be a minute, and we'll get you back to the hospital."

Byron and Juliette bid her good night and allowed Edward a few minutes of privacy as he escorted Tessie to the door. "I want you to promise you'll come back tomorrow evening," Edward cajoled. "I'm not allowing you to leave until I have your word," he stated emphatically.

"I don't know, Edward. I really need to be spending my time with Addie."

"Tell me you haven't enjoyed the adult companionship and some decent food. Tell me it hasn't refreshed you to be away for a few hours. I'm going to expect you here tomorrow evening. Edward's carriage will bring Marie and fetch you back. I know Addie won't care a bit. There's not a child who doesn't love to be with Marie. If Addie is completely unhappy with the arrangement, you send Marie back with the message, and I'll force Byron to allow me a visit with you at the hospital. Do we have a bargain?" he pleaded.

"You are so difficult to refuse, Edward. I have enjoyed the evening. Your sister and niece are so lovely, and of course, you know how much I admire Byron. I guess we have a bargain," she responded, pulling on her gloves and looking up at him.

He seized the opportunity and leaned forward on his crutches, pulling her to him. "Don't back away, my love, or I'll fall on the floor," he whispered in her ear, embracing her. "Oh, Tessie, I've missed you so," he murmured.

"Edward," she began, bending back to meet his eyes but was stopped short as he quickly lowered his head, placing a lingering kiss on her partially open lips. "Edward, you must stop, or I will leave you lying flat on the floor," she breathlessly chastised him. He smiled, gave her one more fleeting kiss, and backed away, knowing his kiss had left its mark.

"Ah, Tessie, you are the woman of my dreams," he told her. "And I intend to have you!"

"I think I'll have some say in the matter," she replied as he opened the front door.

"That you will, that you will," he retorted. "See you tomorrow evening and thank you for coming," he called after her.

Juliette had been right. Addie was fast asleep, and Marie was busy with her embroidery when Tessie returned to the hospital. Addie's exuberance the next day assuaged any feelings of guilt that Tessie had about returning to the Lundstrom's for dinner again that evening. In fact, Addie encouraged her to go. Marie had promised to bring a new game for them to play, and it was obvious she was looking forward to spending more time with the young woman.

"You're sure you don't mind?" Tessie asked for the third time as Marie came walking down the hallway of the hospital.

"No, go," Addie answered. "Marie and I will have fun," she answered, just as Marie entered the room carrying a satchel that immediately caught Addie's attention.

Several hours later, a noise in the hallway caused Marie to look up. Standing in the doorway was a tall, handsome man, a valise in one hand and a gaily wrapped package in the other.

"Charlie!" came the resounding call from Addie. "Oh, Charlie, you came to be with me," the child cried, bounding into his arms.

"And who might you be?" Charlie inquired, looking directly at Marie and noting she was the only other person in the room.

"I'm Marie, an employee of Dr. Lundstrom and his wife," she replied. "Who are you?" she asked, although it was obvious that Addie knew this man well.

"Charlie Banion. A friend of Addie's. Where might Dr. Wilshire be?" he asked, hoping she would be pleased to see him.

"She's gone to the Lundstroms' for dinner. Dr. Lundstrom thought she needed some relaxation away from the hospital, and of course, Edward has driven everyone mad since Dr. Lundstrom wouldn't allow him to leave the house and visit Dr. Wilshire here at the hospital. He's truly smitten with her, and I can certainly understand why. So beautiful and such a fine woman," she confided, not realizing the impact her words were having on Charlie.

"Yes, she is beautiful," Charlie answered. "You know, I'd really like to spend some time alone with Addie, and I'm sure you wouldn't mind having some extra time for yourself. I'll take over your duties here, and you can go ahead and return home," he said, his voice carrying enough authority that Marie knew she had been dismissed.

"Marie, what are you doing home?" Dr. Lundstrom called from the dining room as the young woman entered. Tessie immediately rose from her chair, concern etched on her face.

"Sit down, Dr. Wilshire. Everything is fine. A friend of Addie's is staying with her. She assured me you wouldn't mind a bit. It appeared they wanted to visit privately, and he bid me leave them."

"He? Did you get his name?" Tessie asked, still alarmed at the turn of events.

"Oh, of course. Mrs. Lundstrom would have my hide for such an omission," she answered, giving her mistress a smile. "His name is Charlie Banion. A fine-looking man, I might add. Will you be needing me for anything further this evening, Mrs. Lundstrom?"

"No, nothing else, Marie. Thank you," Juliette responded, noting their guest had turned ghostly pale.

"I really must return to the hospital," Tessie stated, again rising from her chair.

"But you haven't eaten. Sit down and finish your meal. I'll have the driver return you immediately after dinner," Dr. Lundstrom ordered.

She certainly didn't want to insult the doctor. Even though she knew that staying was a mistake, she couldn't afford to offend him. After all, he would be operating on Addie soon. Slowly she sat down and finished the longest meal of her life, dreading the meeting she would soon have with Charlie and knowing what he must be thinking when she didn't immediately return.

Hearing the click of shoes coming down the hallway, Charlie glanced at his pocket watch. It was almost 8:30 P.M. He was sure it must be Tessie. When she hadn't returned shortly after Marie left, he knew she was sending him a message, a message he didn't want to receive. His heart skipped a beat as she entered the room, her cheeks flushed from the cold, even more beautiful than he remembered. He had vowed to keep things civil—not lose his temper. The last thing he wanted was to drive her further into Edward's arms.

"Tessie, it's good to see you," he welcomed, rising from the chair beside Addie's bed. "You look wonderful."

"What are you doing here, Charlie?" Her voice wavered between hostility and dismay.

"Why don't you take off your coat, and I'll explain," he answered warmly, although his first thought had been to ask where she had been when he arrived at the hospital.

"Don't fight. Please don't fight," came Addie's plea from the bed, causing Tessie to feel ashamed of the way she had greeted Charlie. "I love both of you, and I want you both with me," Addie continued. "So, just talk nice and love each other," the child instructed.

"We'll try our best," Charlie answered, giving her a wink. "Why don't we sit down over here? Maybe Addie will be able to get to sleep and won't be able to read our lips quite as easily."

"Folks are missing you in Florence," he began. "Doc Rayburn can't wait for you to return. Says he doesn't know how you ever talked him into coming out of retirement during your absence. And the folks at church, they've all been praying for you and Addie," he continued.

"I'm pleased to hear that, Charlie," she interrupted, "but what I really want to know is why you're in Chicago. You're opposed to all of this, and then without a word, you show up like you belong here."

"I do belong here, Tessie. Addie had John deliver a letter to me asking that I come to Chicago. I have prayed earnestly about the operation and what my role should be. I know we disagree about the surgery, but I hope we both want what is best for Addie, not ourselves. I had just about decided to make the trip, and then I got a wire from Mr. Vance calling a meeting here in Chicago. So, you see, I had to come to Chicago. I guess some folks would say it was Mr. Vance that called me here. I think God called me here," he finished.

"And me too. I called you too," Addie stated from across the room.

"Addie, how were you able to read my lips from over there?" Charlie asked, moving toward her.

"I didn't," she answered. "I listened with my ears."

"What are you telling me? Are you saying you can hear like you used to?" he asked.

"Almost. It's just a little quieter, but it's louder today than yesterday," she responded with a bright smile.

"Addie, why didn't you tell me?" Tessie inquired incredulously.

"Because I knew you wanted to learn all about the operation. I heard you tell Dr. Lundstrom today how excited you were about helping with my operation and that it was a big opportunity. I didn't want to spoil it for you," she answered soulfully.

"Oh, Addie. What I wanted was for you to be able to hear again, and instead I've made you feel that all I was interested in was learning a new surgical technique. Perhaps I was thinking more about myself than you," she answered, tears welling in her eyes.

"Don't cry, Tessie. I wouldn't have let you do the operation. I heard Dr. Lundstrom reminding you about that dizzy stuff I'd have after the surgery. If it hadn't been for that, I might have let you do it, but I don't want to be woozy and throwing up for days," she stated.

Long after Addie had fallen asleep, Tessie wrestled with herself. Before Charlie left for his hotel, the three of them had joined in a prayer of thanks for Addie's restored hearing, but she knew that Addie had spoken the truth. The surgery had become an obsession, and she hadn't wanted anyone or anything attempting to dissuade her. She wanted her way in the matter, not Addie's and certainly not God's. Completely ashamed of herself, she knelt down beside her bed and earnestly prayed for God's forgiveness. Forgiveness for her self-serving attitude after He had entrusted her with the care of this young child, and forgiveness for the way she had treated those who questioned her decision, especially Charlie. Climbing back into bed, she fell into a deep, restful sleep, the best she had had since meeting Edward Buford.

"No one knows exactly what causes things like this to happen," Dr. Lundstrom stated to Tessie. "My guess is that some severe trauma in her life caused her hearing loss. I don't know if it was the fear of surgery that caused her hearing restoration or not," he continued.

"No, it was God. I'm really sure it was," Addie interjected to the group of adults gathered in her room.

"I vote with Addie," Charlie stated.

"And so do I," Tessie remarked.

"Edward asked that you come by the house as soon as possible. He'd like to visit with you. I know you're planning on leaving in the morning, so I told him I'd bring you home with me," Dr. Lundstrom told Tessie.

"I have a meeting to attend so I must be on my way," Charlie stated. "Addie, I'll see you as soon as my meeting is completed," he told the child and walked toward the door.

"I'll see you later too, Charlie," Tessie called after him.

Several hours later Charlie returned. Pulling Addie's coat from the closet, he told her she was certainly well enough to go out for lunch with him. Over the nurse's protest, the two of them met Mr. Vance for an elegant meal in one of the fashionable downtown restaurants. Addie charmed both of them throughout the meal and profusely thanked Mr. Vance for allowing her to come along to such a fancy place. As they were leaving, Addie told Mr. Vance it was nice to meet him and then stated, "You must come to Florence sometime. Our lunch today was very good. But my Johnny's food at the Harvey House is even better." Both men appreciated her remark, knowing she probably spoke the truth.

Tessie was waiting in the hospital room when they returned, and Addie quickly related all the details of the fancy luncheon she had attended. "How was Mr. Vance?" Tessie inquired.

"He's doing just fine. He asked me to send his regrets that you hadn't been available to have lunch with us. And your meeting with Edward, how did that go?" he inquired, knowing he might be overstepping his bounds.

"We can talk about that on the train ride back to Kansas. I assume you're leaving in the morning also?" she inquired, not wanting Addie to be a part of their discussion about the meeting with Edward.

"Yes, in fact, I was hoping you'd agree to leave the hospital now. We can get you and Addie registered at the hotel and at least have an enjoyable dinner together. That is, if you don't have other plans," he offered.

"No other plans. I think you have a grand idea. It will be nice for Addie to see a little of Chicago. I know I'd sleep better in the hotel than this hospital, and it would be fun to have dinner together again," she answered.

For the most part, the trip home was pleasant, although they were all anxious to get back to Florence, making the journey seem longer than anticipated. Charlie proved to be a much more enjoyable traveling companion than Edward, showering attention on both Addie and Tessie. When Addie fell asleep on the seat in front of them, Tessie revealed to Charlie that Edward's intentions had been honorable. He had proposed marriage and wanted her to move to Chicago. He had already discussed the matter with his brother-in-law, and the two of them had agreed that Tessie could join Byron's practice and work at the hospital with him. He wasn't as thrilled about the prospect of having Addie, however. His plans for her were a boarding school in England, where she would attend classes and have occasional visits with them. It would be a much better life than anyone would have ever anticipated for the "poor waif," he had explained to her.

"You know I would never do that to Addie, Charlie," Tessie said, watching as he bristled at the remarks.

"Yes, I know that. I also know you'd never let a man plan your life for you either. Apparently Edward didn't know that quite as well as I do," he said, laughing at her look of mock indignation.

"I really am sorry for all the trouble and pain I've caused you, Charlie. I hope you'll forgive me. I know things can never be the same between us. I've ruined that with my lack of trust in you, but I hope you'll remain our friend," she implored.

"Tessie, I had hoped you knew my feelings for you were deeper than that. Surely you know I'll forgive you. I love you, and with that love comes my understanding and forgiveness. It may take a little time for us to get back to where we were, but I'm certain we will. Hopefully, even further," he said, leaning over to kiss her on the cheek.

"Thank you, Charlie," she whispered, slipping her hand into his.

"Welcome back!" John called out to the trio as they stepped down from the train. "I got your wire saying Addie was fine, and you were coming home today. Told the kitchen help they'd better keep things on schedule 'cause I was coming to meet my friends."

"Johnny," Addie called, rushing to meet her favorite chef. "I can hear now. Isn't it wonderful?"

"You bet it is, little woman. It's good to have you home, all of you," he answered, amazed with Addie's ability to once again hear. "Restores your faith, doesn't it?" he said to the adults.

"It certainly does and then some," Tessie replied. Charlie gave her a knowing look and squeezed her hand, leading them into the station.

"Mary, get yourself over here and take a gander. Looks like Mr. Banion's back in the doctor's good graces again," Cora told her friend. Rushing forward, Mary peeked around Cora's plump figure.

"Wouldn't you just know it!" she seethed.

"I think you'd better give up on this one. It appears to me they're headed for the altar," Cora replied, sounding smug.

"Whose side are you on, anyway?" Mary asked, noting Cora's tone of voice.

"This time I think I'm on that little girl's side. They make a nice-looking family, if you ask me, and there's plenty of other men for you to conquer," her friend answered.

"Well, thanks for nothing," Mary replied, stomping back to her desk, while Cora stood watching the threesome gather their baggage and walk away from the station.

Tessie smiled down at Addie as she tucked her into bed. "I'm glad we're back home," Addie said, after they had finished prayers.

"Me too," Tessie and Charlie replied in unison, causing all three of them to laugh. "You get right to sleep, and tomorrow we'll talk about enrolling you in school. It's going to be such fun for you, with new friends, and I know you'll be an excellent student. I love you, Addie," Tessie lovingly told the child, leaning down to kiss her good night.

"I love you," the child answered, "and you too, Charlie," she said while holding her arms open for a hug.

"I'll make some coffee," Tessie told Charlie as they exited the child's bedroom.

"Sounds great," he replied, walking toward the fireplace to jostle the logs, hopeful that a little more heat would quickly be forthcoming. "Wish John had thought to get this place warmed up a bit before we returned," he called out toward the kitchen.

"John doesn't even have a key to the house, Charlie," she replied.

"If I'd been thinking, I would have wired him. Doc Rayburn could have let him in. Oh well, I didn't think of it, so we'll have to abide the chill for a bit."

"Maybe this will warm you up," Tessie said, handing him a hot cup of coffee.

Taking the cup, he patted the sofa cushion. "Sit down here, next to me," he instructed.

Obediently she seated herself and stared into the fire, her hands wrapped around the steaming cup of coffee. "It's so good to be home. It seems as though I've been gone for months instead of a few weeks," she said, still staring toward the fire.

"Tessie, if you're not too tired, I'd like to talk a little," Charlie stated, hoping she would allow him to continue.

"As long as I can just sit and listen. I'm not sure how much I'll add to the conversation," she replied with a smile.

"I'll expect only a few words here and there," he responded. "On the train, when I told you I loved you, I meant that with all my heart. I also meant what I said about it taking us a little time to heal our wounds. What I would like is for you to accept this," he said, pulling a ring box from his pocket.

"Oh, Charlie," she stammered, "you told me I wouldn't have to think. . ."

"Let me finish. I purchased this ring for you before Christmas. Then with all the problems, I wasn't sure you'd ever agree to be my wife. I've kept it with me since the day I purchased it, hopeful that one day you would accept it. I bought this ring for you. I want you to be my wife, but we need more time. All I'm asking is that you wear this ring as a symbol of our agreement to determine if we're truly meant for each other. If that doesn't happen, you may keep the ring—my gift to you. However, I do feel reasonably certain I'll be placing a wedding band on your finger in the future. Can you agree to my proposal, Tessie?"

She nodded her agreement, holding out her left hand and watching as he slipped the ring on her finger.

"You've made me very happy, Tessie," he said, pulling her close and tenderly enfolding her in his arms. "I don't know what I would have done, had you not agreed."

The mantel clock struck nine, just as he rose from the sofa. "I think, perhaps, I'd better get back over to the Harvey House and make sure they haven't given my room to someone else. Besides, we both need some sleep," he said, walking with her toward the door. "I'll see you in the morning," he called back as she stood in the doorway waving, cold air rushing into the entry.

Two days later, Charlie and Tessie enrolled Addie as Mrs. Landry's newest student at the small schoolhouse several blocks away. Throughout the day, Tessie found herself thinking of the child. In the midst of examining a patient or cleaning her instruments, her mind would wander to Addie and how her day was going. Shortly before the school bell clanged to announce the end of the school day, Charlie arrived at the door.

"I wanted to be here and see how she made out," he told Tessie. "Think I'll wait out here on the porch."

"Charlie, it's cold," she protested.

"I know, but I want to see her face. I'll know how it went when I see her face," he replied.

Tessie smiled and grabbed her coat, pulled it tightly around her, and sat down in the other chair. "I hope she comes quickly," she told him with a grin.

No more had Tessie uttered the words than Addie came skipping down the sidewalk, a smile from ear to ear, holding the hand of another little girl. "Hi," she called out to the couple sitting on the porch "This is my new friend, Ruth," she announced, pulling the youngster up the steps to meet Tessie and Charlie.

"I'd say things went well," Charlie whispered to Tessie and held out his hand to meet Addie's new friend.

In the months that followed, Tessie's medical practice continued to grow, and Addie flourished in the new world unlocked to her. Their days were busy, but Charlie was still required to travel much of the time, and both of them missed him.

It was an especially lovely spring day when Tessie decided to meet Addie after school. Charlie was expected to arrive, and they would walk over to the station and meet him.

"What a pleasant surprise," Charlie exclaimed, walking into the station and giving Addie a big hug while kissing Tessie's cheek. "To what do I owe this unexpected event?"

"It's such a beautiful day; I met Addie after school. We thought it would be nice to greet you here at the station and walk to the house with you," she replied, pleased she had made the decision.

"Just let me drop my bag off with Mrs. Winter in the hotel, and we can be on our way."

They walked slowly, enjoying each other's company as well as the budding trees and flowers. "Is someone sitting on the porch?" Addie asked, squinting to get a better look.

"It does look like there's someone in one of the chairs," Charlie replied as they continued moving toward the house.

"It appears to be a woman and baby. Probably someone with a sick child waiting to see me," Tessie stated, quickening her step.

"No," Addie said, coming to a halt. "It's Lydia."

"It is Lydia," Tessie answered, attempting to conceal her fear. "I wonder what she's doing in Florence," Tessie said, looking toward Charlie.

"Well, she does have a sister here," Charlie reminded her.

"Yes, I know, but she's been gone all this time without a word, and now suddenly she appears on the front porch."

"Don't get alarmed. Let's just remain calm and welcome her," he said, opening the gate, although he noted that Addie hung behind not overly anxious to see her sister.

"Bet you're surprised to see me," Lydia said rising from the chair and adjusting the small child on her hip. "This here's Floyd Jr.," she announced to the three of them.

"Well, he certainly is a fine-looking boy, isn't he?" Charlie observed, glancing at Tessie for confirmation.

"Yes, he is," Tessie replied. "How have you been, Lydia?"

"Well, right now I'm hot and tired. Any chance I could get something to drink and maybe a bite to eat?" she inquired. "Hi, Addie," she said to her sister without so much as a hug, brushing by her to follow Tessie into the house.

It was obvious that Lydia wasn't going to divulge what was on her mind until she was good and ready. She had always been deceptive, and although Tessie had been slow to learn that lesson, she was on guard. Quickly, she prepared cold drinks and arranged some cookies and biscuits on a plate. Returning to the parlor, she found Charlie and Lydia engaged in polite conversation. Addie had disappeared from sight.

"Here you are, Lydia," Tessie stated, offering a glass of lemonade and the plate of cookies.

"I was hoping for something a little more substantial than cookies but guess they'll do for now," she answered, quickly devouring several.

"So how are things going with you and Addie? Must be okay since you didn't put her in an orphanage or get rid of her," Lydia stated, slapping the baby's hand when he reached toward the plate of cookies. Tessie inwardly winced at the punishment.

"They're going fine, Lydia. I've grown to love Addie very much; she's like my own child. I've often wondered how things turned out for you and Floyd."

"Well, it ain't been no bed of roses; that's for sure. Floyd was gone all the time with his sales job, and me, I was home alone with the baby. Then one day Floyd tells me he's met up with someone else, and he's leaving me. I've been trying to make it on my own, but with Floyd Jr., I just can't. That's why I'm here," she announced.

"Why?" Tessie asked, still unclear what the connection might be.

"Because I need someone to take care of Floyd Jr. so I can work. I figured Addie ought to be good for that. If she watches him careful, she could handle him even if she is deaf. So I came to take her off your hands," she stated, as if those were the words Tessie had been waiting to hear.

"Take her off my hands? What are you thinking, Lydia? I'm not going to allow you to take Addie. It was you that made the decision to leave her, and here she'll stay," Tessie snapped in response.

"You've no right to her. She's my blood, my sister. If I say I'm taking her, that's how it will be, and I don't think there's much you can do about it," Lydia retorted.

"Ladies, women," Charlie interrupted. "I think we all need to calm ourselves a bit. Lydia, I'm sure you're tired after your journey from—where did you come from, Lydia?"

"From Kansas City, and I used about all my money just getting here," she answered.

"Whereabouts in Kansas City?" Charlie questioned. "I've spent quite a bit of time in Kansas City myself."

"Not where we were living, I'm sure," she replied, going into detail about the row of shacks where they lived along the riverfront. Charlie listened intently and questioned her for details that she seemed pleased to pass along, wanting all of them to know the poverty in which she had been forced to live.

"Well, I'm sure you and Floyd Jr. are both tired. Why don't I take you down to the Harvey House and get you a room? There's plenty of time to discuss this tomorrow after you've had a good night of rest," he counseled.

"I'm not going to change my mind about this no matter if we discuss it now or in the morning. Besides, I can't spare the money for a hotel room," she said, looking around the house as though the accommodations there would be just fine.

"Well, I'll be more than happy to pay for your room, Lydia," Charlie offered. "I'll talk with Mrs. Winter and have it put on my bill, your meals too. That way you don't have to worry," he said, leading her toward the front door.

"Mrs. Winter? Is that old fuddy-duddy still around? Are any of the women I worked with still there?" she inquired excitedly, never giving another thought to Tessie or Addie.

"Is she gone?" Addie asked, peeking around the corner.

"Yes, for the moment anyway," Tessie responded. Addie flew into her arms and clung for dear life.

"You won't let her take me, will you?" the child tearfully questioned. "I don't want to go with her. She doesn't care about me; she just wants me to watch her baby. I don't know anything about taking care of babies, do I?" she asked, hoping that particular fact would change the situation.

"I don't want you to worry about this, Addie. Charlie is coming back, and we're going to find a way to work things out. Charlie always has good ideas, and I'm sure he'll think of some way to convince Lydia you should stay with me," she soothingly answered, just as Charlie entered the front door.

"Did you get her settled?"

"I'm not sure settled is the word," he answered. "I got her a room, but she found a couple of waitresses she had worked with before. When I left, she was busy drinking coffee and visiting with them. I'm afraid poor Floyd Jr. is in for a night of it. She'll probably keep him up until all hours while she gossips with the women."

"Tessie said you always have good ideas and that you'll figure out a plan so Lydia will go away. You can do that, can't you, Charlie?" Addie interrupted, her voice trembling.

"Addie, I can't promise to make Lydia leave, but I'll do everything I can possibly think of to keep you with Tessie—and me," he added. "I think it might be better if we cancel our plans for dinner at the Harvey House this evening. How about going to the café downtown? They have some pretty good food too."

"I think that's an excellent idea," Tessie responded, and Addie shook her head affirmatively.

After Addie had gone to bed, Tessie and Charlie sat on the front porch, wanting to be sure she didn't overhear their conversation, which was something they were having to get used to. It occurred to Tessie that they hadn't even told Lydia that Addie's hearing had been restored—not that Lydia would have particularly cared unless it was of benefit to her.

"We're going to have to handle this very carefully, Tessie. I understand your anger and your fear because I have those same feelings, but Lydia isn't going to back down just because we tell her. I'd like to get this resolved as quickly and painlessly as possible, but I'm afraid if I offer her a sum of money, she'll keep coming back for more. I think we must come up with a permanent solution that will benefit her, Floyd Jr., and the three of us, especially Addie."

"I agree with everything you've said, although I do have trouble holding my temper. Her audacity truly offends me, thinking she can just waltz back into Addie's life and turn it upside down whenever it suits her fancy. Have you thought of a plan that she might agree to?" Tessie questioned, trying to calm herself.

"I have an idea she's not been entirely truthful with us, and we'll need time to verify what she's told us. It's going to be difficult to placate her if she becomes suspicious, but in order to discover the truth, I'm going to have to leave town. In the morning I'll tell Lydia that I must leave town on business, which is true enough, and request that she wait until I return to make a final decision regarding Addie."

"Do you really think she'll agree to that?" Tessie inquired.

"If I offer to pay the tab for her little vacation at the Harvey House, I think she'll agree. We may have to offer babysitting services if she wants to go out partying with her friends," he said, giving her a lopsided smile.

"I'd keep him the whole time you're gone if it would help. Speaking of which, how long do you think you'll be gone?" Tessie asked.

"If everything goes as planned, I should be back in two or three days at the most, but in the event this fails, we'll have to come up with an alternate plan. You might give that some consideration and prayer while I'm gone. I hope you trust me to handle this," he stated.

"I trust you implicitly, Charlie," she answered.

"In that case, I think it's about time we added a wedding band to that engagement ring," he said with a wink. "Perhaps you could spend a little time making wedding plans too?" he continued, with a question in his voice.

"Perhaps I could," she answered, looking into his gray eyes.

Gently, he pulled her to him and slowly lowered his head. "I love you, Tessie Wilshire," he said and then gently kissed her. "I'll stop by tomorrow after I've talked to Lydia, but for now I'd better get back over to the hotel," he said, walking toward the door.

Encircling her in his arms, he smiled down at her. "We'll see this through,

Tessie. Things will work out—you'll see," he said, kissing her gently on the lips.

"I know you're right. I'll try to quit worrying and start praying," she responded, hoping God would lead Charlie in the right direction.

"Good! I'll see you sometime tomorrow morning," he replied. "Now, I'd really better be on my way."

Tessie watched as he walked toward the Harvey House. *He is truly a marvelous man. How did I ever consider anyone else?* she thought to herself.

The next morning Charlie arrived shortly after ten o'clock. "Things are looking like they might work out. I've convinced Lydia to sit tight as my guest at the hotel, and she seems willing to do that. She was complaining about the baby, and I told her if she needed a brief respite, you would most likely agree to care for him so long as it didn't interfere with office hours," he said almost apologetically.

"Charlie, that's fine. I said I didn't mind, and I don't. It's the very least I can do while you're off tracking down information," she told him.

"My train leaves in half an hour so I can't stay, but if Lydia attempts to take Addie, rely upon John for assistance. I've filled him in, and he said he'll keep an eye on her over at the hotel. He'll have no problem getting information from the waitresses about what Lydia's telling them."

"I'm glad you thought of John as a resource. He's been a trusted friend, and Addie loves him so much. I know he would do anything to help her," she stated, pleased to know that she would have an ally while Charlie was gone.

"It seems all I do is leave you, but I must get over to the station," he said.

She reached up and placed her hands on either side of his face. "I love you, Charlie Banion," she sighed.

"You're not making it any easier for me to leave," he said, leaning down and ardently kissing her. Quickly, he moved away. "If I don't make an exit now, I may never go," he told her and bounded down the steps with a wave.

Lydia lost little time making her way back to visit Tessie, causing Addie to hide in her room immediately upon her sister's arrival. "This kid is drivin' me crazy," she stated, plopping Floyd Jr. on the floor. "Mr. Banion said you'd watch after him while he was gone, so I brought his clothes and things," she said, dropping a satchel beside the baby.

"Lydia, Mr. Banion told you I would watch the baby so long as it didn't interfere with my office hours. I have patients to see and certainly can't watch your baby. If you want to go somewhere this evening with your friends, bring him back then," Tessie said, trying to keep her voice friendly.

"I guess if I can't leave him, I'll have to take Addie over to the hotel with me so she can watch after him. I'm planning on enjoying this little holiday," she stated in a menacing voice. "I think I've got the trump card, Dr. Wilshire. What's it gonna be, Addie at the hotel or Floyd Jr. at your house?"

"Floyd Jr. at my house," Tessie answered. "You certainly seem to have no qualms about disposing of the people in your life, do you, Lydia?"

"Nobody ever had much problem disposing of me either," she angrily retorted. "Are you keeping him or not?"

"I said I would. When will you be back?"

"Mr. Banion said he would be gone a couple of days. Guess I'll be back when he is," she retorted and walked out, slamming the door behind her, frightening Floyd Jr., who began to wail. Addie, who had been listening to the conversation, came running out in need of consolation just as a patient walked into the office. Tessie wasn't sure where to turn first.

Tessie took Addie and Floyd Jr. into the office with her, and within a short time Addie had become fond of the baby and was entertaining him. By the end of the day, he was in love with Addie, and she was in love with him. He held his chubby arms out for Addie, not Tessie, and in no time she was diapering and feeding him as if she had been doing it all her life.

"Don't get too attached, Addie. Lydia will be back in no time, and Floyd Jr. will be gone. Enjoy him while you can, but remember he'll be leaving soon," she reminded the child, fearful that the baby's departure would be difficult.

"I know, I know," Addie would answer and immediately begin hugging and kissing Floyd Jr., who was thoroughly enjoying the continuous attention.

Two days later Charlie returned.

Chapter 12

Addie peeked through the lace curtains, watching as Lydia sauntered toward the front door with a smug look on her face. "She's coming," the child called out in a hushed voice.

"It's all right," Tessie reassured her. Floyd Jr. was in Addie's arms, much cleaner than when he had arrived, although his clothing was tattered and permanently stained from lack of care. *He is a sweet child,* Tessie thought, watching him play with Addie's hair.

Tessie opened the front door just as Lydia had raised her hand to knock. "Couldn't wait for me to get here, could you? Now, you know how it feels, being tied down to a kid all the time," she greeted in a taunting voice.

"It's nice to see you, Lydia," Tessie responded, ignoring the hateful remark. "As soon as Charlie arrives, we'll have dinner," she offered.

Lydia seated herself on the sofa and stared after Addie, who was headed for the backyard carrying the baby. Tessie had expected the baby to miss his mother and show excitement at her reappearance, but that didn't occur. Floyd Jr. clung to Addie, who appeared to be his preference, at least for the time being. Lydia didn't seem to mind, however, showing no interest in either of the children.

"She seems different somehow. Probably 'cause she's living the good life here with you—but not for much longer. She'll soon remember what it's like to do without all this finery," Lydia stated smugly.

Tessie inwardly grimaced at the thought of Addie being required to live with Lydia. It was obvious that she would be reduced to servant status and once again become the brunt of Lydia's bitterness and resentment.

"Where is Mr. Banion anyway? He told me to be here at five o'clock. I'm not waiting around forever. Maybe he ran out on you, just like Floyd did to me. Men have a way of doing that," Lydia retorted above the rumbling of the evening train as it pulled into the station.

"I'll be just a few moments. I need to check things in the kitchen," Tessie replied, her palms wet with perspiration.

Where can he be? she thought, not sure how much longer Lydia would remain. She stood there envisioning Lydia grabbing Addie and whisking her off into the night, never to be seen again. *Stop this nonsense,* she admonished herself, quickly bowing her head in prayer to ask God's forgiveness for not trusting this matter to His care. "Father, I know there is no problem You can't handle, if we'll just remember to ask and place our trust in You. I'm doing that now and will cease this useless worrying." No sooner had she uttered the prayer than the command in I Peter 5:7, came to mind: "Casting all your care upon him; for he careth for you." An awareness of God's peace was now with her as she returned to the parlor.

Walking into the room, Tessie stood back as the front and back doors opened simultaneously. "Charlie! Floyd!" came cries from the assembling group.

"What's he doing here?" Lydia fumed, pointing her finger in Floyd's direction. Floyd Jr. began crying, wriggling in Addie's arms in an attempt to reach his father.

"Here, I'll take him, Addie. How's Daddy's boy?" Floyd crooned to his son. "How are you, Addie?" he asked, tousling her hair and giving her a genuine smile.

"I'm just fine, Floyd. I can hear again," Addie told him.

"Why that's wonder—"

"What do you mean, you can hear? Nobody told me anything about you hearing? Were you just playacting for more attention, you little brat? You always got the best of everything, even now," the older sister enviously raved.

"Stop it, Lydia! Stop it, right now. Mr. Banion knows all about what's going on between the two of us. I even told him about not wanting to leave Addie but that you insisted on running off, away from Florence, away from Addie, away from everything. Even when I offered to quit my sales job and stay in Florence so Addie could live with us, you wouldn't agree. You had to go to the big city. Well, you've been there, Lydia. Now, what? Are you going to ruin everyone else's life, deciding what you want next?"

"You know, I think it might be best if we all just relaxed a bit and had dinner. We can talk after we've eaten," Tessie suggested, not wanting a full-fledged battle to take place in front of the children.

"That's a good idea. I could eat a horse," Charlie replied.

"You could? Not me. I'd never eat a horse," Addie giggled back.

"You would if you were hungry enough," Lydia angrily shot back at the child.

Addie moved closer to Charlie, feeling the need of his protection against this woman who was so full of hate. *Why does my sister despise me so,* Addie wondered, as they sat down at the table.

Tessie's roasted chicken, mashed potatoes and peas, butterhorn rolls, and apple cobbler were eaten in formidable silence. Charlie and Tessie made feeble attempts at dinner conversation, only to be cut short by Lydia's caustic rebuttals. Floyd held the baby, spooning mashed potatoes into the child's mouth, unable to conceal his embarrassment.

None of them failed to note Floyd's compassionate nature with his son.

Whereas Lydia slapped and hollered, Floyd praised and coaxed. When Lydia was annoyed with the baby's antics, Floyd was delighted. It was obvious he loved his son, and it was obvious that Lydia had woven a tale of lies.

After dinner, with Floyd Jr., asleep in his father's lap and Addie in her bedroom, Lydia admitted that Floyd had not run off and left her.

"But why did you do this, Lydia? I just do not understand," Floyd questioned.

"I don't think you really want to know, Floyd."

"Yes, I do. How can we fix this unless I know what's going on?"

"I don't think you can fix it, Floyd, but here goes," she replied. "I can't stand being tied down to the baby all day. He gets on my nerves. You get to be gone, out seeing other people and come home, and all you do is play with him. All I do is cook and clean. I want some fun out of life, Floyd. Can't you understand that?"

"If the baby is such a problem for you, why'd you bring him? Why didn't you just slip away at night and leave him with me? You could have left him, just like you left your sister," he retorted.

"To tell the truth, I thought about that. Long and hard. But, then I decided upon this plan, which would've worked if you hadn't gone and found him," she fumed at Charlie. "Speaking of which, just how did you know where to find Floyd?"

"You gave me enough information about where you lived that it didn't take much investigating to find him. All I had to do was ask a few people to do a little inquiring."

She glowered at him, hating his ability to outsmart her and ruin her plans.

"You still haven't told us about your great plan," Floyd insisted.

"Oh, what's the difference? I might as well tell you. Everything's spoiled now anyway. I figured if I said I was taking Addie and going to make her take care of Floyd Jr. while I was working, Dr. Wilshire would offer me money so she could keep Addie. I wasn't going to take the money right away. Thought I'd find someplace a ways off, over to Marion or Lost Springs, and get a job. Make her real lonely for wonderful little Addie until she offered me as much money as I wanted. Then I'd give her back, take Floyd Jr. back to you, and be off to make a life for myself. Not a bad plan until Mr. Banion stuck his nose in the middle of it."

"Lydia," Floyd whispered, "how could you ever think of doing something so cruel and mean-spirited to people who have loved you and tried to be kind?" he asked in disbelief. "I don't even know this person. . .this creature who would plot to hurt others so ruthlessly, without a thought for them. Your own flesh and blood, Lydia, your sister, your own son, me, Dr. Wilshire, Mr. Banion, all people who have loved you or tried to help—and all you want to do is inflict pain on us. Why, Lydia, why?" A tear overflowed and rolled down his cheek.

"Stop it, Floyd. Quit acting like such a whining fool, crying like your kid. Why don't you grow up and see what life is really like? I've had to. I really got nothing more to say to any of you. Since you're so all-fired in love with that kid, you figure out how to take care of him and hold down a job. Me? I'm gonna start over and never look back. Don't any of you ever come looking for me either. You're all a part of my life that never existed. My life's starting the minute I walk out this door," she replied, with a loathing look aimed at all of them.

They watched as she rose from the chair and stormed out the front door, never giving a second look at her husband or child.

"What's gotten into her? I just don't understand," Floyd said to no one in particular.

"It's not what's gotten into her, Floyd, it's what hasn't. She's looking for good times and money to take care of filling the void in her life, but she'll find out that they won't cure what ails her. The hole Lydia feels inside, that desperate longing to be accepted and loved, needs to be filled, and only God can heal her. The pain will cling to her like an undesired affliction until she turns to the One who loves her in spite of all her shortcomings," Tessie told him.

"What are you going to do, Floyd?" Addie asked. The adults had wondered the same thing but didn't broach the question.

"Right now, I think the baby and I need to be with family until I get things sorted out. I think I'll head back to Ohio. I can stop in Kansas City and close out the apartment, then go see my folks. I'll leave my address with you and our landlord in Kansas City. In case Lydia decides she wants to come back, she'll need to know where to find us," he stated hopefully.

Charlie and Tessie agreed that Ohio sounded like a good place for a fresh start. His parents were still there to help with Floyd Jr. and being settled in one place would allow him the opportunity to spend more time with his son.

"You're always welcome to come visit with us, Floyd," Tessie told the young man. "Addie has become very attached to Floyd Jr. in the short time he's been here, and I know she's going to miss him. We all will," she added.

"I'll keep in touch with you. I'm not real good at letter writing, but I'll try. You'll let me know if you hear from Lydia, won't you?" he asked.

"Of course, we will. If she contacts us, we'll be sure that she receives your address," Tessie reassured him.

"Guess I'd better get over to the hotel. I need to make train reservations and get some sleep before we leave in the morning. I really appreciate what you've all done for me and the baby. Especially you, Mr. Banion. If you hadn't come and found me, I hate to think of what Lydia might have done," he told them. "I'm sure glad you folks decided to keep Addie. She'll have a good life with you. Lydia would destroy her," he stated sadly, before walking out the door.

The next morning Tessie, Charlie, and Addie watched as Floyd boarded the train, with the baby in his arms. He looked forlorn and dejected, but his smile returned when he gazed down at his son. He kissed the baby's rosy cheek and whispered to him, "Who knows what will happen? Maybe one day God will open your mama's heart, and she'll come back to us."

"I've made a decision," Charlie told his two favorite women as they walked home.

"What might that be?" Tessie asked.

"I think the three of us need to sit down and do some serious planning for a wedding. You two women aren't getting things moving toward the church quick enough to suit me," he stated with mock indignation.

"Charlie, it's only been a few days since you told me to start making plans, and we have had a few major interruptions in our life," Tessie retorted.

"Don't worry, Charlie. Tessie has her wedding gown ready to go. She had it even before you asked her to get married," Addie told him.

"Is that so? Pretty sure of yourself, were you?" he teased.

Tessie felt a blush rise in her cheeks. "It's not what you're thinking at all. One day when Addie and I were talking, I mentioned that when I got married I would wear my Aunt Phiney's wedding dress. So, you see, I wasn't being presumptuous," she told him, as they walked onto the porch and he leaned down to kiss her.

"You can be just as presumptuous as you like, Dr. Wilshire, as long as it's me you're marrying in that dress. So, when's the date? Have you talked to the preacher? What about a special dress for Addie? Shall we get married here in Florence, or do you want to go home? How about a big cake? What do you think, Addie? A really, really big cake?" Charlie asked, clasping his outstretched hands and forming his arms into a huge circle.

Addie laughed at him, for his good mood was contagious. "We'll need to make another quilt," the child informed them.

"Why do we need another quilt?" Charlie inquired when Tessie nodded her head, agreeing with the child.

"So we can weave you into the family, just like me," Addie replied.

"I'm all for that, just as long as you wait until after the wedding to make it!" Charlie told the two of them.

"I think that's one thing that can wait," Tessie agreed.

"Well, this can't," he replied, pulling her into his arms and kissing her thoroughly while Addie sat on the front steps giggling, unable to conceal her happiness.

JUDITH McCOY MILLER
Judith makes her home in Kansas with her family. Intrigued by the law, Judy is a certified legal assistant currently employed as a compliance analyst with the Kansas Insurance Department. After ignoring an "urge" to write for approximately two years, Judy quit thinking about what she had to say and began writing it. She has been extremely blessed. Her first two books earned her the honor of being selected Heartsong's favorite new author in 1997.

A Letter to Our Readers

Dear Readers:

In order that we might better contribute to your reading enjoyment, we would appreciate you taking a few minutes to respond to the following questions. When completed, please return to the following: Fiction Editor, Barbour Publishing, Inc., P.O. Box 719, Uhrichsville, OH 44683.

1. Did you enjoy reading *Kansas?*
   ❑ Very much—I would like to see more books like this.
   ❑ Moderately—I would have enjoyed it more if ______________

____

____

2. What influenced your decision to purchase this book?
   (Check those that apply.)
   ❑ Cover ❑ Back cover copy ❑ Title ❑ Price
   ❑ Friends ❑ Publicity ❑ Other

3. Which story was your favorite?
   ❑ *Beyond Today* ❑ *Threads of Love*
   ❑ *The House on Windridge* ❑ *Woven Threads*

4. Please check your age range:
   ❑ Under 18 ❑ 18–24 ❑ 25–34
   ❑ 35–45 ❑ 46–55 ❑ Over 55

5. How many hours per week do you read? ______________

Name ______________________________________

Occupation __________________________________

Address ____________________________________

City ________________ State __________ Zip __________